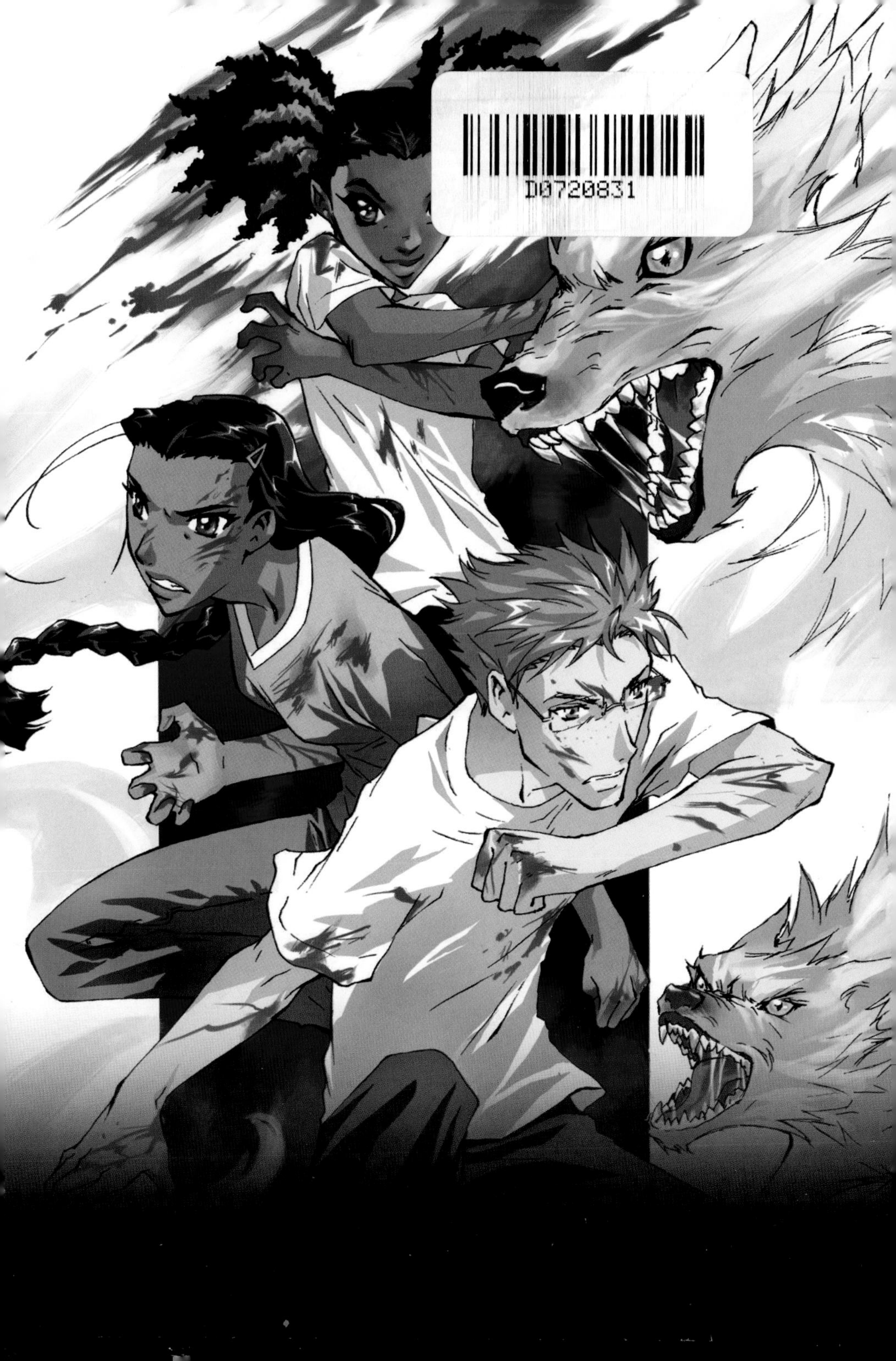

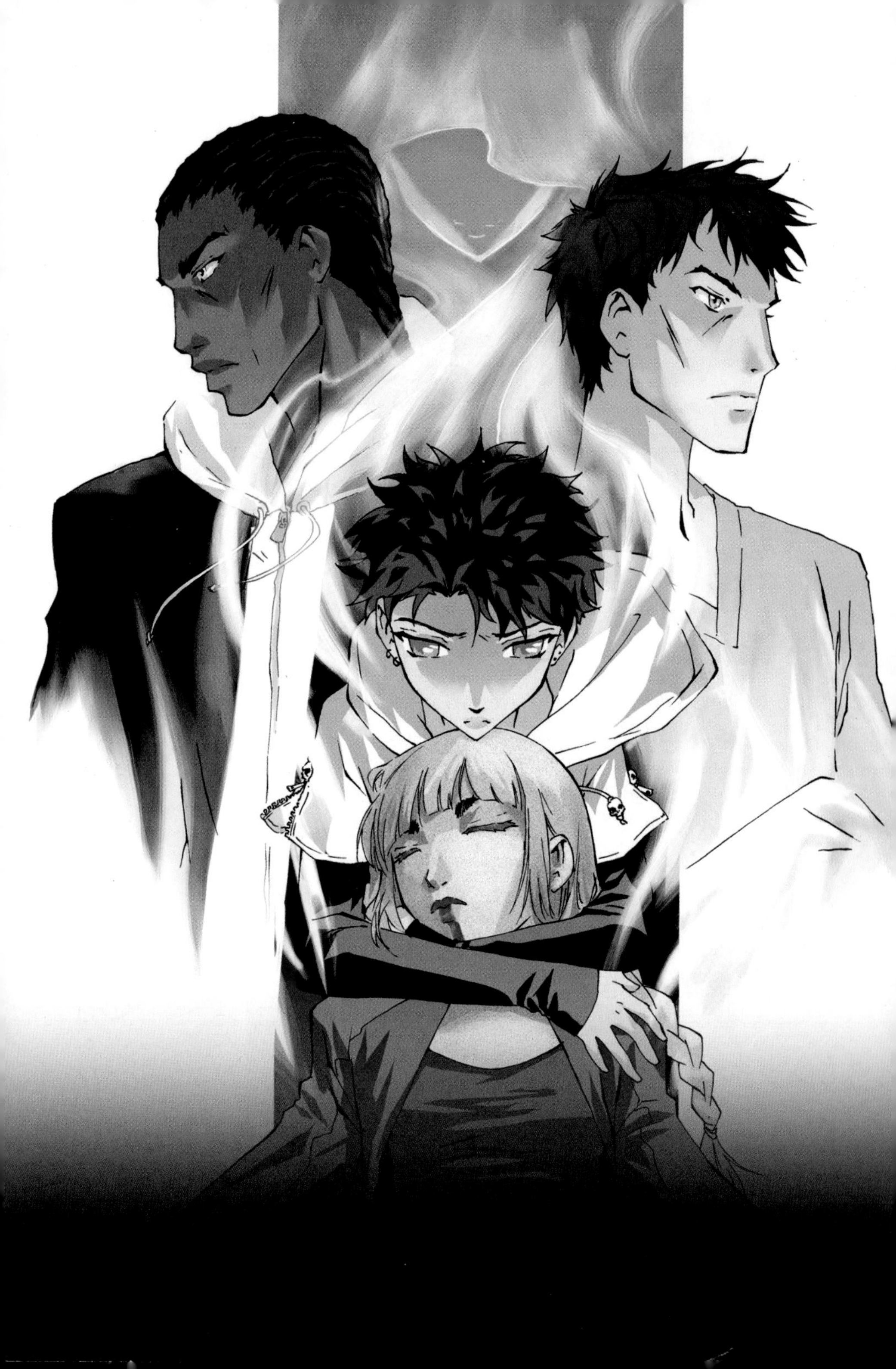

Nightschool

The Weirn Books

Collector's Edition 2

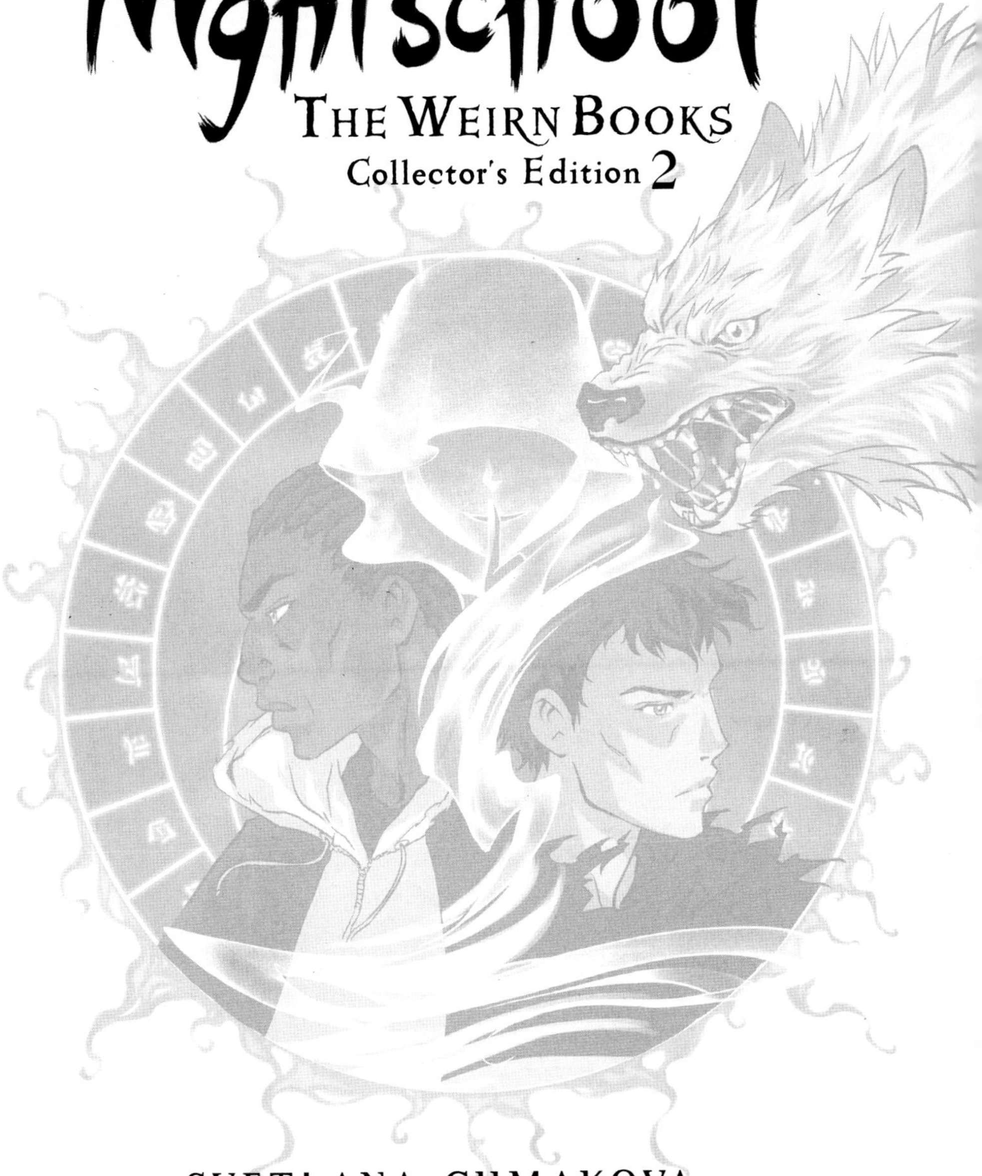

SVETLANA CHMAKOVA

Yen Press

Contents

Chapter 13

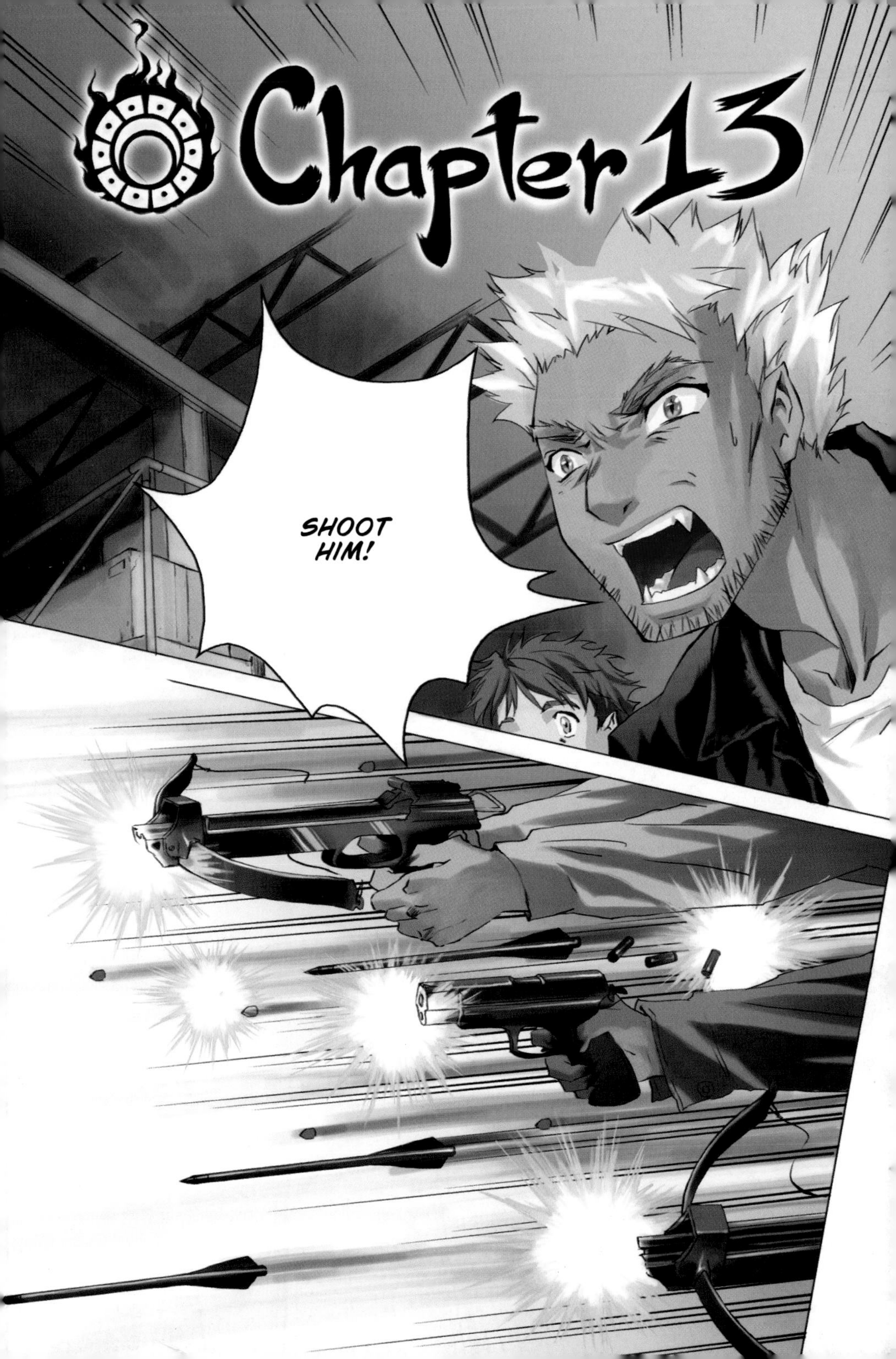
SHOOT HIM!

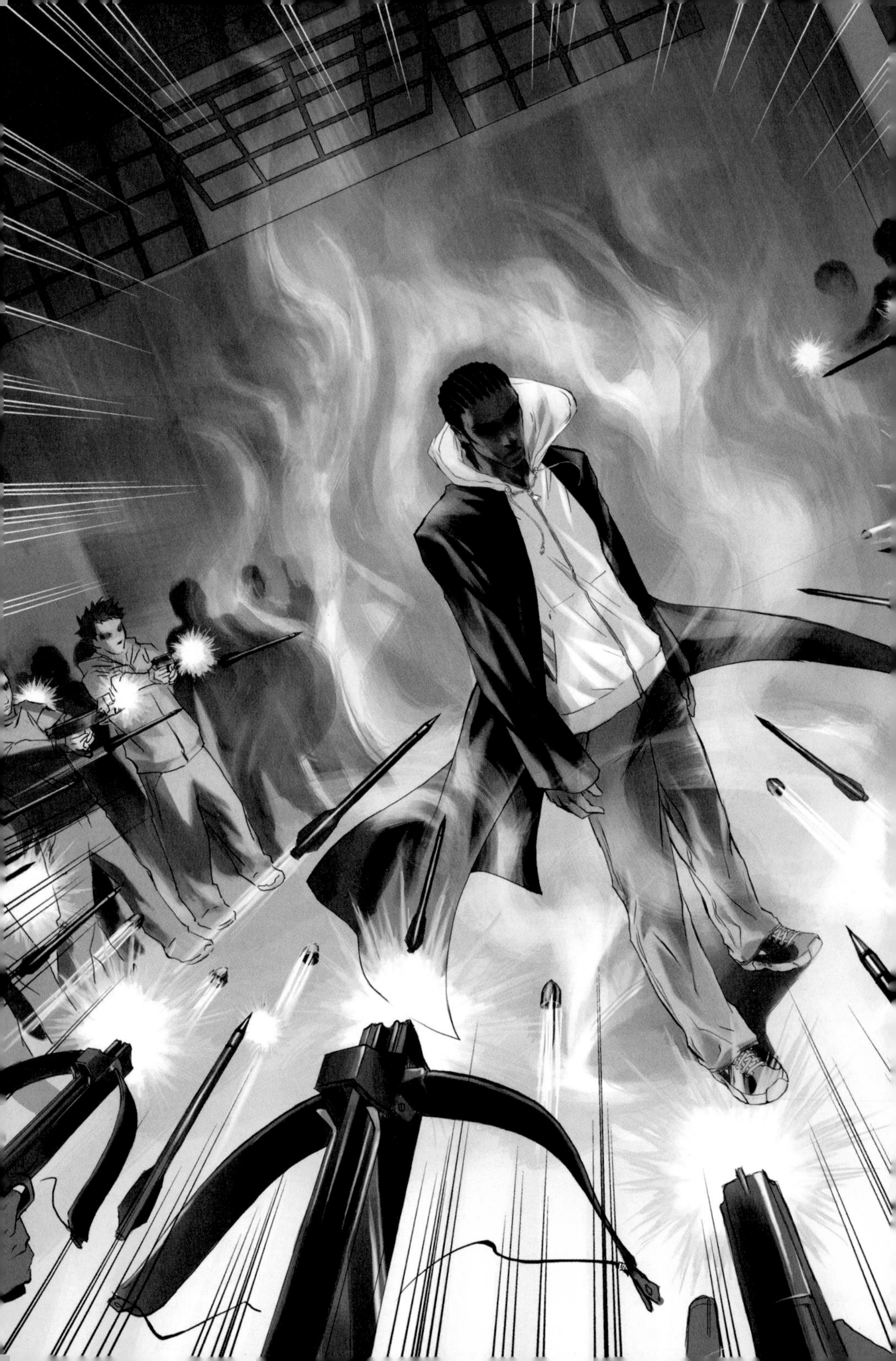

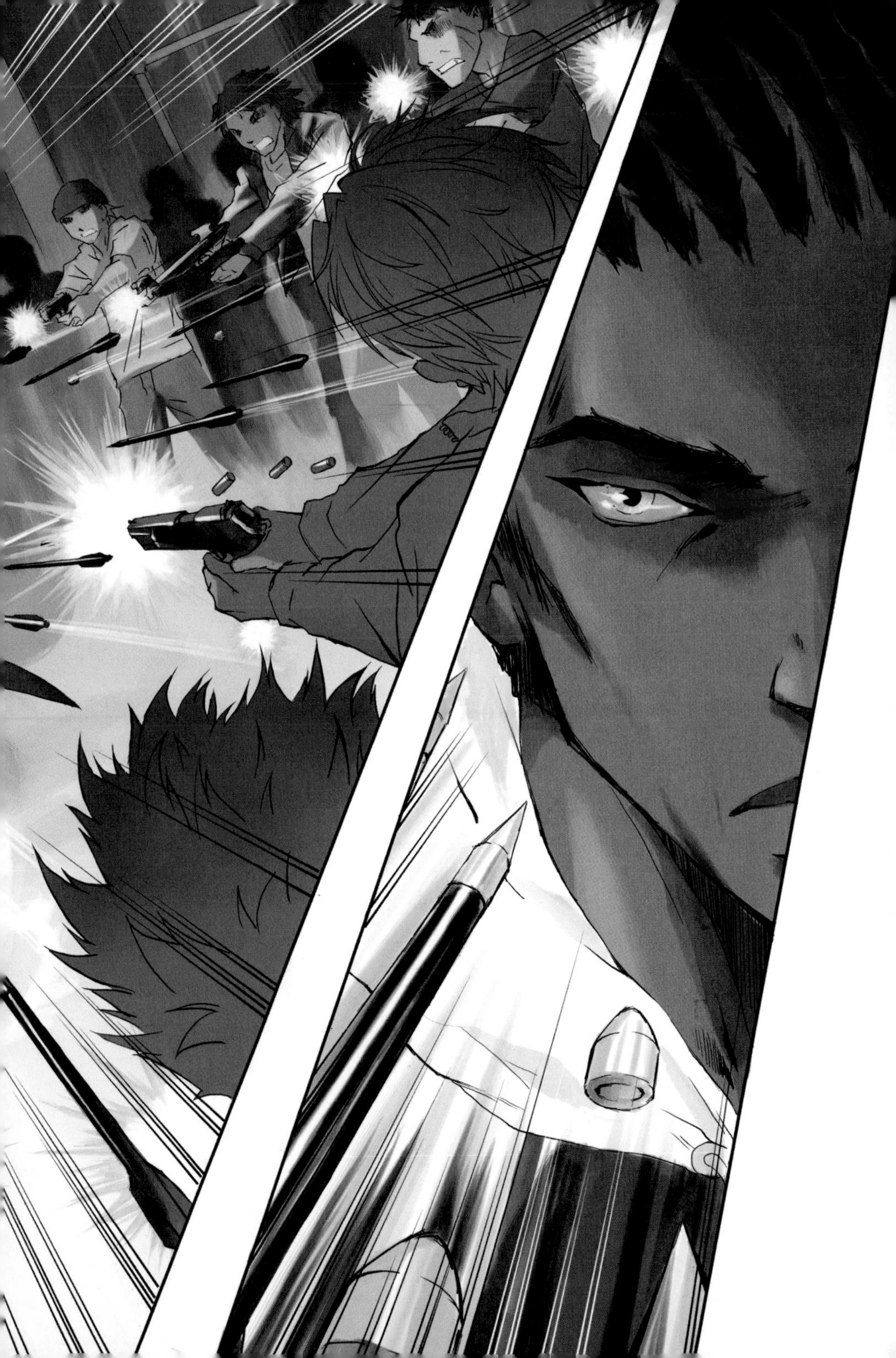

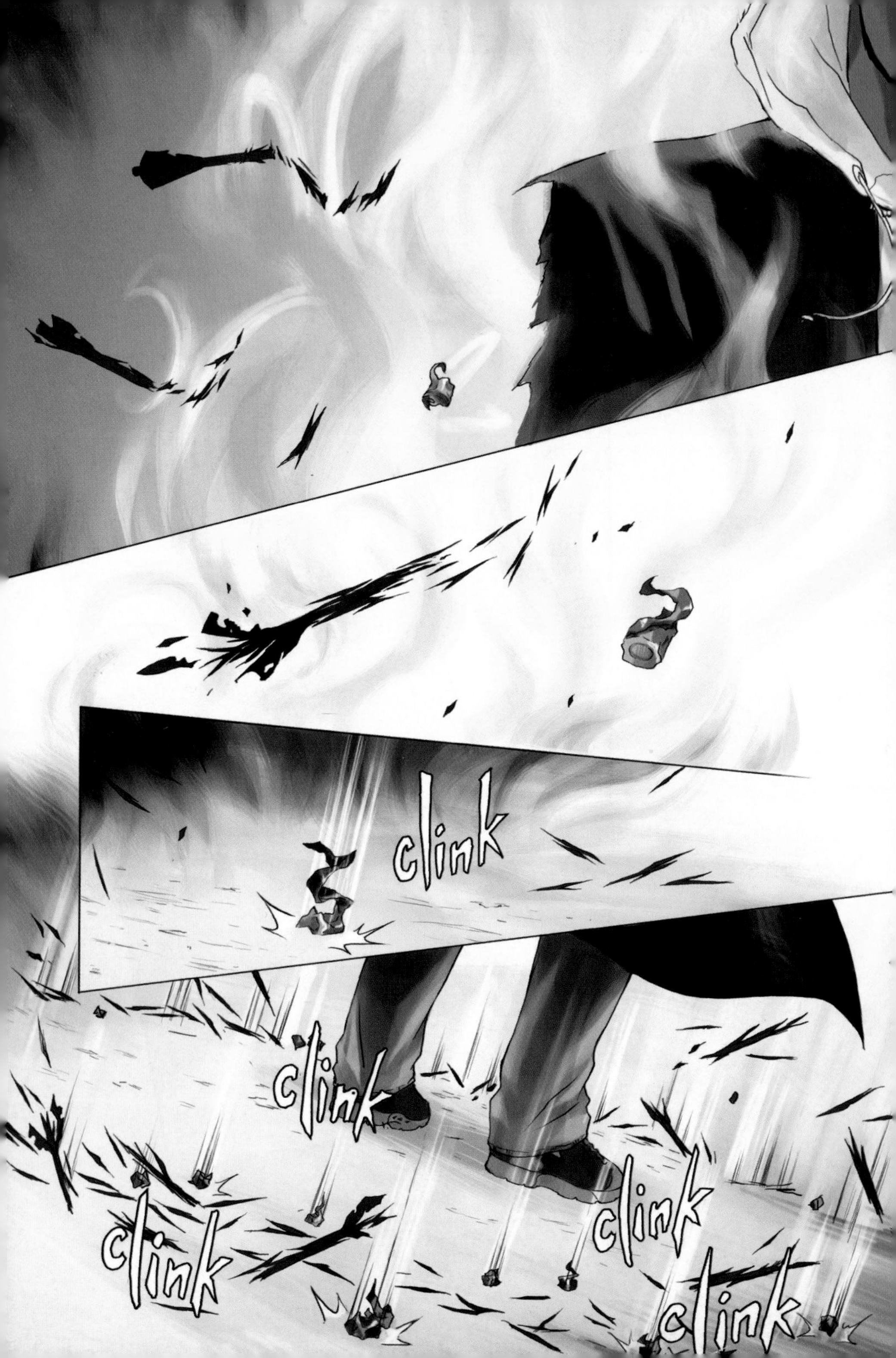
clink
clink
clink
clink
clink

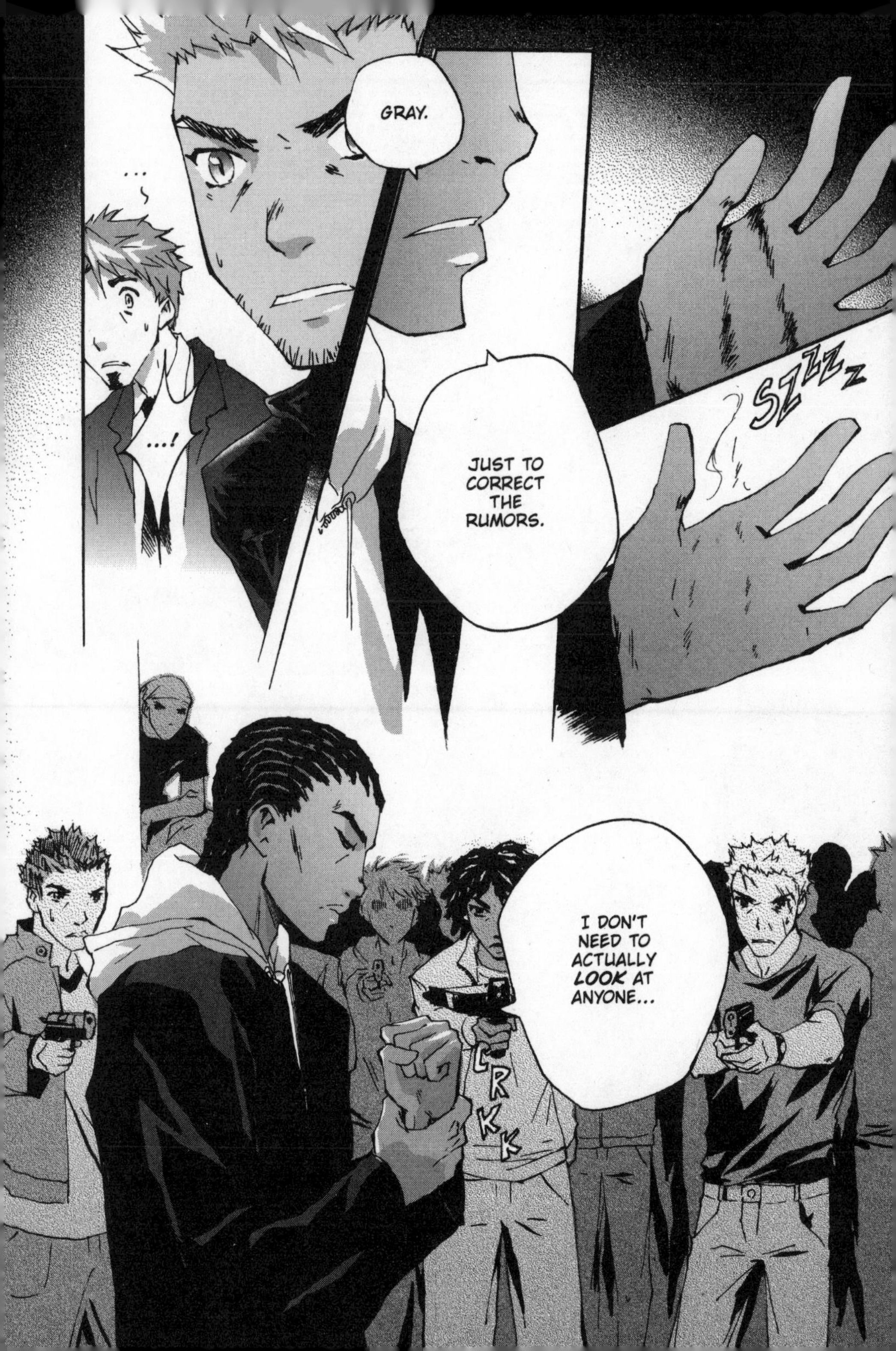
...
...!
GRAY.
JUST TO CORRECT THE RUMORS.
SZZZZ
I DON'T NEED TO ACTUALLY LOOK AT ANYONE...
CRKK

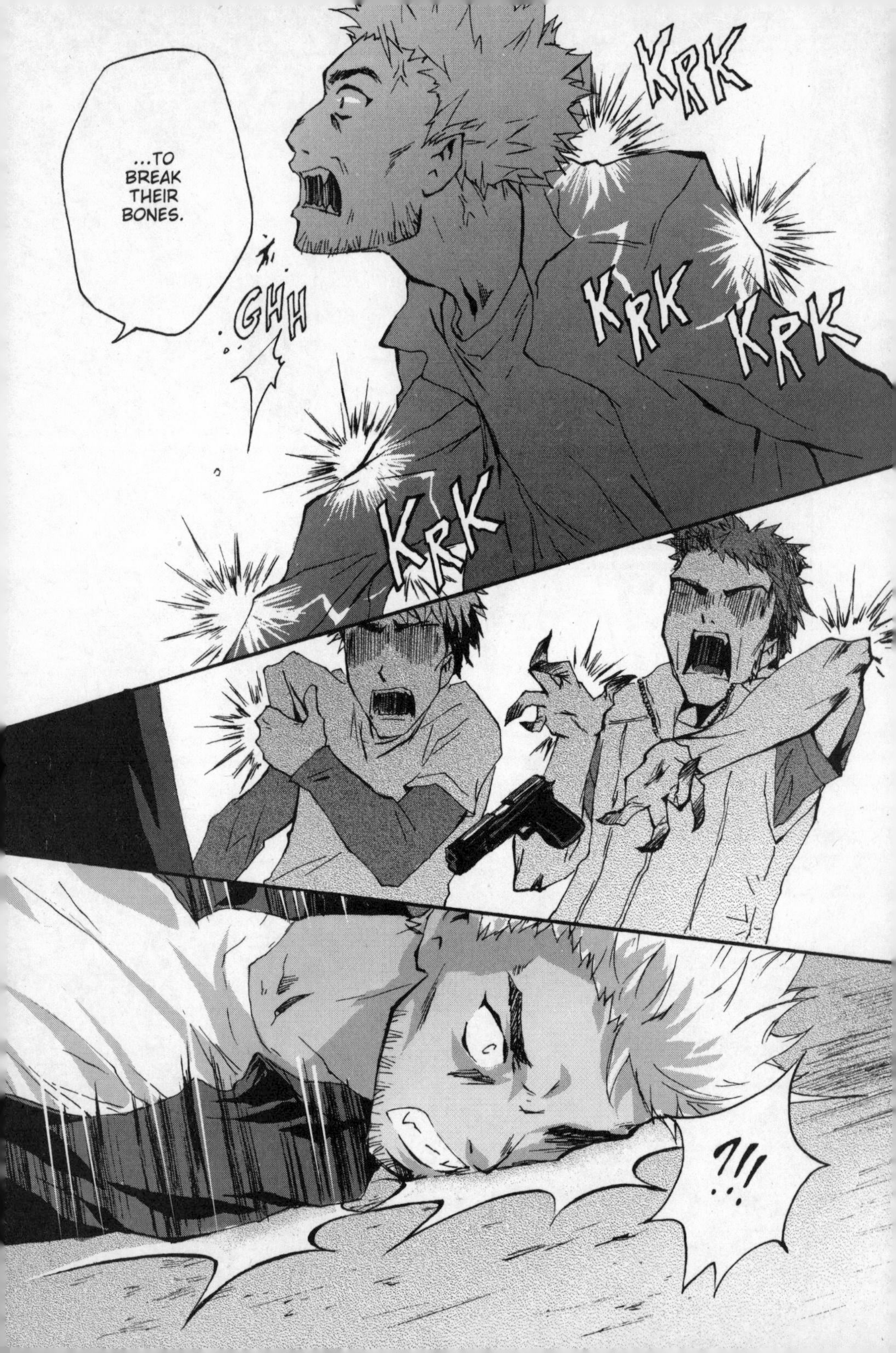
...TO BREAK THEIR BONES.
KRK
GHH
KRK
KRK
KRK
?!!

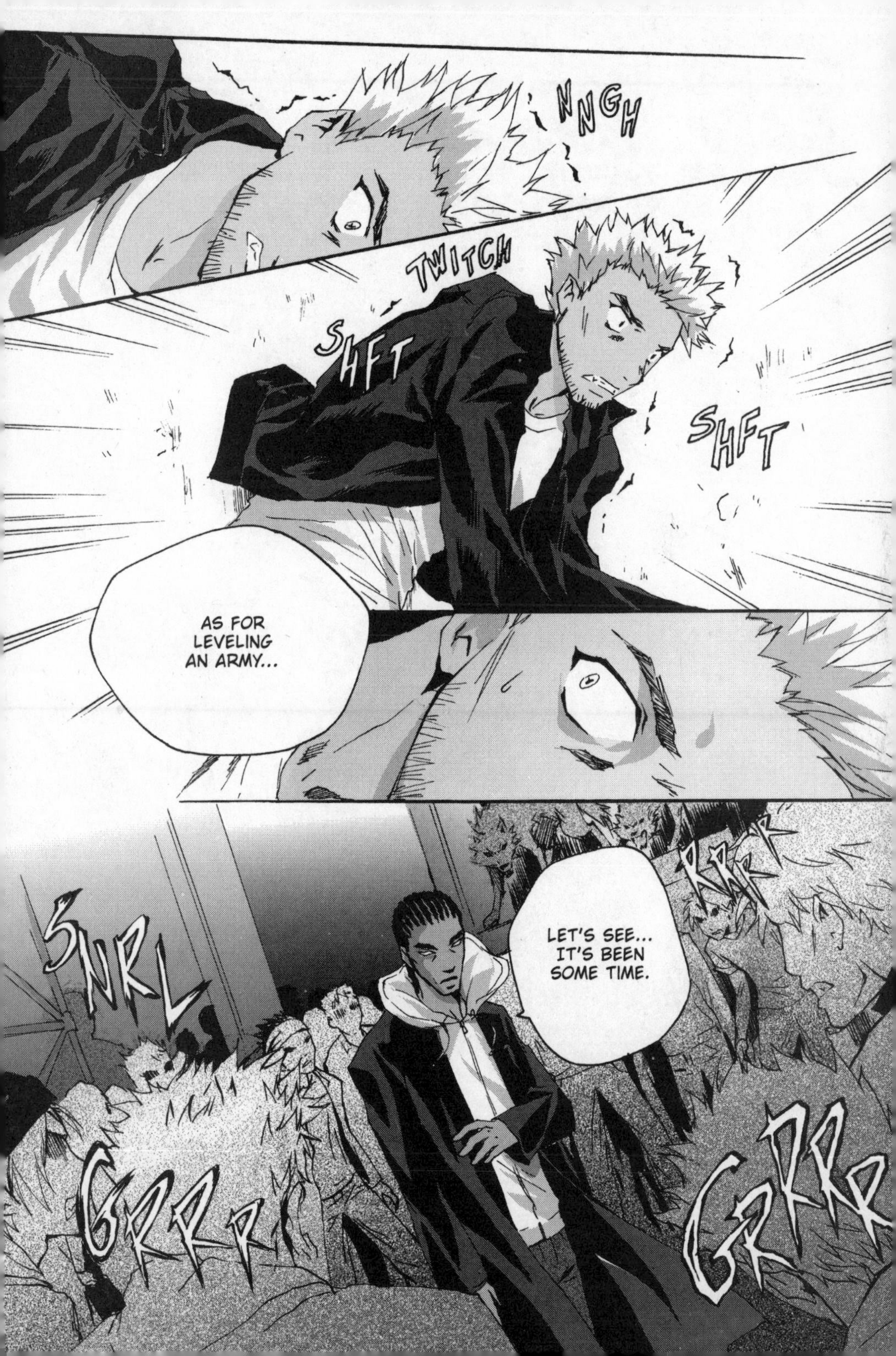
NNGH
TWITCH
SHFT
SHFT
AS FOR LEVELING AN ARMY...
SNRL
LET'S SEE... IT'S BEEN SOME TIME.
RRR
GRRR
GRRR

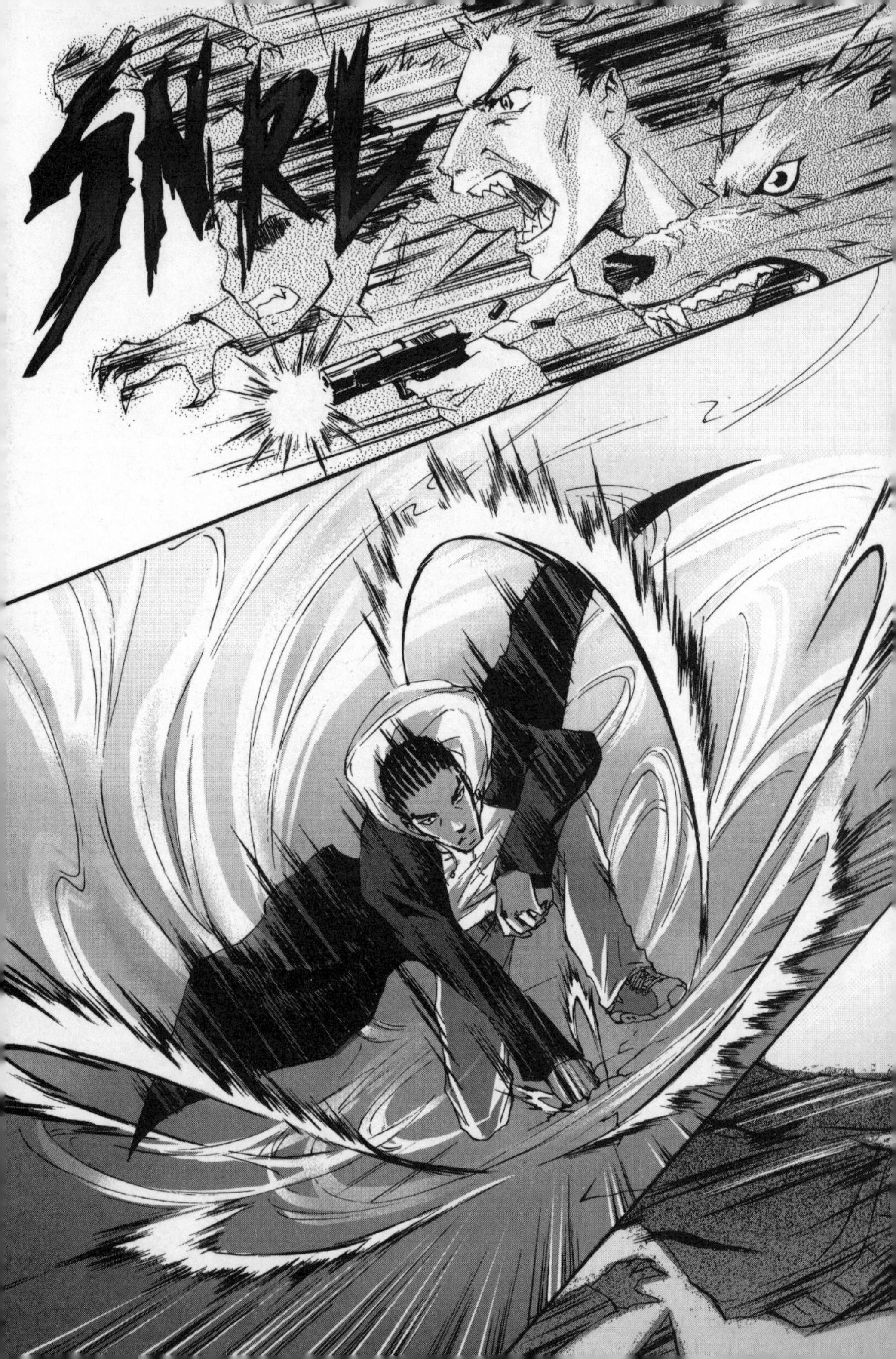
SNRL

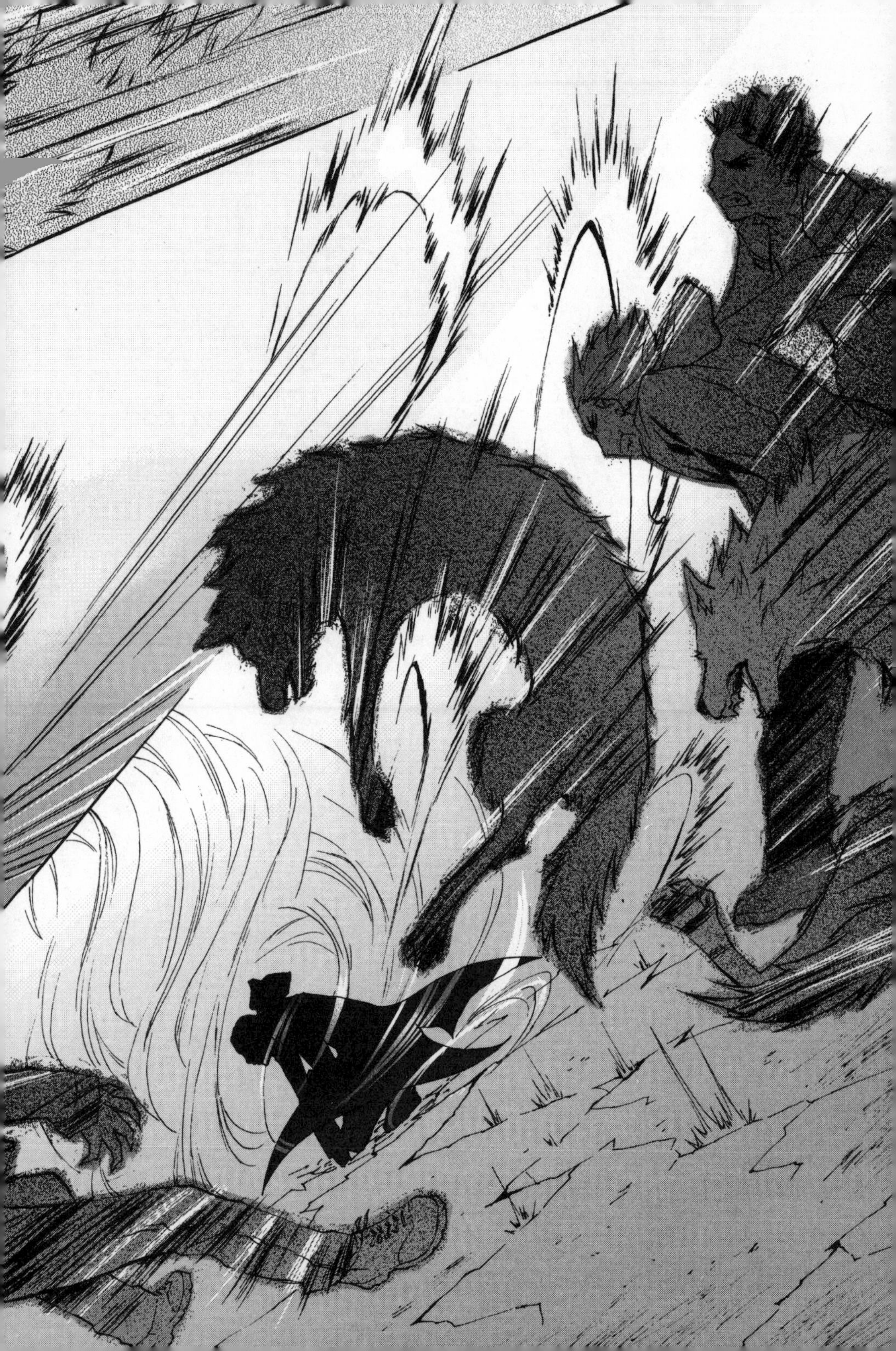

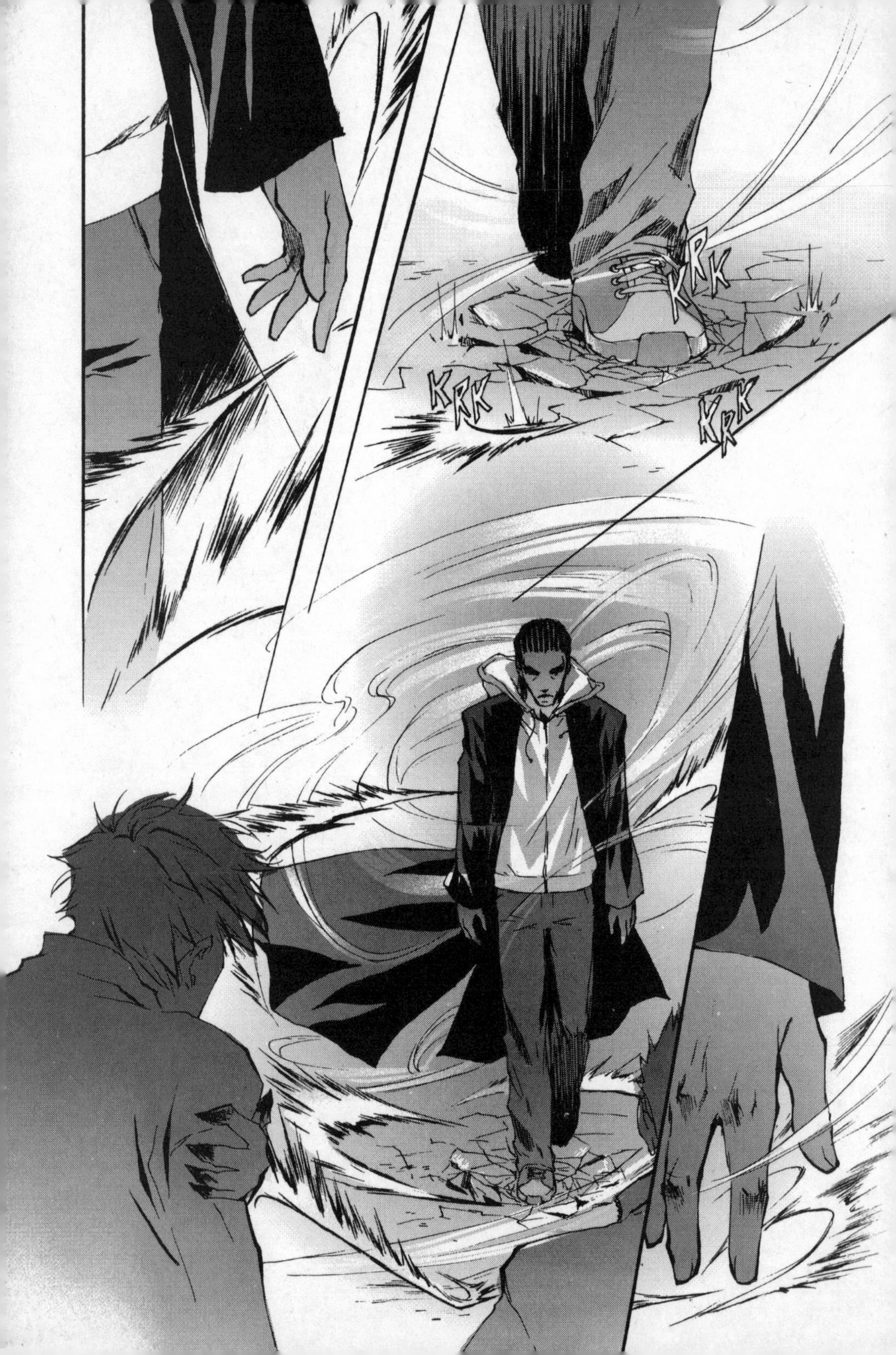
KRK
KRK
KRK

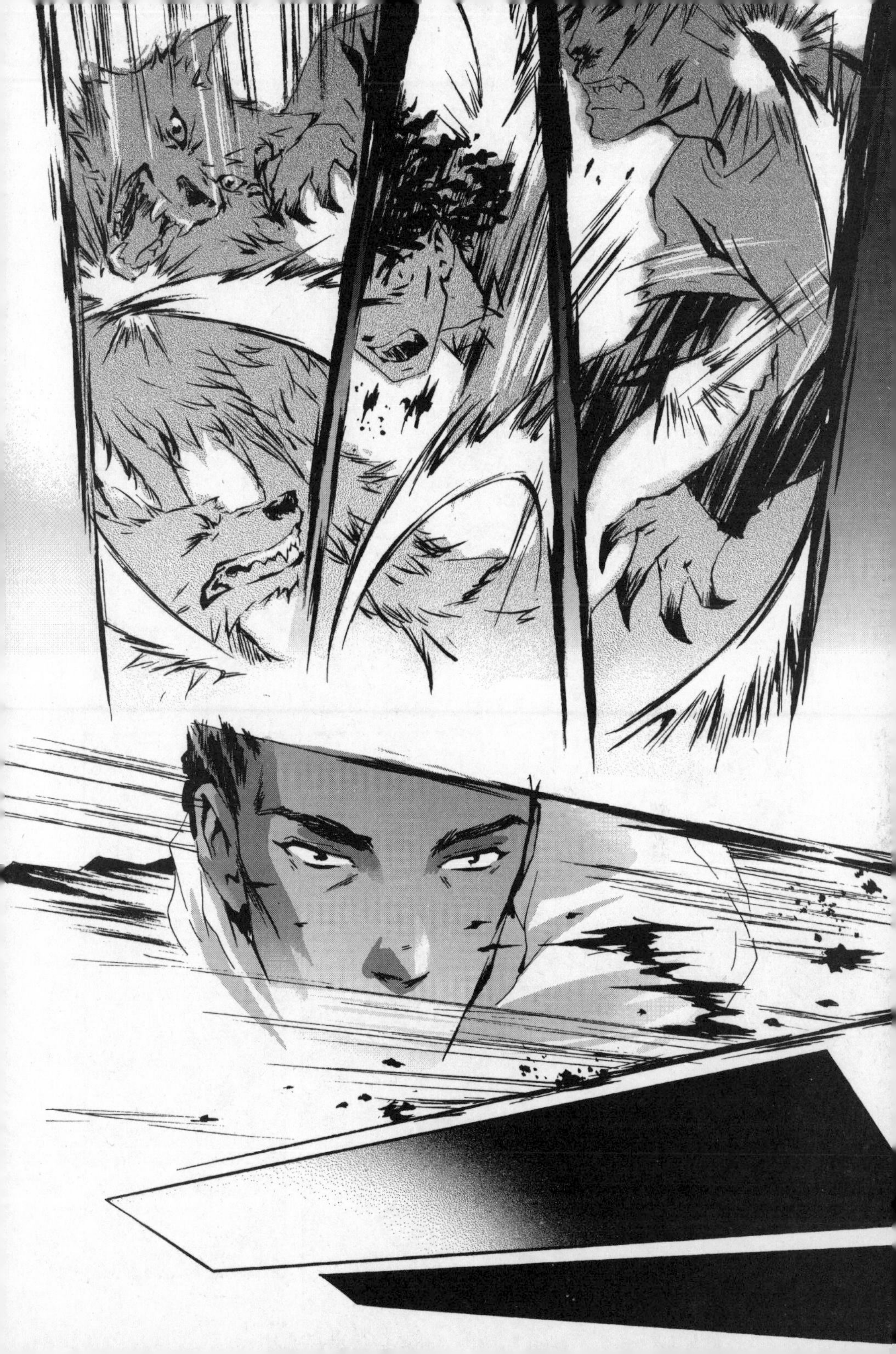

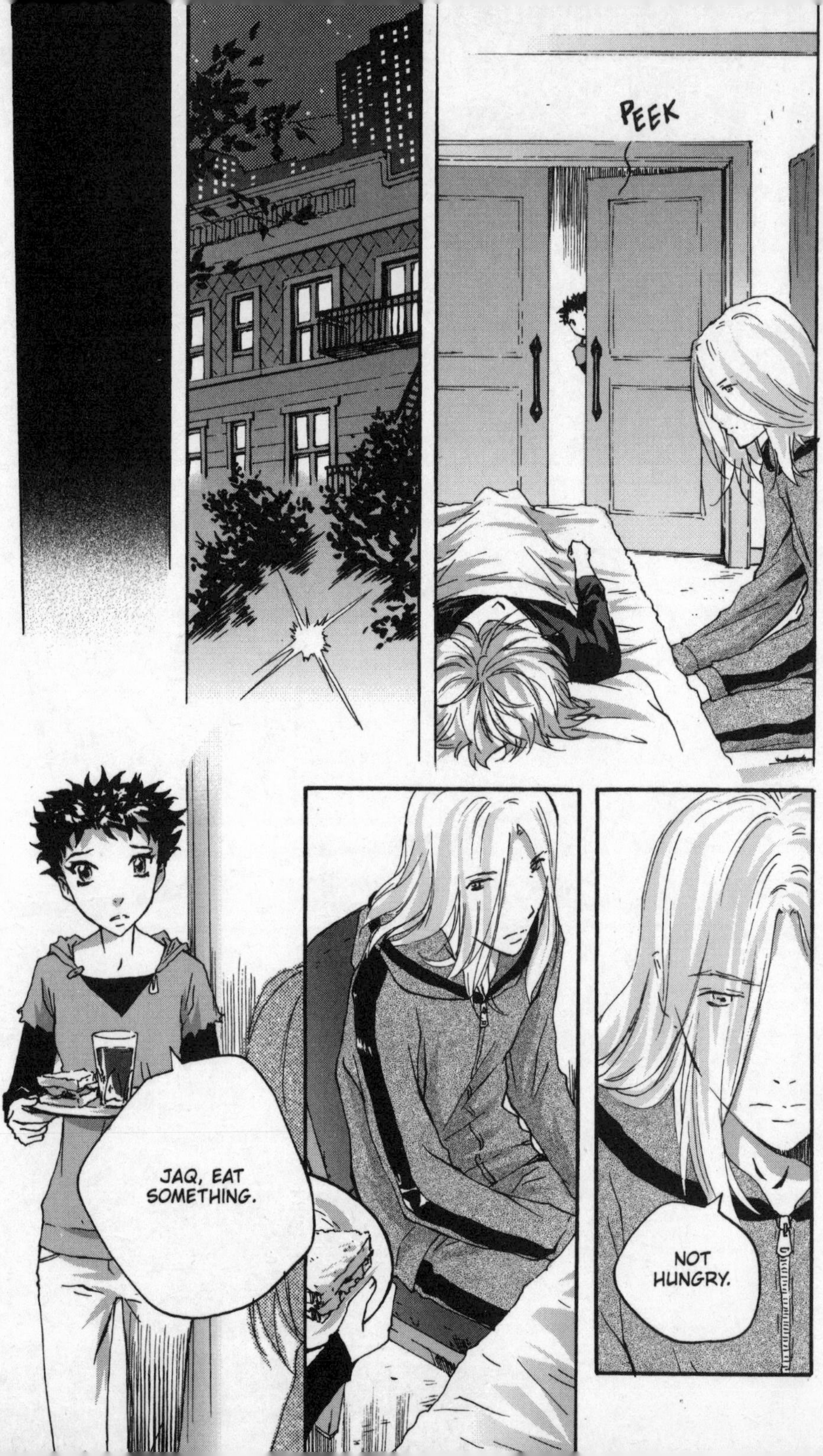
PEEK
JAQ, EAT SOMETHING.
NOT HUNGRY.

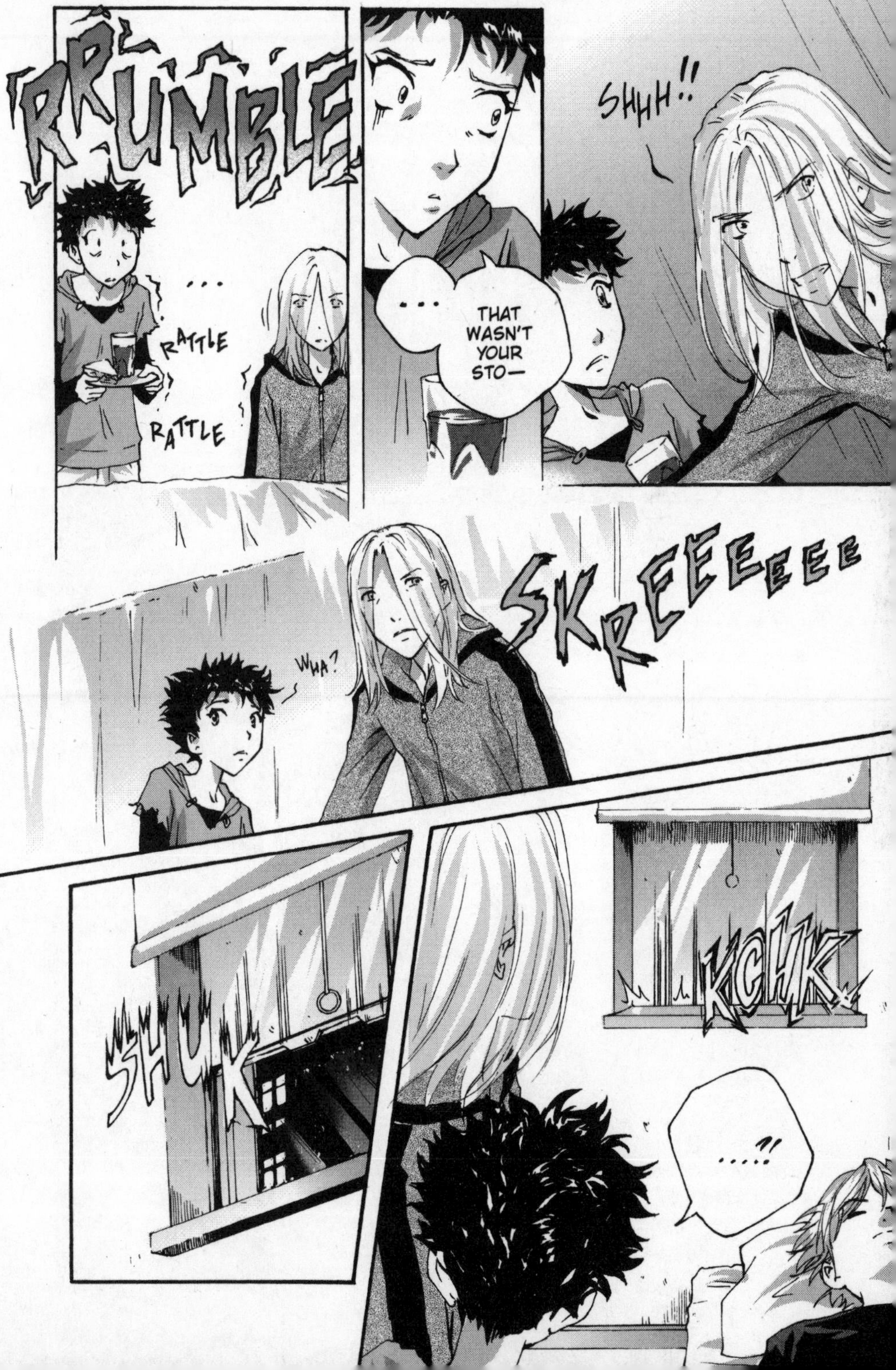
RRUMBLE
...
RATTLE
RATTLE
...
THAT WASN'T YOUR STO—
SHHH!!
SKREEEEEE
WHA?
SHUK
KCHK
....?!

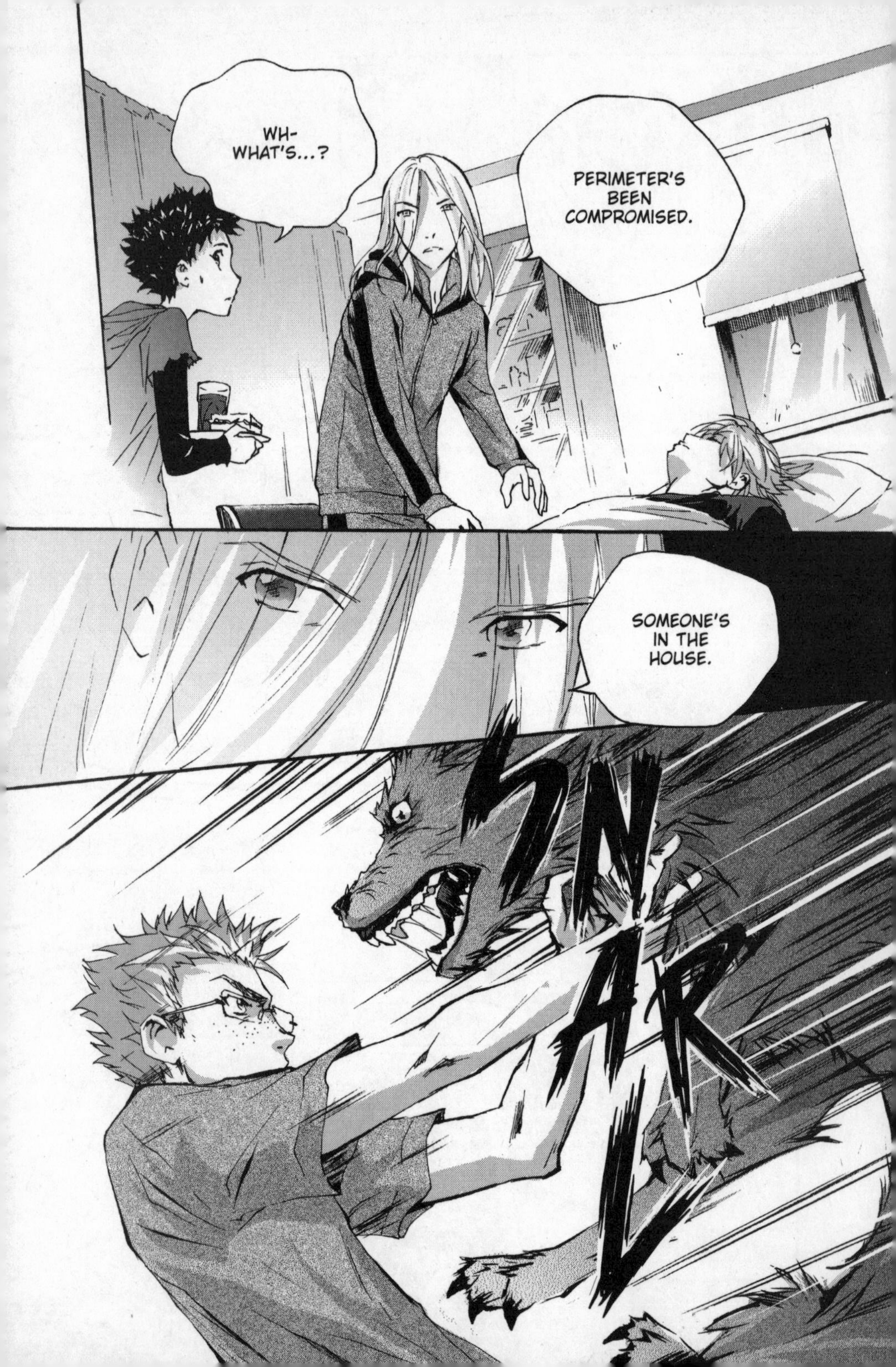
WH- WHAT'S...?
PERIMETER'S BEEN COMPROMISED.
SOMEONE'S IN THE HOUSE.
SNARL

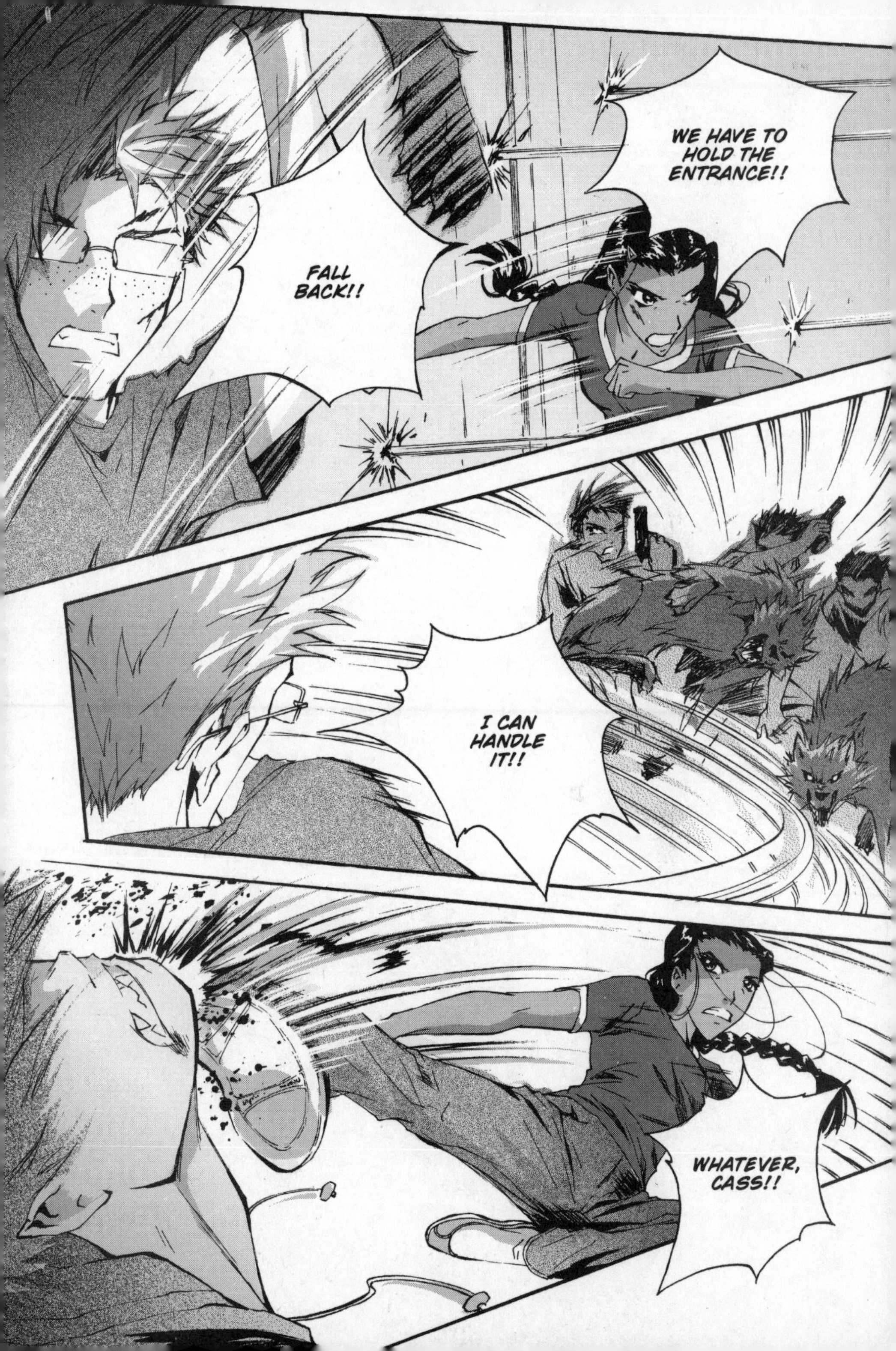
FALL BACK!!
WE HAVE TO HOLD THE ENTRANCE!!
I CAN HANDLE IT!!
WHATEVER, CASS!!

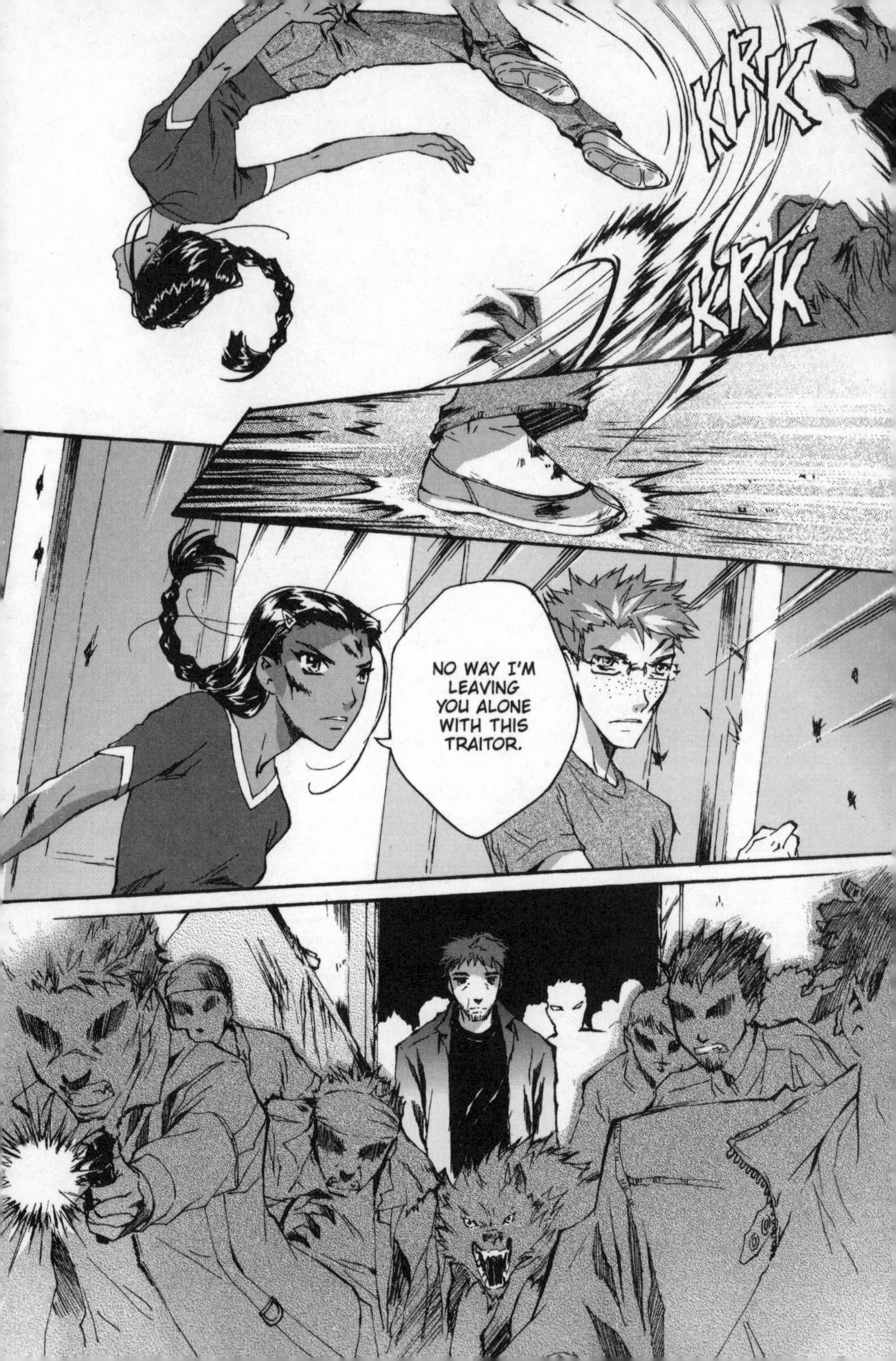
KRK
KRK
NO WAY I'M LEAVING YOU ALONE WITH THIS TRAITOR.

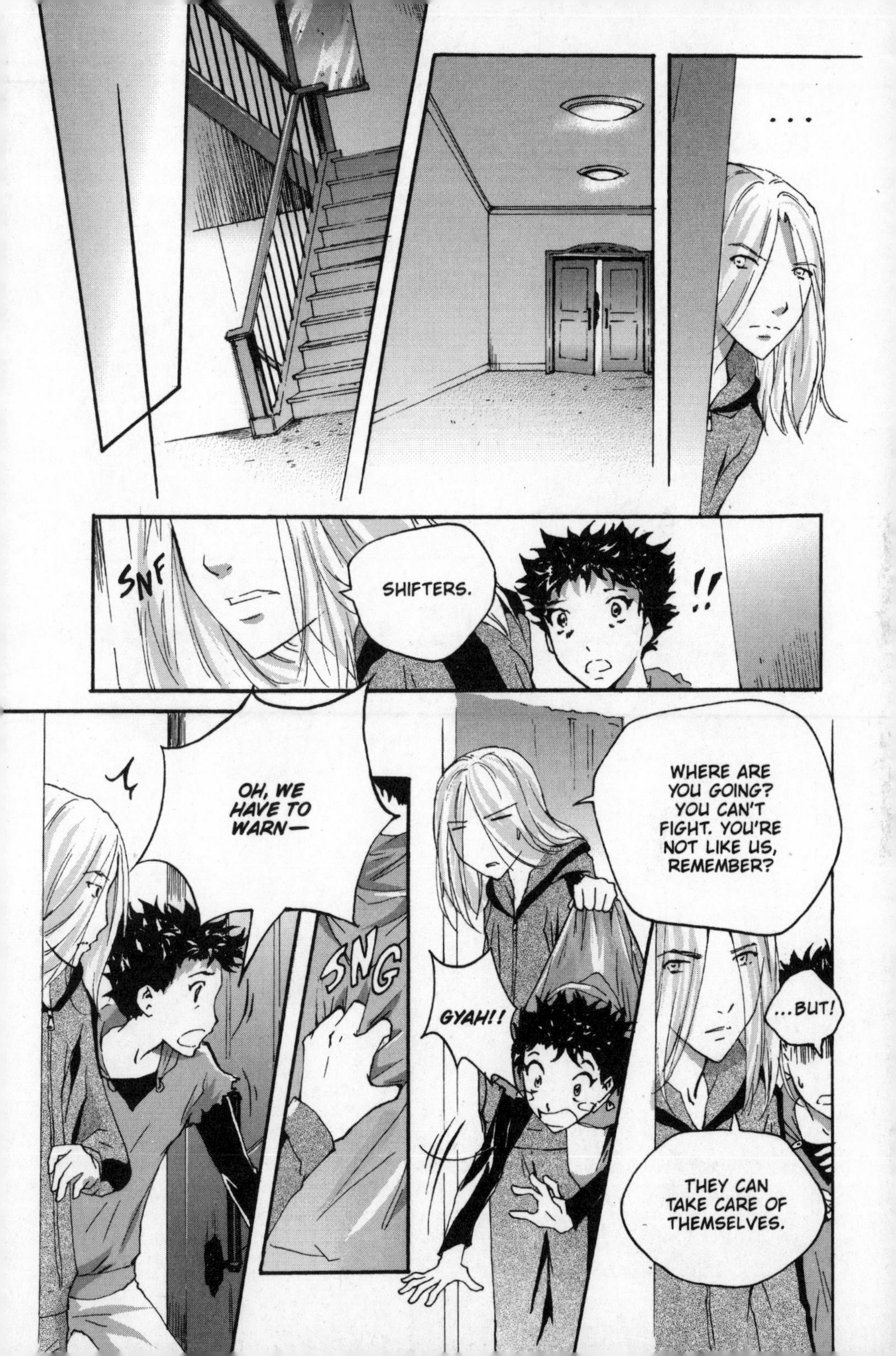
...
SNF
SHIFTERS.
!!
OH, WE HAVE TO WARN—
SNG
WHERE ARE YOU GOING? YOU CAN'T FIGHT. YOU'RE NOT LIKE US, REMEMBER?
GYAH!!
...BUT!
THEY CAN TAKE CARE OF THEMSELVES.

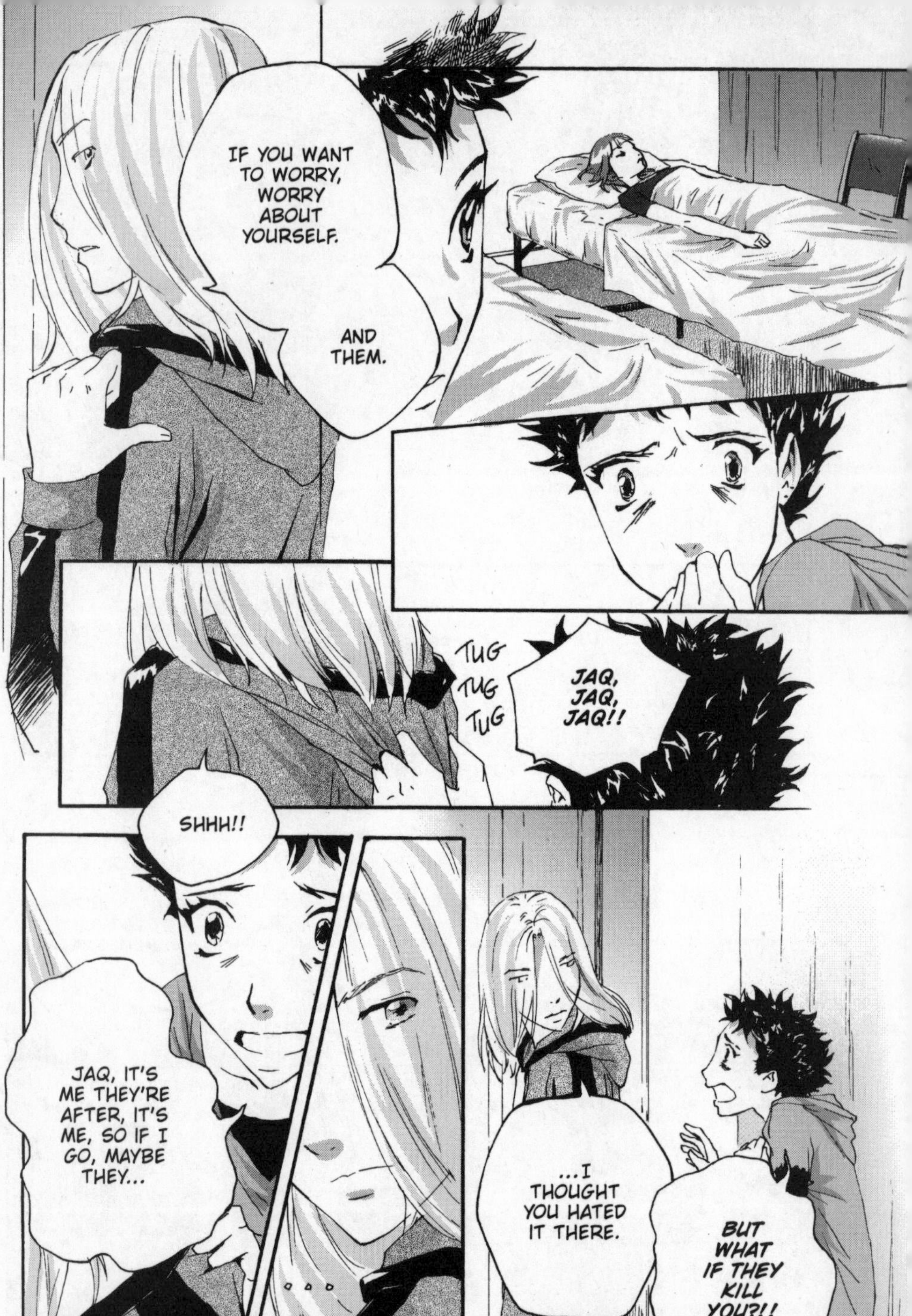
IF YOU WANT TO WORRY, WORRY ABOUT YOURSELF.
AND THEM.
TUG TUG TUG
JAQ, JAQ, JAQ!!
SHHH!!
JAQ, IT'S ME THEY'RE AFTER, IT'S ME, SO IF I GO, MAYBE THEY...
...
...I THOUGHT YOU HATED IT THERE.
BUT WHAT IF THEY KILL YOU?!!

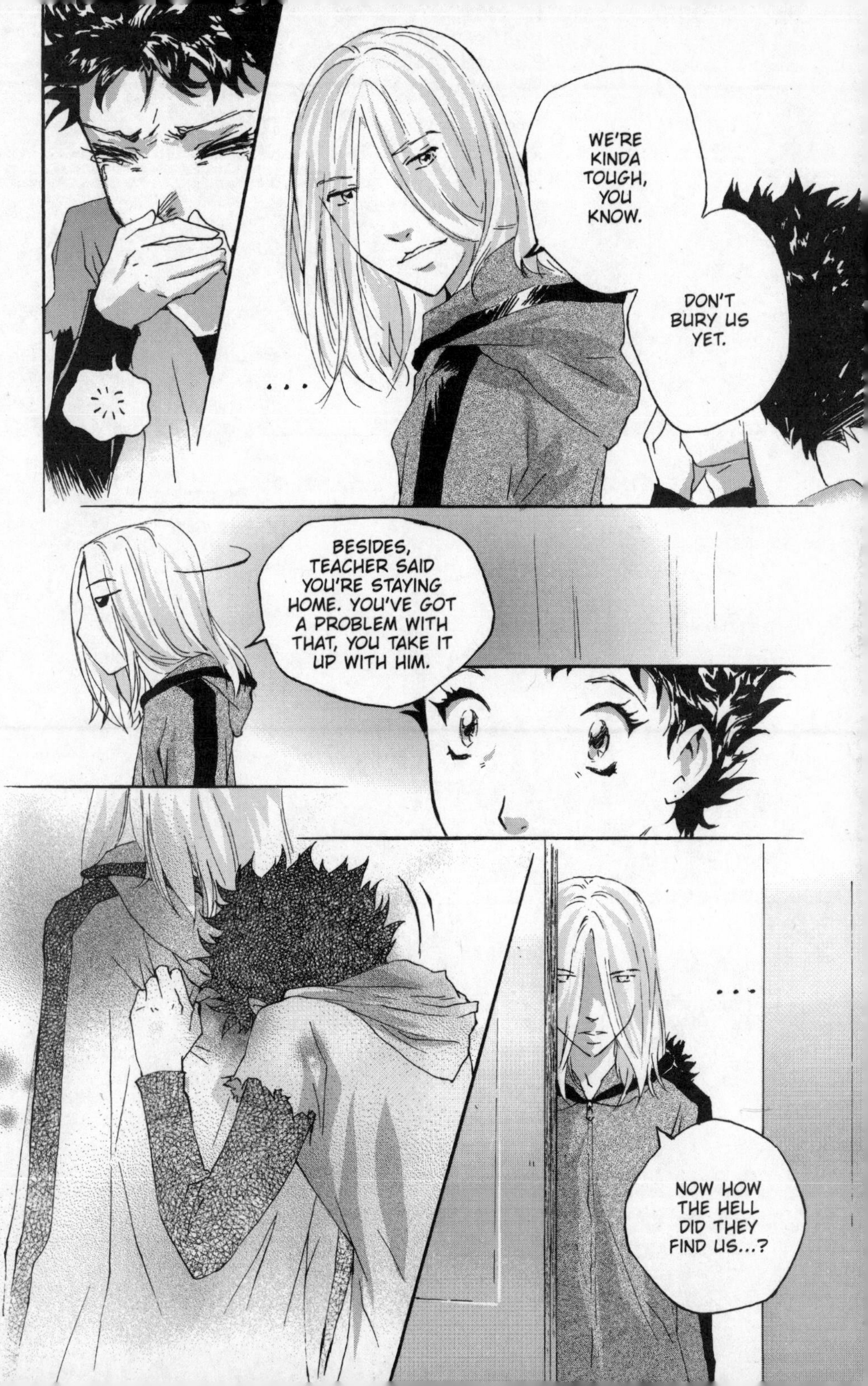
...
WE'RE KINDA TOUGH, YOU KNOW.
DON'T BURY US YET.
BESIDES, TEACHER SAID YOU'RE STAYING HOME. YOU'VE GOT A PROBLEM WITH THAT, YOU TAKE IT UP WITH HIM.
...
NOW HOW THE HELL DID THEY FIND US...?

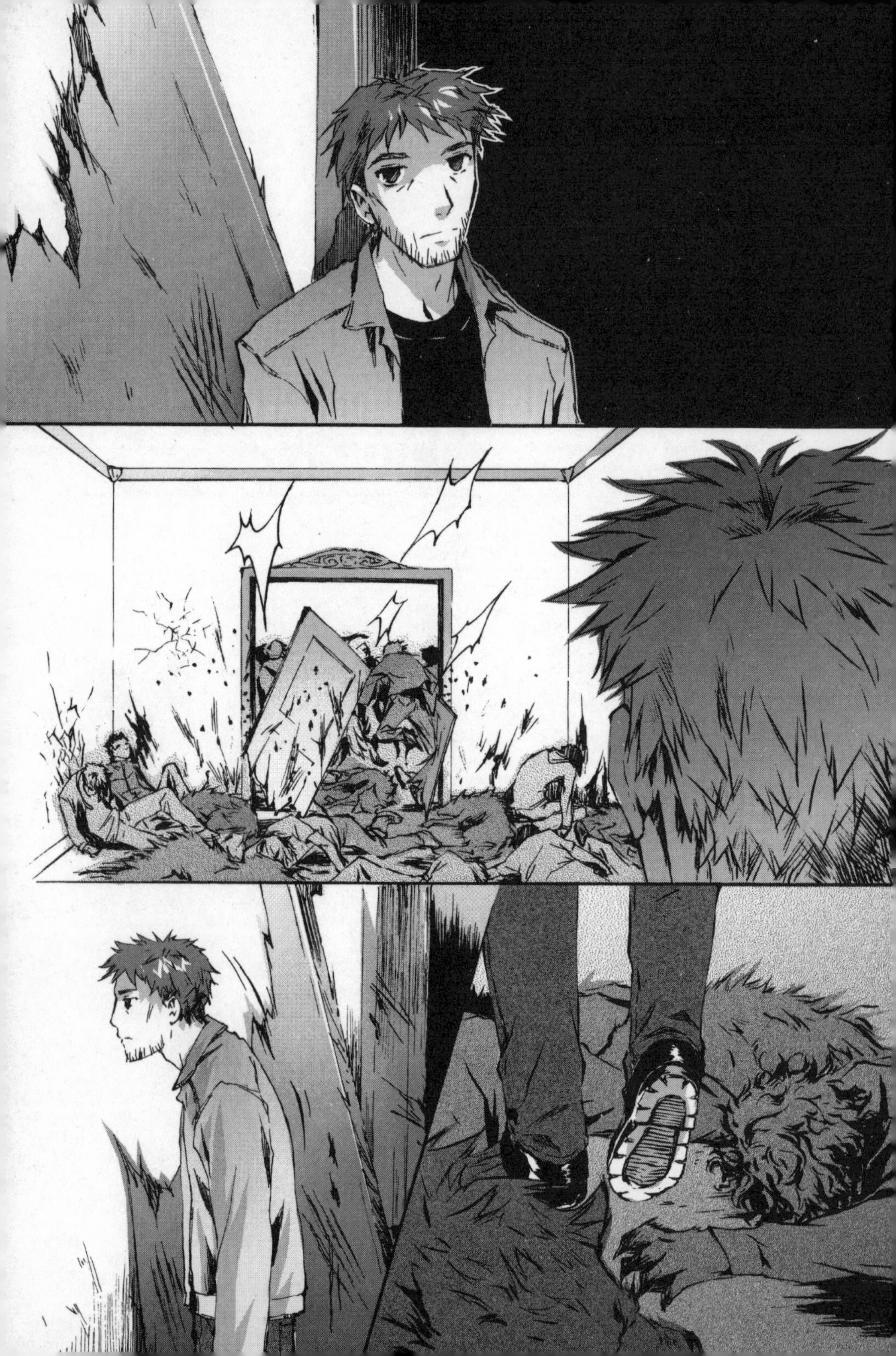

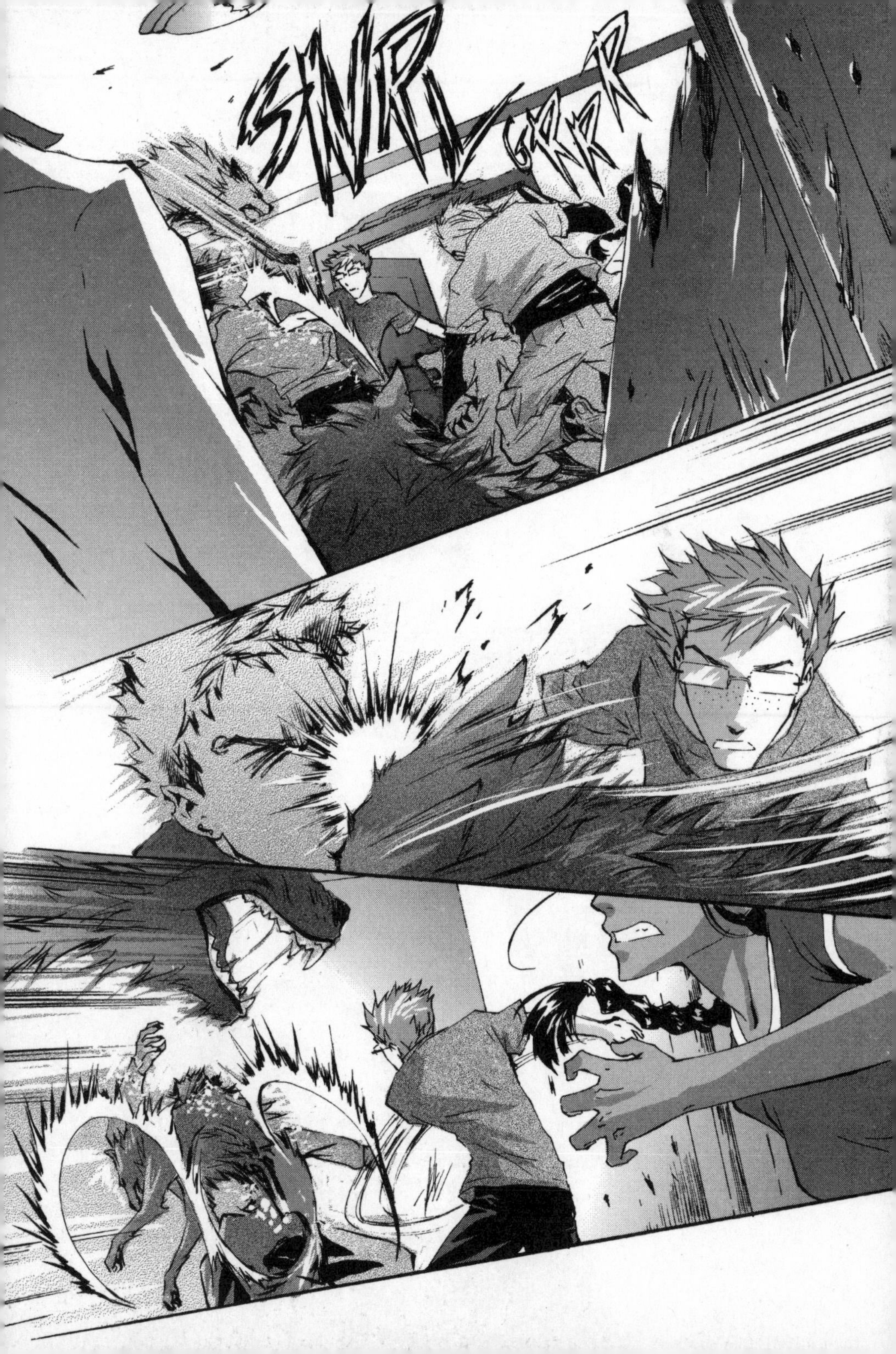
SNRL
GRRR

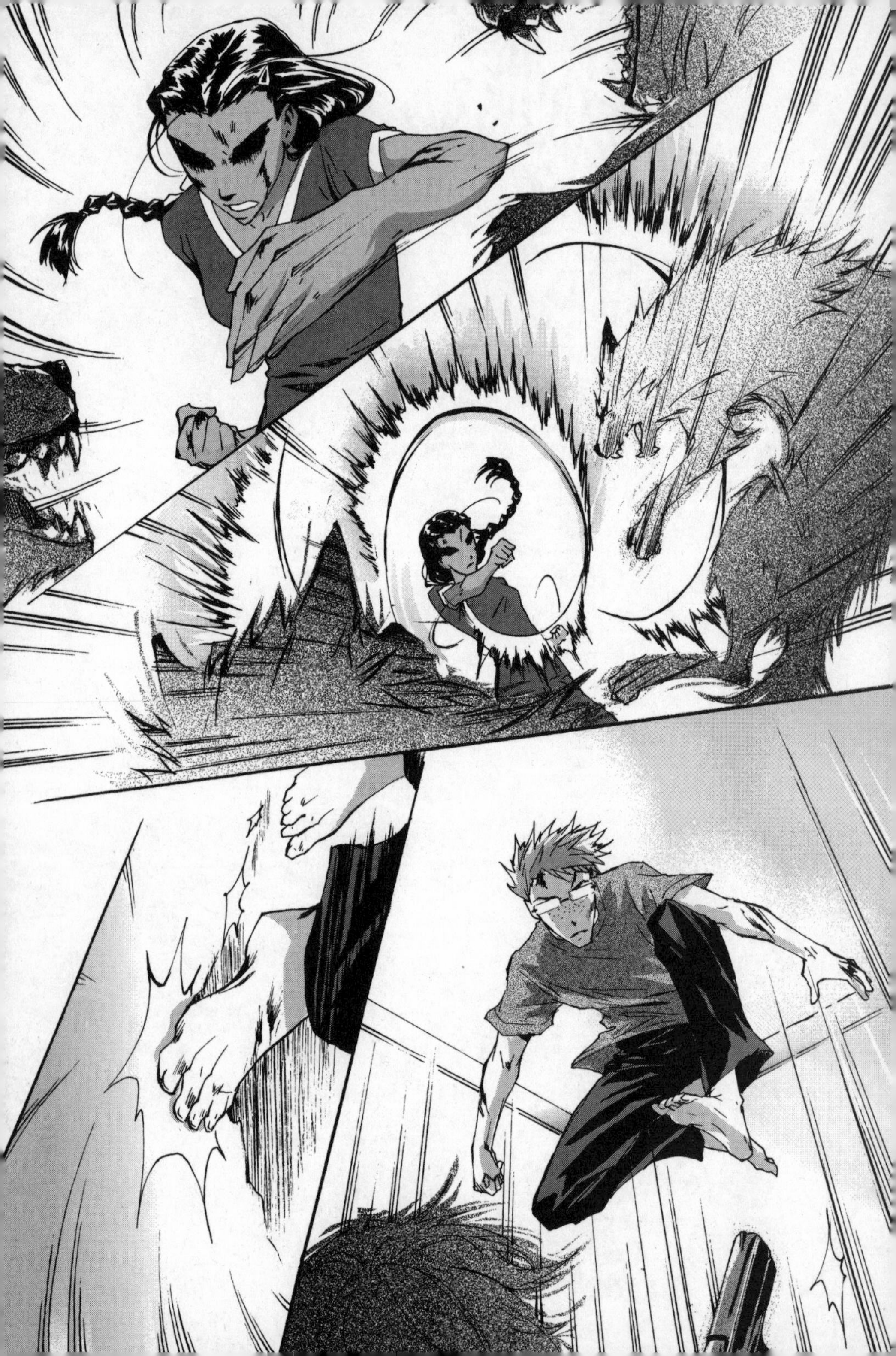

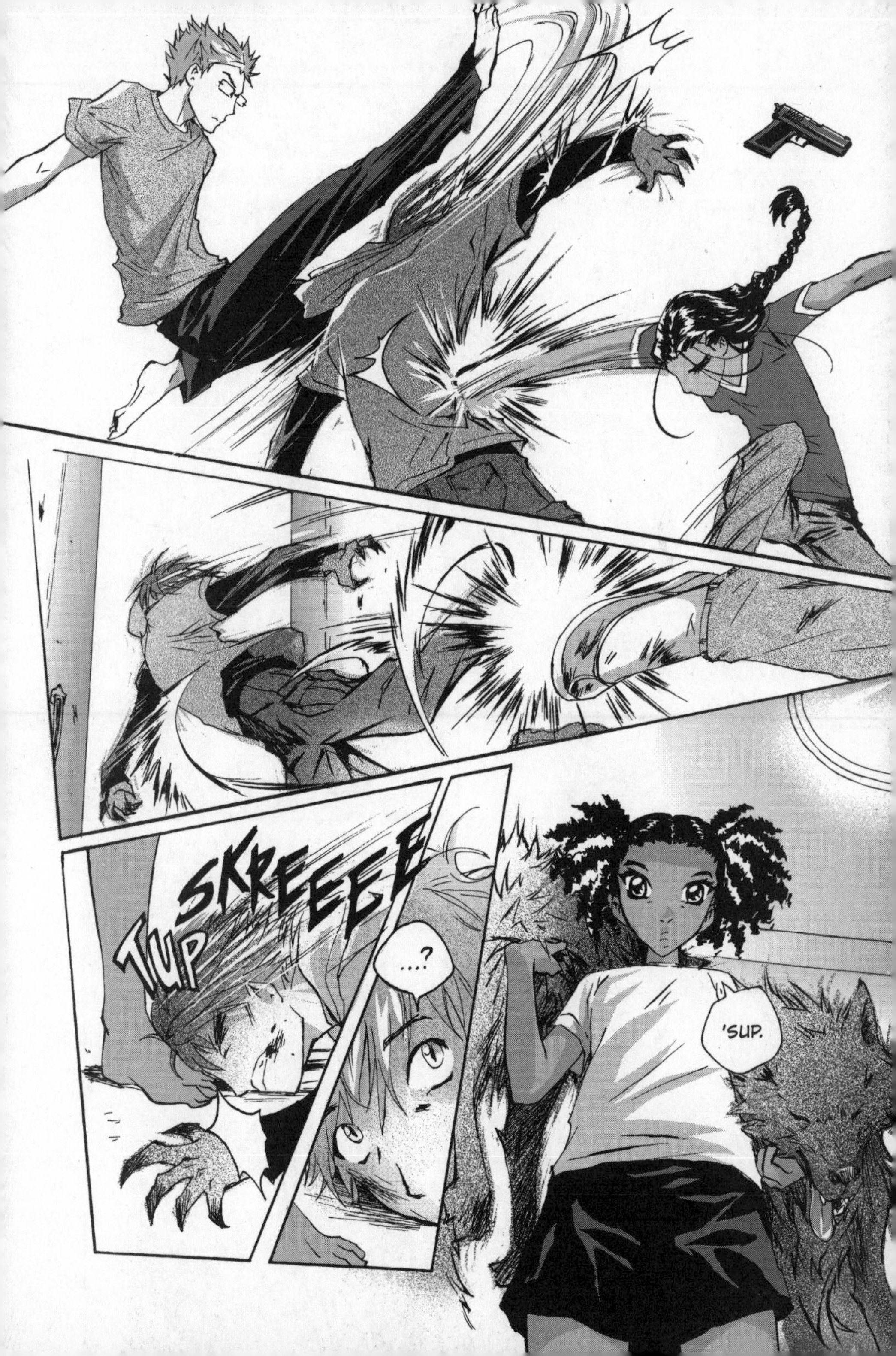
TUP
SKREEEEE
...?
'SUP.

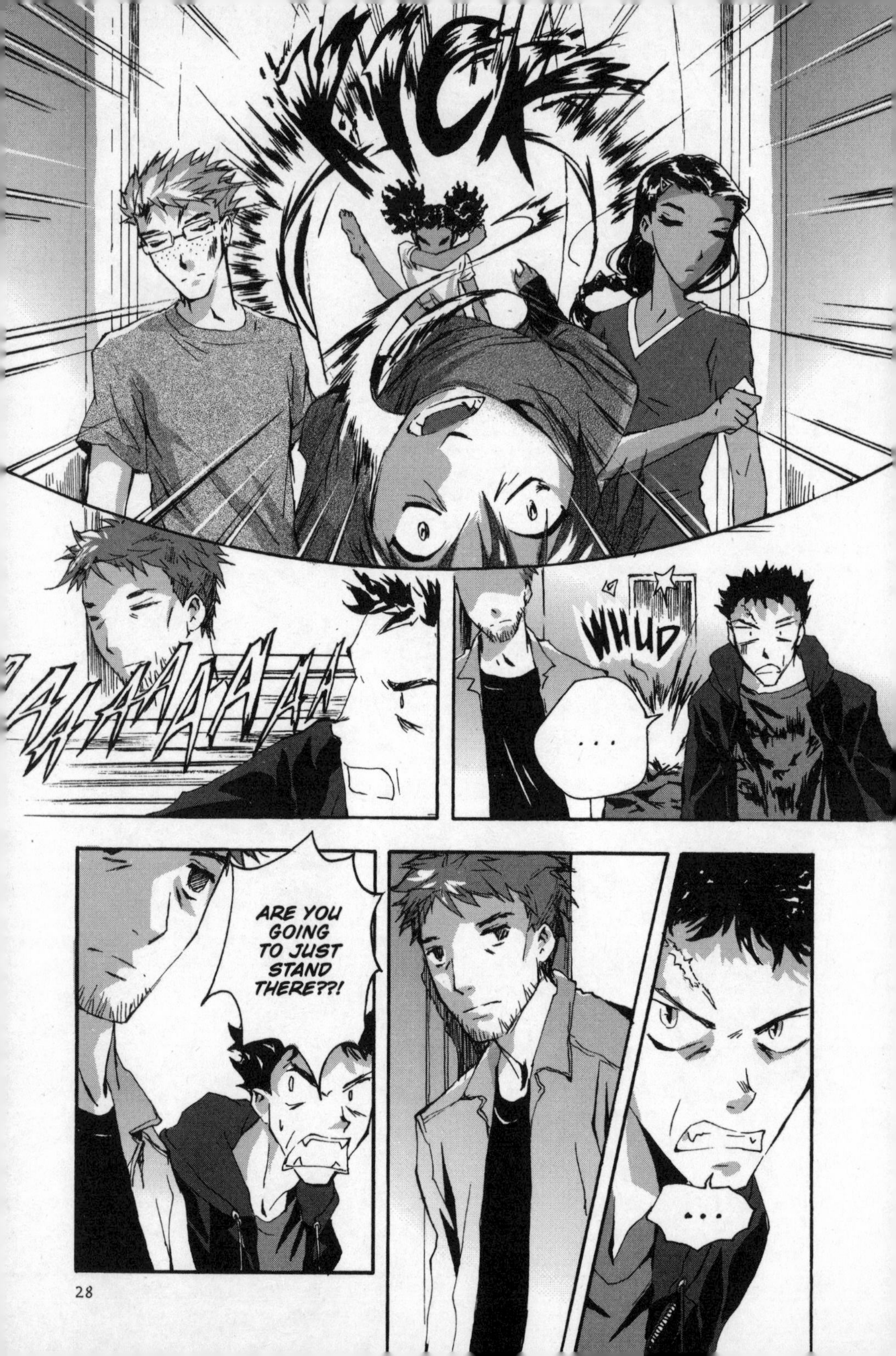
WHACK
WHUD
...
ARE YOU GOING TO JUST STAND THERE??!
...

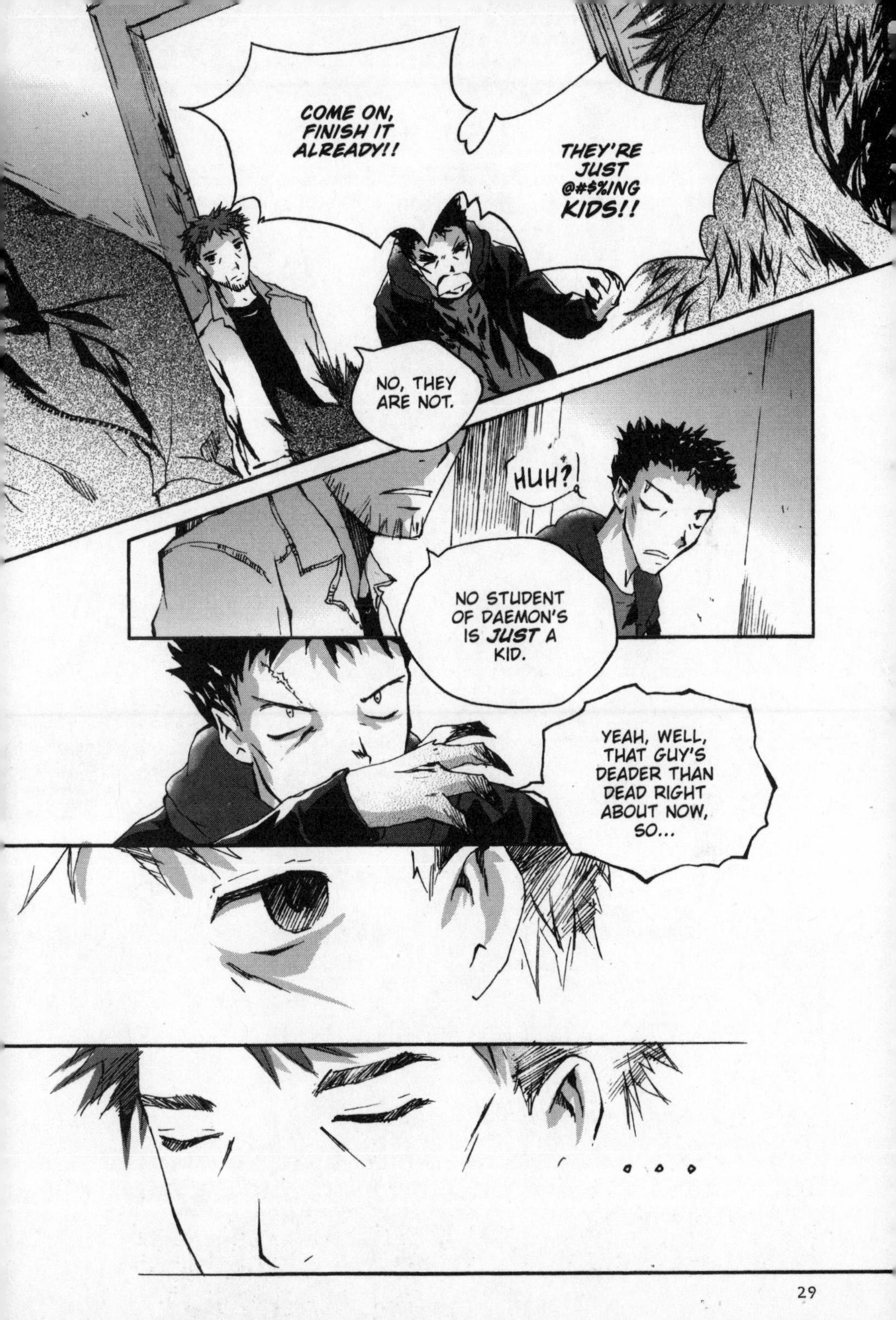
COME ON, FINISH IT ALREADY!!
THEY'RE JUST @#$%ING KIDS!!
NO, THEY ARE NOT.
HUH?!
NO STUDENT OF DAEMON'S IS JUST A KID.
YEAH, WELL, THAT GUY'S DEADER THAN DEAD RIGHT ABOUT NOW, SO...
...

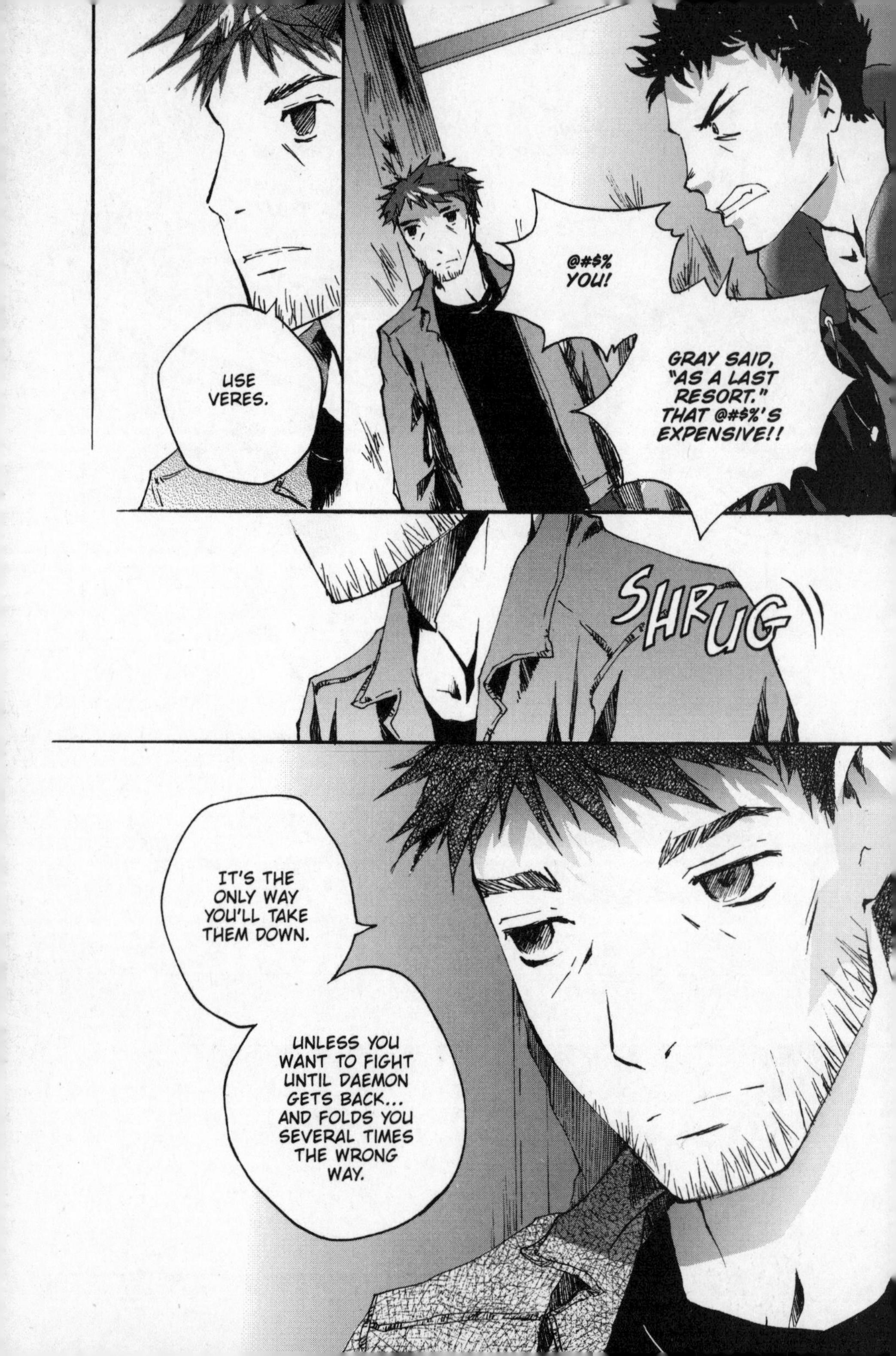
USE VERES.
@#$% YOU!
GRAY SAID, "AS A LAST RESORT." THAT @#$%'S EXPENSIVE!!
SHRUG
IT'S THE ONLY WAY YOU'LL TAKE THEM DOWN.
UNLESS YOU WANT TO FIGHT UNTIL DAEMON GETS BACK... AND FOLDS YOU SEVERAL TIMES THE WRONG WAY.

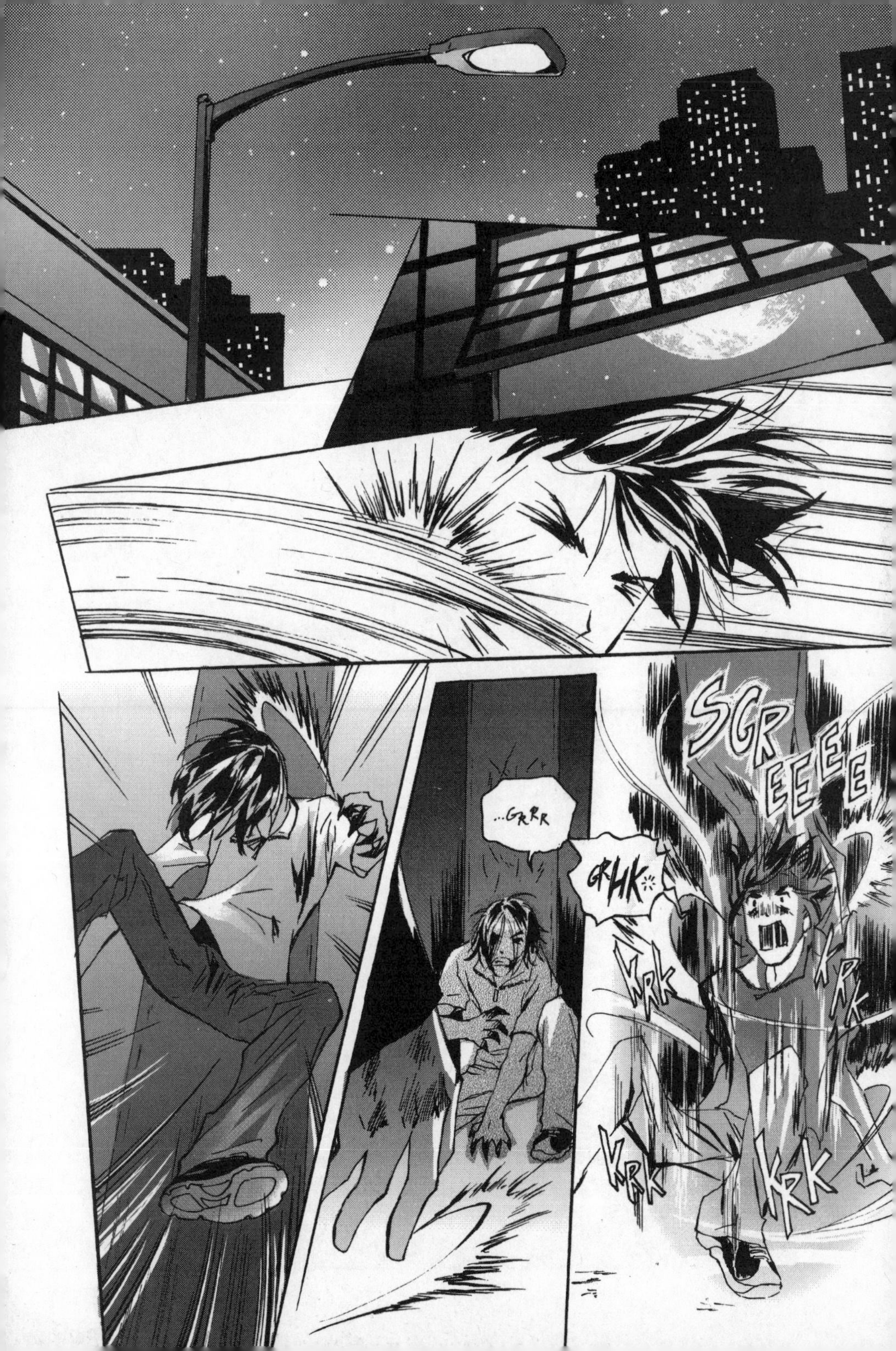
...GRRR
GRHK
SGREEEEE
KRK
KRK
KRK
KRK

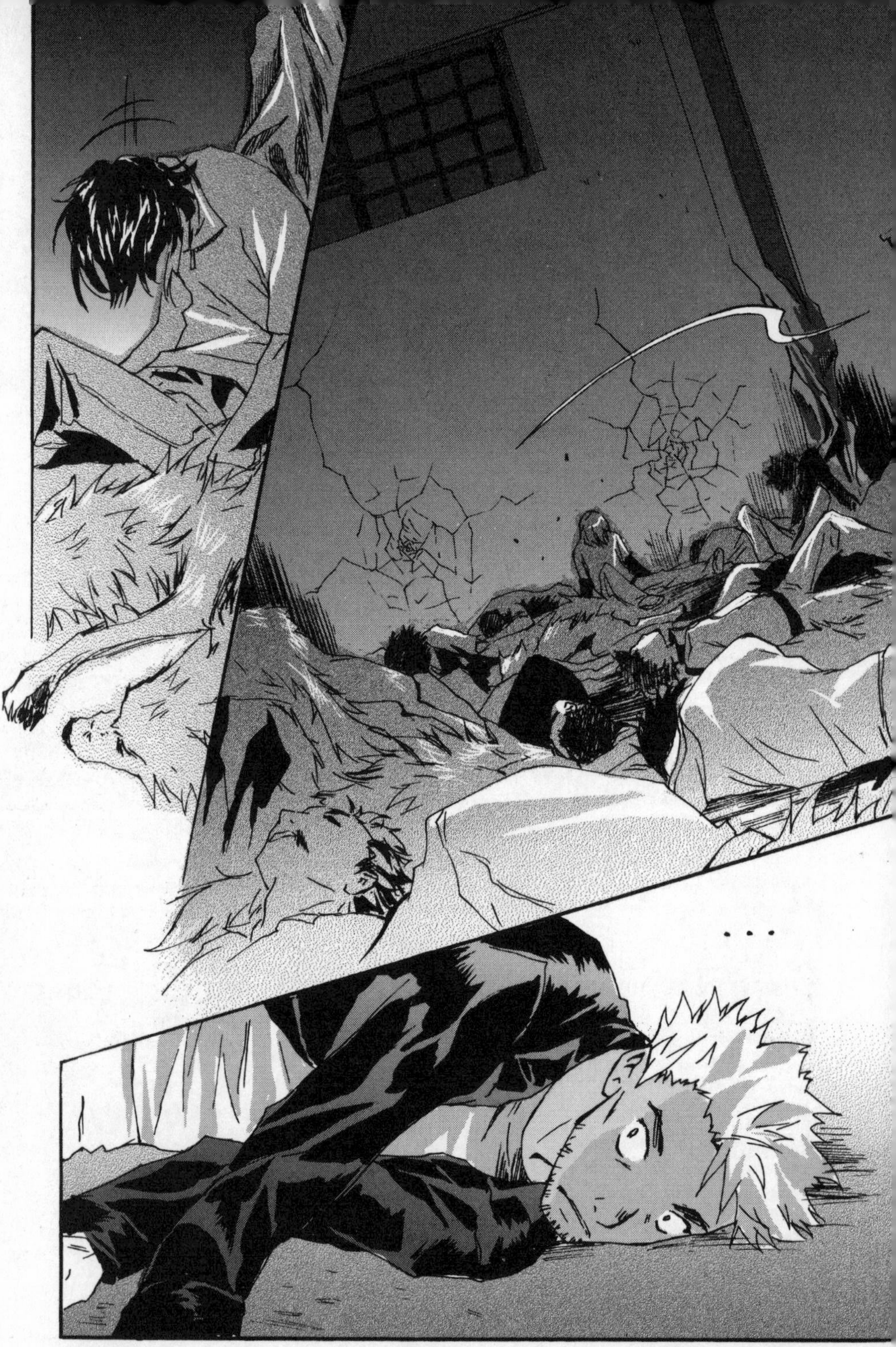
...

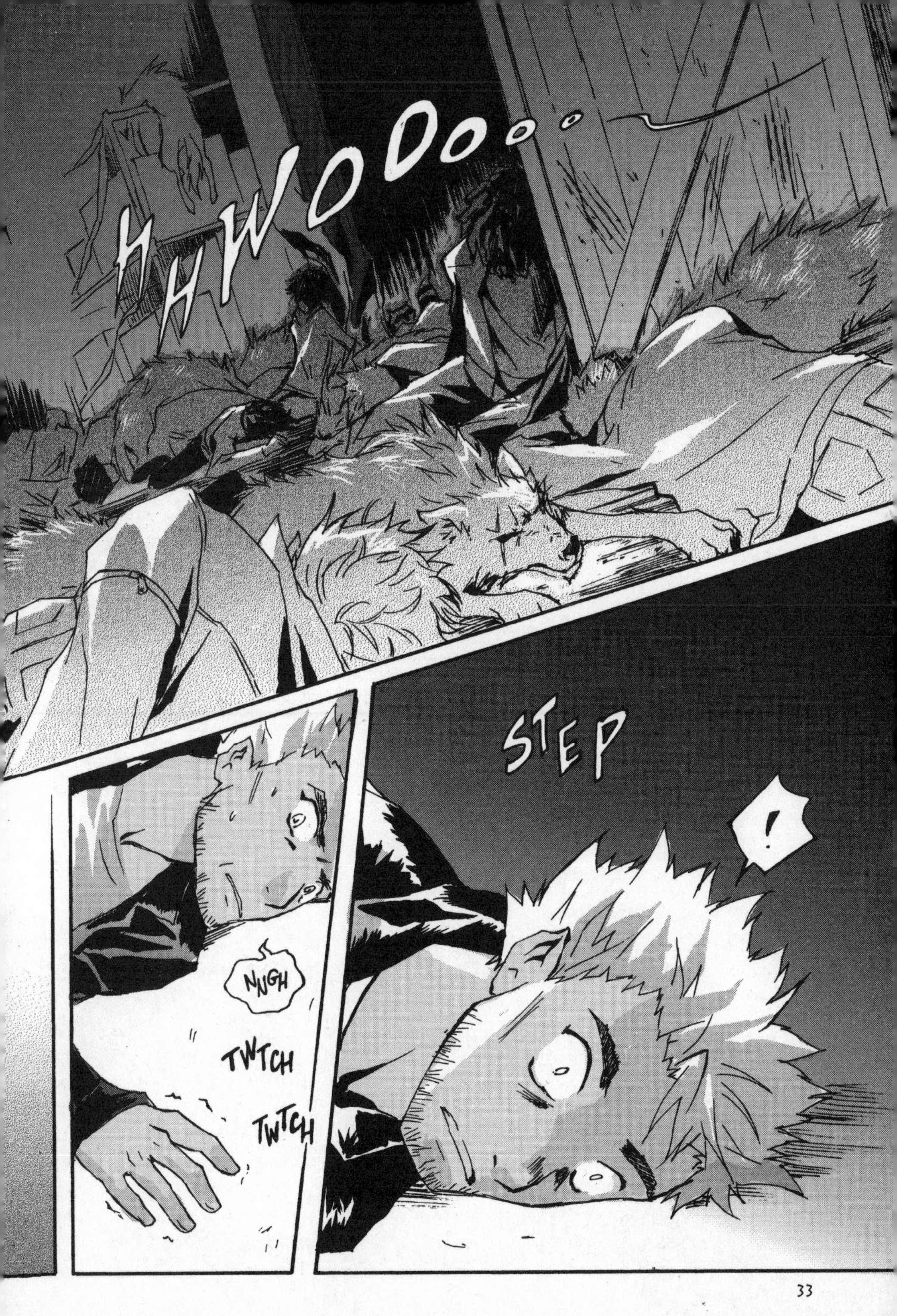
HWOOoo...
STEP
!
NNGH
TWTCH
TWTCH

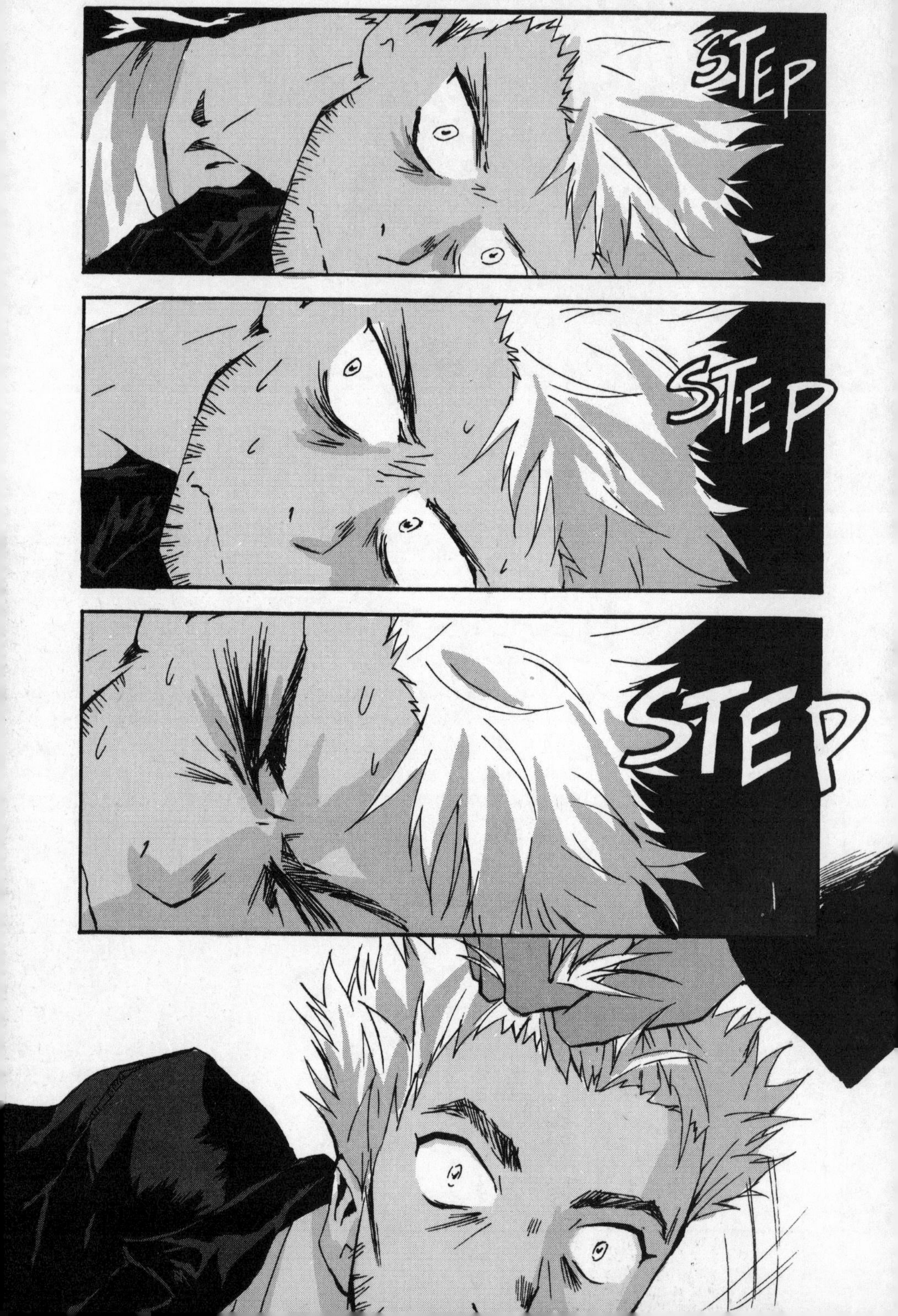
STEP
STEP
STEP

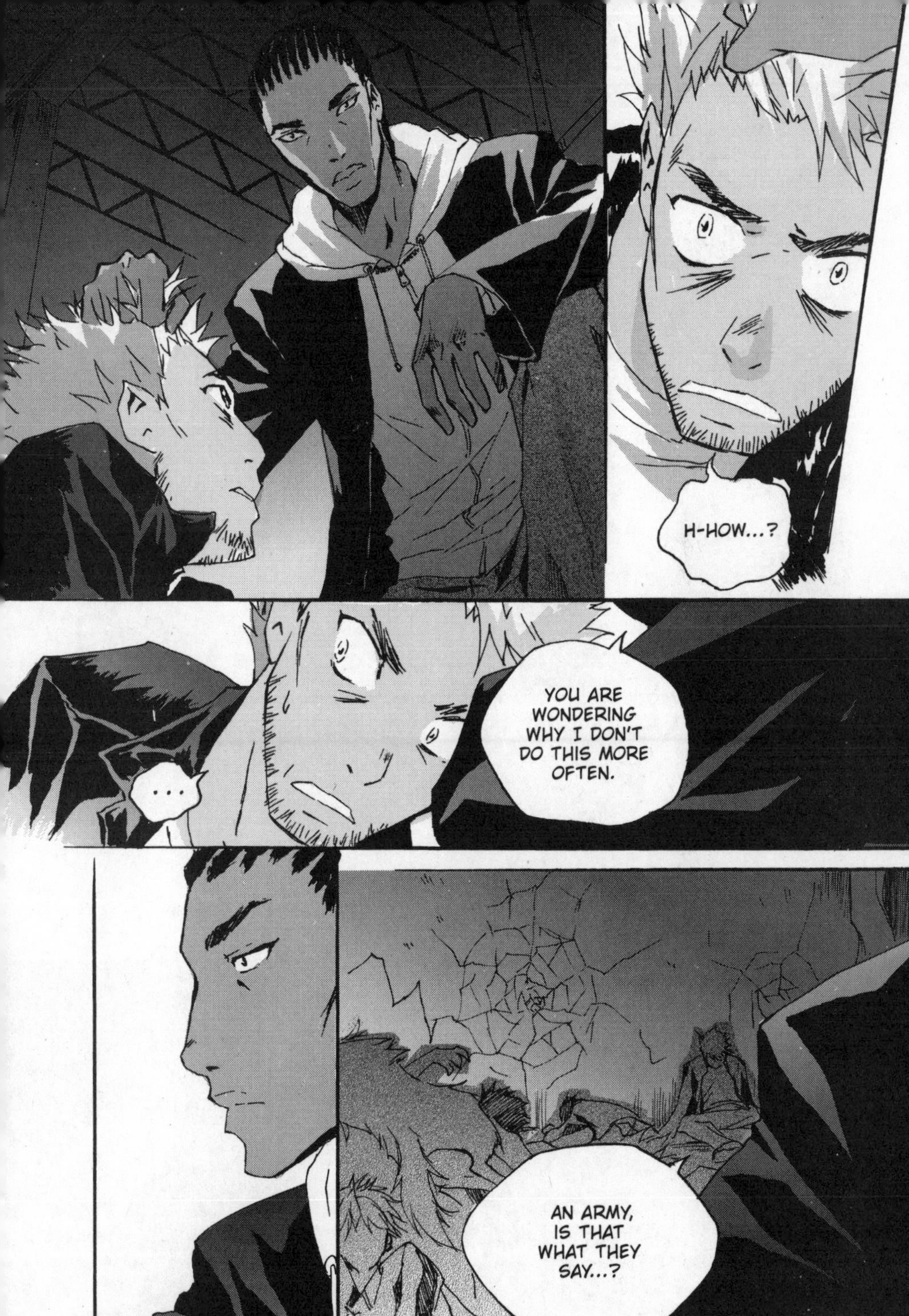
H-HOW...?
...
YOU ARE WONDERING WHY I DON'T DO THIS MORE OFTEN.
AN ARMY, IS THAT WHAT THEY SAY...?

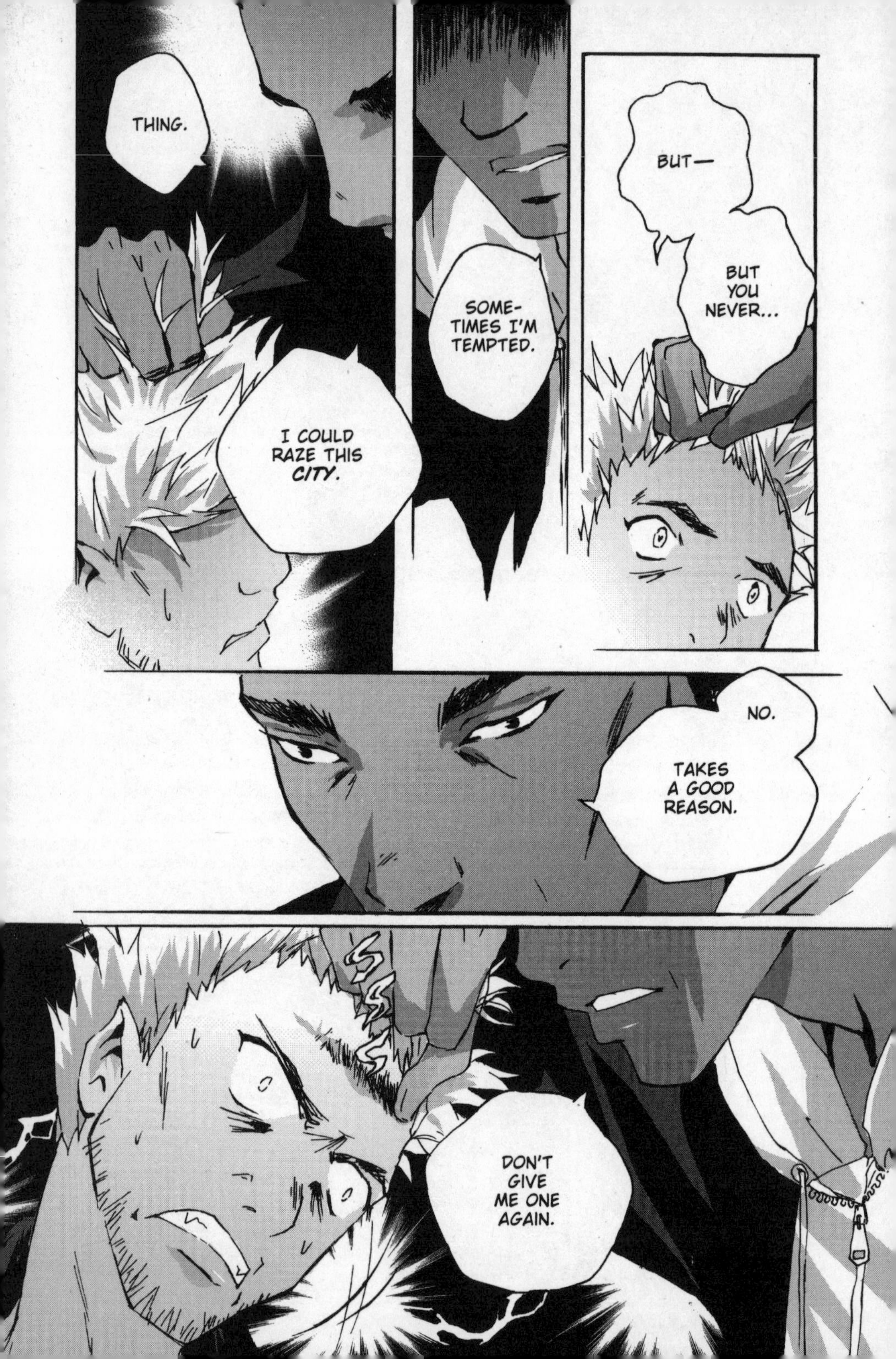
THING.
I COULD RAZE THIS *CITY*.
SOME-TIMES I'M TEMPTED.
BUT—
BUT YOU NEVER...
NO.
TAKES A GOOD REASON.
DON'T GIVE ME ONE AGAIN.

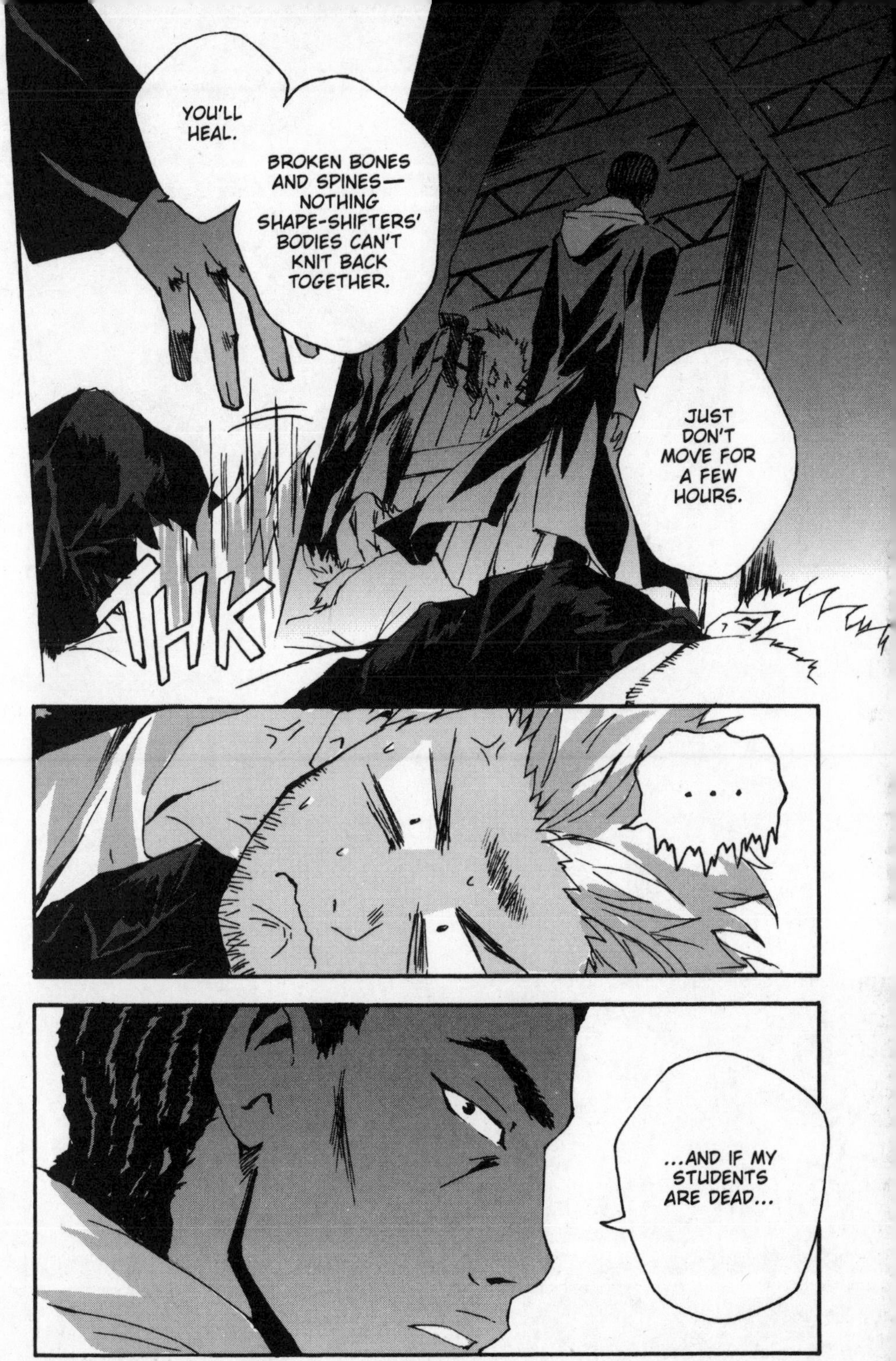
YOU'LL HEAL.
BROKEN BONES AND SPINES— NOTHING SHAPE-SHIFTERS' BODIES CAN'T KNIT BACK TOGETHER.
JUST DON'T MOVE FOR A FEW HOURS.
THK
...
...AND IF MY STUDENTS ARE DEAD...

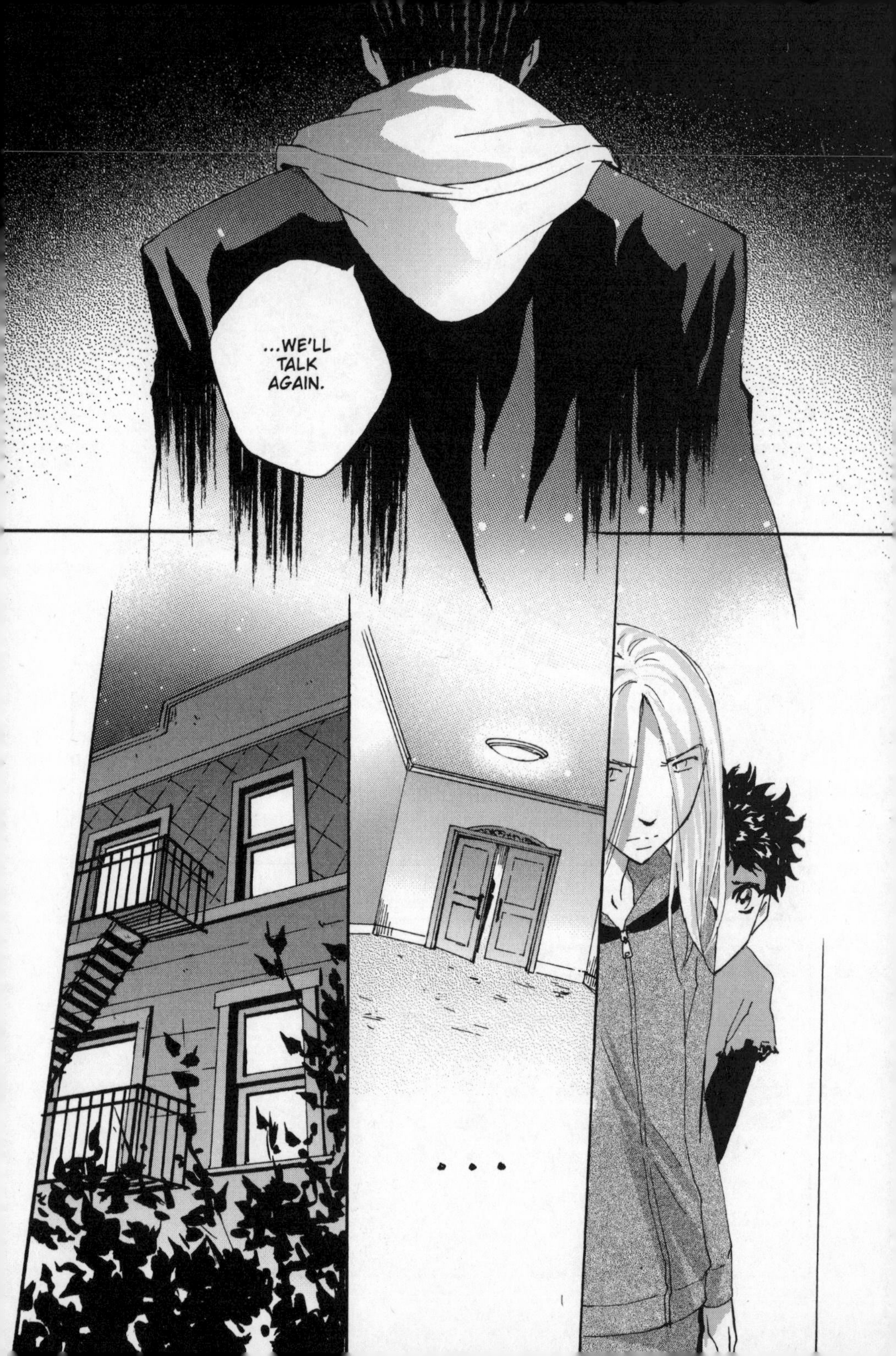
...WE'LL TALK AGAIN.
. . .

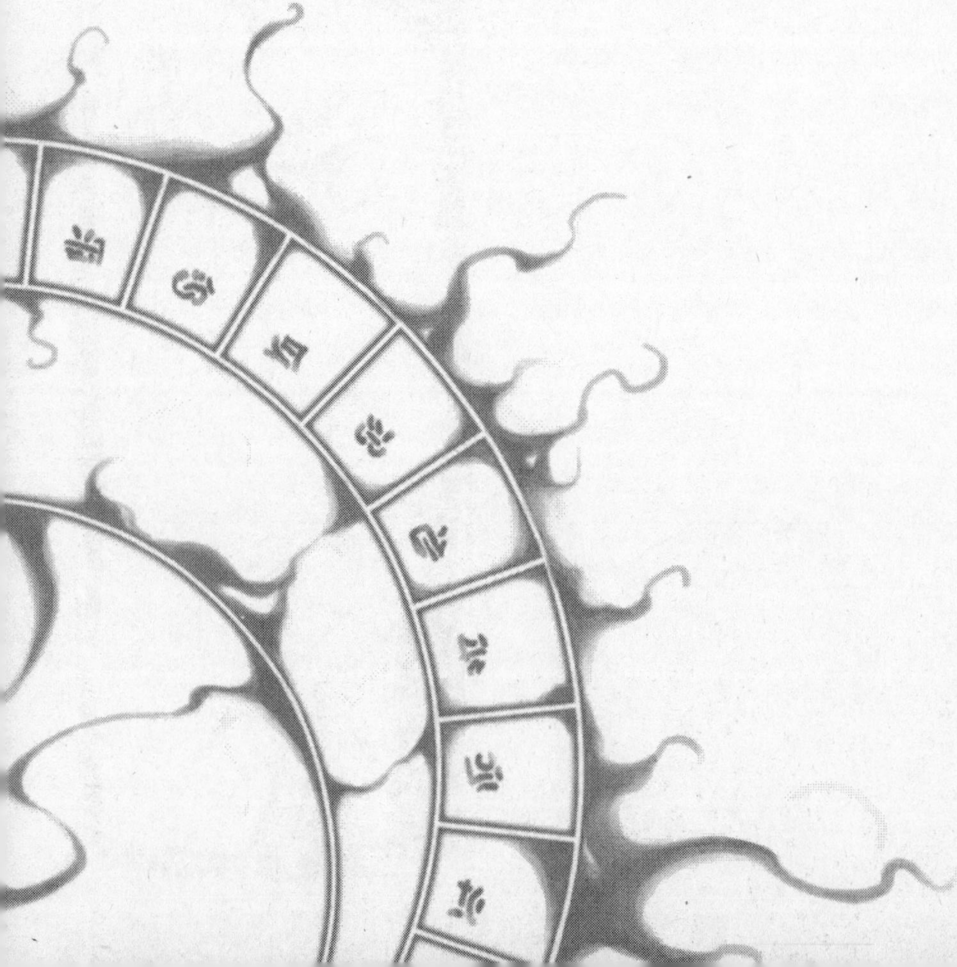

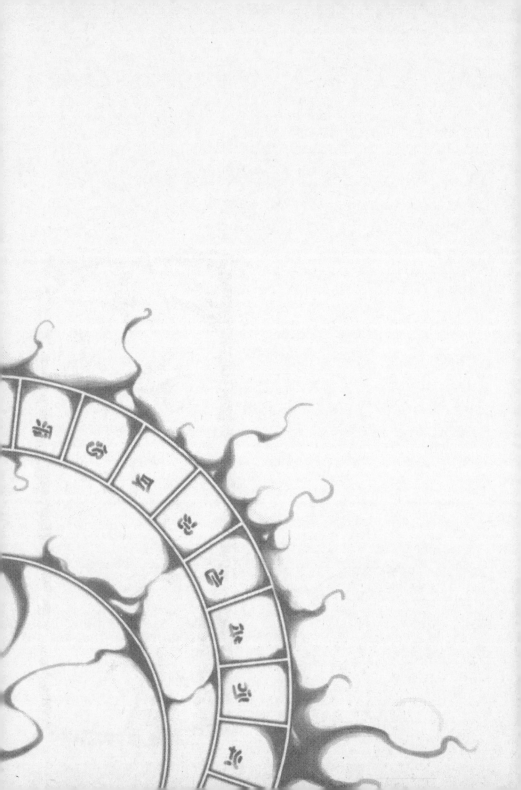

Chapter 14

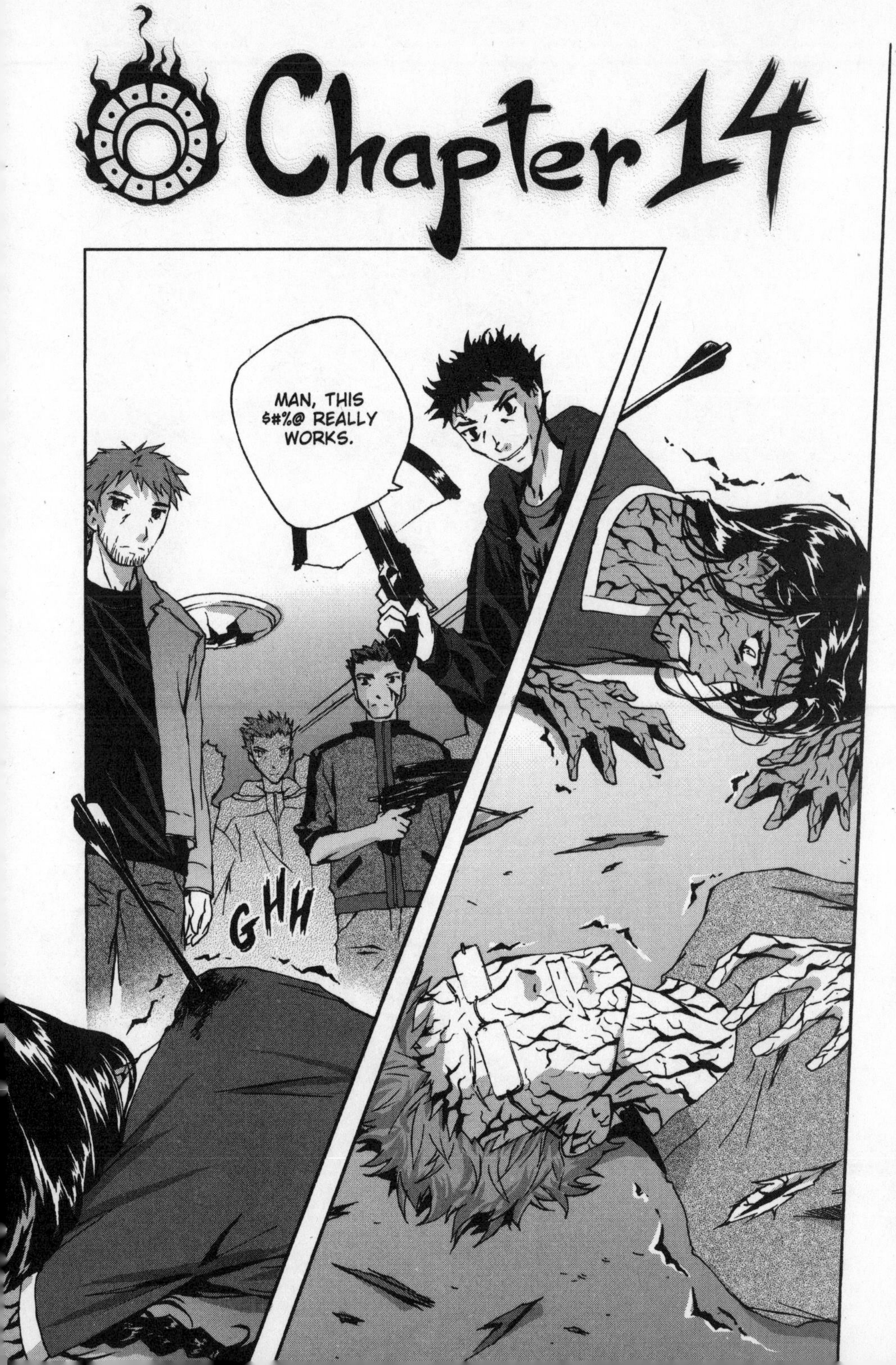
MAN, THIS $#%@ REALLY WORKS.
GHH

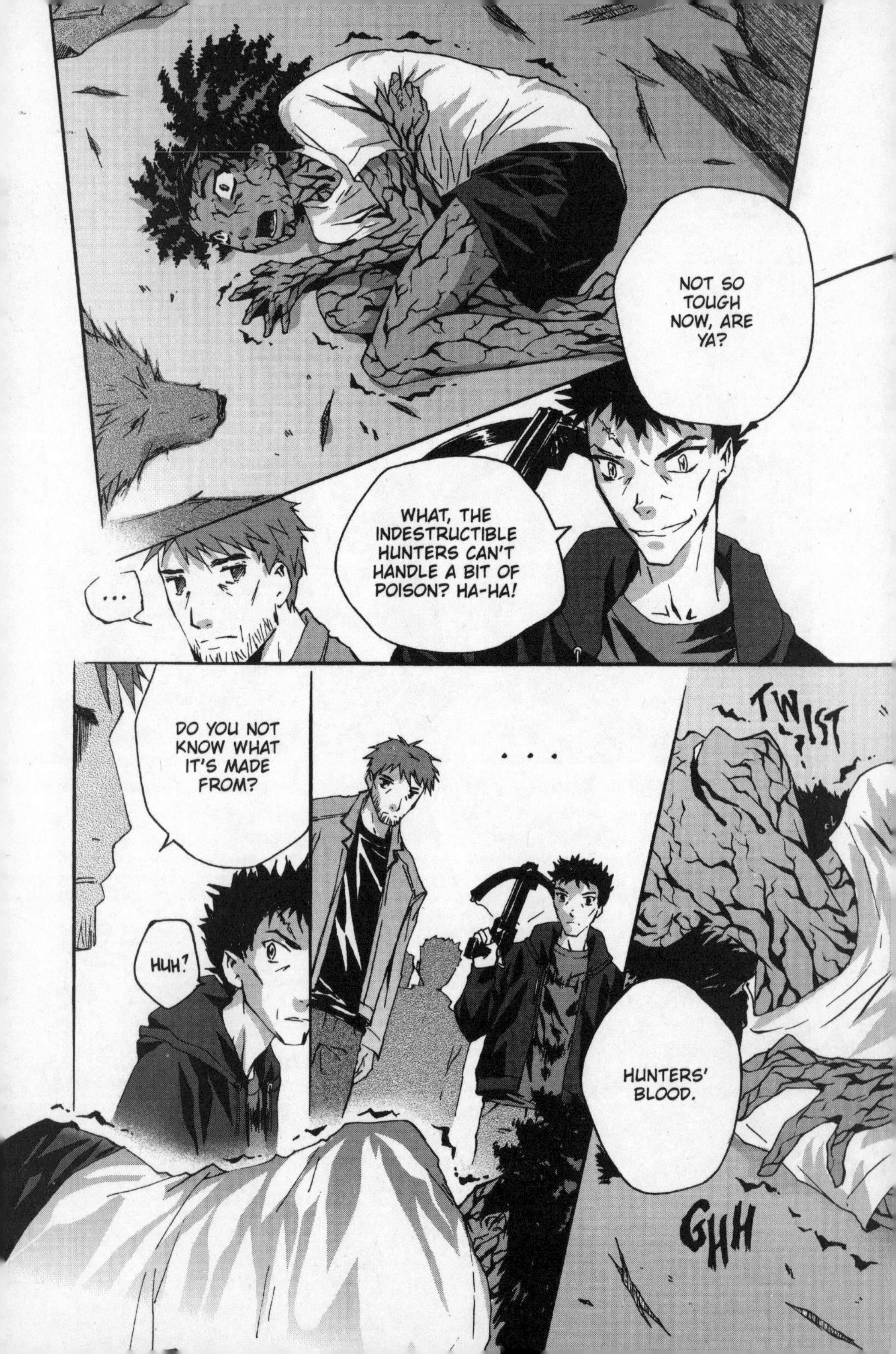

NOT SO TOUGH NOW, ARE YA?
...
WHAT, THE INDESTRUCTIBLE HUNTERS CAN'T HANDLE A BIT OF POISON? HA-HA!
DO YOU NOT KNOW WHAT IT'S MADE FROM?
HUH?
• • •
TWIST
HUNTERS' BLOOD.
GHH

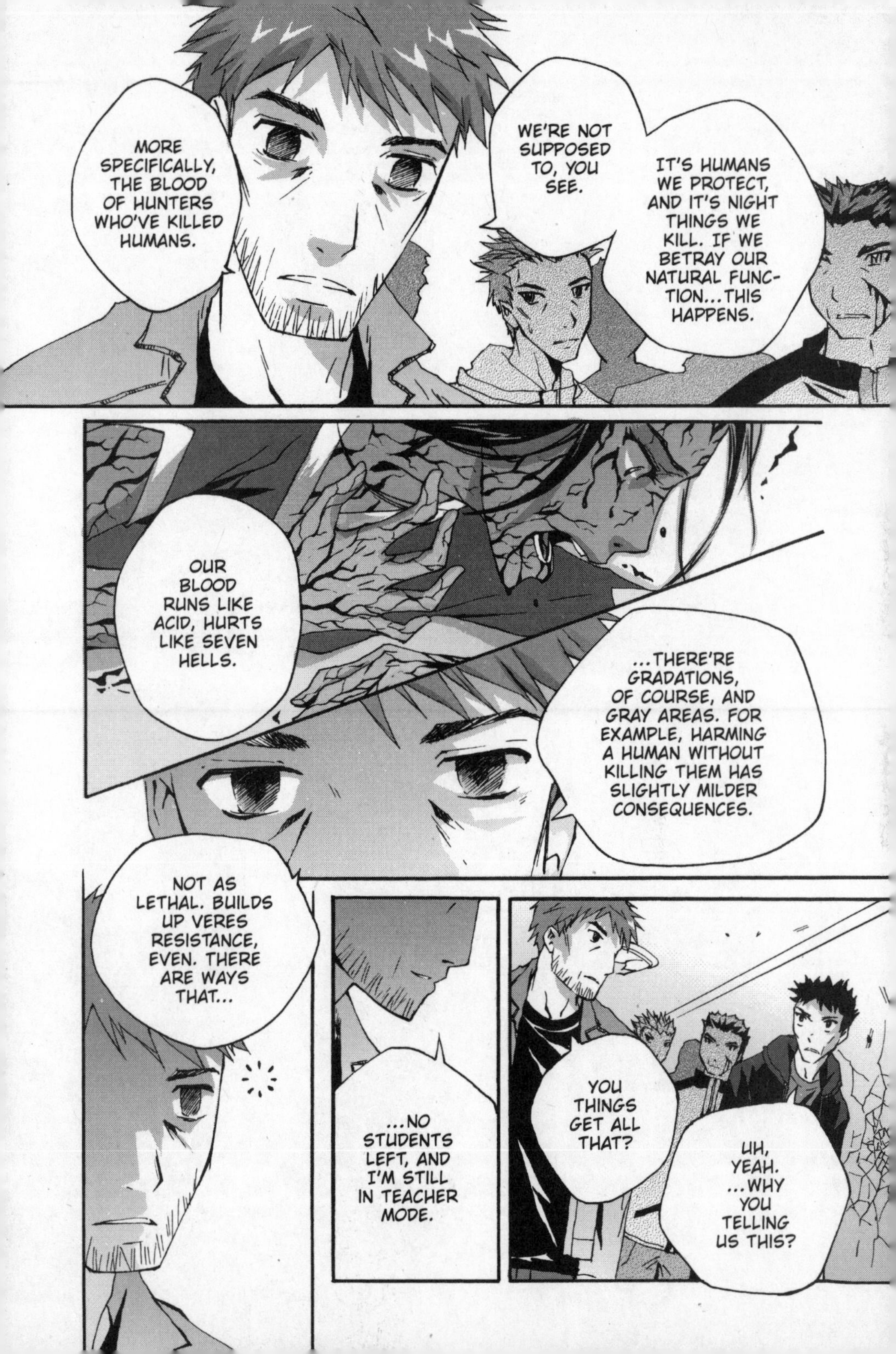
MORE SPECIFICALLY, THE BLOOD OF HUNTERS WHO'VE KILLED HUMANS.
WE'RE NOT SUPPOSED TO, YOU SEE.
IT'S HUMANS WE PROTECT, AND IT'S NIGHT THINGS WE KILL. IF WE BETRAY OUR NATURAL FUNCTION...THIS HAPPENS.
OUR BLOOD RUNS LIKE ACID, HURTS LIKE SEVEN HELLS.
...THERE'RE GRADATIONS, OF COURSE, AND GRAY AREAS. FOR EXAMPLE, HARMING A HUMAN WITHOUT KILLING THEM HAS SLIGHTLY MILDER CONSEQUENCES.
NOT AS LETHAL. BUILDS UP VERES RESISTANCE, EVEN. THERE ARE WAYS THAT...
...NO STUDENTS LEFT, AND I'M STILL IN TEACHER MODE.
YOU THINGS GET ALL THAT?
UH, YEAH. ...WHY YOU TELLING US THIS?

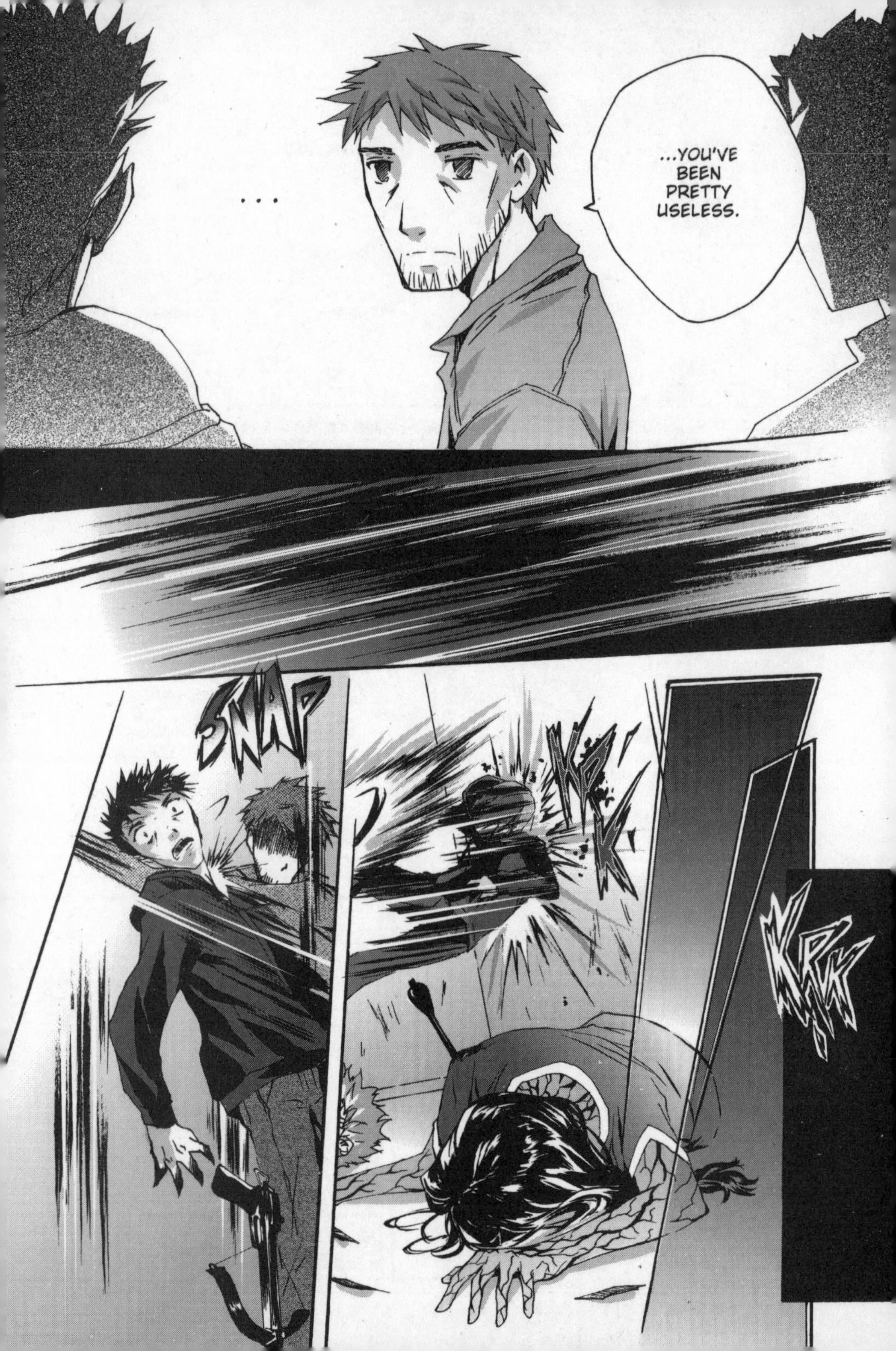
...
...YOU'VE BEEN PRETTY USELESS.
SNAP

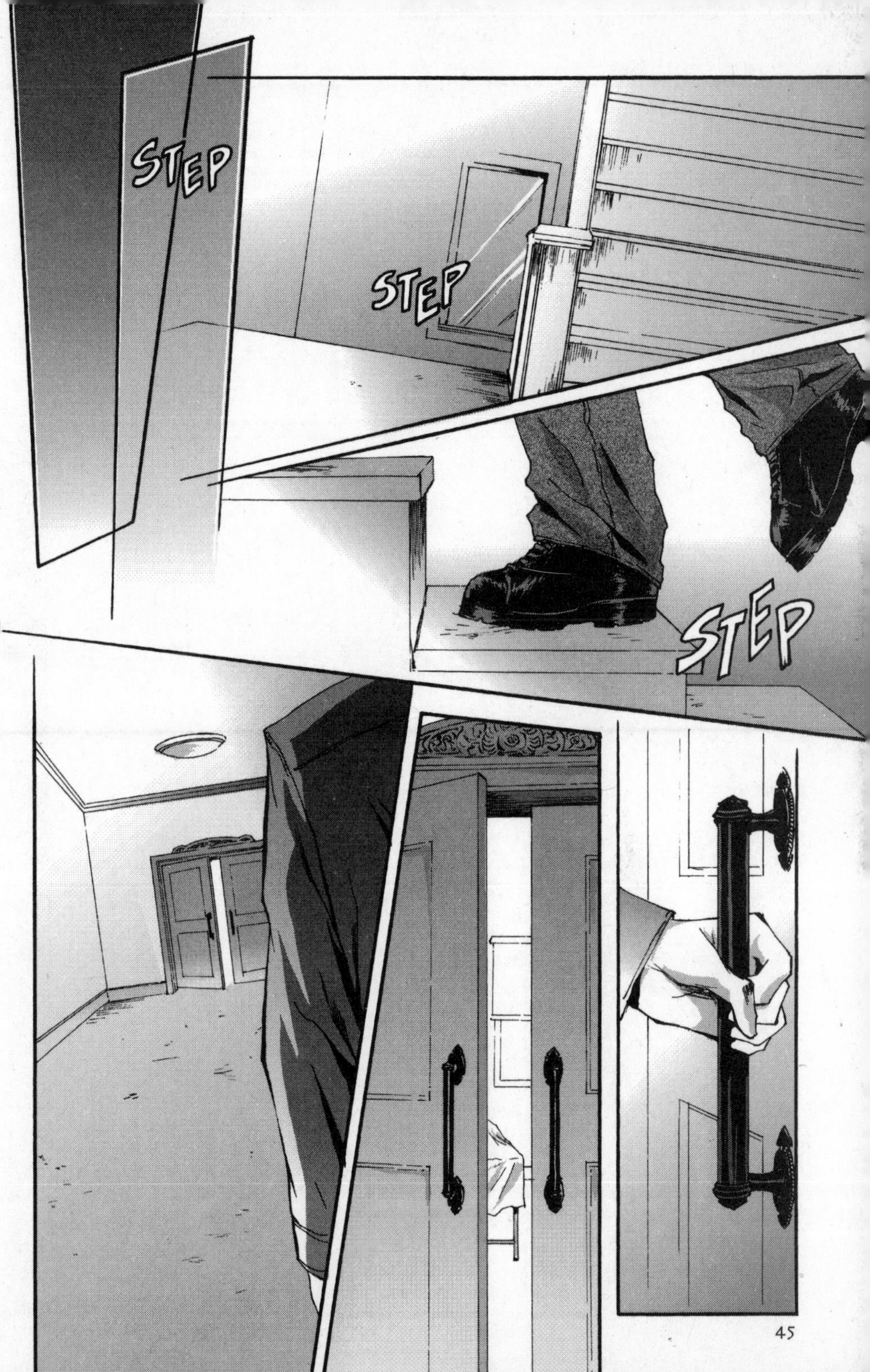
STEP
STEP
STEP

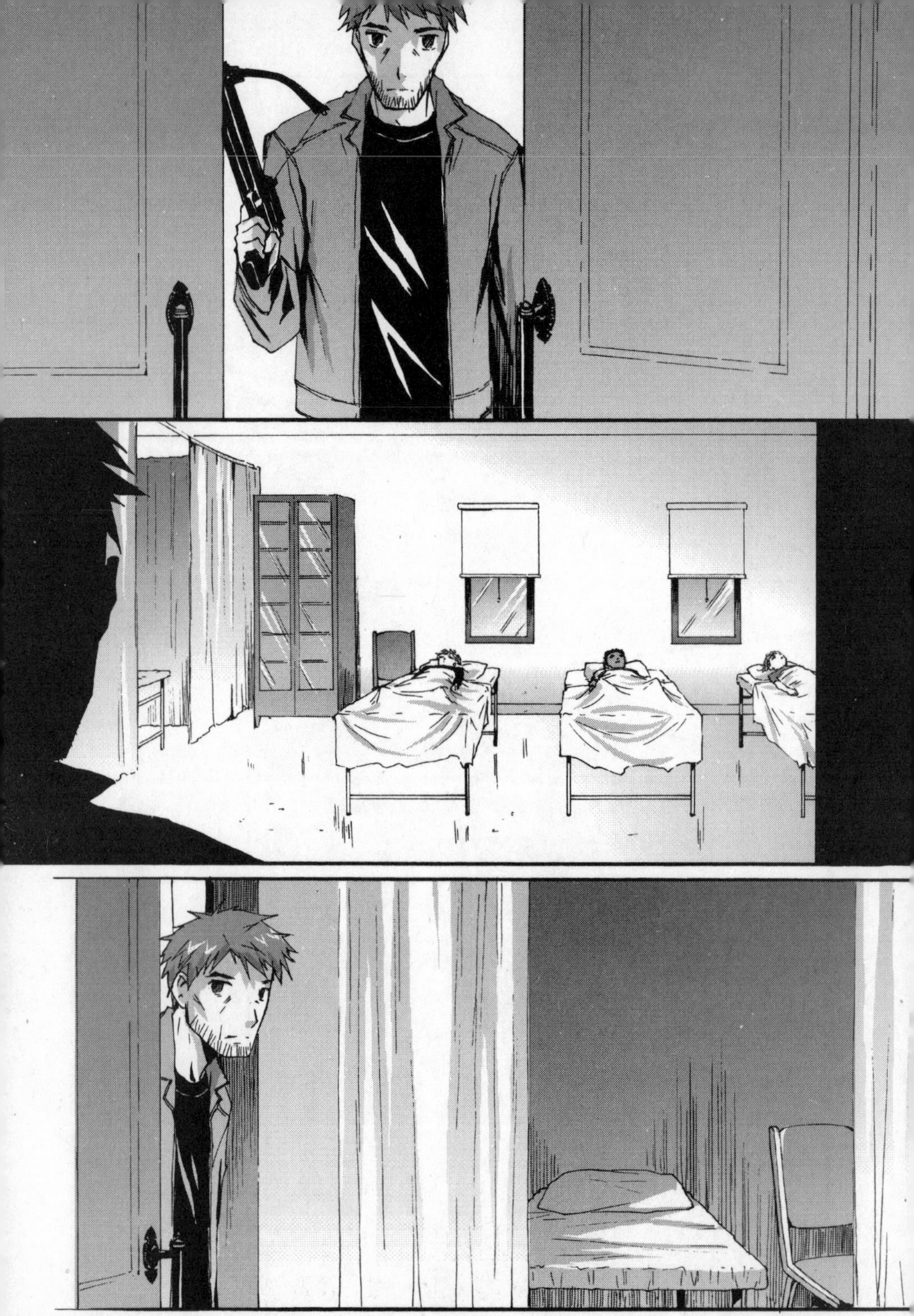

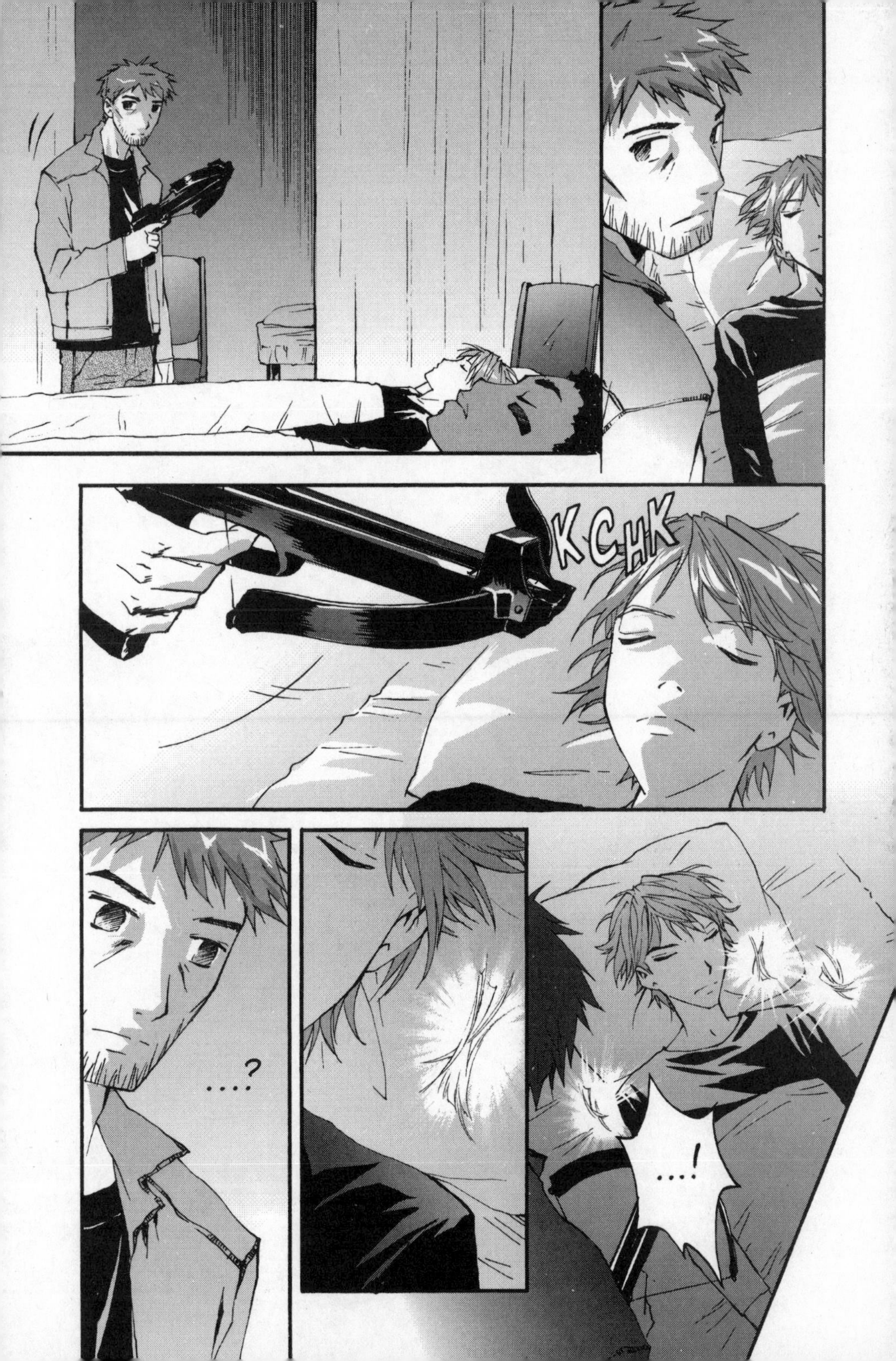
KCHK
...?
...!

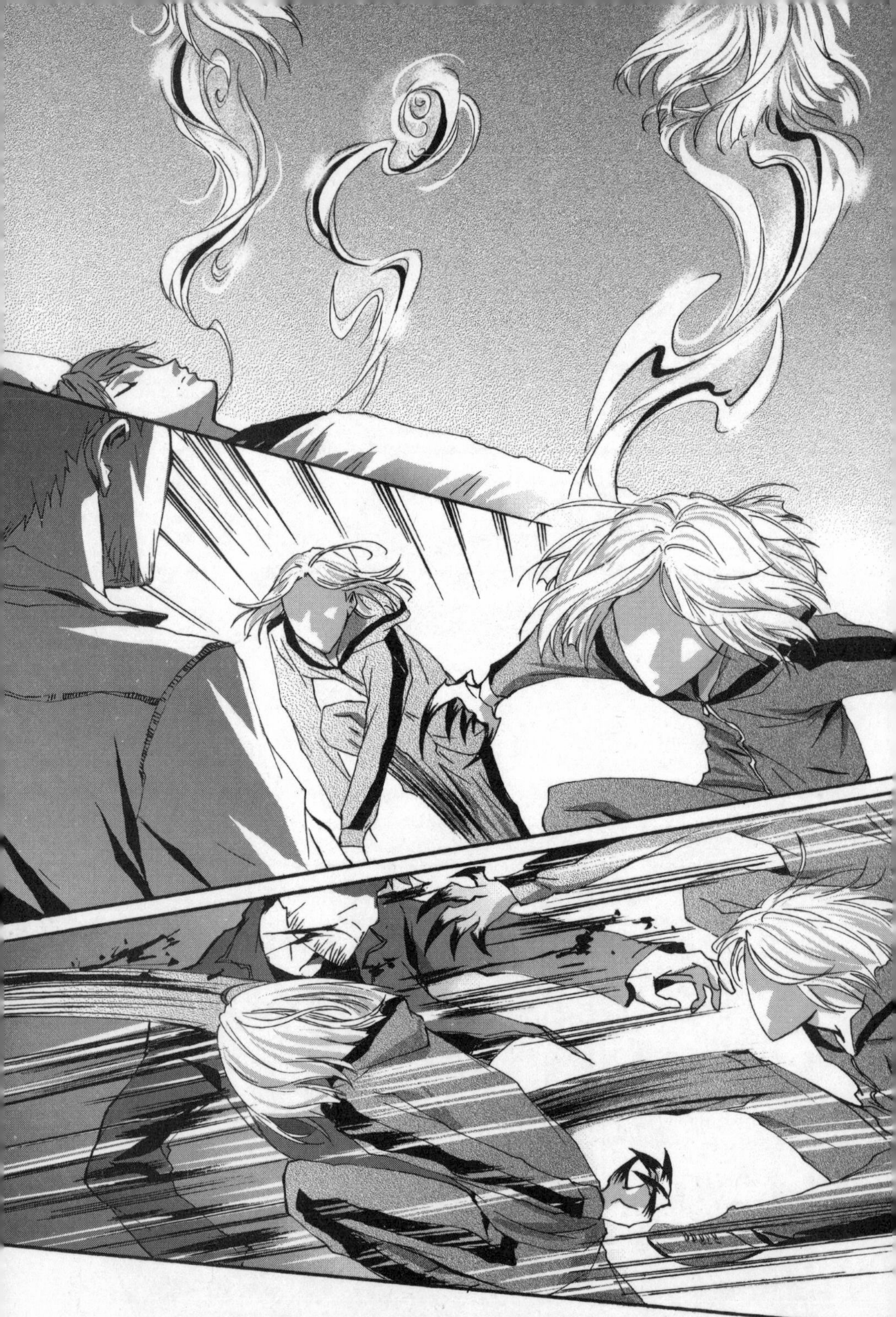

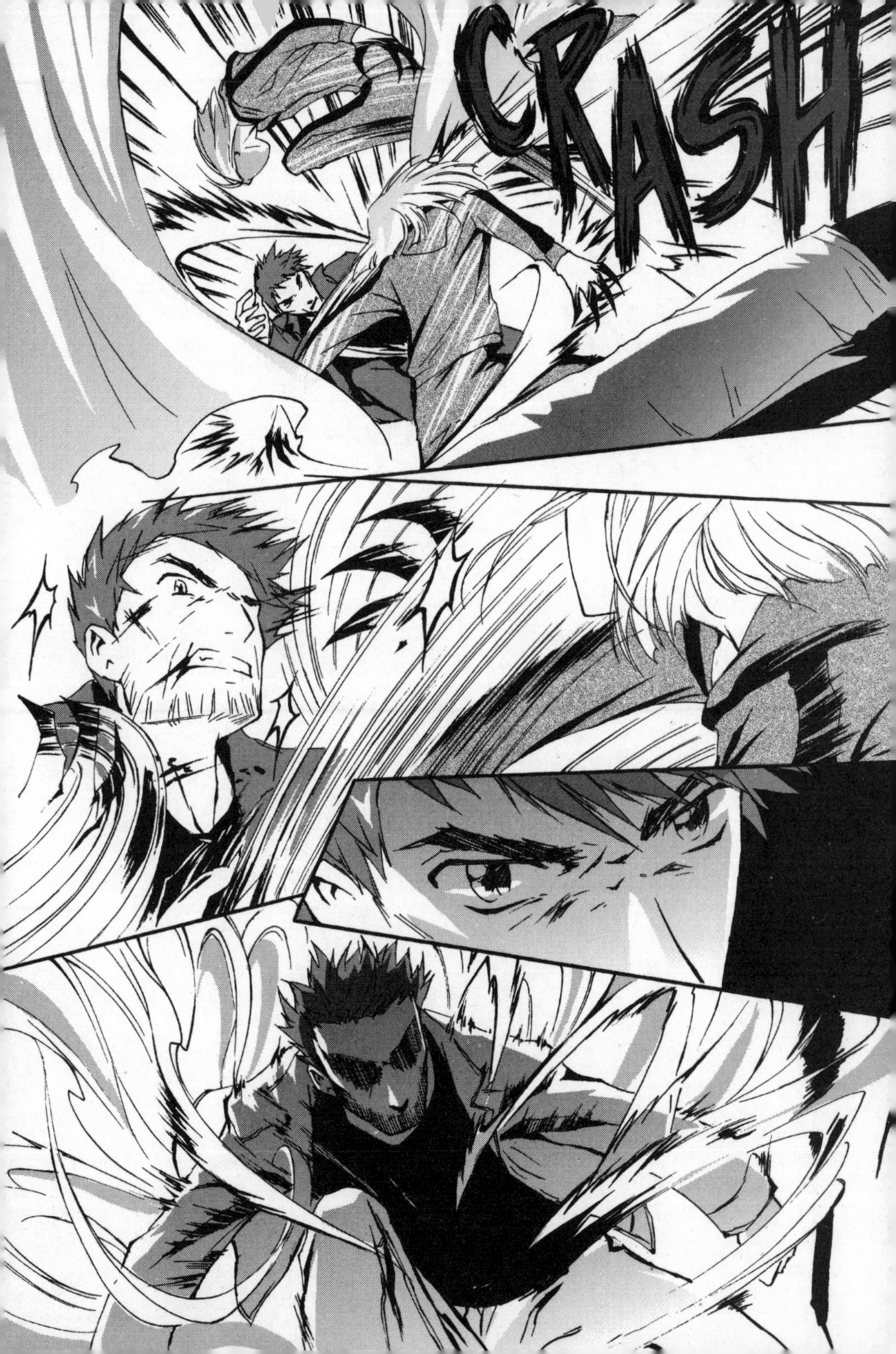
CRASH

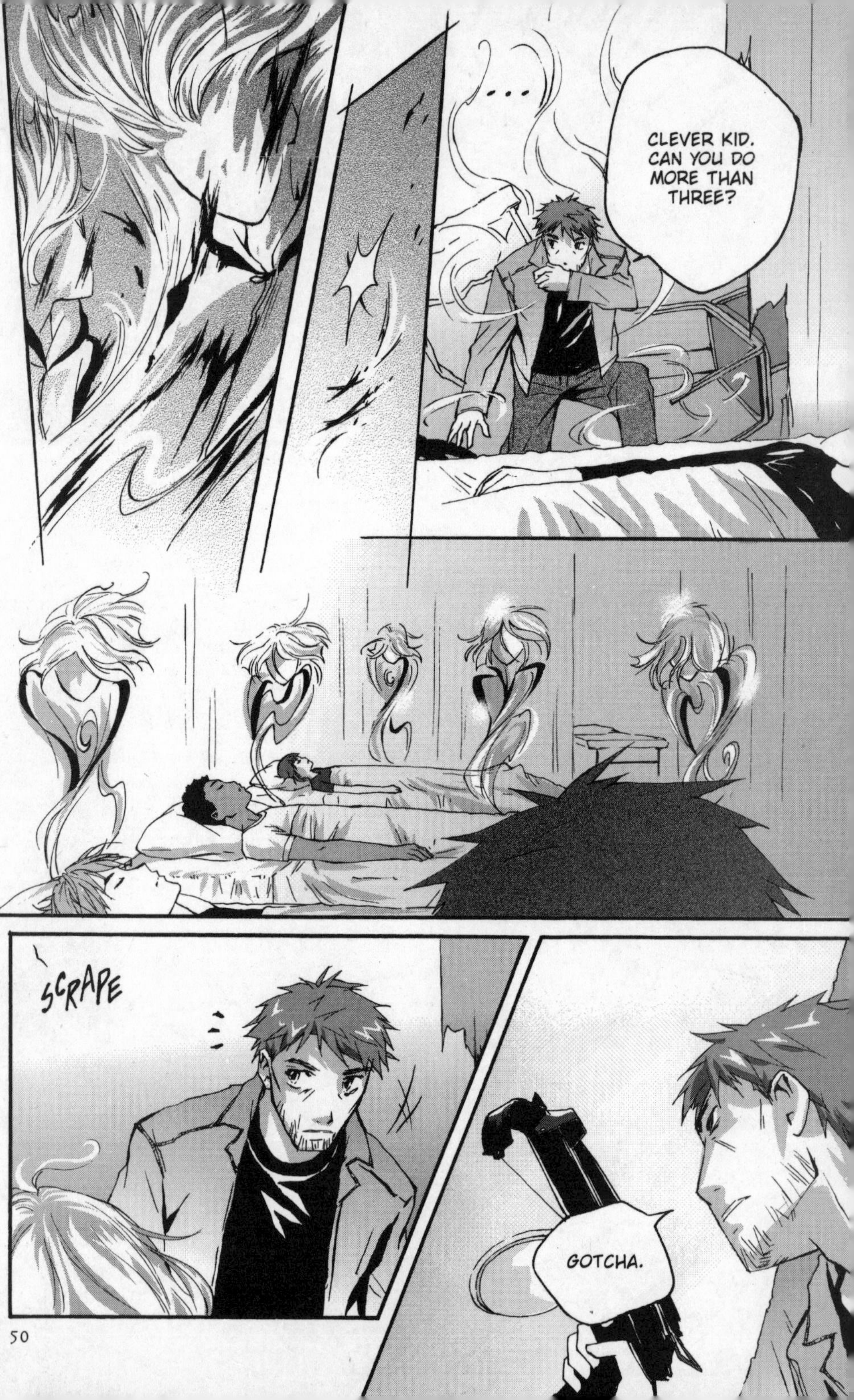
...
CLEVER KID. CAN YOU DO MORE THAN THREE?
SCRAPE
GOTCHA.

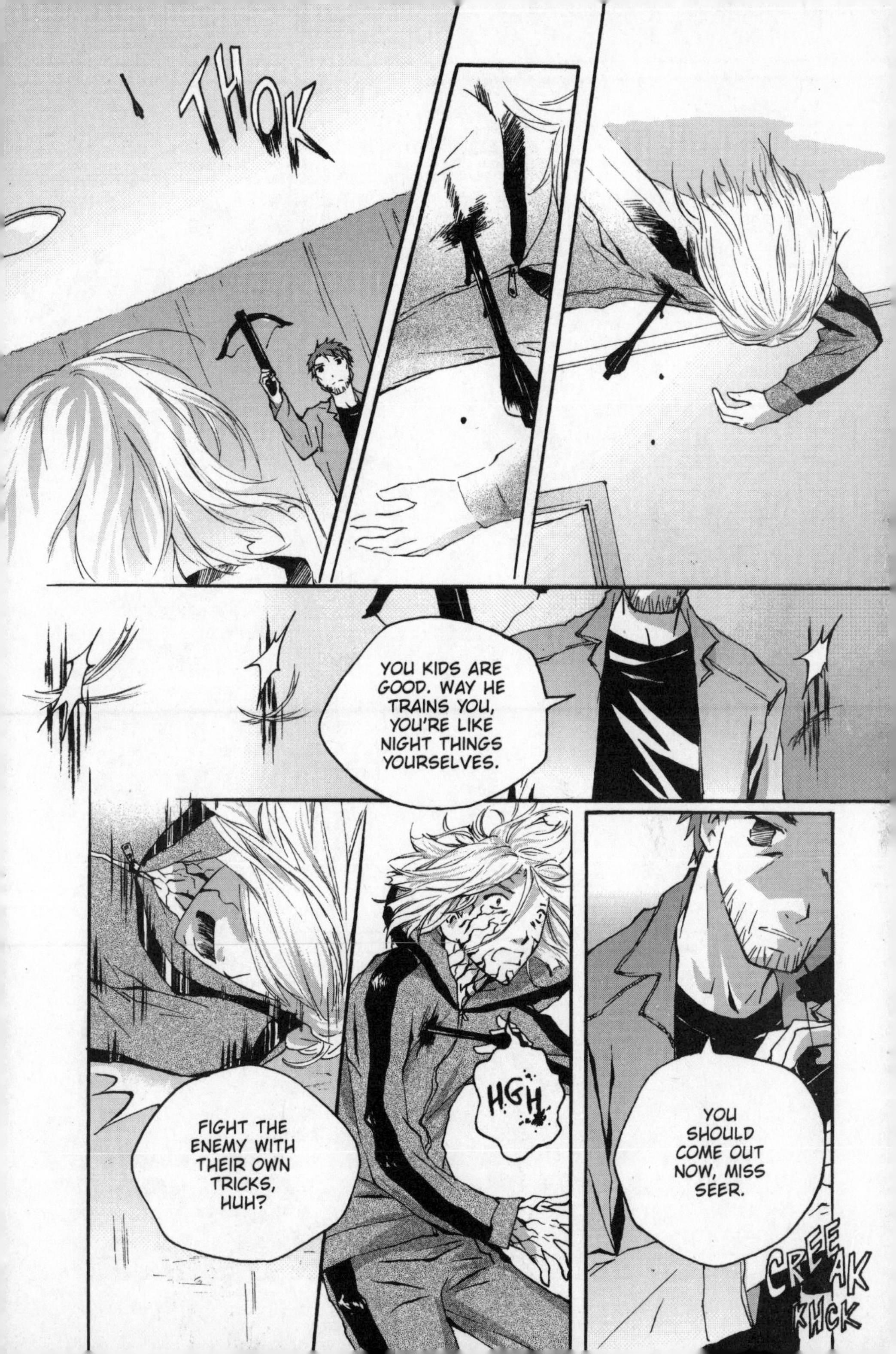
THOK
YOU KIDS ARE GOOD. WAY HE TRAINS YOU, YOU'RE LIKE NIGHT THINGS YOURSELVES.
FIGHT THE ENEMY WITH THEIR OWN TRICKS, HUH?
HGH
YOU SHOULD COME OUT NOW, MISS SEER.
CREEAK
KHCK

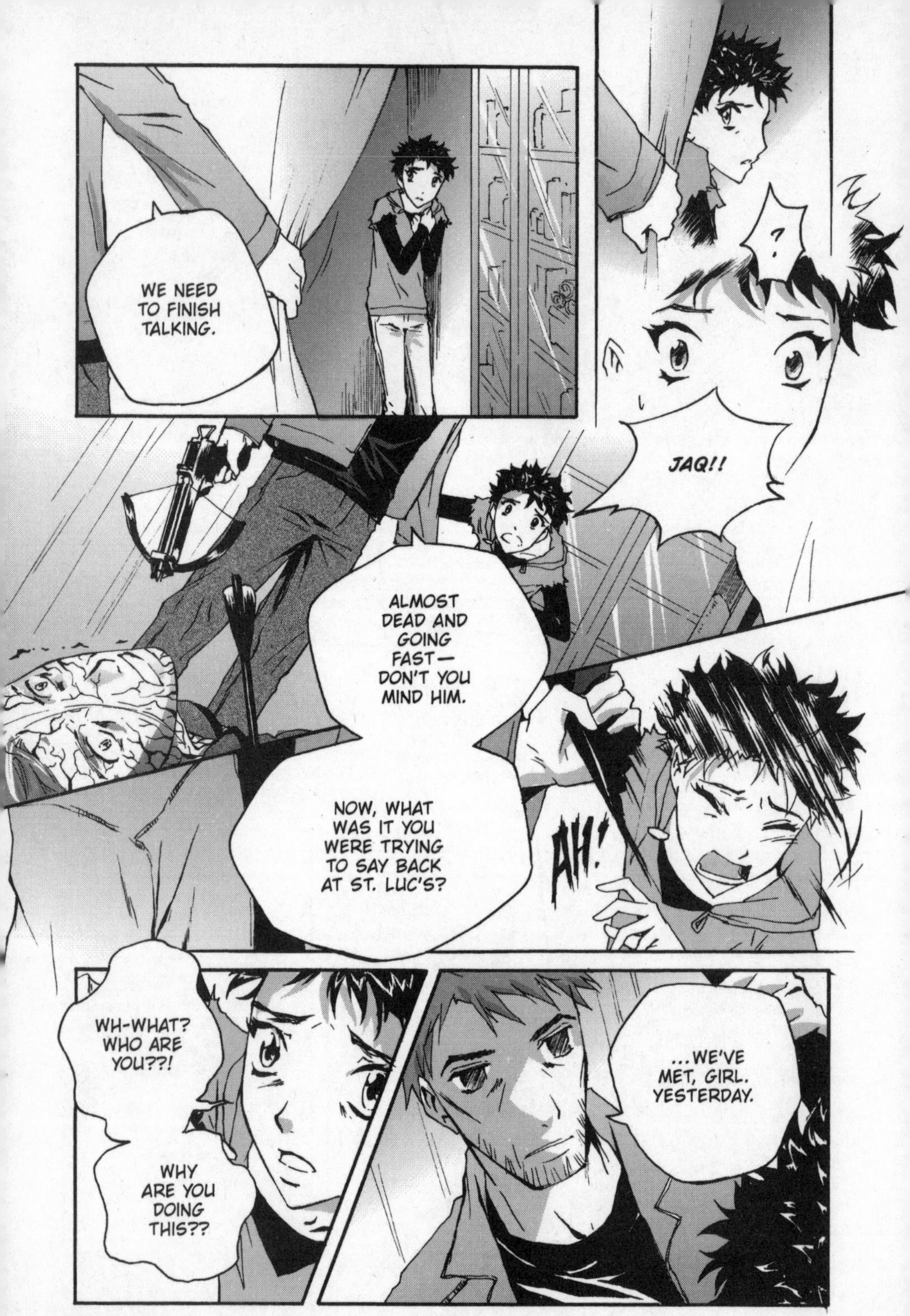
WE NEED TO FINISH TALKING.
?
JAQ!!
ALMOST DEAD AND GOING FAST— DON'T YOU MIND HIM.
NOW, WHAT WAS IT YOU WERE TRYING TO SAY BACK AT ST. LUC'S?
AH!
WH-WHAT? WHO ARE YOU??!
WHY ARE YOU DOING THIS??
...WE'VE MET, GIRL. YESTERDAY.

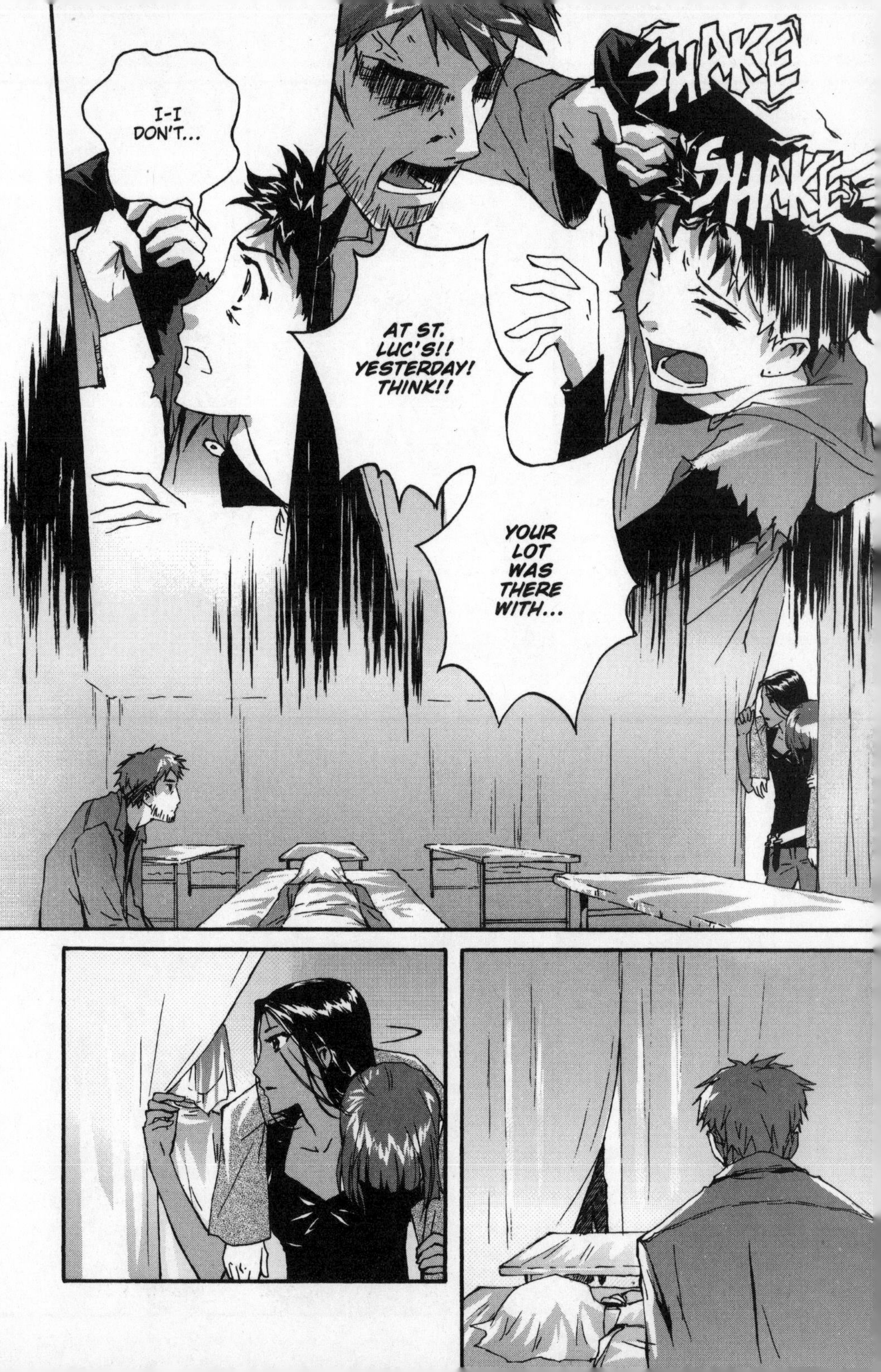
I-I DON'T...
SHAKE
SHAKE
AT ST. LUC'S!! YESTERDAY! THINK!!
YOUR LOT WAS THERE WITH...

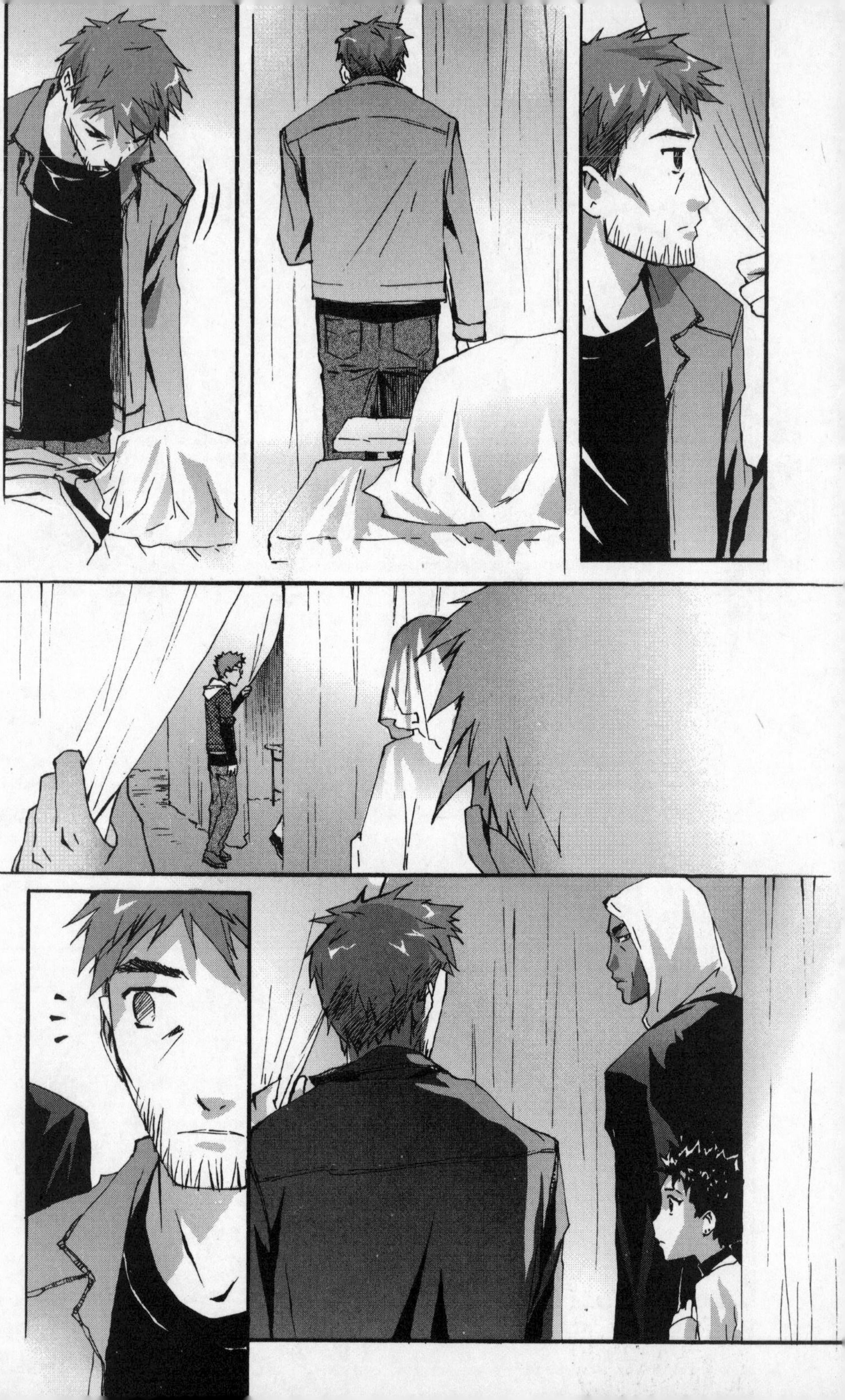

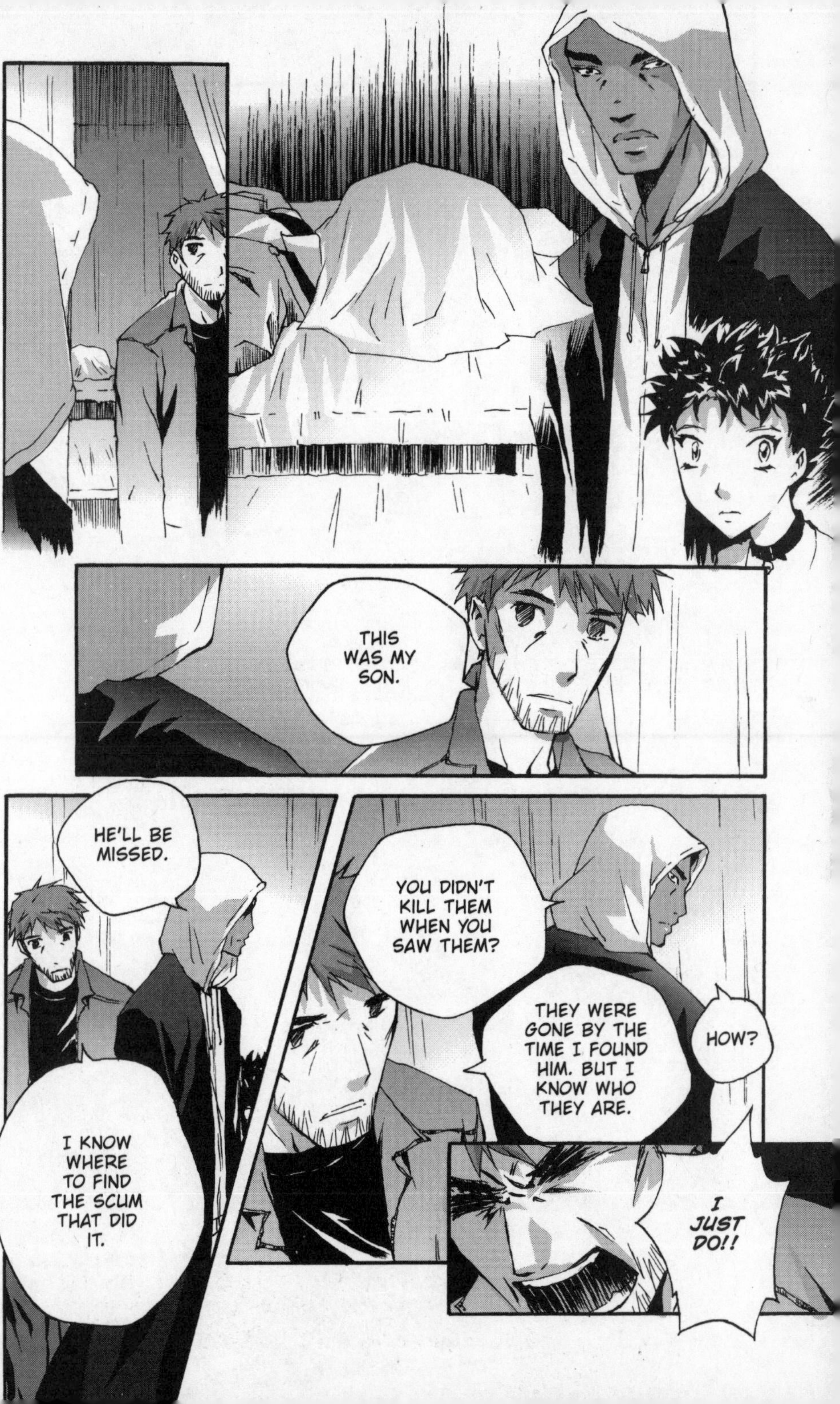
THIS WAS MY SON.
HE'LL BE MISSED.
I KNOW WHERE TO FIND THE SCUM THAT DID IT.
YOU DIDN'T KILL THEM WHEN YOU SAW THEM?
THEY WERE GONE BY THE TIME I FOUND HIM. BUT I KNOW WHO THEY ARE.
HOW?
I JUST DO!!

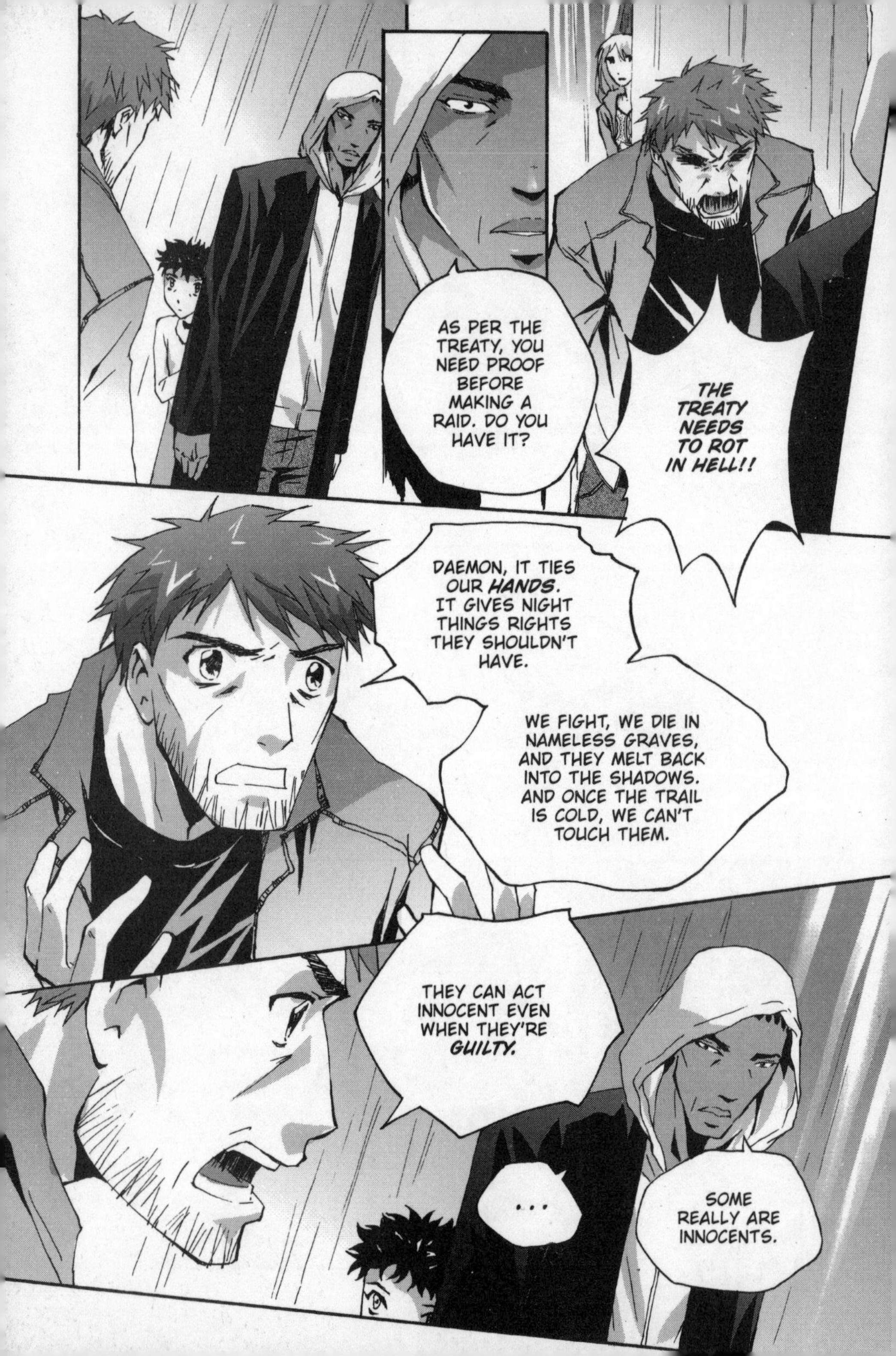
AS PER THE TREATY, YOU NEED PROOF BEFORE MAKING A RAID. DO YOU HAVE IT?
THE TREATY NEEDS TO ROT IN HELL!!
DAEMON, IT TIES OUR HANDS. IT GIVES NIGHT THINGS RIGHTS THEY SHOULDN'T HAVE.
WE FIGHT, WE DIE IN NAMELESS GRAVES, AND THEY MELT BACK INTO THE SHADOWS. AND ONCE THE TRAIL IS COLD, WE CAN'T TOUCH THEM.
THEY CAN ACT INNOCENT EVEN WHEN THEY'RE GUILTY.
...
SOME REALLY ARE INNOCENTS.

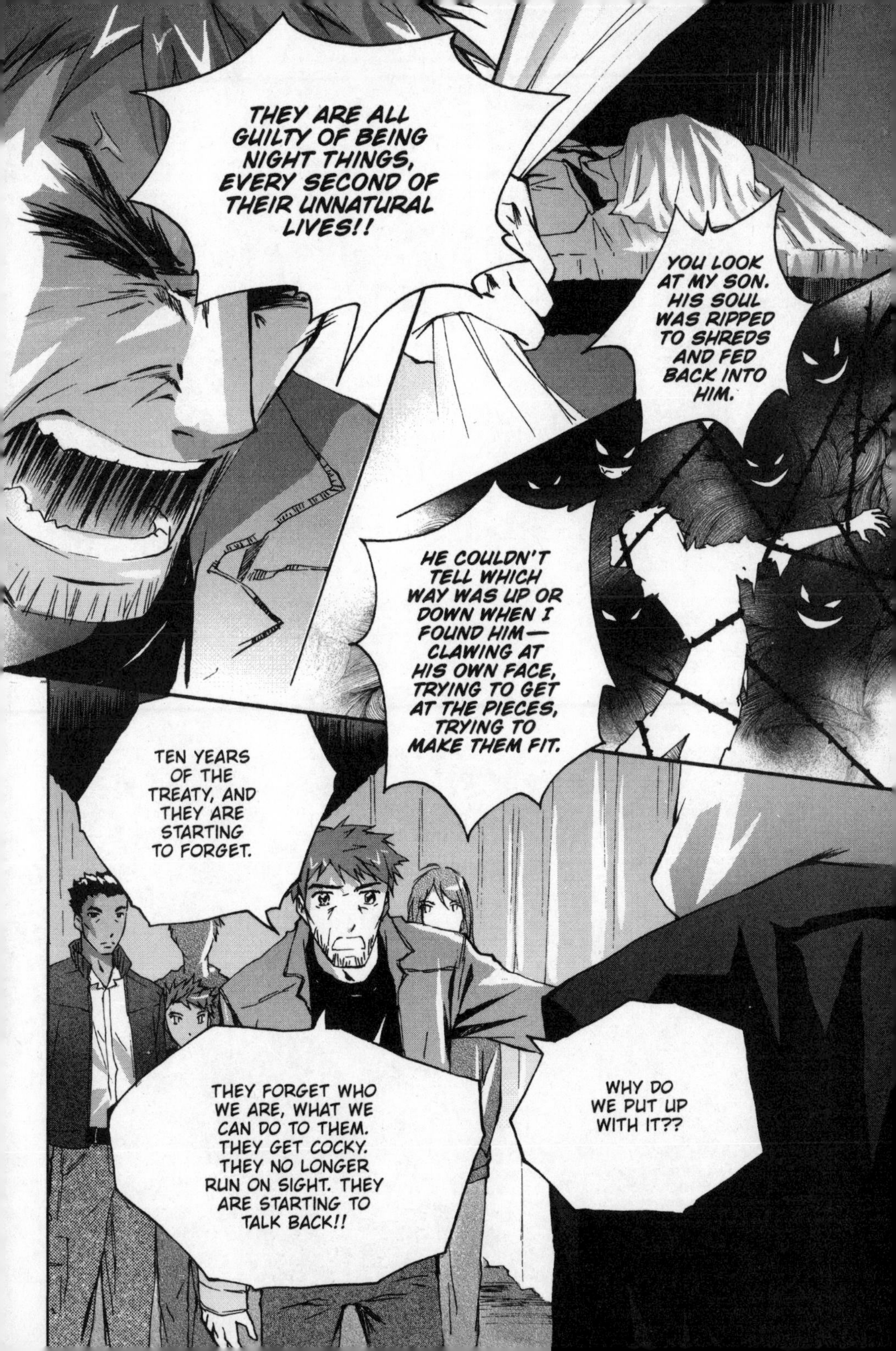
THEY ARE ALL GUILTY OF BEING NIGHT THINGS, EVERY SECOND OF THEIR UNNATURAL LIVES!!
YOU LOOK AT MY SON. HIS SOUL WAS RIPPED TO SHREDS AND FED BACK INTO HIM.
HE COULDN'T TELL WHICH WAY WAS UP OR DOWN WHEN I FOUND HIM— CLAWING AT HIS OWN FACE, TRYING TO GET AT THE PIECES, TRYING TO MAKE THEM FIT.
TEN YEARS OF THE TREATY, AND THEY ARE STARTING TO FORGET.
THEY FORGET WHO WE ARE, WHAT WE CAN DO TO THEM. THEY GET COCKY. THEY NO LONGER RUN ON SIGHT. THEY ARE STARTING TO TALK BACK!!
WHY DO WE PUT UP WITH IT??

BECAUSE WE'RE SUPPOSED TO BE THE GOOD GUYS.

...

THE TREATY SAVES LIVES. I AM SORRY ONE WASN'T YOUR SON'S.

HE DIED LIKE A HUNTER.

AS WILL WE ALL.

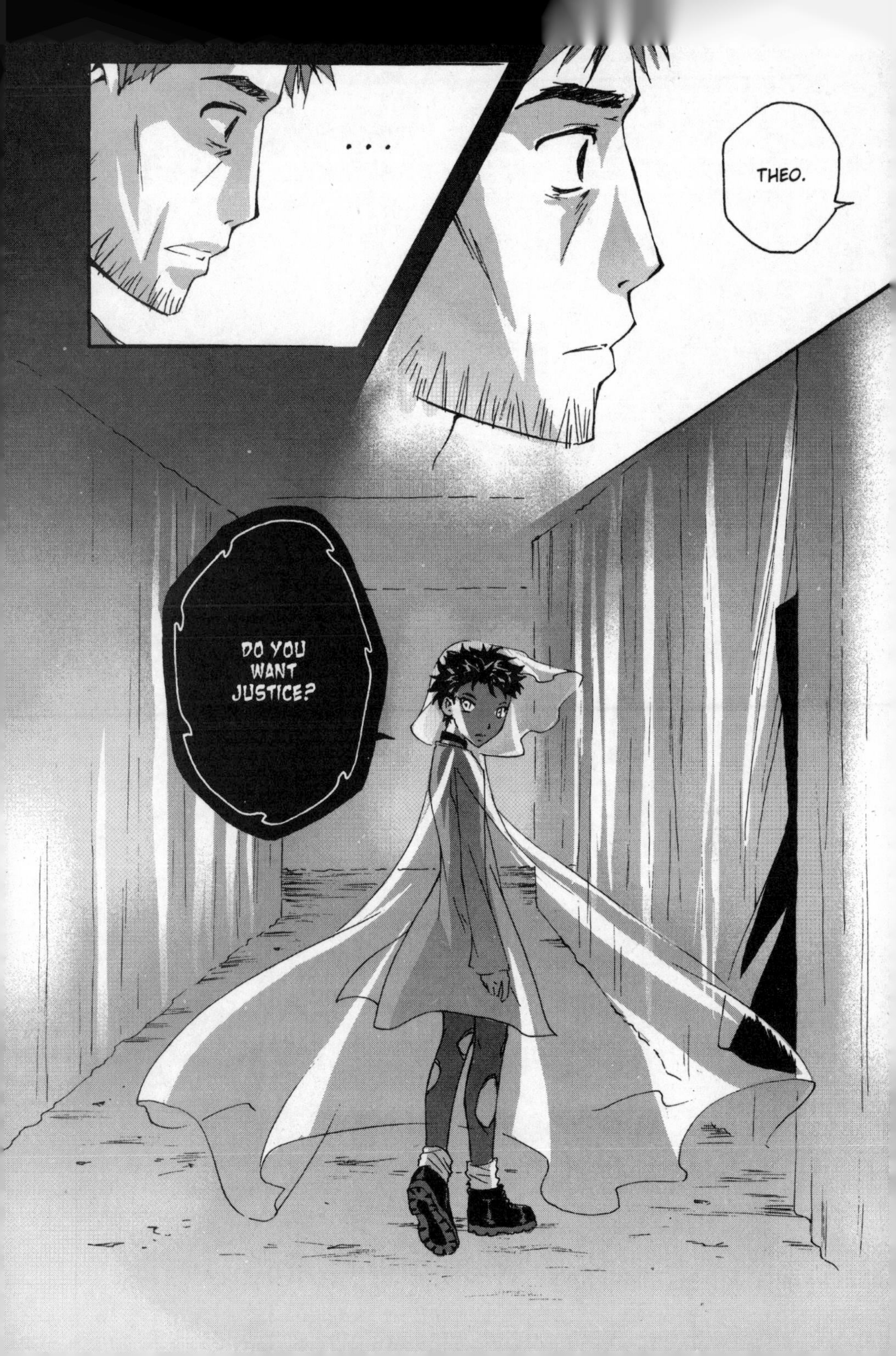
. . .
THEO.
DO YOU WANT JUSTICE?

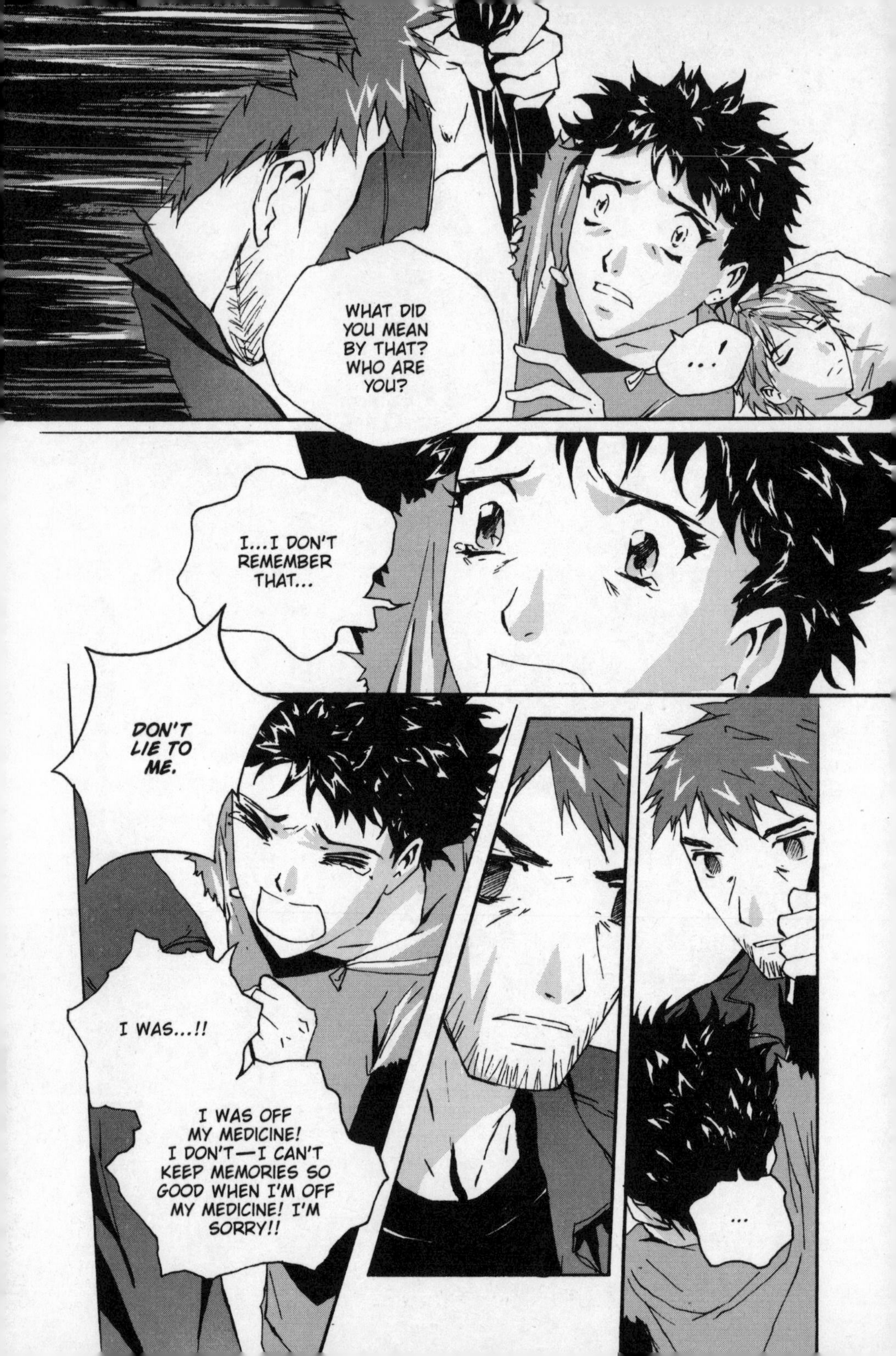
WHAT DID YOU MEAN BY THAT? WHO ARE YOU?
...
I...I DON'T REMEMBER THAT...
DON'T LIE TO ME.
I WAS...!!
I WAS OFF MY MEDICINE! I DON'T—I CAN'T KEEP MEMORIES SO GOOD WHEN I'M OFF MY MEDICINE! I'M SORRY!!
...

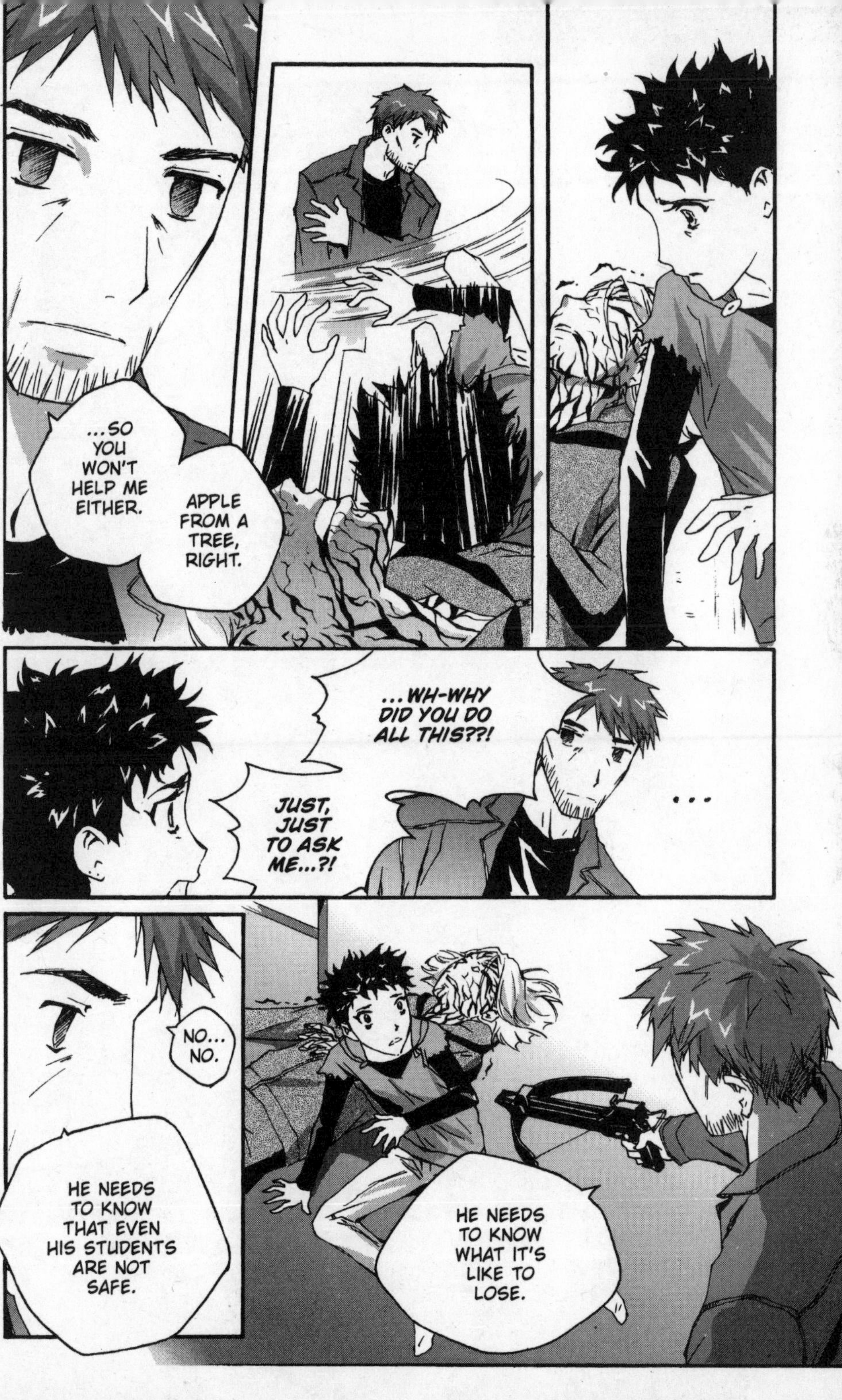
...SO YOU WON'T HELP ME EITHER.
APPLE FROM A TREE, RIGHT.
...WH-WHY DID YOU DO ALL THIS??!
JUST, JUST TO ASK ME...?!
...
NO... NO.
HE NEEDS TO KNOW THAT EVEN HIS STUDENTS ARE NOT SAFE.
HE NEEDS TO KNOW WHAT IT'S LIKE TO LOSE.

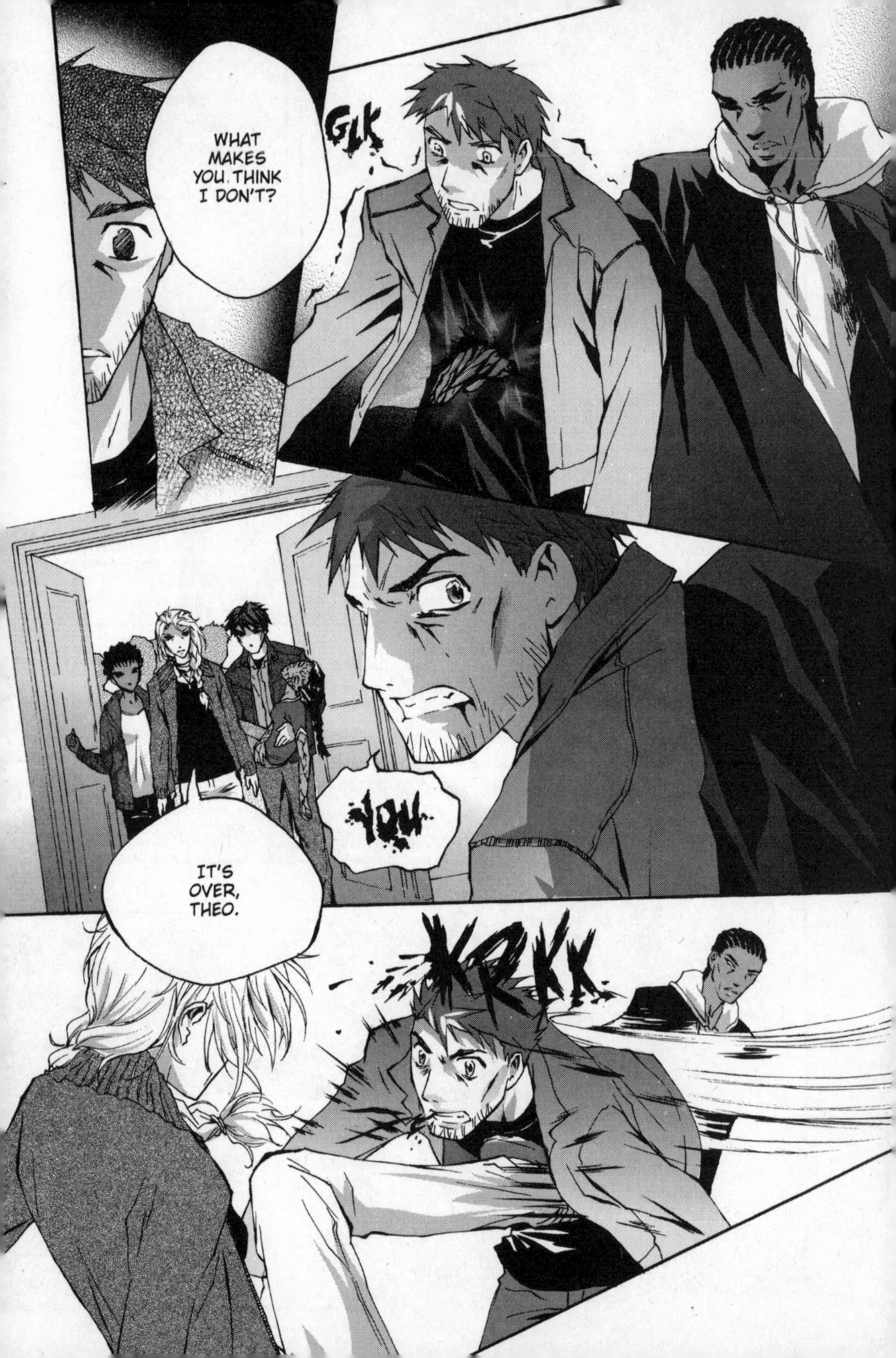
WHAT MAKES YOU THINK I DON'T?
GLK
YOU
IT'S OVER, THEO.
KRKK

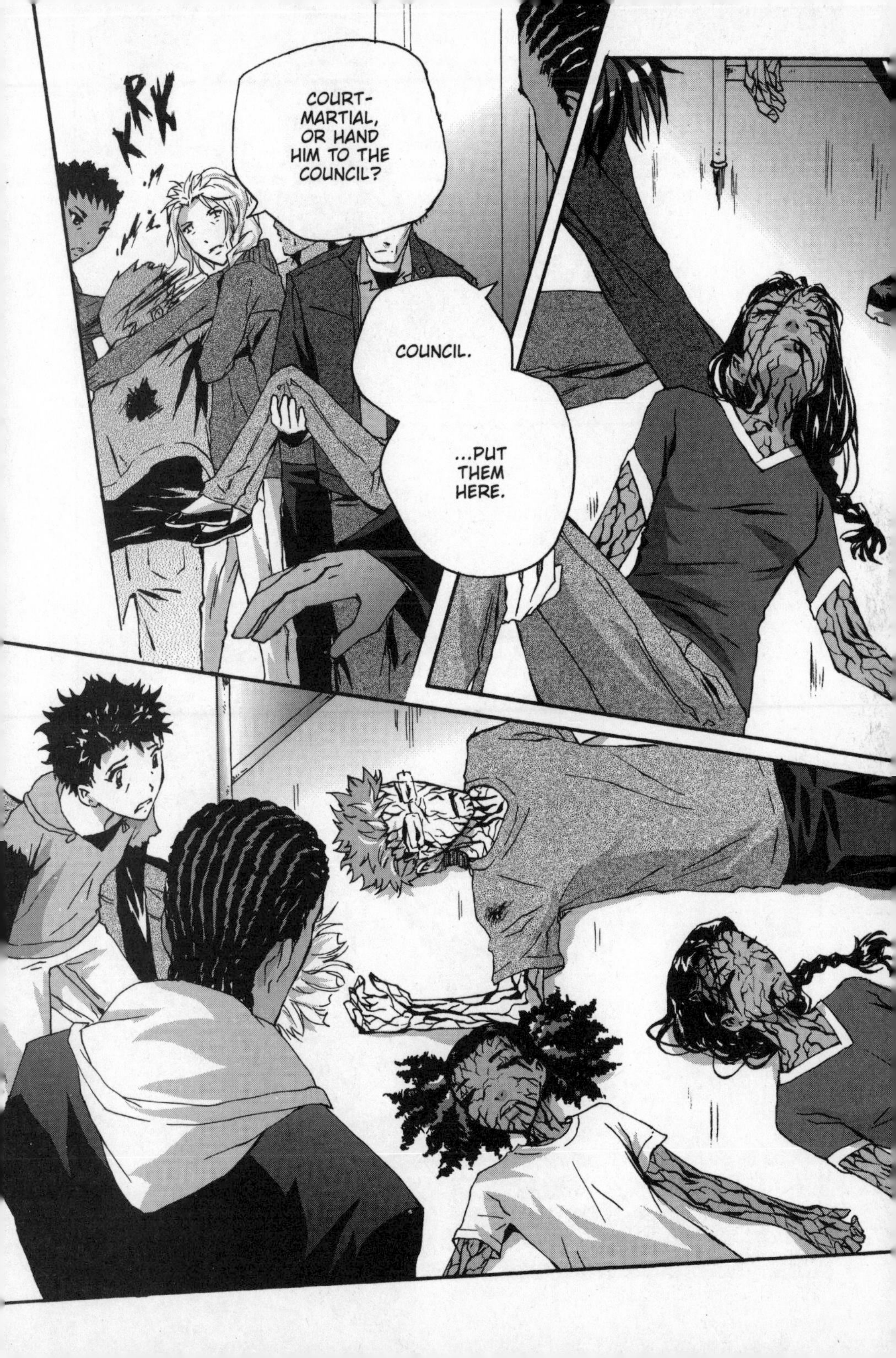
KRK
COURT-MARTIAL, OR HAND HIM TO THE COUNCIL?
COUNCIL.
...PUT THEM HERE.

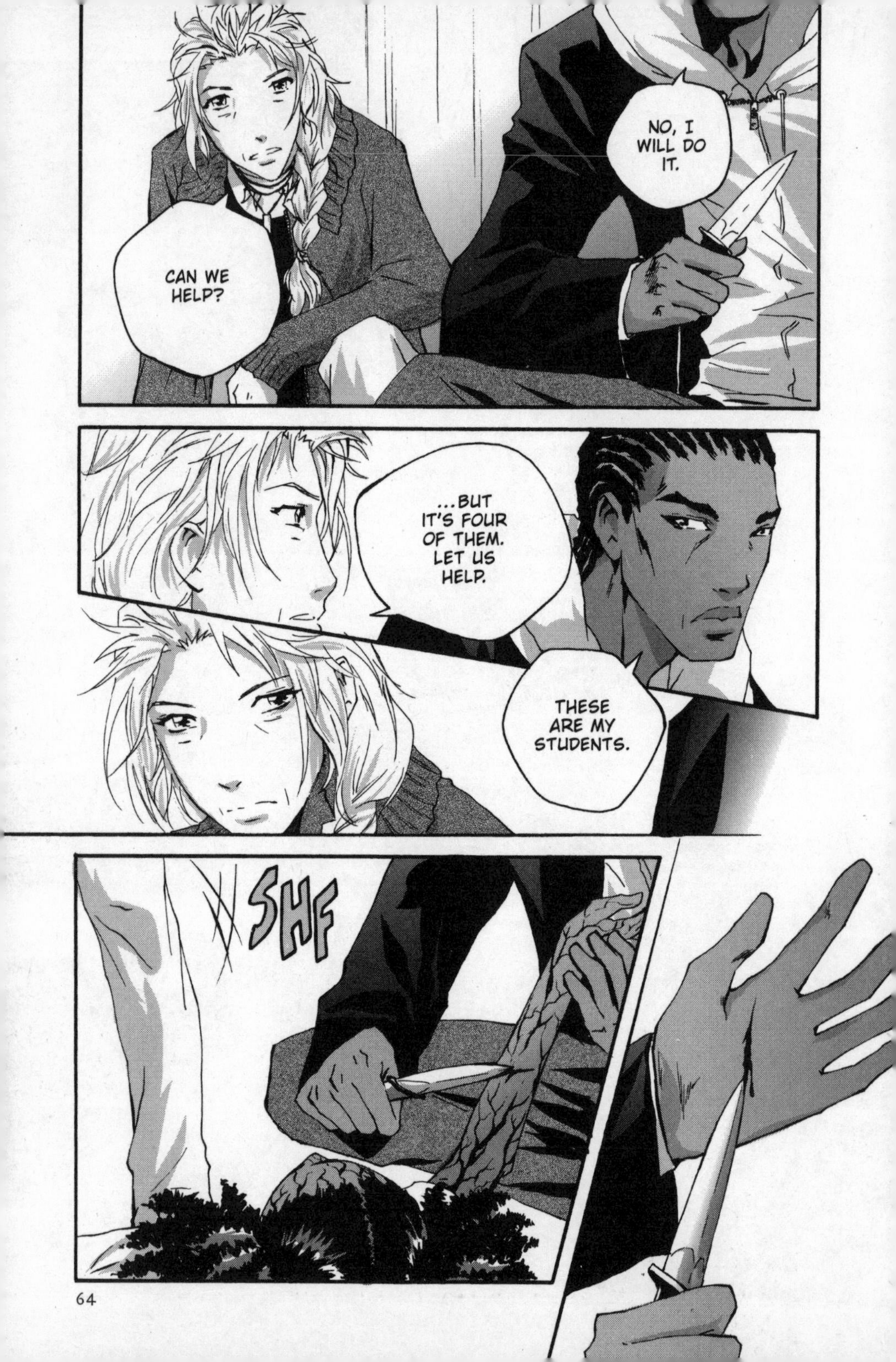
CAN WE HELP?
NO, I WILL DO IT.
...BUT IT'S FOUR OF THEM. LET US HELP.
THESE ARE MY STUDENTS.
SHF

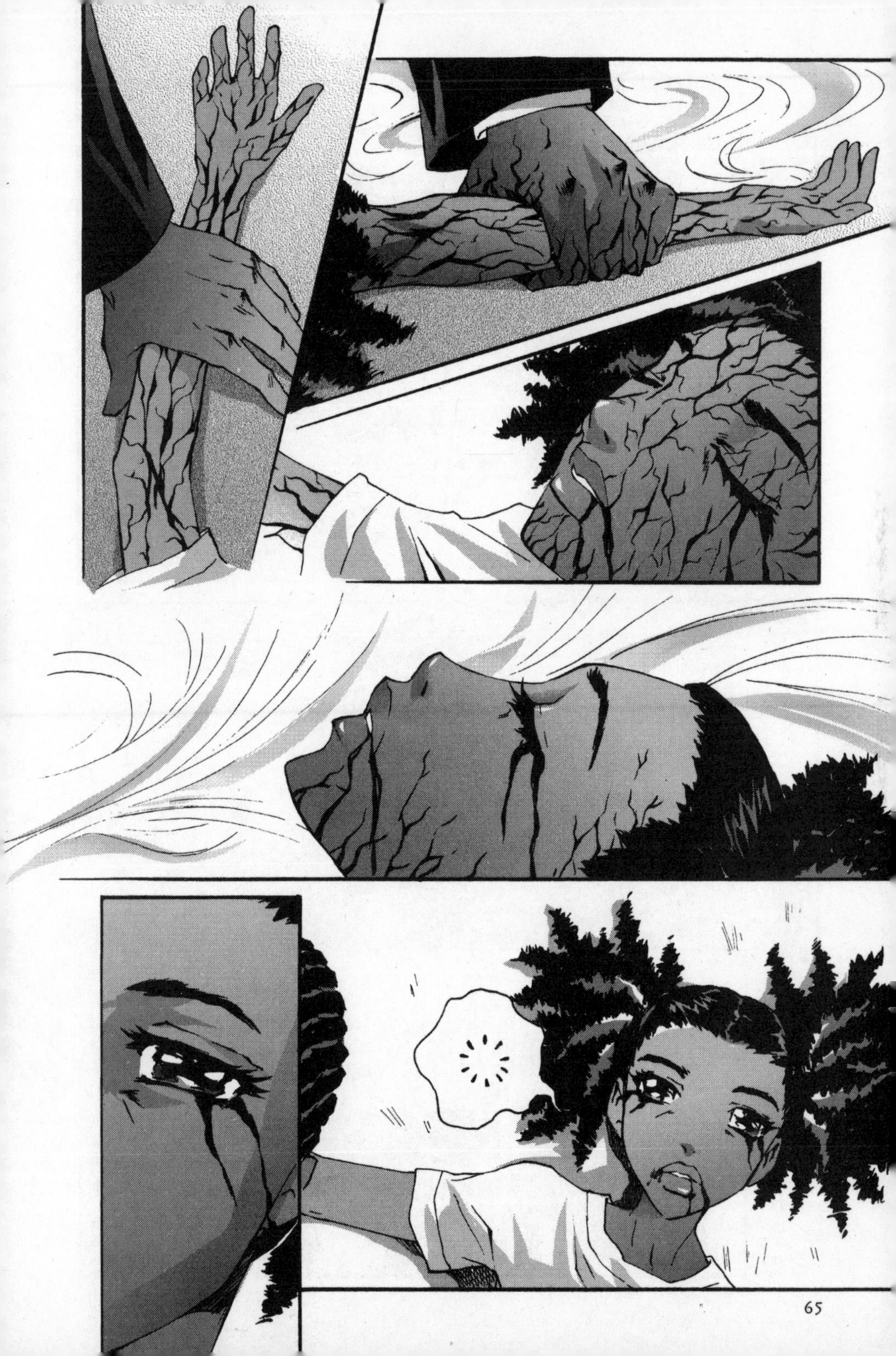

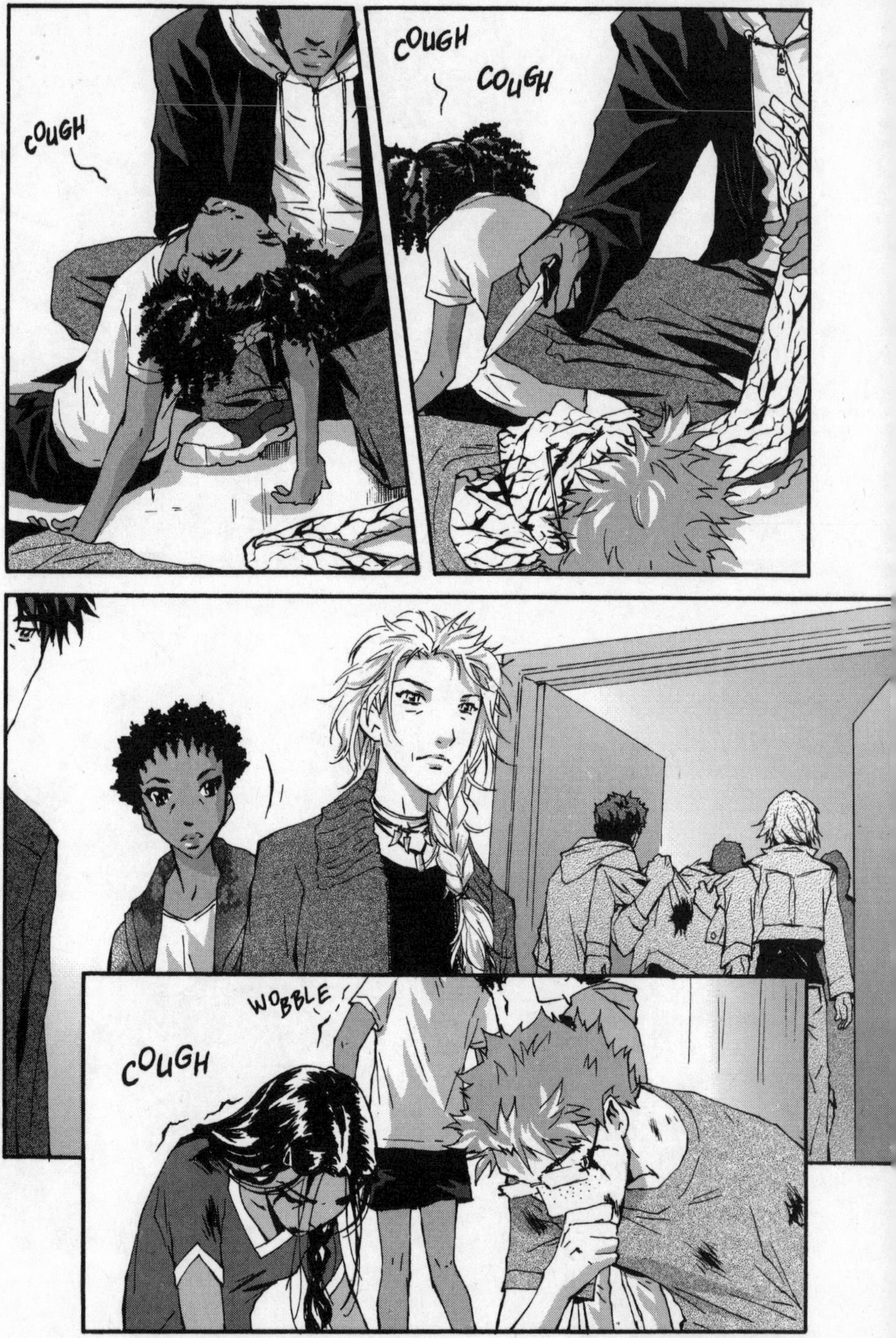
COUGH
COUGH
COUGH
WOBBLE
COUGH

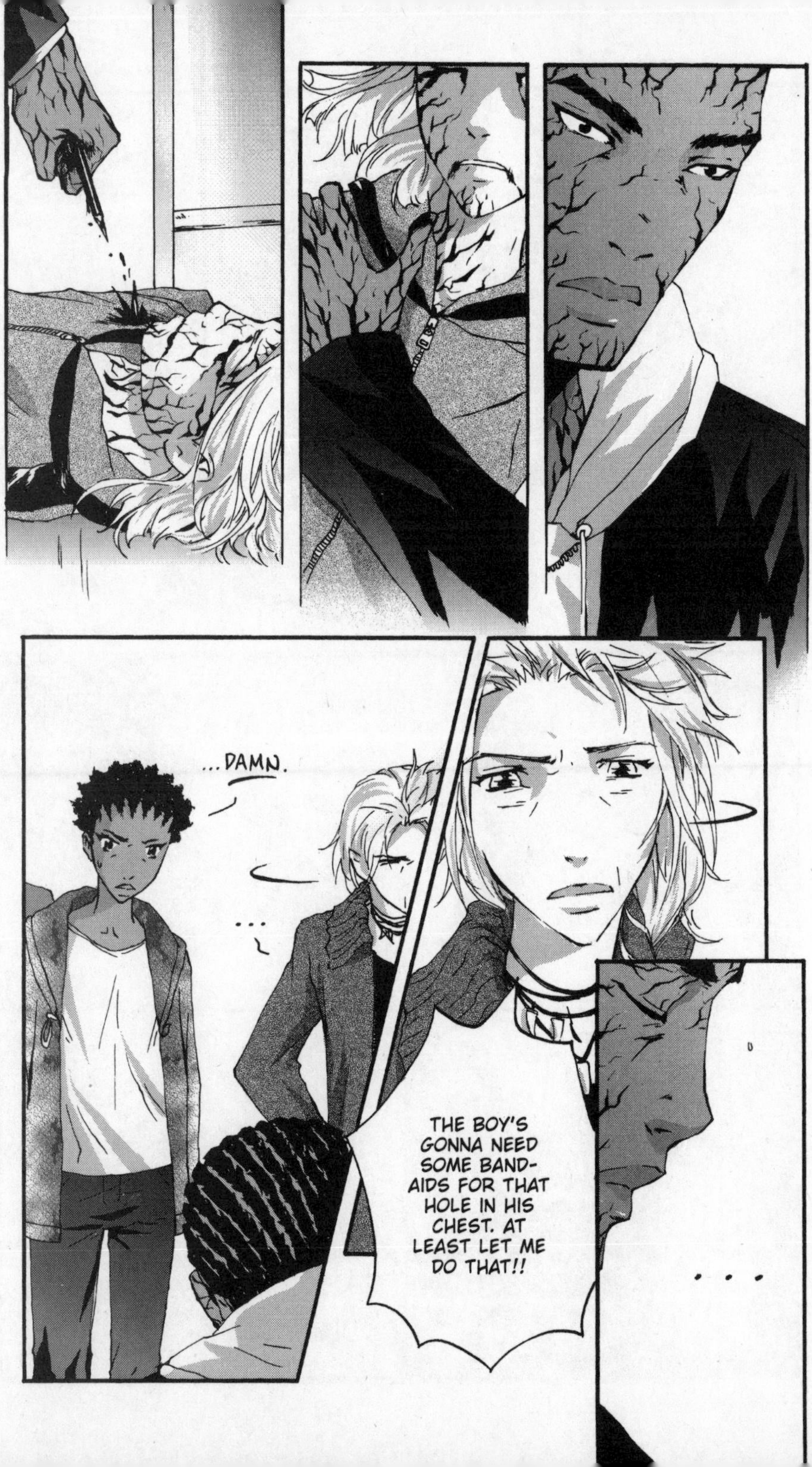
...DAMN.
...
THE BOY'S GONNA NEED SOME BAND-AIDS FOR THAT HOLE IN HIS CHEST. AT LEAST LET ME DO THAT!!
...

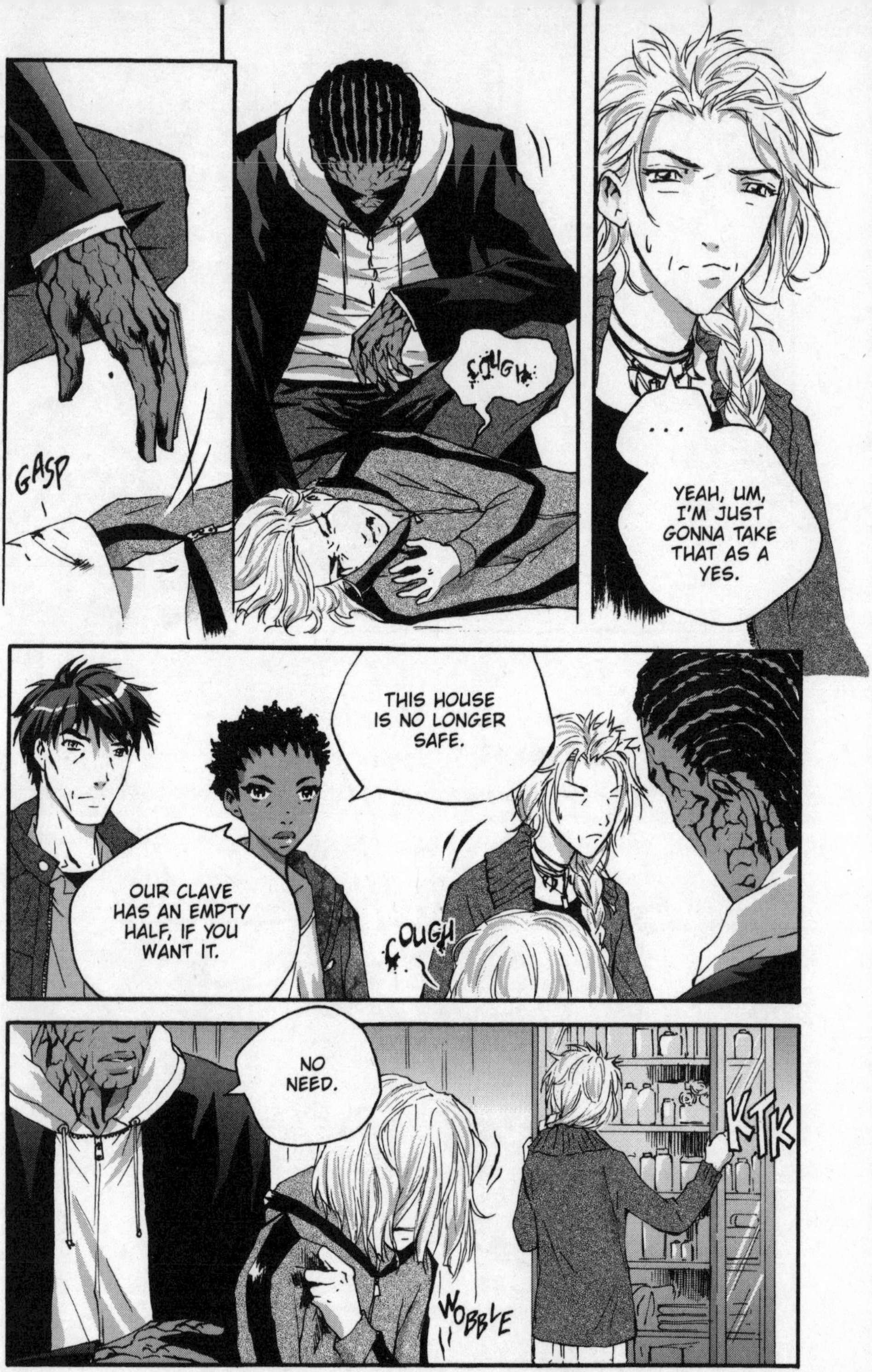

GASP
COUGH
...
YEAH, UM, I'M JUST GONNA TAKE THAT AS A YES.
THIS HOUSE IS NO LONGER SAFE.
OUR CLAVE HAS AN EMPTY HALF, IF YOU WANT IT.
COUGH
NO NEED.
KTK
WOBBLE

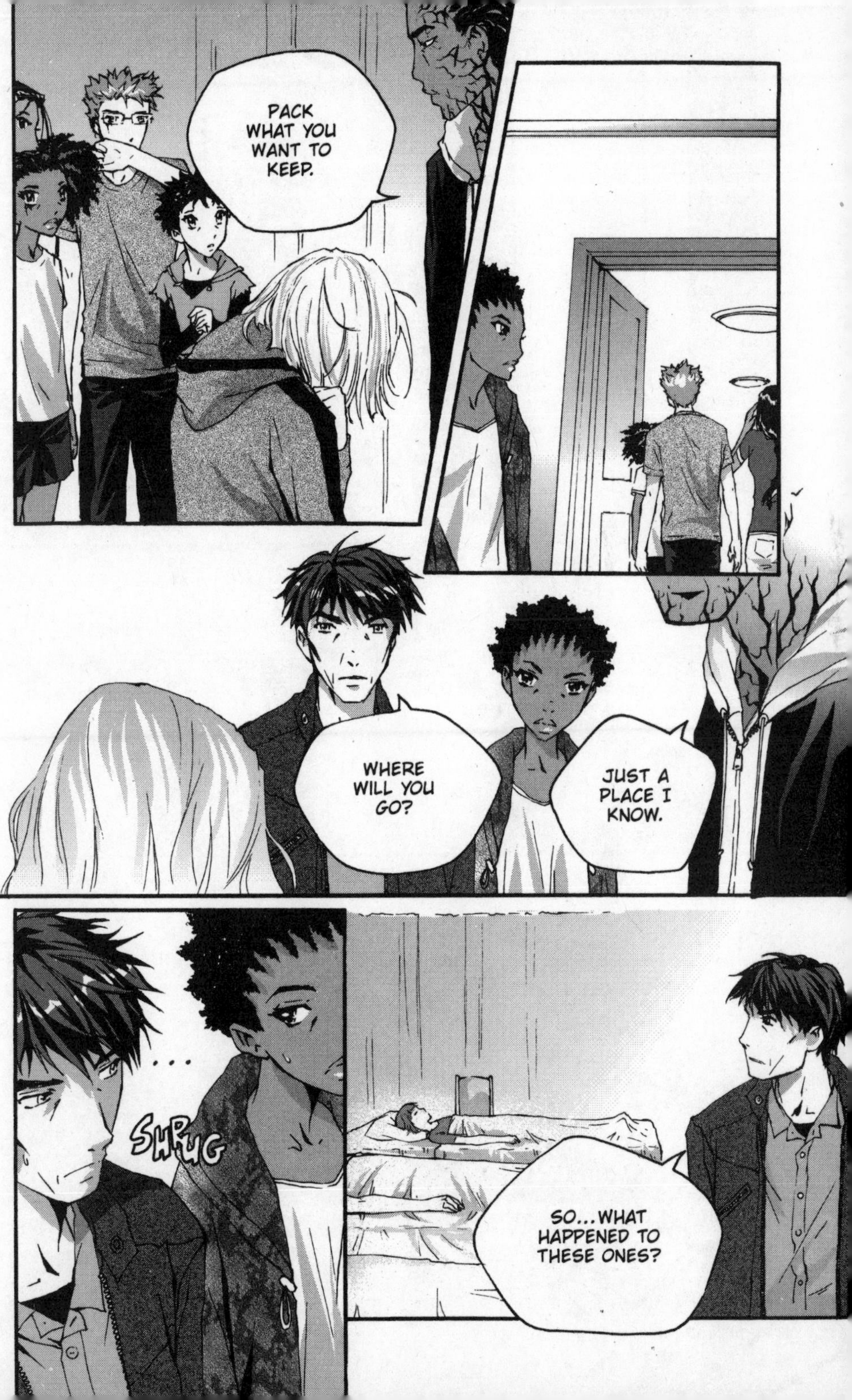
PACK WHAT YOU WANT TO KEEP.
WHERE WILL YOU GO?
JUST A PLACE I KNOW.
...
SHRUG
SO...WHAT HAPPENED TO THESE ONES?

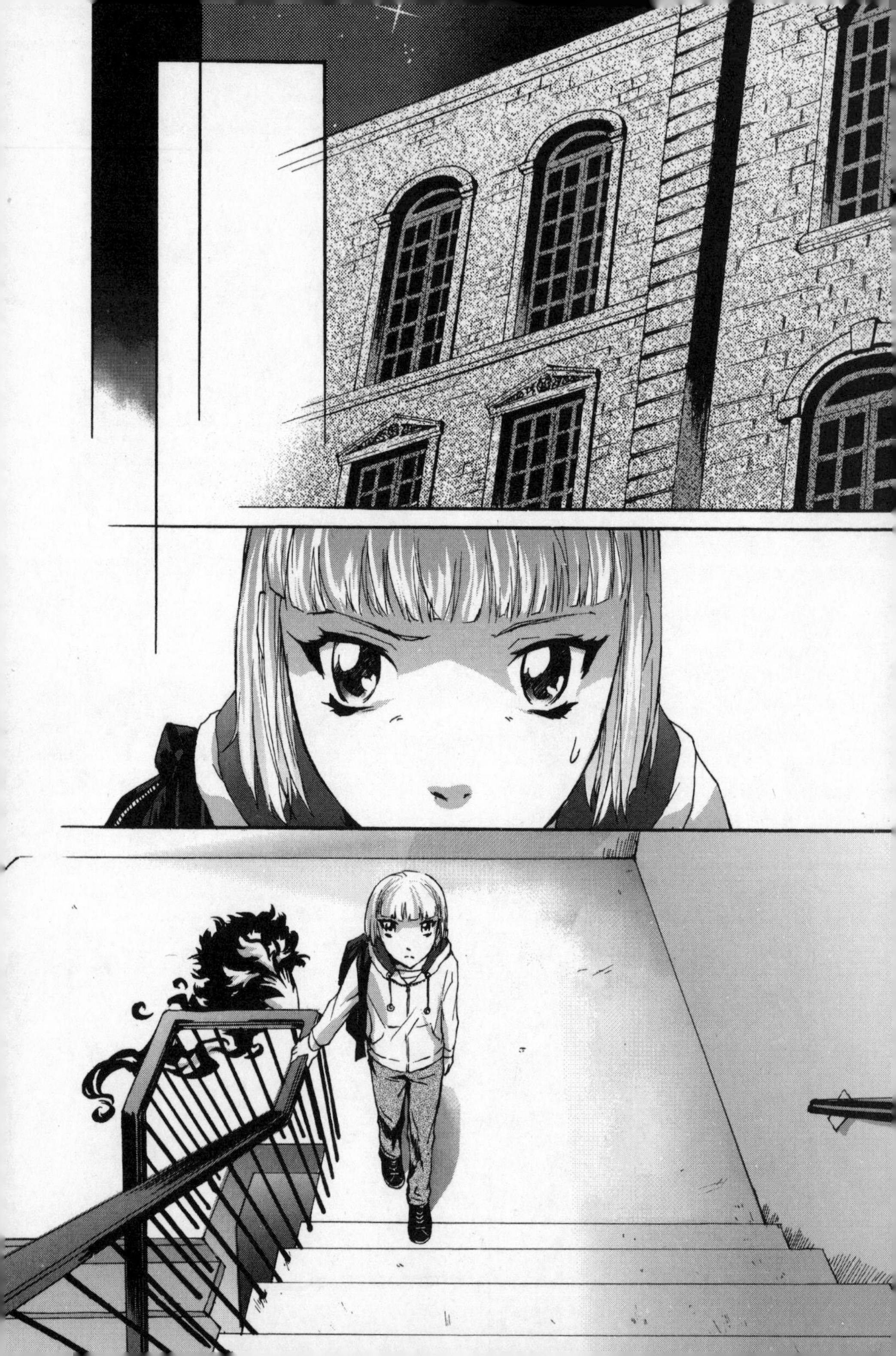

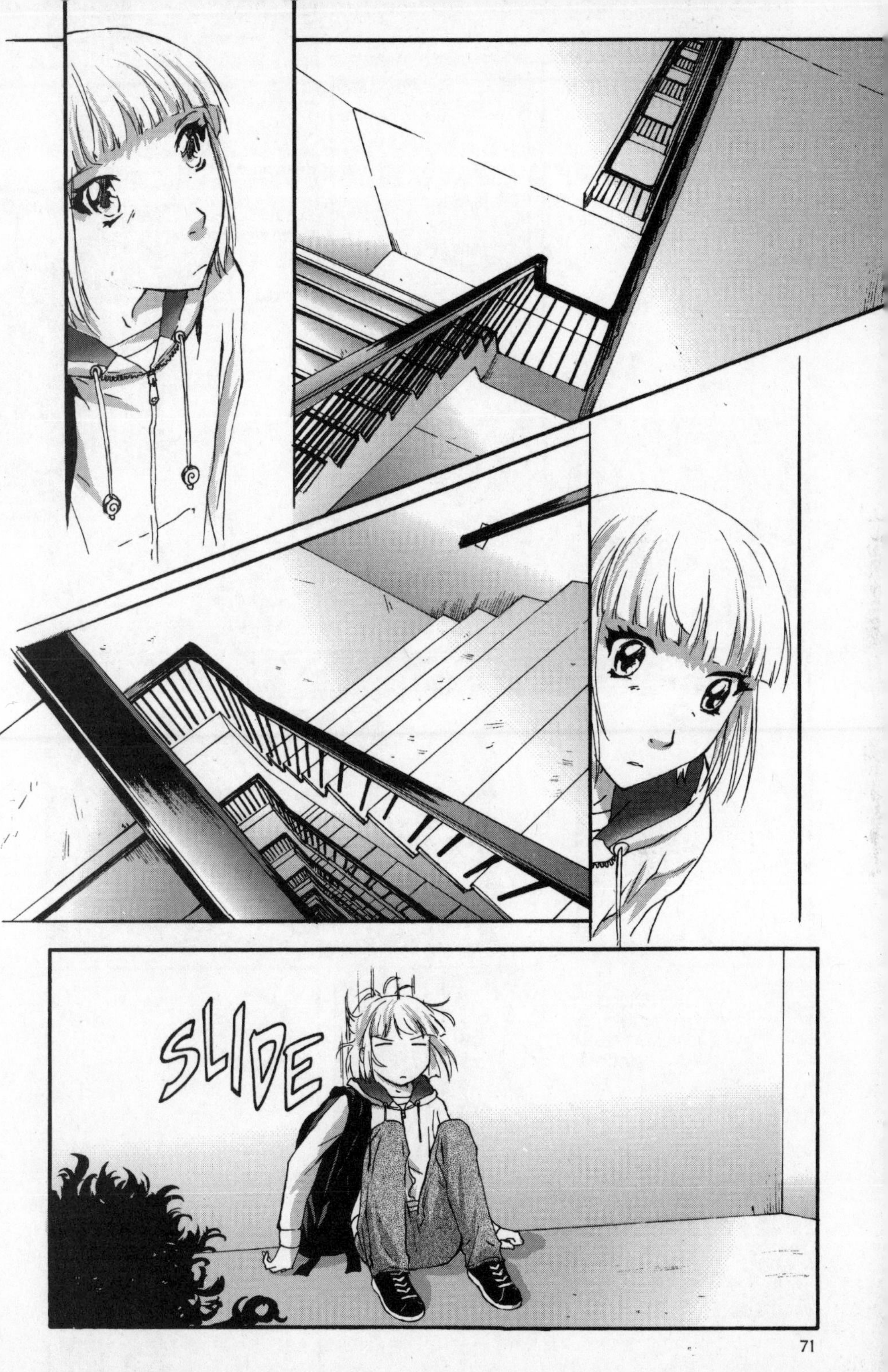
SLIDE

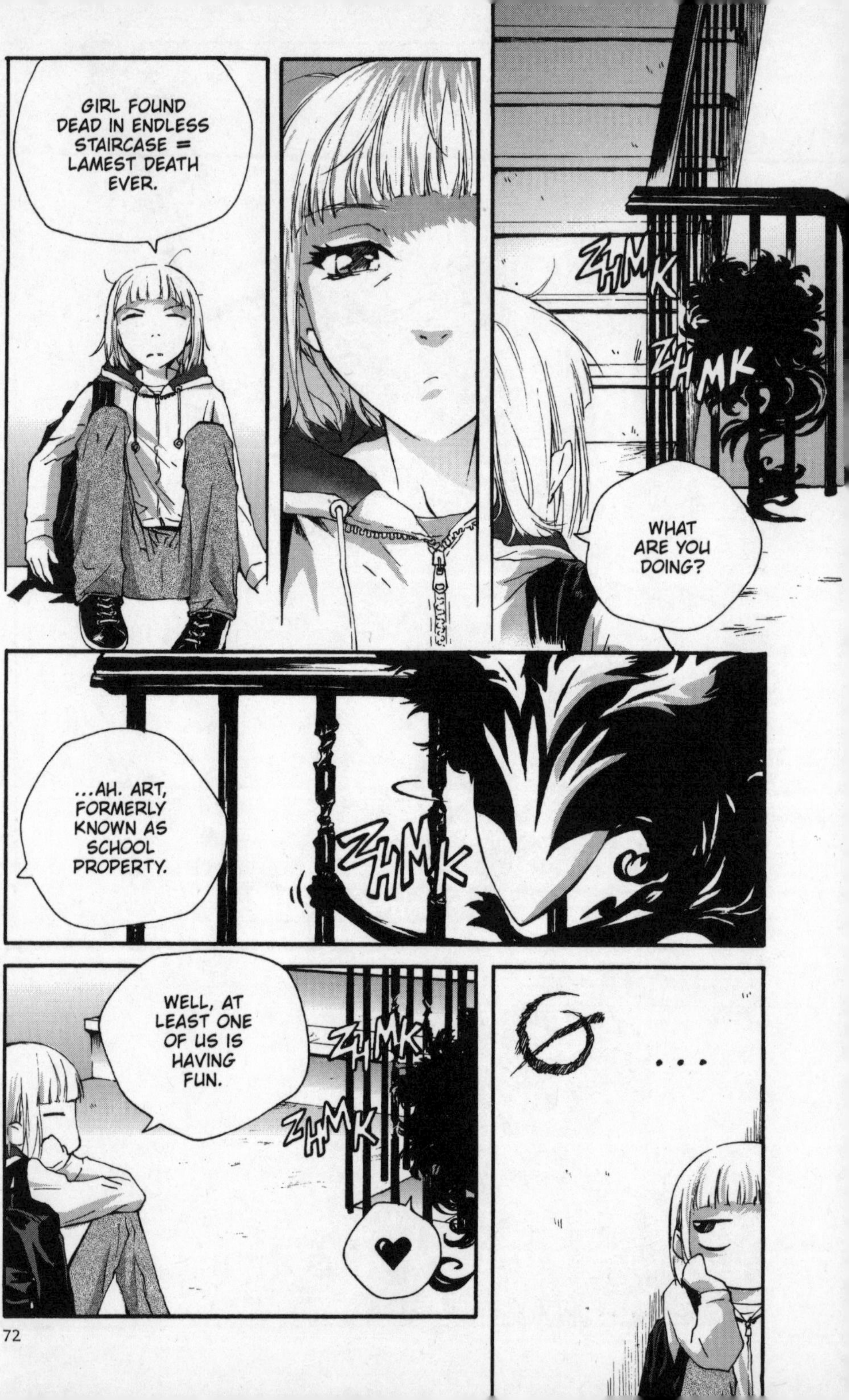
GIRL FOUND DEAD IN ENDLESS STAIRCASE = LAMEST DEATH EVER.
ZHMK
ZHMK
WHAT ARE YOU DOING?
...AH. ART, FORMERLY KNOWN AS SCHOOL PROPERTY.
ZHMK
WELL, AT LEAST ONE OF US IS HAVING FUN.
ZHMK
ZHMK
...

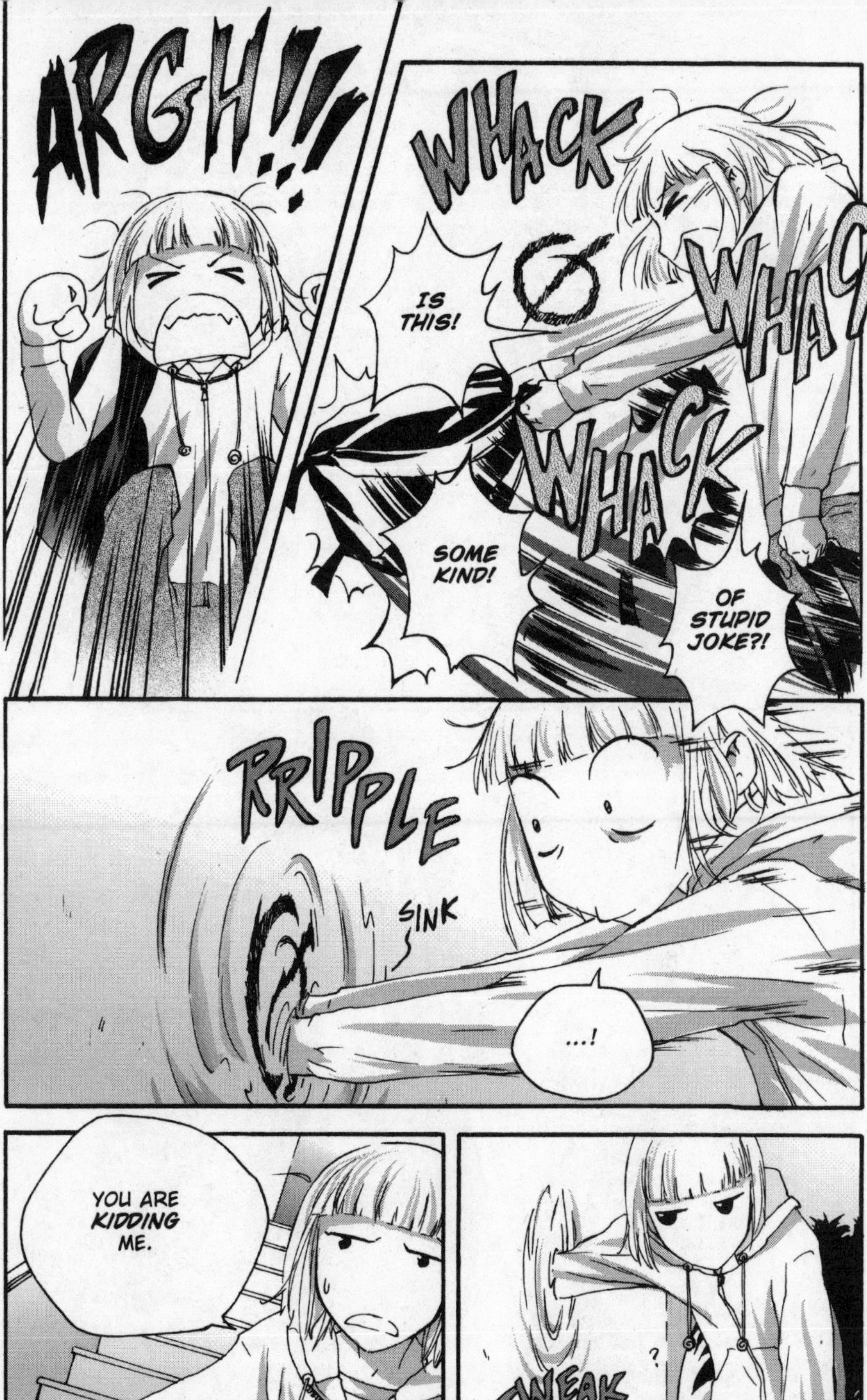
ARGH!!!
WHACK
IS THIS!
WHACK
WHACK
SOME KIND!
OF STUPID JOKE?!
RRIPPLE
SINK
...!
YOU ARE KIDDING ME.
?
TWEAK TWEAK

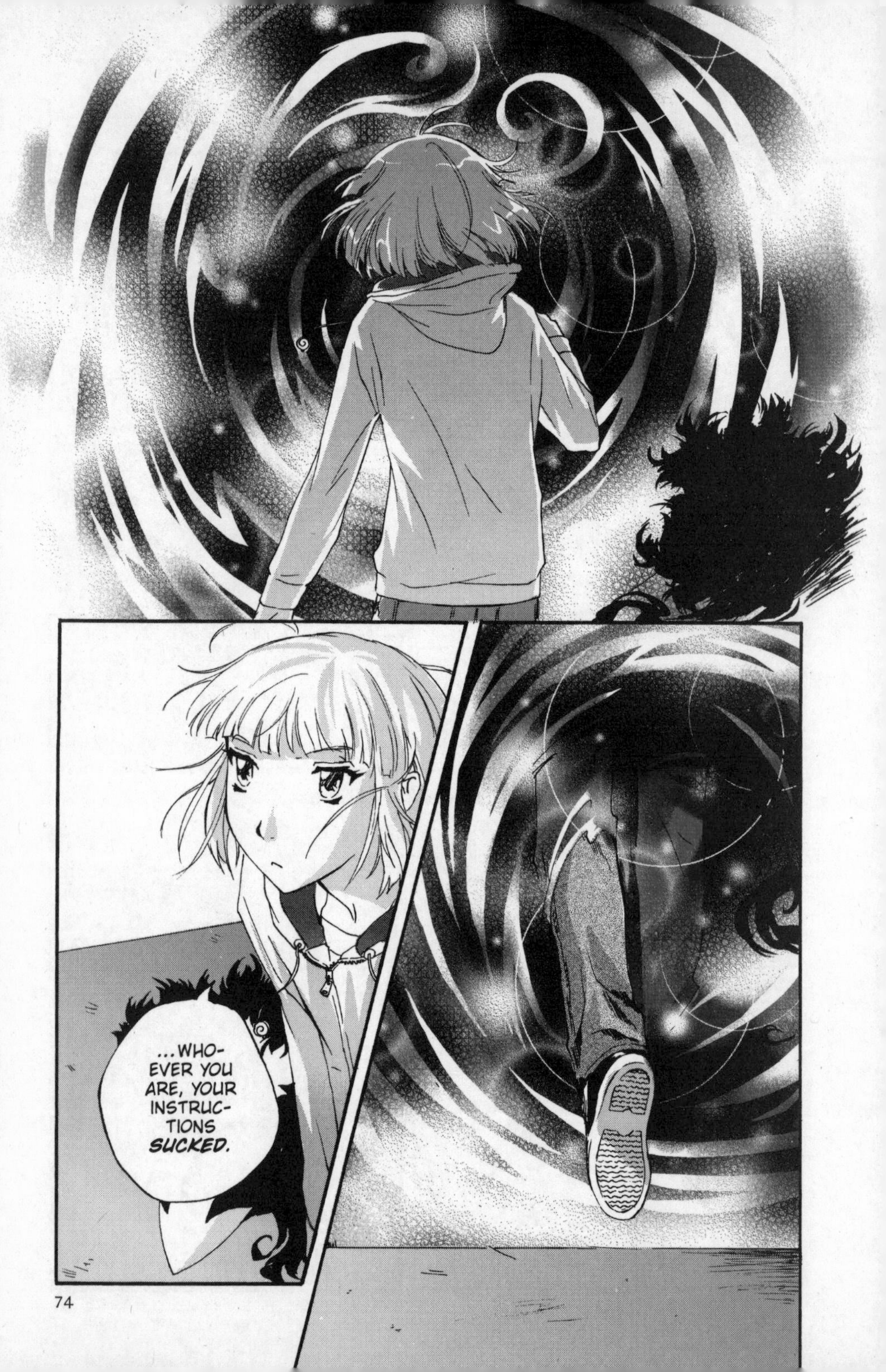
...WHO-EVER YOU ARE, YOUR INSTRUC-TIONS SUCKED.

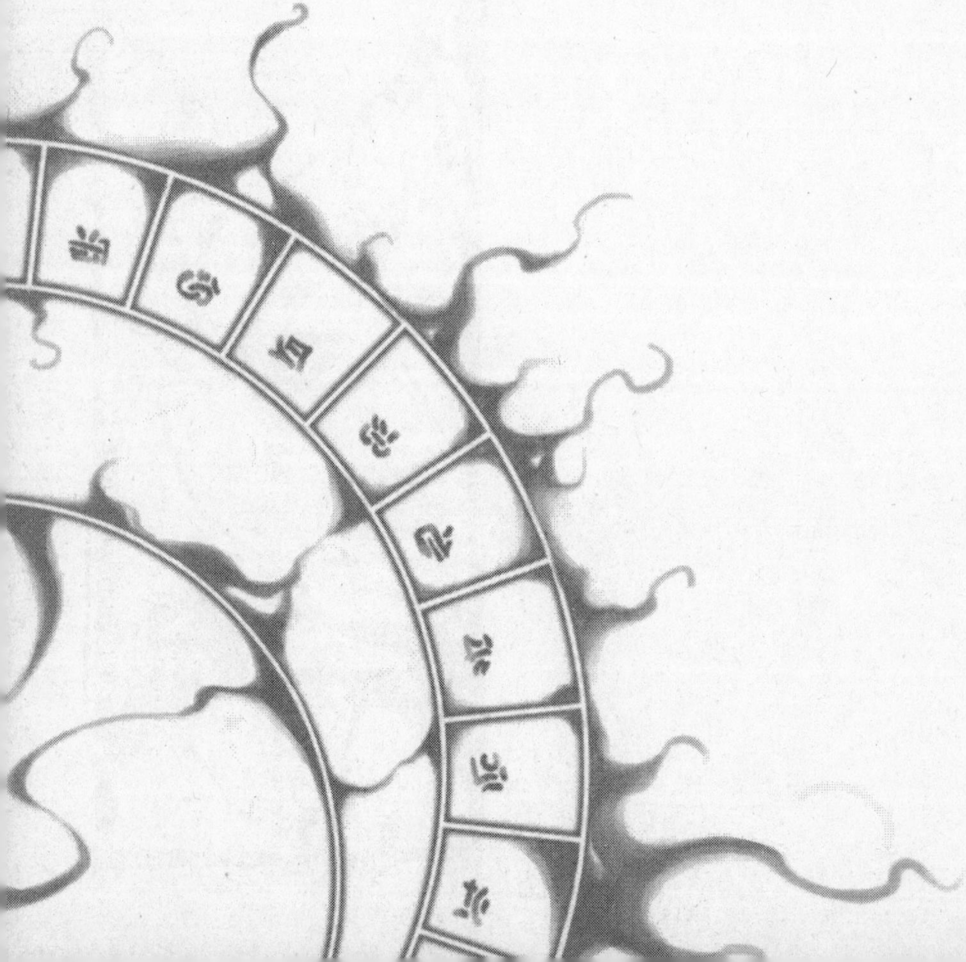

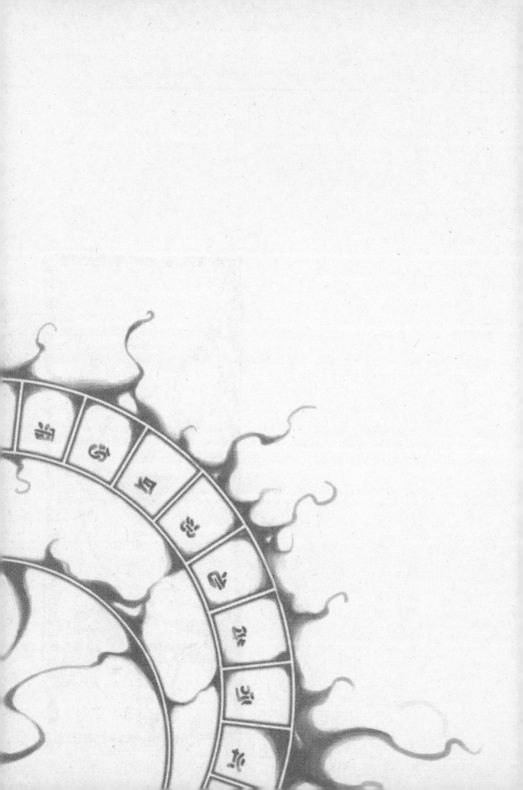

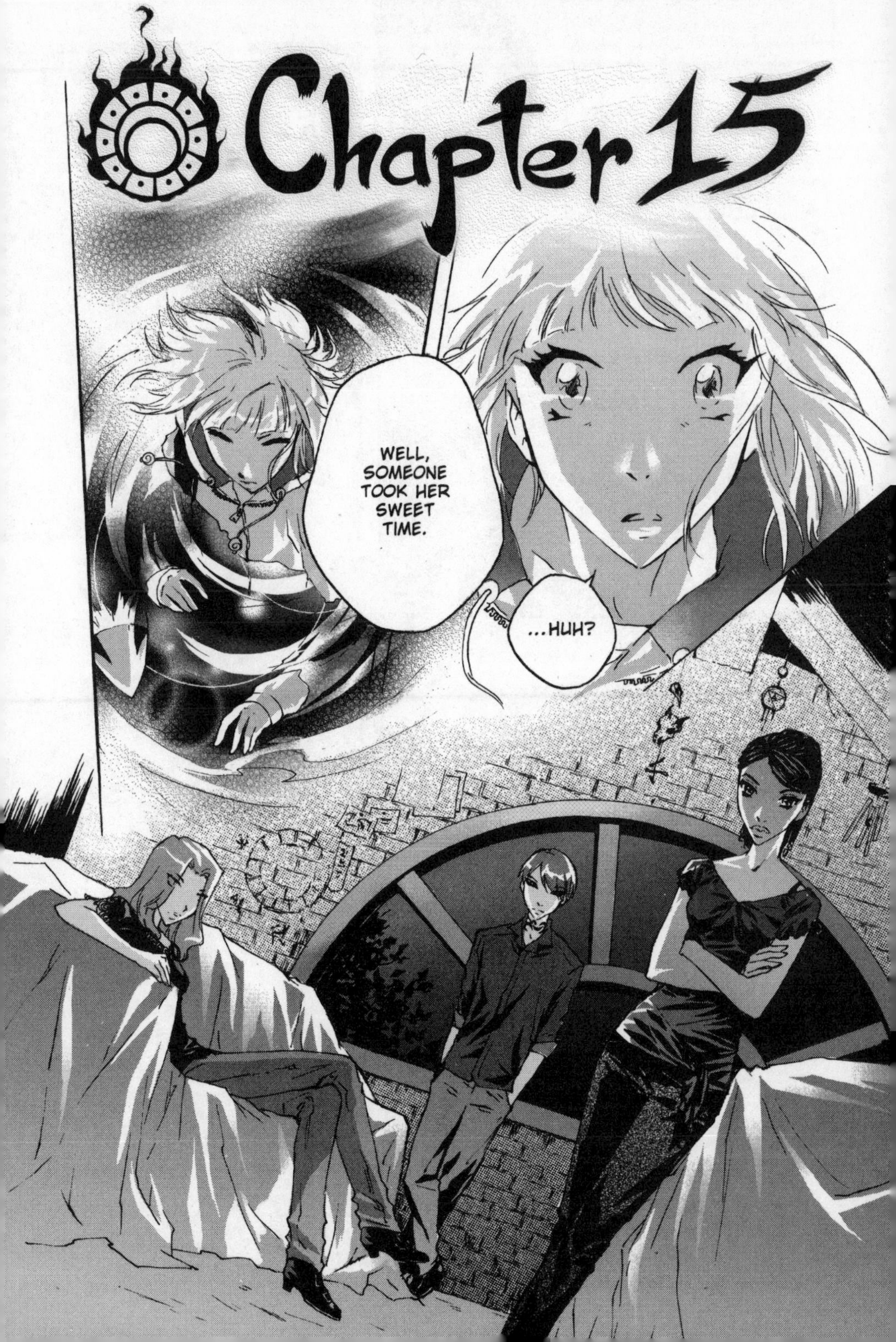
Chapter 15
WELL, SOMEONE TOOK HER SWEET TIME.
...HUH?

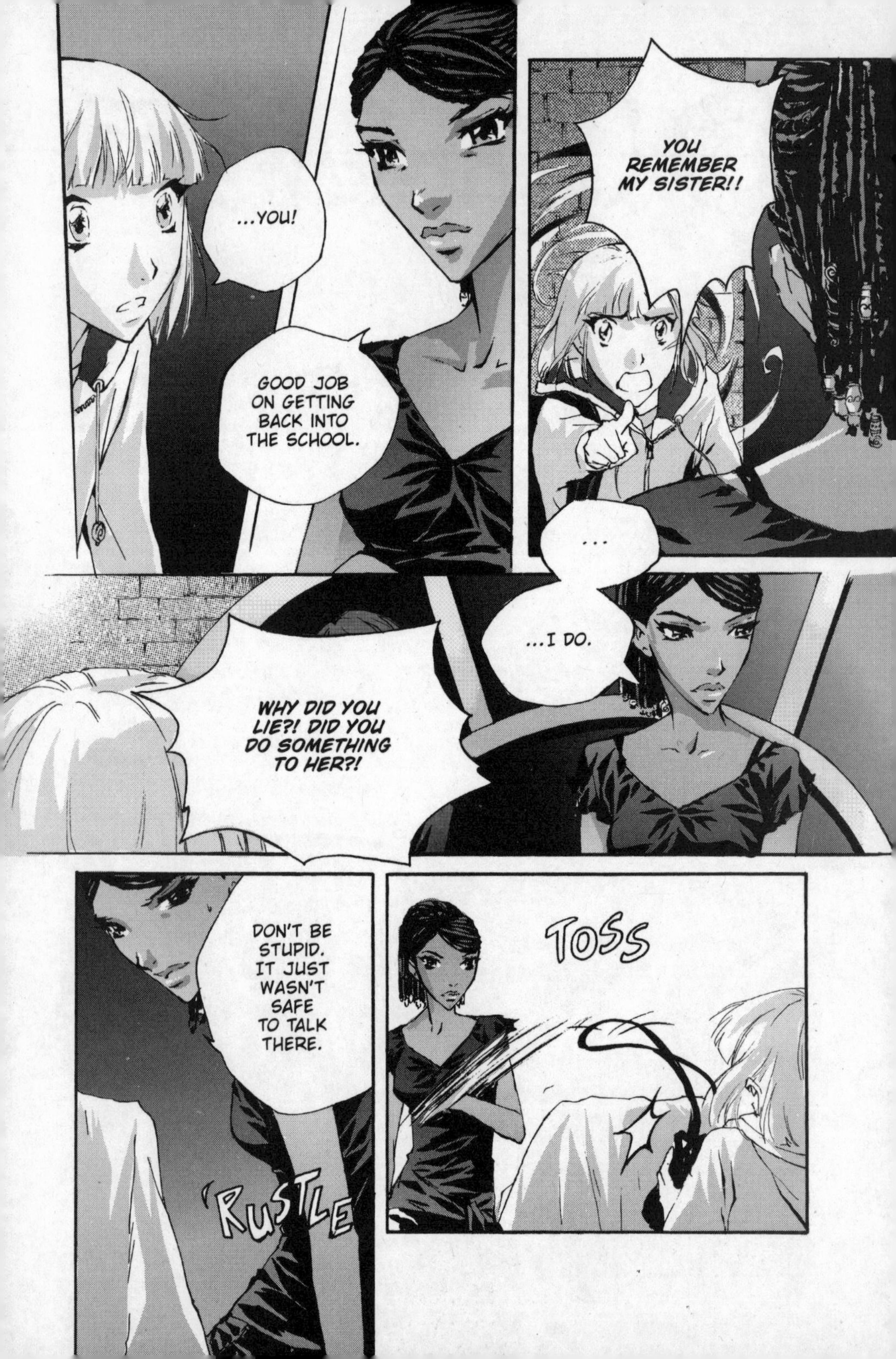
...YOU!
GOOD JOB ON GETTING BACK INTO THE SCHOOL.
YOU REMEMBER MY SISTER!!
...
WHY DID YOU LIE?! DID YOU DO SOMETHING TO HER?!
...I DO.
DON'T BE STUPID. IT JUST WASN'T SAFE TO TALK THERE.
RUSTLE
TOSS

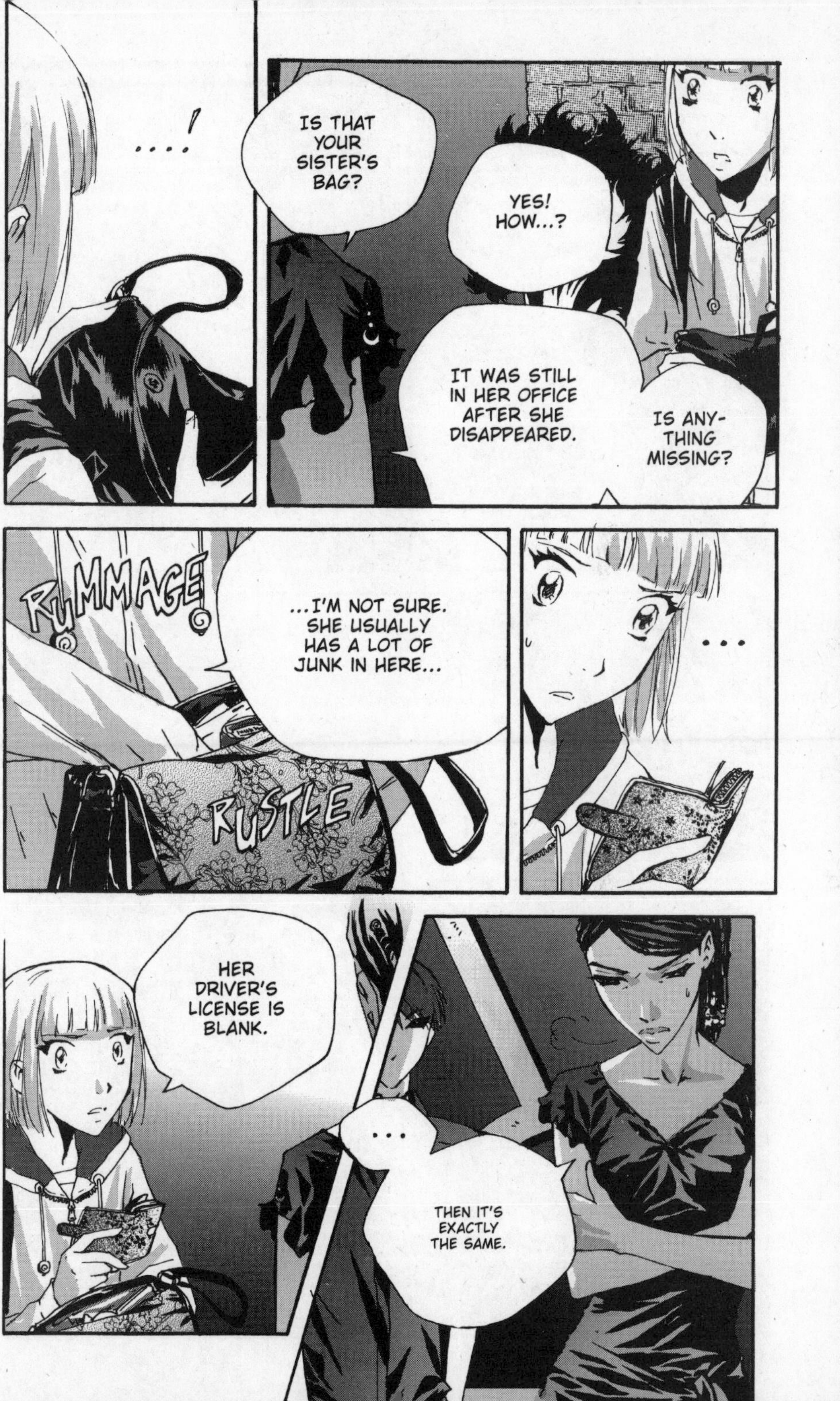
....!
IS THAT YOUR SISTER'S BAG?
YES! HOW...?
IT WAS STILL IN HER OFFICE AFTER SHE DISAPPEARED.
IS ANY-THING MISSING?
RUMMAGE
...I'M NOT SURE. SHE USUALLY HAS A LOT OF JUNK IN HERE...
RUSTLE
...
HER DRIVER'S LICENSE IS BLANK.
...
THEN IT'S EXACTLY THE SAME.

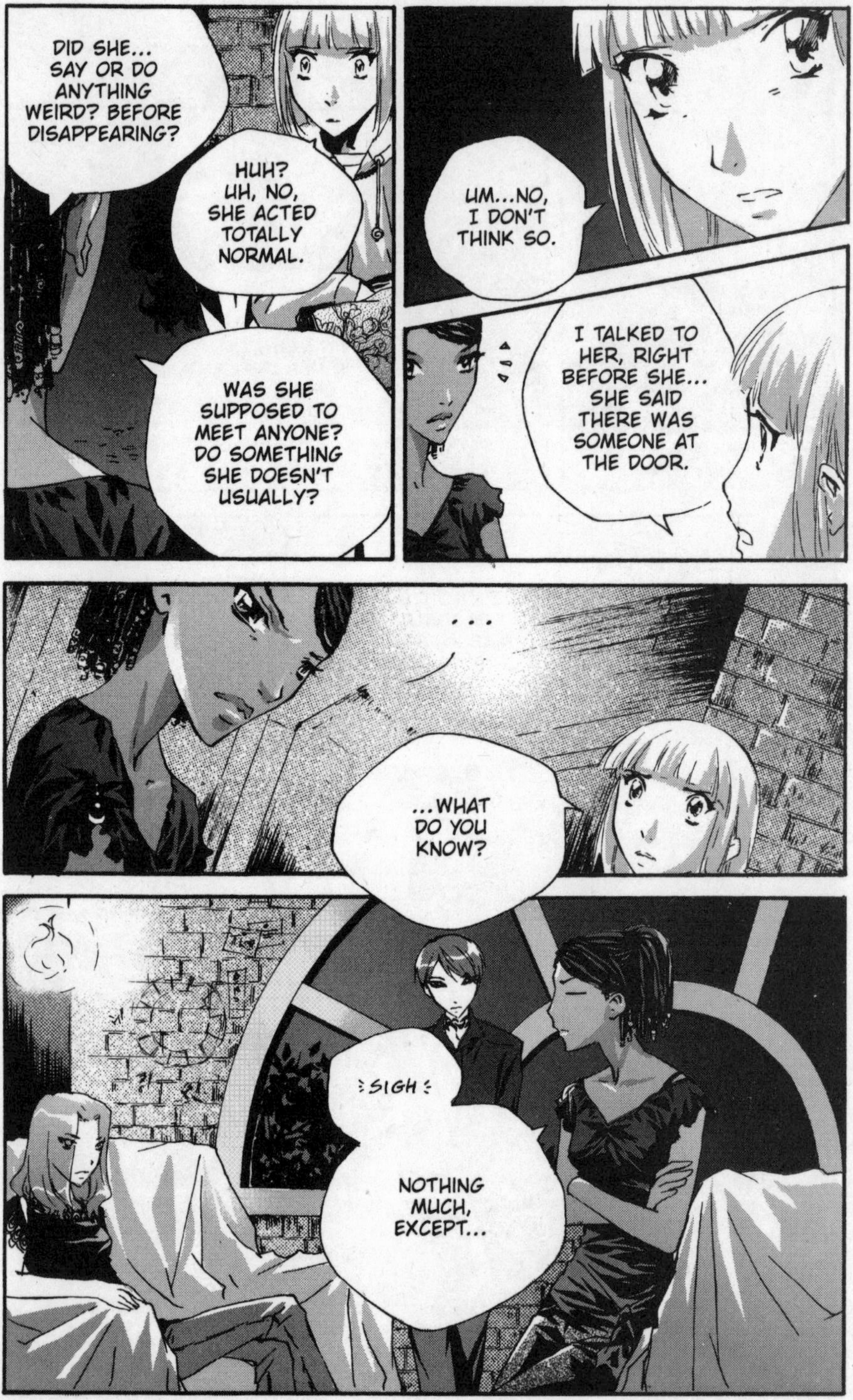
DID SHE... SAY OR DO ANYTHING WEIRD? BEFORE DISAPPEARING?
HUH? UH, NO, SHE ACTED TOTALLY NORMAL.
WAS SHE SUPPOSED TO MEET ANYONE? DO SOMETHING SHE DOESN'T USUALLY?
UM...NO, I DON'T THINK SO.
I TALKED TO HER, RIGHT BEFORE SHE... SHE SAID THERE WAS SOMEONE AT THE DOOR.
...
...WHAT DO YOU KNOW?
SIGH
NOTHING MUCH, EXCEPT...

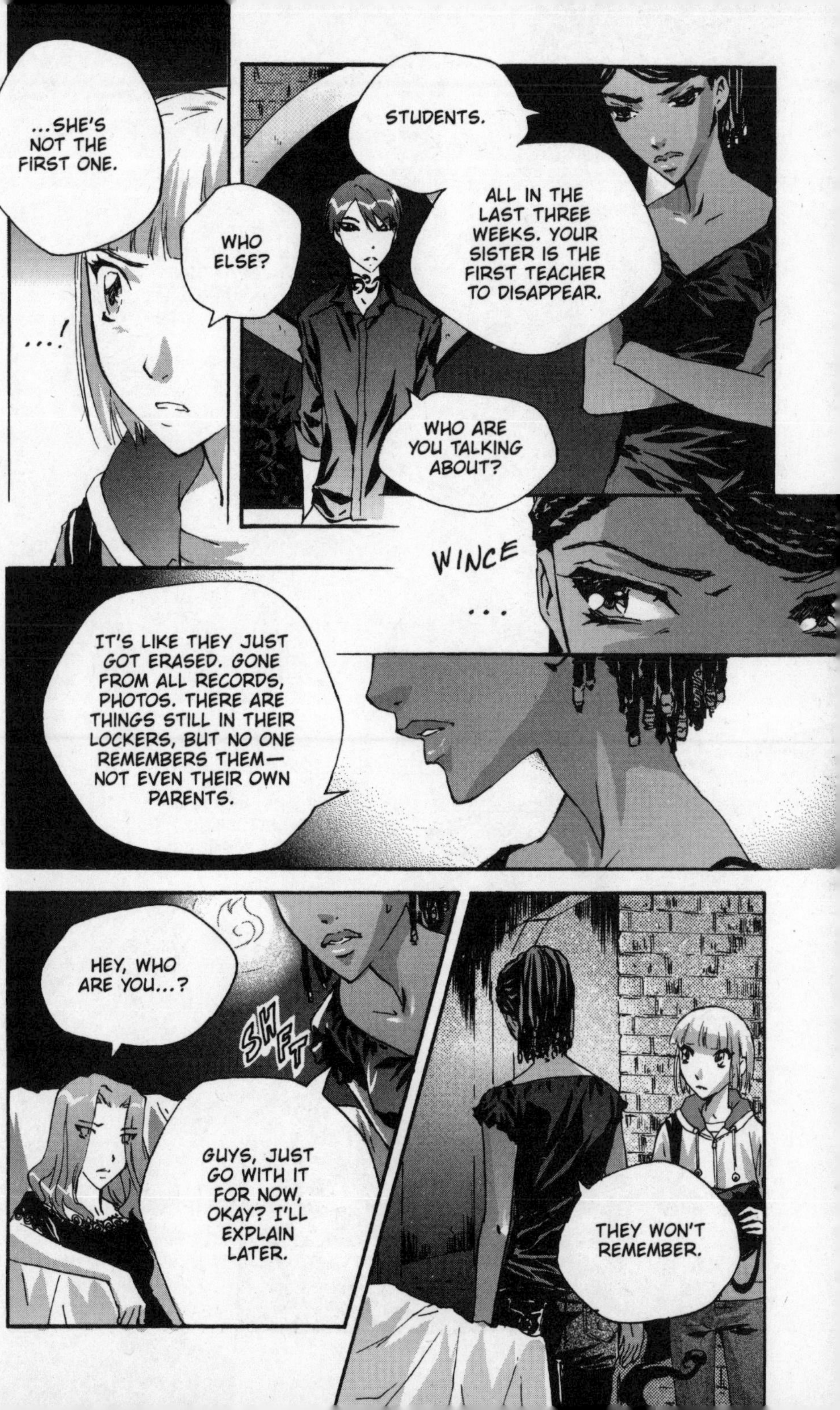
...SHE'S NOT THE FIRST ONE.
...!
WHO ELSE?
STUDENTS.
ALL IN THE LAST THREE WEEKS. YOUR SISTER IS THE FIRST TEACHER TO DISAPPEAR.
WHO ARE YOU TALKING ABOUT?
WINCE
...
IT'S LIKE THEY JUST GOT ERASED. GONE FROM ALL RECORDS, PHOTOS. THERE ARE THINGS STILL IN THEIR LOCKERS, BUT NO ONE REMEMBERS THEM—NOT EVEN THEIR OWN PARENTS.
HEY, WHO ARE YOU...?
SHFT
GUYS, JUST GO WITH IT FOR NOW, OKAY? I'LL EXPLAIN LATER.
THEY WON'T REMEMBER.

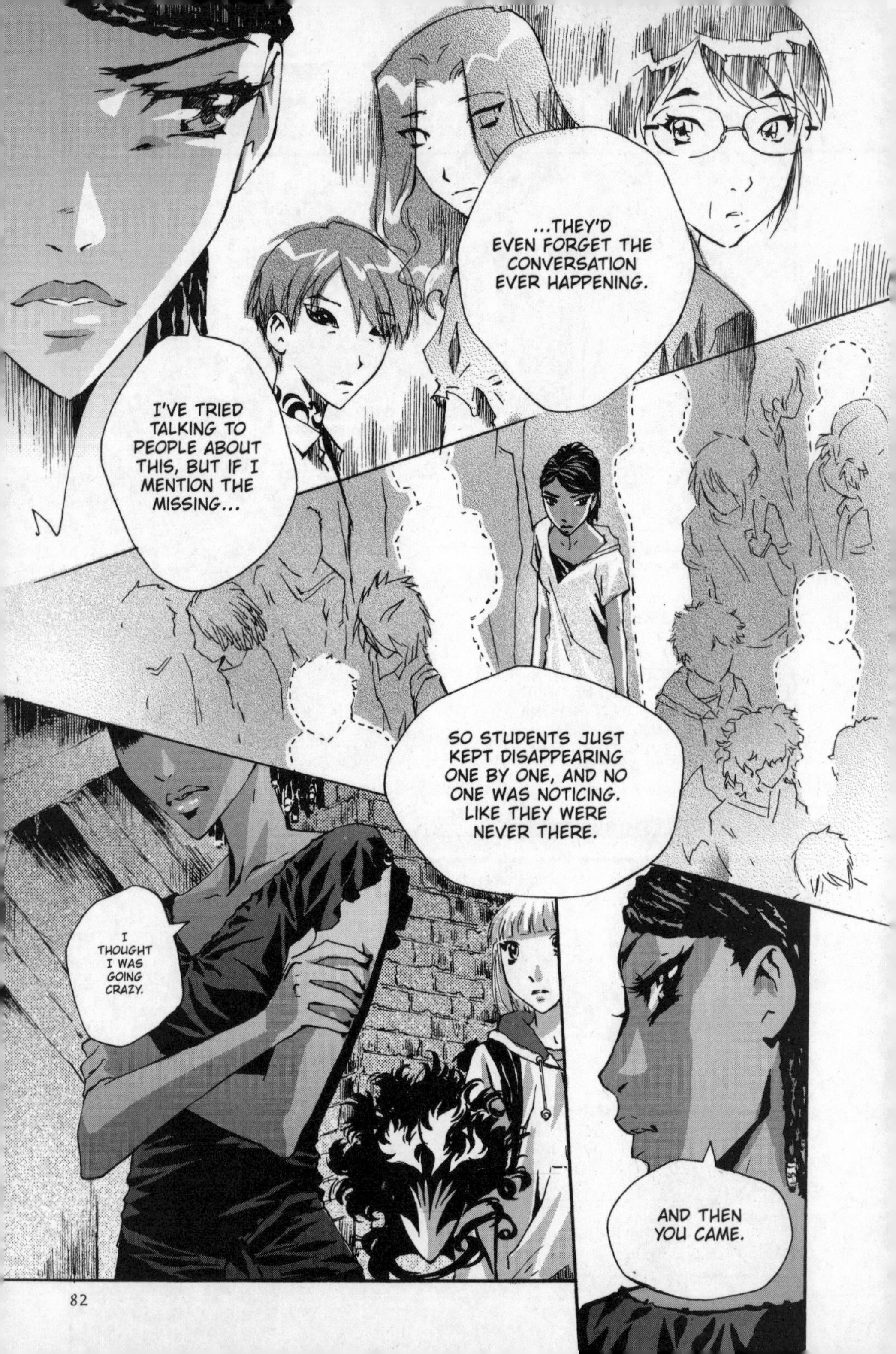
I'VE TRIED TALKING TO PEOPLE ABOUT THIS, BUT IF I MENTION THE MISSING...
...THEY'D EVEN FORGET THE CONVERSATION EVER HAPPENING.
SO STUDENTS JUST KEPT DISAPPEARING ONE BY ONE, AND NO ONE WAS NOTICING. LIKE THEY WERE NEVER THERE.
I THOUGHT I WAS GOING CRAZY.
AND THEN YOU CAME.

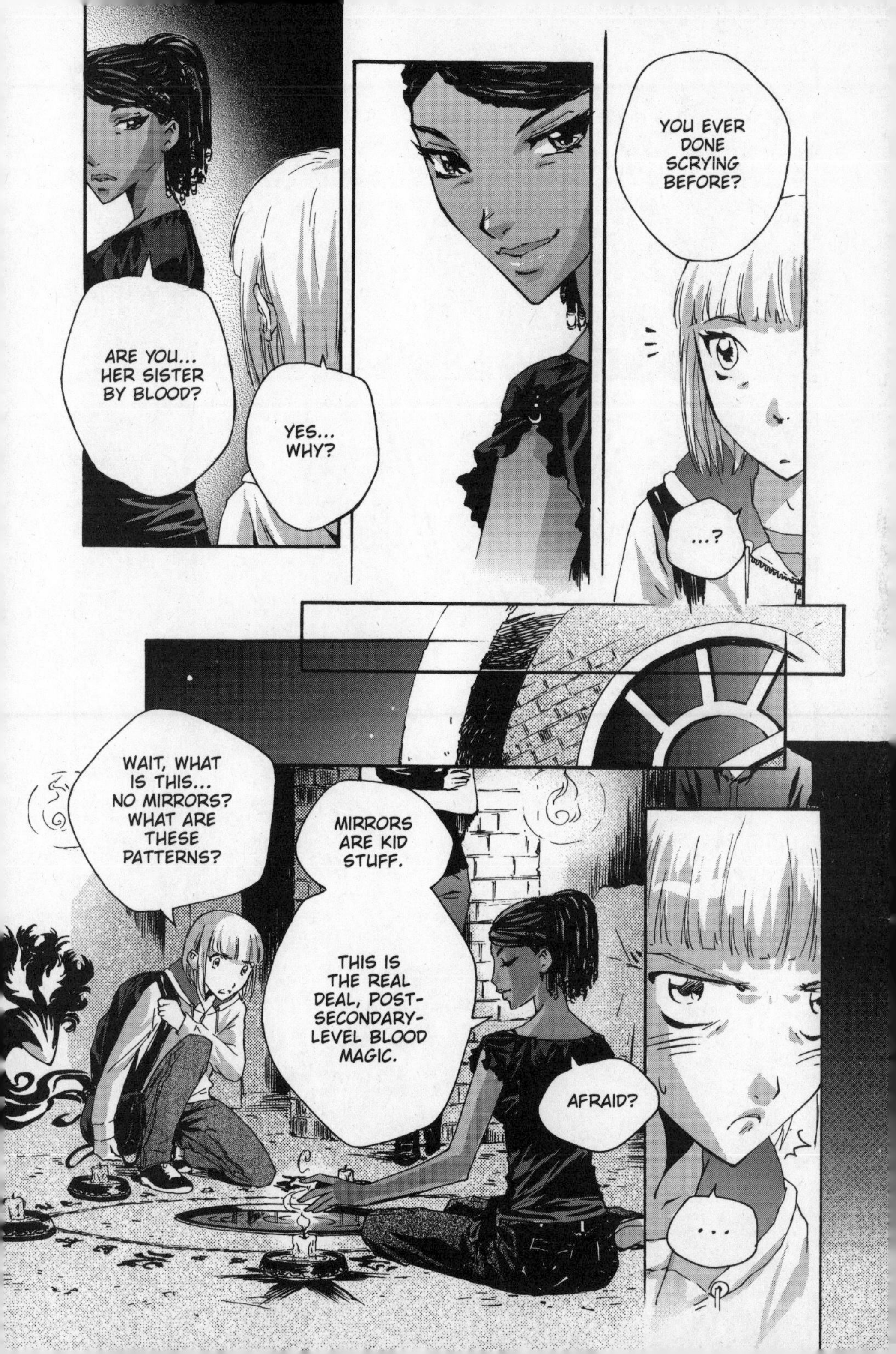
ARE YOU... HER SISTER BY BLOOD?
YES... WHY?
YOU EVER DONE SCRYING BEFORE?
...?
WAIT, WHAT IS THIS... NO MIRRORS? WHAT ARE THESE PATTERNS?
MIRRORS ARE KID STUFF.
THIS IS THE REAL DEAL, POST-SECONDARY-LEVEL BLOOD MAGIC.
AFRAID?
...

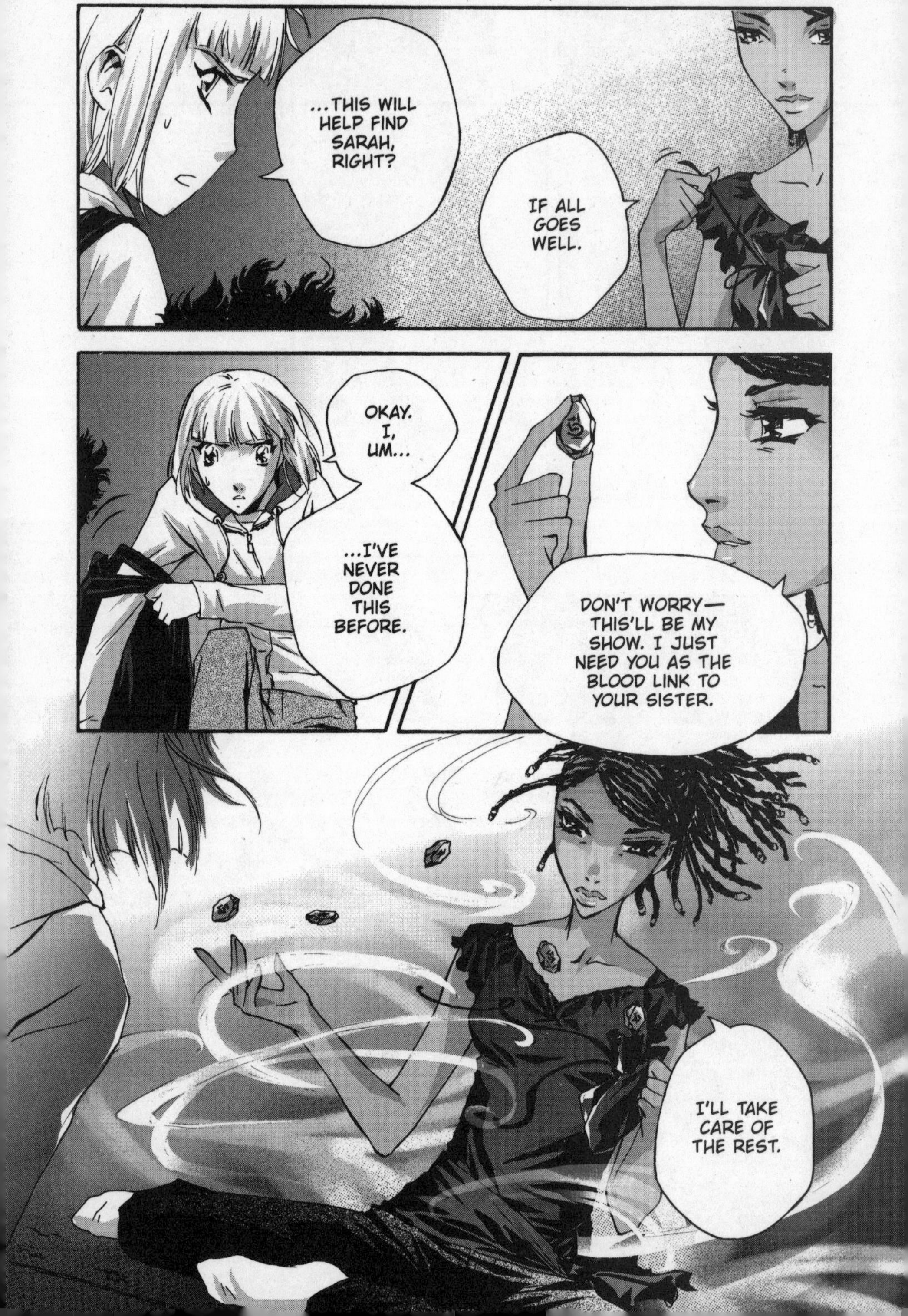
...THIS WILL HELP FIND SARAH, RIGHT?
IF ALL GOES WELL.
OKAY. I, UM...
...I'VE NEVER DONE THIS BEFORE.
DON'T WORRY—THIS'LL BE MY SHOW. I JUST NEED YOU AS THE BLOOD LINK TO YOUR SISTER.
I'LL TAKE CARE OF THE REST.

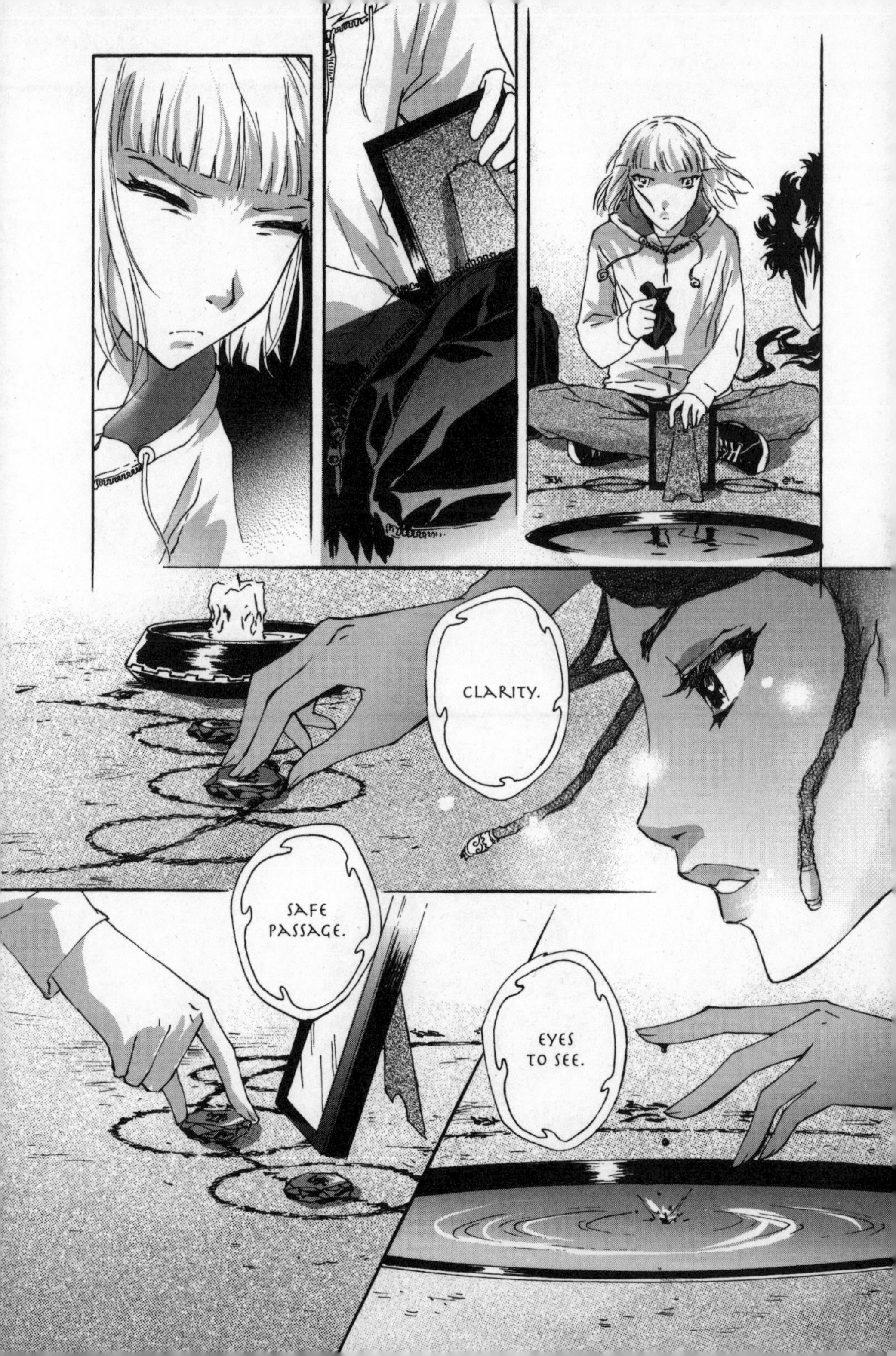
CLARITY.
SAFE PASSAGE.
EYES TO SEE.

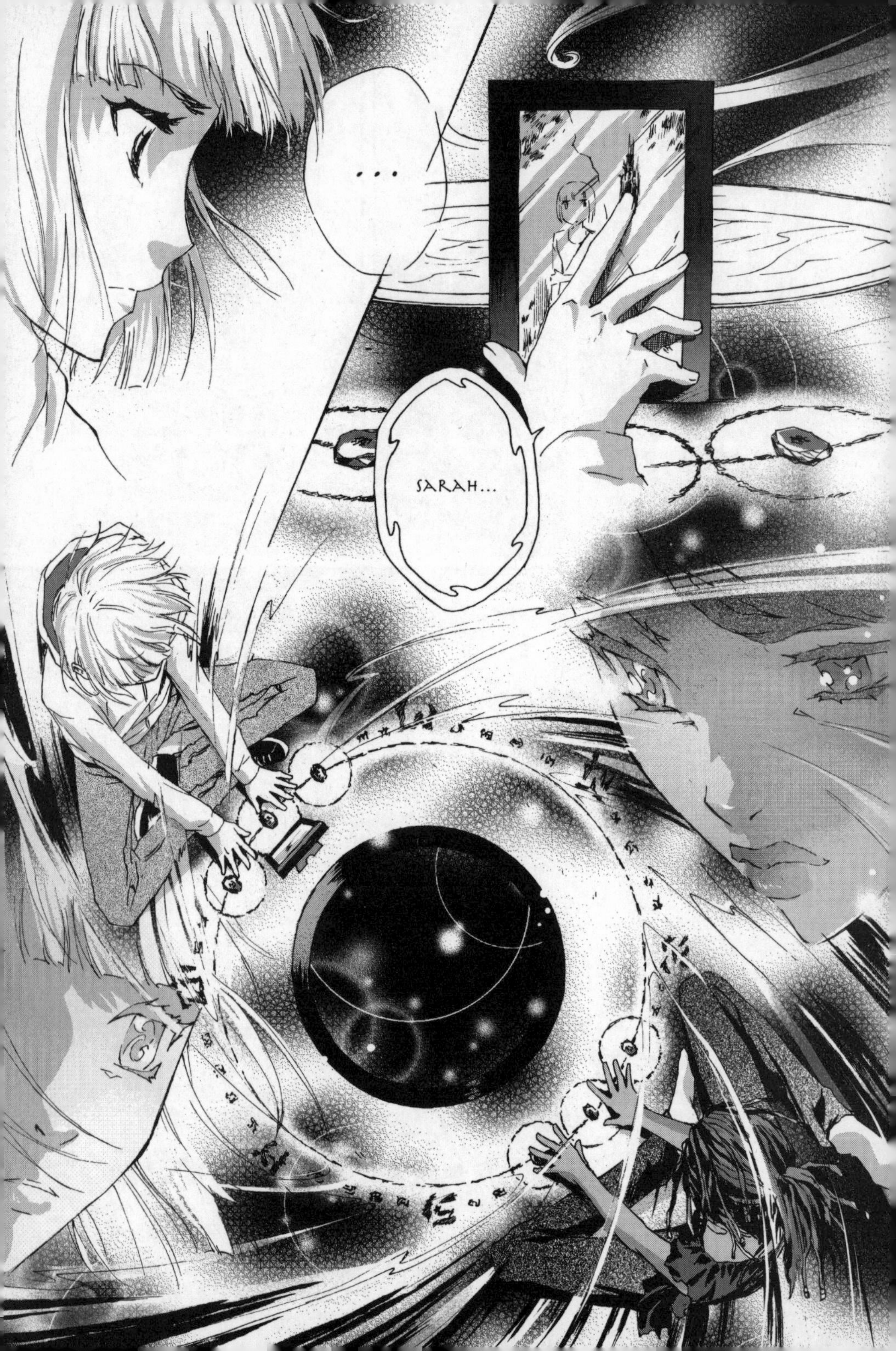
...
SARAH...

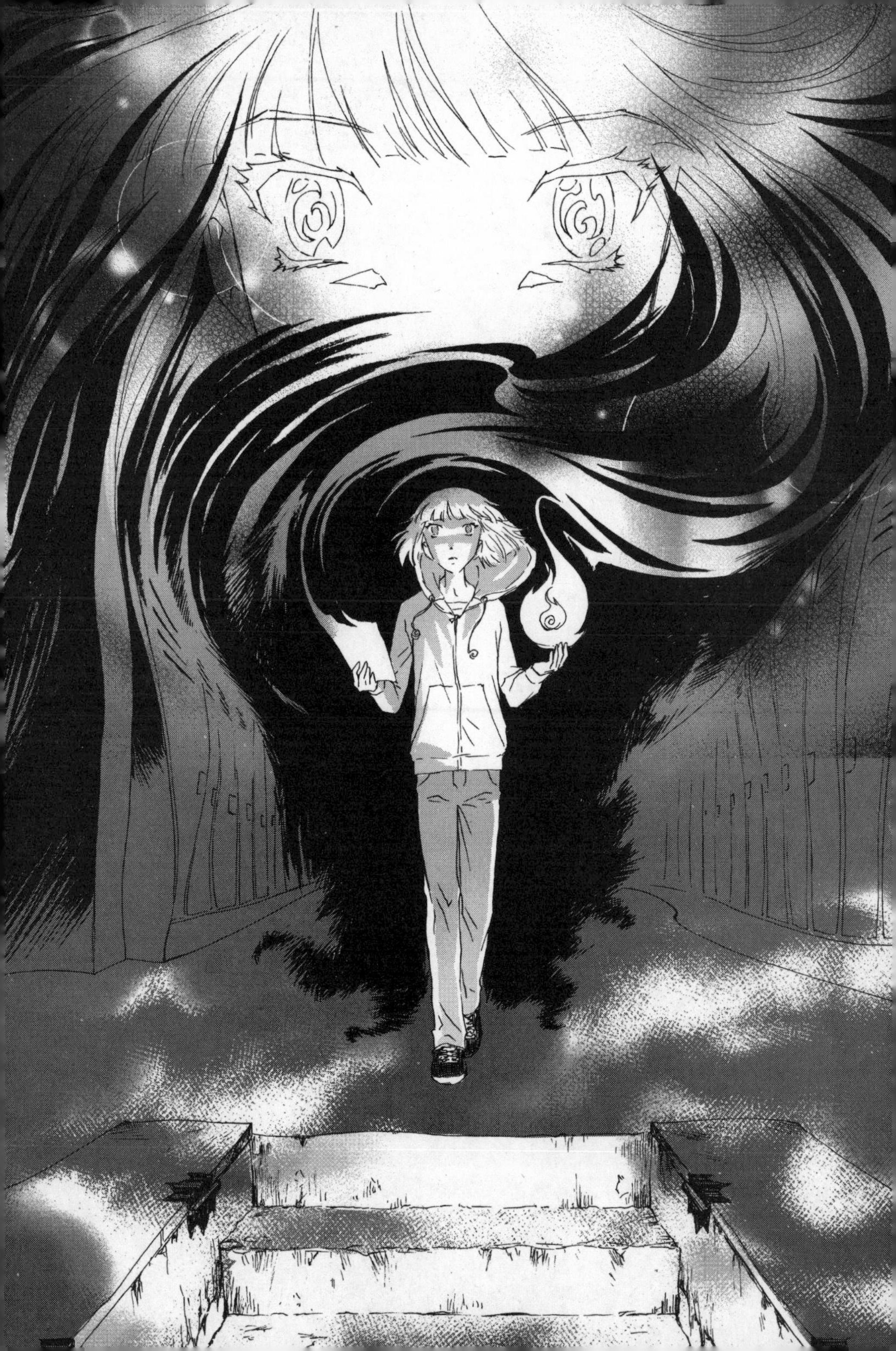

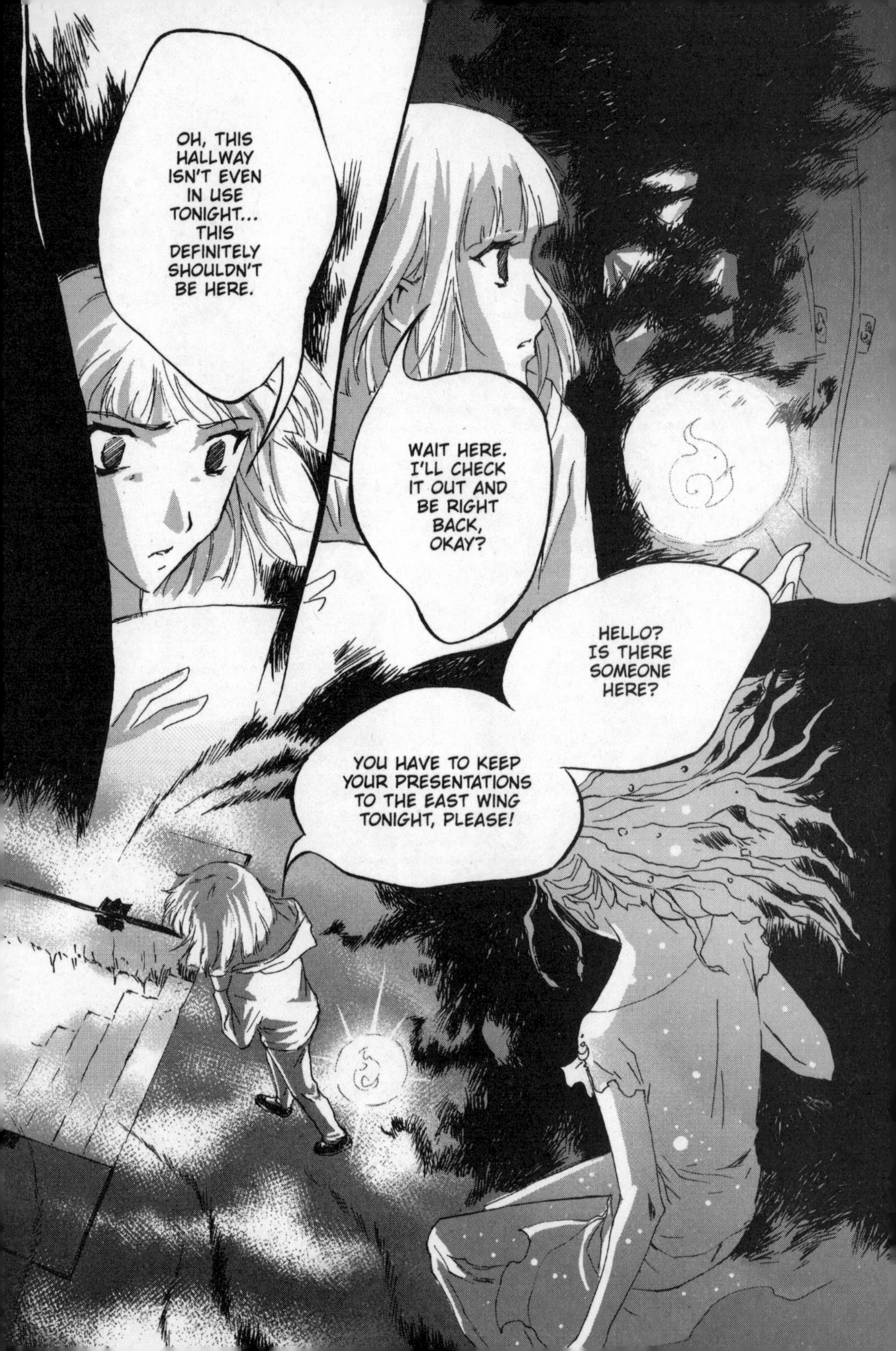
OH, THIS HALLWAY ISN'T EVEN IN USE TONIGHT... THIS DEFINITELY SHOULDN'T BE HERE.
WAIT HERE. I'LL CHECK IT OUT AND BE RIGHT BACK, OKAY?
HELLO? IS THERE SOMEONE HERE?
YOU HAVE TO KEEP YOUR PRESENTATIONS TO THE EAST WING TONIGHT, PLEASE!

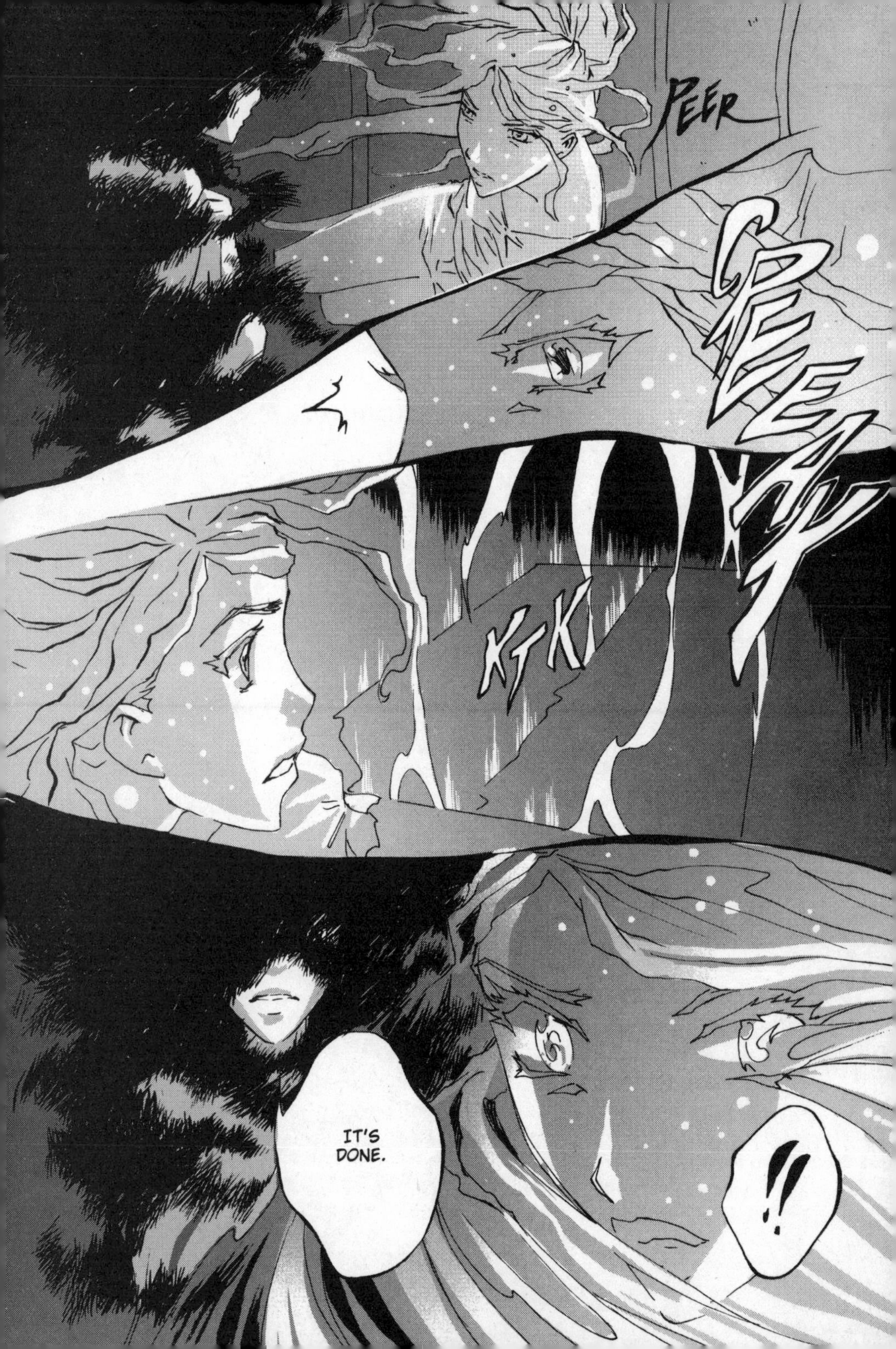
PEER
CREEAK
KTK
IT'S DONE.
!!

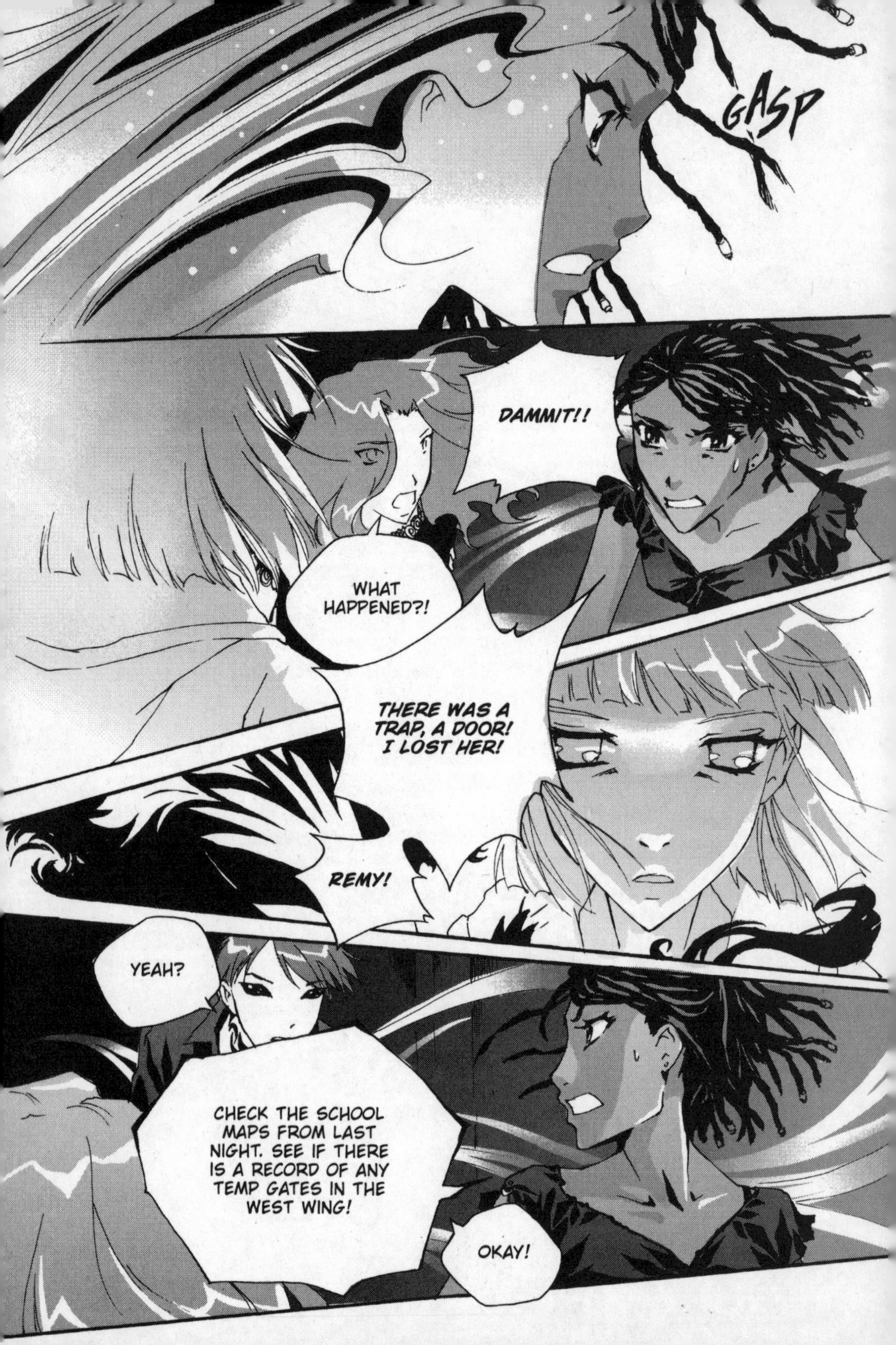
GASP
DAMMIT!!
WHAT HAPPENED?!
THERE WAS A TRAP, A DOOR! I LOST HER!
REMY!
YEAH?
CHECK THE SCHOOL MAPS FROM LAST NIGHT. SEE IF THERE IS A RECORD OF ANY TEMP GATES IN THE WEST WING!
OKAY!

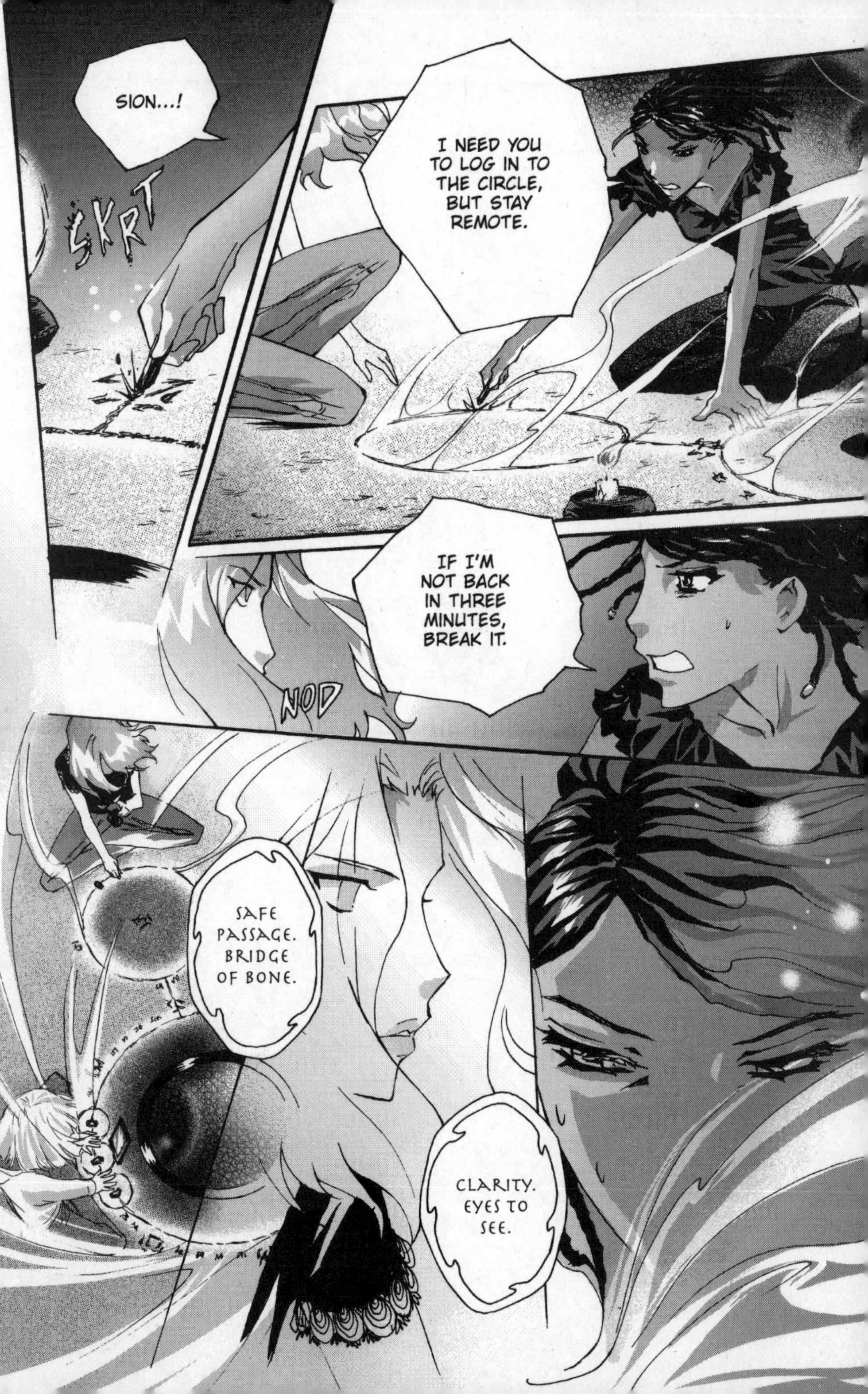
SION...!
SKRT
I NEED YOU TO LOG IN TO THE CIRCLE, BUT STAY REMOTE.
NOD
IF I'M NOT BACK IN THREE MINUTES, BREAK IT.
SAFE PASSAGE. BRIDGE OF BONE.
CLARITY. EYES TO SEE.

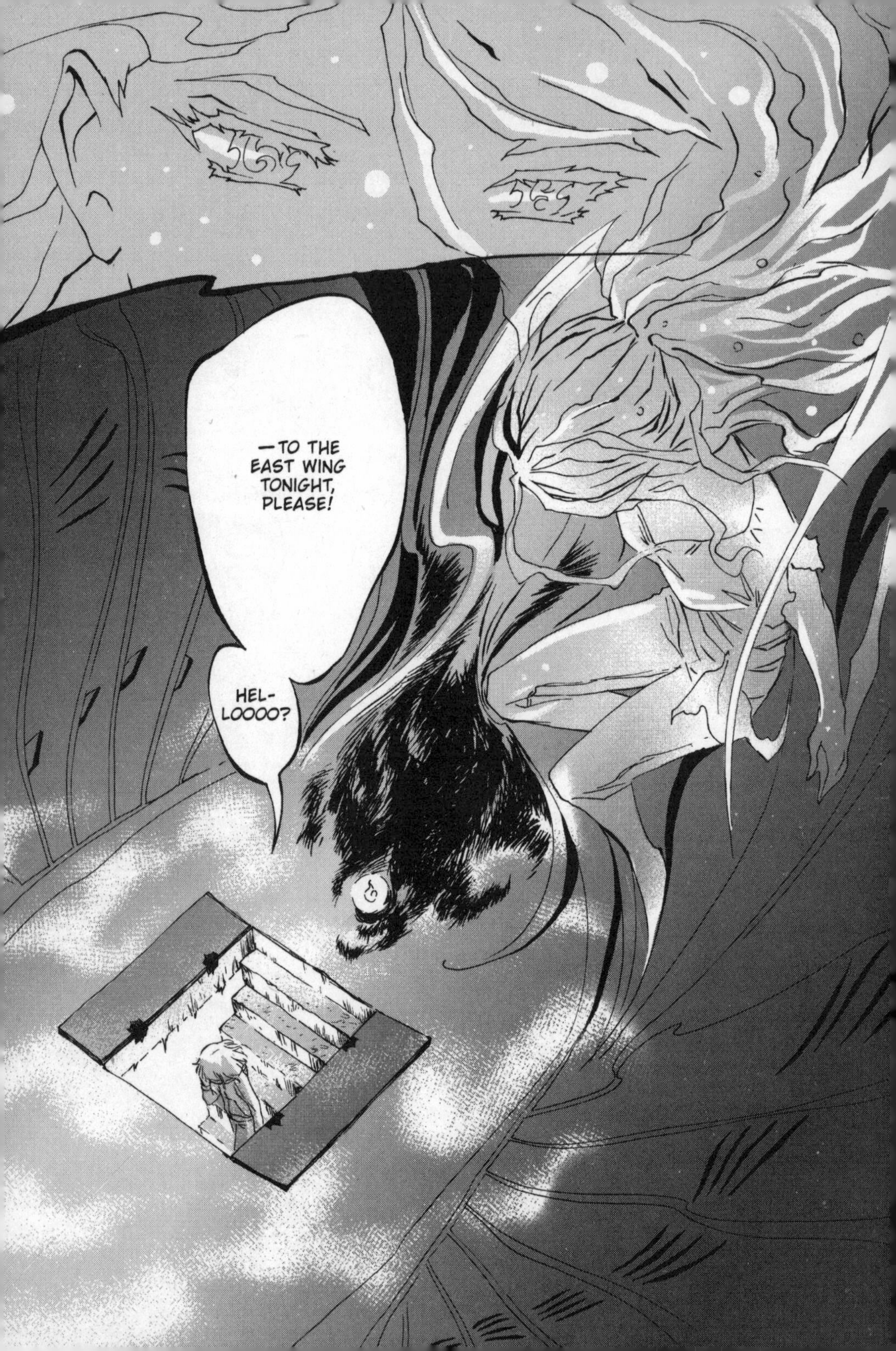
—TO THE EAST WING TONIGHT, PLEASE!
HEL-LOOOO?

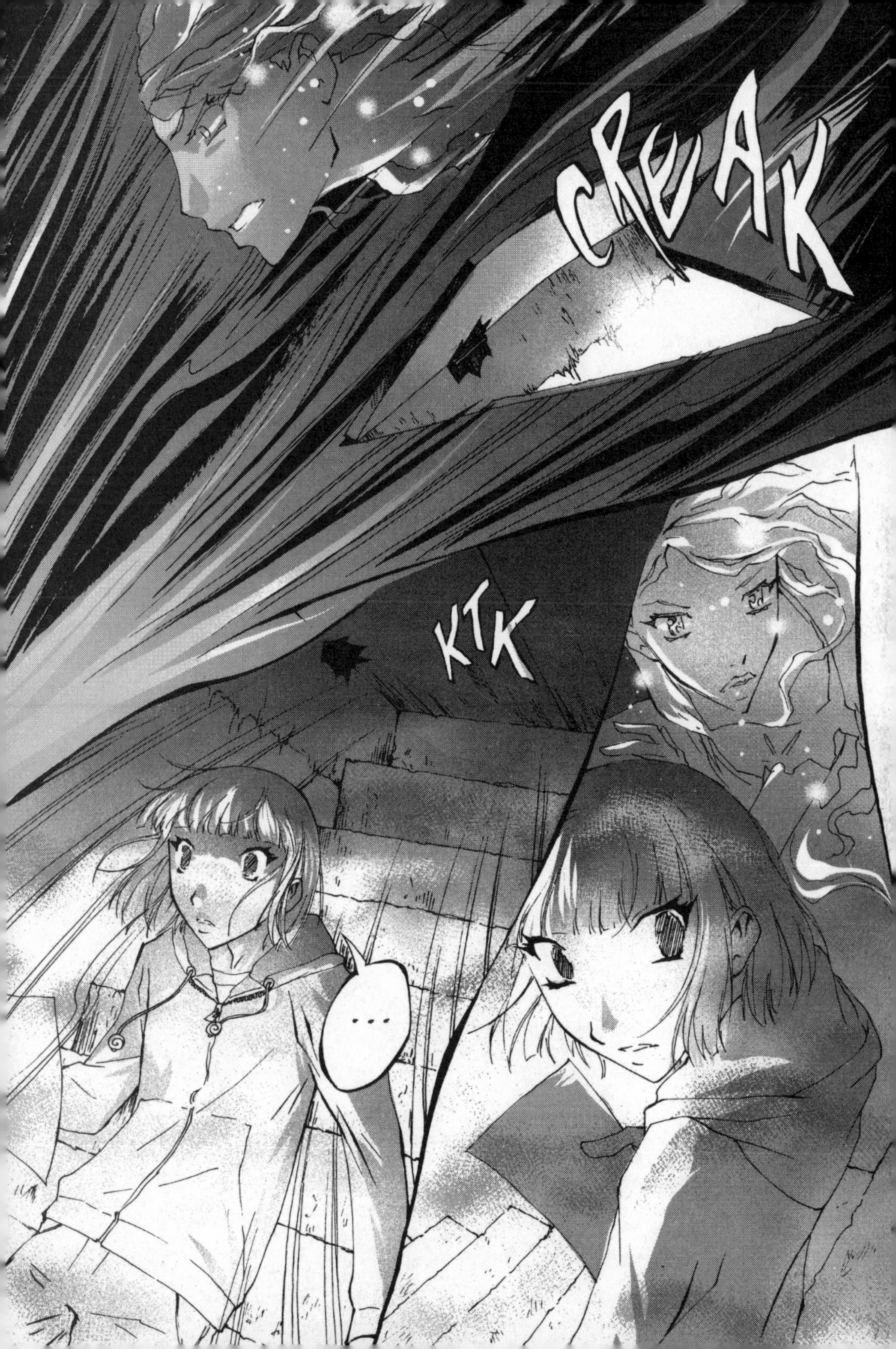
CREAK
KTK
...

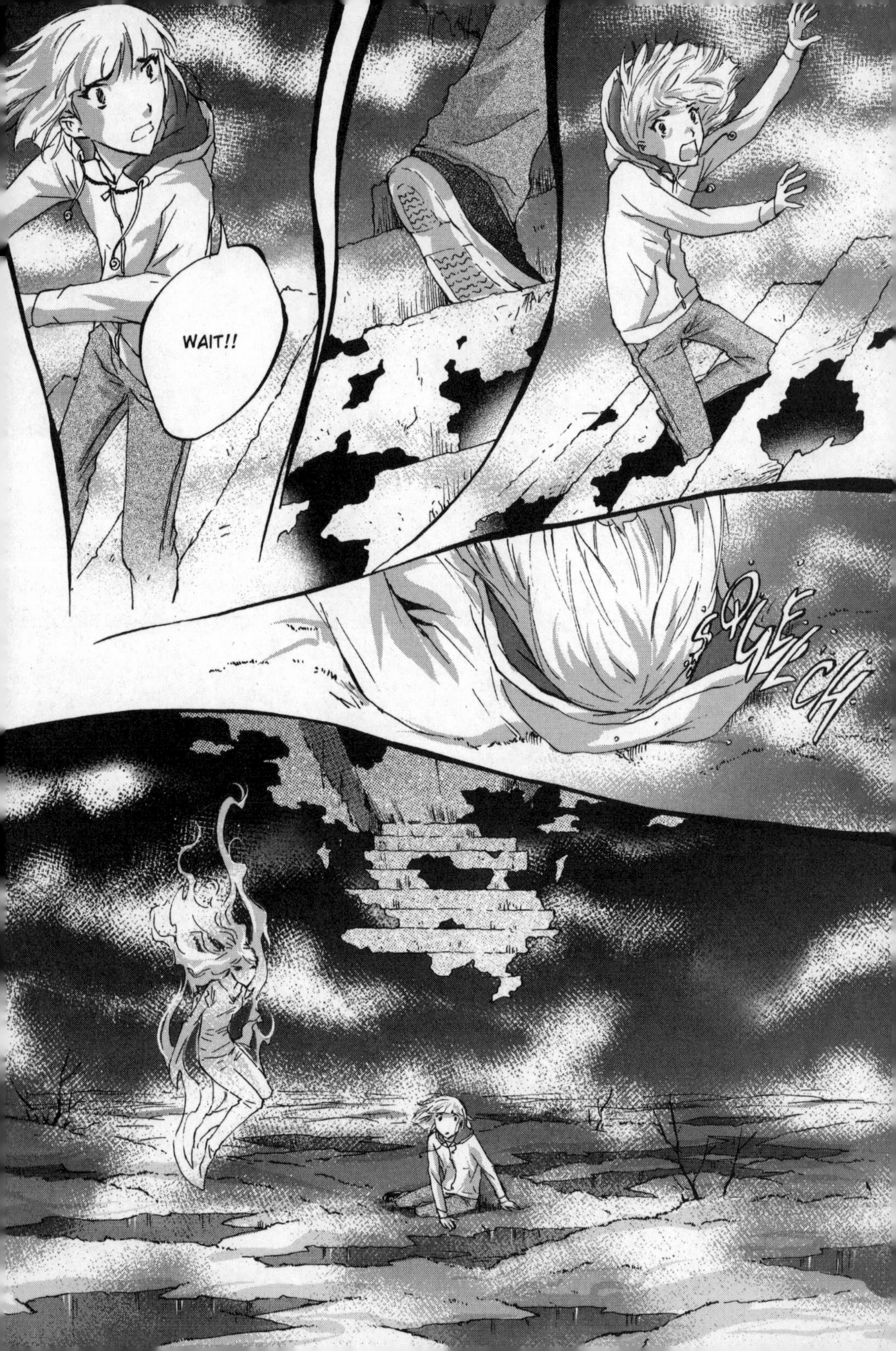
WAIT!!
SQUELCH

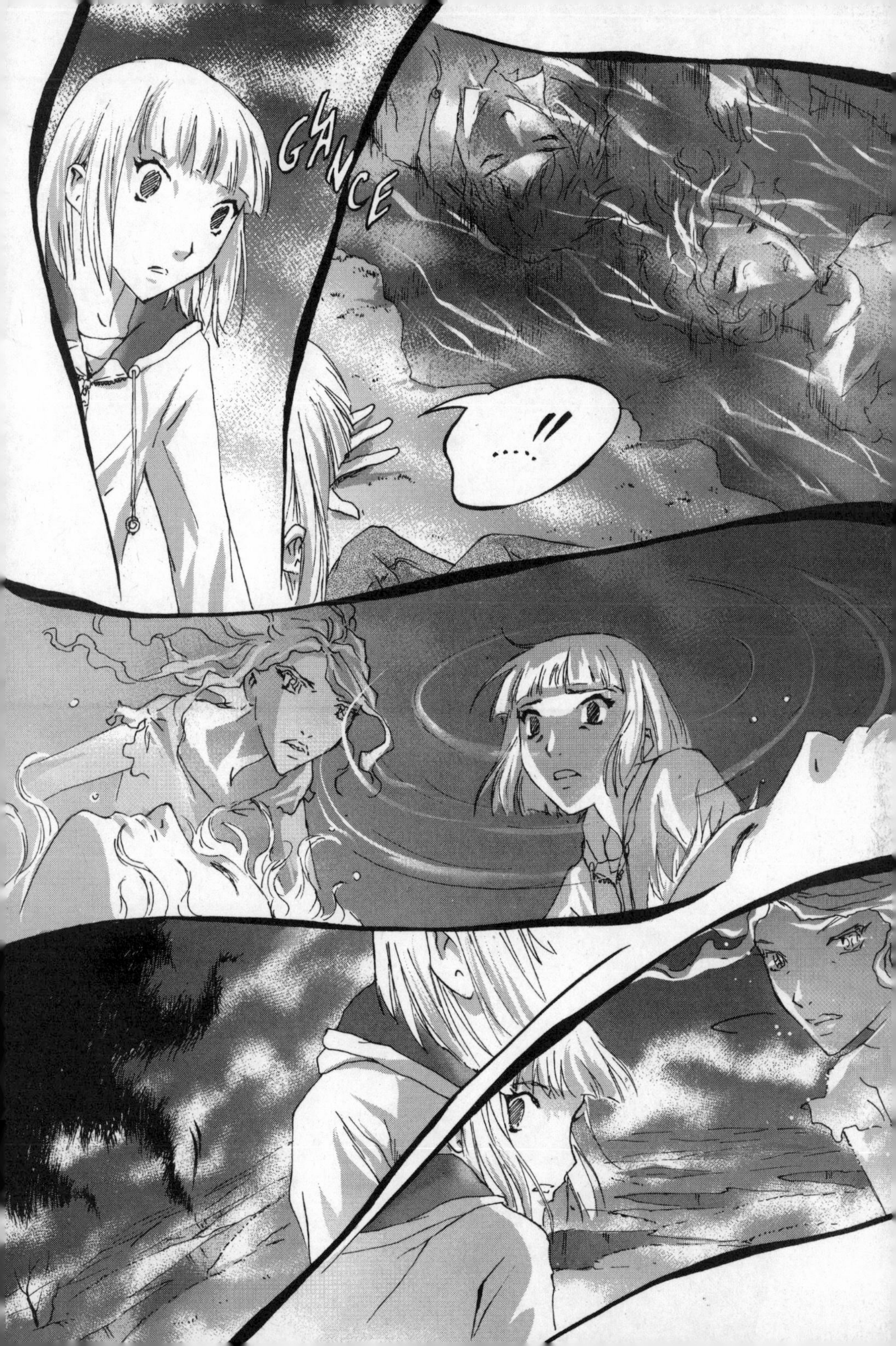
GLANCE
......!!

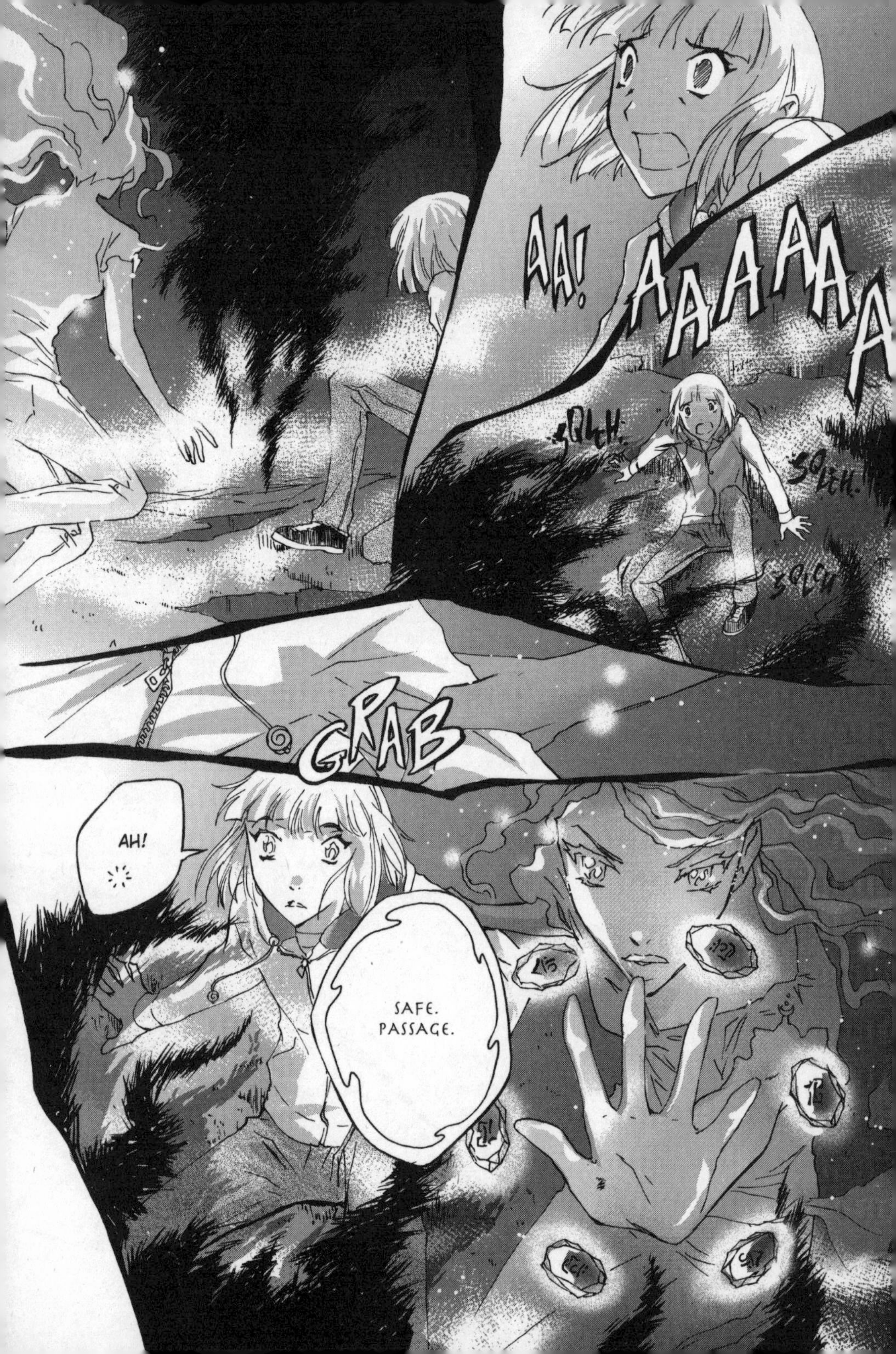
AA! AAAAAA
SQLCH.
SQLCH.
SQLCH
GRAB
AH!
SAFE. PASSAGE.

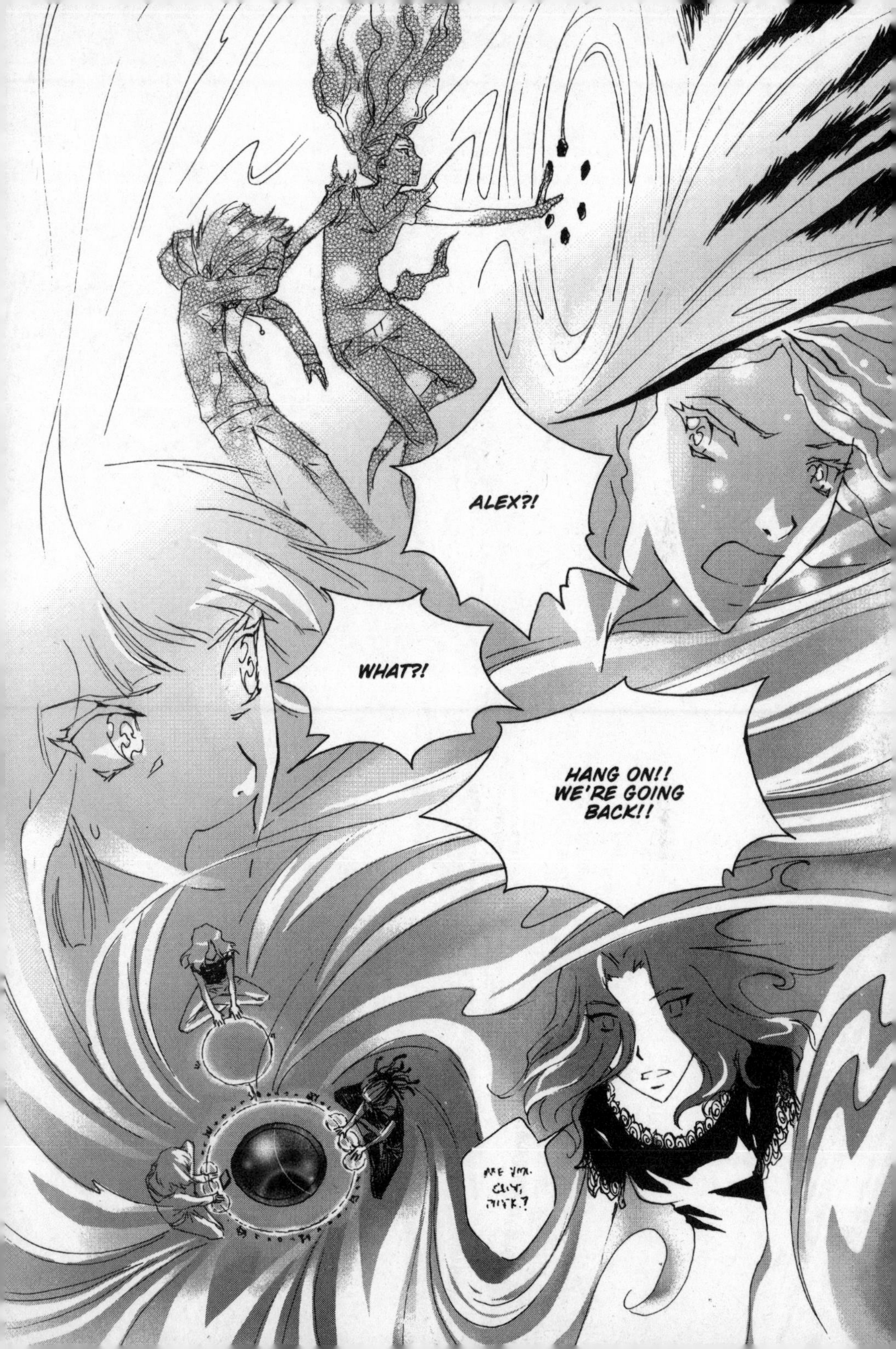
ALEX?!
WHAT?!
HANG ON!! WE'RE GOING BACK!!

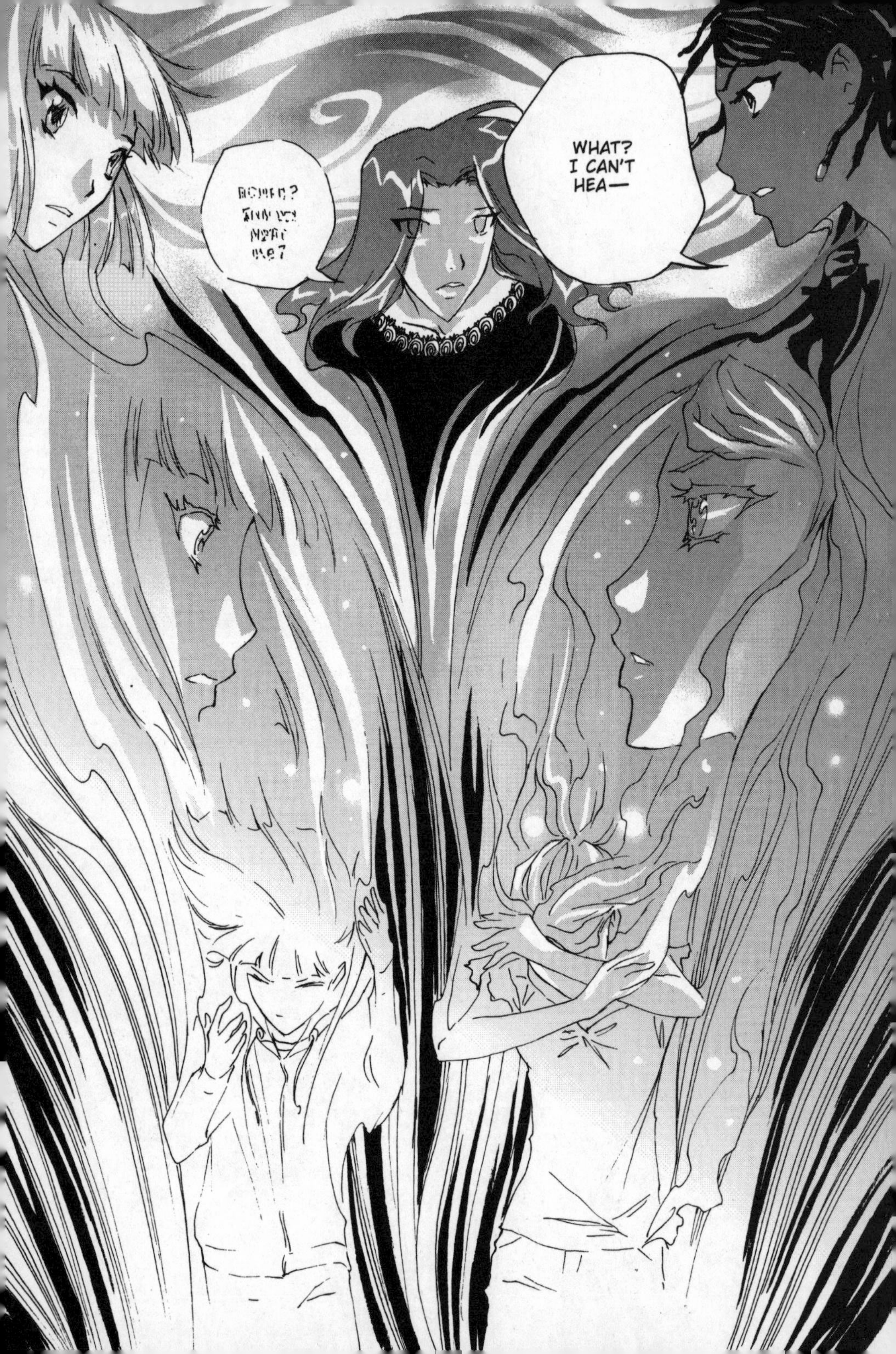
WHAT? I CAN'T HEA—

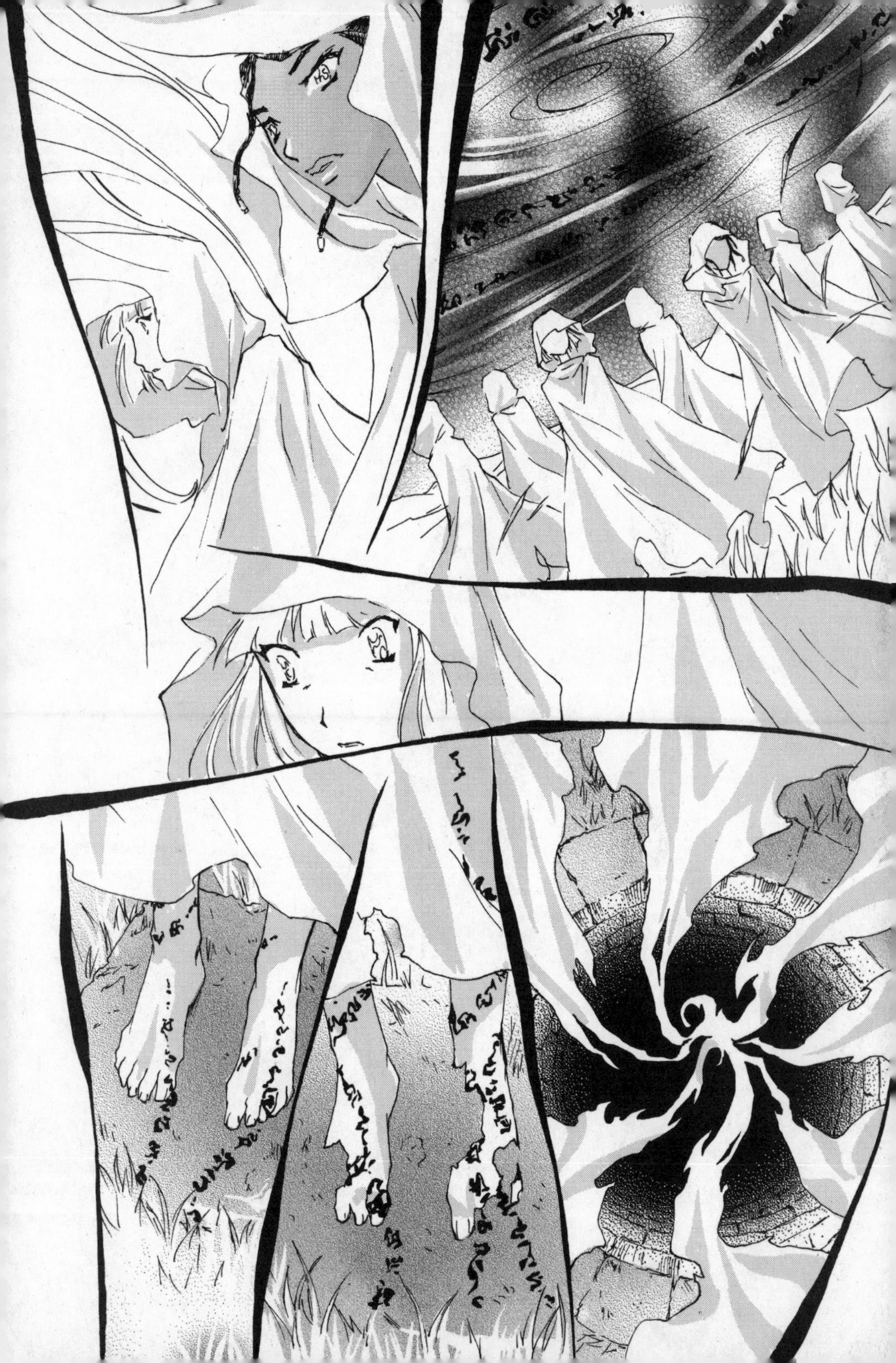

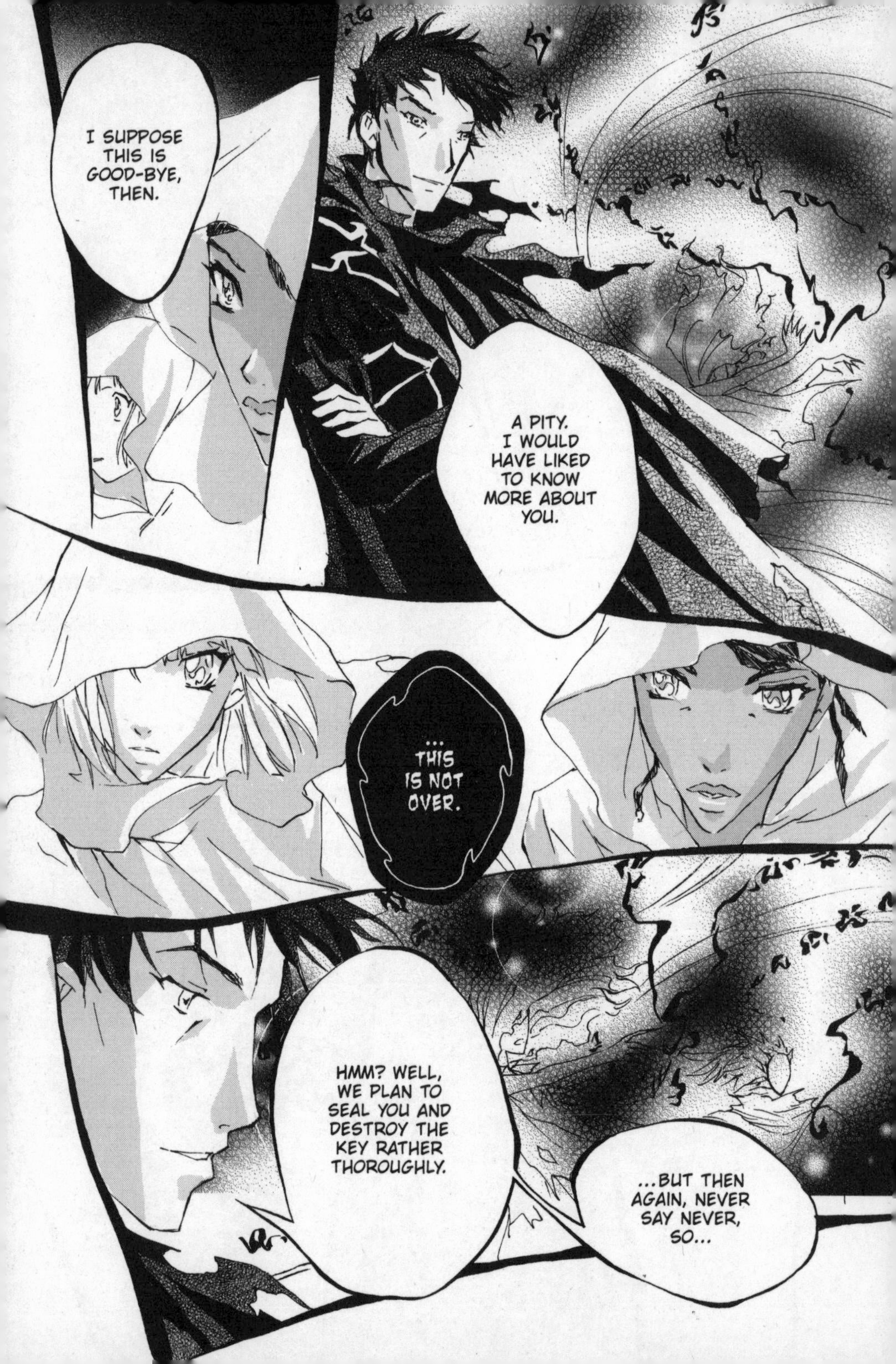
I SUPPOSE THIS IS GOOD-BYE, THEN.
A PITY. I WOULD HAVE LIKED TO KNOW MORE ABOUT YOU.
... THIS IS NOT OVER.
HMM? WELL, WE PLAN TO SEAL YOU AND DESTROY THE KEY RATHER THOROUGHLY.
...BUT THEN AGAIN, NEVER SAY NEVER, SO...

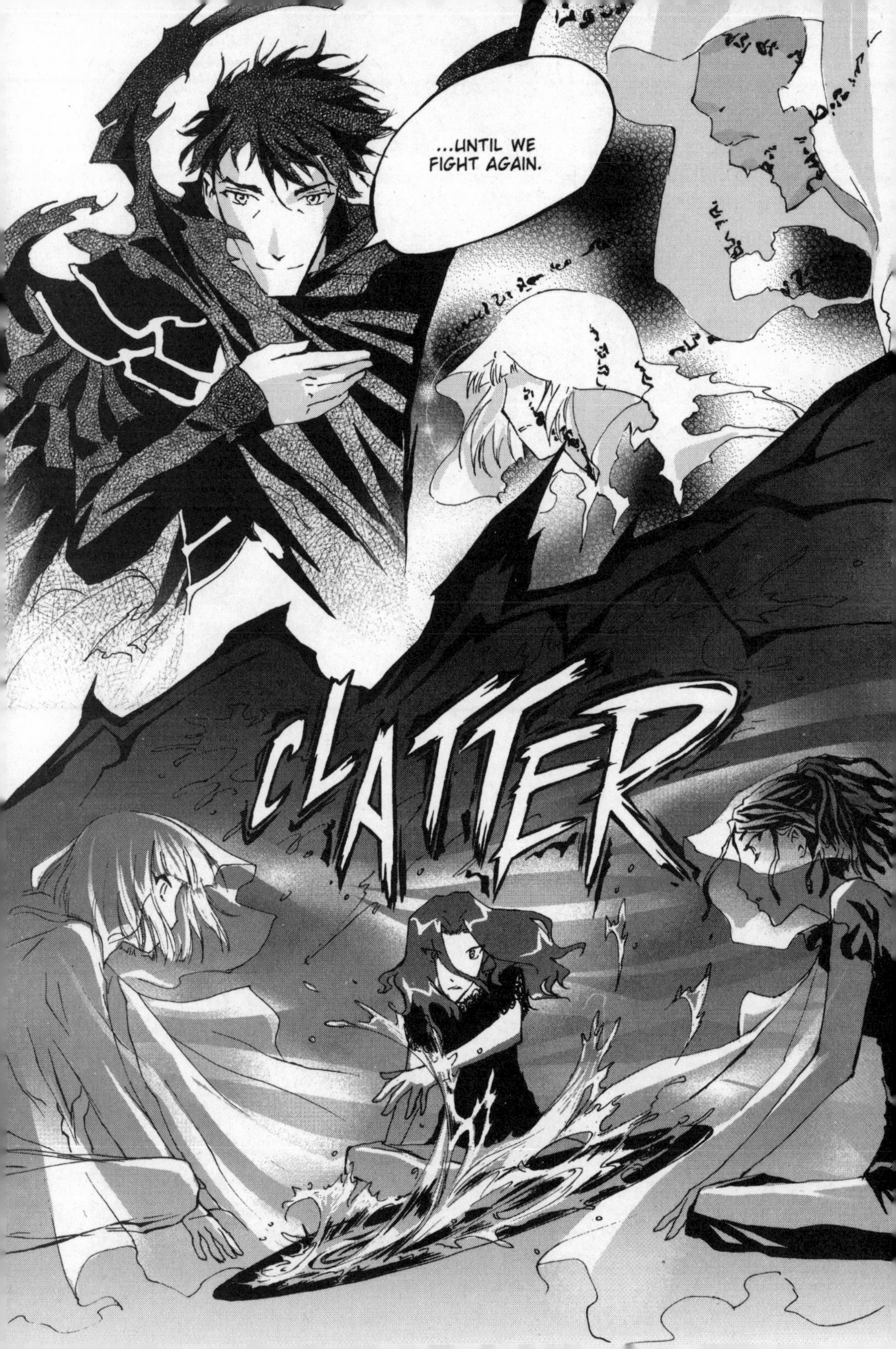
...UNTIL WE FIGHT AGAIN.
CLATTER

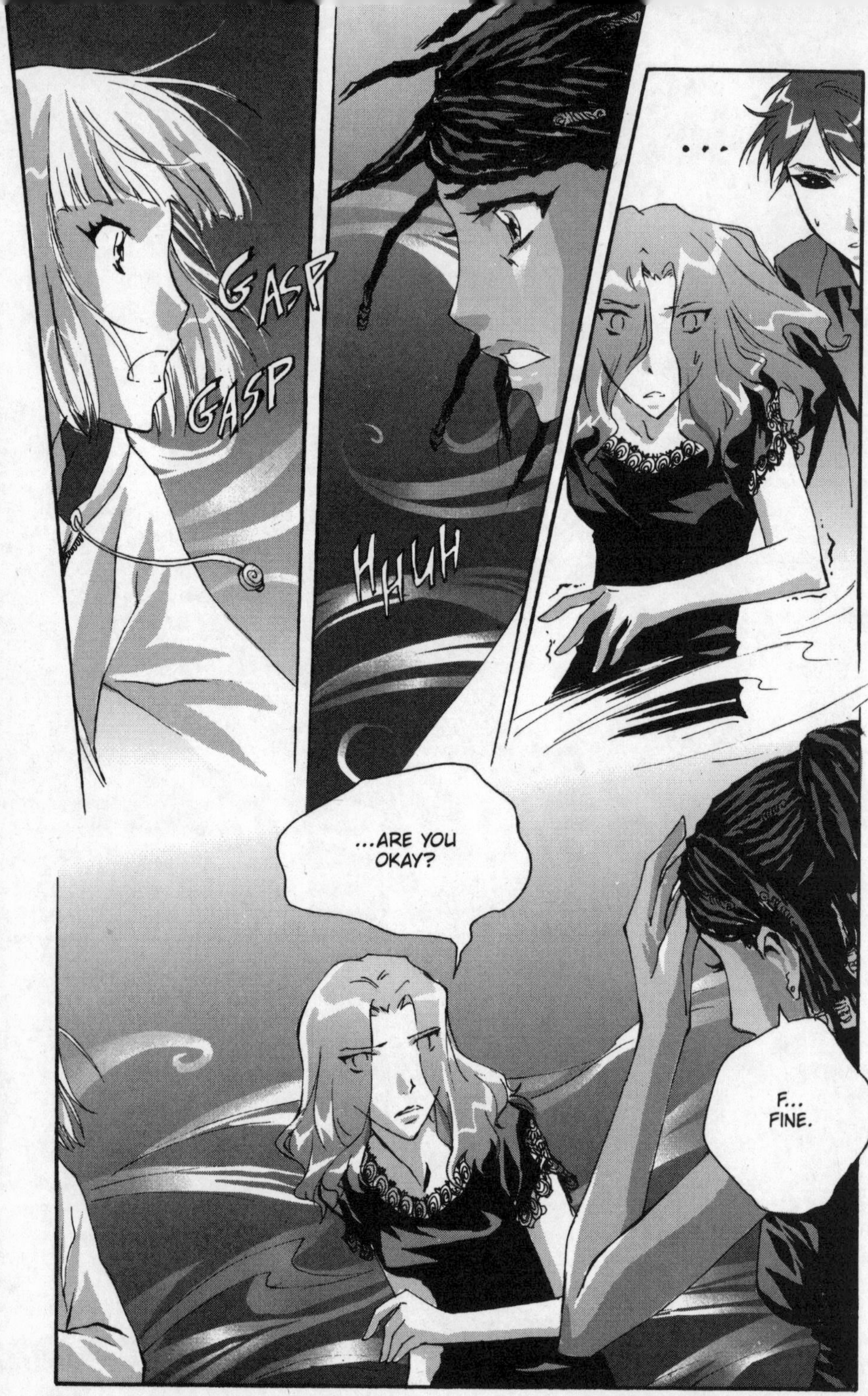
GASP
GASP
HHUH
...
...ARE YOU OKAY?
F... FINE.

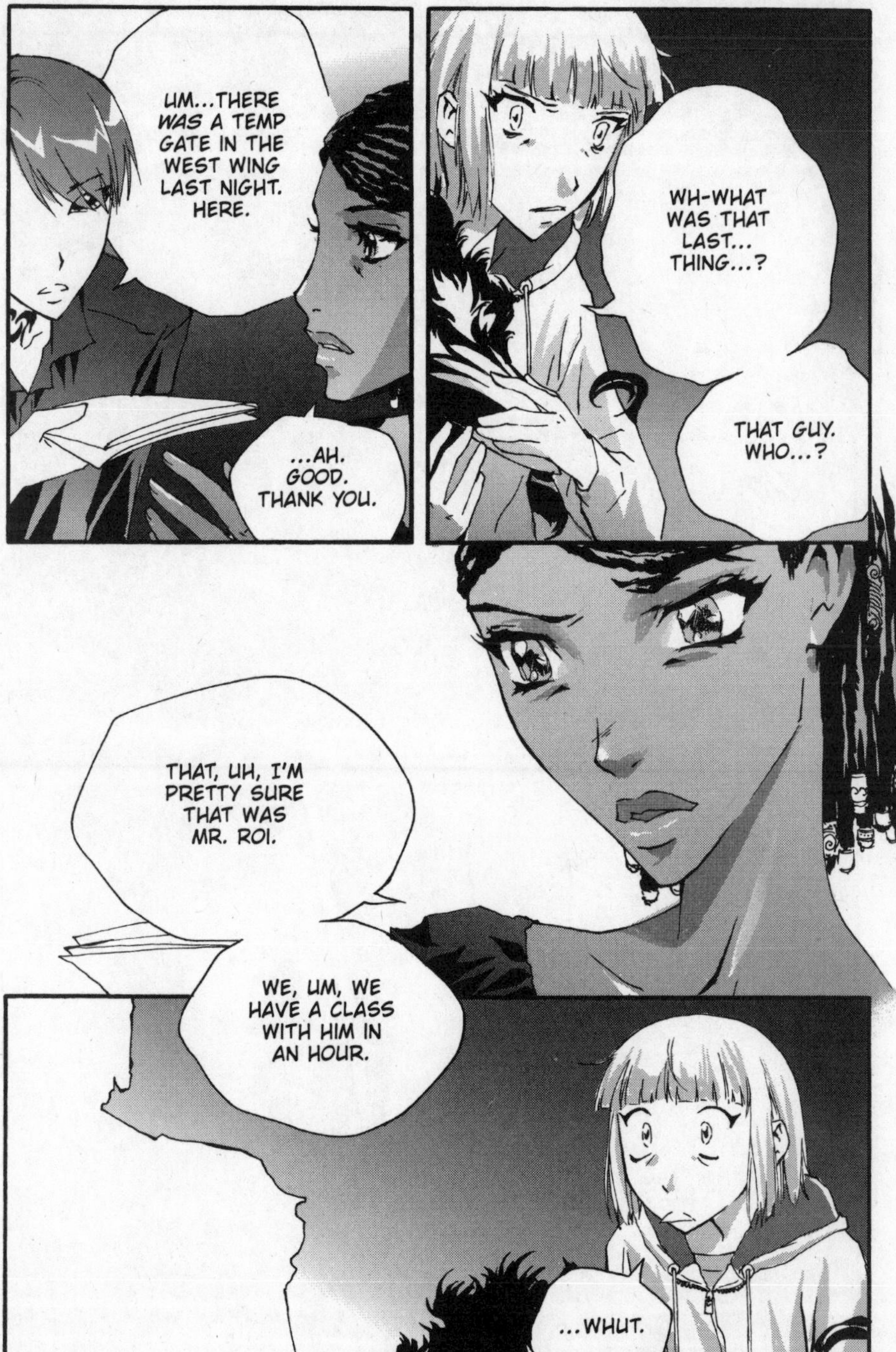
UM...THERE WAS A TEMP GATE IN THE WEST WING LAST NIGHT. HERE.
...AH. GOOD. THANK YOU.
WH-WHAT WAS THAT LAST... THING...?
THAT GUY. WHO...?
THAT, UH, I'M PRETTY SURE THAT WAS MR. ROI.
WE, UM, WE HAVE A CLASS WITH HIM IN AN HOUR.
...WHUT.

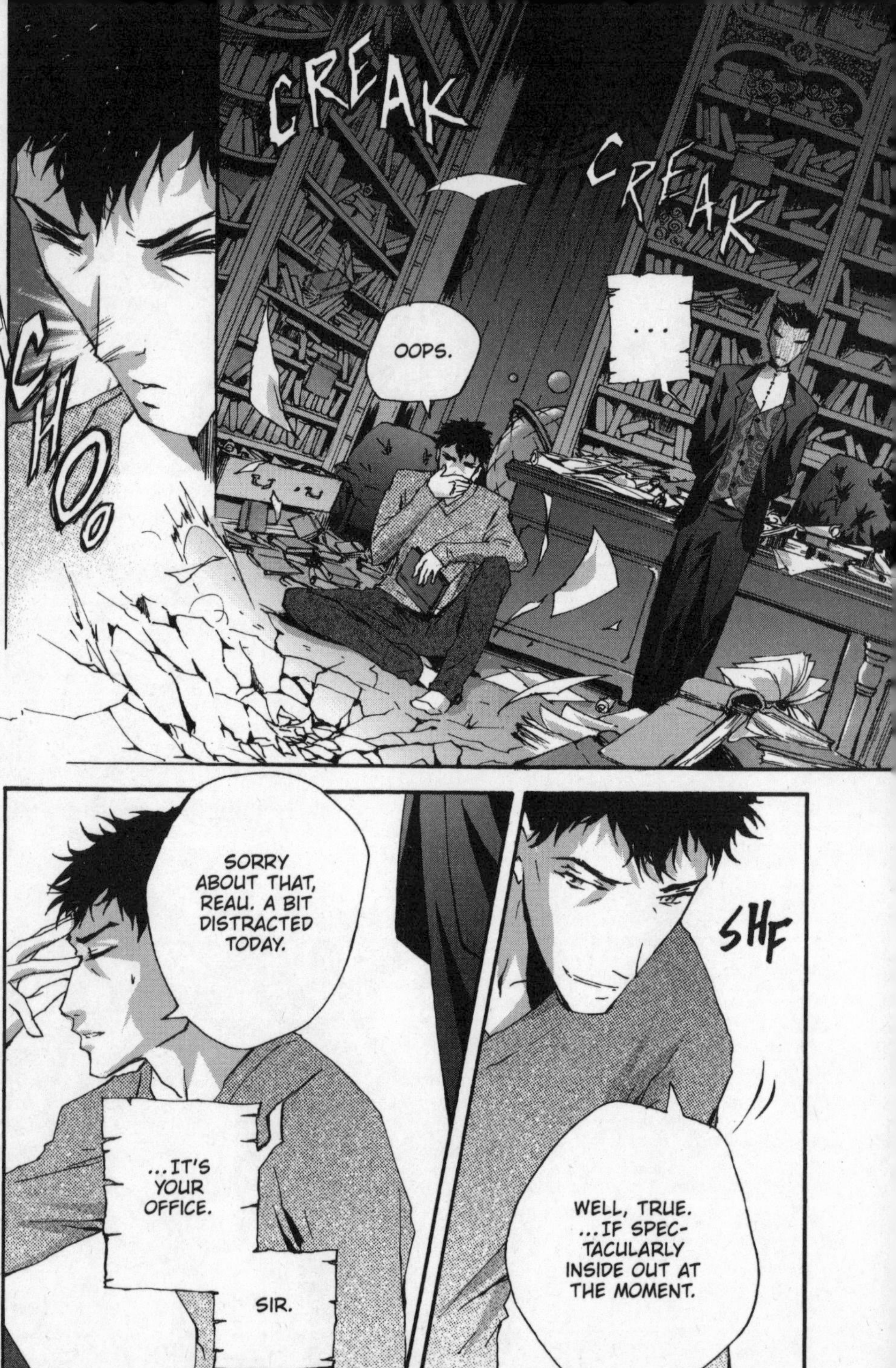
CREAK
CREAK
ACHOO
OOPS.
...
SORRY ABOUT THAT, REAU. A BIT DISTRACTED TODAY.
...IT'S YOUR OFFICE.
SIR.
SHF
WELL, TRUE. ...IF SPEC-TACULARLY INSIDE OUT AT THE MOMENT.

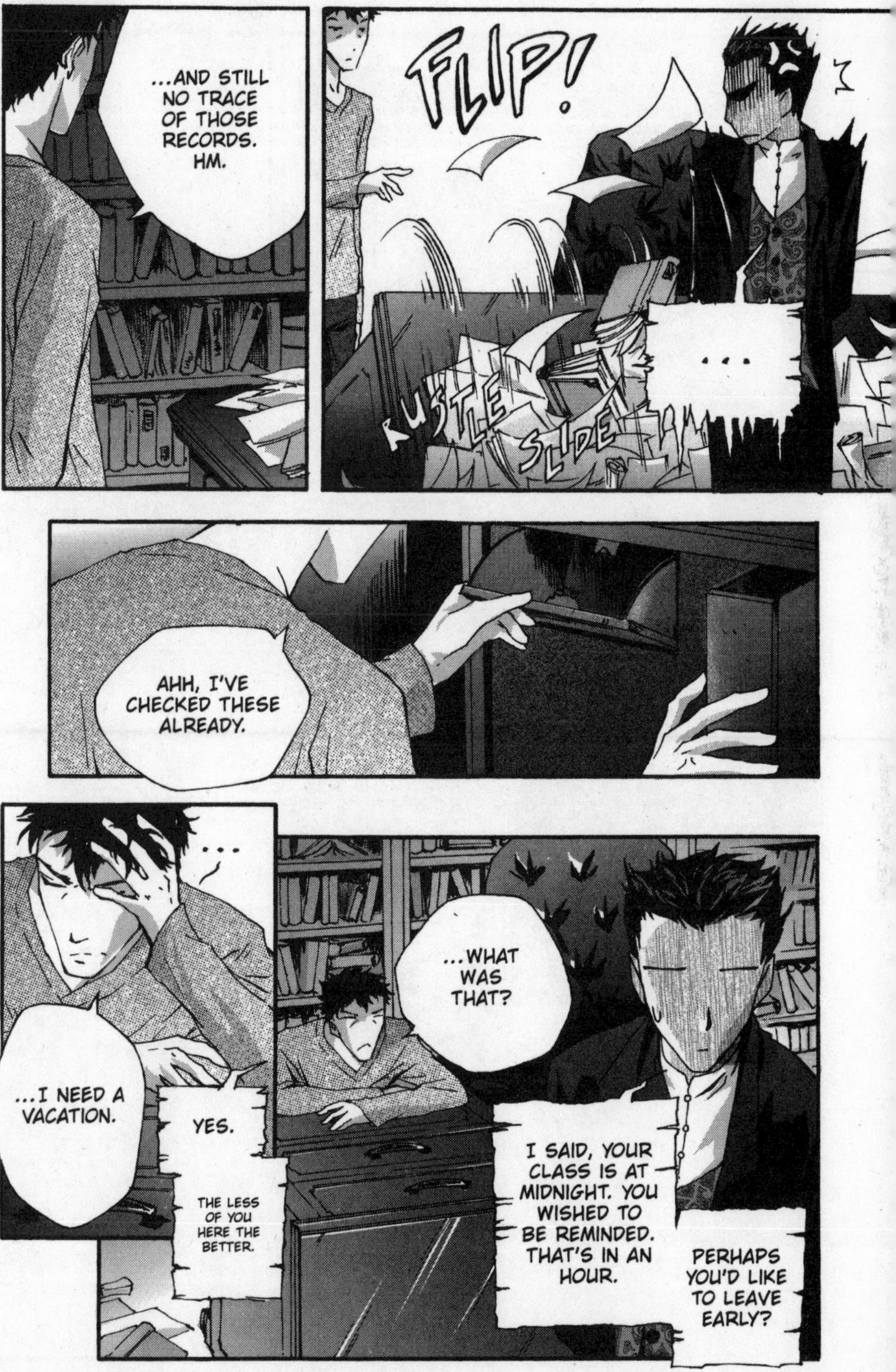
...AND STILL NO TRACE OF THOSE RECORDS. HM.
FLIP!
RUSTLE
SLIDE
...
AHH, I'VE CHECKED THESE ALREADY.
...
...I NEED A VACATION.
...WHAT WAS THAT?
YES.
THE LESS OF YOU HERE THE BETTER.
I SAID, YOUR CLASS IS AT MIDNIGHT. YOU WISHED TO BE REMINDED. THAT'S IN AN HOUR.
PERHAPS YOU'D LIKE TO LEAVE EARLY?

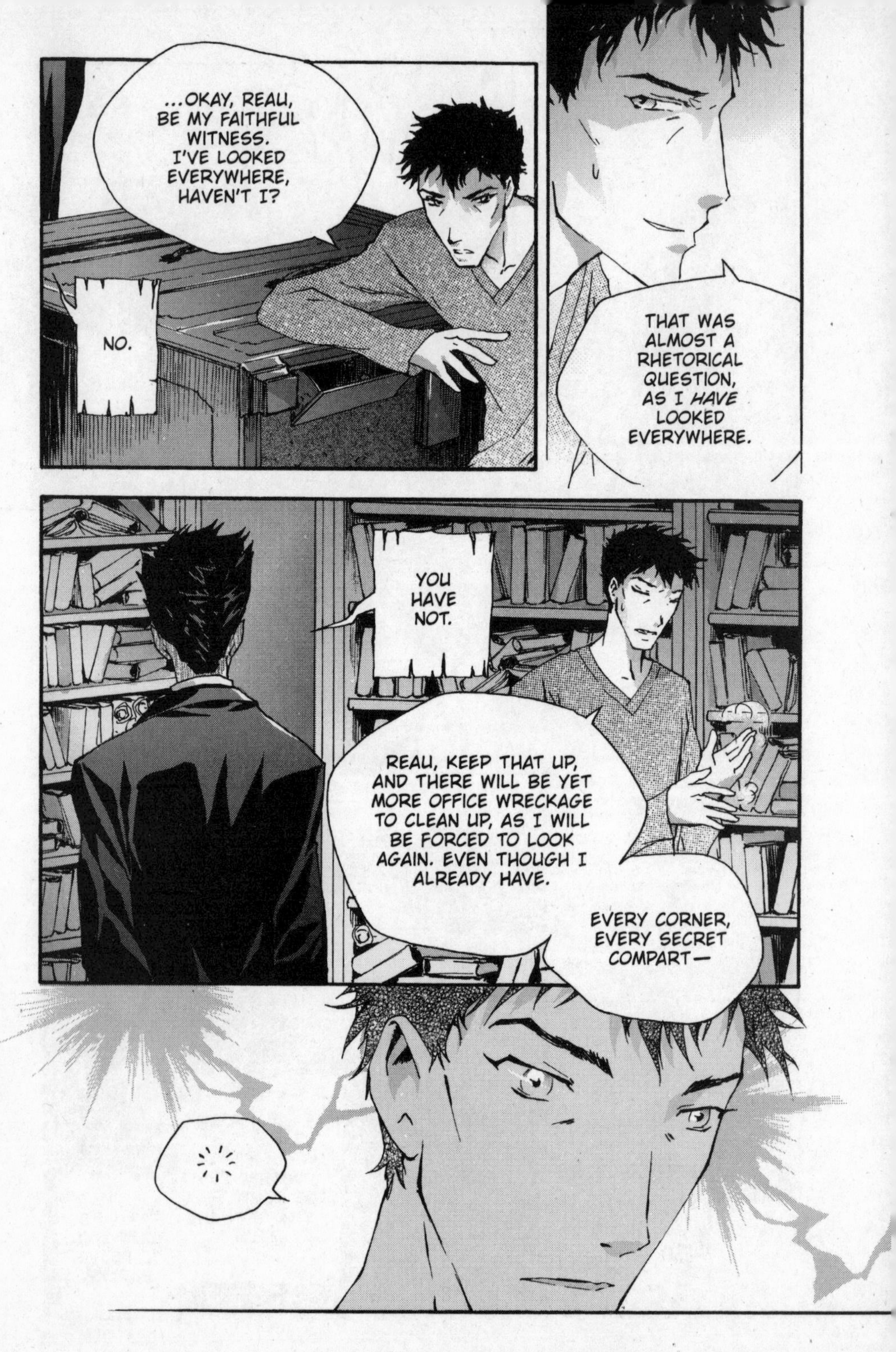
...OKAY, REAU, BE MY FAITHFUL WITNESS. I'VE LOOKED EVERYWHERE, HAVEN'T I?
NO.
THAT WAS ALMOST A RHETORICAL QUESTION, AS I *HAVE* LOOKED EVERYWHERE.
YOU HAVE NOT.
REAU, KEEP THAT UP, AND THERE WILL BE YET MORE OFFICE WRECKAGE TO CLEAN UP, AS I WILL BE FORCED TO LOOK AGAIN. EVEN THOUGH I ALREADY HAVE.
EVERY CORNER, EVERY SECRET COMPART—

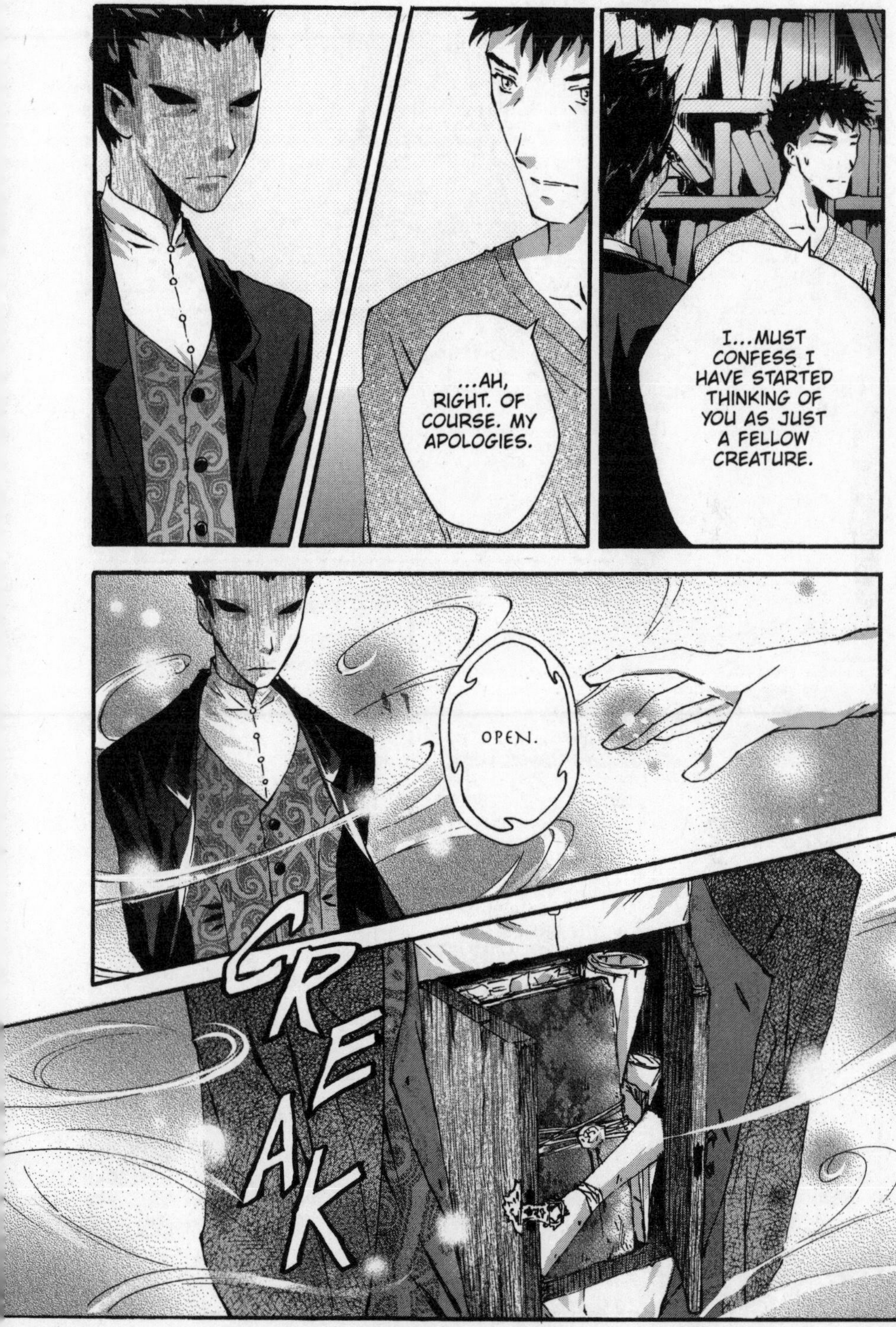
...AH, RIGHT. OF COURSE. MY APOLOGIES.
I...MUST CONFESS I HAVE STARTED THINKING OF YOU AS JUST A FELLOW CREATURE.
OPEN.
CREAK

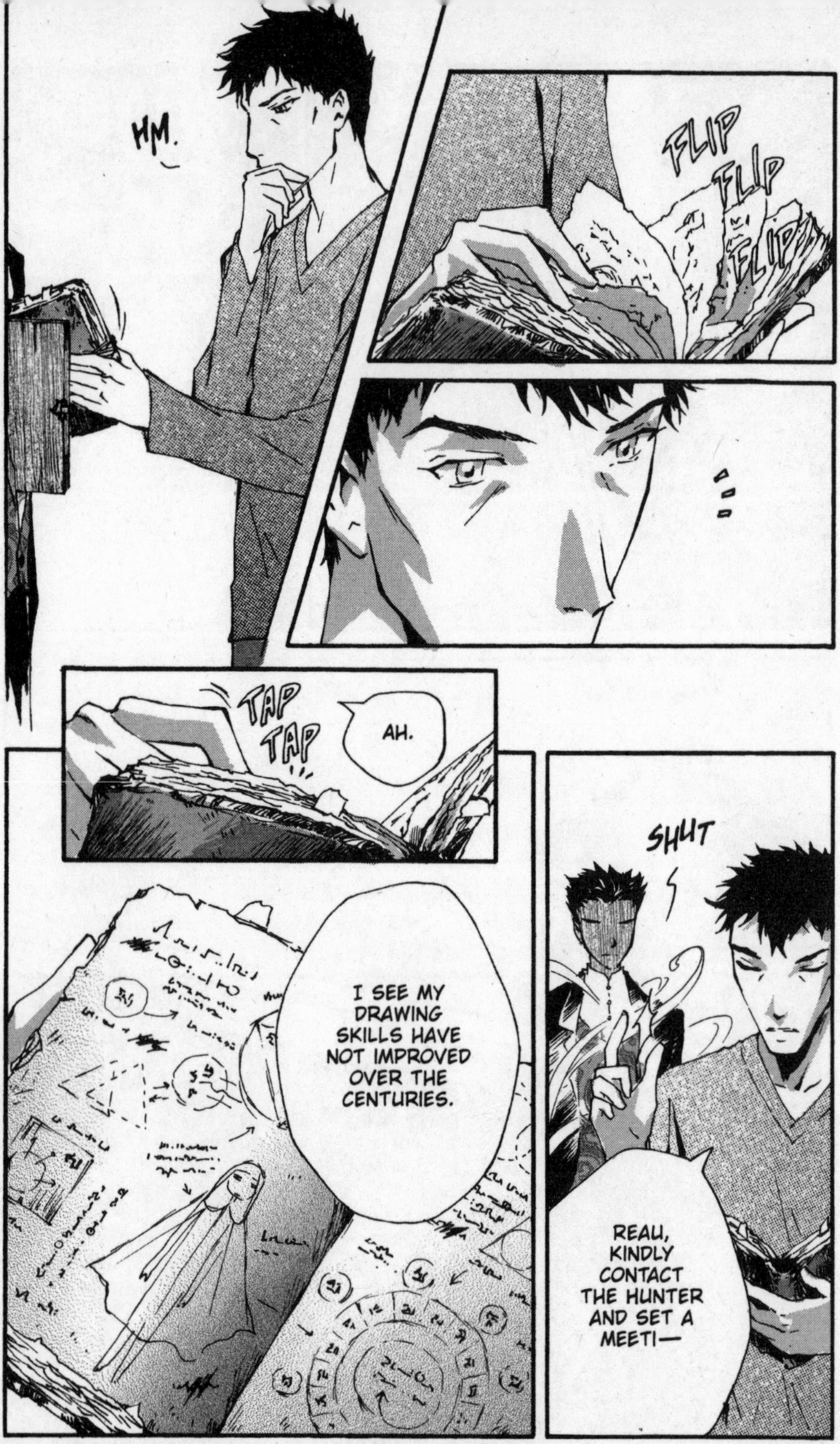

HM.
FLIP
FLIP
FLIP
TAP
TAP
AH.
I SEE MY DRAWING SKILLS HAVE NOT IMPROVED OVER THE CENTURIES.
SHUT
REAU, KINDLY CONTACT THE HUNTER AND SET A MEETI—

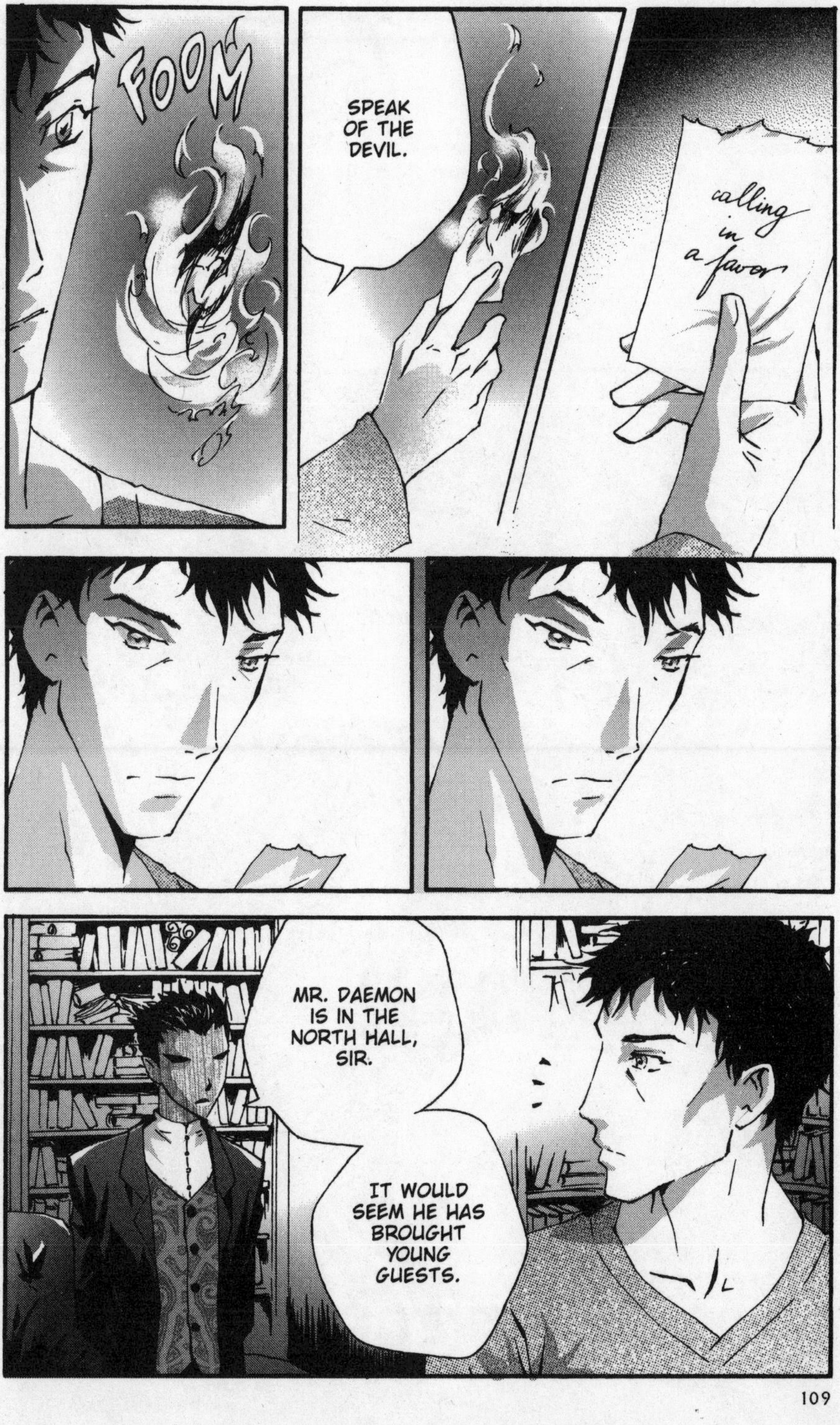
FOOM
SPEAK OF THE DEVIL.
calling in a favor
MR. DAEMON IS IN THE NORTH HALL, SIR.
IT WOULD SEEM HE HAS BROUGHT YOUNG GUESTS.

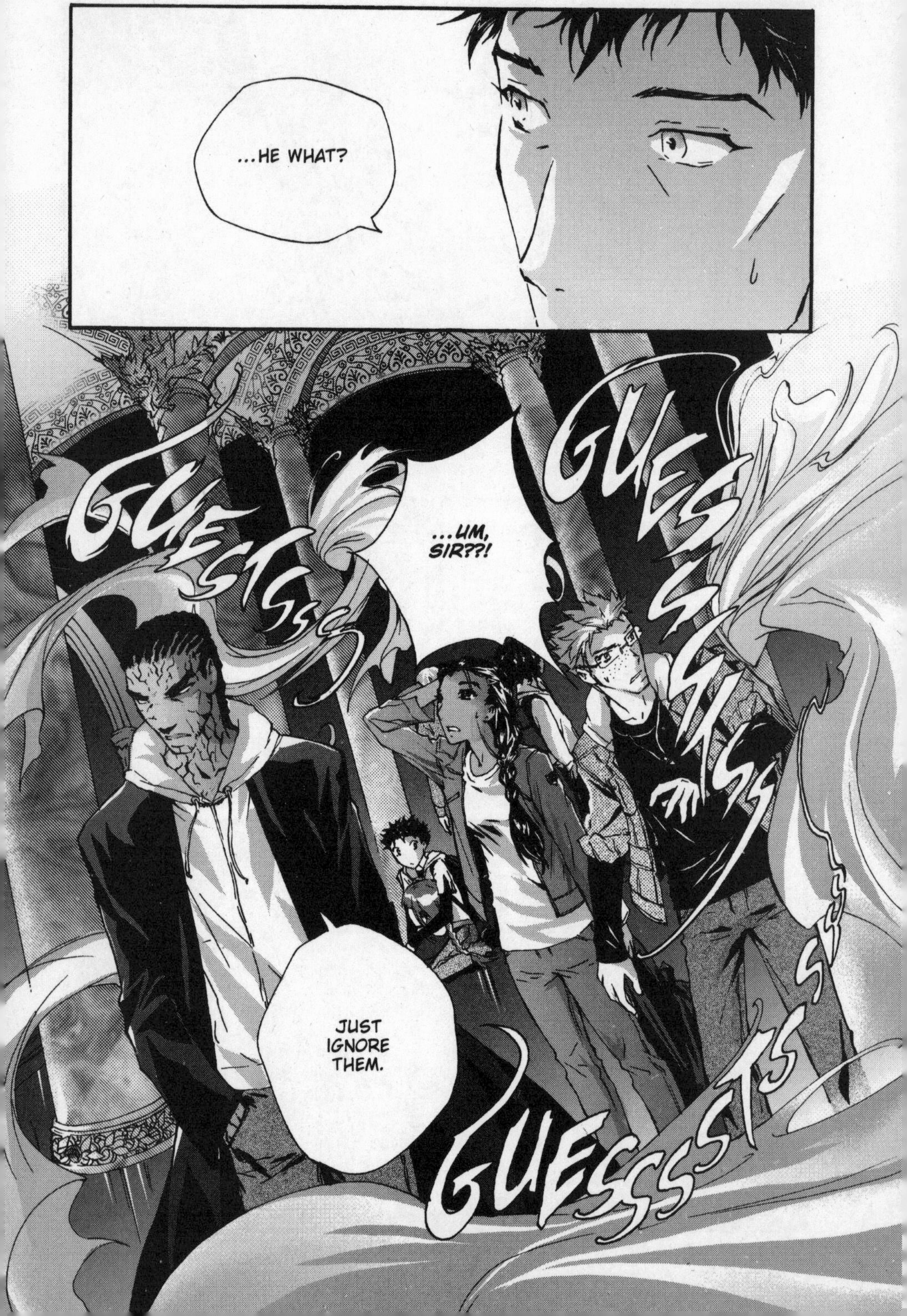
...HE WHAT?
GUESTSSS
...UM, SIR??!
GUESSSSSS
JUST IGNORE THEM.
GUESSSSTS

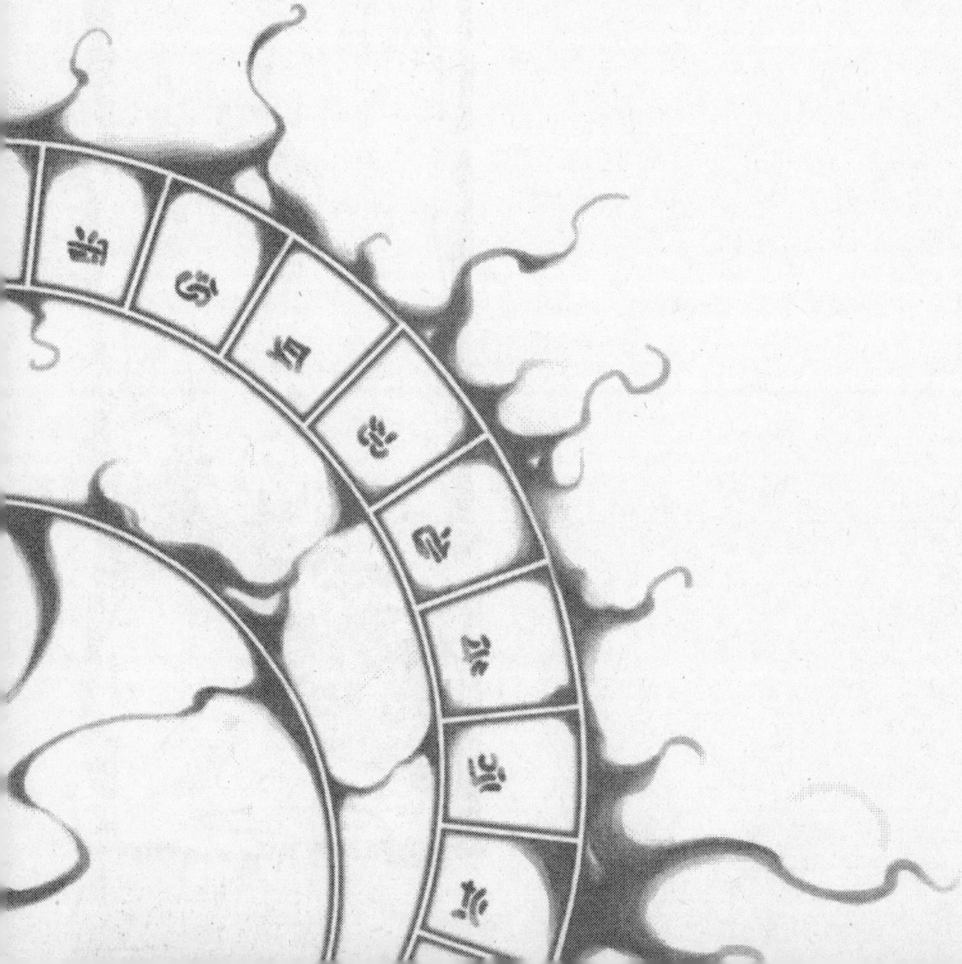

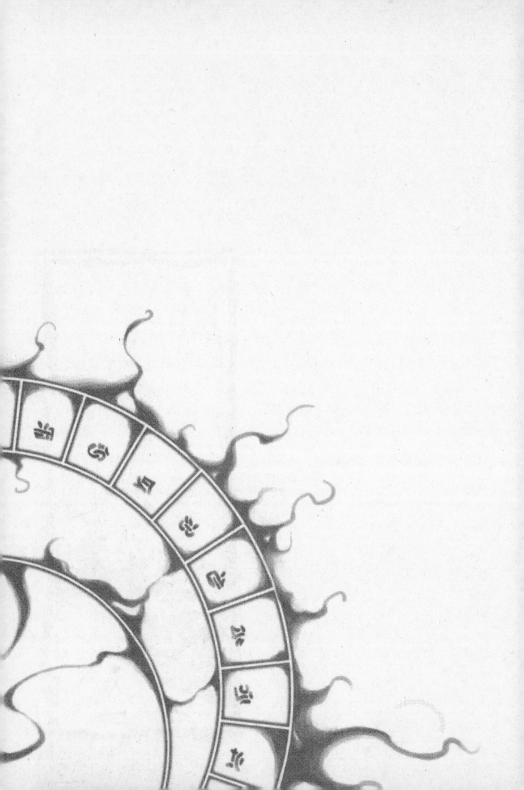

Chapter 16

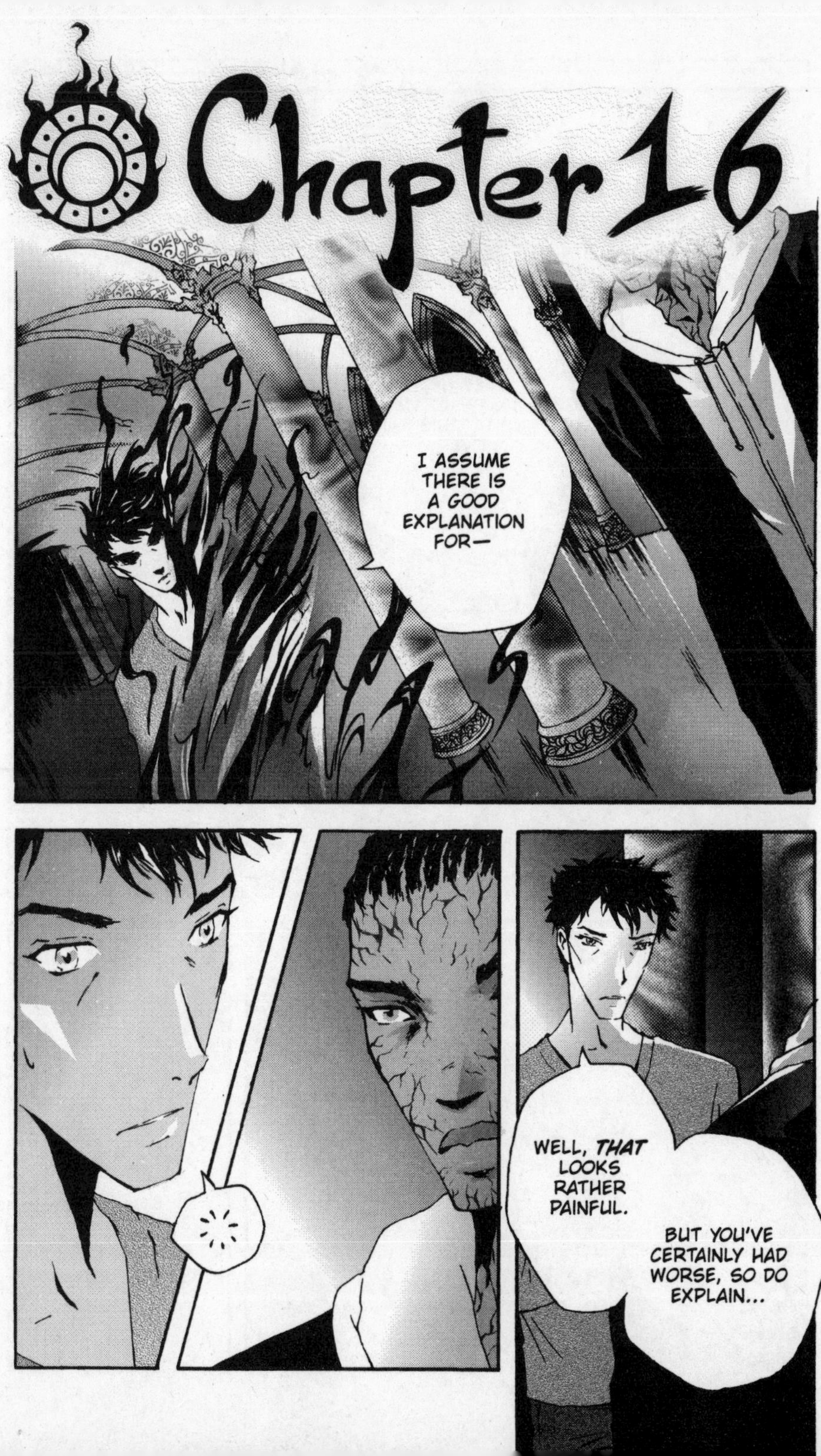
I ASSUME THERE IS A GOOD EXPLANATION FOR—
WELL, *THAT* LOOKS RATHER PAINFUL.
BUT YOU'VE CERTAINLY HAD WORSE, SO DO EXPLAIN...

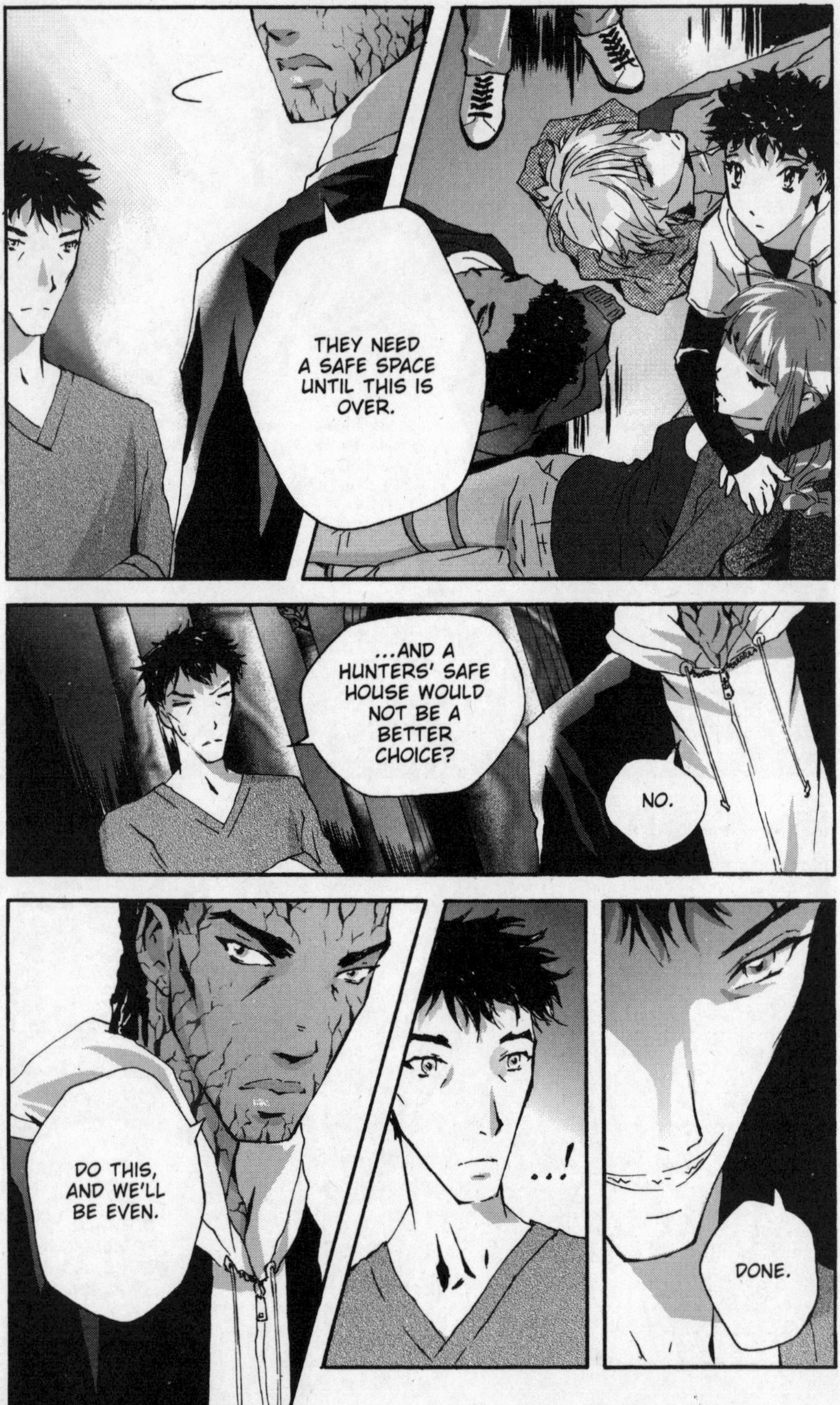
THEY NEED A SAFE SPACE UNTIL THIS IS OVER.
...AND A HUNTERS' SAFE HOUSE WOULD NOT BE A BETTER CHOICE?
NO.
DO THIS, AND WE'LL BE EVEN.
...!
DONE.

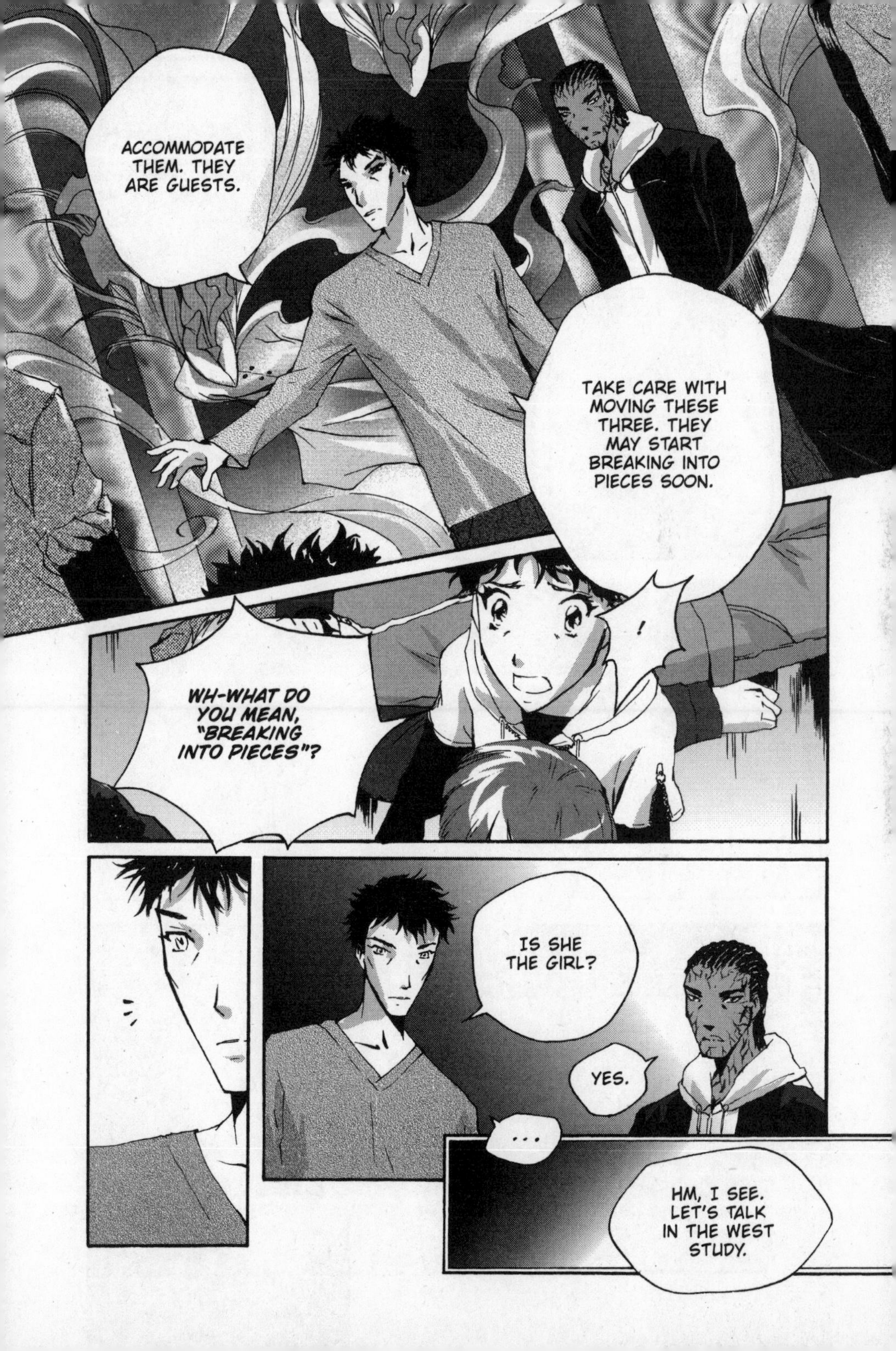
ACCOMMODATE THEM. THEY ARE GUESTS.
TAKE CARE WITH MOVING THESE THREE. THEY MAY START BREAKING INTO PIECES SOON.
!
WH-WHAT DO YOU MEAN, "BREAKING INTO PIECES"?
IS SHE THE GIRL?
YES.
...
HM, I SEE. LET'S TALK IN THE WEST STUDY.

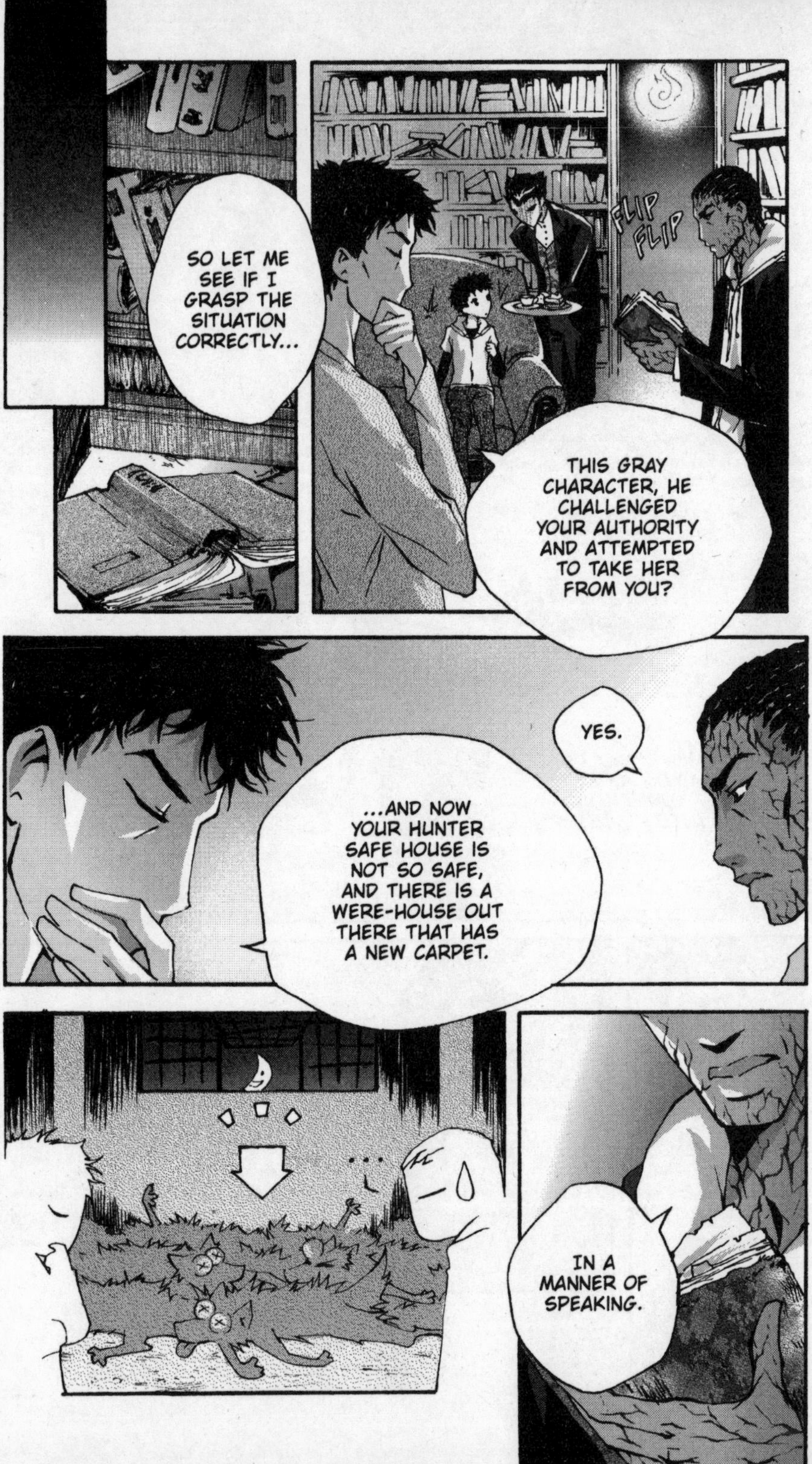
SO LET ME SEE IF I GRASP THE SITUATION CORRECTLY...
FLIP FLIP
THIS GRAY CHARACTER, HE CHALLENGED YOUR AUTHORITY AND ATTEMPTED TO TAKE HER FROM YOU?
...AND NOW YOUR HUNTER SAFE HOUSE IS NOT SO SAFE, AND THERE IS A WERE-HOUSE OUT THERE THAT HAS A NEW CARPET.
YES.
...
IN A MANNER OF SPEAKING.

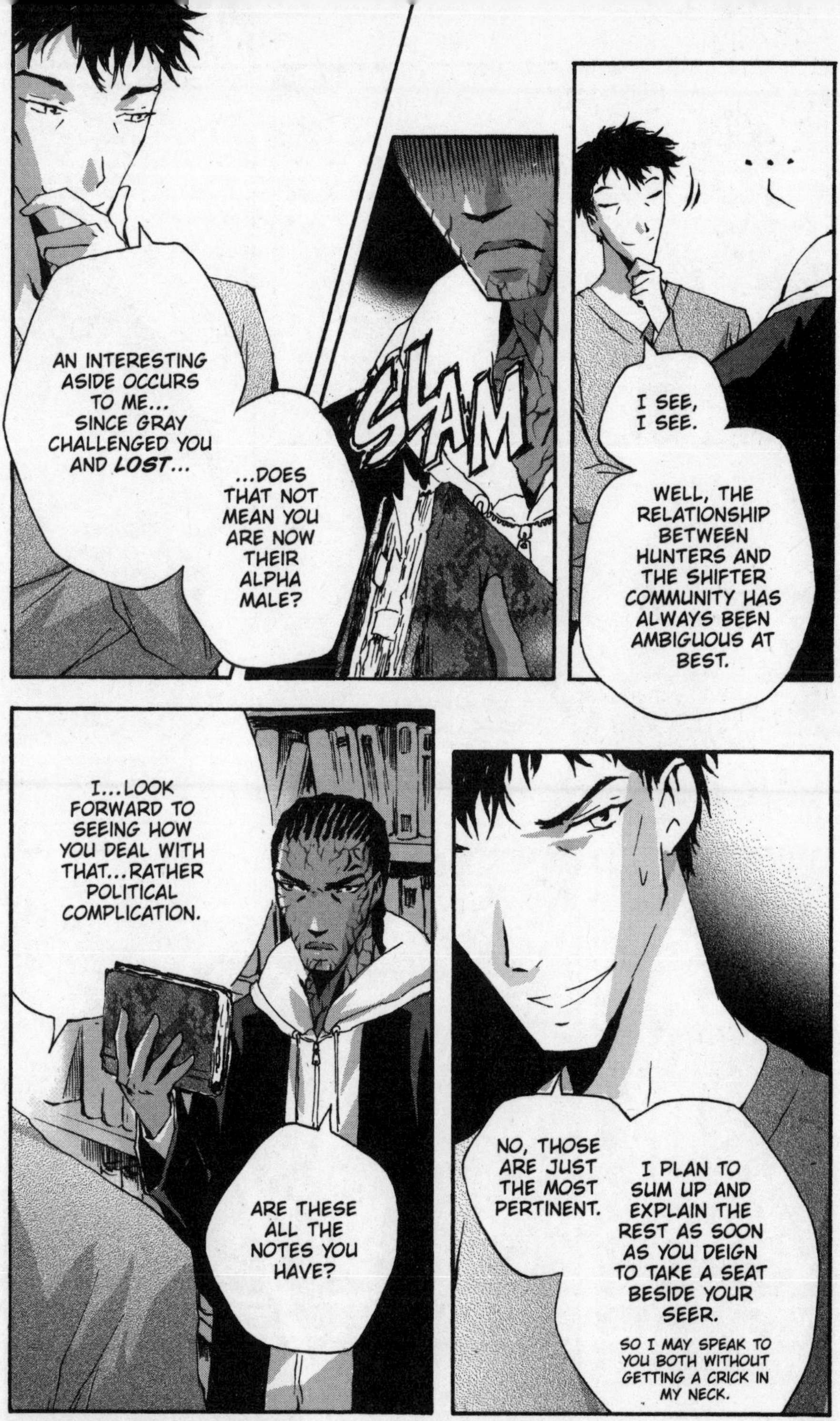
AN INTERESTING ASIDE OCCURS TO ME... SINCE GRAY CHALLENGED YOU AND *LOST*...
...DOES THAT NOT MEAN YOU ARE NOW THEIR ALPHA MALE?
SLAM
. . .
I SEE, I SEE.
WELL, THE RELATIONSHIP BETWEEN HUNTERS AND THE SHIFTER COMMUNITY HAS ALWAYS BEEN AMBIGUOUS AT BEST.
I...LOOK FORWARD TO SEEING HOW YOU DEAL WITH THAT...RATHER POLITICAL COMPLICATION.
ARE THESE ALL THE NOTES YOU HAVE?
NO, THOSE ARE JUST THE MOST PERTINENT.
I PLAN TO SUM UP AND EXPLAIN THE REST AS SOON AS YOU DEIGN TO TAKE A SEAT BESIDE YOUR SEER.
SO I MAY SPEAK TO YOU BOTH WITHOUT GETTING A CRICK IN MY NECK.

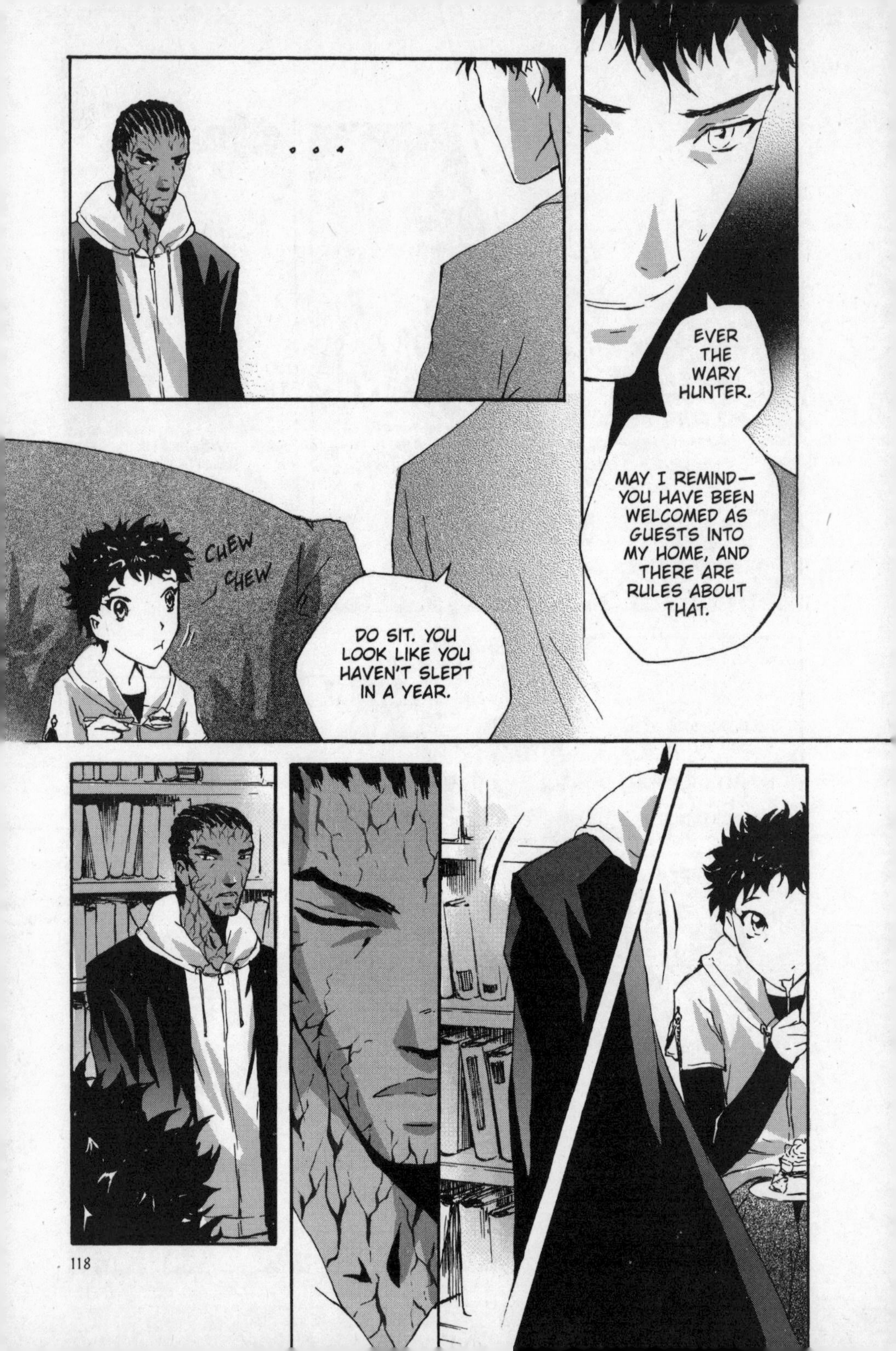
EVER THE WARY HUNTER.
...
MAY I REMIND— YOU HAVE BEEN WELCOMED AS GUESTS INTO MY HOME, AND THERE ARE RULES ABOUT THAT.
DO SIT. YOU LOOK LIKE YOU HAVEN'T SLEPT IN A YEAR.
CHEW CHEW

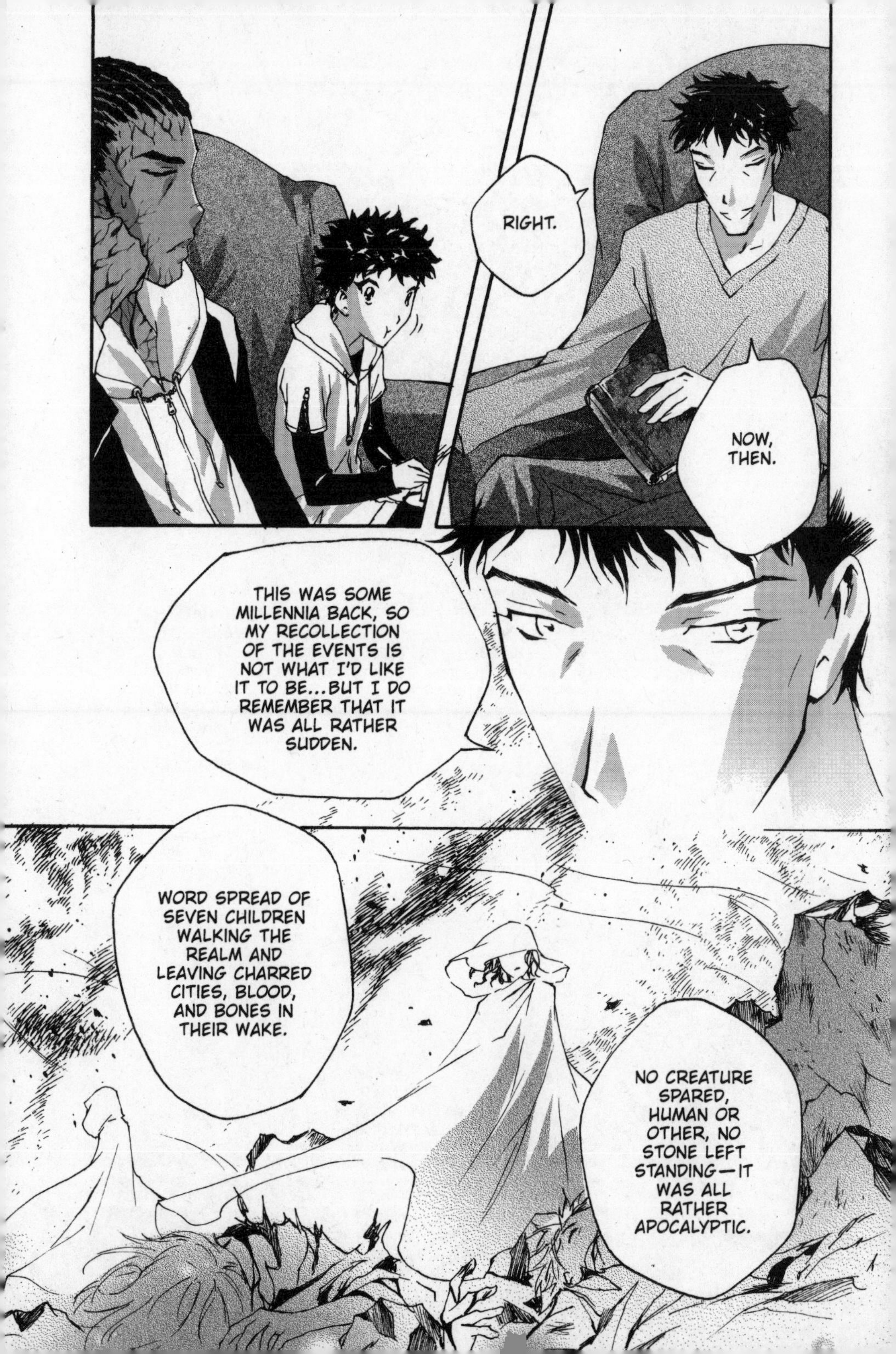
RIGHT.
NOW, THEN.
THIS WAS SOME MILLENNIA BACK, SO MY RECOLLECTION OF THE EVENTS IS NOT WHAT I'D LIKE IT TO BE...BUT I DO REMEMBER THAT IT WAS ALL RATHER SUDDEN.
WORD SPREAD OF SEVEN CHILDREN WALKING THE REALM AND LEAVING CHARRED CITIES, BLOOD, AND BONES IN THEIR WAKE.
NO CREATURE SPARED, HUMAN OR OTHER, NO STONE LEFT STANDING—IT WAS ALL RATHER APOCALYPTIC.

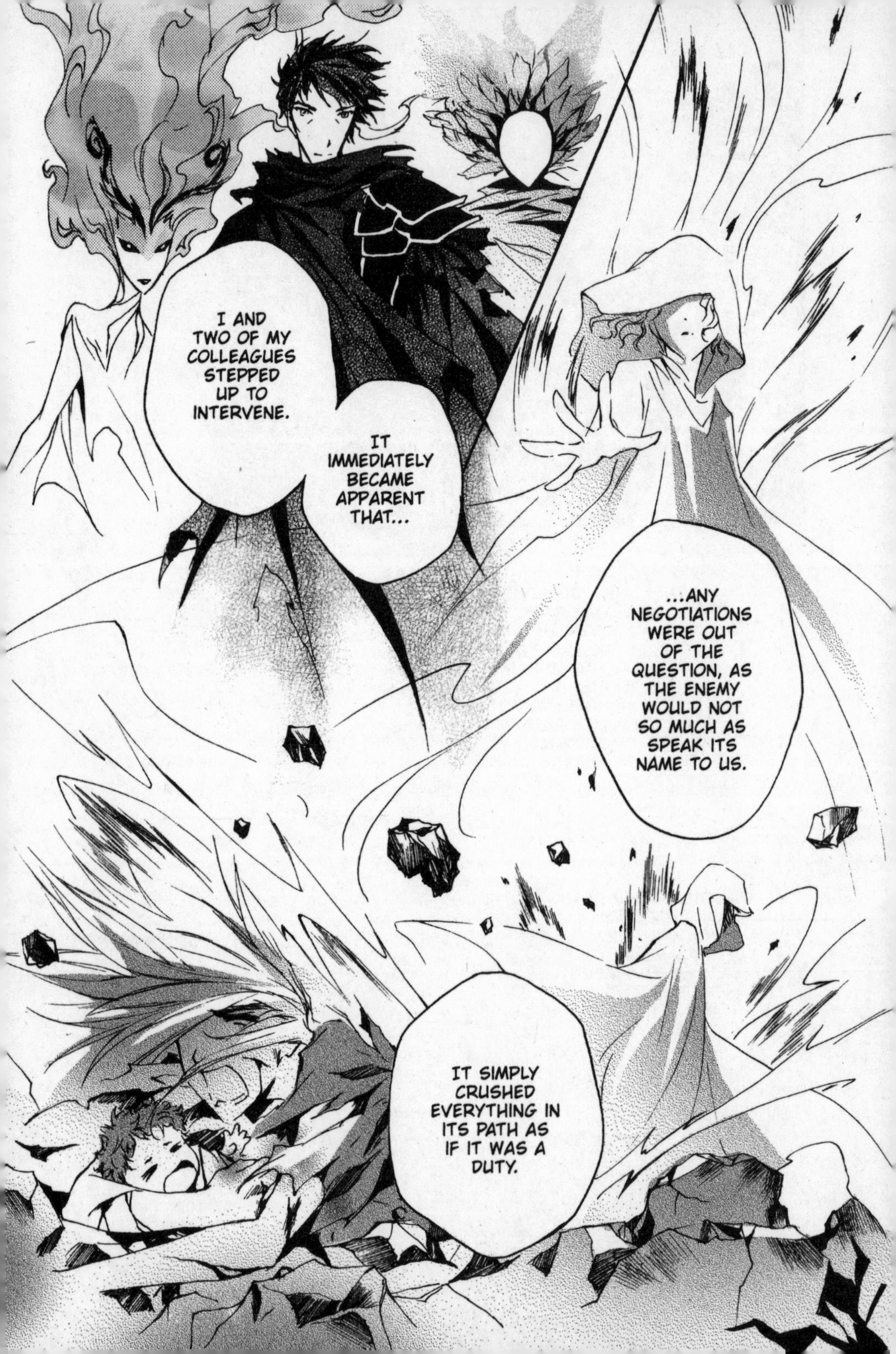

I AND TWO OF MY COLLEAGUES STEPPED UP TO INTERVENE.
IT IMMEDIATELY BECAME APPARENT THAT...
...ANY NEGOTIATIONS WERE OUT OF THE QUESTION, AS THE ENEMY WOULD NOT SO MUCH AS SPEAK ITS NAME TO US.
IT SIMPLY CRUSHED EVERYTHING IN ITS PATH AS IF IT WAS A DUTY.

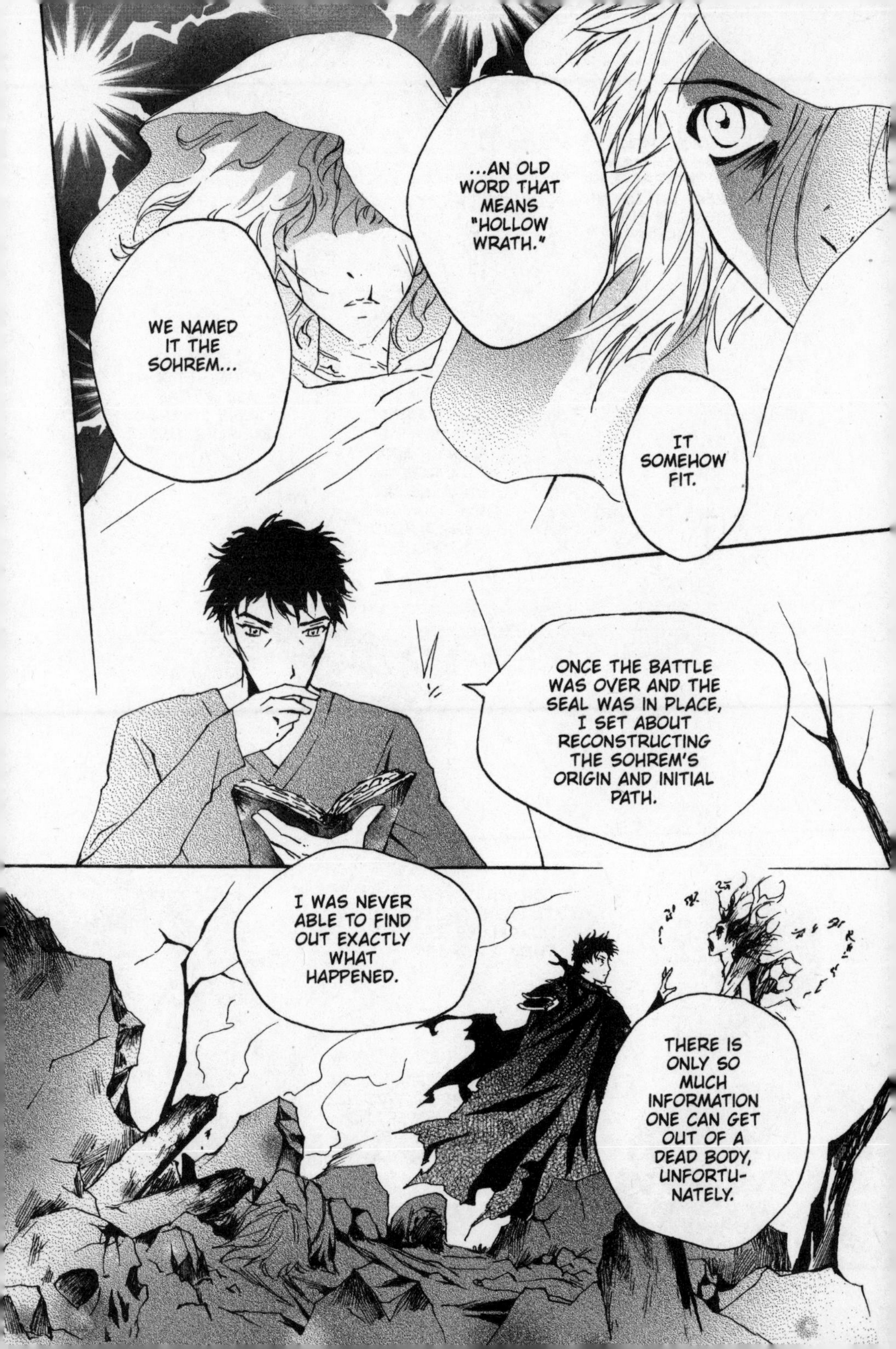
WE NAMED IT THE SOHREM...
...AN OLD WORD THAT MEANS "HOLLOW WRATH."
IT SOMEHOW FIT.
ONCE THE BATTLE WAS OVER AND THE SEAL WAS IN PLACE, I SET ABOUT RECONSTRUCTING THE SOHREM'S ORIGIN AND INITIAL PATH.
I WAS NEVER ABLE TO FIND OUT EXACTLY WHAT HAPPENED.
THERE IS ONLY SO MUCH INFORMATION ONE CAN GET OUT OF A DEAD BODY, UNFORTU-NATELY.

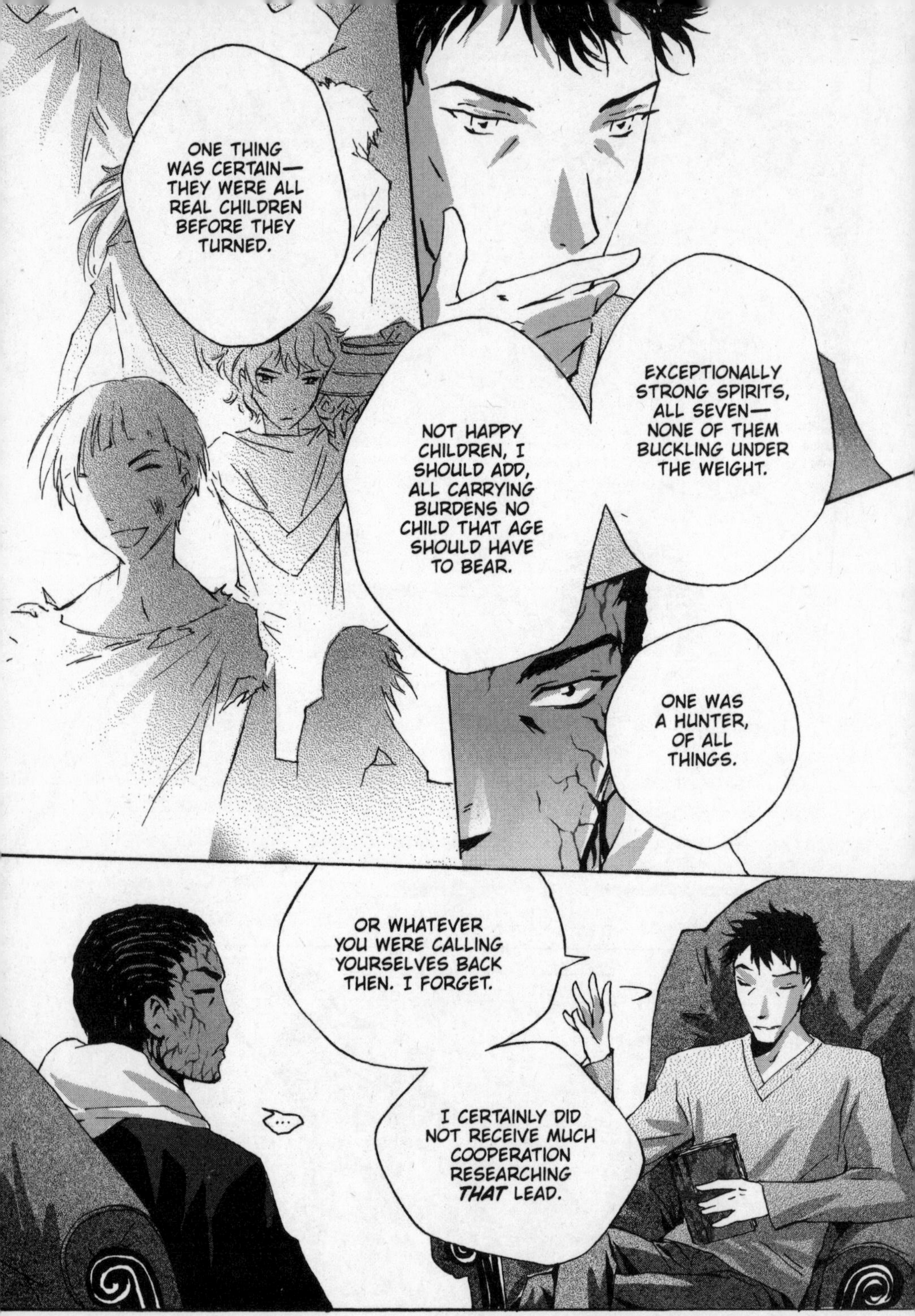
ONE THING WAS CERTAIN— THEY WERE ALL REAL CHILDREN BEFORE THEY TURNED.
NOT HAPPY CHILDREN, I SHOULD ADD, ALL CARRYING BURDENS NO CHILD THAT AGE SHOULD HAVE TO BEAR.
EXCEPTIONALLY STRONG SPIRITS, ALL SEVEN— NONE OF THEM BUCKLING UNDER THE WEIGHT.
ONE WAS A HUNTER, OF ALL THINGS.
OR WHATEVER YOU WERE CALLING YOURSELVES BACK THEN. I FORGET.
...
I CERTAINLY DID NOT RECEIVE MUCH COOPERATION RESEARCHING *THAT* LEAD.

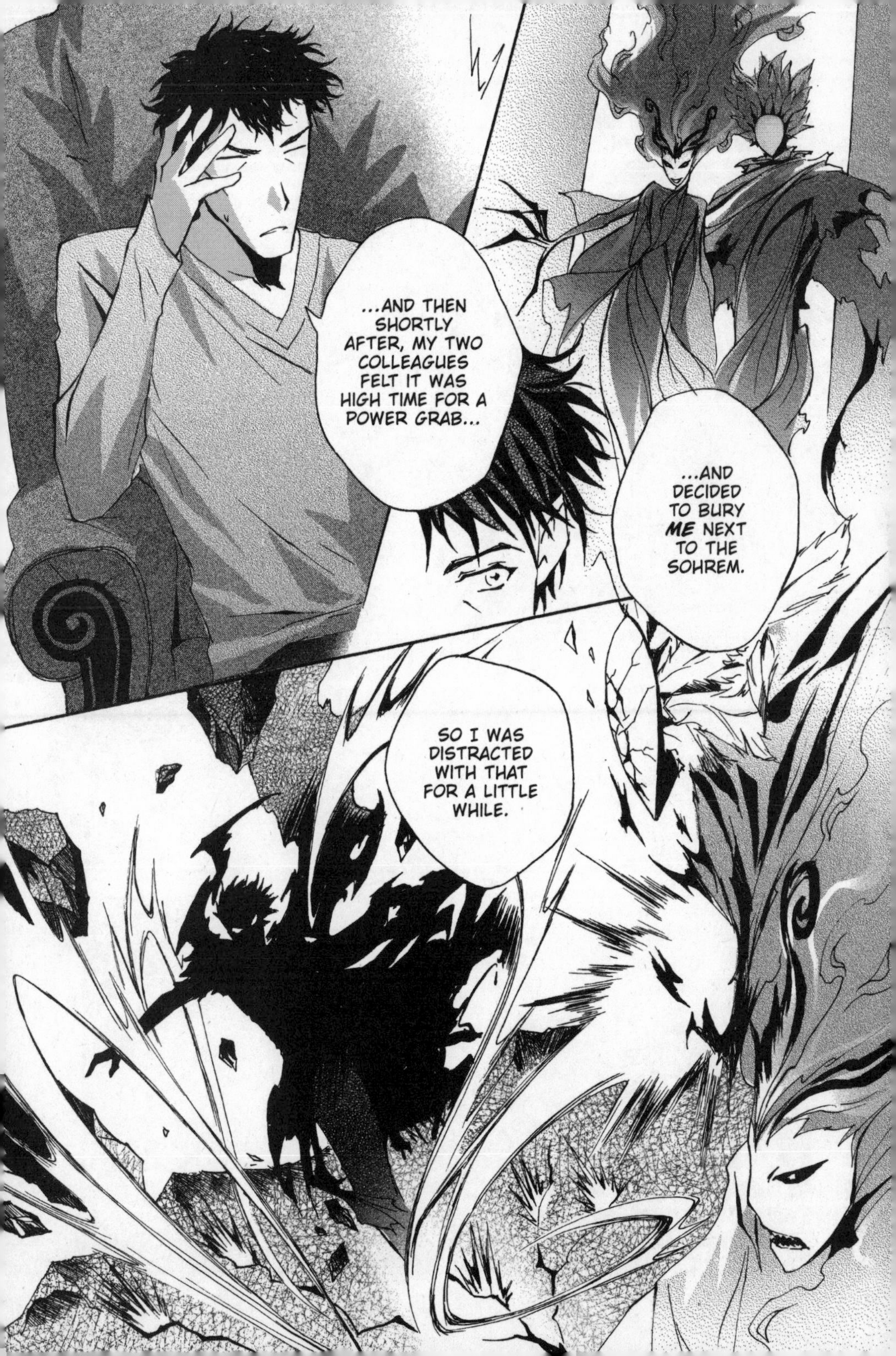
...AND THEN SHORTLY AFTER, MY TWO COLLEAGUES FELT IT WAS HIGH TIME FOR A POWER GRAB...
...AND DECIDED TO BURY *ME* NEXT TO THE SOHREM.
SO I WAS DISTRACTED WITH THAT FOR A LITTLE WHILE.

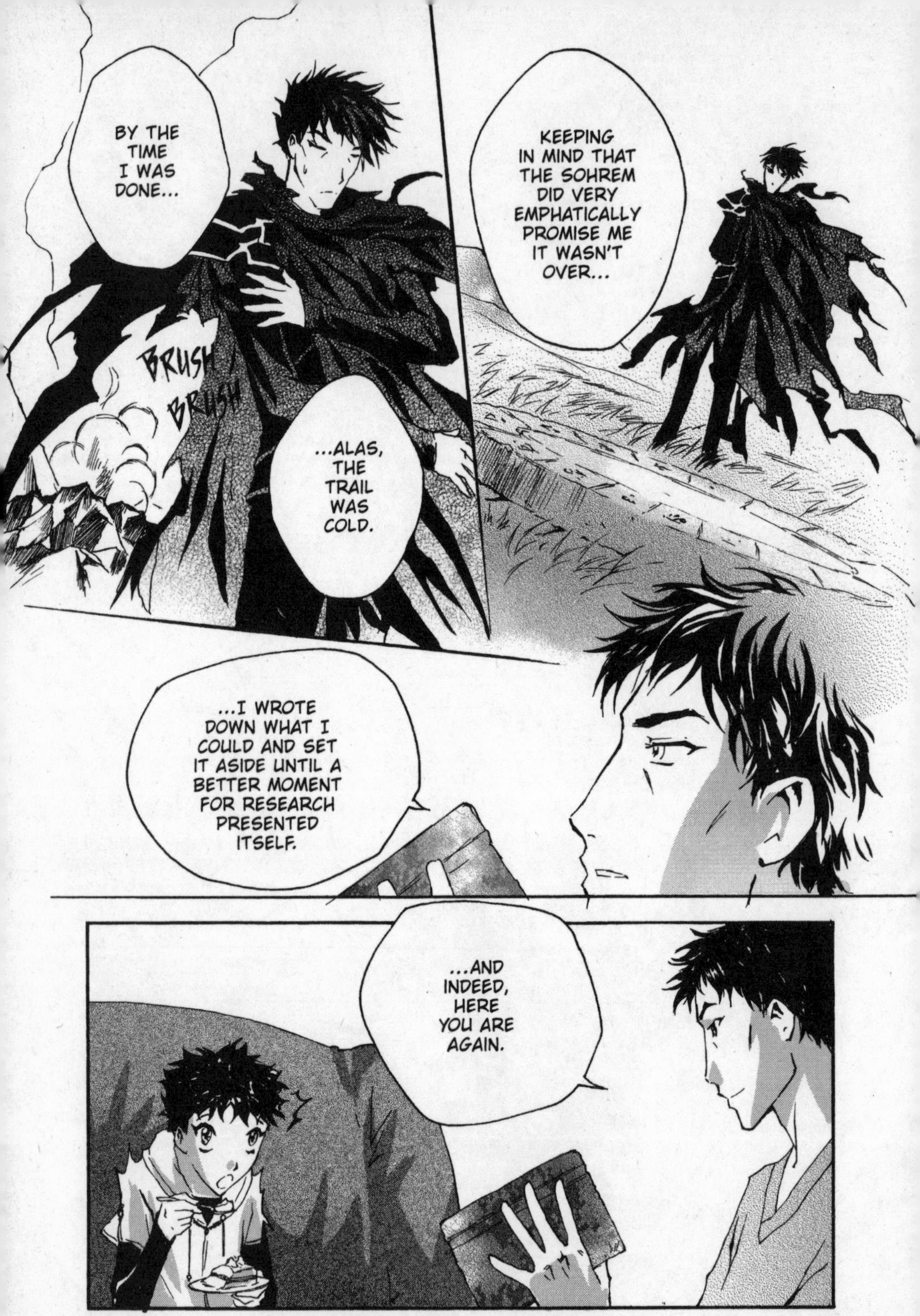

BY THE TIME I WAS DONE...
BRUSH BRUSH
...ALAS, THE TRAIL WAS COLD.
KEEPING IN MIND THAT THE SOHREM DID VERY EMPHATICALLY PROMISE ME IT WASN'T OVER...
...I WROTE DOWN WHAT I COULD AND SET IT ASIDE UNTIL A BETTER MOMENT FOR RESEARCH PRESENTED ITSELF.
...AND INDEED, HERE YOU ARE AGAIN.

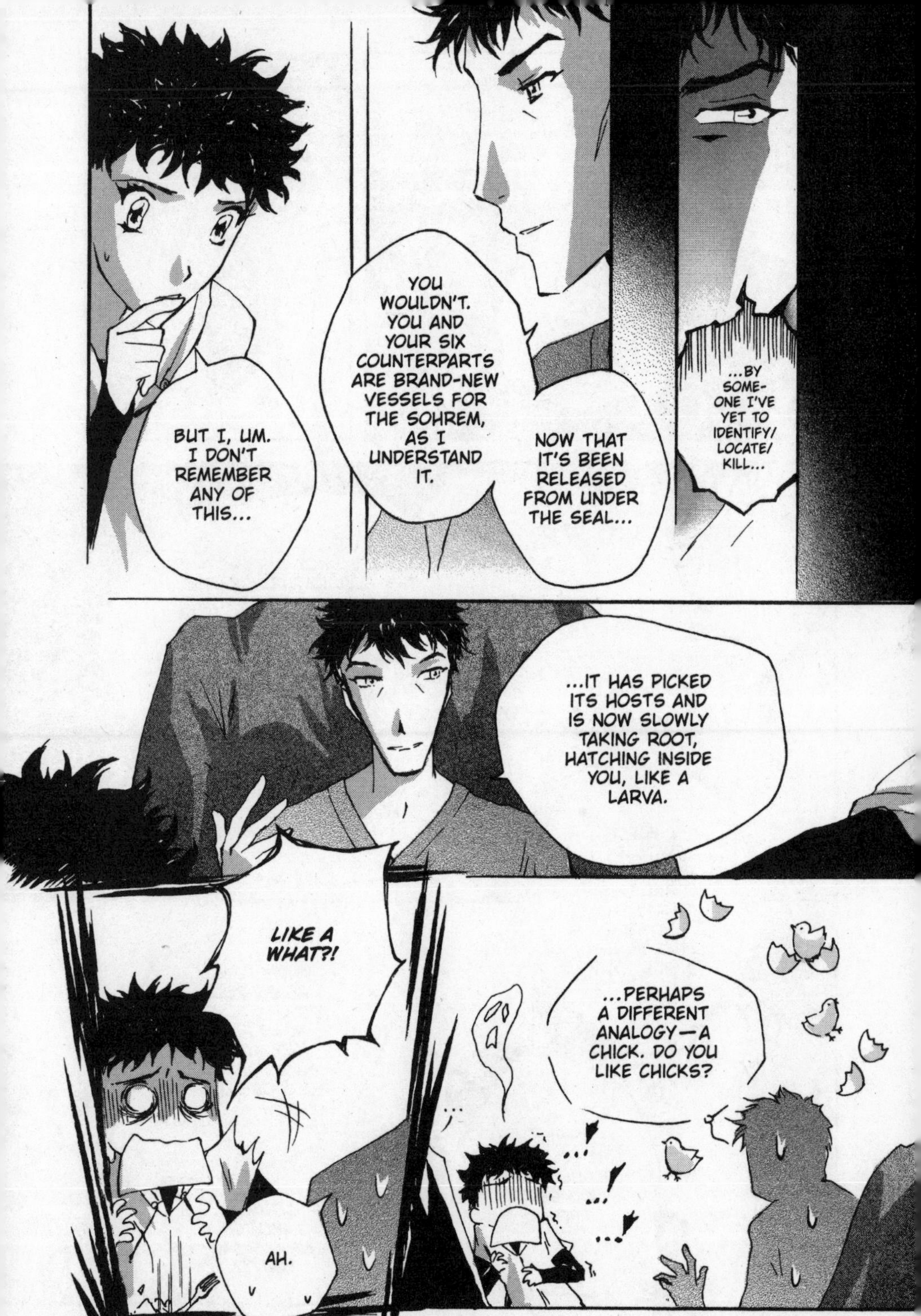
BUT I, UM. I DON'T REMEMBER ANY OF THIS...
YOU WOULDN'T. YOU AND YOUR SIX COUNTERPARTS ARE BRAND-NEW VESSELS FOR THE SOHREM, AS I UNDERSTAND IT.
NOW THAT IT'S BEEN RELEASED FROM UNDER THE SEAL...
...BY SOME-ONE I'VE YET TO IDENTIFY/LOCATE/KILL...
...IT HAS PICKED ITS HOSTS AND IS NOW SLOWLY TAKING ROOT, HATCHING INSIDE YOU, LIKE A LARVA.
LIKE A WHAT?!
AH.
...PERHAPS A DIFFERENT ANALOGY—A CHICK. DO YOU LIKE CHICKS?

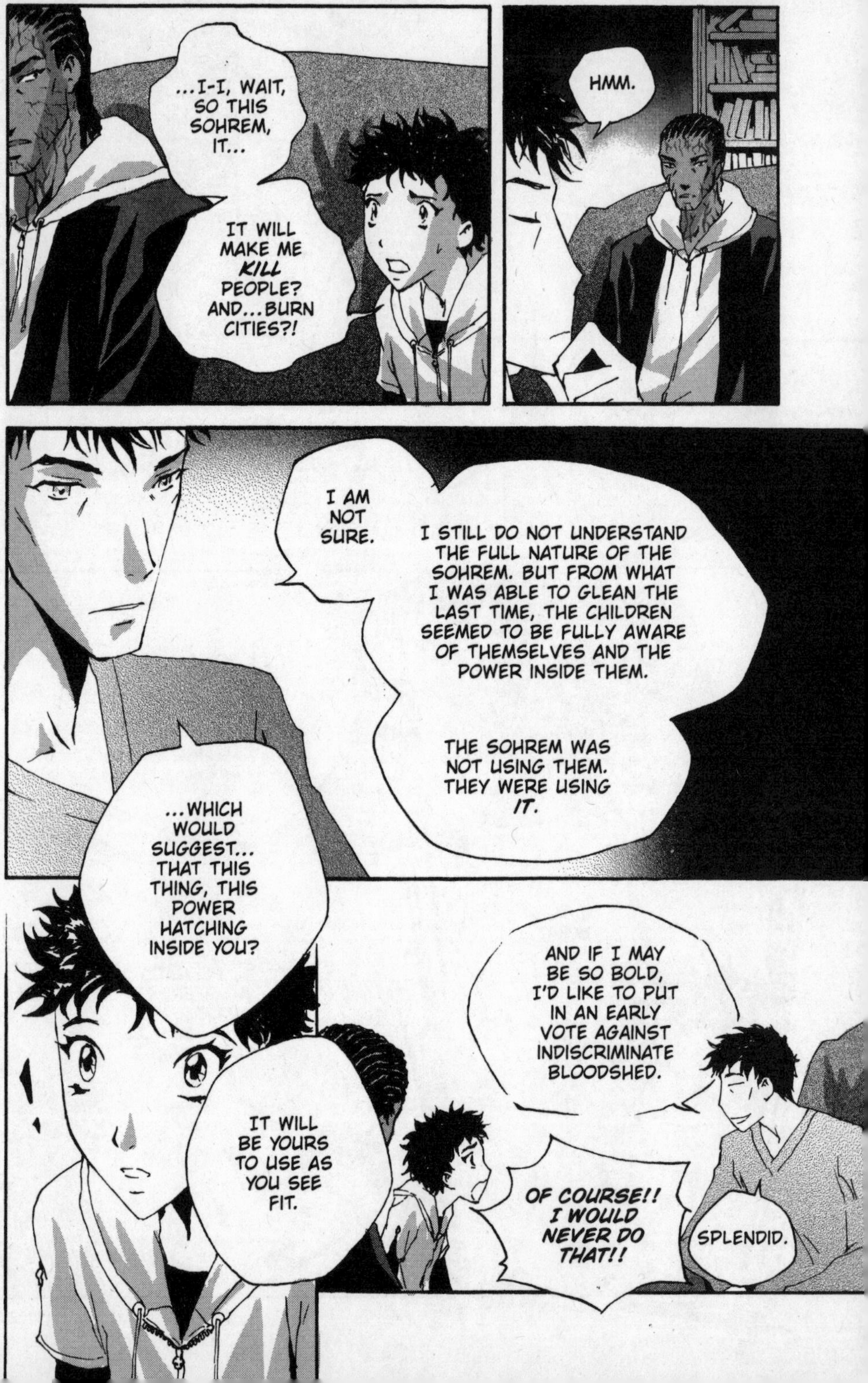
...I-I, WAIT, SO THIS SOHREM, IT...
IT WILL MAKE ME KILL PEOPLE? AND...BURN CITIES?!
HMM.
I AM NOT SURE.
I STILL DO NOT UNDERSTAND THE FULL NATURE OF THE SOHREM. BUT FROM WHAT I WAS ABLE TO GLEAN THE LAST TIME, THE CHILDREN SEEMED TO BE FULLY AWARE OF THEMSELVES AND THE POWER INSIDE THEM.
THE SOHREM WAS NOT USING THEM. THEY WERE USING IT.
...WHICH WOULD SUGGEST... THAT THIS THING, THIS POWER HATCHING INSIDE YOU?
IT WILL BE YOURS TO USE AS YOU SEE FIT.
AND IF I MAY BE SO BOLD, I'D LIKE TO PUT IN AN EARLY VOTE AGAINST INDISCRIMINATE BLOODSHED.
OF COURSE!! I WOULD NEVER DO THAT!!
SPLENDID.

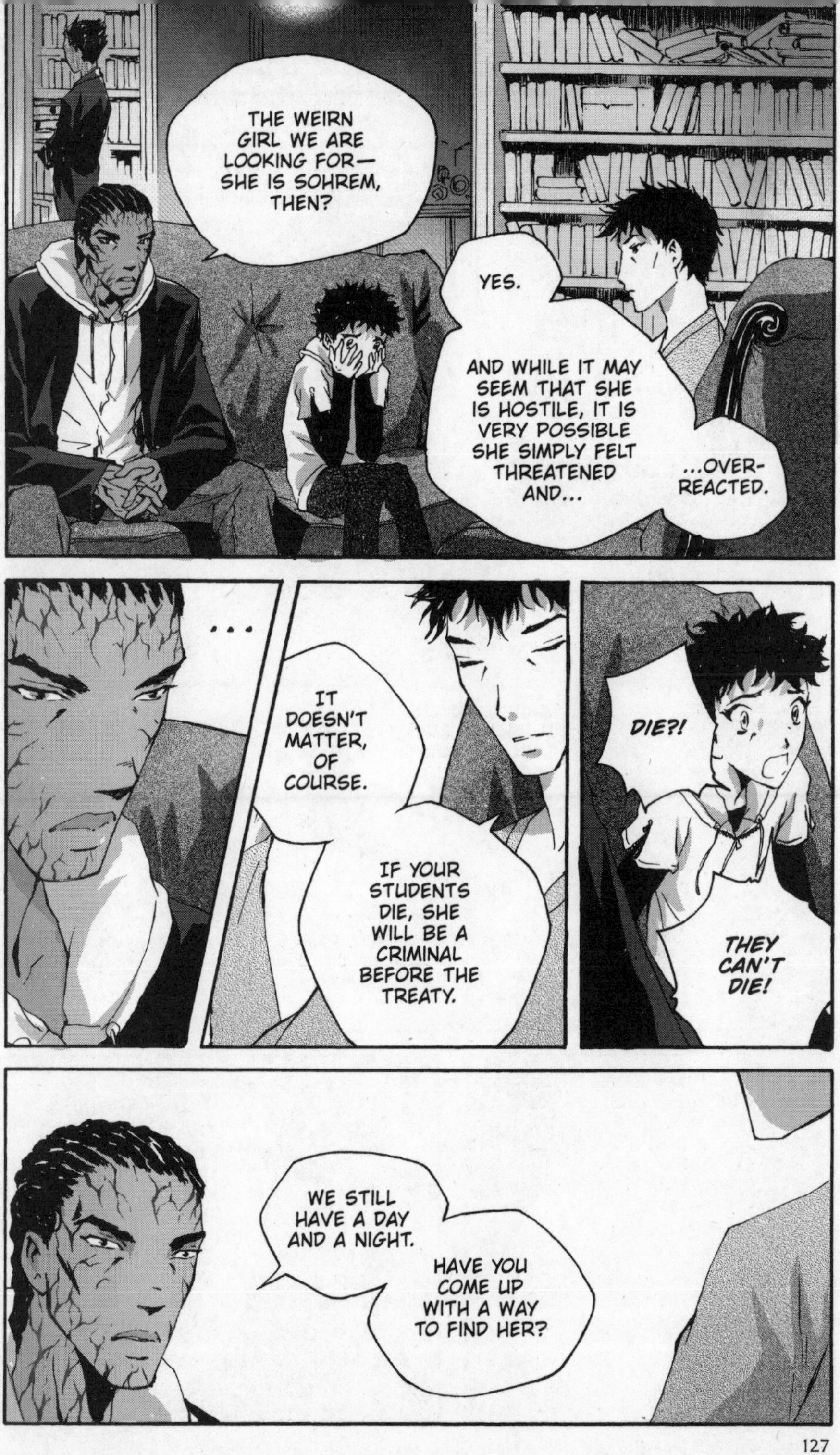
THE WEIRN GIRL WE ARE LOOKING FOR— SHE IS SOHREM, THEN?
YES.
AND WHILE IT MAY SEEM THAT SHE IS HOSTILE, IT IS VERY POSSIBLE SHE SIMPLY FELT THREATENED AND...
...OVER-REACTED.
...
IT DOESN'T MATTER, OF COURSE.
IF YOUR STUDENTS DIE, SHE WILL BE A CRIMINAL BEFORE THE TREATY.
DIE?!
THEY CAN'T DIE!
WE STILL HAVE A DAY AND A NIGHT.
HAVE YOU COME UP WITH A WAY TO FIND HER?

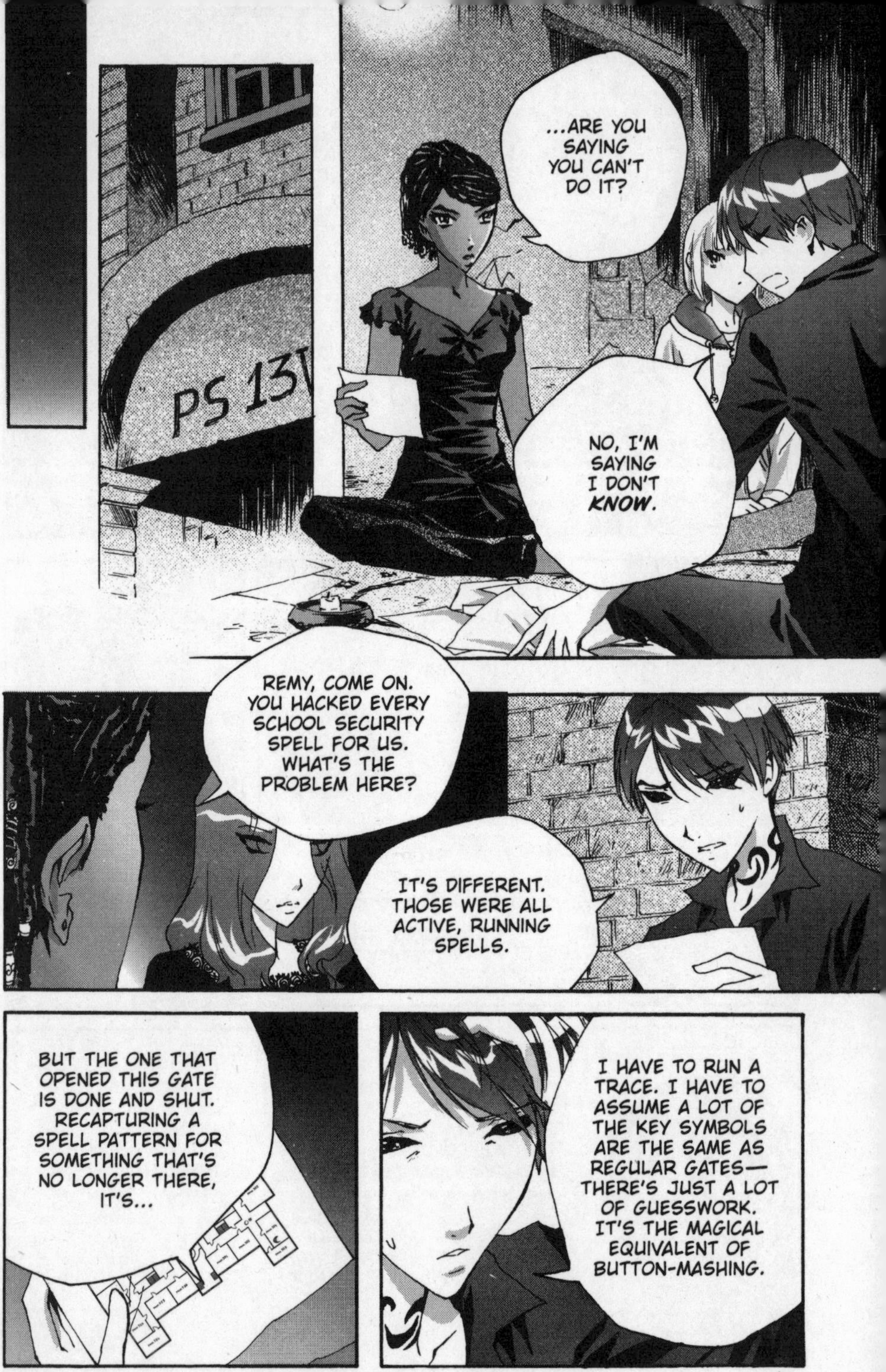
...ARE YOU SAYING YOU CAN'T DO IT?
NO, I'M SAYING I DON'T *KNOW*.
PS 13
REMY, COME ON. YOU HACKED EVERY SCHOOL SECURITY SPELL FOR US. WHAT'S THE PROBLEM HERE?
IT'S DIFFERENT. THOSE WERE ALL ACTIVE, RUNNING SPELLS.
BUT THE ONE THAT OPENED THIS GATE IS DONE AND SHUT. RECAPTURING A SPELL PATTERN FOR SOMETHING THAT'S NO LONGER THERE, IT'S...
I HAVE TO RUN A TRACE. I HAVE TO ASSUME A LOT OF THE KEY SYMBOLS ARE THE SAME AS REGULAR GATES—THERE'S JUST A LOT OF GUESSWORK. IT'S THE MAGICAL EQUIVALENT OF BUTTON-MASHING.

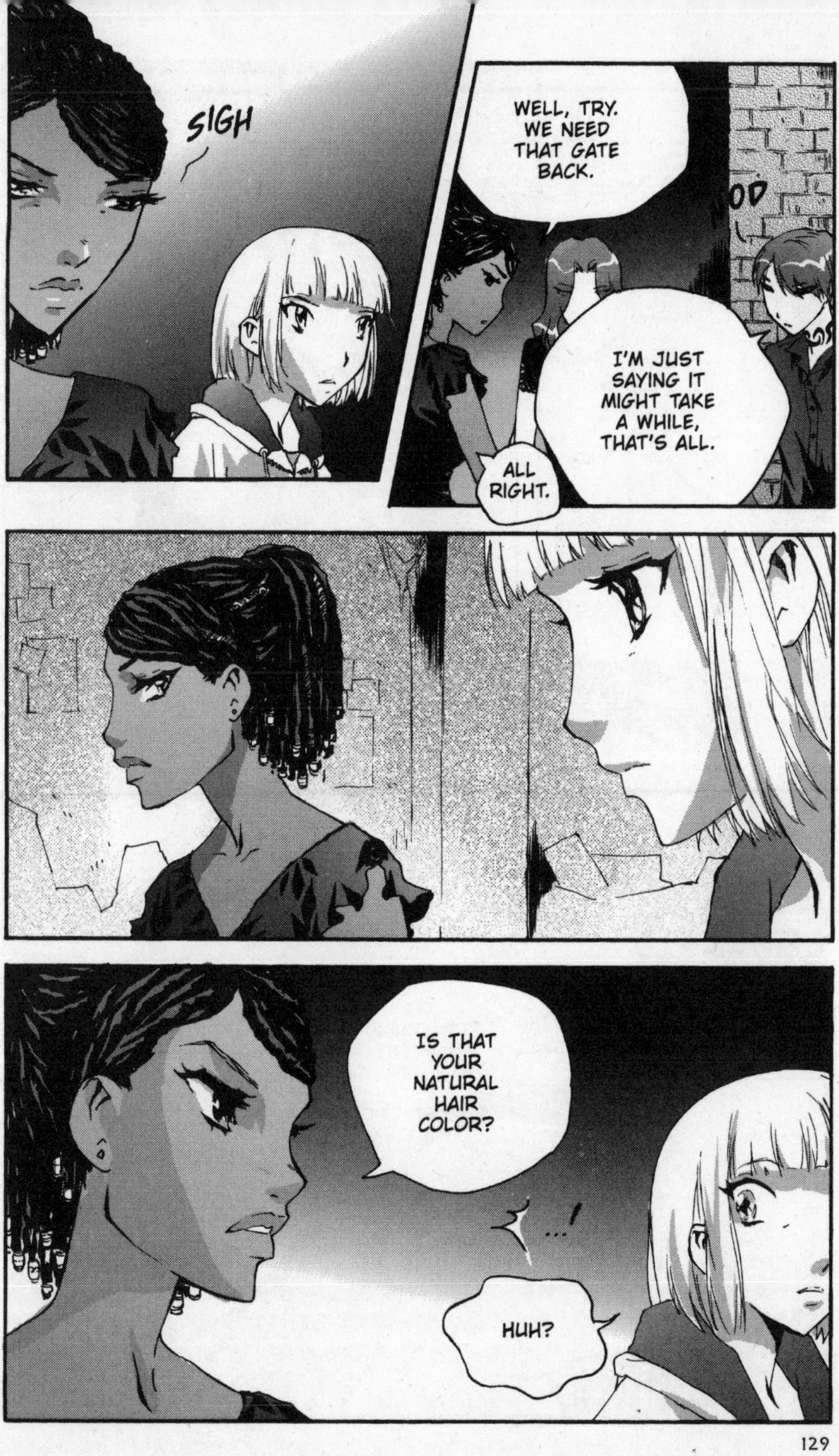
SIGH
WELL, TRY. WE NEED THAT GATE BACK.
NOD
I'M JUST SAYING IT MIGHT TAKE A WHILE, THAT'S ALL.
ALL RIGHT.
IS THAT YOUR NATURAL HAIR COLOR?
...!
HUH?

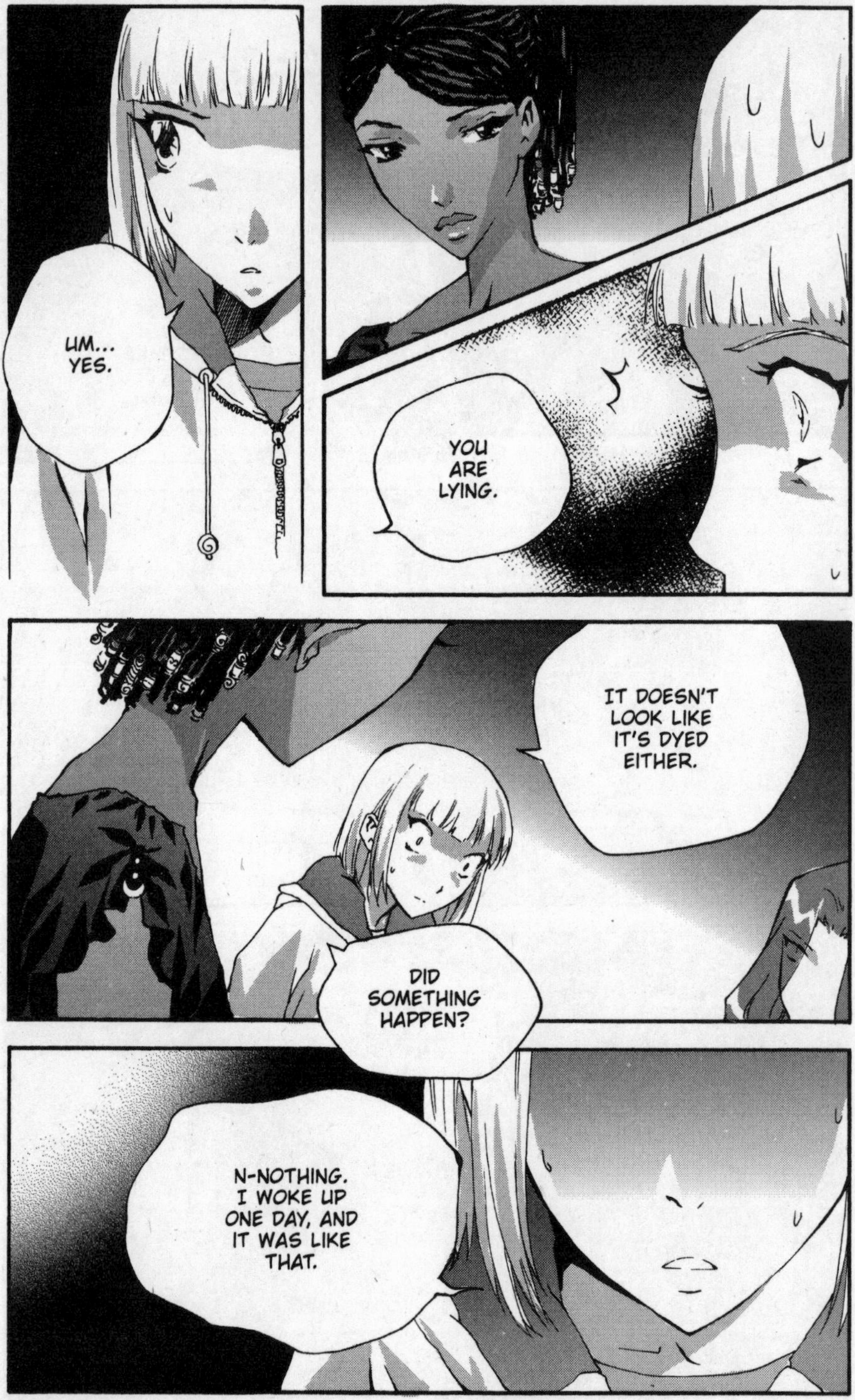
UM... YES.
YOU ARE LYING.
IT DOESN'T LOOK LIKE IT'S DYED EITHER.
DID SOMETHING HAPPEN?
N-NOTHING. I WOKE UP ONE DAY, AND IT WAS LIKE THAT.

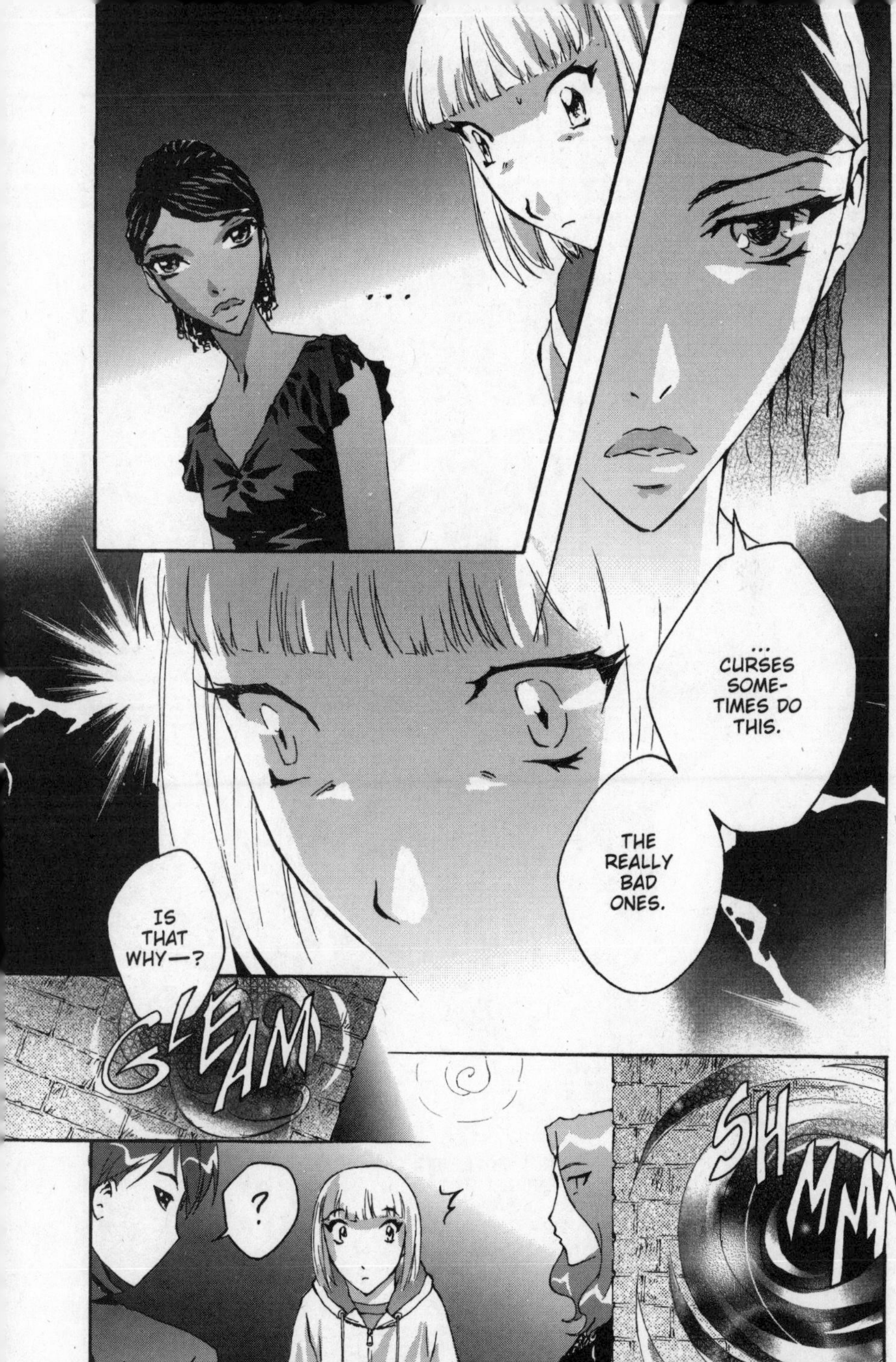
...
...CURSES SOMETIMES DO THIS.
THE REALLY BAD ONES.
IS THAT WHY—?
GLEAM
?
SHMMM

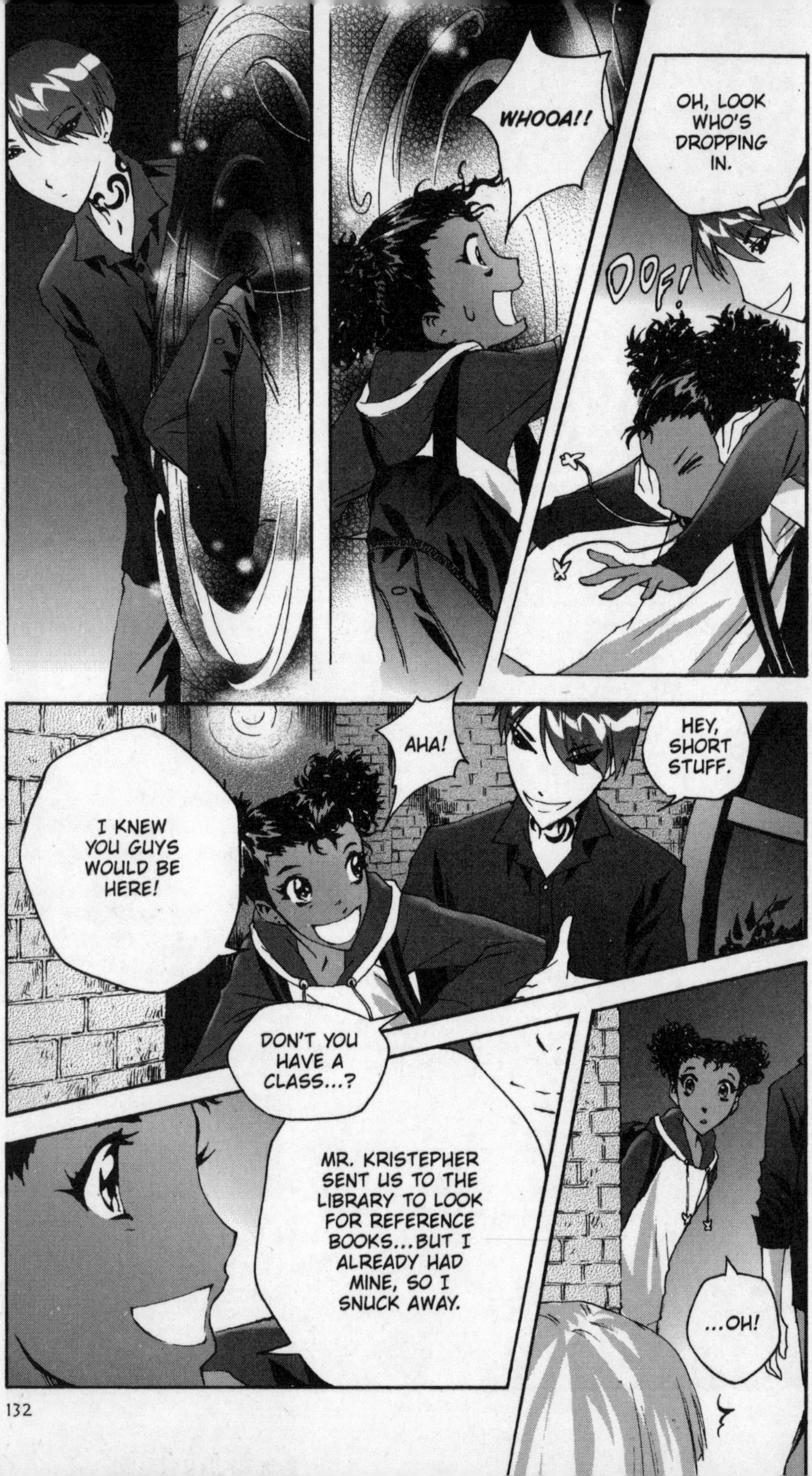
WHOOA!!
OH, LOOK WHO'S DROPPING IN.
OOF!
AHA!
I KNEW YOU GUYS WOULD BE HERE!
HEY, SHORT STUFF.
DON'T YOU HAVE A CLASS...?
MR. KRISTEPHER SENT US TO THE LIBRARY TO LOOK FOR REFERENCE BOOKS...BUT I ALREADY HAD MINE, SO I SNUCK AWAY.
...OH!

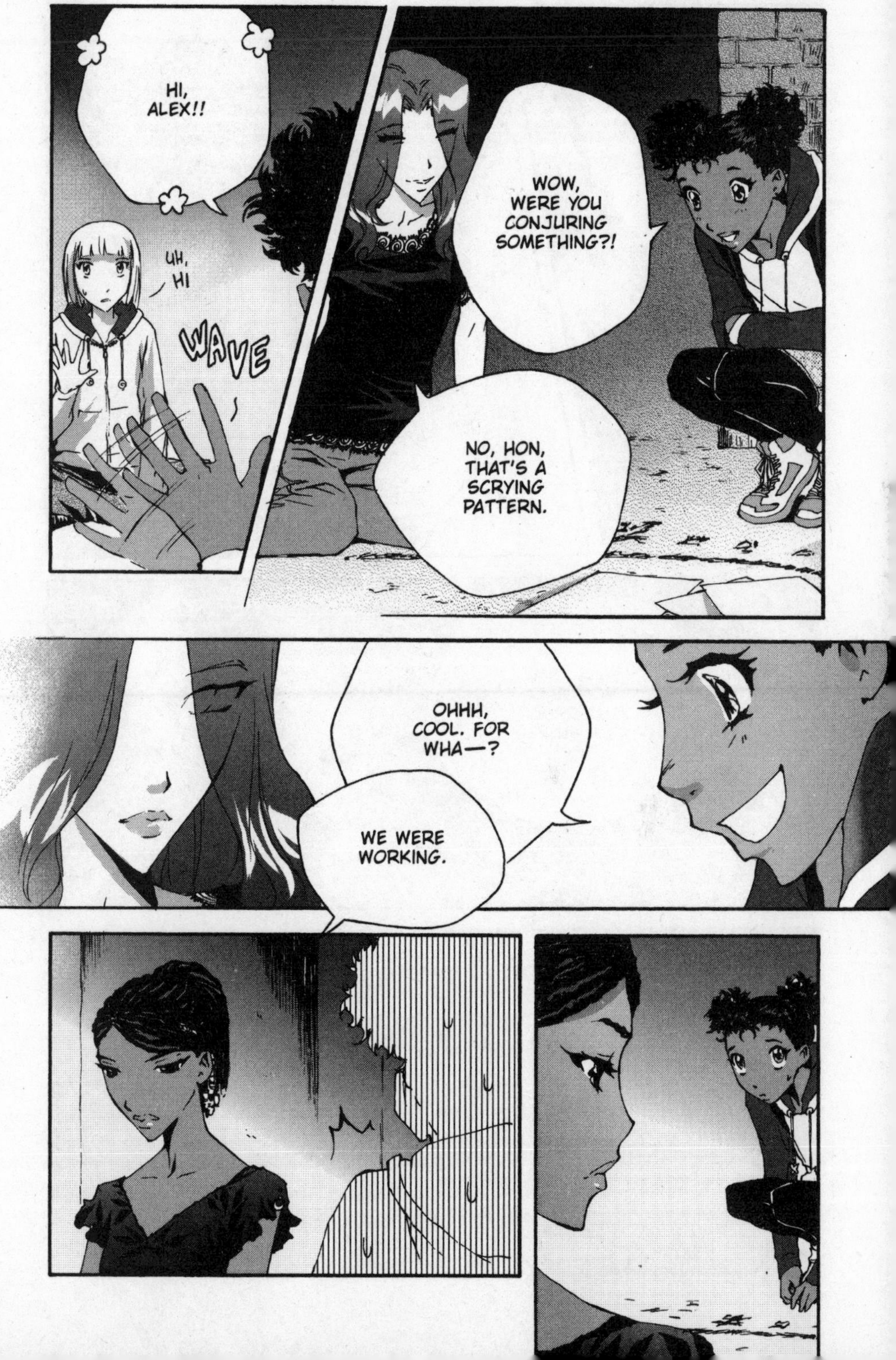
HI, ALEX!!
UH, HI
WAVE
WOW, WERE YOU CONJURING SOMETHING?!
NO, HON, THAT'S A SCRYING PATTERN.
OHHH, COOL. FOR WHA—?
WE WERE WORKING.

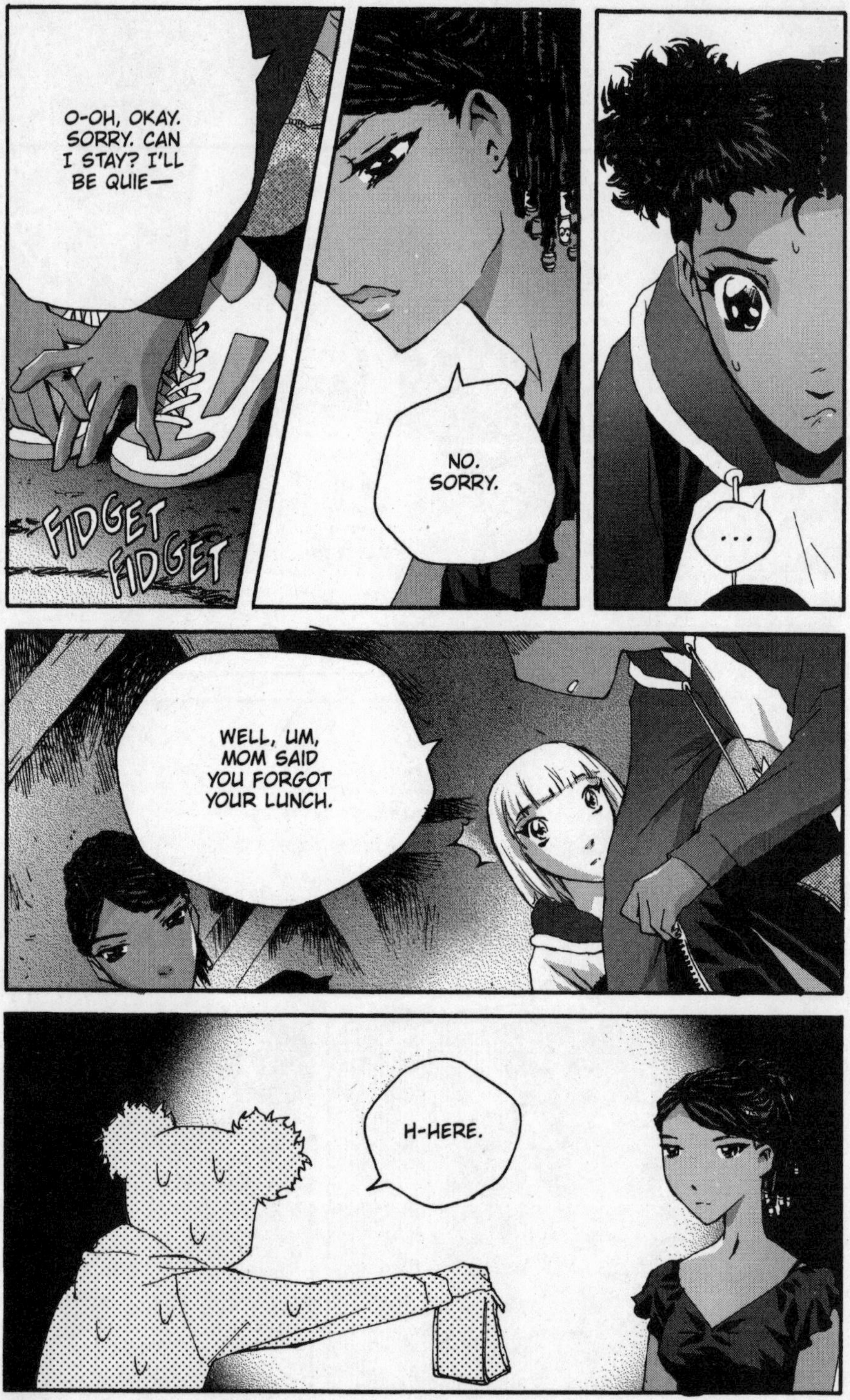
O-OH, OKAY. SORRY. CAN I STAY? I'LL BE QUIE—
FIDGET FIDGET
NO. SORRY.
...
WELL, UM, MOM SAID YOU FORGOT YOUR LUNCH.
H-HERE.

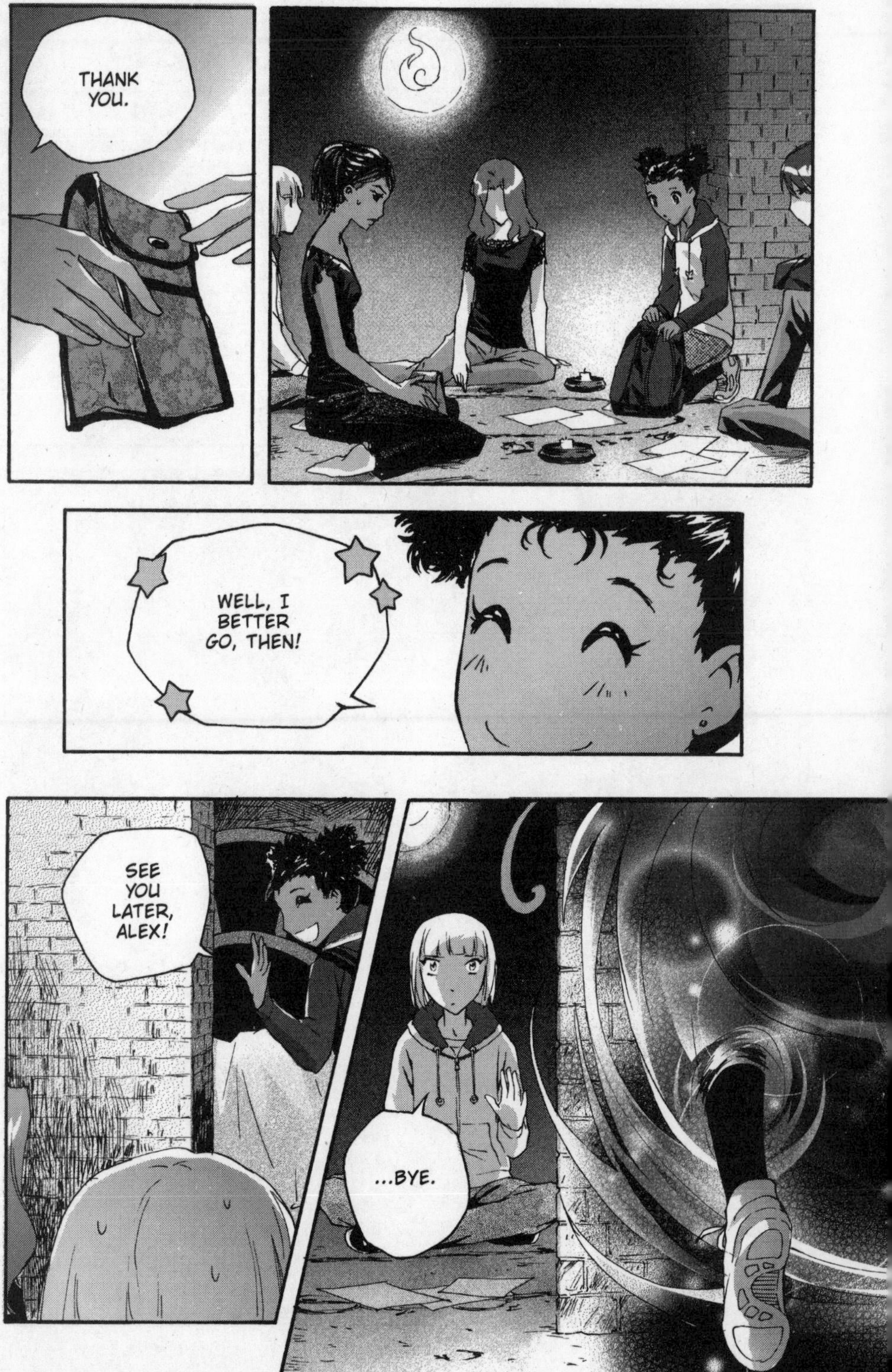
THANK YOU.
WELL, I BETTER GO, THEN!
SEE YOU LATER, ALEX!
...BYE.

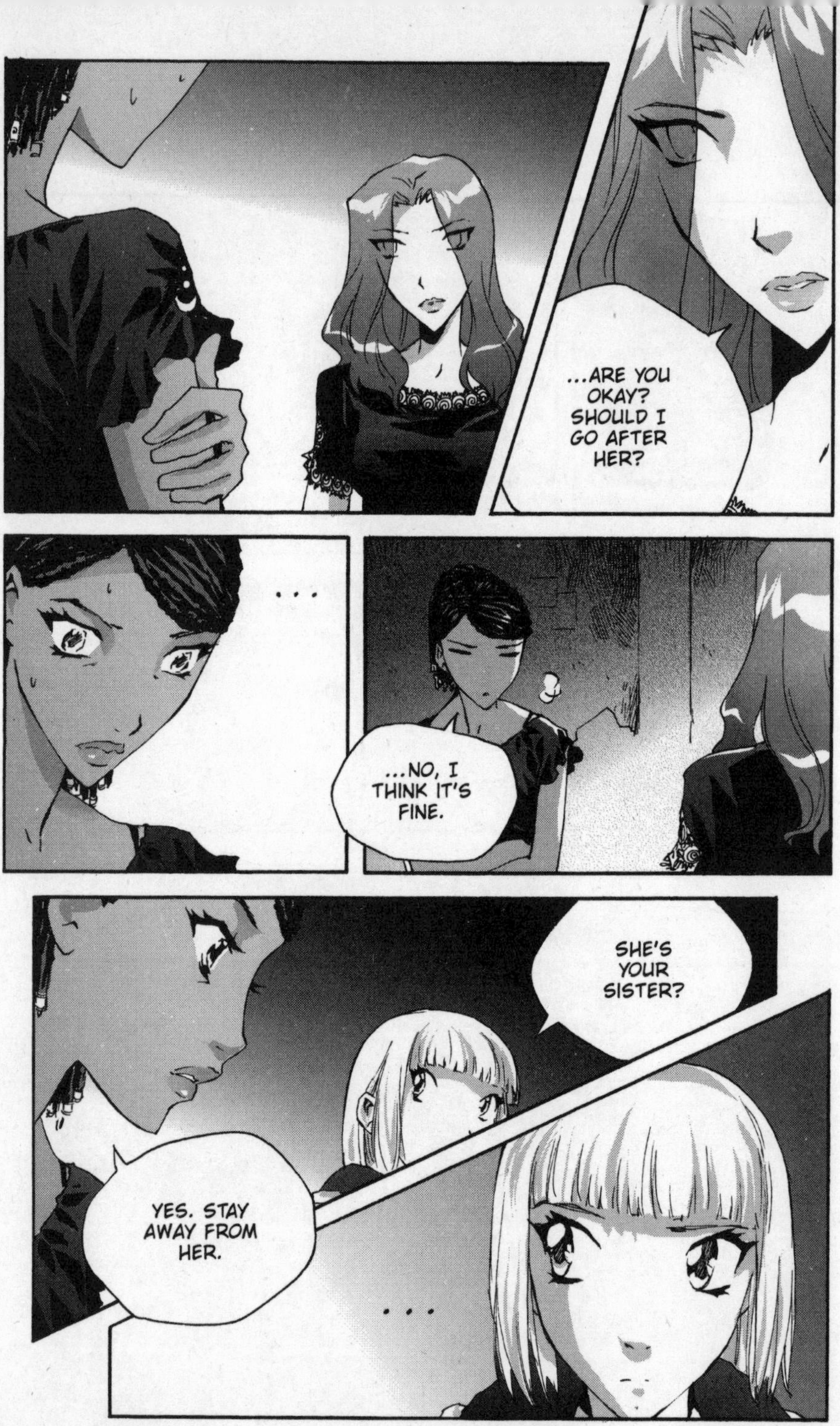
...ARE YOU OKAY? SHOULD I GO AFTER HER?
...
...NO, I THINK IT'S FINE.
SHE'S YOUR SISTER?
YES. STAY AWAY FROM HER.
...

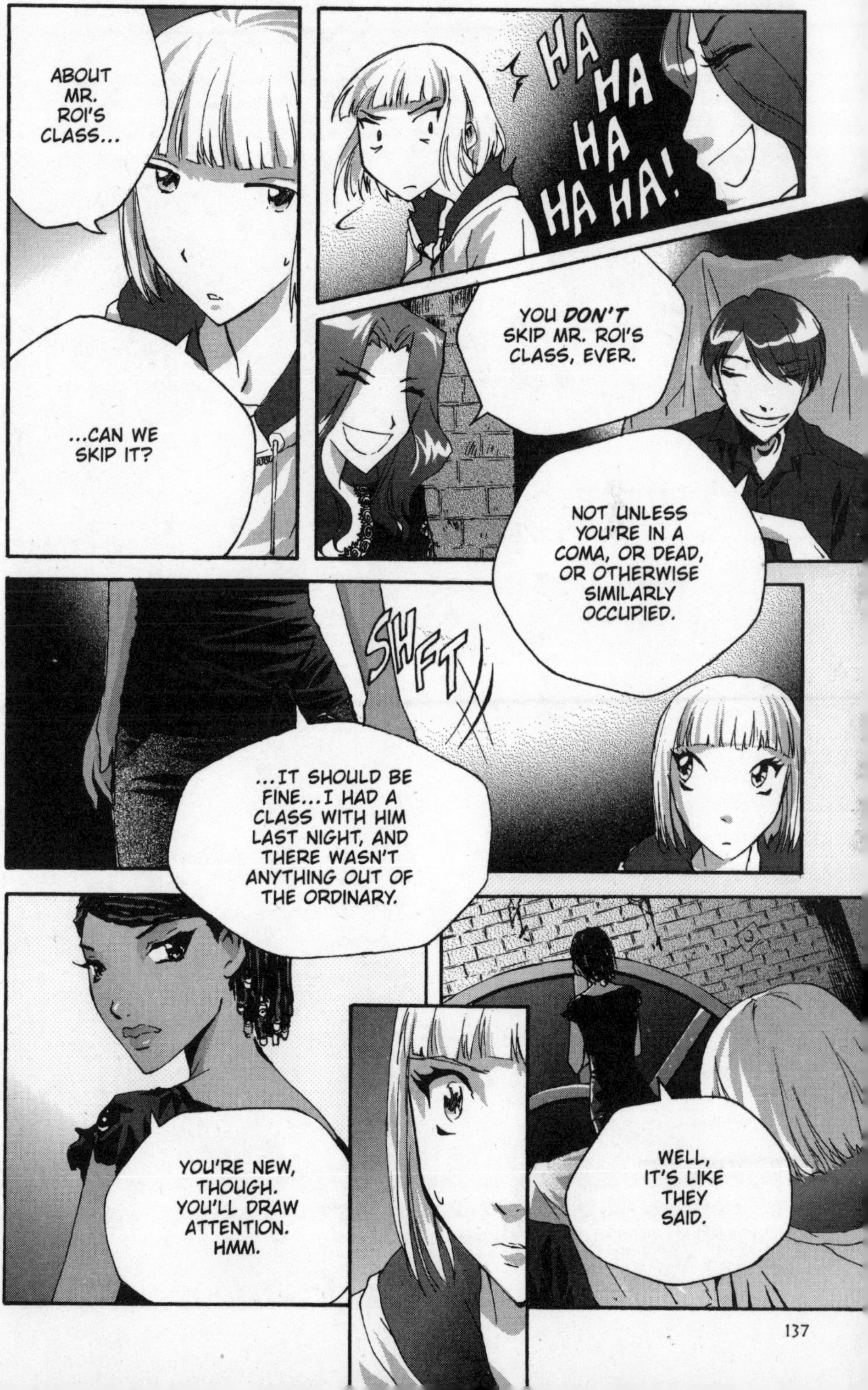
ABOUT MR. ROI'S CLASS...
...CAN WE SKIP IT?
HA HA HA HA HA!
YOU *DON'T* SKIP MR. ROI'S CLASS, EVER.
NOT UNLESS YOU'RE IN A COMA, OR DEAD, OR OTHERWISE SIMILARLY OCCUPIED.
SHFT
...IT SHOULD BE FINE...I HAD A CLASS WITH HIM LAST NIGHT, AND THERE WASN'T ANYTHING OUT OF THE ORDINARY.
YOU'RE NEW, THOUGH. YOU'LL DRAW ATTENTION. HMM.
WELL, IT'S LIKE THEY SAID.

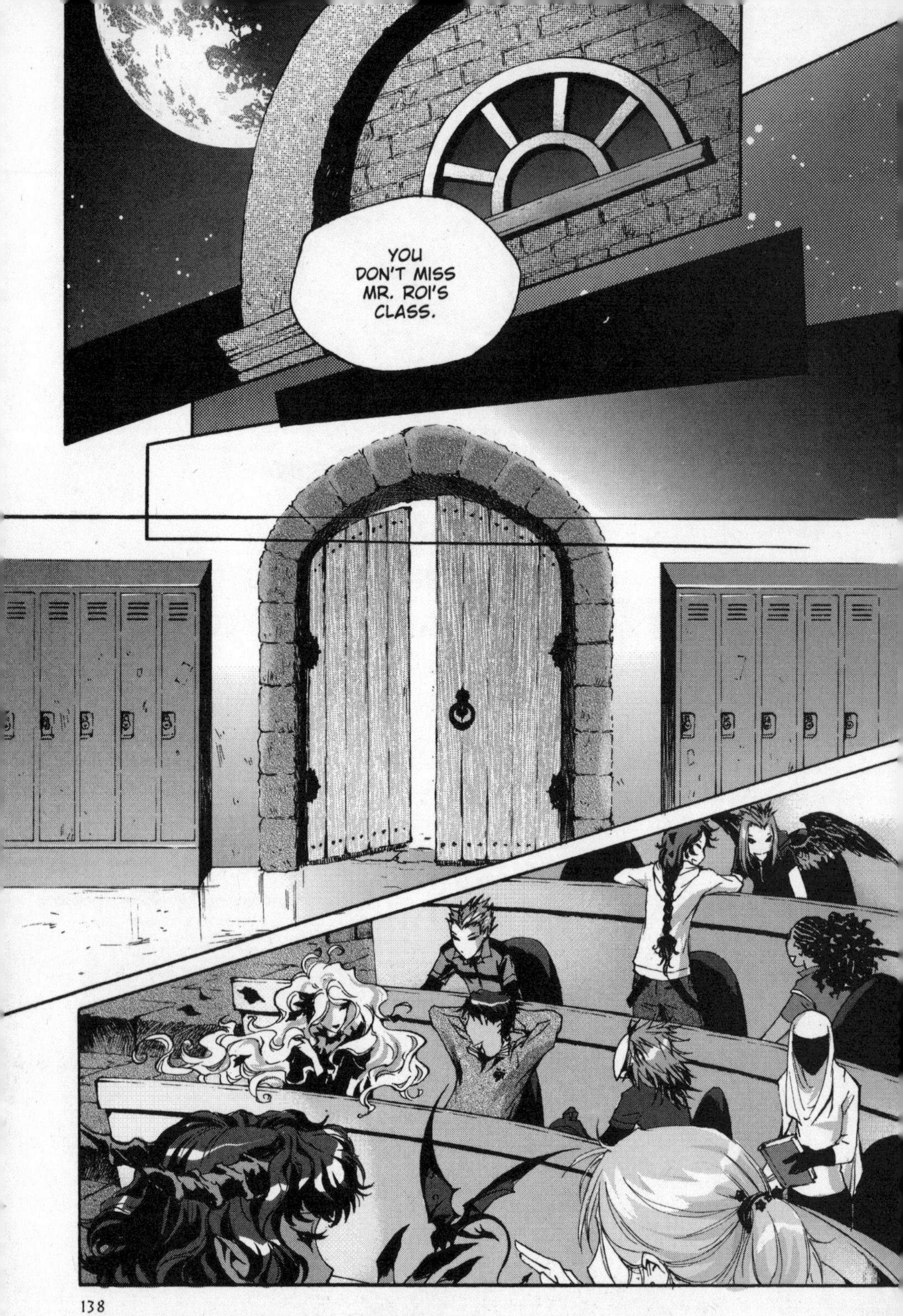
YOU DON'T MISS MR. ROI'S CLASS.

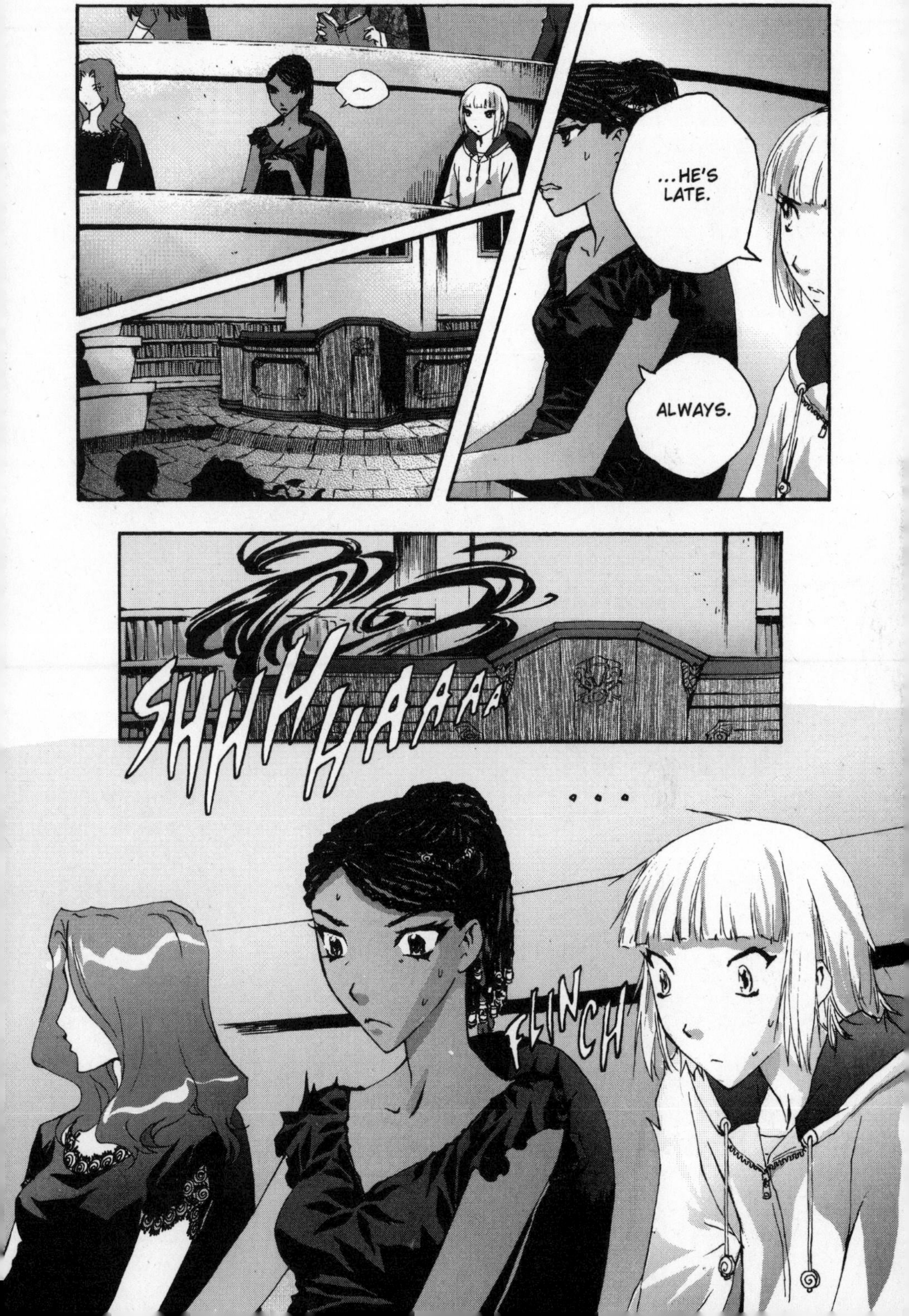
~
...HE'S LATE.
ALWAYS.
SHHHHAAAAA
...
FLINCH

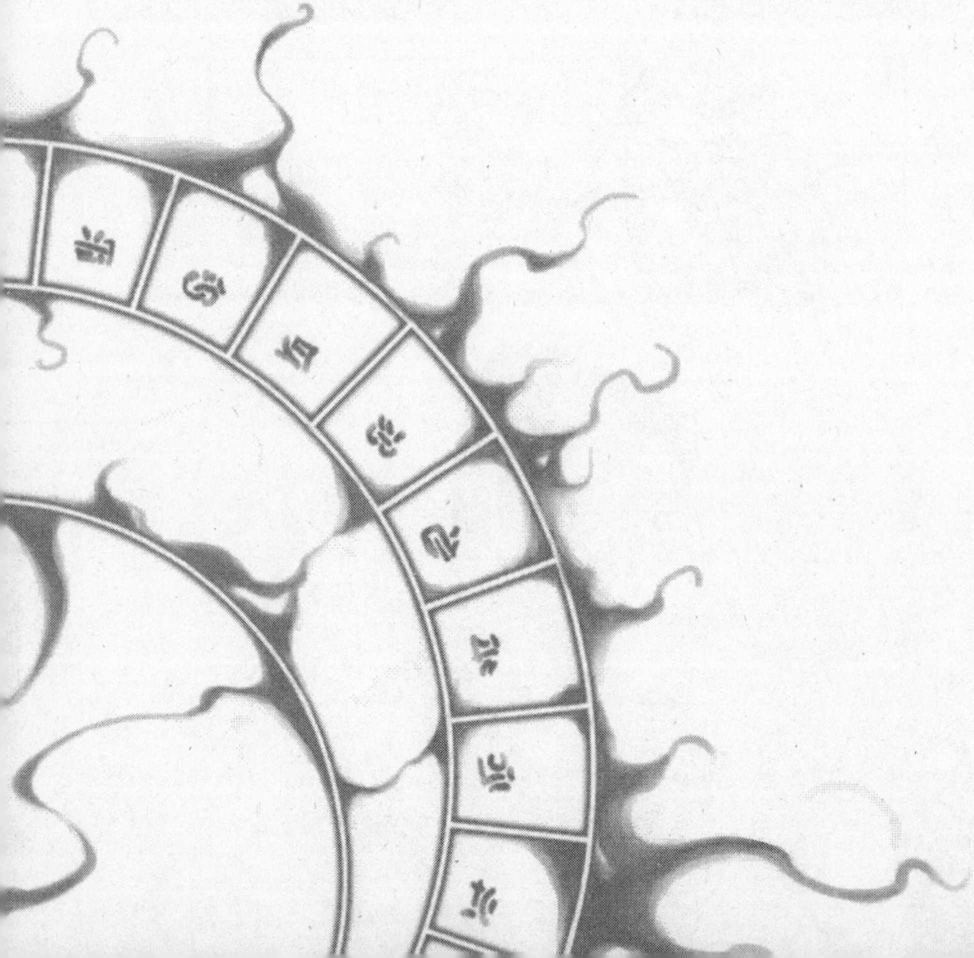

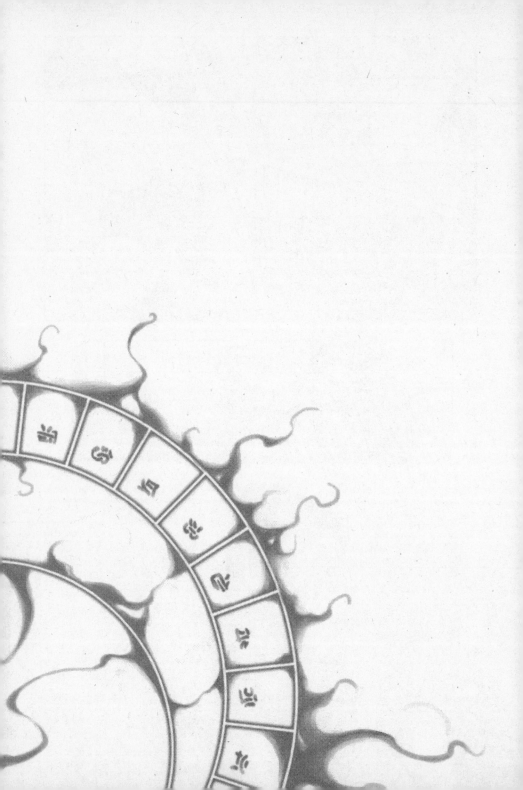

Chapter 17

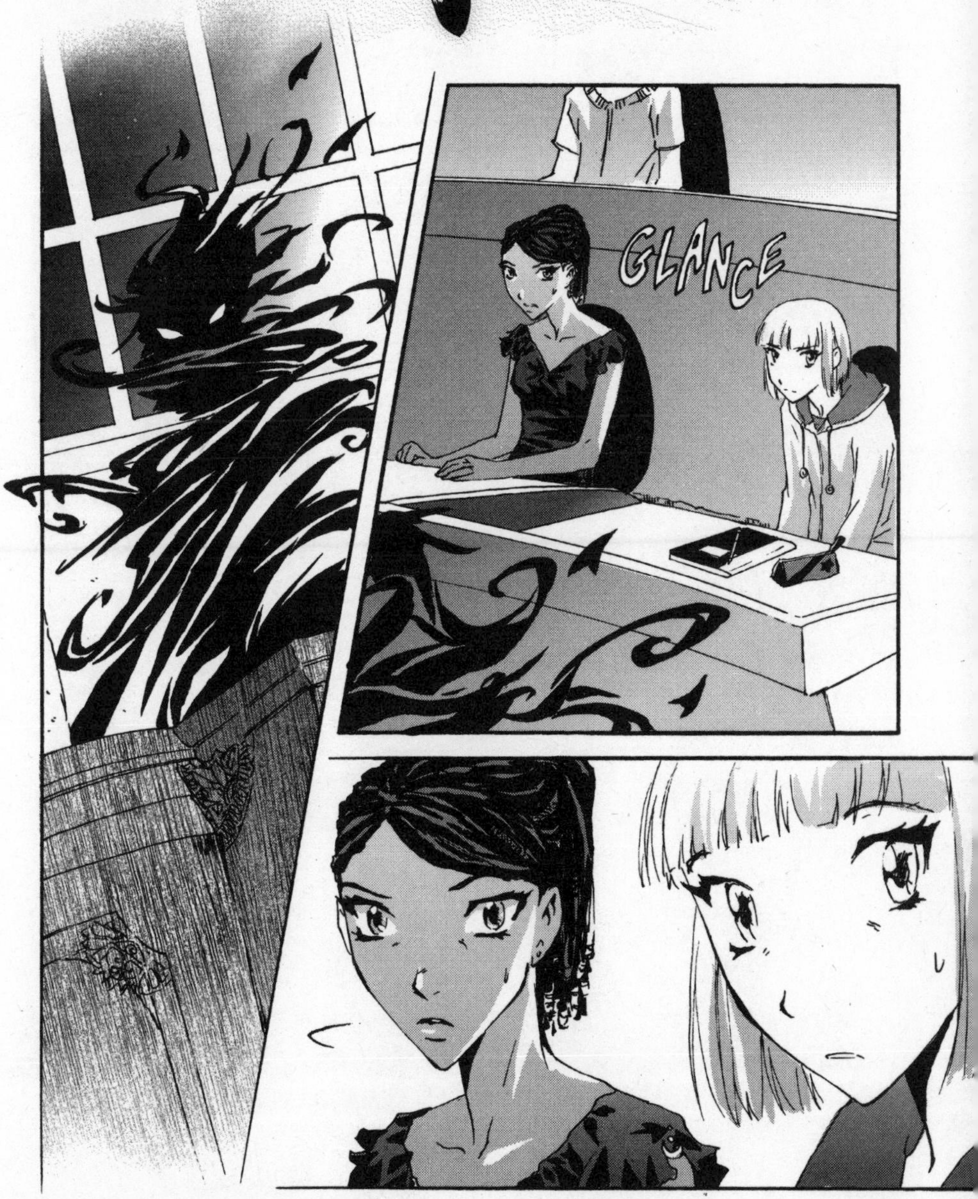
GLANCE

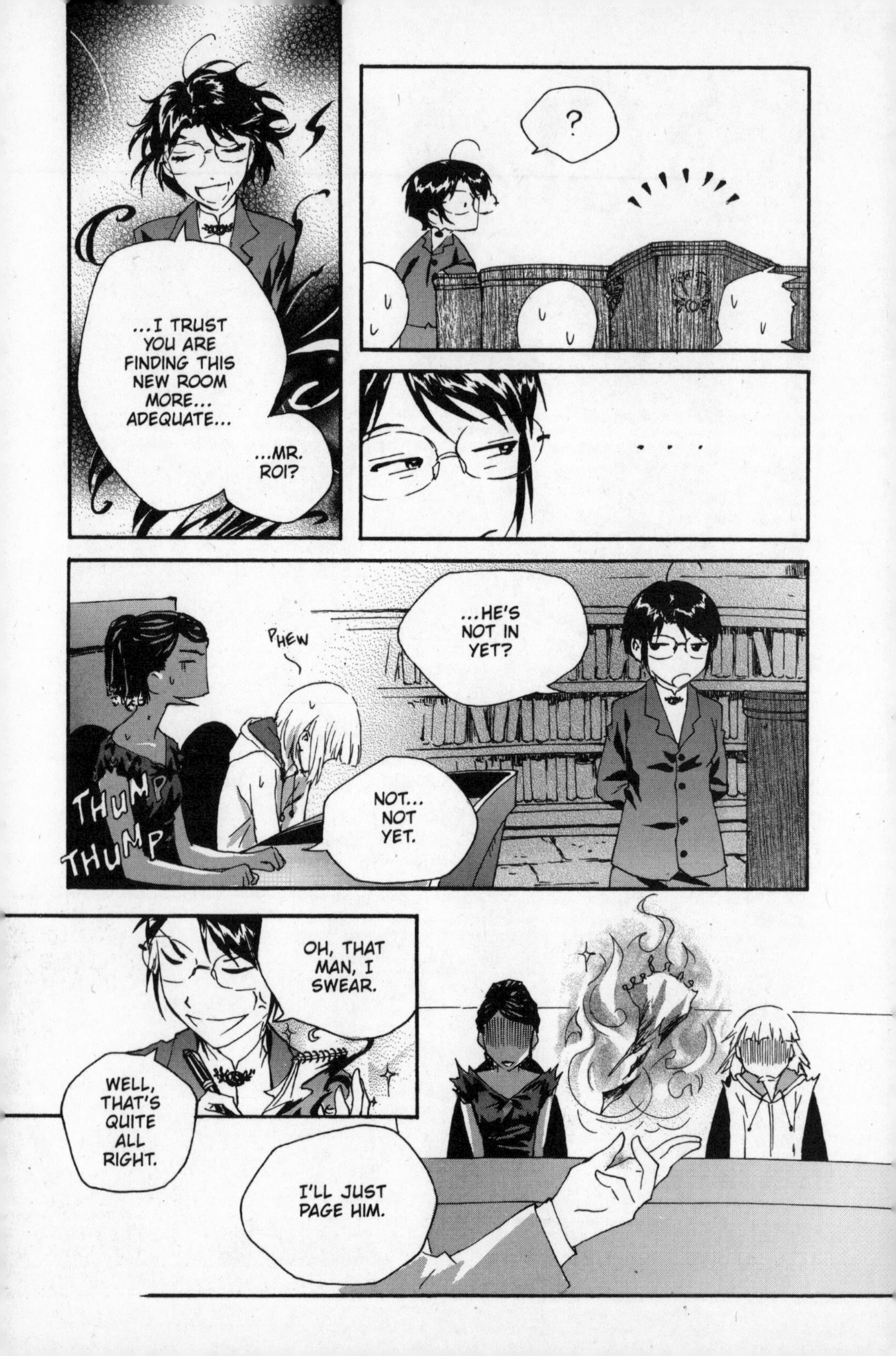
...I TRUST YOU ARE FINDING THIS NEW ROOM MORE... ADEQUATE...
...MR. ROI?
?
. . .
PHEW
...HE'S NOT IN YET?
THUMP THUMP
NOT... NOT YET.
OH, THAT MAN, I SWEAR.
WELL, THAT'S QUITE ALL RIGHT.
I'LL JUST PAGE HIM.

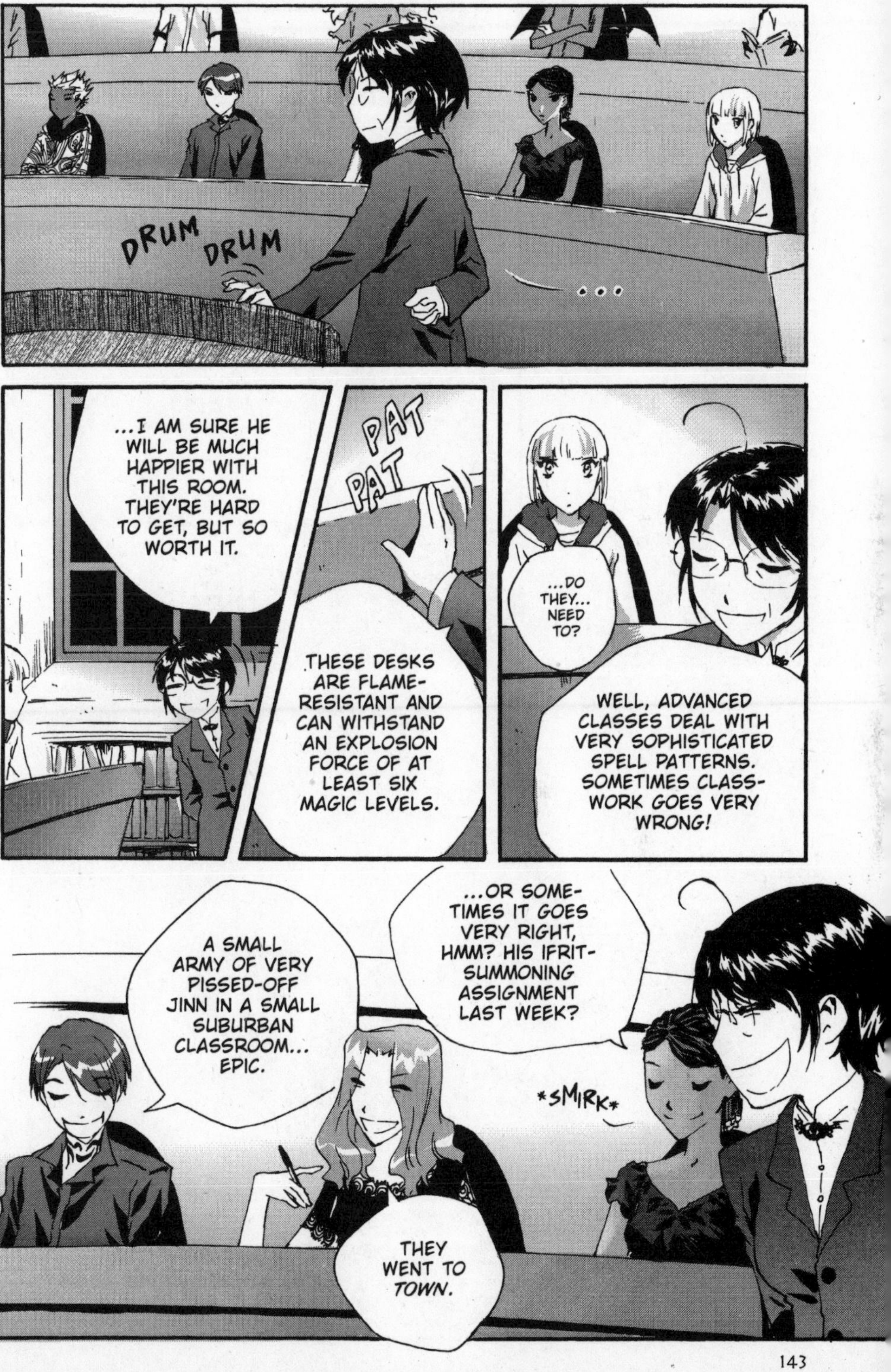

DRUM DRUM
...
...I AM SURE HE WILL BE MUCH HAPPIER WITH THIS ROOM. THEY'RE HARD TO GET, BUT SO WORTH IT.
PAT PAT
THESE DESKS ARE FLAME-RESISTANT AND CAN WITHSTAND AN EXPLOSION FORCE OF AT LEAST SIX MAGIC LEVELS.
...DO THEY... NEED TO?
WELL, ADVANCED CLASSES DEAL WITH VERY SOPHISTICATED SPELL PATTERNS. SOMETIMES CLASS-WORK GOES VERY WRONG!
A SMALL ARMY OF VERY PISSED-OFF JINN IN A SMALL SUBURBAN CLASSROOM... EPIC.
...OR SOME-TIMES IT GOES VERY RIGHT, HMM? HIS IFRIT-SUMMONING ASSIGNMENT LAST WEEK?
SMIRK
THEY WENT TO *TOWN*.

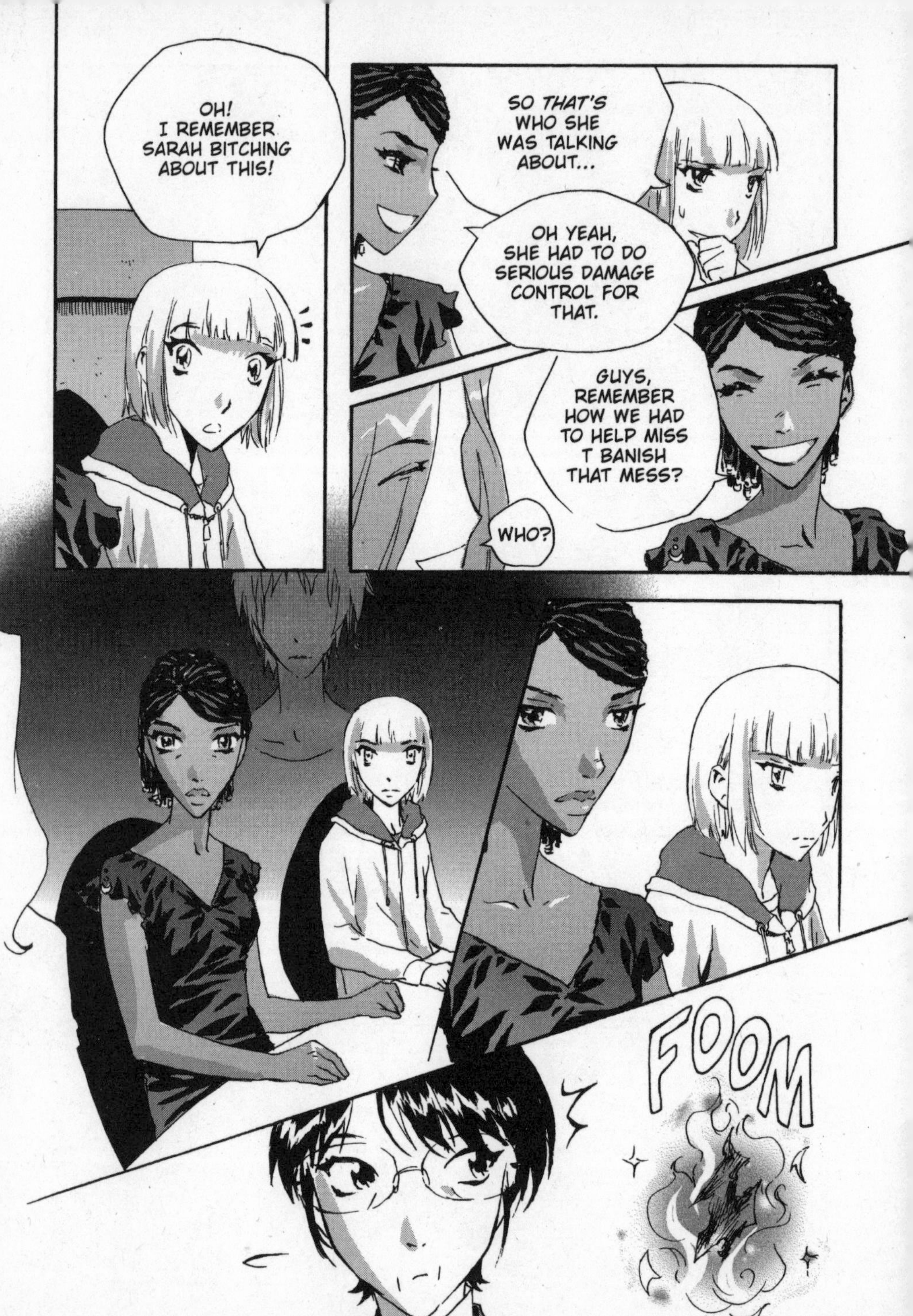
OH! I REMEMBER SARAH BITCHING ABOUT THIS!
SO *THAT'S* WHO SHE WAS TALKING ABOUT...
OH YEAH, SHE HAD TO DO SERIOUS DAMAGE CONTROL FOR THAT.
WHO?
GUYS, REMEMBER HOW WE HAD TO HELP MISS T BANISH THAT MESS?
FOOM

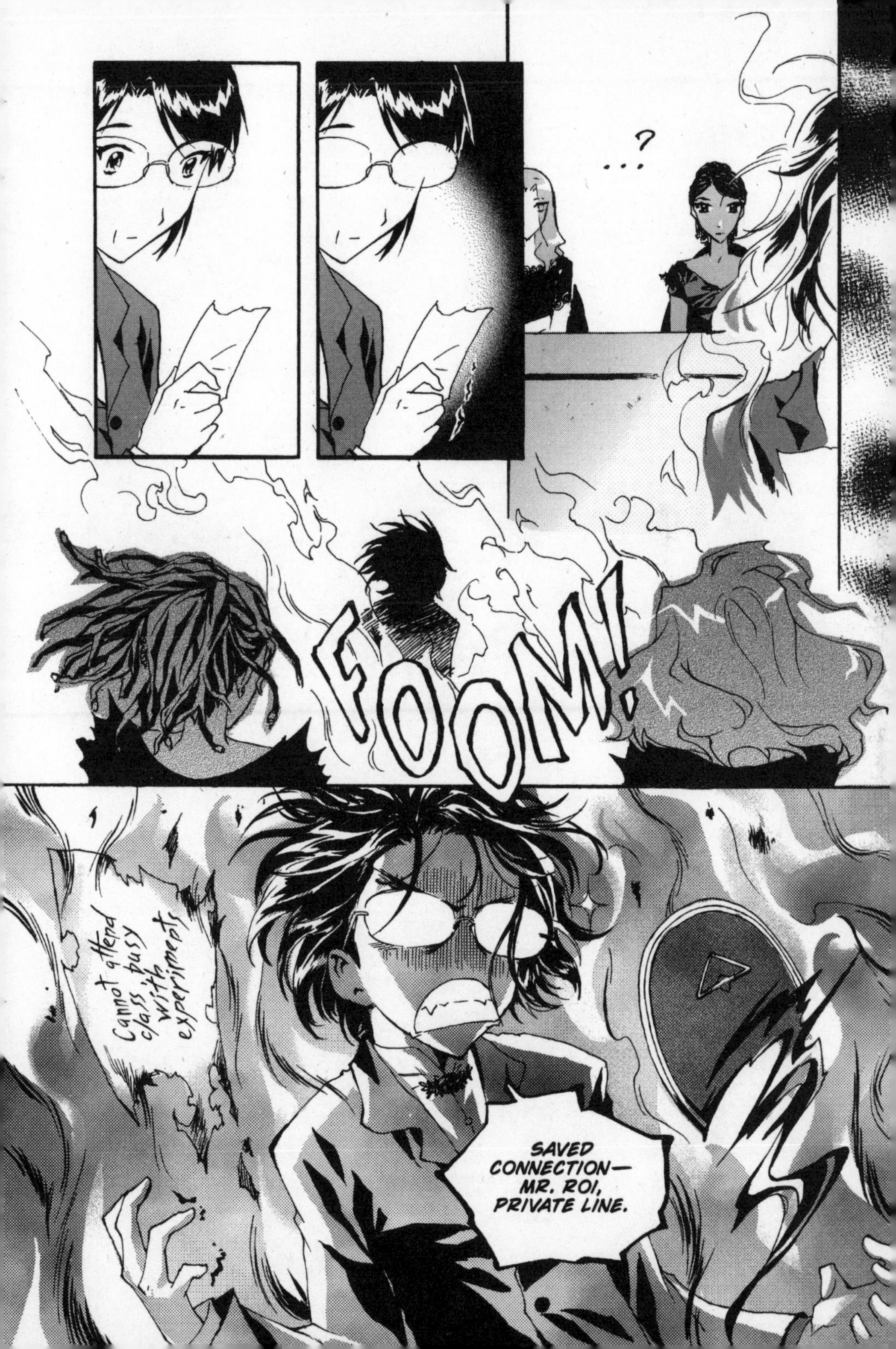
...?
FOOM!
Cannot attend class, busy with experiments
SAVED CONNECTION— MR. ROI, PRIVATE LINE.

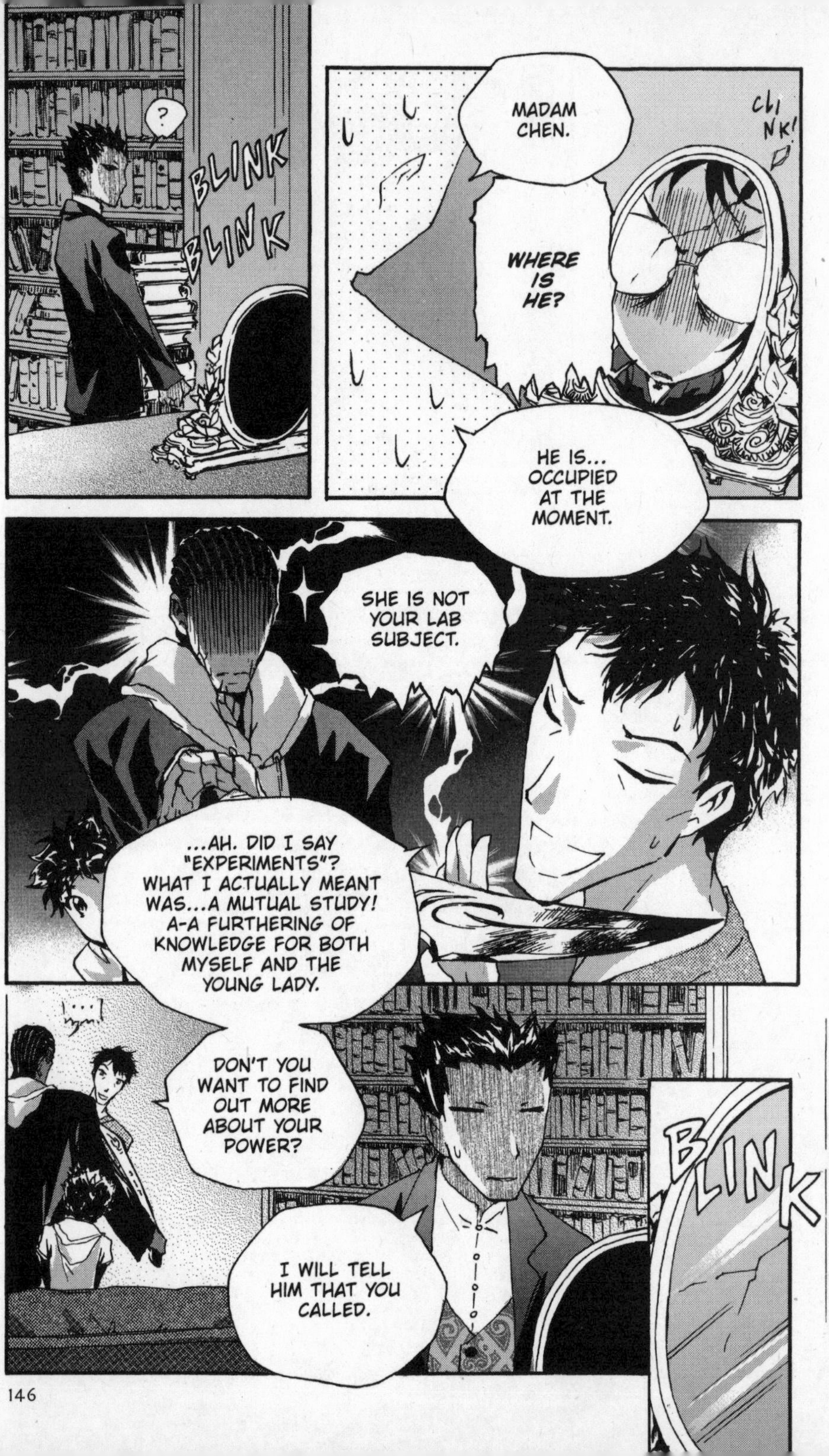
?
BLINK
BLINK
MADAM CHEN.
CLINK!
WHERE IS HE?
HE IS... OCCUPIED AT THE MOMENT.
SHE IS NOT YOUR LAB SUBJECT.
...AH. DID I SAY "EXPERIMENTS"? WHAT I ACTUALLY MEANT WAS...A MUTUAL STUDY! A-A FURTHERING OF KNOWLEDGE FOR BOTH MYSELF AND THE YOUNG LADY.
...
DON'T YOU WANT TO FIND OUT MORE ABOUT YOUR POWER?
I WILL TELL HIM THAT YOU CALLED.
BLINK

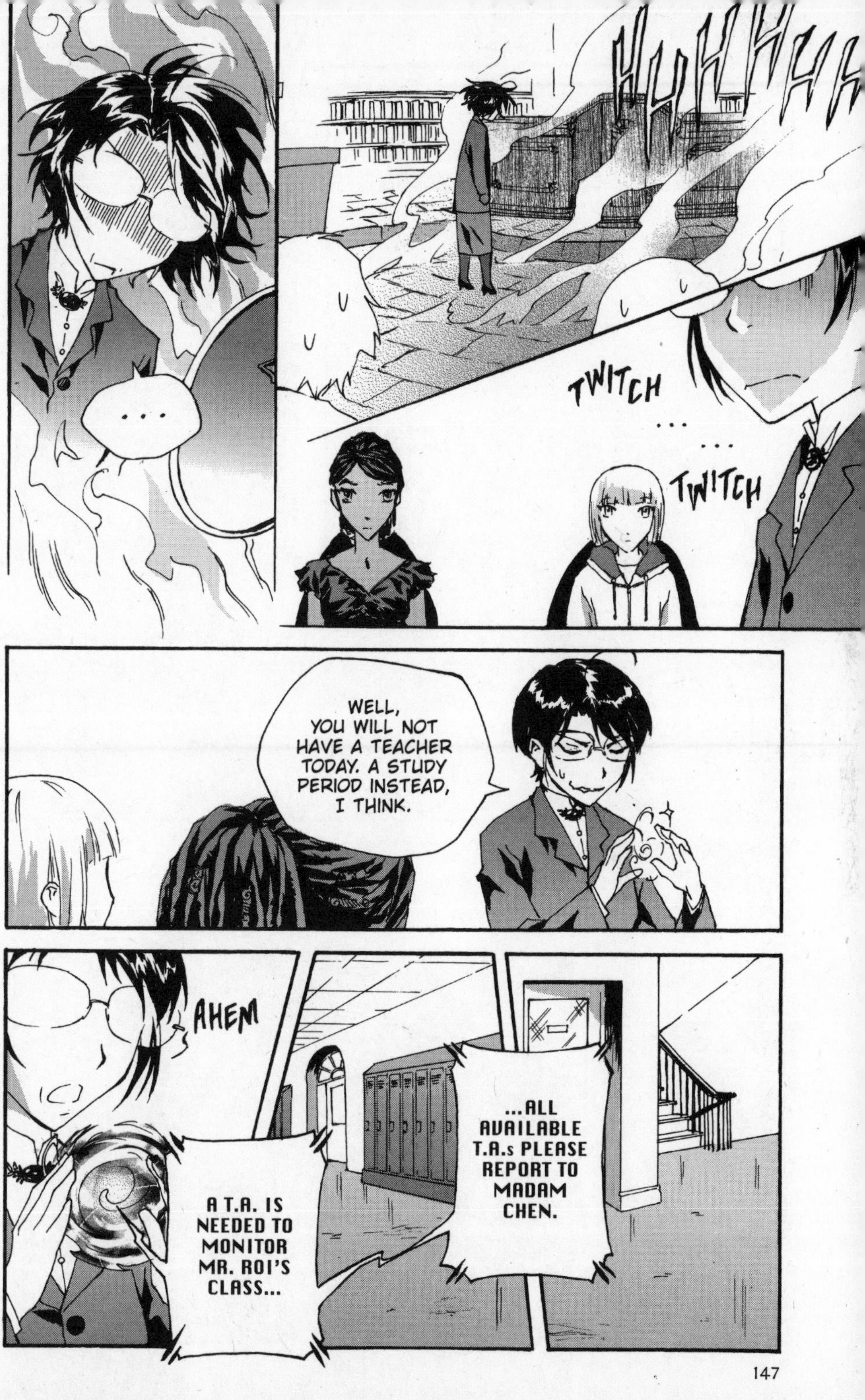
...
TWITCH
...
...
TWITCH
WELL, YOU WILL NOT HAVE A TEACHER TODAY. A STUDY PERIOD INSTEAD, I THINK.
AHEM
A T.A. IS NEEDED TO MONITOR MR. ROI'S CLASS...
...ALL AVAILABLE T.A.s PLEASE REPORT TO MADAM CHEN.

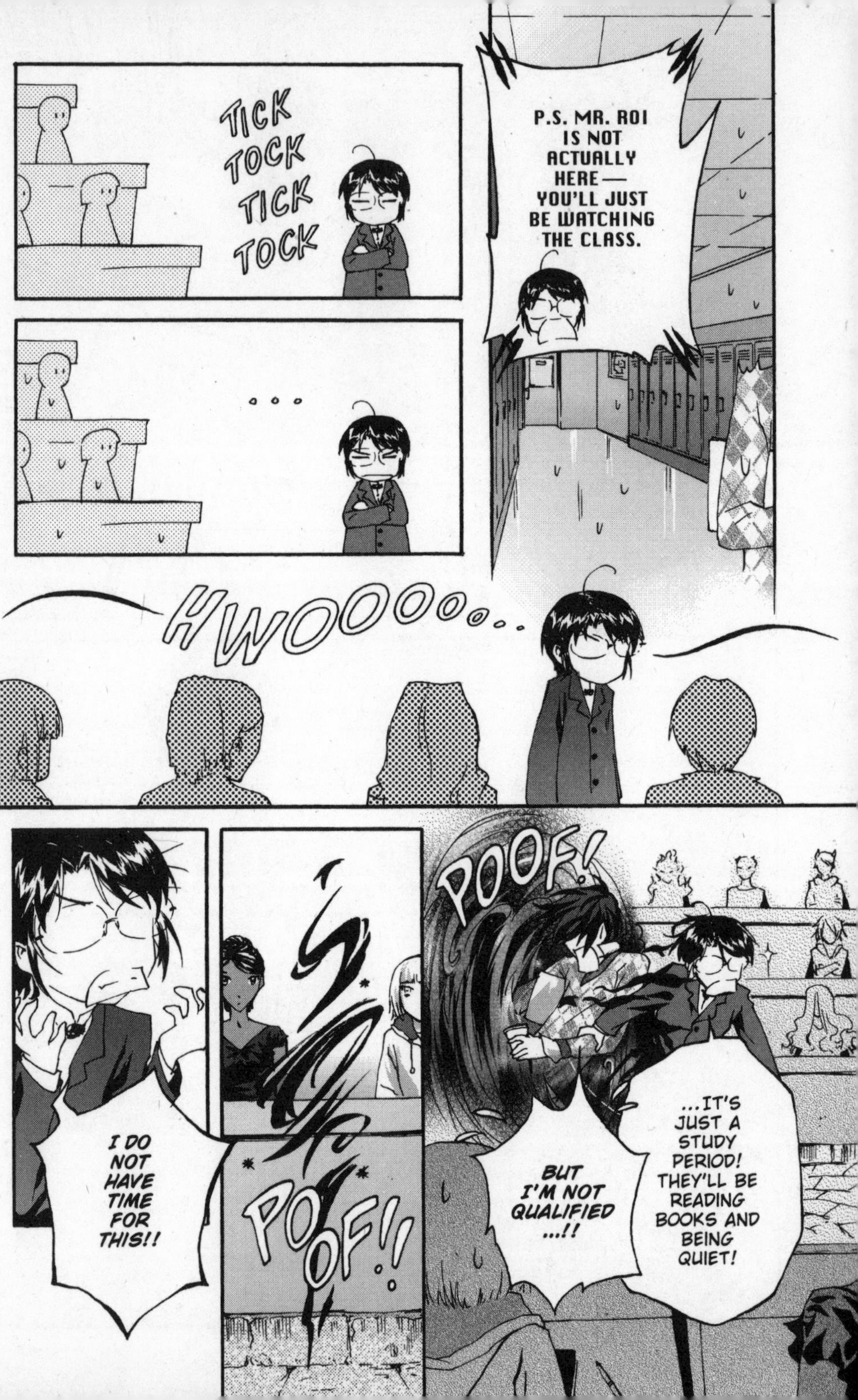
TICK TOCK TICK TOCK
. . .
P.S. MR. ROI IS NOT ACTUALLY HERE— YOU'LL JUST BE WATCHING THE CLASS.
HWOOOOo...
I DO NOT HAVE TIME FOR THIS!!
POOF!!
POOF!
BUT I'M NOT QUALIFIED ...!!
...IT'S JUST A STUDY PERIOD! THEY'LL BE READING BOOKS AND BEING QUIET!

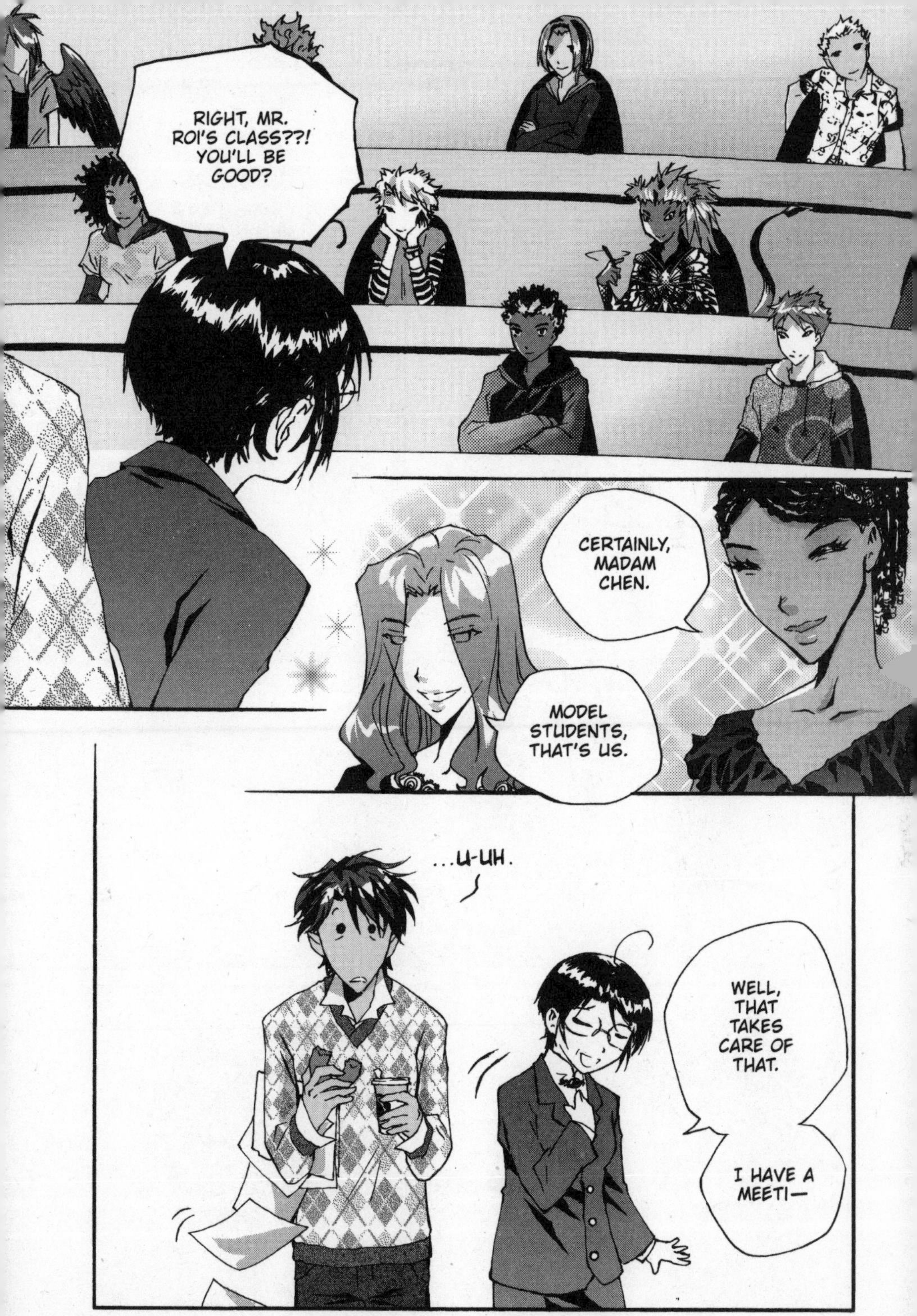

RIGHT, MR. ROI'S CLASS??! YOU'LL BE GOOD?
CERTAINLY, MADAM CHEN.
MODEL STUDENTS, THAT'S US.
...U-UH.
WELL, THAT TAKES CARE OF THAT.
I HAVE A MEETI—

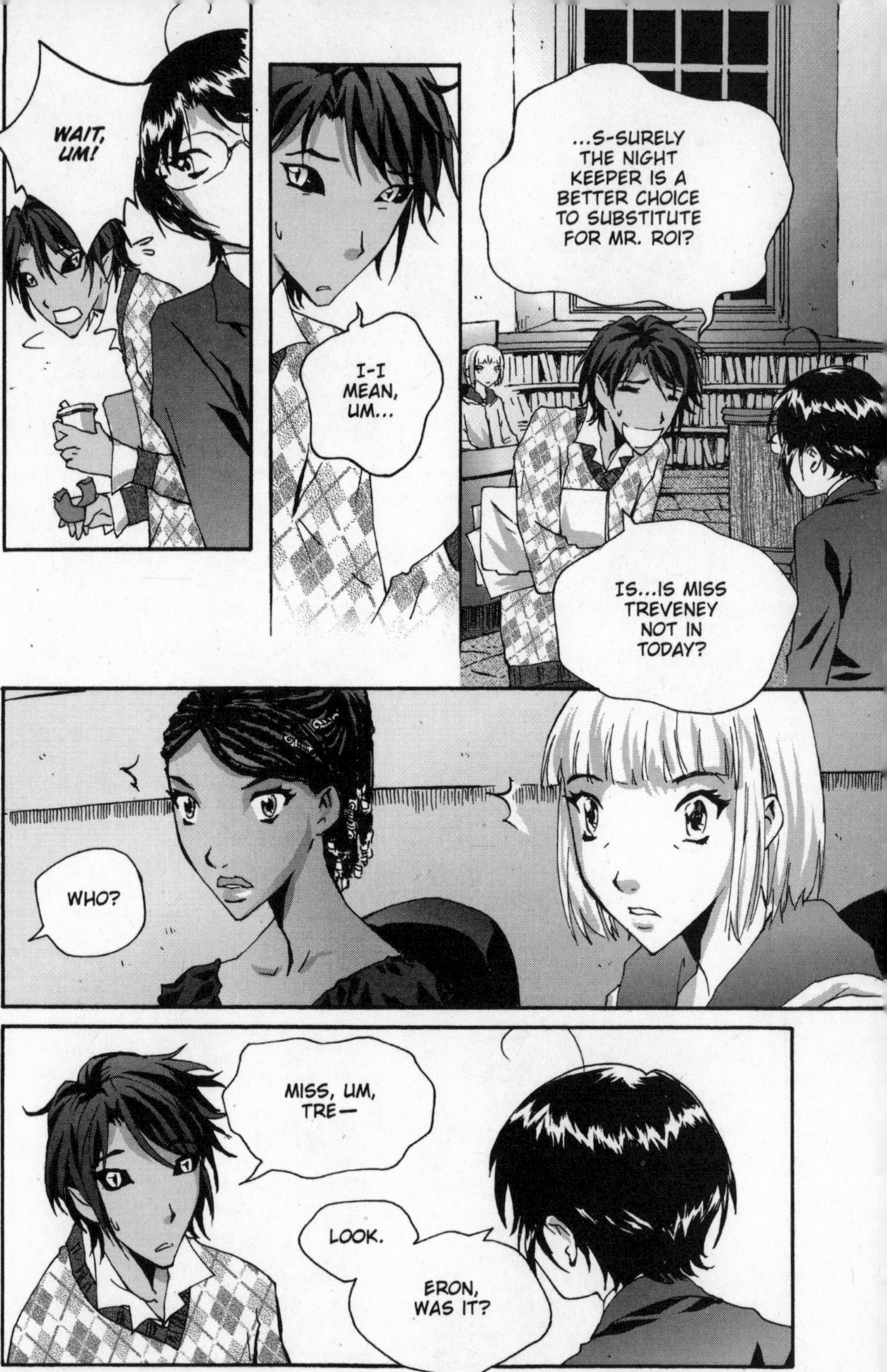
WAIT, UM!
I-I MEAN, UM...
...S-SURELY THE NIGHT KEEPER IS A BETTER CHOICE TO SUBSTITUTE FOR MR. ROI?
IS...IS MISS TREVENEY NOT IN TODAY?
WHO?
MISS, UM, TRE—
LOOK.
ERON, WAS IT?

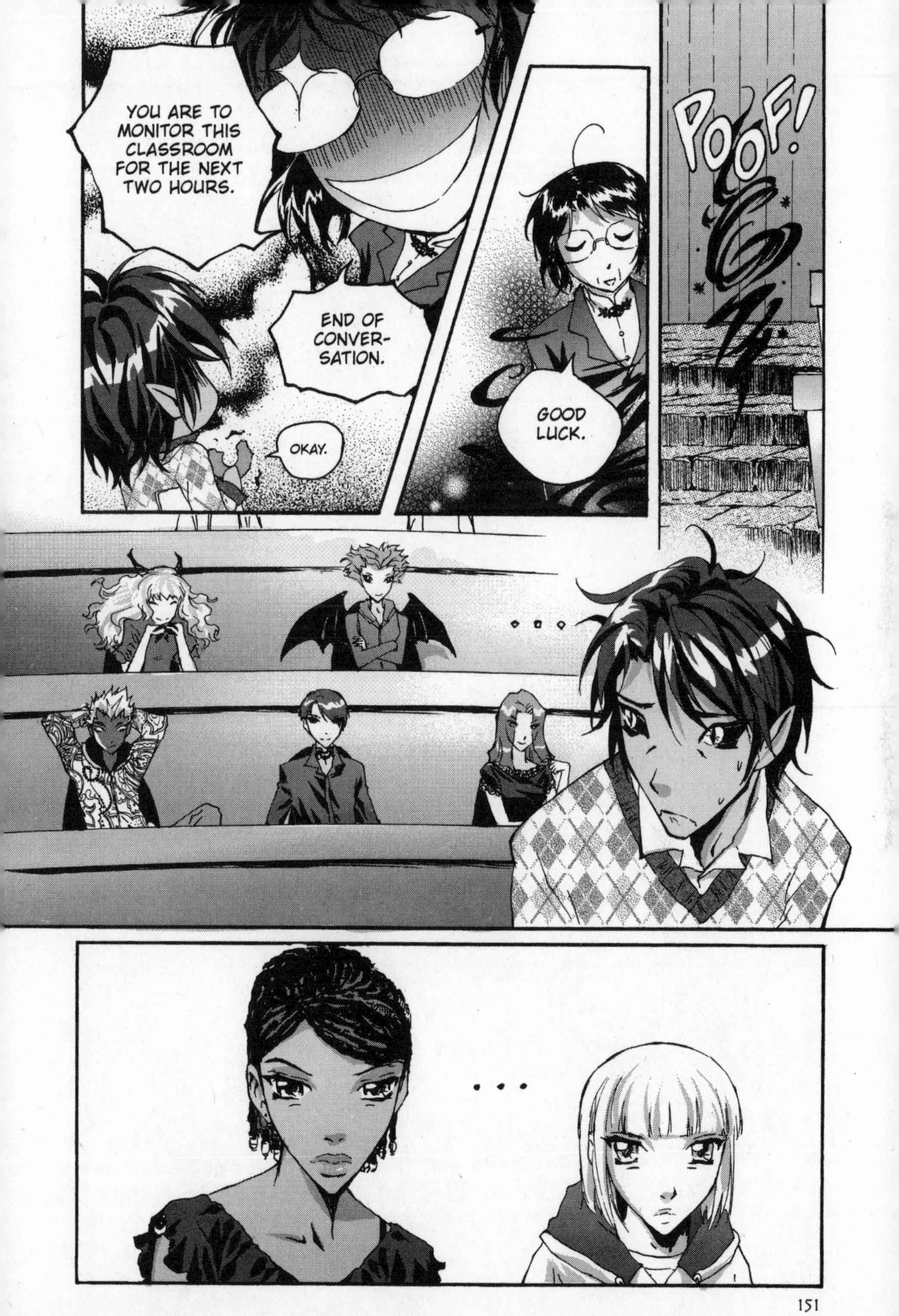
YOU ARE TO MONITOR THIS CLASSROOM FOR THE NEXT TWO HOURS.
END OF CONVER-SATION.
OKAY.
GOOD LUCK.
POOF!
...
...

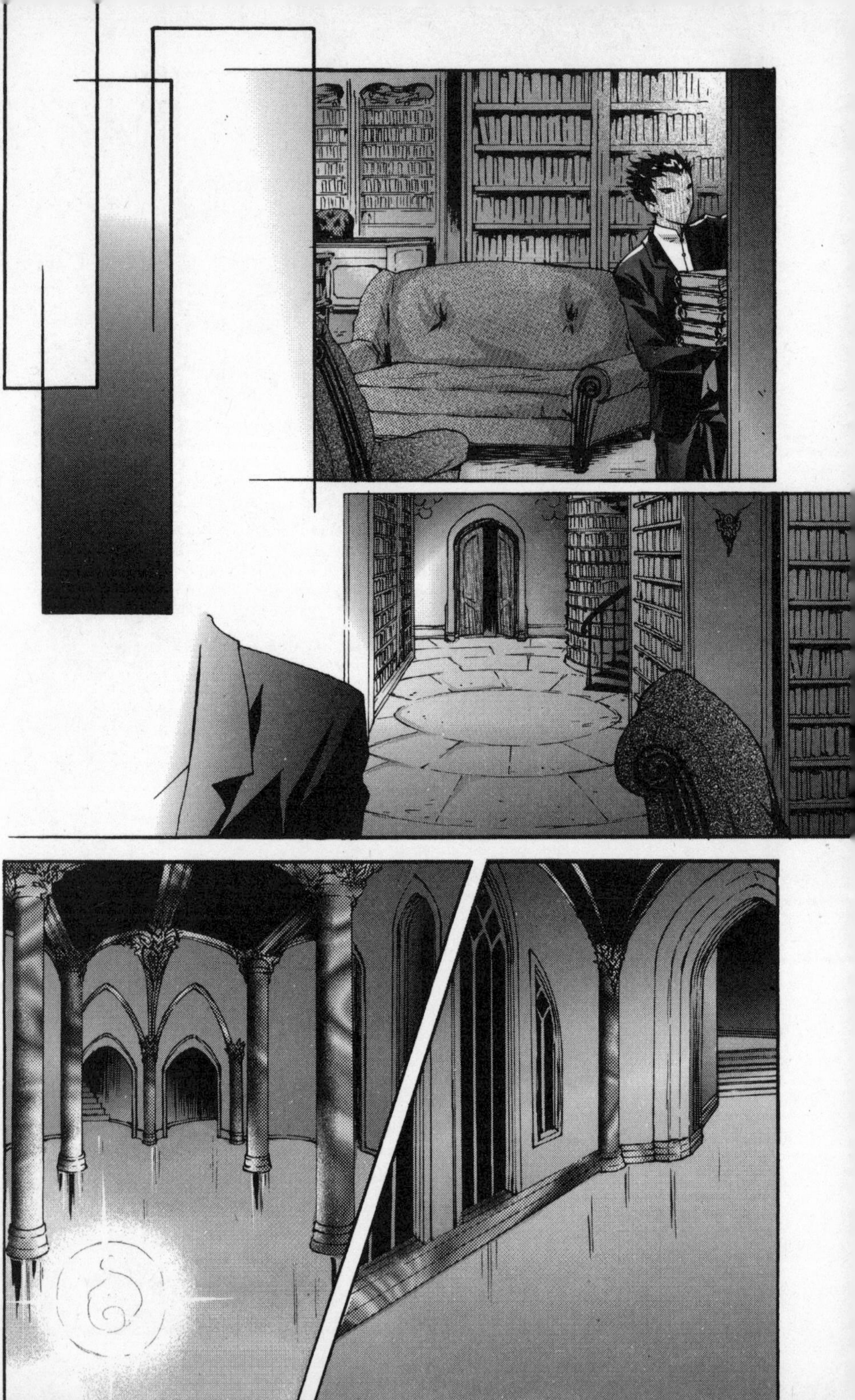

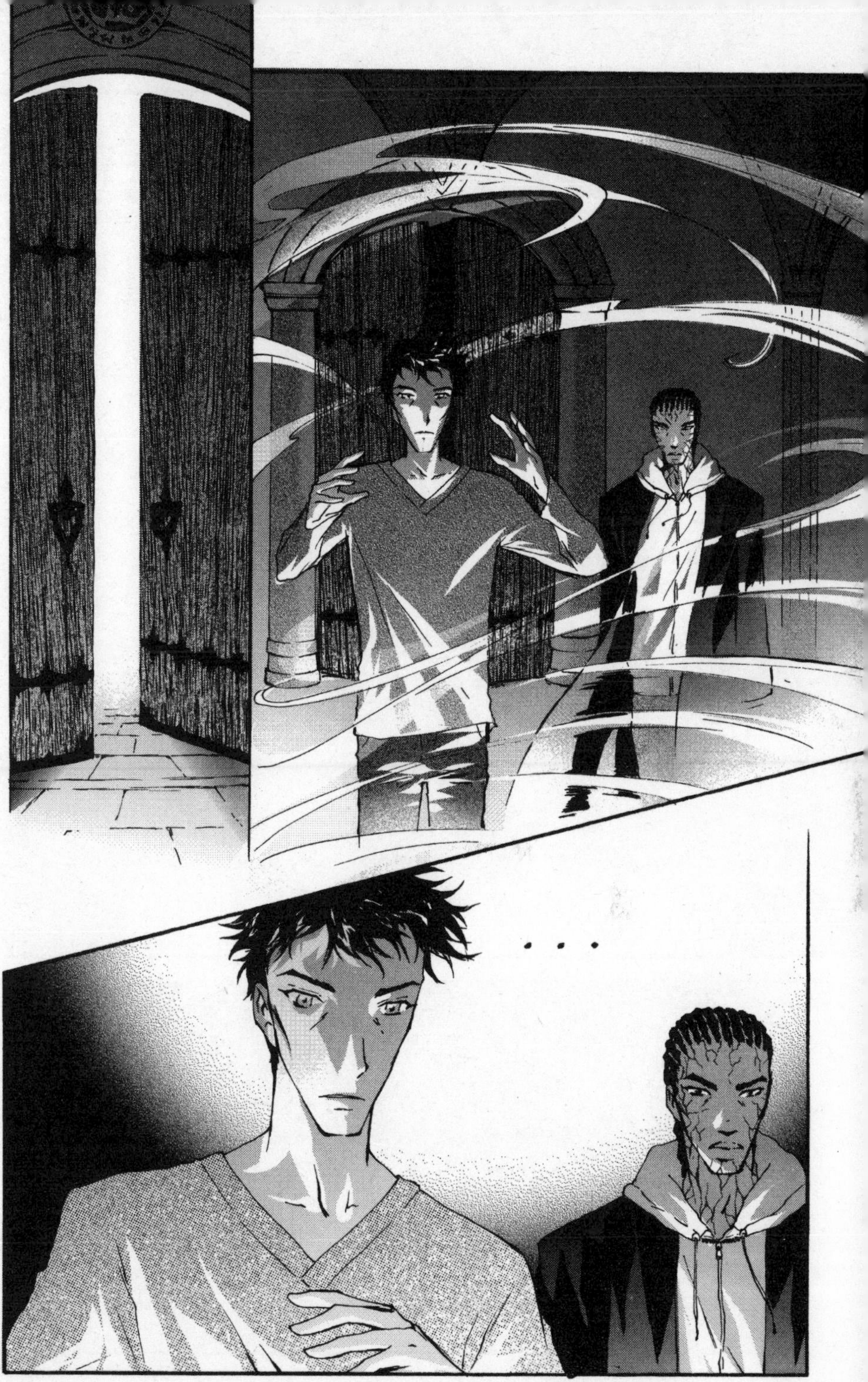
...

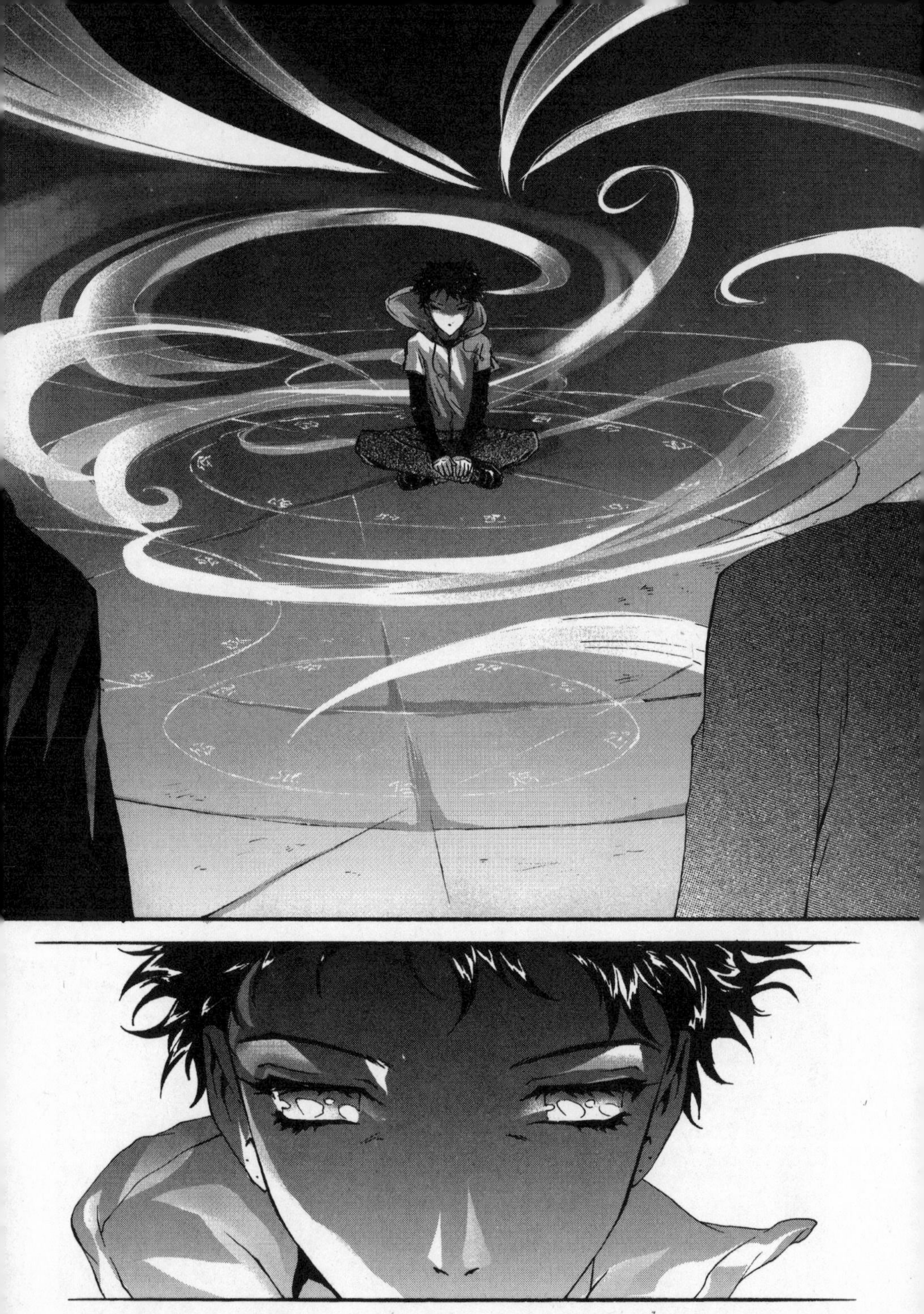

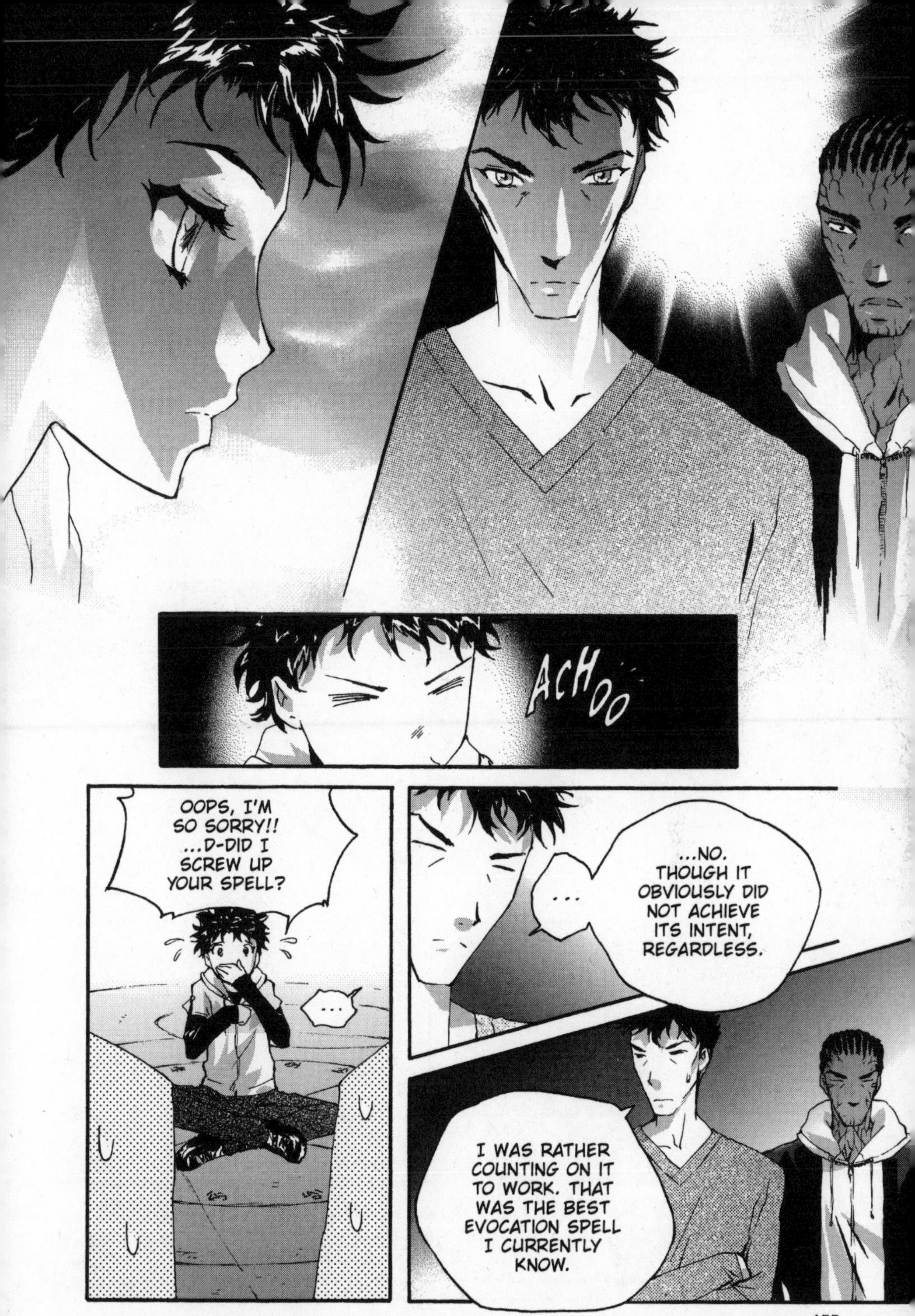
ACHOO
OOPS, I'M SO SORRY!! ...D-DID I SCREW UP YOUR SPELL?
...
...
...NO. THOUGH IT OBVIOUSLY DID NOT ACHIEVE ITS INTENT, REGARDLESS.
I WAS RATHER COUNTING ON IT TO WORK. THAT WAS THE BEST EVOCATION SPELL I CURRENTLY KNOW.

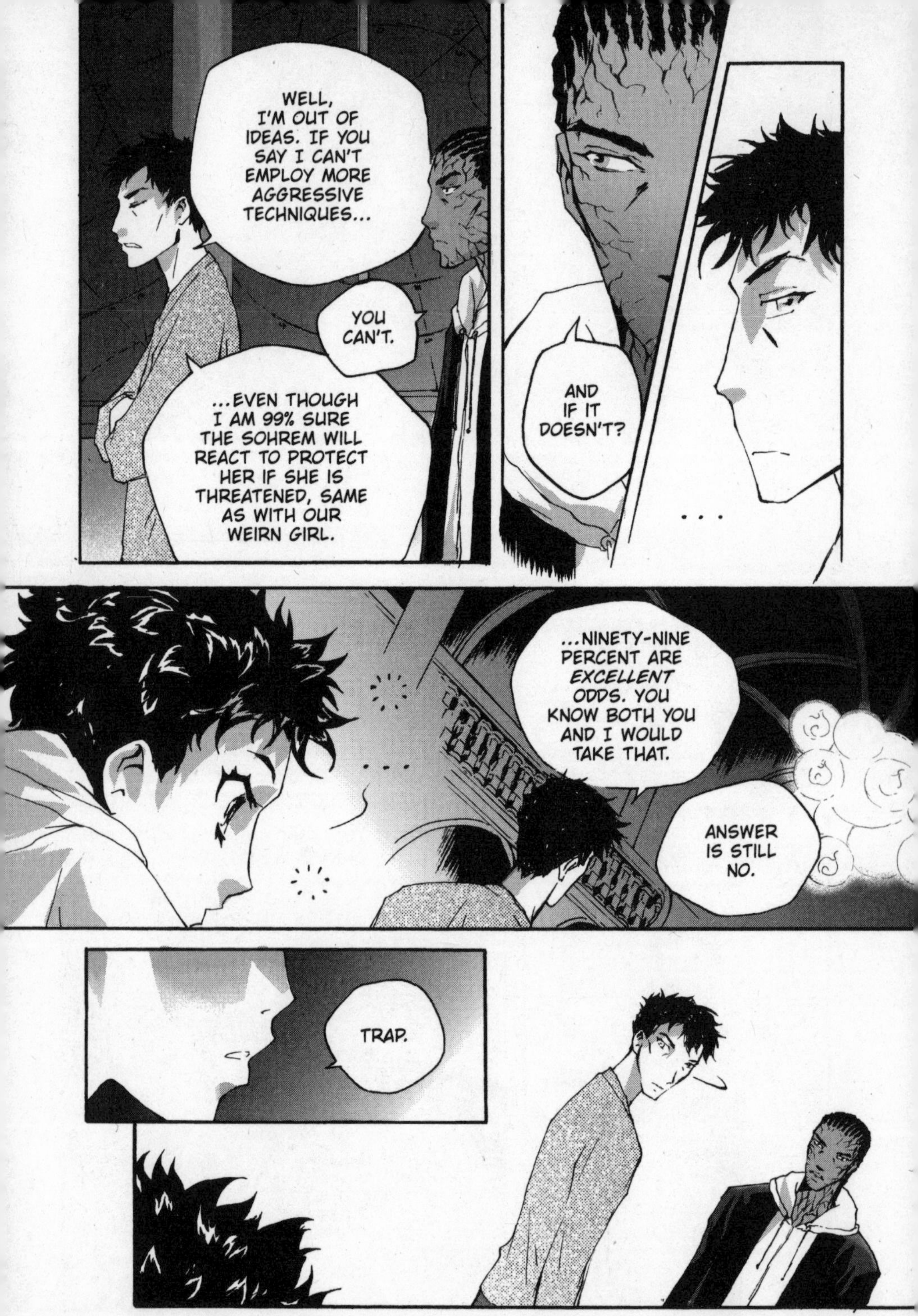
WELL, I'M OUT OF IDEAS. IF YOU SAY I CAN'T EMPLOY MORE AGGRESSIVE TECHNIQUES...
YOU CAN'T.
...EVEN THOUGH I AM 99% SURE THE SOHREM WILL REACT TO PROTECT HER IF SHE IS THREATENED, SAME AS WITH OUR WEIRN GIRL.
AND IF IT DOESN'T?
...
...
...NINETY-NINE PERCENT ARE *EXCELLENT* ODDS. YOU KNOW BOTH YOU AND I WOULD TAKE THAT.
ANSWER IS STILL NO.
TRAP.

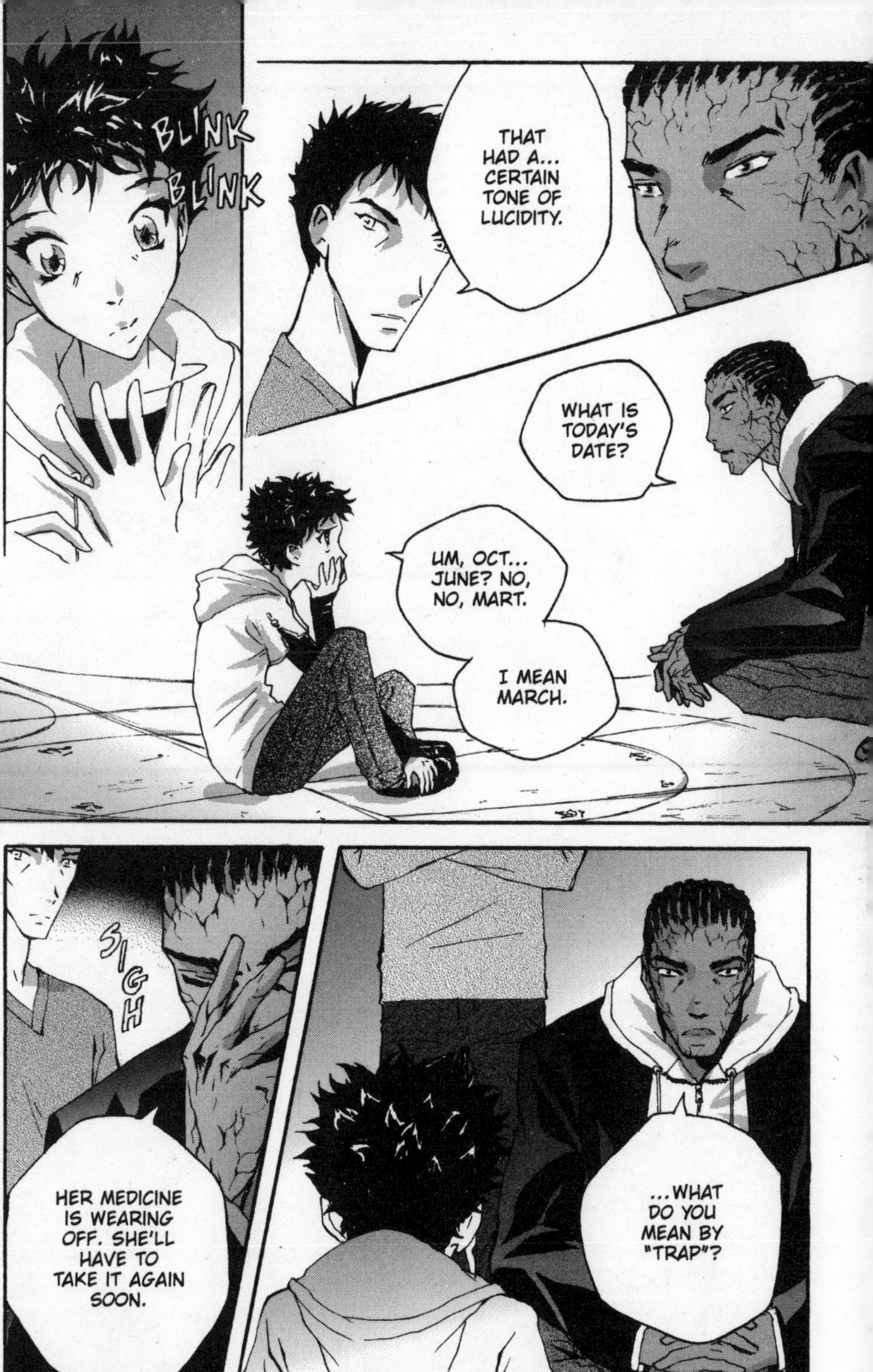
BLINK BLINK
THAT HAD A... CERTAIN TONE OF LUCIDITY.
WHAT IS TODAY'S DATE?
UM, OCT... JUNE? NO, NO, MART.
I MEAN MARCH.
SIGH
HER MEDICINE IS WEARING OFF. SHE'LL HAVE TO TAKE IT AGAIN SOON.
...WHAT DO YOU MEAN BY "TRAP"?

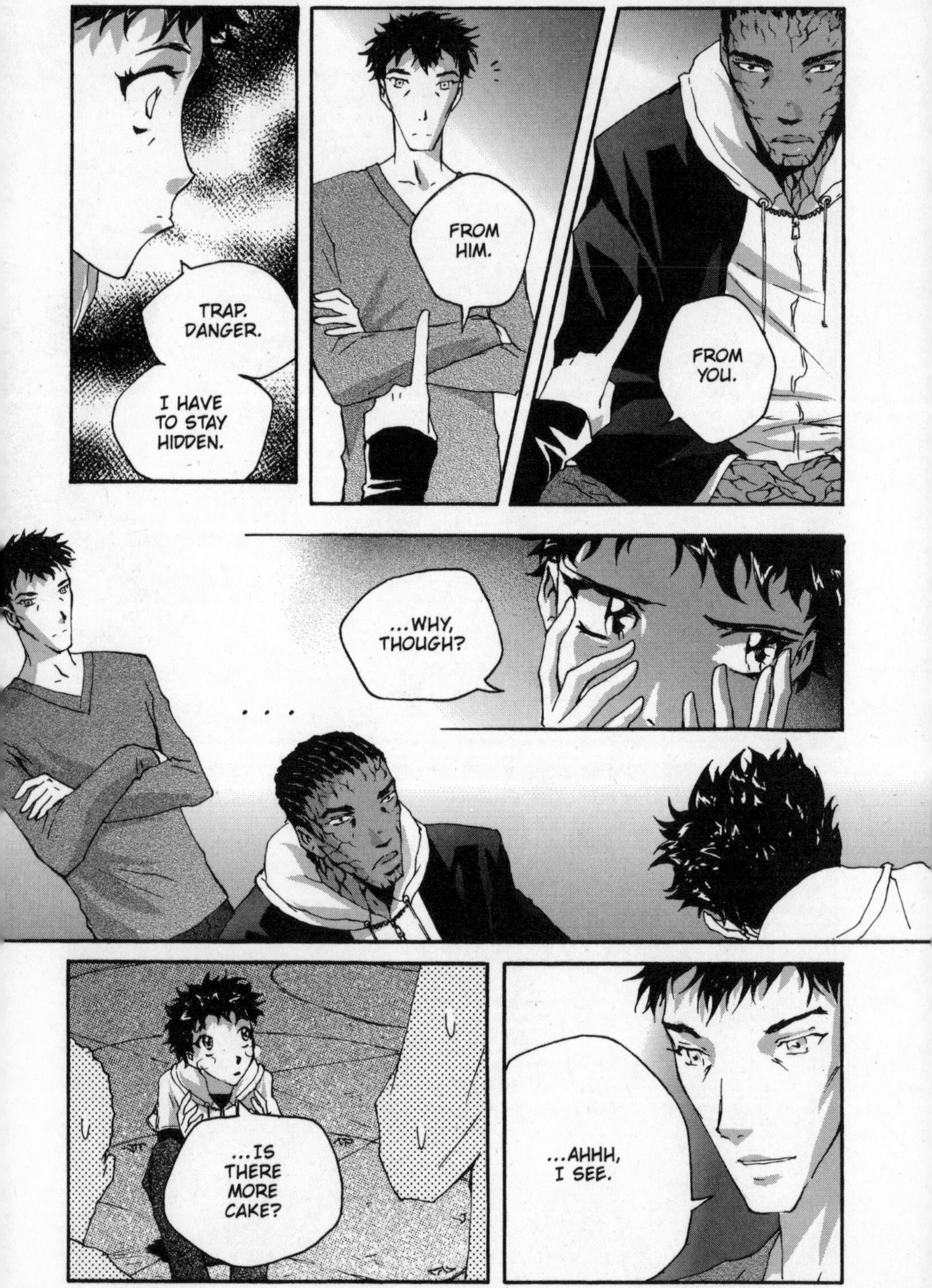
TRAP. DANGER.
I HAVE TO STAY HIDDEN.
FROM HIM.
FROM YOU.
...WHY, THOUGH?
. . .
...IS THERE MORE CAKE?
...AHHH, I SEE.

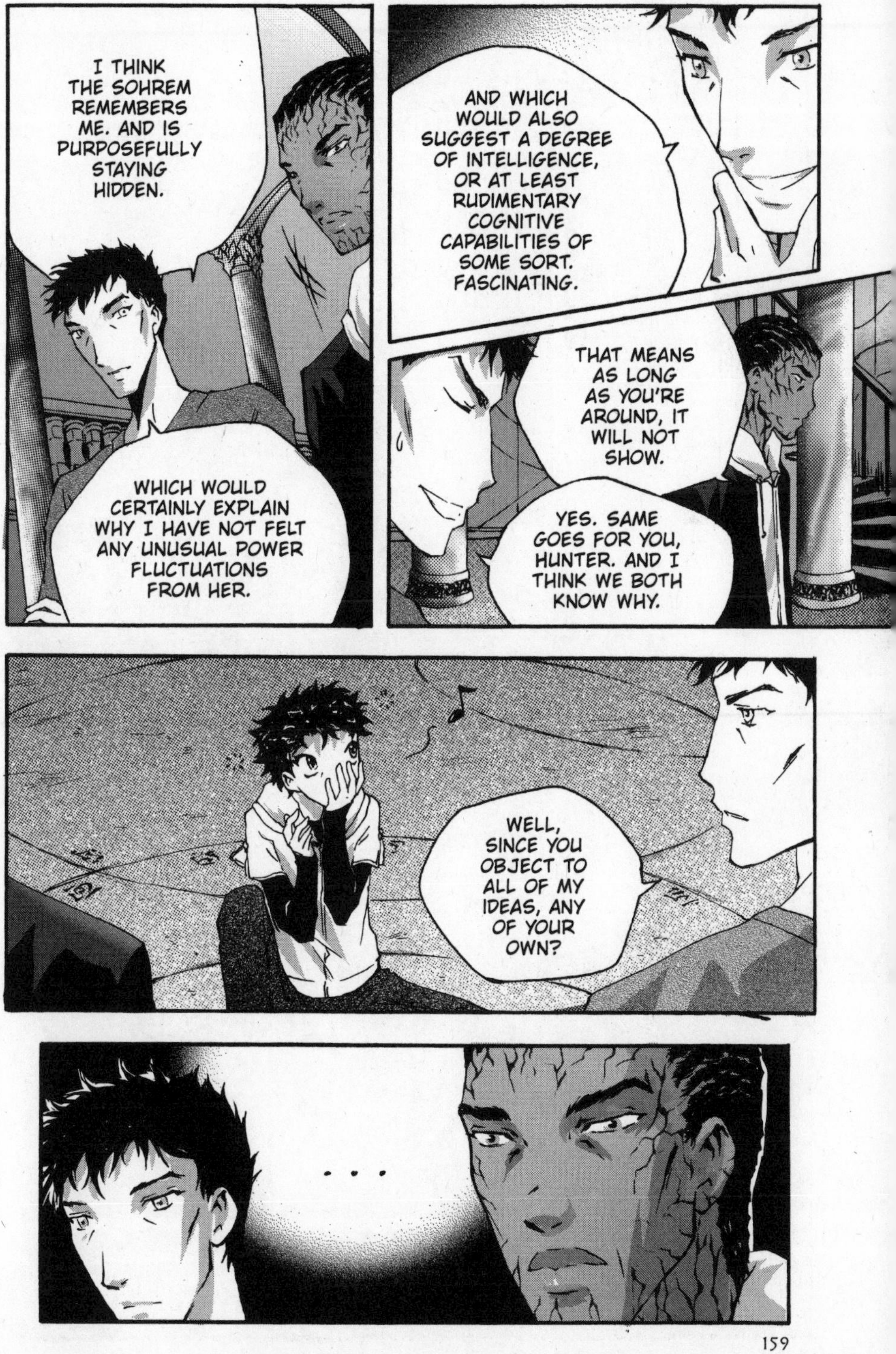

I THINK THE SOHREM REMEMBERS ME. AND IS PURPOSEFULLY STAYING HIDDEN.
WHICH WOULD CERTAINLY EXPLAIN WHY I HAVE NOT FELT ANY UNUSUAL POWER FLUCTUATIONS FROM HER.
AND WHICH WOULD ALSO SUGGEST A DEGREE OF INTELLIGENCE, OR AT LEAST RUDIMENTARY COGNITIVE CAPABILITIES OF SOME SORT. FASCINATING.
THAT MEANS AS LONG AS YOU'RE AROUND, IT WILL NOT SHOW.
YES. SAME GOES FOR YOU, HUNTER. AND I THINK WE BOTH KNOW WHY.
WELL, SINCE YOU OBJECT TO ALL OF MY IDEAS, ANY OF YOUR OWN?
. . .

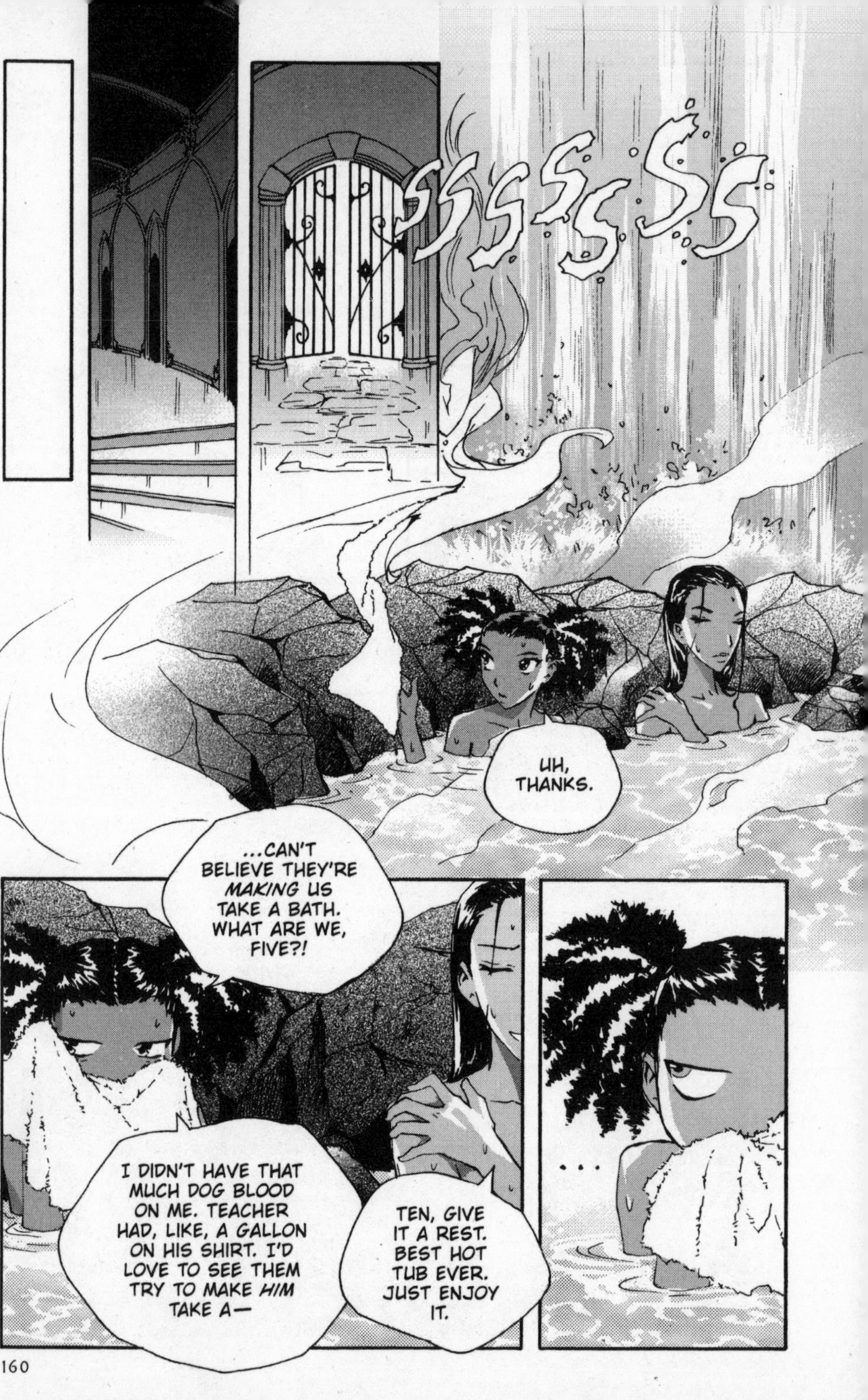
SSSSSSS
UH, THANKS.
...CAN'T BELIEVE THEY'RE *MAKING* US TAKE A BATH. WHAT ARE WE, FIVE?!
I DIDN'T HAVE THAT MUCH DOG BLOOD ON ME. TEACHER HAD, LIKE, A GALLON ON HIS SHIRT. I'D LOVE TO SEE THEM TRY TO MAKE *HIM* TAKE A—
TEN, GIVE IT A REST. BEST HOT TUB EVER. JUST ENJOY IT.
...

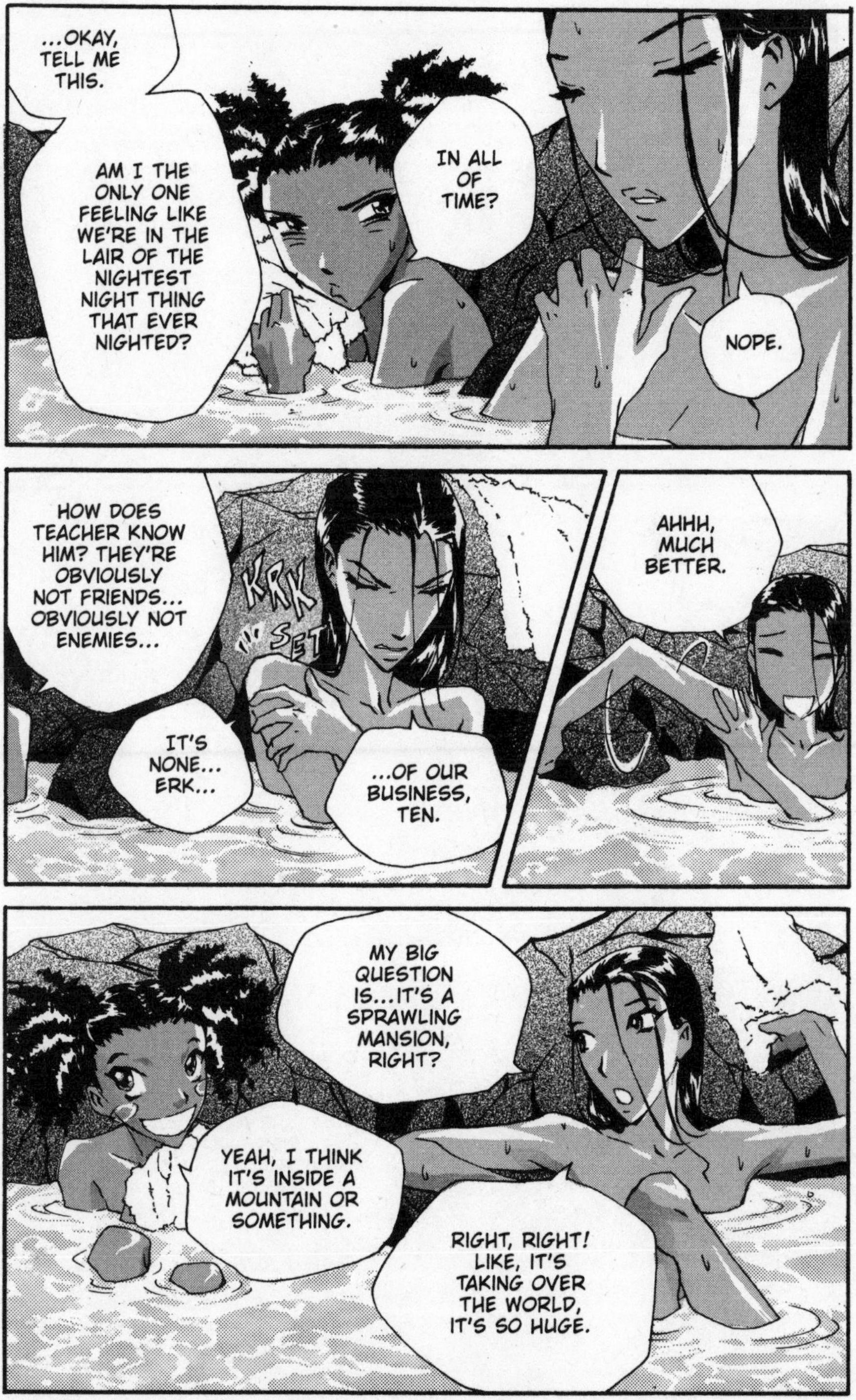
...OKAY, TELL ME THIS.
AM I THE ONLY ONE FEELING LIKE WE'RE IN THE LAIR OF THE NIGHTEST NIGHT THING THAT EVER NIGHTED?
IN ALL OF TIME?
NOPE.
HOW DOES TEACHER KNOW HIM? THEY'RE OBVIOUSLY NOT FRIENDS... OBVIOUSLY NOT ENEMIES...
KRK
SET
IT'S NONE... ERK...
...OF OUR BUSINESS, TEN.
AHHH, MUCH BETTER.
MY BIG QUESTION IS...IT'S A SPRAWLING MANSION, RIGHT?
YEAH, I THINK IT'S INSIDE A MOUNTAIN OR SOMETHING.
RIGHT, RIGHT! LIKE, IT'S TAKING OVER THE WORLD, IT'S SO HUGE.

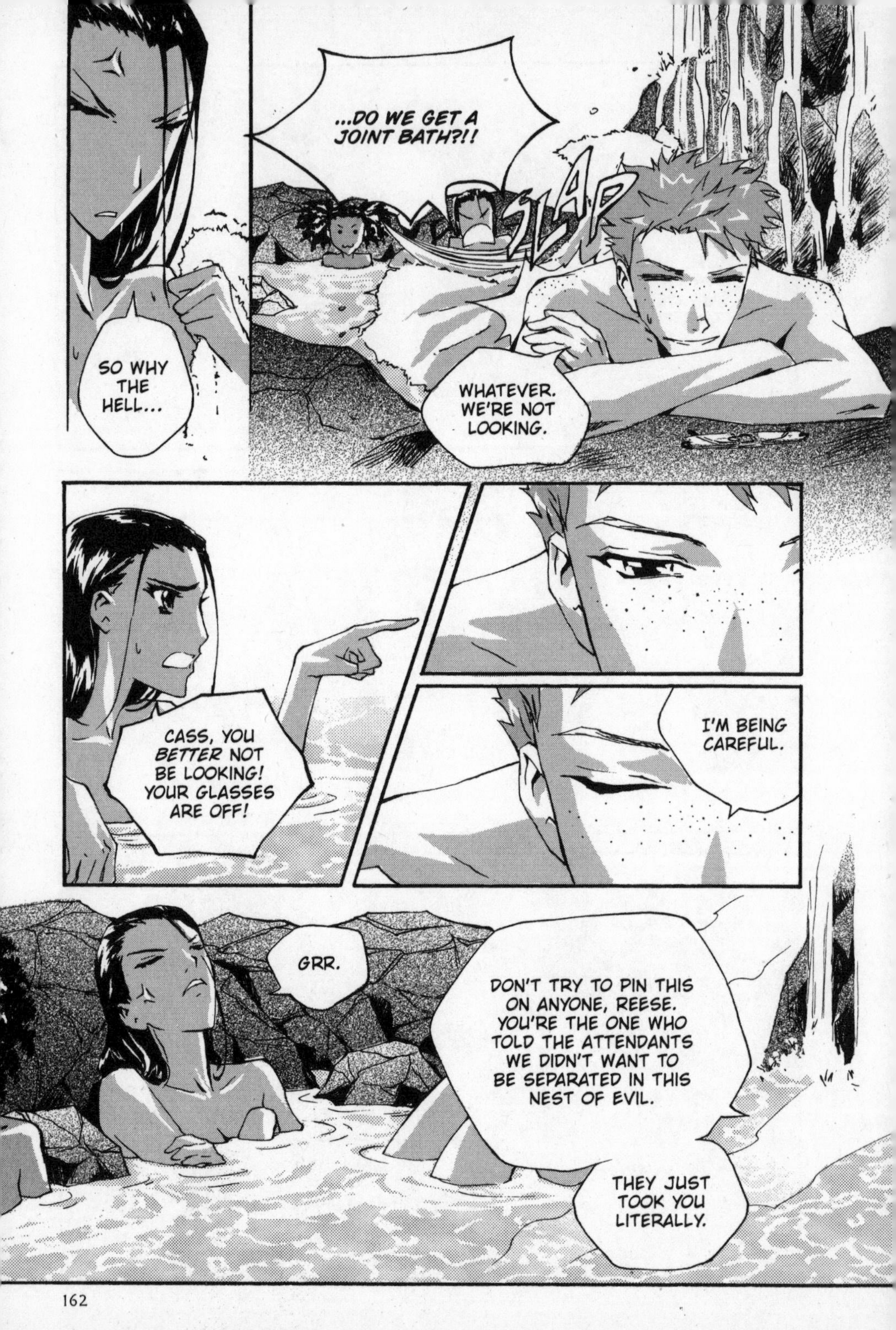
SO WHY THE HELL...
...DO WE GET A JOINT BATH?!!
SLAP
WHATEVER. WE'RE NOT LOOKING.
CASS, YOU *BETTER* NOT BE LOOKING! YOUR GLASSES ARE OFF!
I'M BEING CAREFUL.
GRR.
DON'T TRY TO PIN THIS ON ANYONE, REESE. YOU'RE THE ONE WHO TOLD THE ATTENDANTS WE DIDN'T WANT TO BE SEPARATED IN THIS NEST OF EVIL.
THEY JUST TOOK YOU LITERALLY.

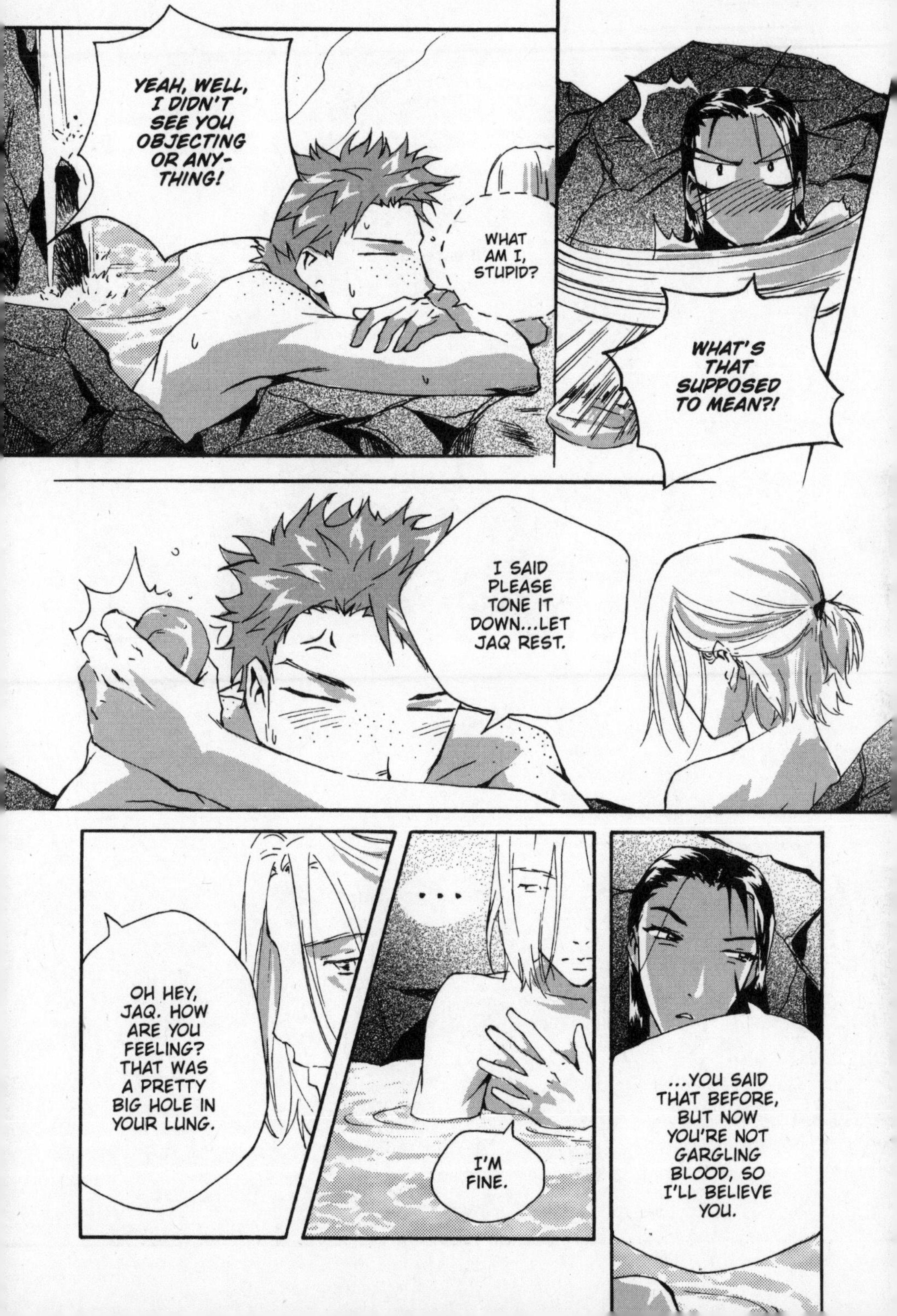

YEAH, WELL, I DIDN'T SEE YOU OBJECTING OR ANY-THING!
WHAT AM I, STUPID?
WHAT'S THAT SUPPOSED TO MEAN?!
I SAID PLEASE TONE IT DOWN...LET JAQ REST.
OH HEY, JAQ. HOW ARE YOU FEELING? THAT WAS A PRETTY BIG HOLE IN YOUR LUNG.
...
I'M FINE.
...YOU SAID THAT BEFORE, BUT NOW YOU'RE NOT GARGLING BLOOD, SO I'LL BELIEVE YOU.

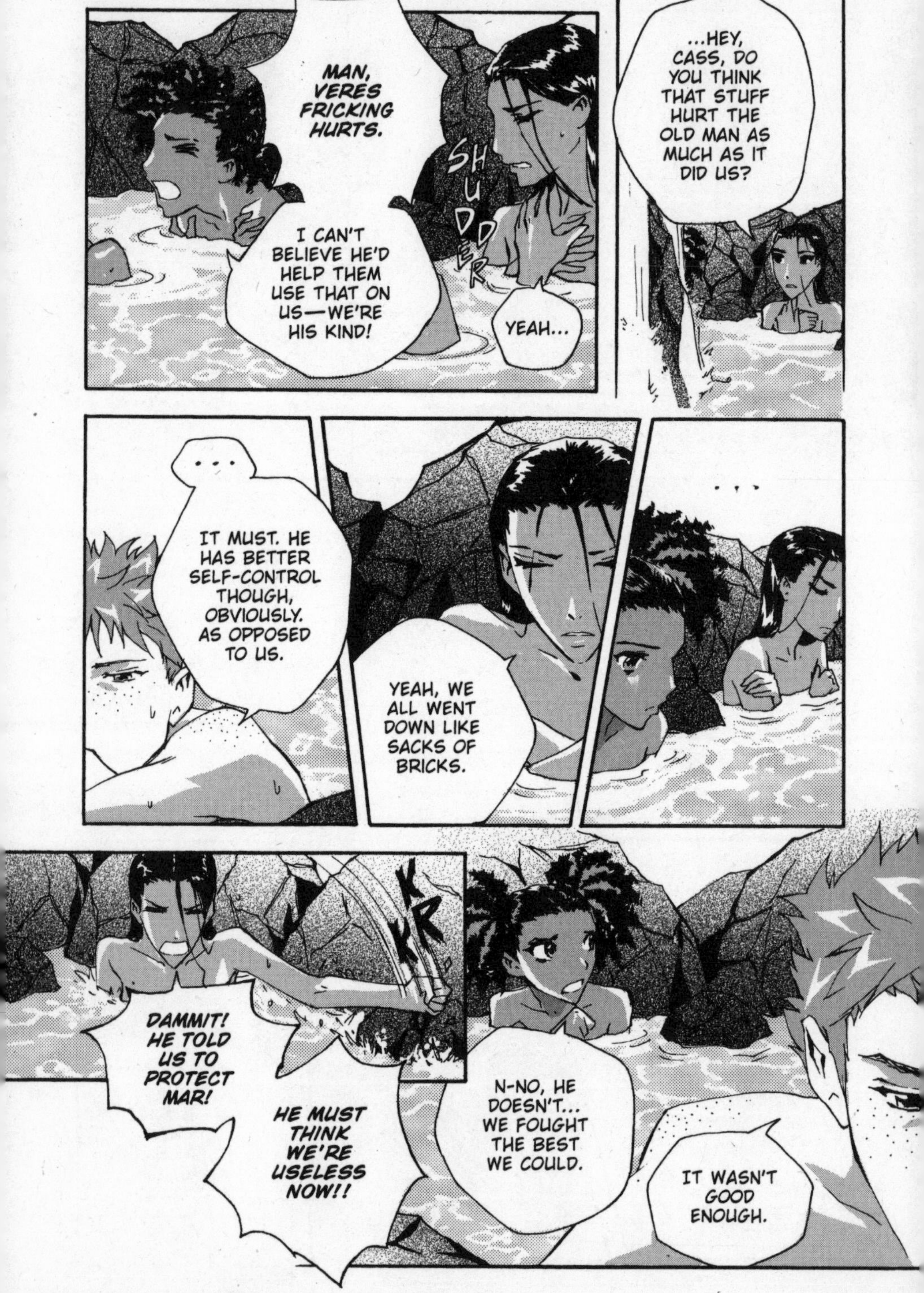
MAN, VERES FRICKING HURTS.
I CAN'T BELIEVE HE'D HELP THEM USE THAT ON US—WE'RE HIS KIND!
SHUDDER
YEAH...
...HEY, CASS, DO YOU THINK THAT STUFF HURT THE OLD MAN AS MUCH AS IT DID US?
...
IT MUST. HE HAS BETTER SELF-CONTROL THOUGH, OBVIOUSLY. AS OPPOSED TO US.
YEAH, WE ALL WENT DOWN LIKE SACKS OF BRICKS.
...
DAMMIT! HE TOLD US TO PROTECT MAR!
KRKK
HE MUST THINK WE'RE USELESS NOW!!
N-NO, HE DOESN'T... WE FOUGHT THE BEST WE COULD.
IT WASN'T GOOD ENOUGH.

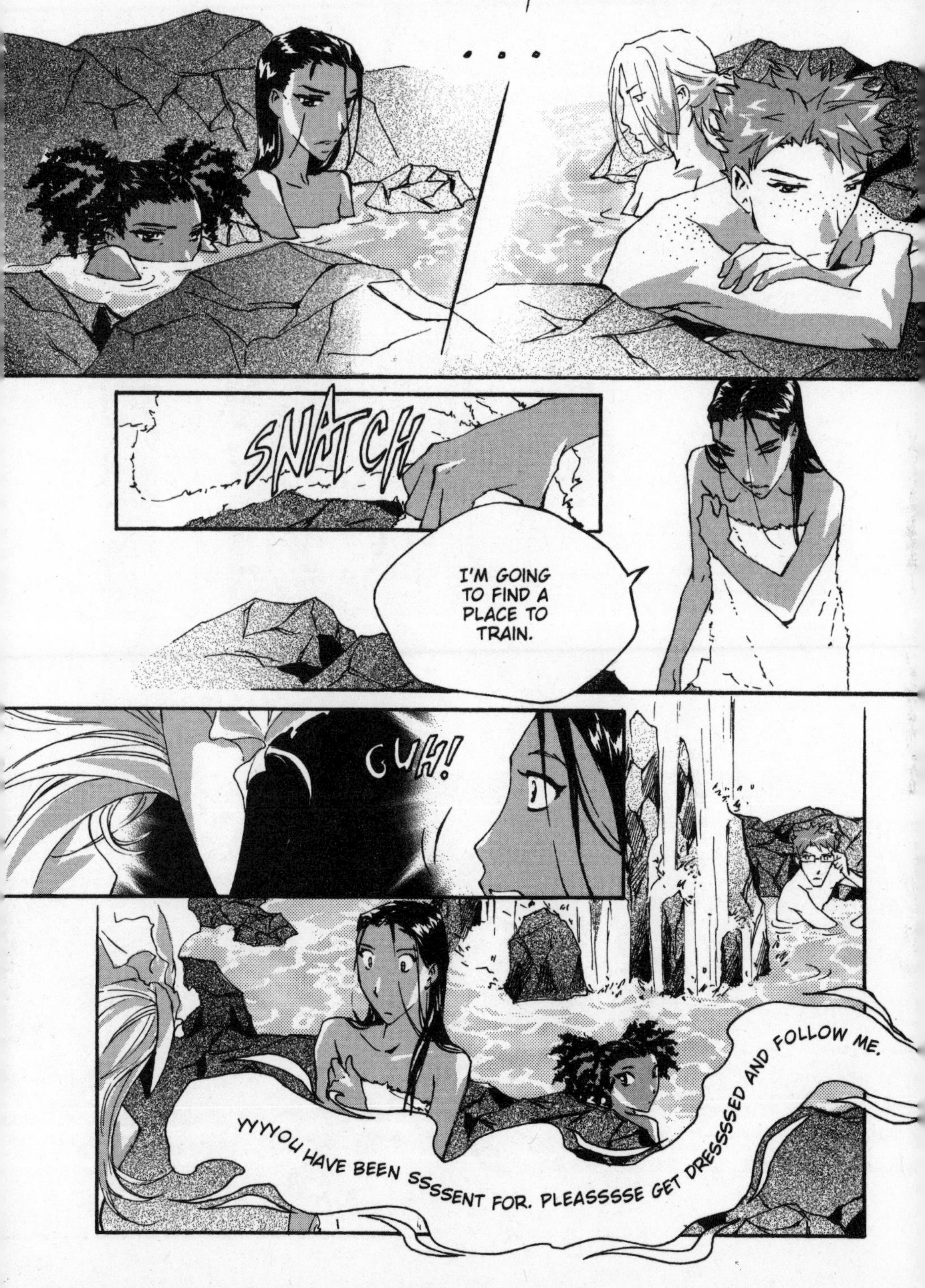
...
SNATCH
I'M GOING TO FIND A PLACE TO TRAIN.
GUH!
YYYYOU HAVE BEEN SSSSENT FOR. PLEASSSSE GET DRESSSSED AND FOLLOW ME.

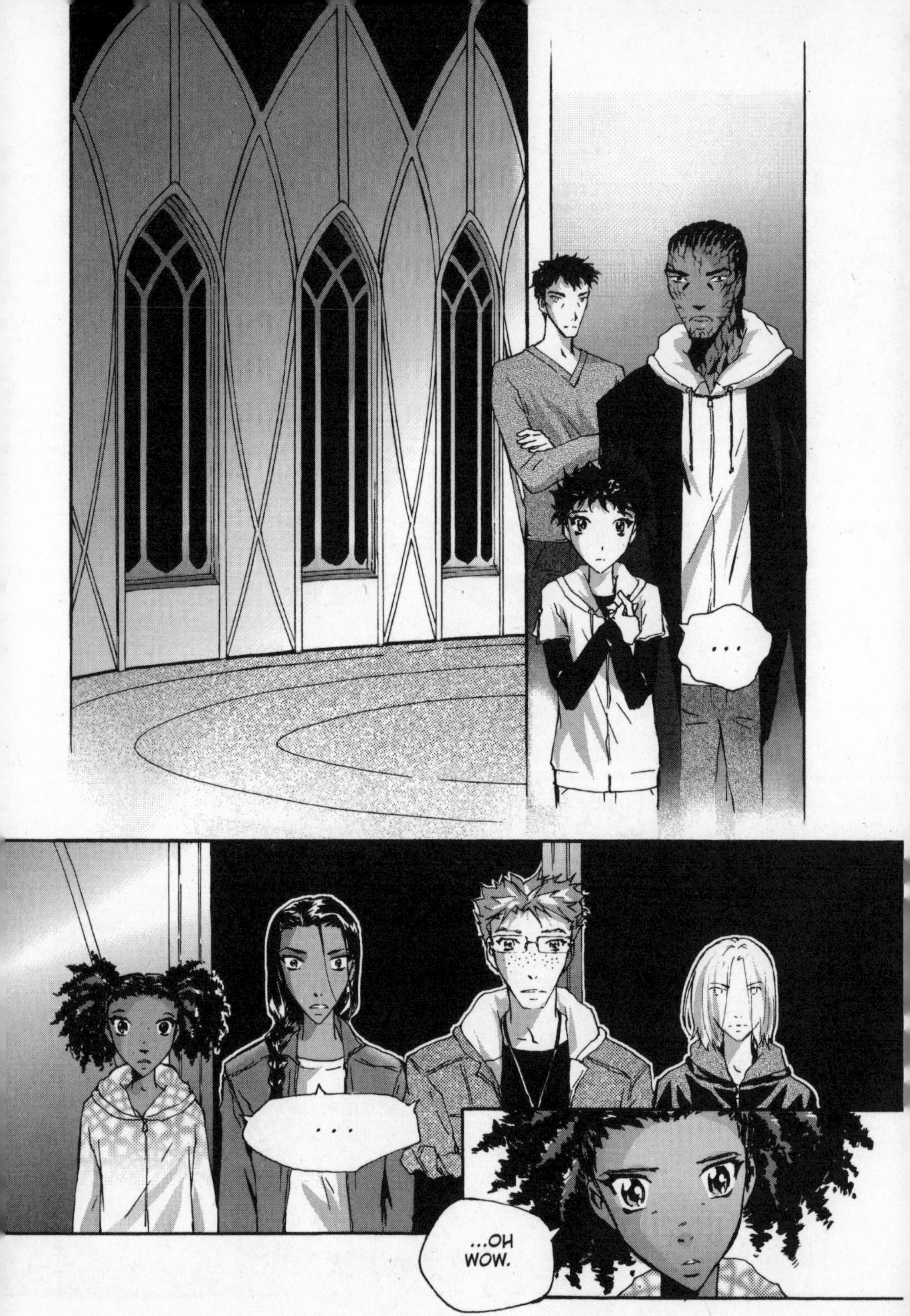
...
...
...OH WOW.

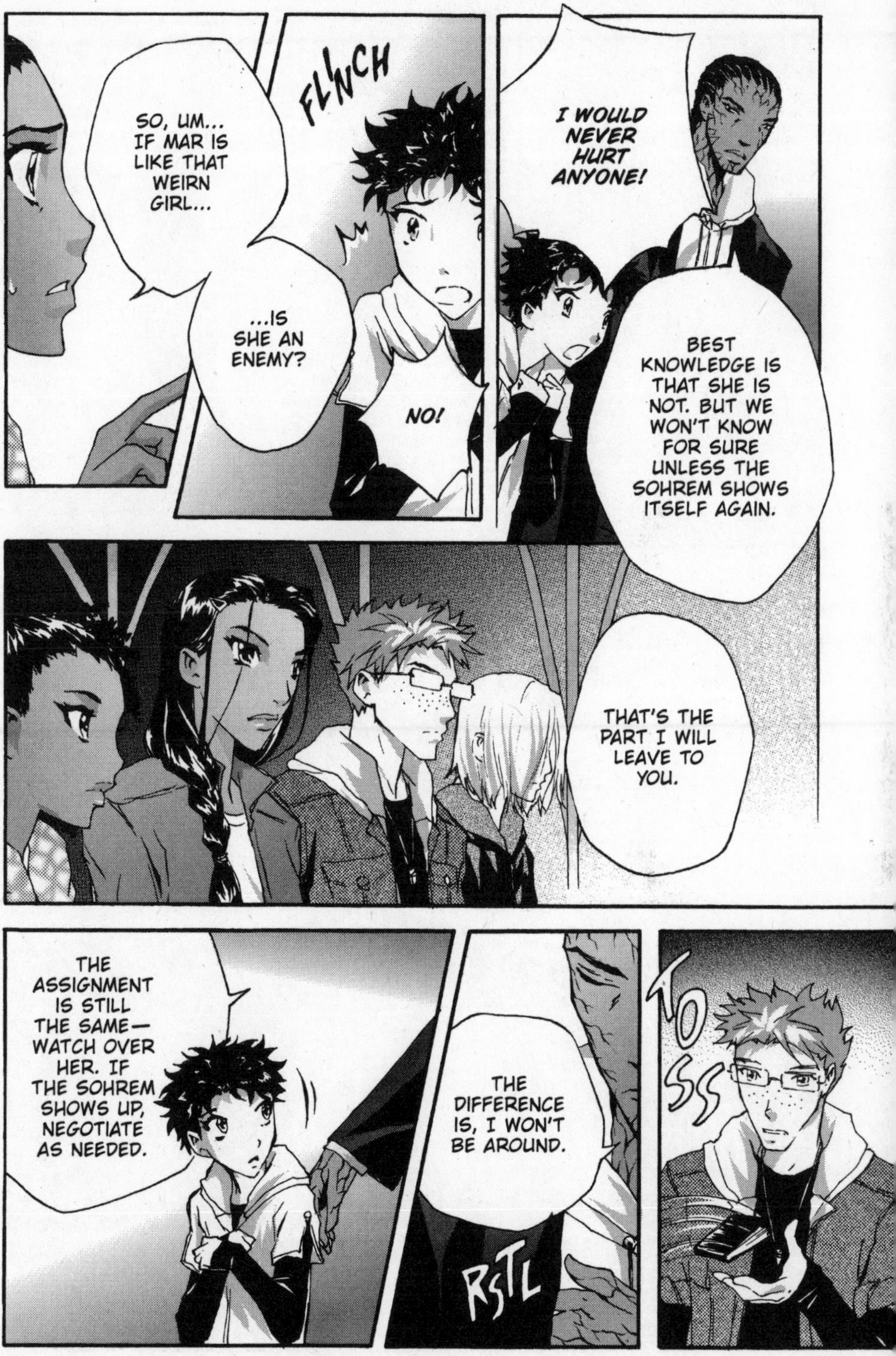

SO, UM... IF MAR IS LIKE THAT WEIRN GIRL...
...IS SHE AN ENEMY?
FLINCH
NO!
I WOULD NEVER HURT ANYONE!
BEST KNOWLEDGE IS THAT SHE IS NOT. BUT WE WON'T KNOW FOR SURE UNLESS THE SOHREM SHOWS ITSELF AGAIN.
THAT'S THE PART I WILL LEAVE TO YOU.
THE ASSIGNMENT IS STILL THE SAME—WATCH OVER HER. IF THE SOHREM SHOWS UP, NEGOTIATE AS NEEDED.
THE DIFFERENCE IS, I WON'T BE AROUND.
RSTL
TOSS

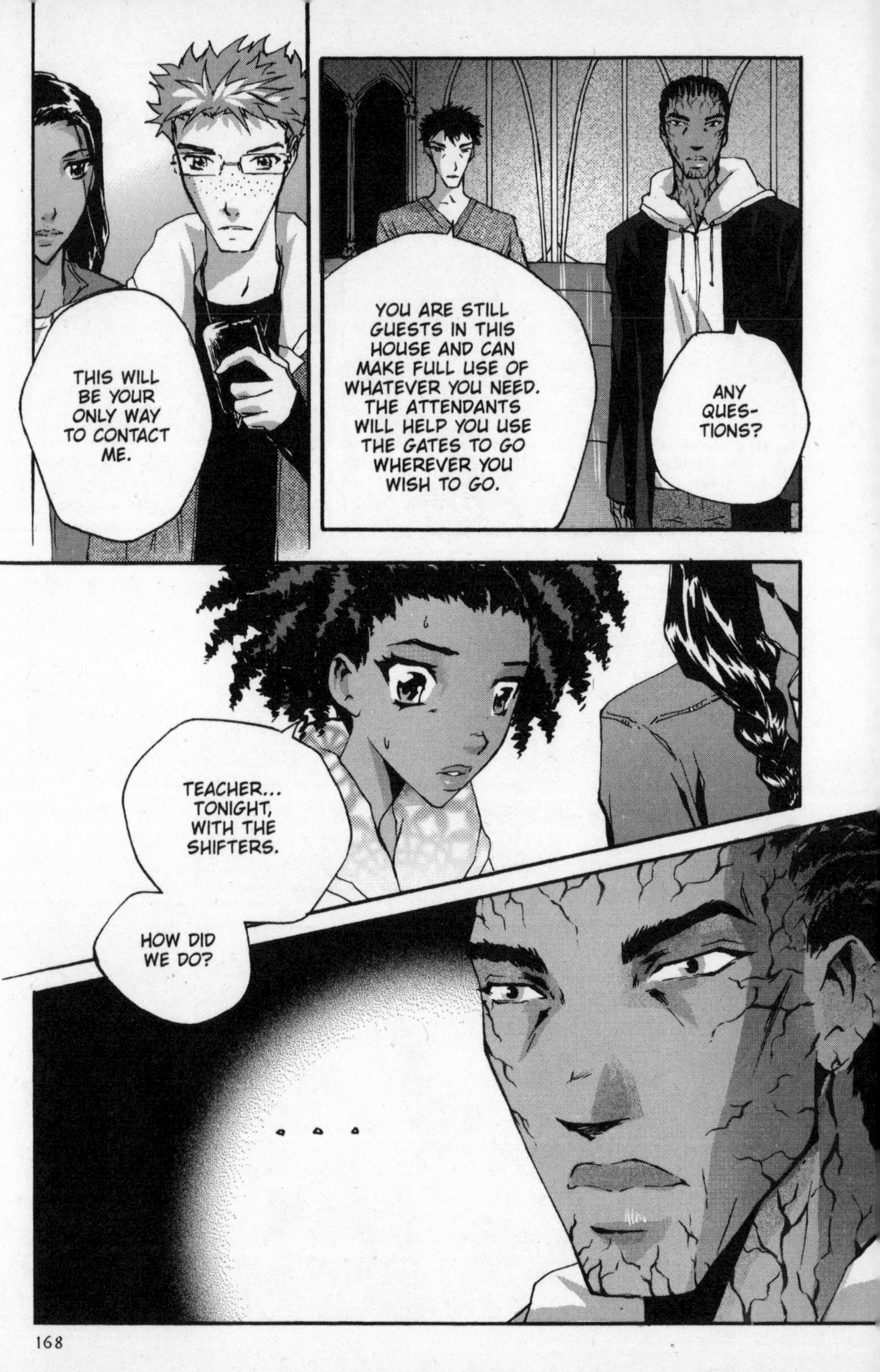
THIS WILL BE YOUR ONLY WAY TO CONTACT ME.
YOU ARE STILL GUESTS IN THIS HOUSE AND CAN MAKE FULL USE OF WHATEVER YOU NEED. THE ATTENDANTS WILL HELP YOU USE THE GATES TO GO WHEREVER YOU WISH TO GO.
ANY QUESTIONS?
TEACHER... TONIGHT, WITH THE SHIFTERS.
HOW DID WE DO?
...

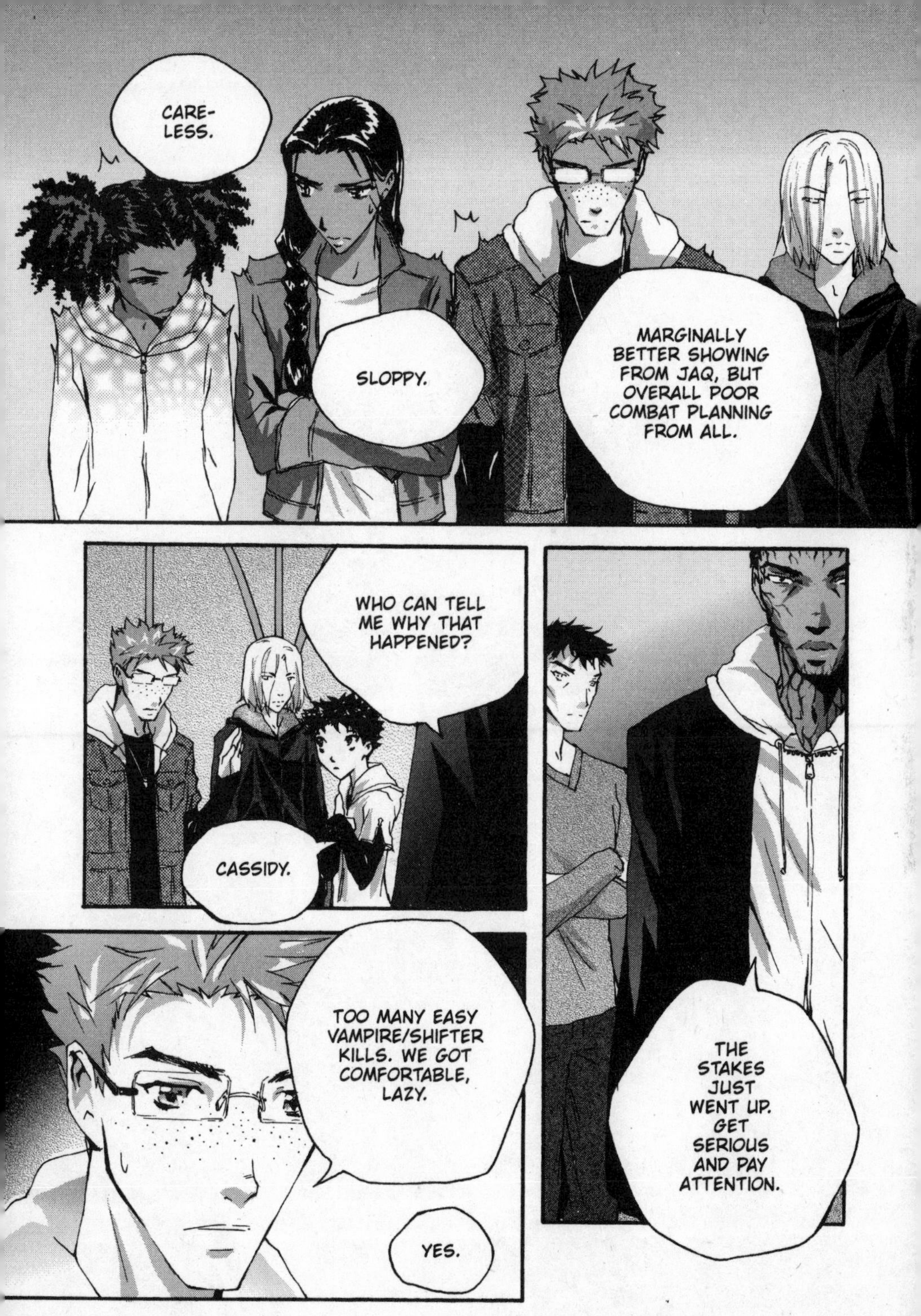
CARE-LESS.
SLOPPY.
MARGINALLY BETTER SHOWING FROM JAQ, BUT OVERALL POOR COMBAT PLANNING FROM ALL.
WHO CAN TELL ME WHY THAT HAPPENED?
CASSIDY.
TOO MANY EASY VAMPIRE/SHIFTER KILLS. WE GOT COMFORTABLE, LAZY.
YES.
THE STAKES JUST WENT UP. GET SERIOUS AND PAY ATTENTION.

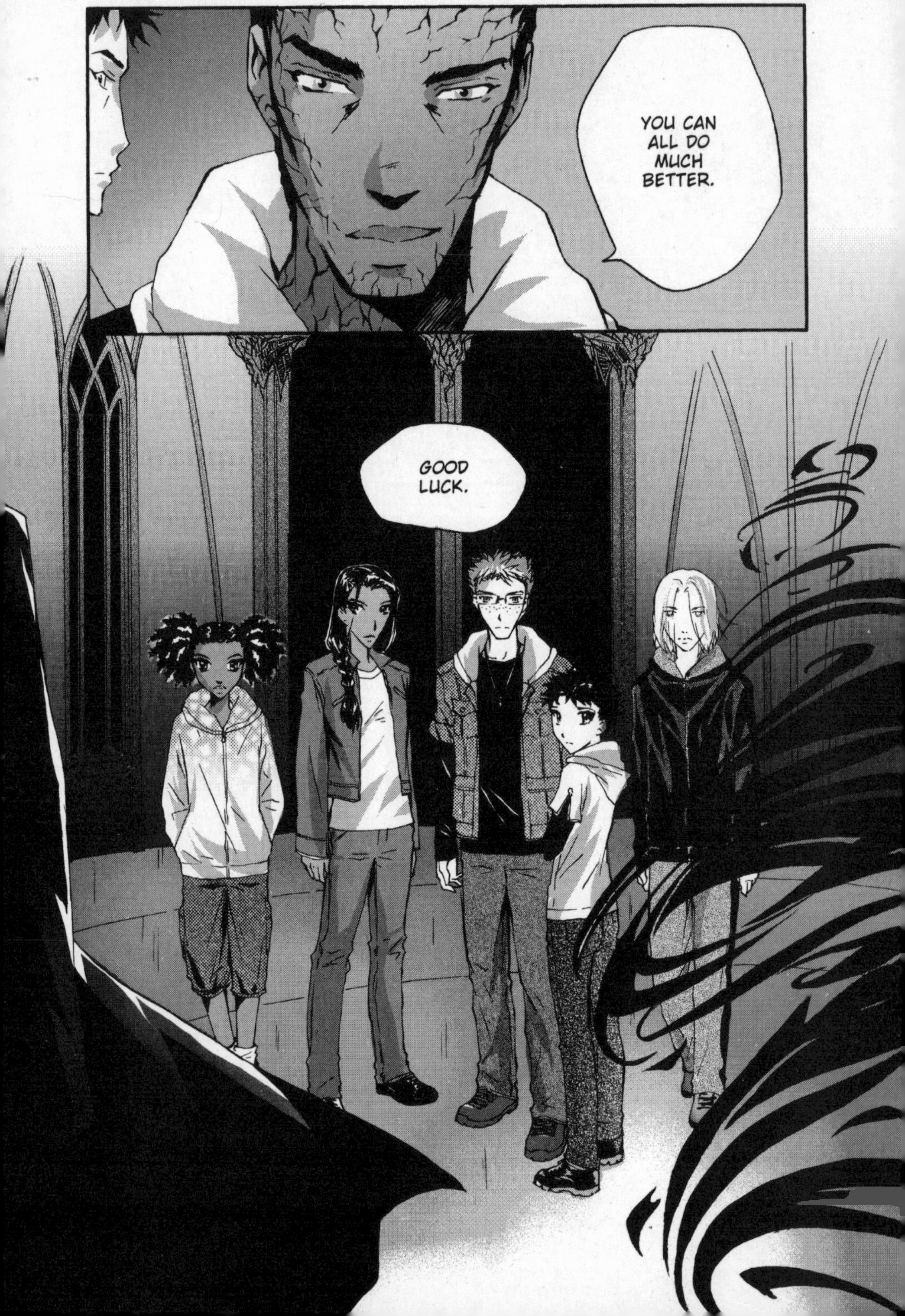
YOU CAN ALL DO MUCH BETTER.
GOOD LUCK.

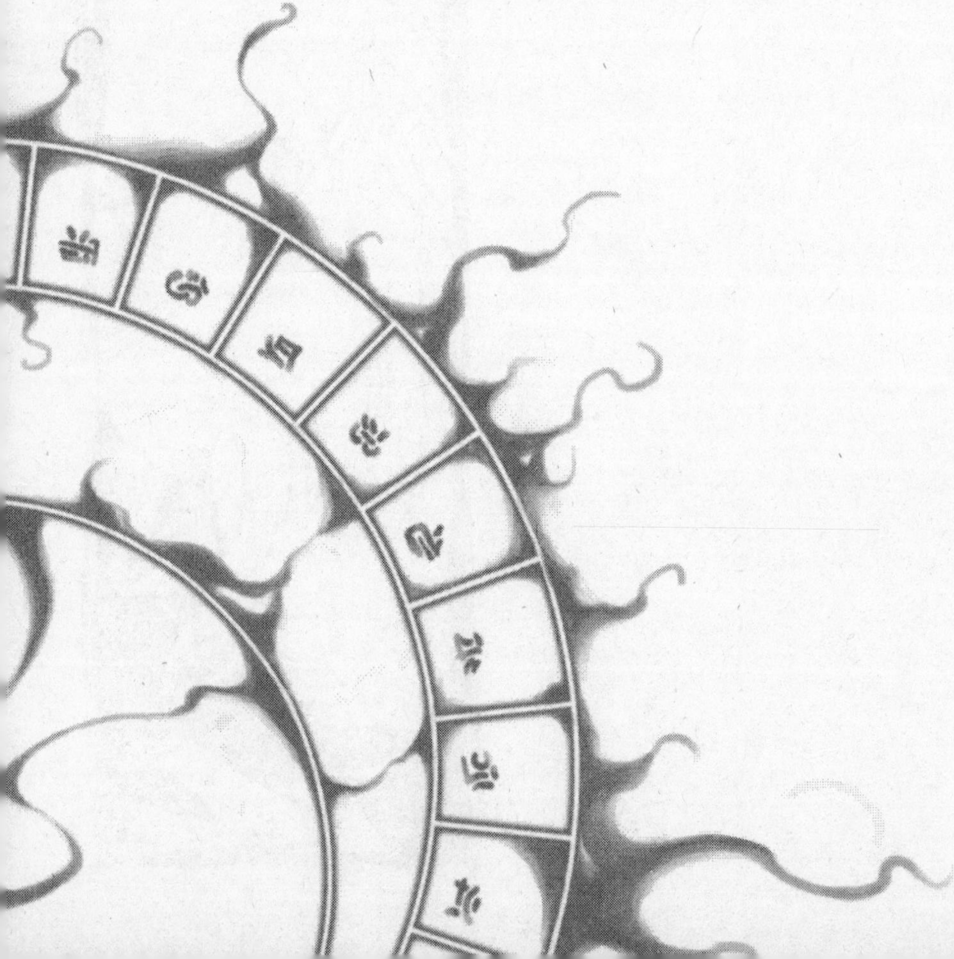

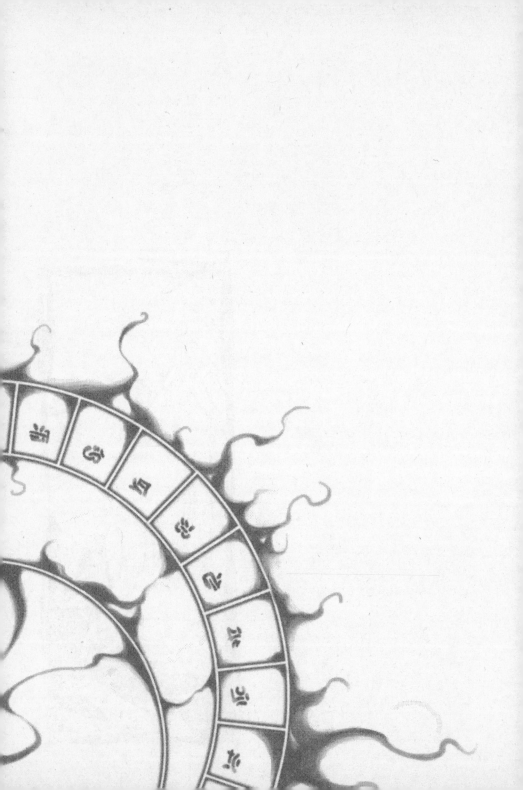

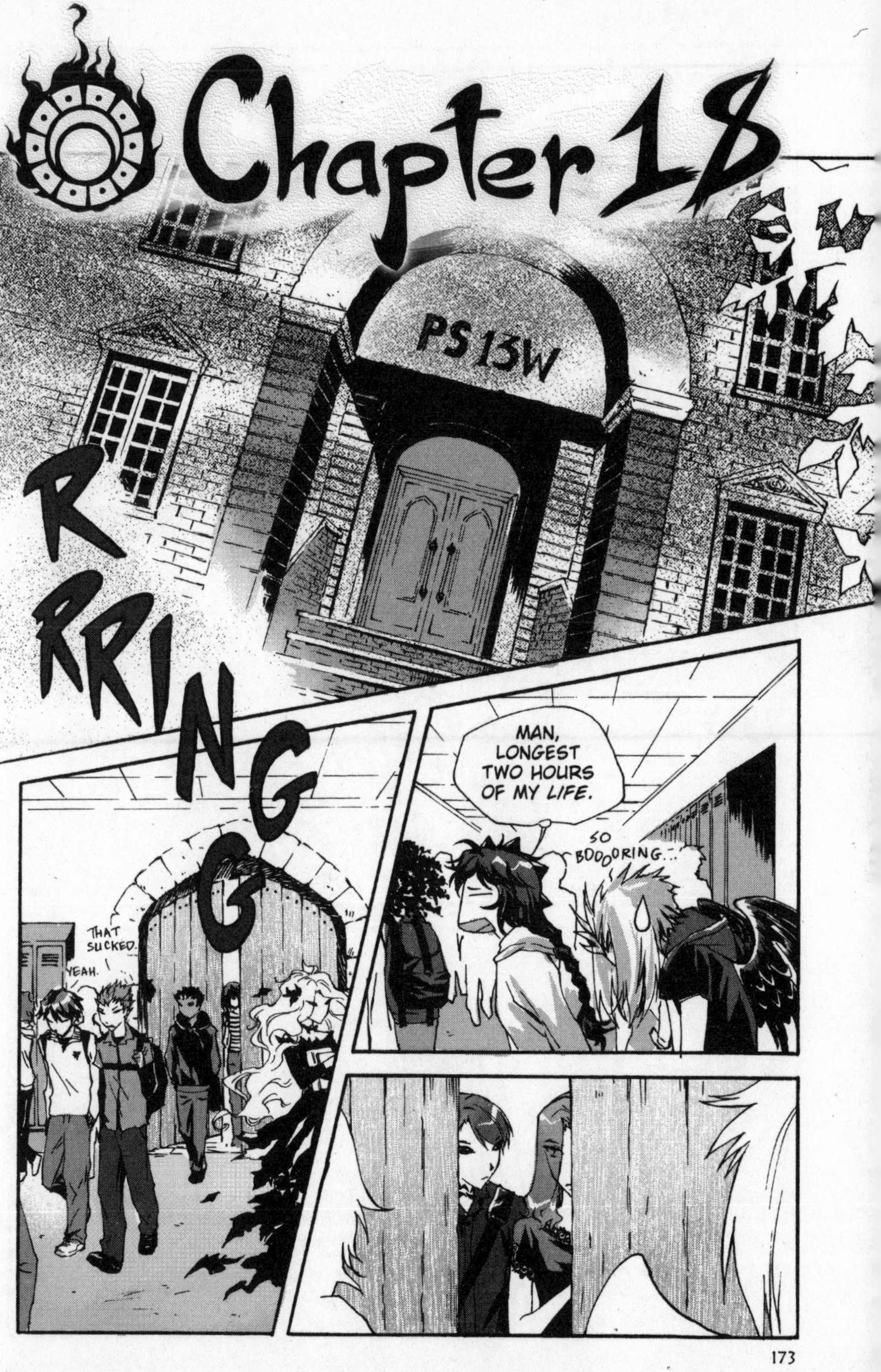
Chapter 18
PS 13W
R RRING G
THAT SUCKED.
YEAH.
MAN, LONGEST TWO HOURS OF MY LIFE.
SO BOOOORING...

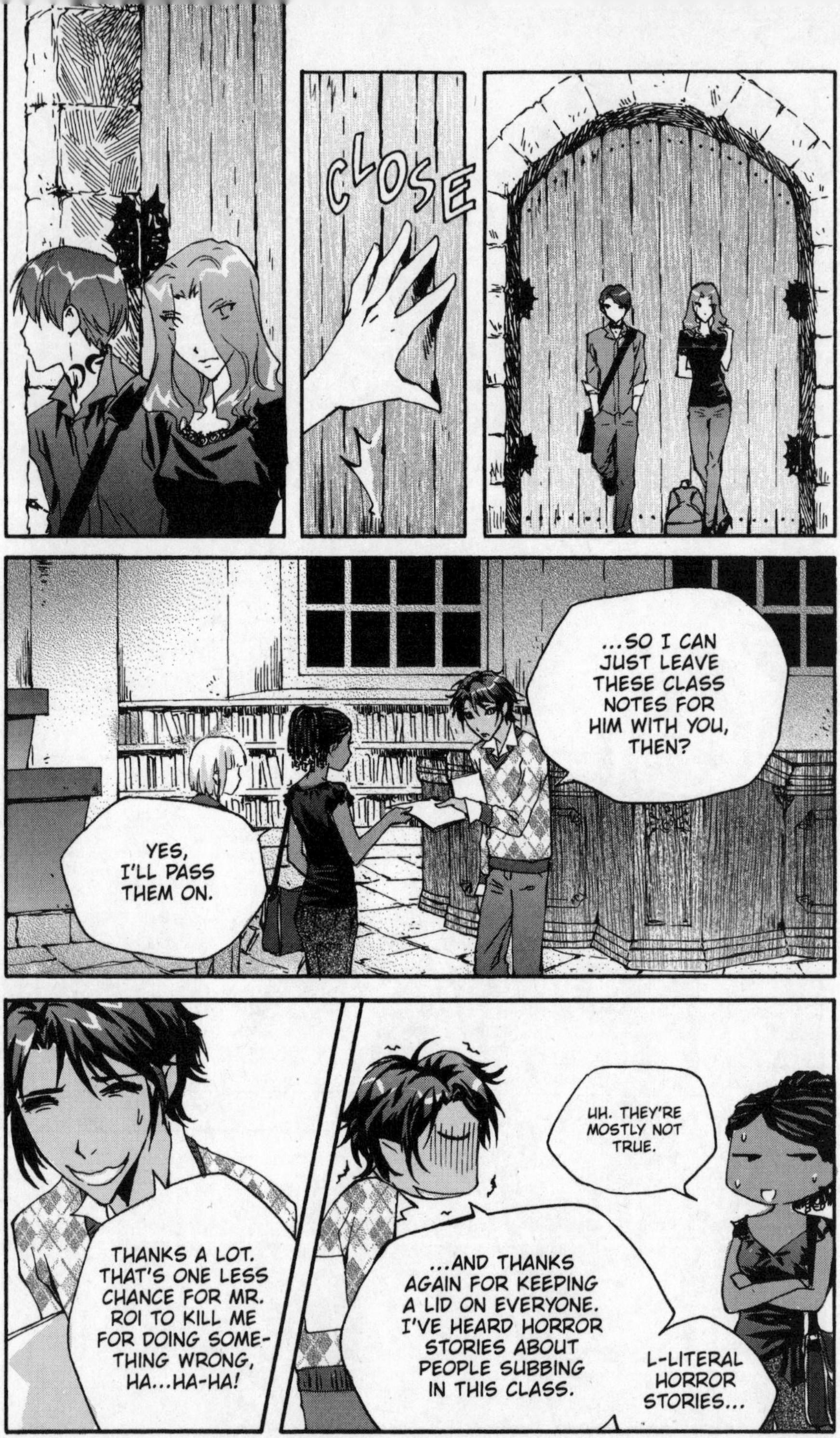
CLOSE
...SO I CAN JUST LEAVE THESE CLASS NOTES FOR HIM WITH YOU, THEN?
YES, I'LL PASS THEM ON.
THANKS A LOT. THAT'S ONE LESS CHANCE FOR MR. ROI TO KILL ME FOR DOING SOME-THING WRONG, HA...HA-HA!
...AND THANKS AGAIN FOR KEEPING A LID ON EVERYONE. I'VE HEARD HORROR STORIES ABOUT PEOPLE SUBBING IN THIS CLASS.
UH. THEY'RE MOSTLY NOT TRUE.
L-LITERAL HORROR STORIES...

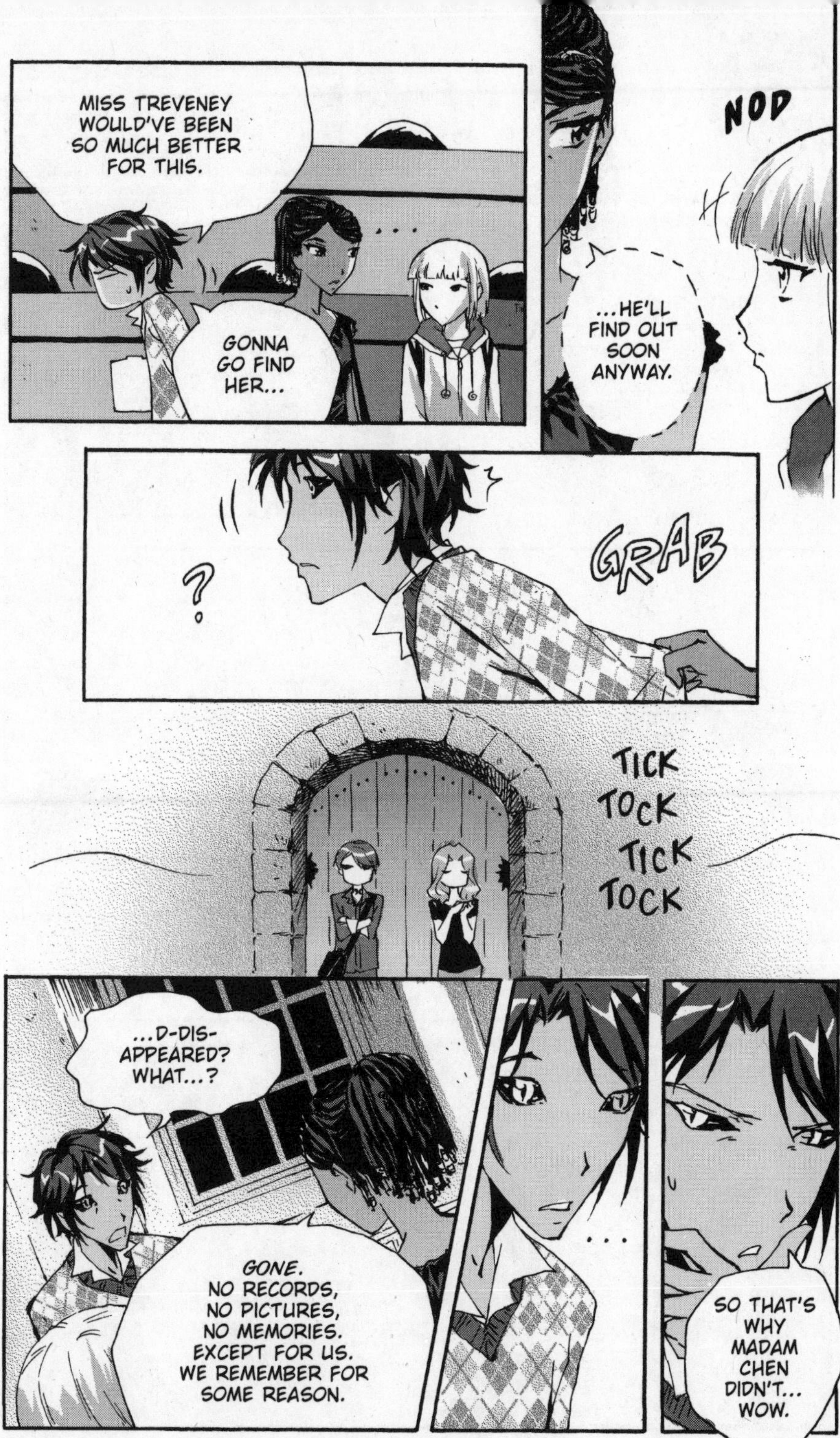

MISS TREVENEY WOULD'VE BEEN SO MUCH BETTER FOR THIS.
...
GONNA GO FIND HER...
NOD
...HE'LL FIND OUT SOON ANYWAY.
?
GRAB
TICK TOCK TICK TOCK
...D-DIS-APPEARED? WHAT...?
GONE. NO RECORDS, NO PICTURES, NO MEMORIES. EXCEPT FOR US. WE REMEMBER FOR SOME REASON.
...
SO THAT'S WHY MADAM CHEN DIDN'T... WOW.

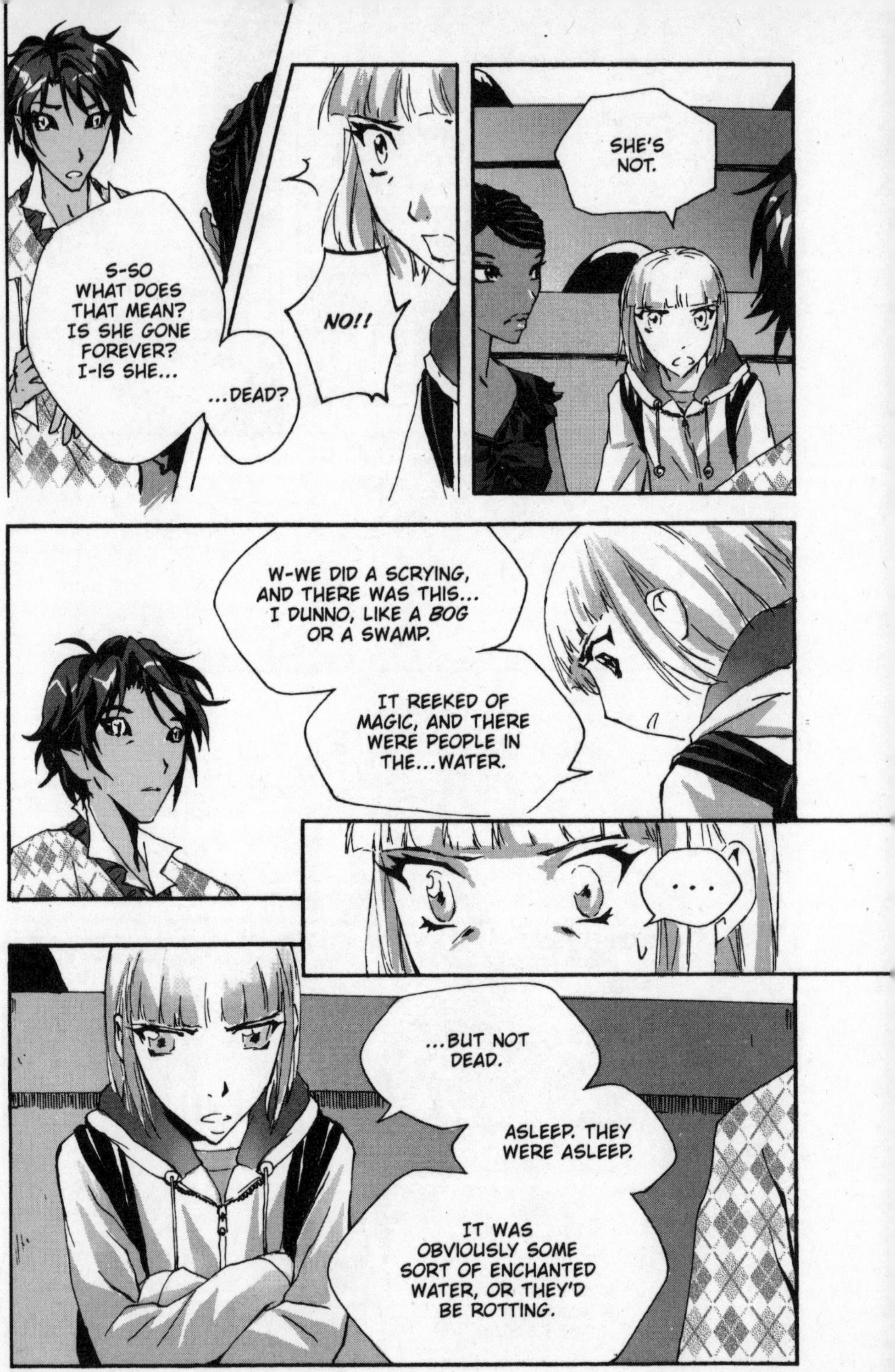
S-SO WHAT DOES THAT MEAN? IS SHE GONE FOREVER? I-IS SHE...
...DEAD?
NO!!
SHE'S NOT.
W-WE DID A SCRYING, AND THERE WAS THIS... I DUNNO, LIKE A *BOG* OR A SWAMP.
IT REEKED OF MAGIC, AND THERE WERE PEOPLE IN THE...WATER.
...
...BUT NOT DEAD.
ASLEEP. THEY WERE ASLEEP.
IT WAS OBVIOUSLY SOME SORT OF ENCHANTED WATER, OR THEY'D BE ROTTING.

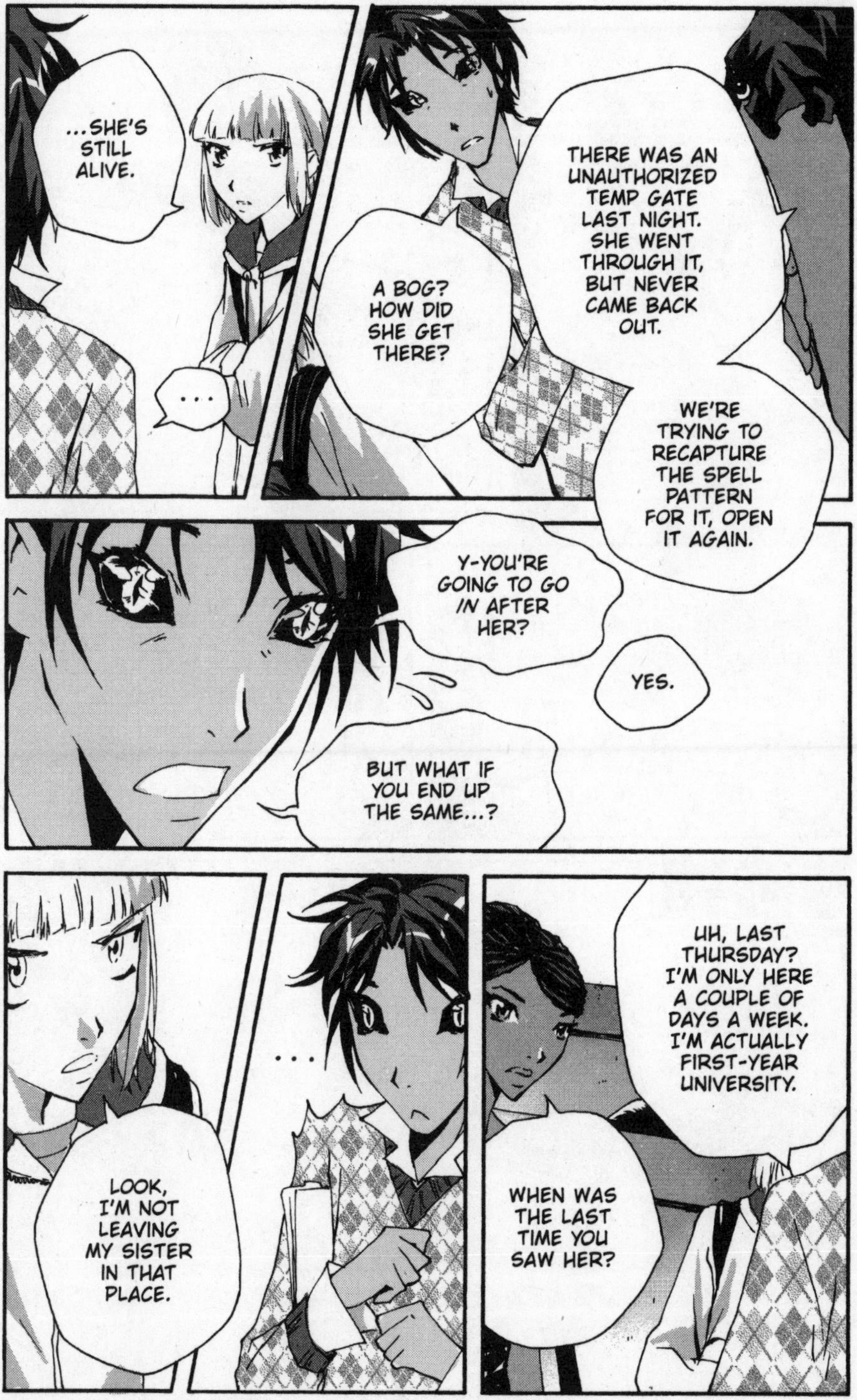
...SHE'S STILL ALIVE.
...
A BOG? HOW DID SHE GET THERE?
THERE WAS AN UNAUTHORIZED TEMP GATE LAST NIGHT. SHE WENT THROUGH IT, BUT NEVER CAME BACK OUT.
WE'RE TRYING TO RECAPTURE THE SPELL PATTERN FOR IT, OPEN IT AGAIN.
Y-YOU'RE GOING TO GO *IN* AFTER HER?
YES.
BUT WHAT IF YOU END UP THE SAME...?
LOOK, I'M NOT LEAVING MY SISTER IN THAT PLACE.
...
WHEN WAS THE LAST TIME YOU SAW HER?
UH, LAST THURSDAY? I'M ONLY HERE A COUPLE OF DAYS A WEEK. I'M ACTUALLY FIRST-YEAR UNIVERSITY.

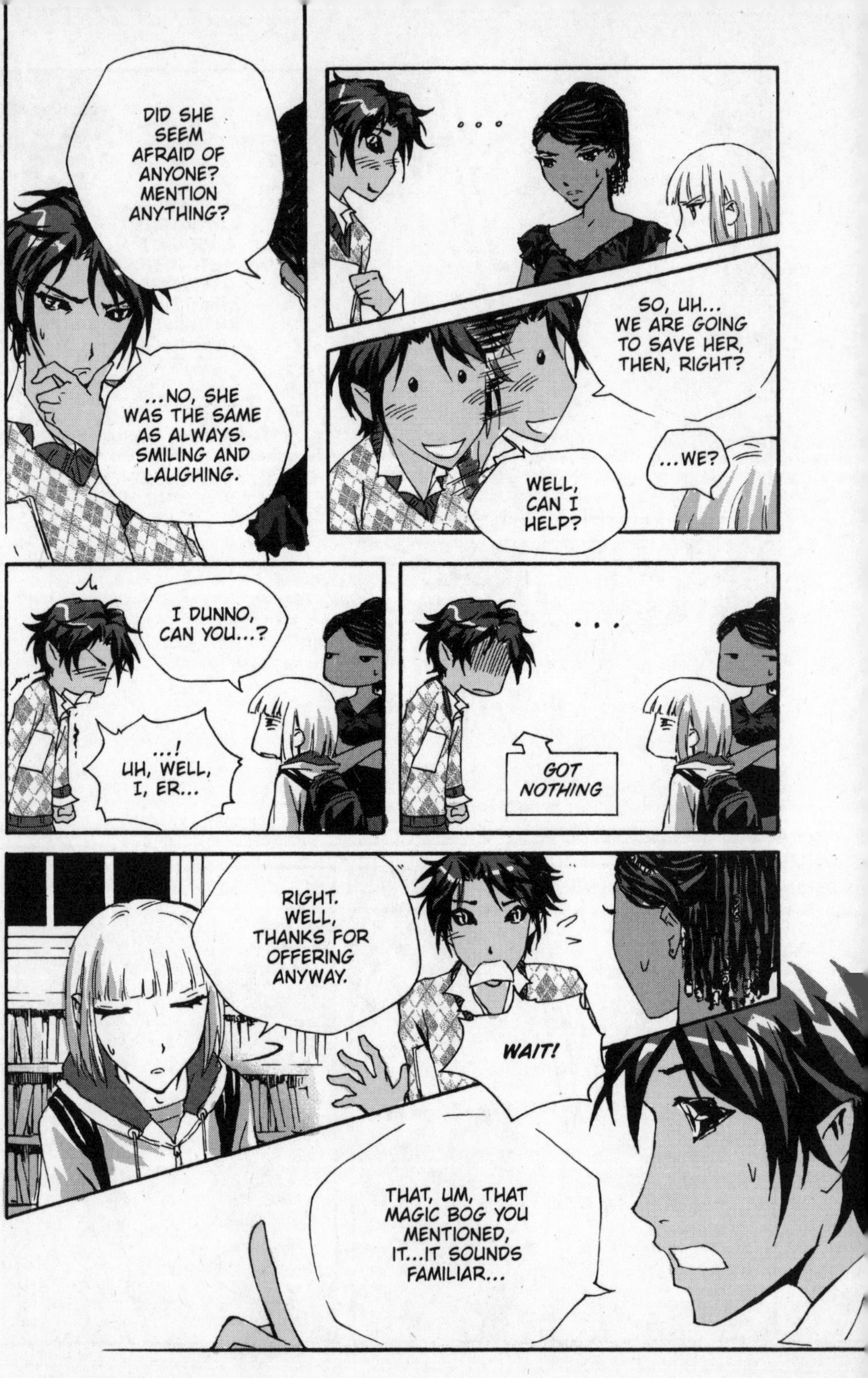
DID SHE SEEM AFRAID OF ANYONE? MENTION ANYTHING?
...NO, SHE WAS THE SAME AS ALWAYS. SMILING AND LAUGHING.
...
SO, UH... WE ARE GOING TO SAVE HER, THEN, RIGHT?
...WE?
WELL, CAN I HELP?
I DUNNO, CAN YOU...?
...! UH, WELL, I, ER...
...
GOT NOTHING
RIGHT. WELL, THANKS FOR OFFERING ANYWAY.
WAIT!
THAT, UM, THAT MAGIC BOG YOU MENTIONED, IT...IT SOUNDS FAMILIAR...

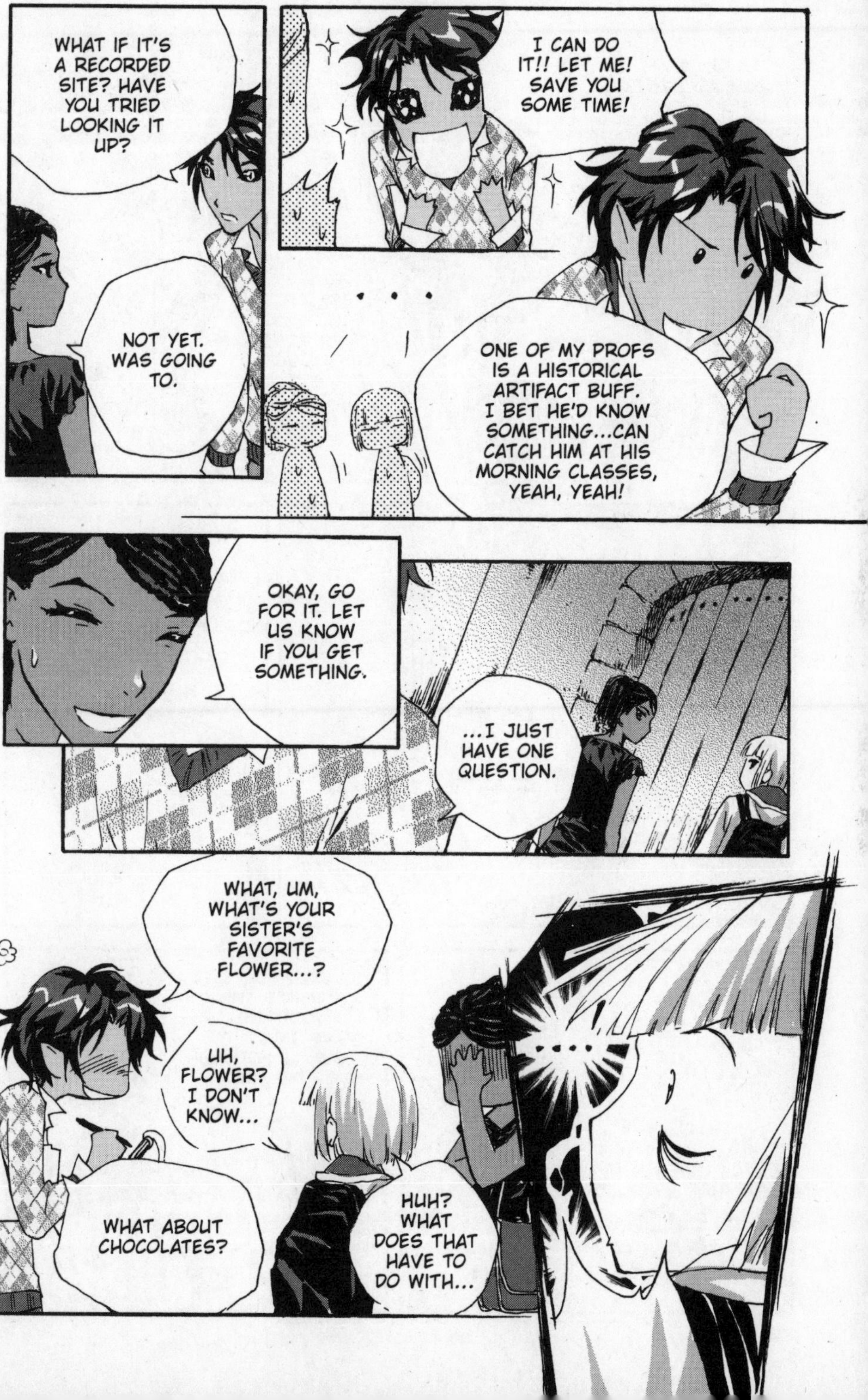
WHAT IF IT'S A RECORDED SITE? HAVE YOU TRIED LOOKING IT UP?
NOT YET. WAS GOING TO.
I CAN DO IT!! LET ME! SAVE YOU SOME TIME!
...
ONE OF MY PROFS IS A HISTORICAL ARTIFACT BUFF. I BET HE'D KNOW SOMETHING...CAN CATCH HIM AT HIS MORNING CLASSES, YEAH, YEAH!
OKAY, GO FOR IT. LET US KNOW IF YOU GET SOMETHING.
...I JUST HAVE ONE QUESTION.
WHAT, UM, WHAT'S YOUR SISTER'S FAVORITE FLOWER...?
UH, FLOWER? I DON'T KNOW...
WHAT ABOUT CHOCOLATES?
HUH? WHAT DOES THAT HAVE TO DO WITH...
....

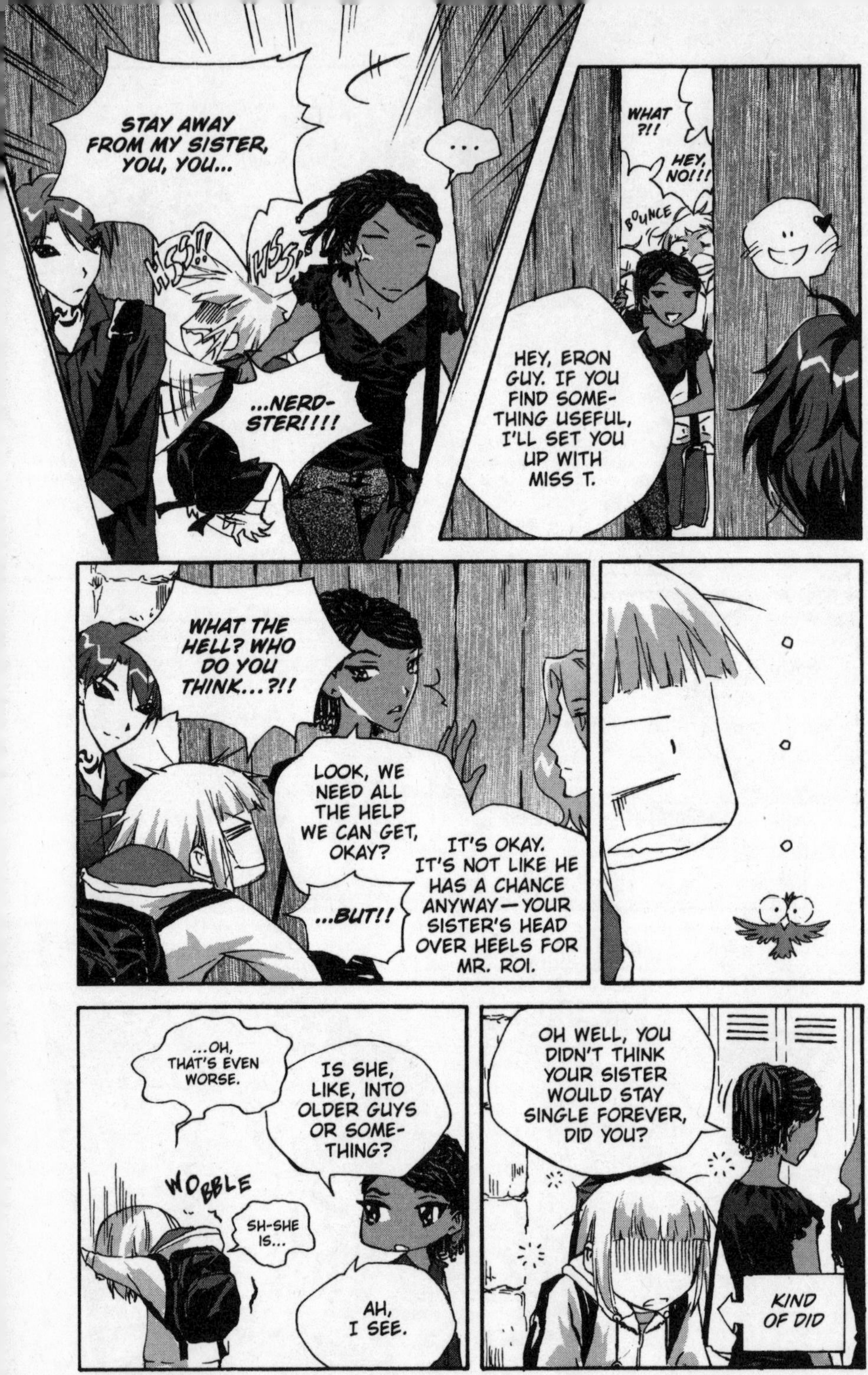
STAY AWAY FROM MY SISTER, YOU, YOU...
HSS!!
HSS!!
...NERD-STER!!!!
...
WHAT ?!!
HEY, NO!!!
BOUNCE
HEY, ERON GUY. IF YOU FIND SOME-THING USEFUL, I'LL SET YOU UP WITH MISS T.
WHAT THE HELL? WHO DO YOU THINK...?!!
LOOK, WE NEED ALL THE HELP WE CAN GET, OKAY?
...BUT!!
IT'S OKAY. IT'S NOT LIKE HE HAS A CHANCE ANYWAY—YOUR SISTER'S HEAD OVER HEELS FOR MR. ROI.
...OH, THAT'S EVEN WORSE.
IS SHE, LIKE, INTO OLDER GUYS OR SOME-THING?
WOBBLE
SH-SHE IS...
AH, I SEE.
OH WELL, YOU DIDN'T THINK YOUR SISTER WOULD STAY SINGLE FOREVER, DID YOU?
KIND OF DID

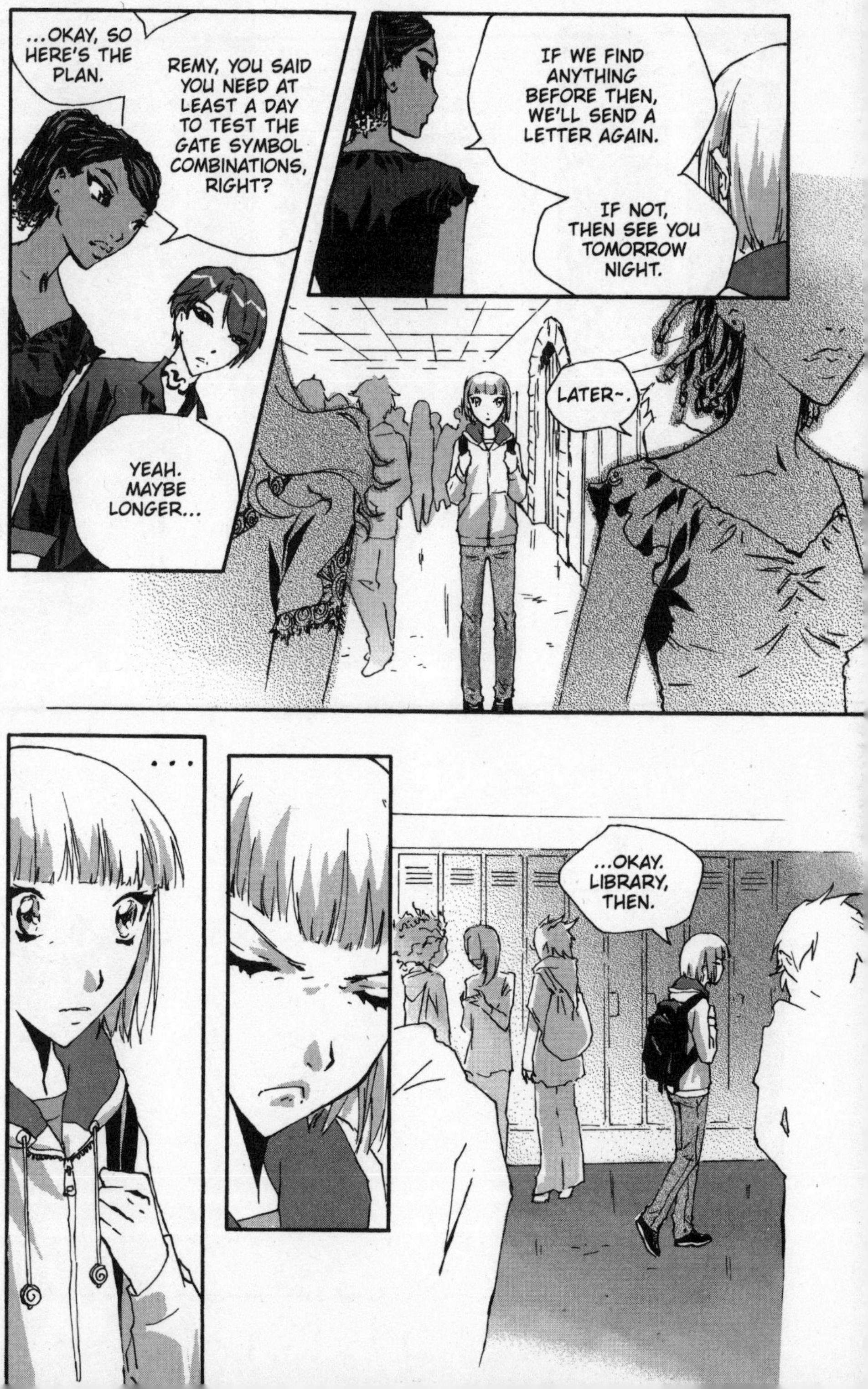
...OKAY, SO HERE'S THE PLAN.
REMY, YOU SAID YOU NEED AT LEAST A DAY TO TEST THE GATE SYMBOL COMBINATIONS, RIGHT?
YEAH. MAYBE LONGER...
IF WE FIND ANYTHING BEFORE THEN, WE'LL SEND A LETTER AGAIN.
IF NOT, THEN SEE YOU TOMORROW NIGHT.
LATER~.
...
...OKAY. LIBRARY, THEN.

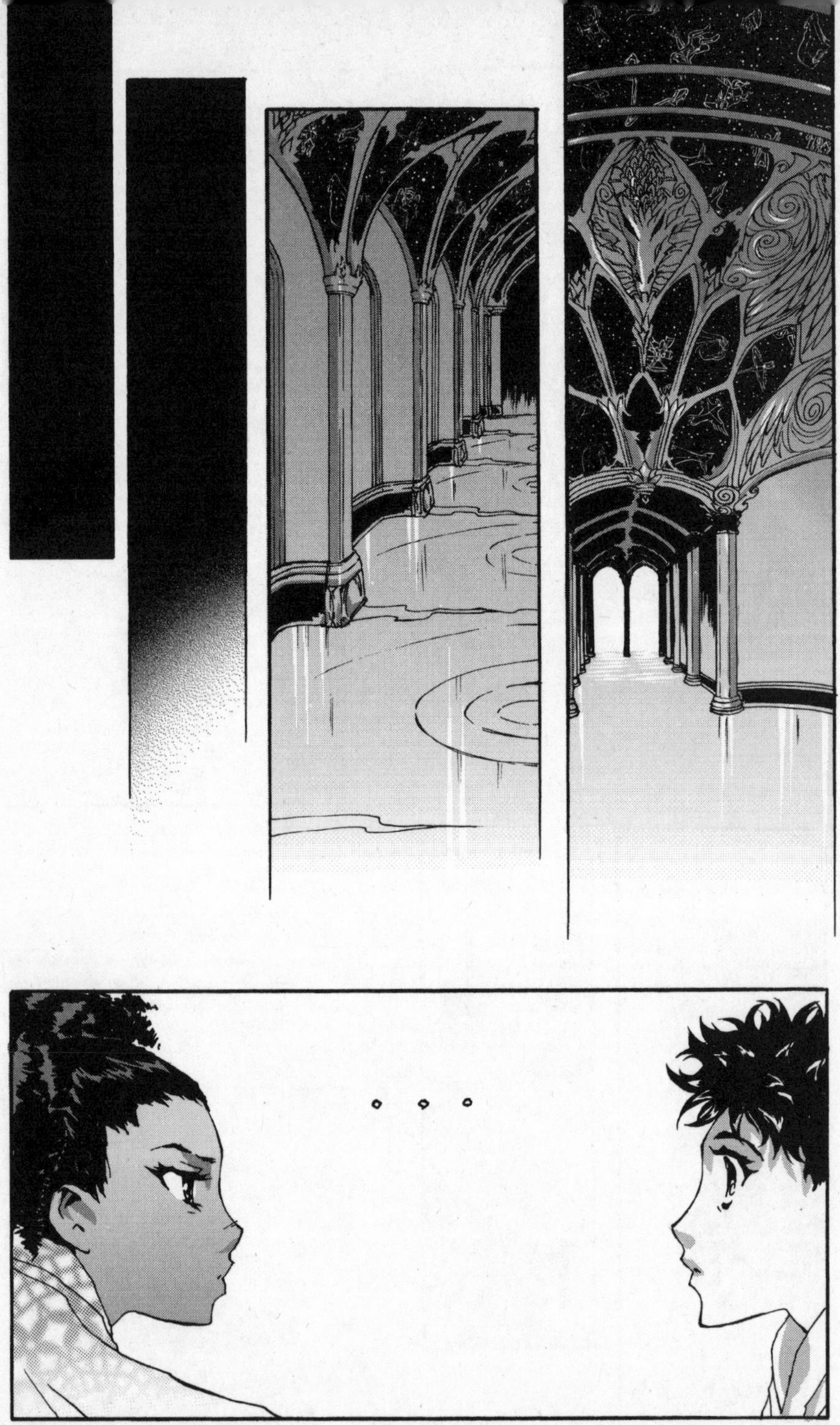
。。。

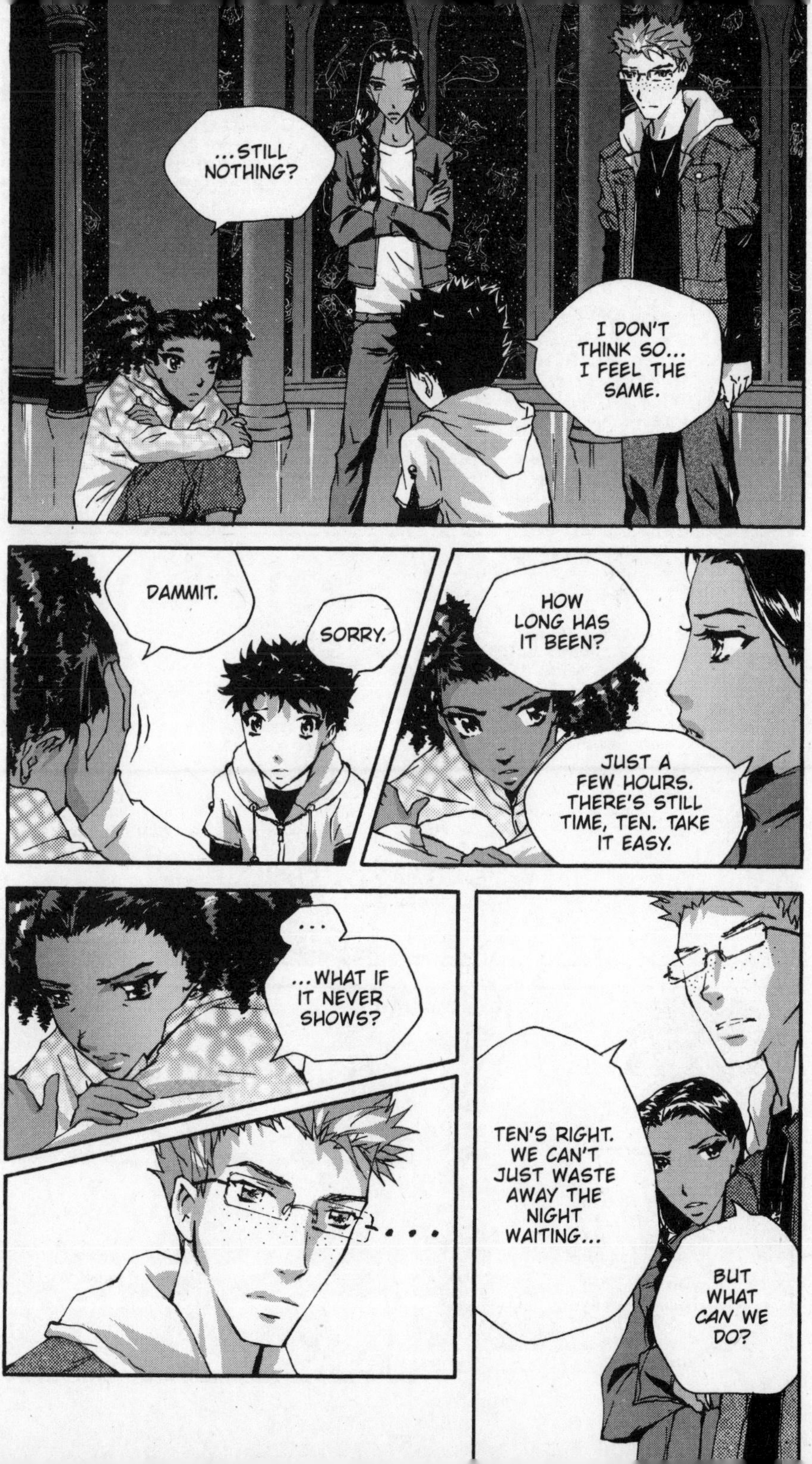
...STILL NOTHING?
I DON'T THINK SO... I FEEL THE SAME.
DAMMIT.
SORRY.
HOW LONG HAS IT BEEN?
JUST A FEW HOURS. THERE'S STILL TIME, TEN. TAKE IT EASY.
...
...WHAT IF IT NEVER SHOWS?
...
TEN'S RIGHT. WE CAN'T JUST WASTE AWAY THE NIGHT WAITING...
BUT WHAT CAN WE DO?

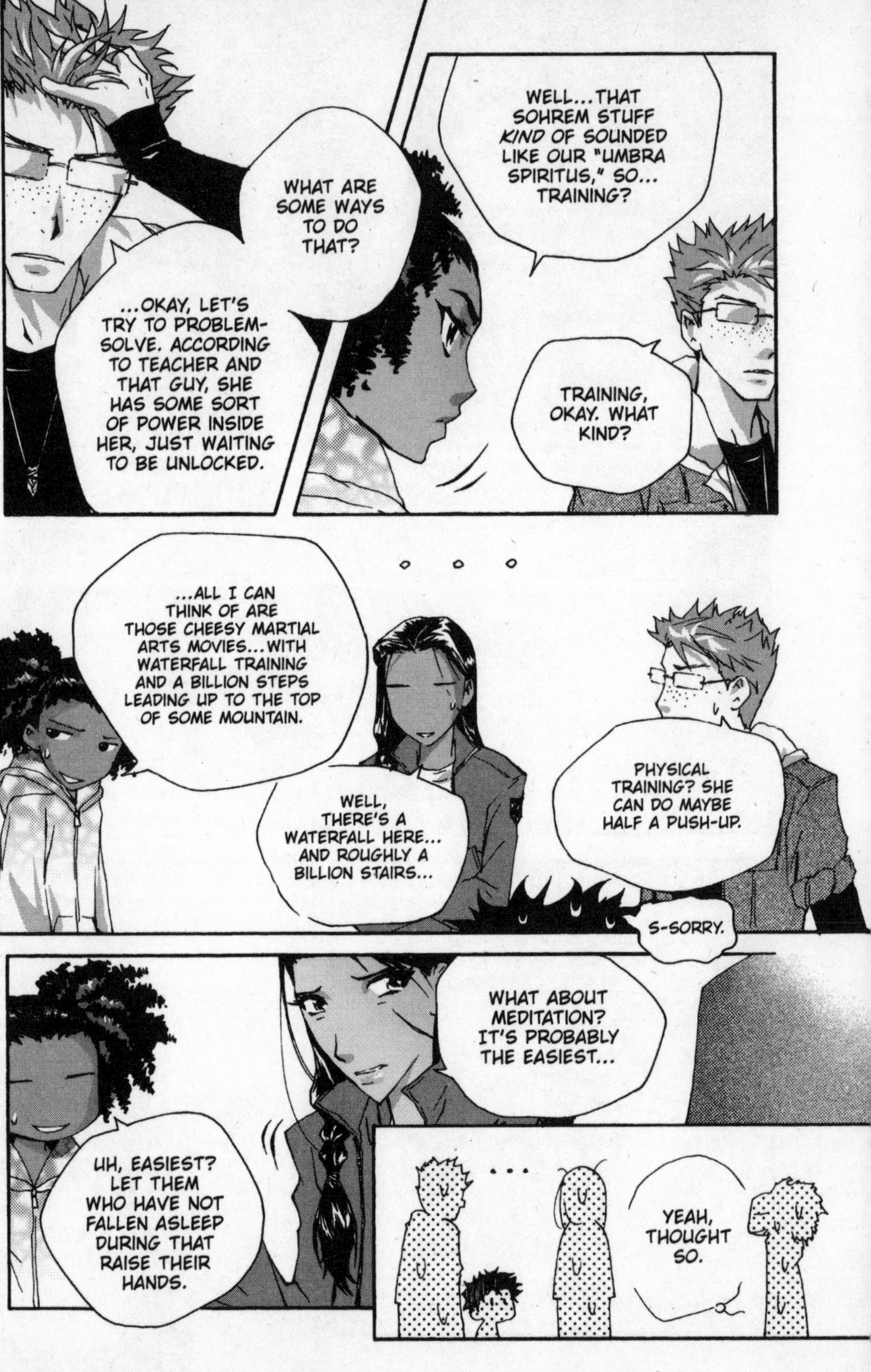
...OKAY, LET'S TRY TO PROBLEM-SOLVE. ACCORDING TO TEACHER AND THAT GUY, SHE HAS SOME SORT OF POWER INSIDE HER, JUST WAITING TO BE UNLOCKED.
WHAT ARE SOME WAYS TO DO THAT?
WELL...THAT SOHREM STUFF *KIND* OF SOUNDED LIKE OUR "UMBRA SPIRITUS," SO... TRAINING?
TRAINING, OKAY. WHAT KIND?
...ALL I CAN THINK OF ARE THOSE CHEESY MARTIAL ARTS MOVIES...WITH WATERFALL TRAINING AND A BILLION STEPS LEADING UP TO THE TOP OF SOME MOUNTAIN.
WELL, THERE'S A WATERFALL HERE... AND ROUGHLY A BILLION STAIRS...
PHYSICAL TRAINING? SHE CAN DO MAYBE HALF A PUSH-UP.
S-SORRY.
WHAT ABOUT MEDITATION? IT'S PROBABLY THE EASIEST...
UH, EASIEST? LET THEM WHO HAVE NOT FALLEN ASLEEP DURING THAT RAISE THEIR HANDS.
...
YEAH, THOUGHT SO.

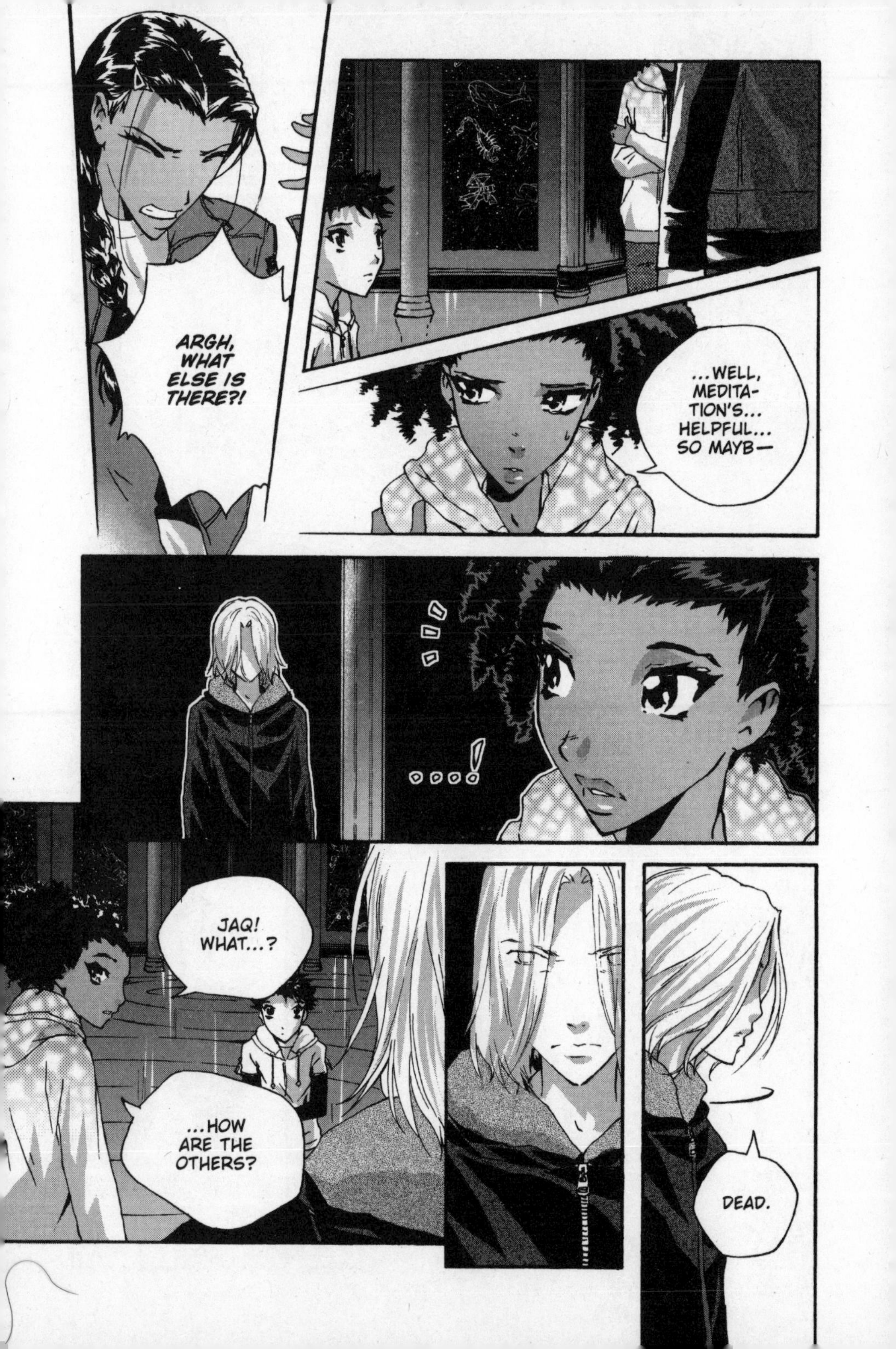
ARGH, WHAT ELSE IS THERE?!
...WELL, MEDITA-TION'S... HELPFUL... SO MAYB—
...!
JAQ! WHAT...?
...HOW ARE THE OTHERS?
DEAD.

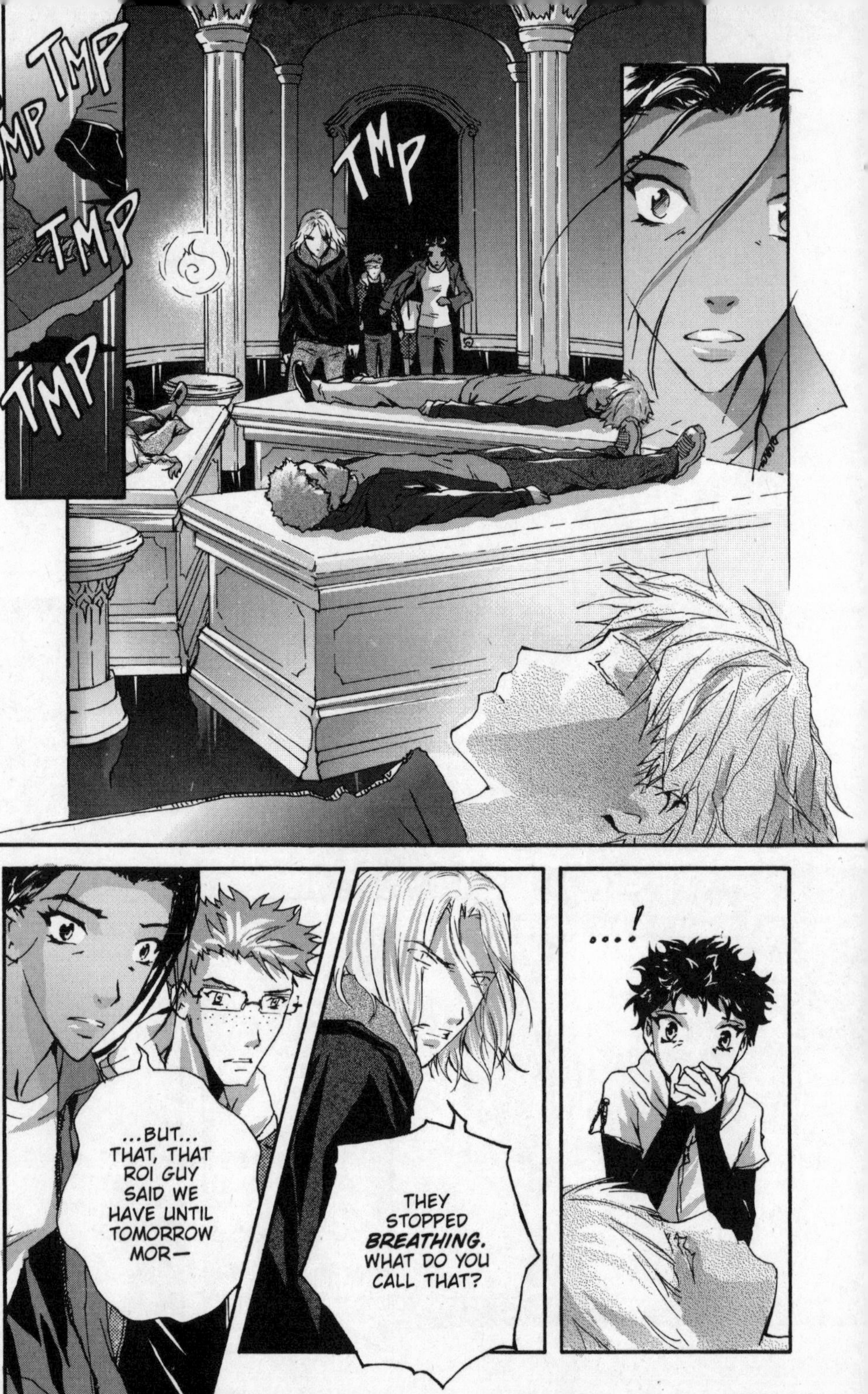

TMP TMP
TMP
TMP
TMP
...BUT... THAT, THAT ROI GUY SAID WE HAVE UNTIL TOMORROW MOR—
THEY STOPPED BREATHING. WHAT DO YOU CALL THAT?
...!

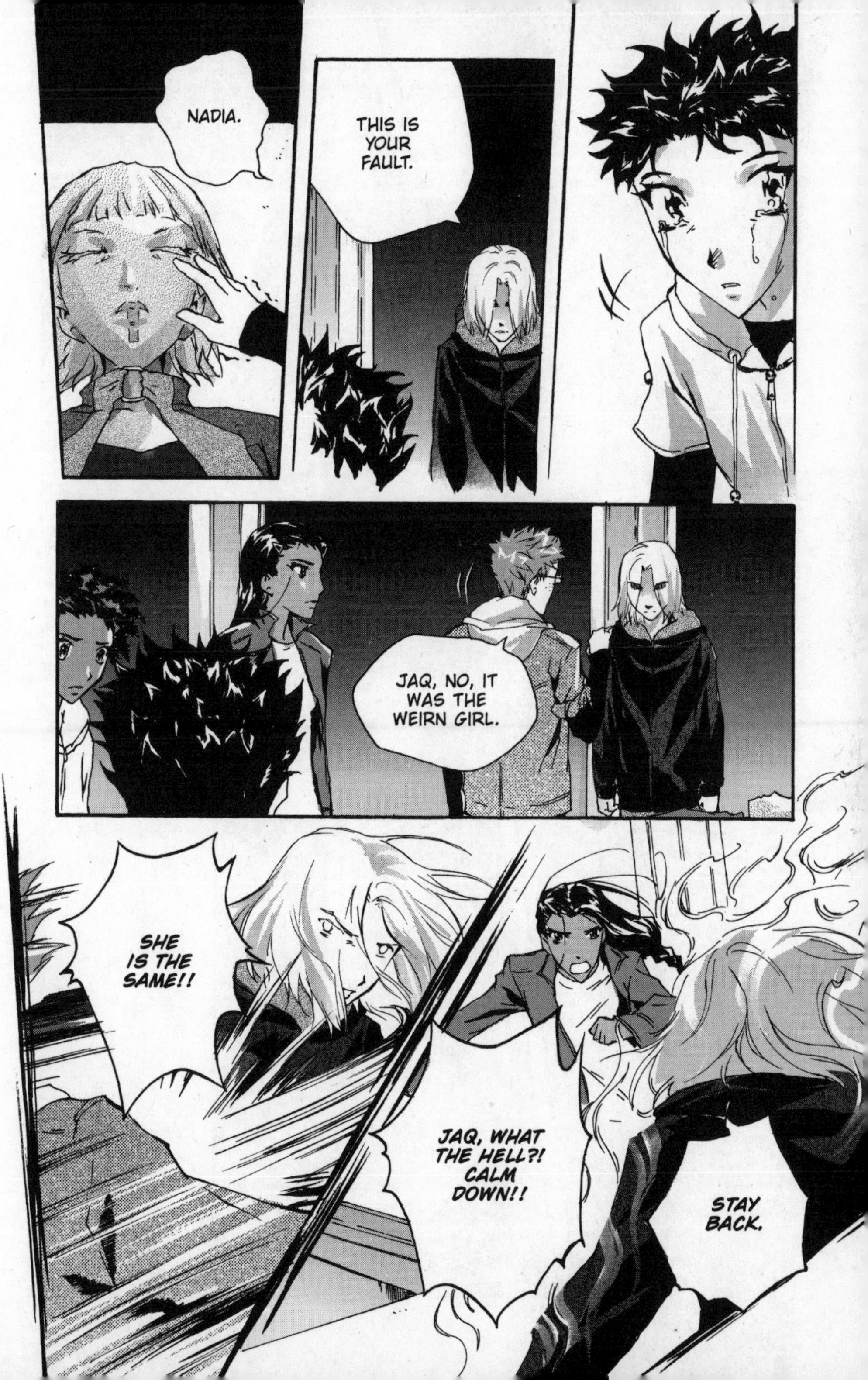
NADIA.
THIS IS YOUR FAULT.
JAQ, NO, IT WAS THE WEIRN GIRL.
SHE IS THE SAME!!
JAQ, WHAT THE HELL?! CALM DOWN!!
STAY BACK.

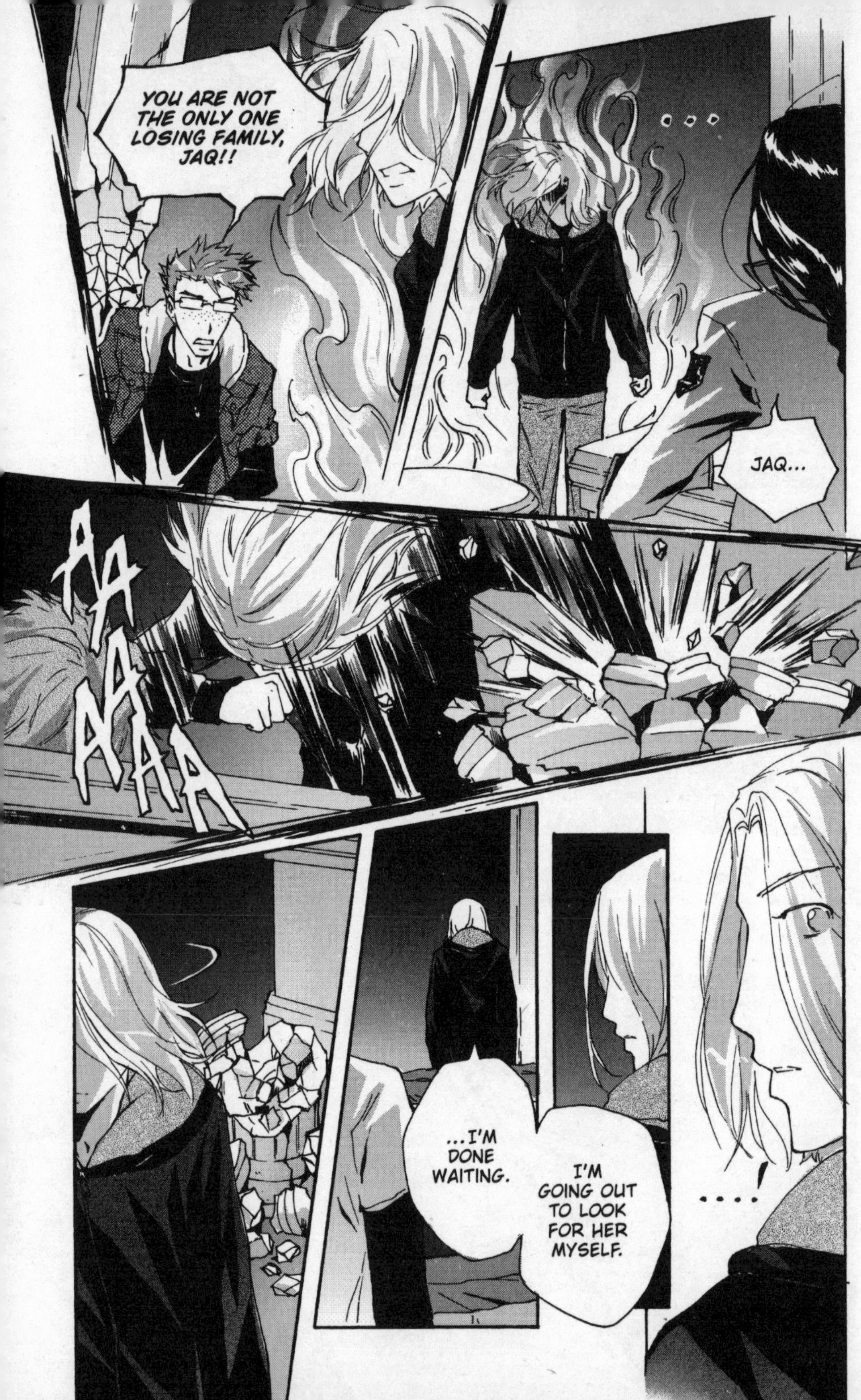
YOU ARE NOT THE ONLY ONE LOSING FAMILY, JAQ!!
...
JAQ...
AAAAAAA
...I'M DONE WAITING.
I'M GOING OUT TO LOOK FOR HER MYSELF.
....!

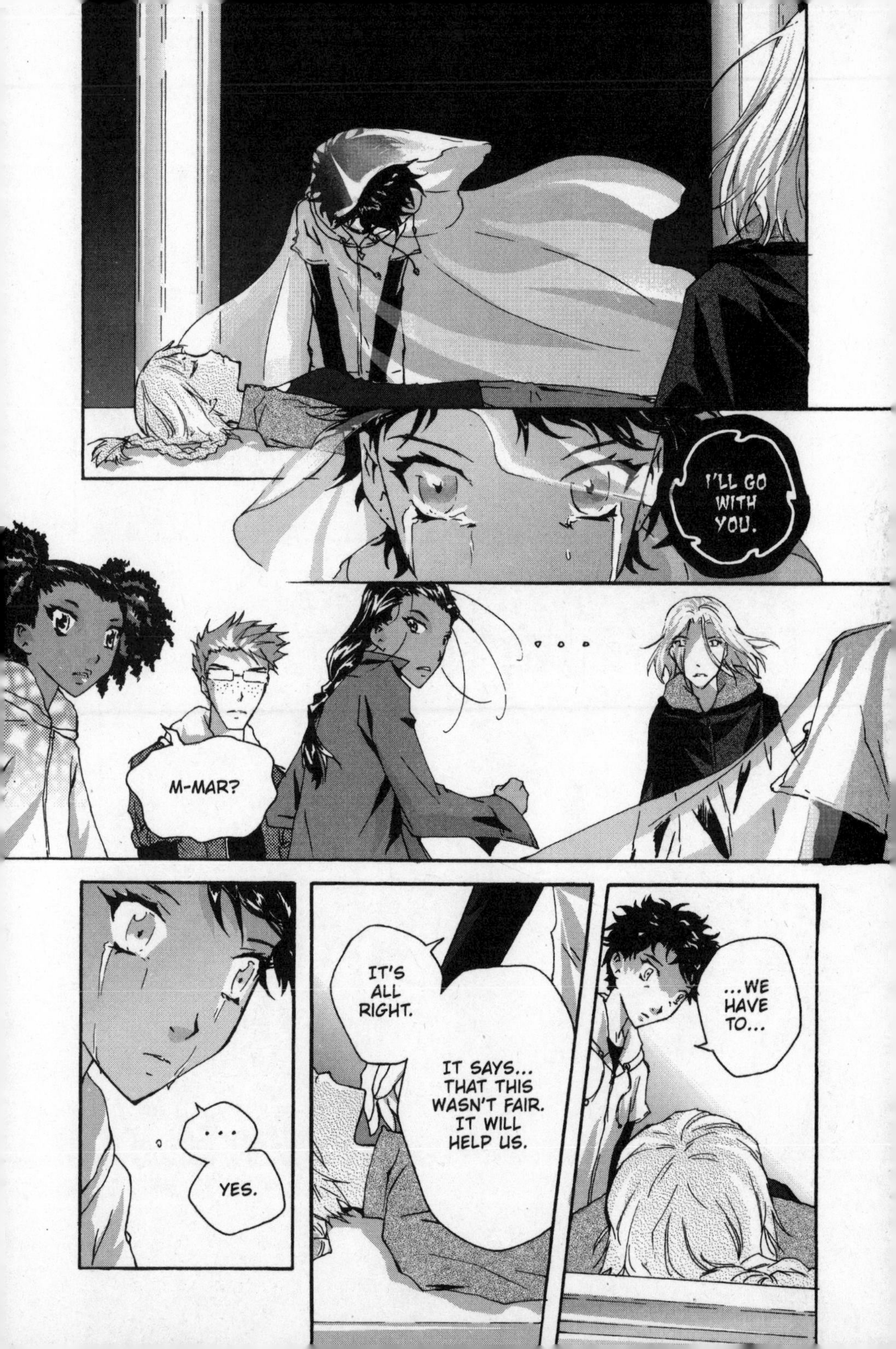
I'LL GO WITH YOU.
M-MAR?
...
...
YES.
IT'S ALL RIGHT.
IT SAYS... THAT THIS WASN'T FAIR. IT WILL HELP US.
...WE HAVE TO...

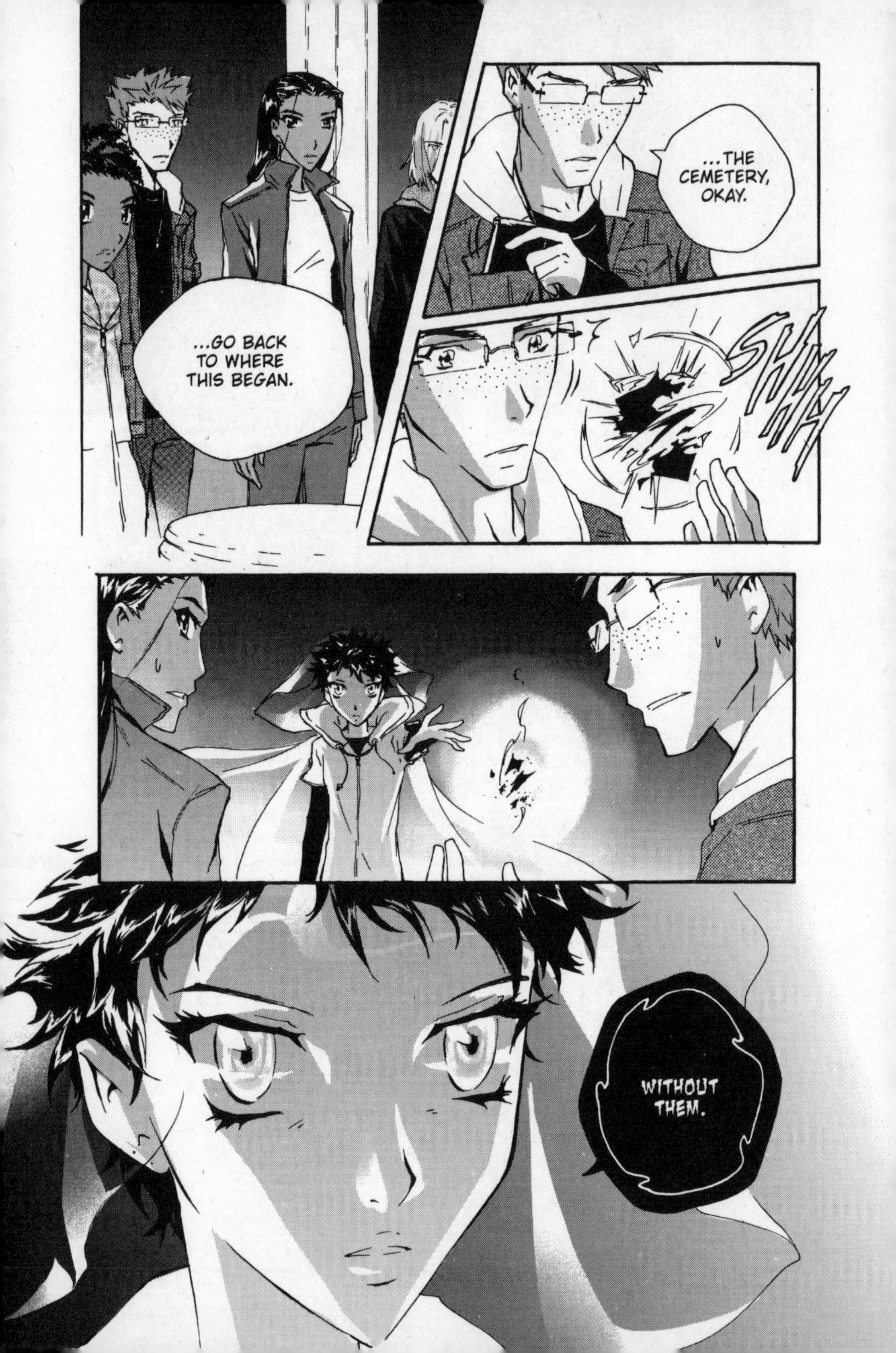
...GO BACK TO WHERE THIS BEGAN.
...THE CEMETERY, OKAY.
SHHH
WITHOUT THEM.

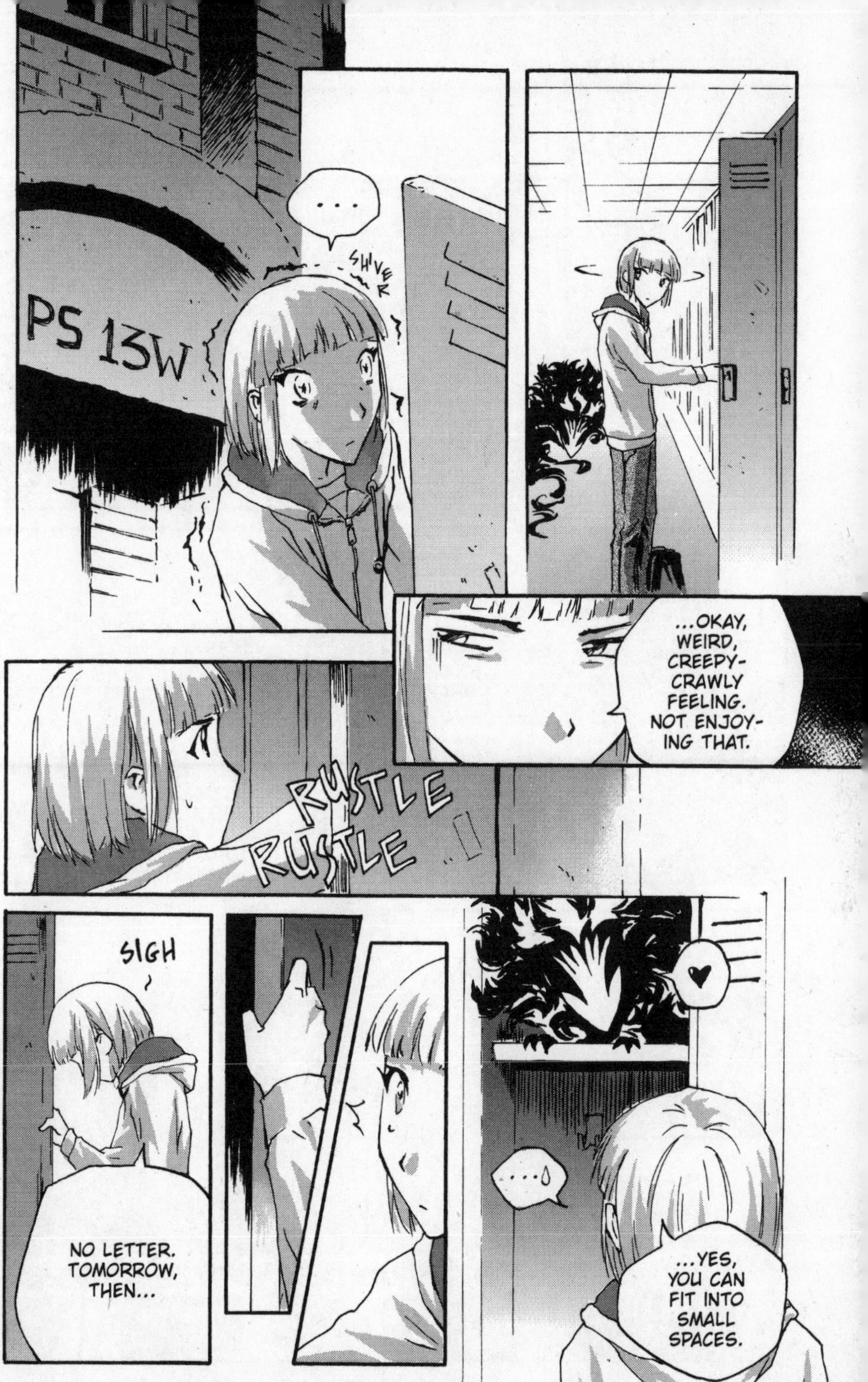
PS 13W
...
SHIVER
...OKAY, WEIRD, CREEPY-CRAWLY FEELING. NOT ENJOYING THAT.
RUSTLE RUSTLE
SIGH
NO LETTER. TOMORROW, THEN...
♥
...
...YES, YOU CAN FIT INTO SMALL SPACES.

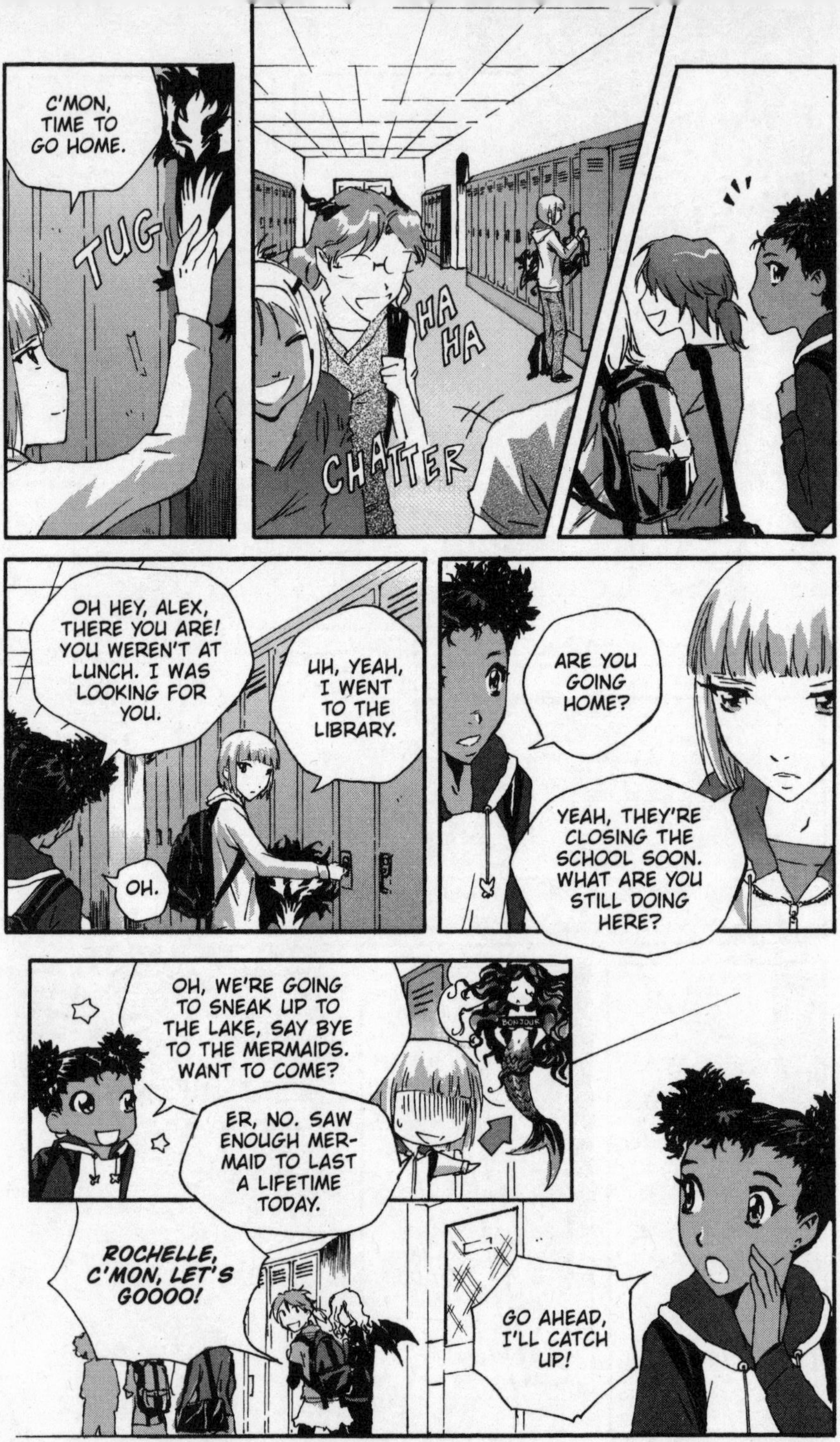
C'MON, TIME TO GO HOME.
TUG
!
HA HA
CHATTER
OH HEY, ALEX, THERE YOU ARE! YOU WEREN'T AT LUNCH. I WAS LOOKING FOR YOU.
UH, YEAH, I WENT TO THE LIBRARY.
OH.
ARE YOU GOING HOME?
YEAH, THEY'RE CLOSING THE SCHOOL SOON. WHAT ARE YOU STILL DOING HERE?
OH, WE'RE GOING TO SNEAK UP TO THE LAKE, SAY BYE TO THE MERMAIDS. WANT TO COME?
BONJOUR
ER, NO. SAW ENOUGH MER-MAID TO LAST A LIFETIME TODAY.
ROCHELLE, C'MON, LET'S GOOOO!
GO AHEAD, I'LL CATCH UP!

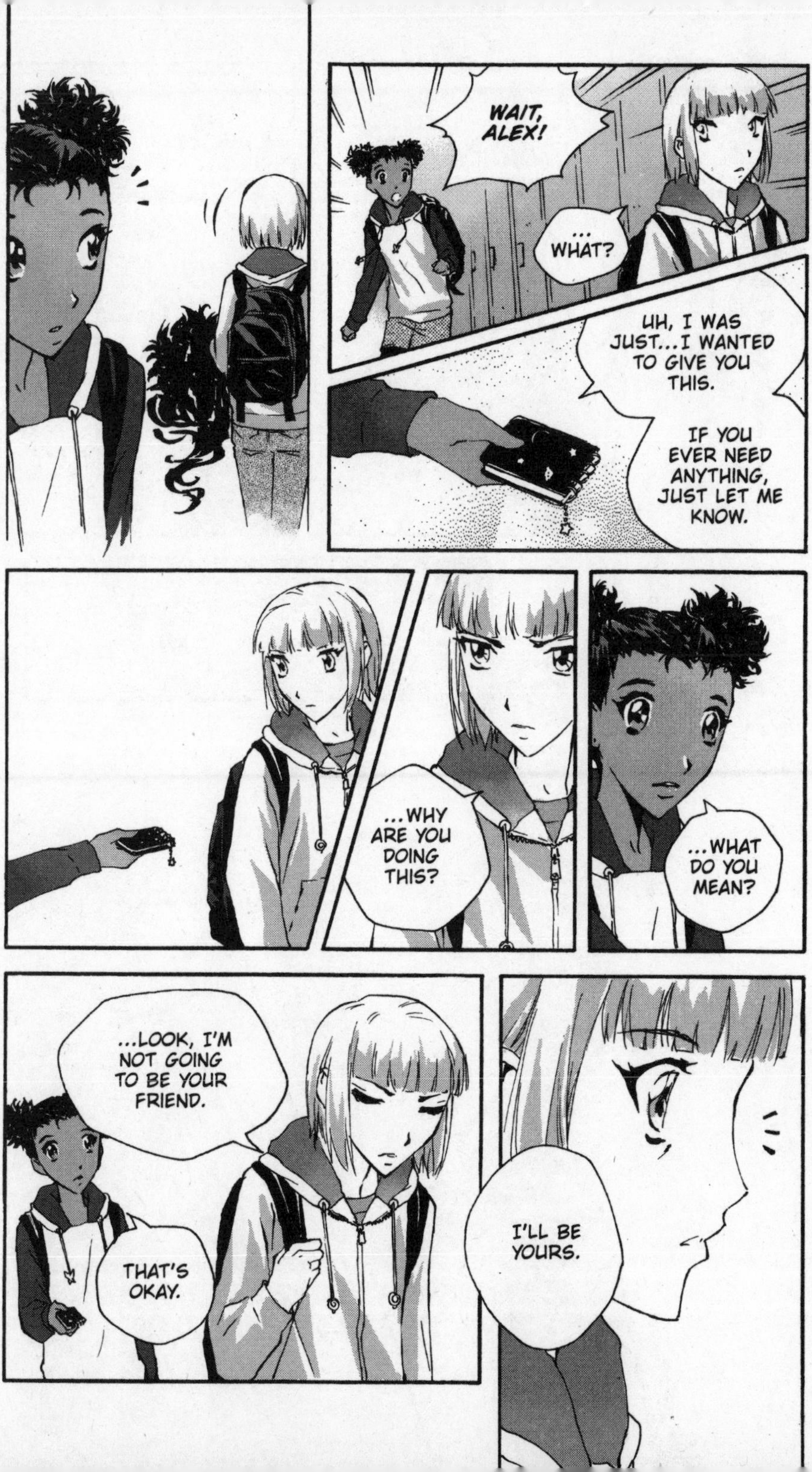
WAIT, ALEX!
...WHAT?
UH, I WAS JUST...I WANTED TO GIVE YOU THIS.
IF YOU EVER NEED ANYTHING, JUST LET ME KNOW.
...WHY ARE YOU DOING THIS?
...WHAT DO YOU MEAN?
...LOOK, I'M NOT GOING TO BE YOUR FRIEND.
THAT'S OKAY.
I'LL BE YOURS.

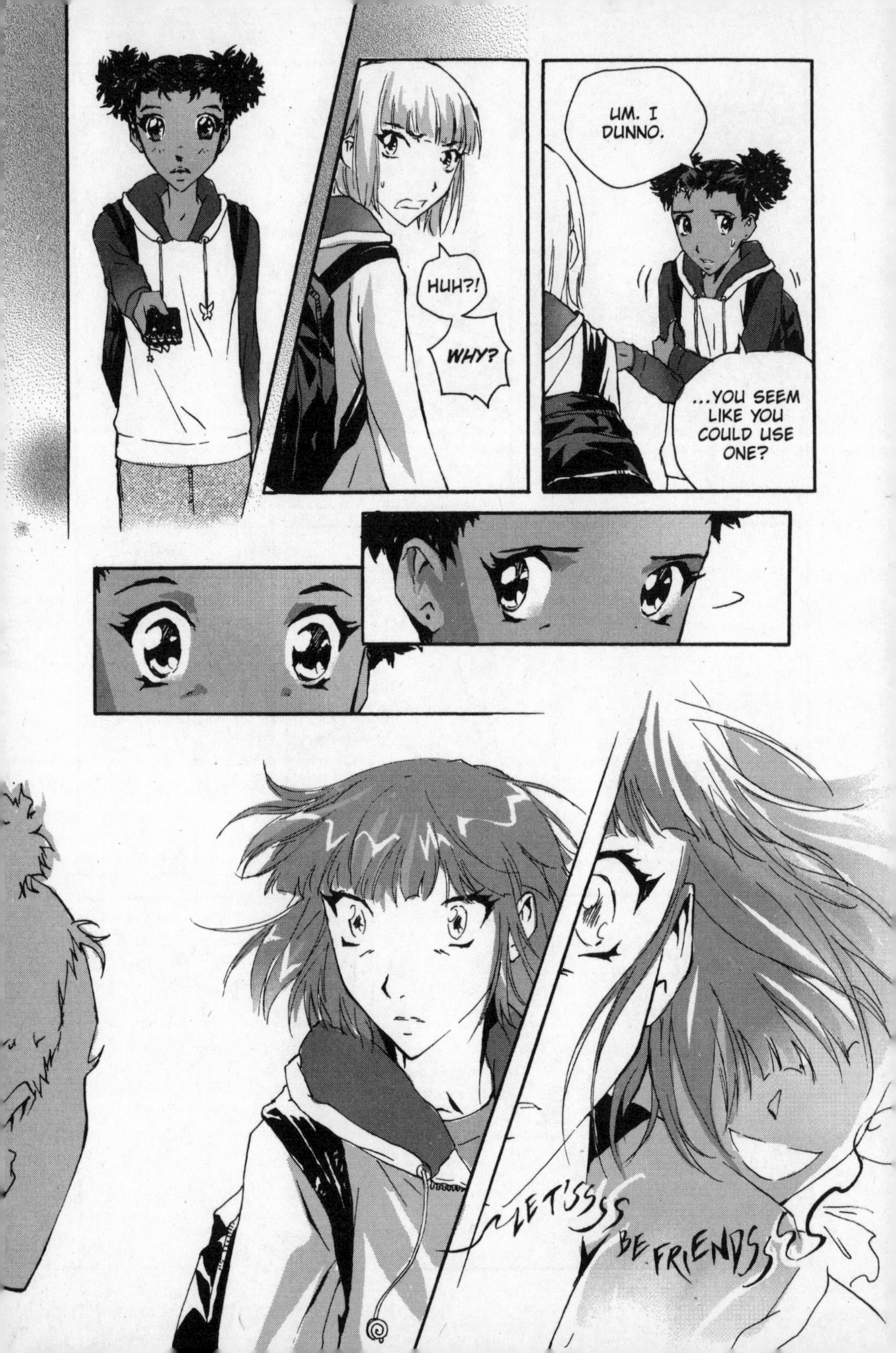
HUH?!
WHY?
UM. I DUNNO.
...YOU SEEM LIKE YOU COULD USE ONE?
LET'SSSS BE FRIENDSSSS

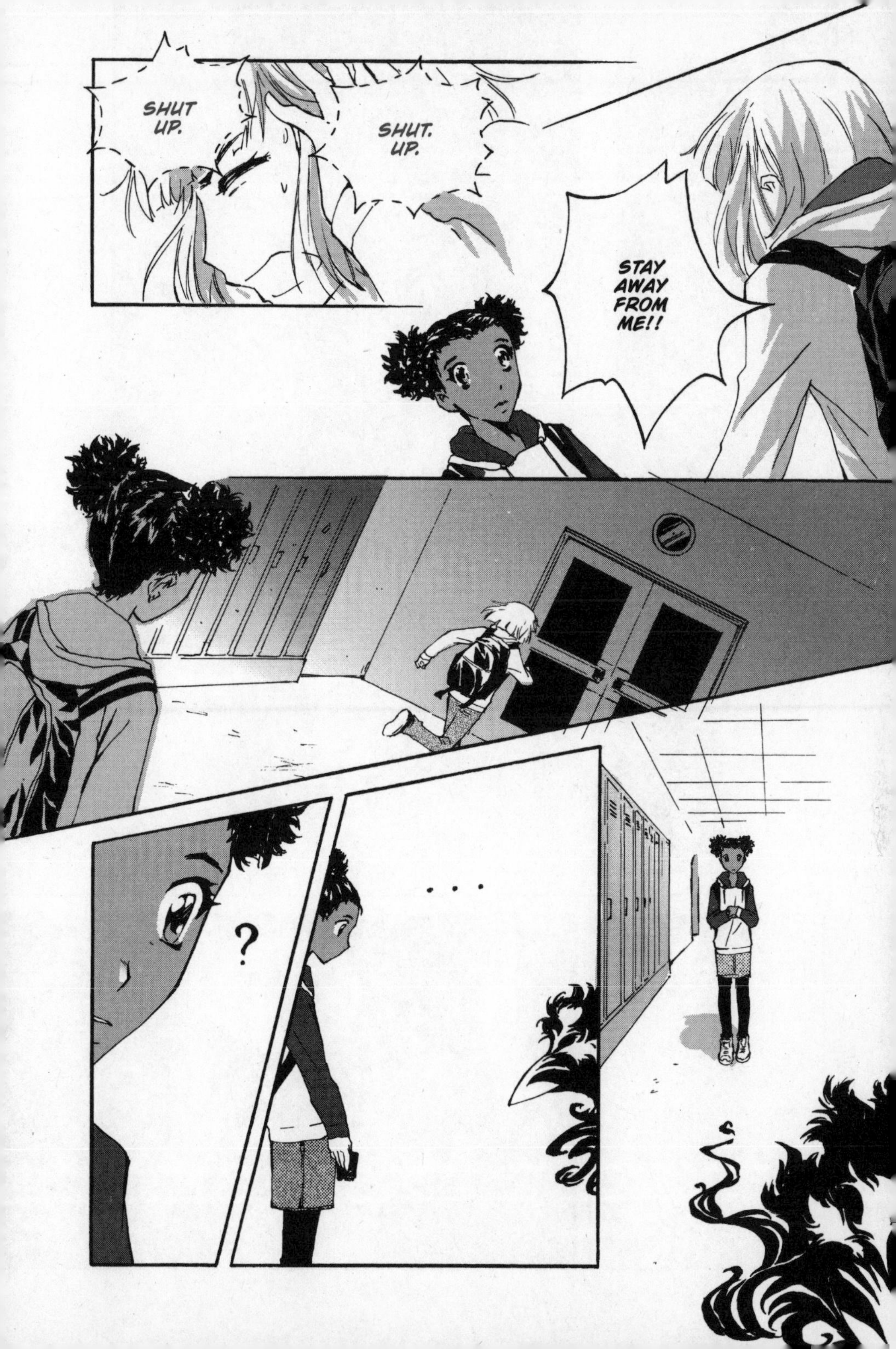
SHUT UP.
SHUT. UP.
STAY AWAY FROM ME!!
?
. . .

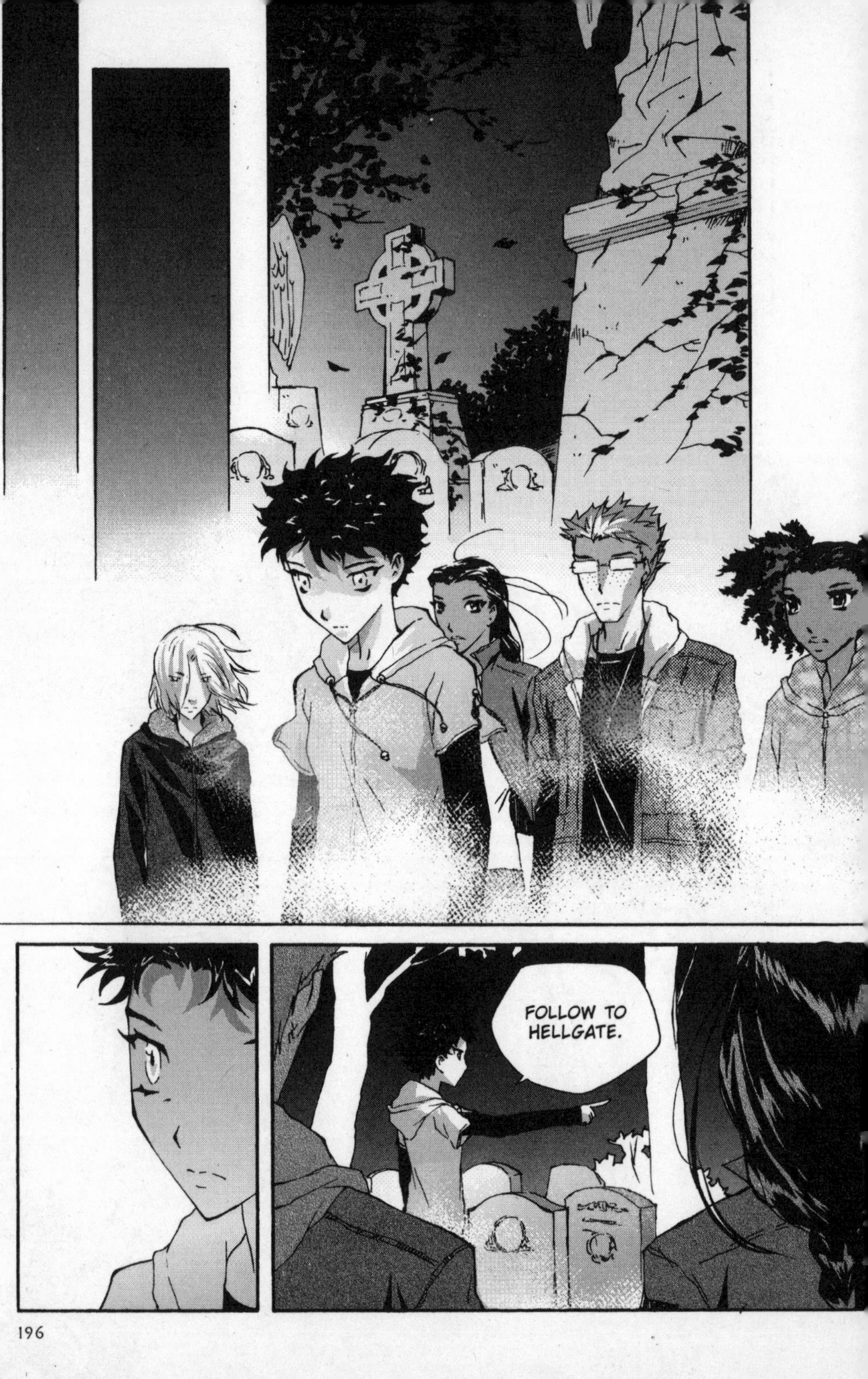
FOLLOW TO
HELLGATE.

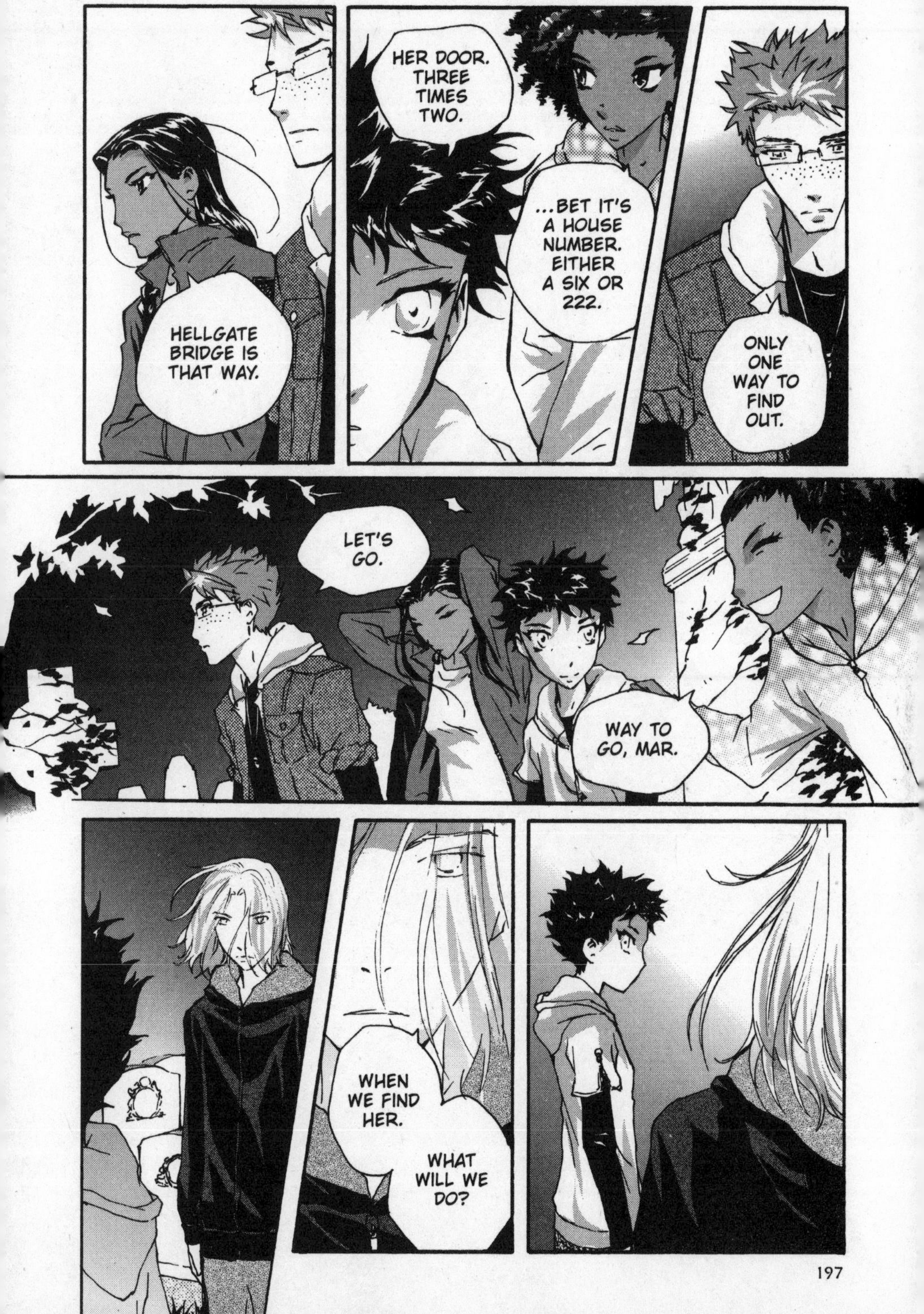
HELLGATE BRIDGE IS THAT WAY.
HER DOOR. THREE TIMES TWO.
...BET IT'S A HOUSE NUMBER. EITHER A SIX OR 222.
ONLY ONE WAY TO FIND OUT.
LET'S GO.
WAY TO GO, MAR.
WHEN WE FIND HER.
WHAT WILL WE DO?

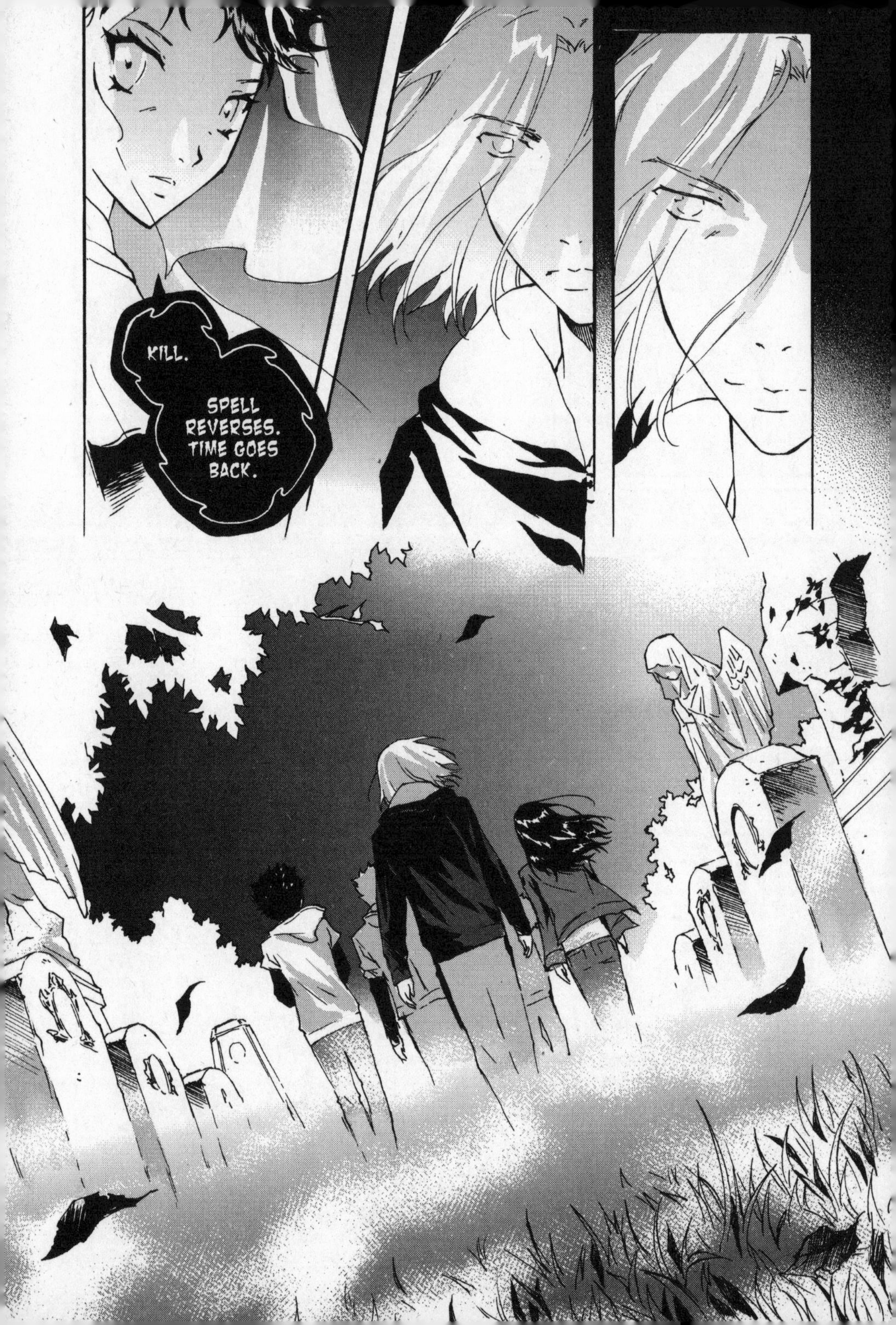
KILL.
SPELL REVERSES. TIME GOES BACK.

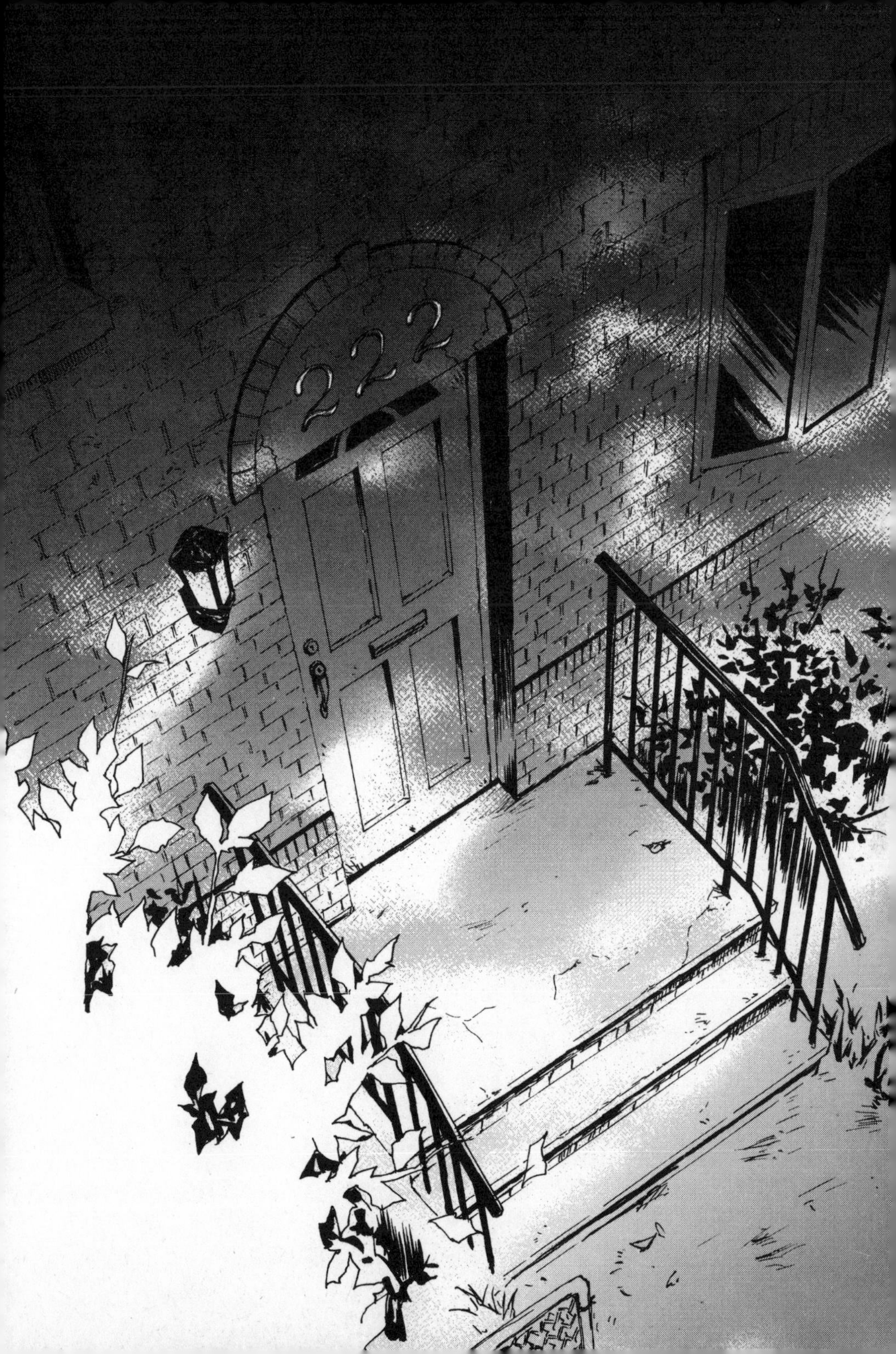
222

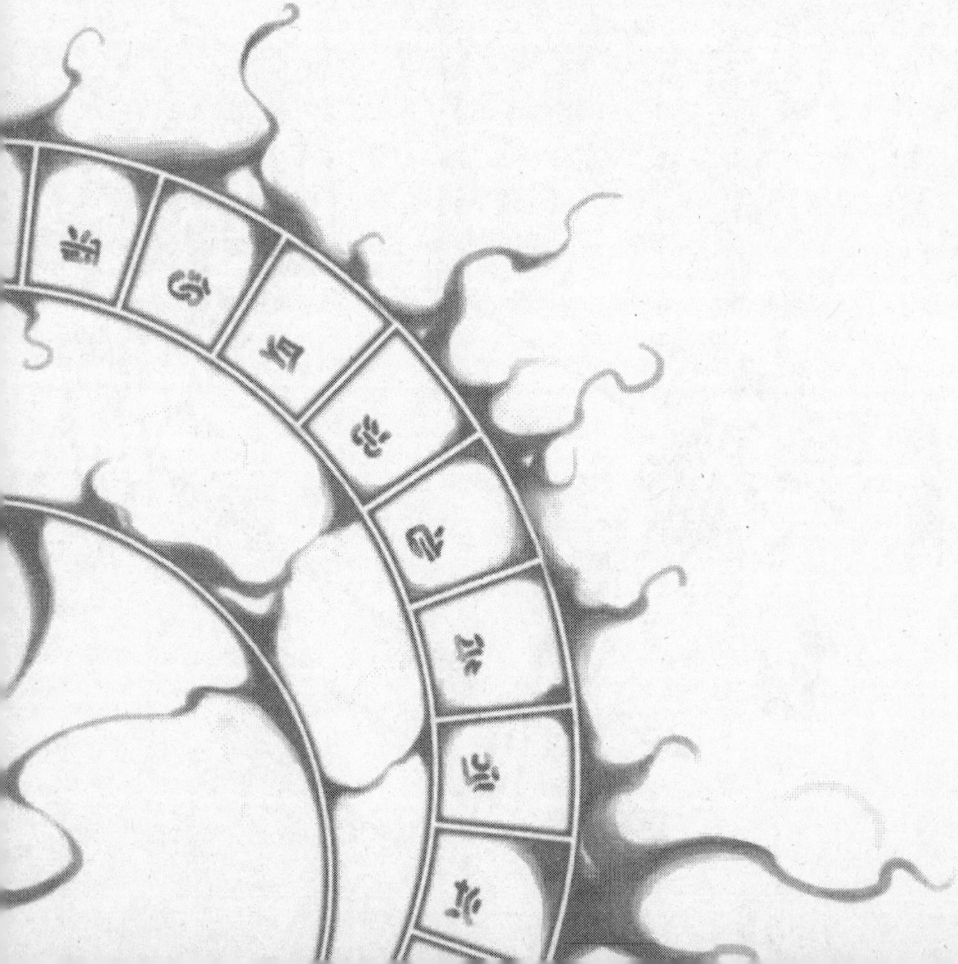

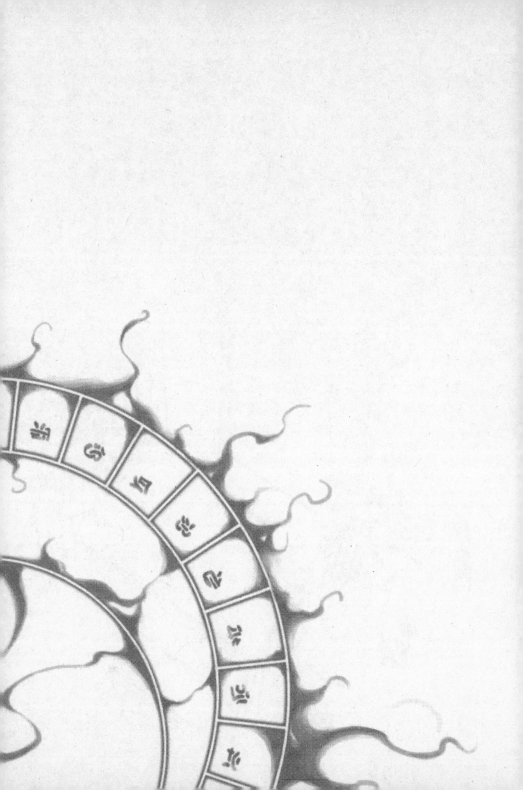

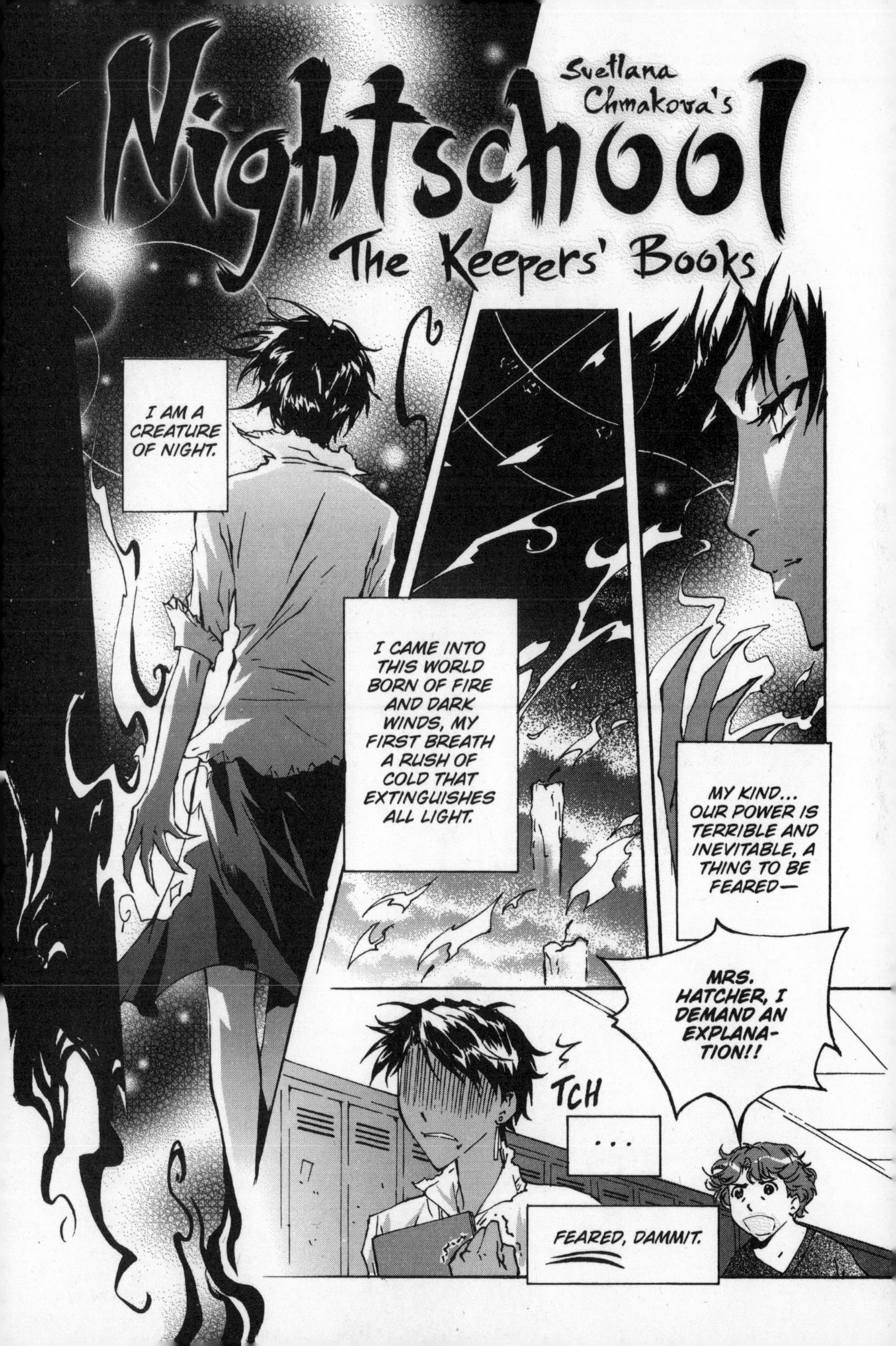
Svetlana Chmakova's
Nightschool
The Keepers' Books
I AM A CREATURE OF NIGHT.
I CAME INTO THIS WORLD BORN OF FIRE AND DARK WINDS, MY FIRST BREATH A RUSH OF COLD THAT EXTINGUISHES ALL LIGHT.
MY KIND... OUR POWER IS TERRIBLE AND INEVITABLE, A THING TO BE FEARED—
MRS. HATCHER, I DEMAND AN EXPLANA-TION!!
TCH
...
FEARED, DAMMIT.

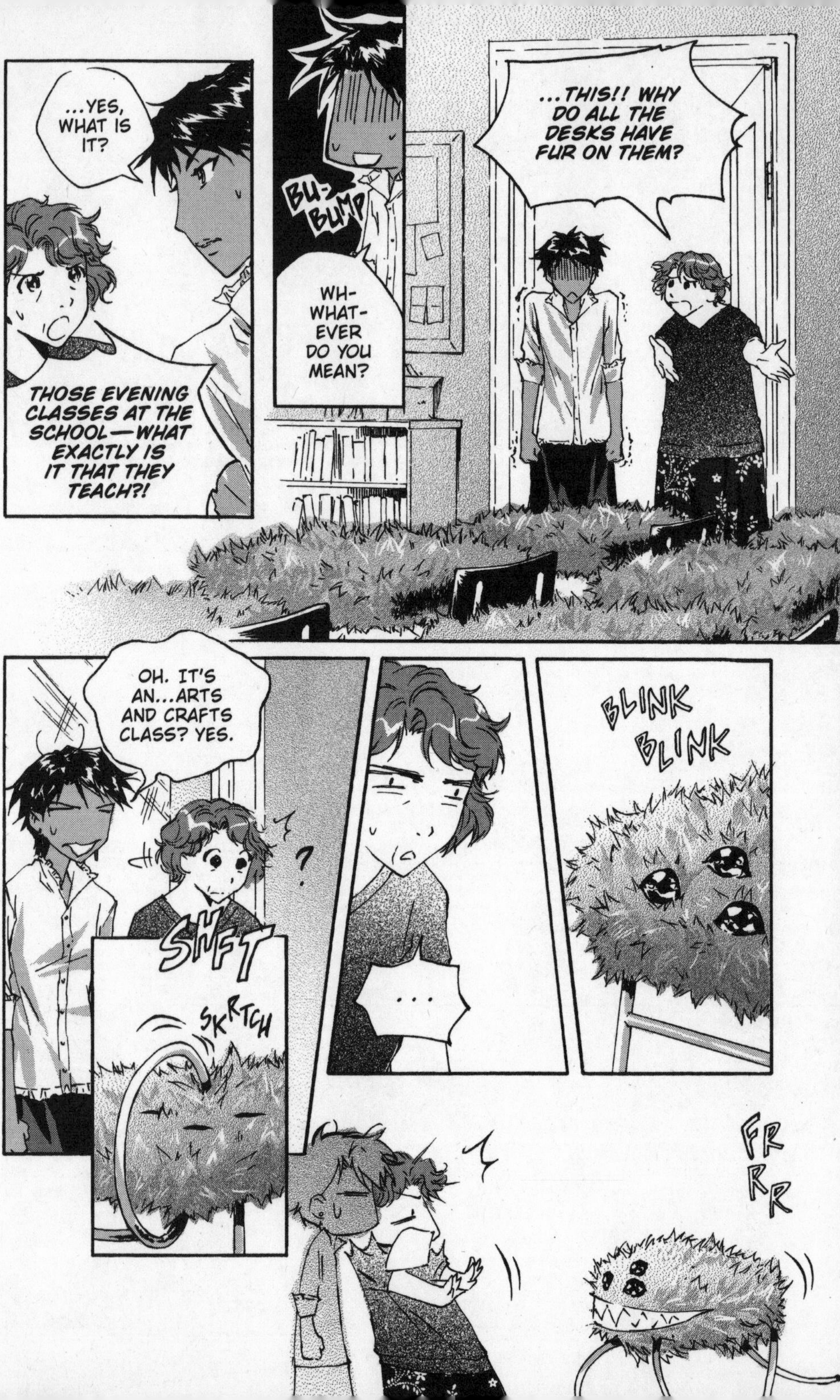
...YES, WHAT IS IT?
THOSE EVENING CLASSES AT THE SCHOOL—WHAT EXACTLY IS IT THAT THEY TEACH?!
BU-BUMP
WH-WHAT-EVER DO YOU MEAN?
...THIS!! WHY DO ALL THE DESKS HAVE FUR ON THEM?
OH. IT'S AN...ARTS AND CRAFTS CLASS? YES.
?
SHFT
SKRTCH
...
BLINK BLINK
FRRR

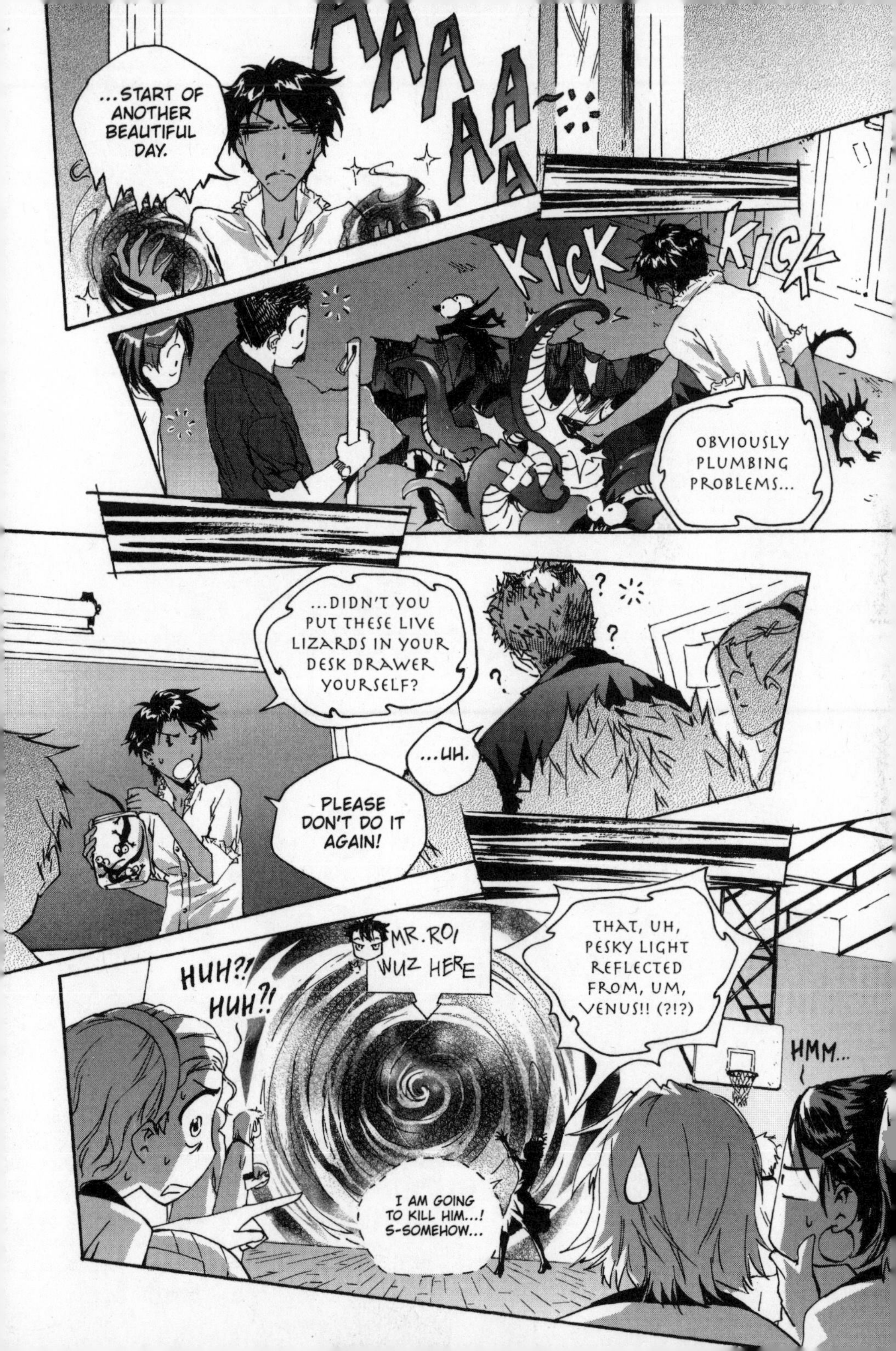
...START OF ANOTHER BEAUTIFUL DAY.
AAAAAAA~
KICK
KICK
OBVIOUSLY PLUMBING PROBLEMS...
...DIDN'T YOU PUT THESE LIVE LIZARDS IN YOUR DESK DRAWER YOURSELF?
...UH.
PLEASE DON'T DO IT AGAIN!
HUH?!
HUH?!
MR. ROI WUZ HERE
THAT, UH, PESKY LIGHT REFLECTED FROM, UM, VENUS!! (?!?)
HMM...
I AM GOING TO KILL HIM...! S-SOMEHOW...

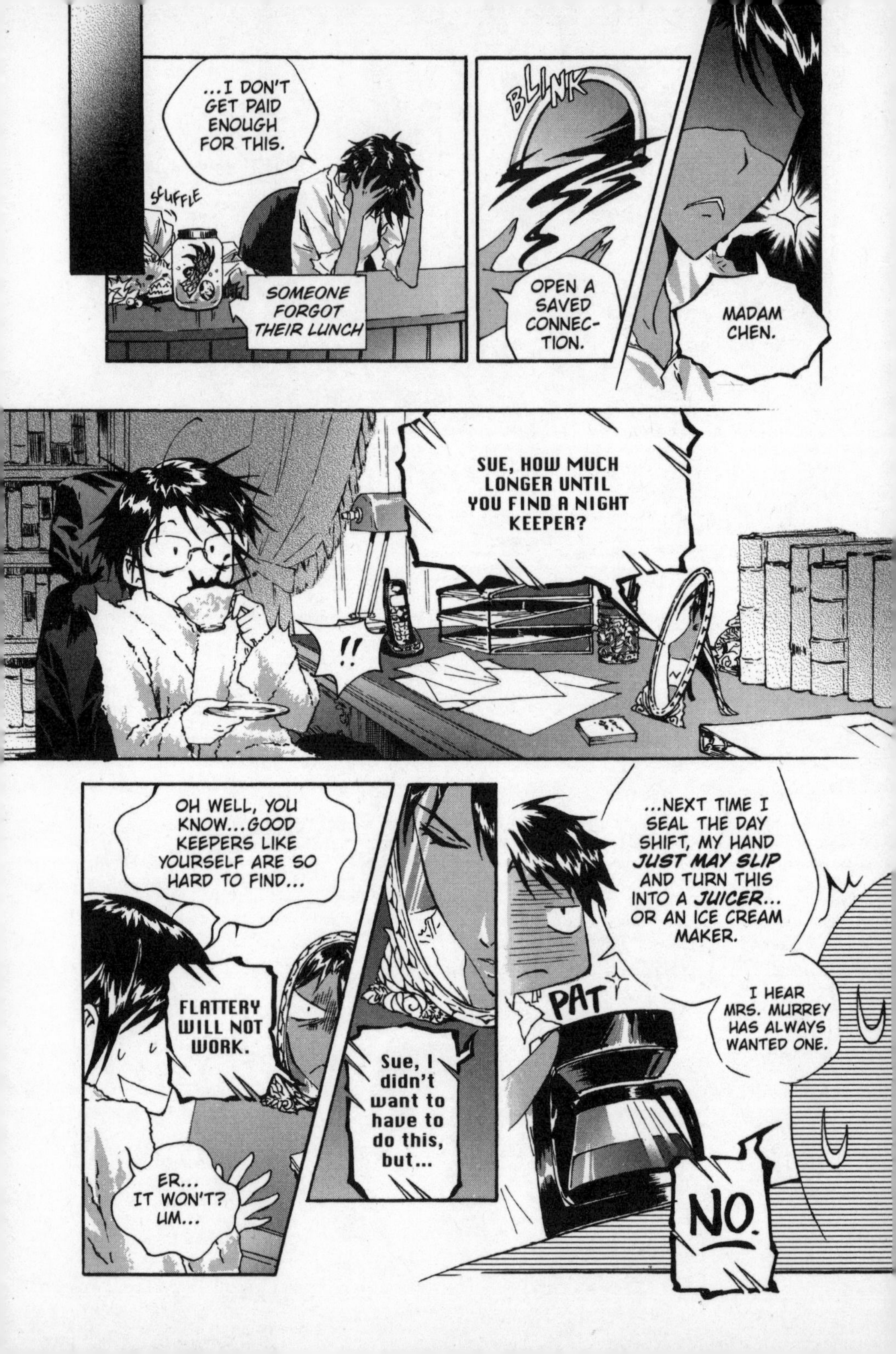

...I DON'T GET PAID ENOUGH FOR THIS.
SCUFFLE
SOMEONE FORGOT THEIR LUNCH
BLINK
OPEN A SAVED CONNEC- TION.
MADAM CHEN.
SUE, HOW MUCH LONGER UNTIL YOU FIND A NIGHT KEEPER?
!!
OH WELL, YOU KNOW...GOOD KEEPERS LIKE YOURSELF ARE SO HARD TO FIND...
FLATTERY WILL NOT WORK.
ER... IT WON'T? UM...
Sue, I didn't want to have to do this, but...
...NEXT TIME I SEAL THE DAY SHIFT, MY HAND JUST MAY SLIP AND TURN THIS INTO A JUICER... OR AN ICE CREAM MAKER.
PAT
I HEAR MRS. MURREY HAS ALWAYS WANTED ONE.
NO.

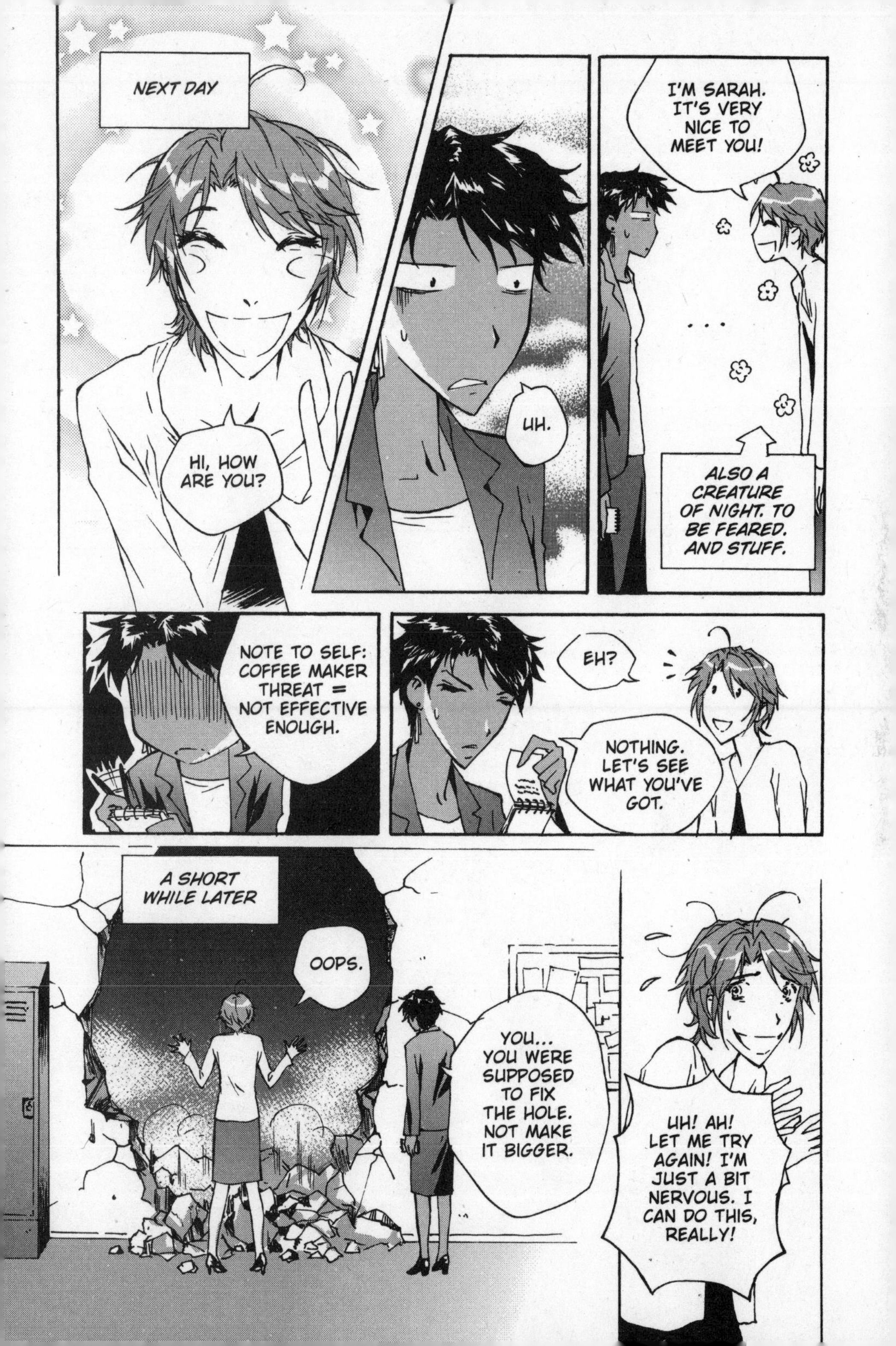
NEXT DAY
HI, HOW ARE YOU?
UH.
I'M SARAH. IT'S VERY NICE TO MEET YOU!
...
ALSO A CREATURE OF NIGHT. TO BE FEARED. AND STUFF.
NOTE TO SELF: COFFEE MAKER THREAT = NOT EFFECTIVE ENOUGH.
EH?
NOTHING. LET'S SEE WHAT YOU'VE GOT.
A SHORT WHILE LATER
OOPS.
YOU... YOU WERE SUPPOSED TO FIX THE HOLE. NOT MAKE IT BIGGER.
UH! AH! LET ME TRY AGAIN! I'M JUST A BIT NERVOUS. I CAN DO THIS, REALLY!

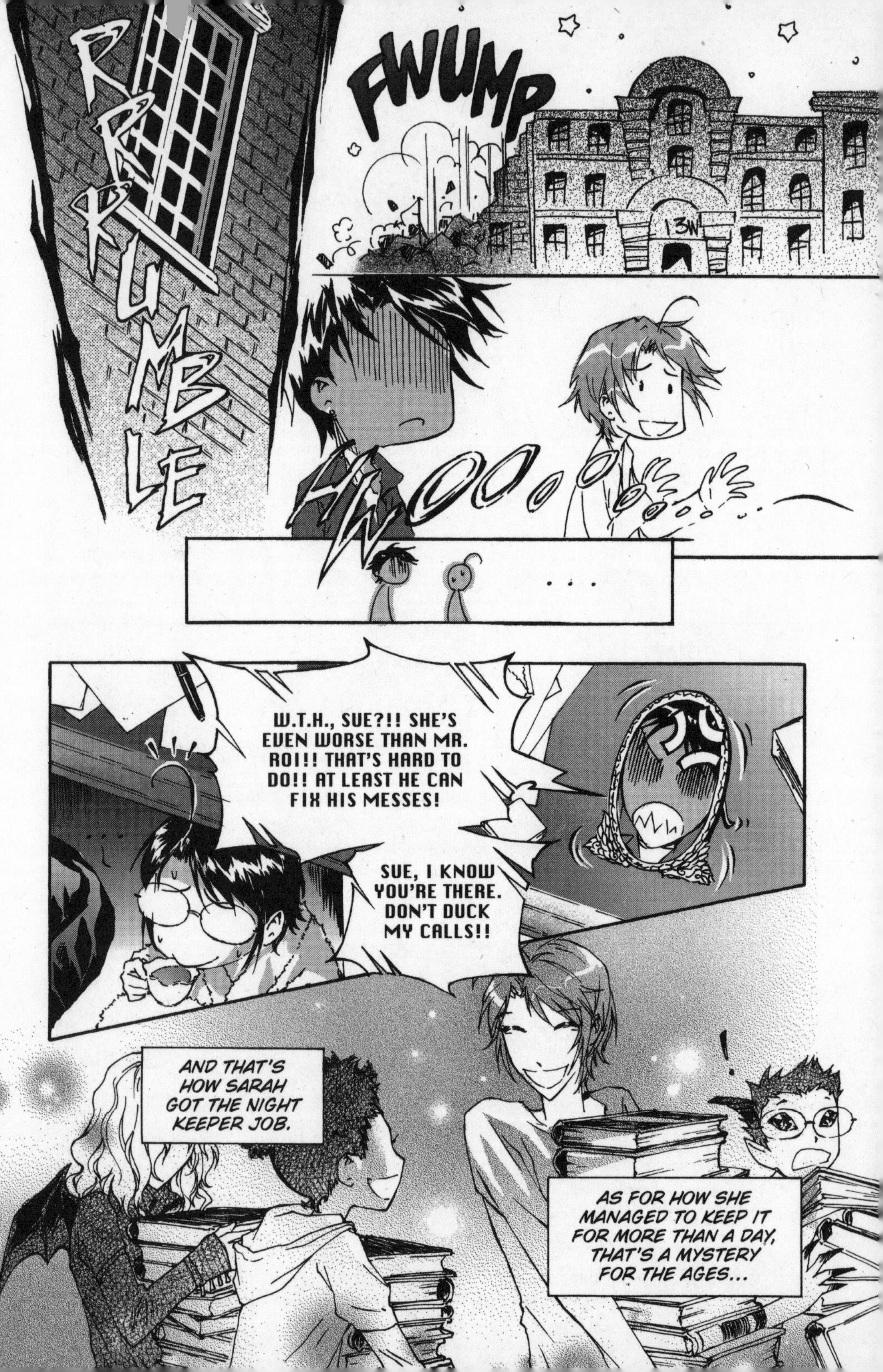
RRRRUMBLE
FWUMP
HWOOOOooo
...
W.T.H., SUE?!! SHE'S EVEN WORSE THAN MR. ROI!! THAT'S HARD TO DO!! AT LEAST HE CAN FIX HIS MESSES!
SUE, I KNOW YOU'RE THERE. DON'T DUCK MY CALLS!!
AND THAT'S HOW SARAH GOT THE NIGHT KEEPER JOB.
!
AS FOR HOW SHE MANAGED TO KEEP IT FOR MORE THAN A DAY, THAT'S A MYSTERY FOR THE AGES...

BONUS

NEXT VOLUME! ANSWERS! AND ALL THE BIG SHOWDOWNS AND BATTLES! ***SO EXCITED***. AS FOR LIFE UPDATES, WELL, NOT MUCH HAS HAPPENED SINCE THE LAST VOLUME (HALF A YEAR AGO), BUT HERE ARE A FEW HIGHLIGHTS:

I ACCIDENTALLY KILLED TWO PLANTS IN MY STUDIO.

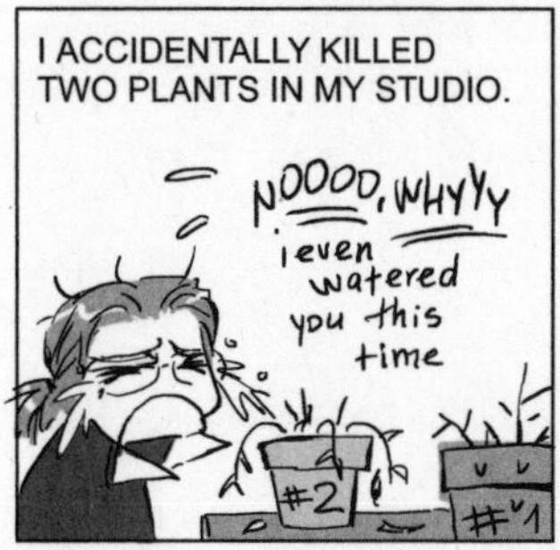

NOOOO, WHYYY
i even watered you this time
#2
#1

LEARNED TO MAKE CREAM OF BROCCOLI SOUP.

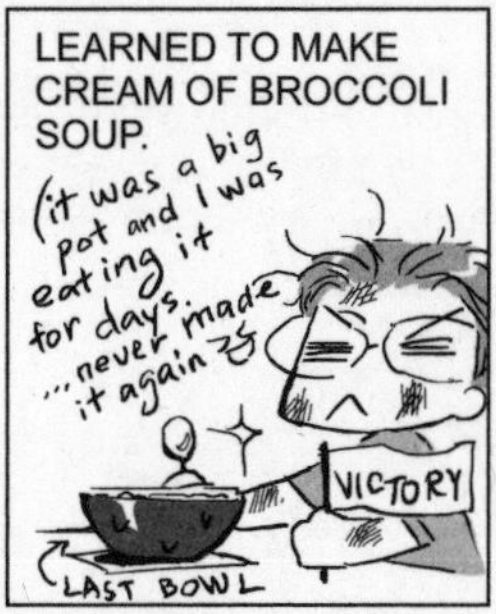

(it was a big pot and I was eating it for days. ...never made it again
VICTORY
LAST BOWL

WENT TO JAPAN AND LEARNED HOW TO SAY 'W.T.H.' IN JAPANESE WITH A KANSAI ACCENT.

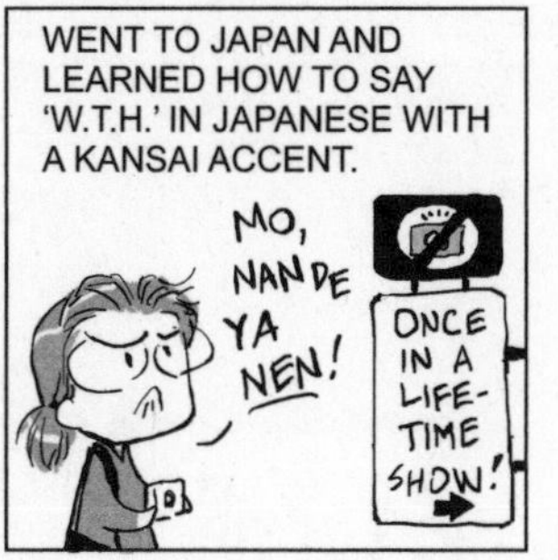

MO, NANDE YA NEN!
ONCE IN A LIFE-TIME SHOW!

...BTW, ON THE TOPIC OF SAYING THINGS IN DIFFERENT LANGUAGES!! I COMPLETELY FORGOT TO INCLUDE THE TRANSLATIONS OF THE NON-ENGLISH PHRASES FROM VOLUME 2!! SO IF YOU WONDERED, HERE THEY ARE NOW:

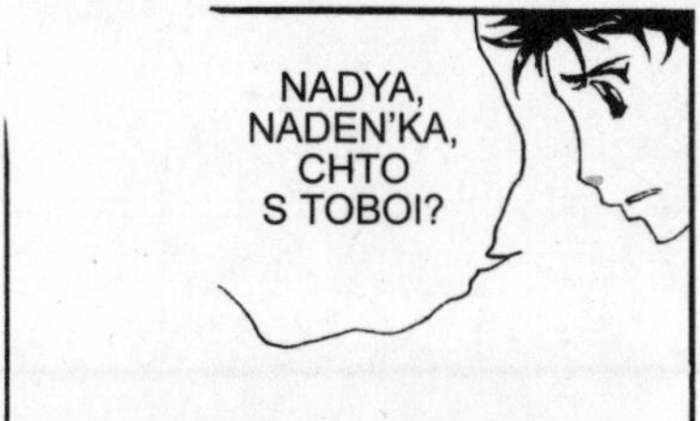

NADYA, NADEN'KA, CHTO S TOBOI?

Noh's real name is Nadezhda, or Nadya for short. "Naden'ka" is another form of the same, but with extra affection. What Marina is asking translates to, "What's with you?" meaning, "What's wrong?"

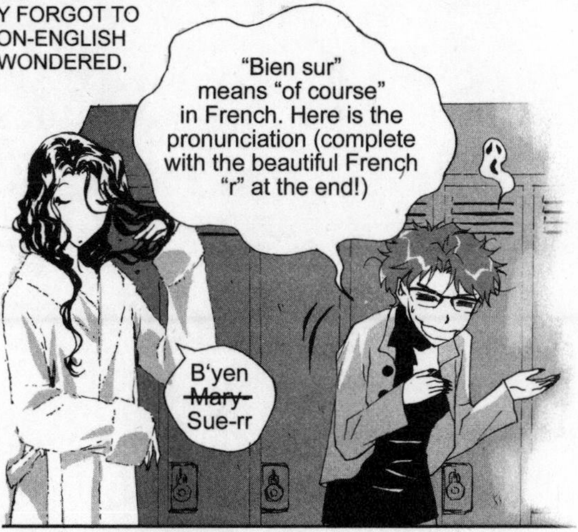

"Bien sur" means "of course" in French. Here is the pronunciation (complete with the beautiful French "r" at the end!)
B'yen ~~Mary~~ Sue-rr

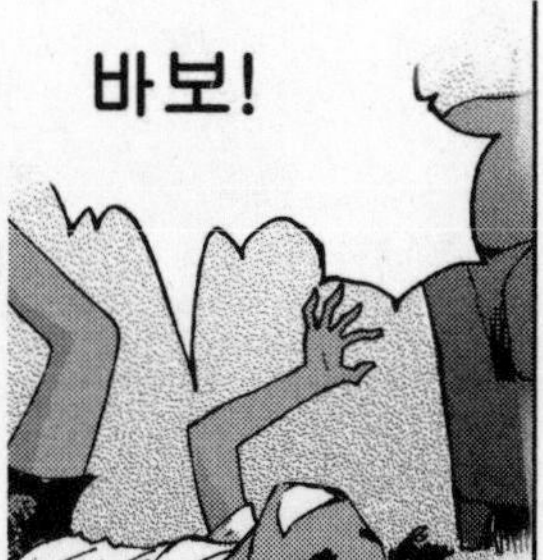

바보!

What Ten has to say about Marina criticizing her choice of studying material...is a Korean word similar to "jerk" or "idiot," though much milder in meaning. This can be jokingly said to a friend and is pronounced "babo"!

The translation of Ten's homework:
1: Die! (Ju-goh-rah)
2: Unbelievable... (Mael-toh-an-dwea)
3. How can that be? (O-doh-ke Ee-run-il-ee)

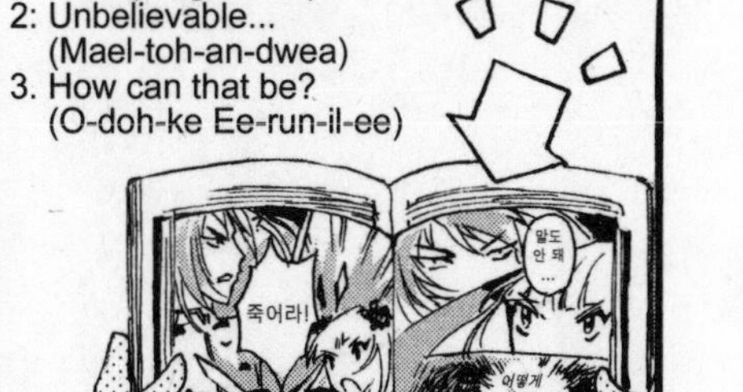

말도 안 돼 ...
죽어라!
어떻게 이런 일이...

HOPE THIS HELPS!! BIG THANKS TO TANIA BISWAS FOR HELP WITH THE FRENCH AND TO JUYOUN FOR PROVIDING MY NONEXISTENT KOREAN! :D

FANART!

We've received some truly wonderful fan art for the Fan Art contest again, thanks, you guys!!! I am so glad I'm not the one judging these things – I'd never be able to choose! XD The following pages are the entries that our hardworking judges have picked as winners. Please enjoy!

And what's this, below?! That's...

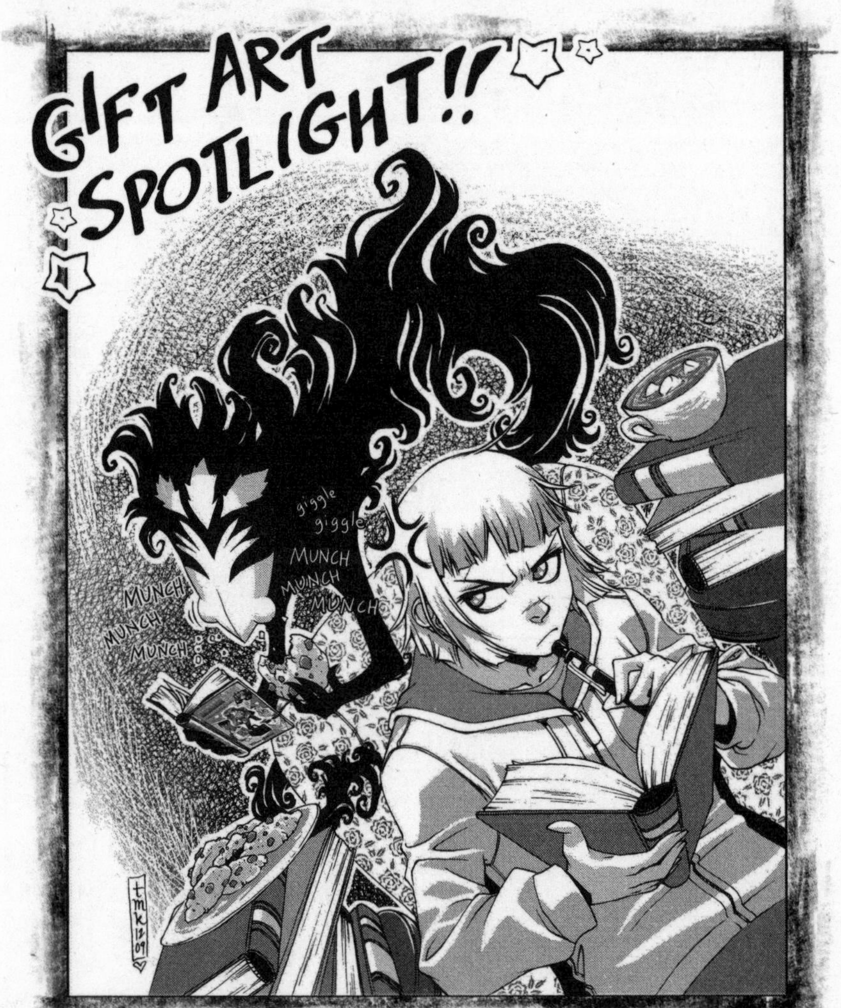
GIFT ART SPOTLIGHT!!
giggle giggle
MUNCH MUNCH MUNCH
MUNCH MUNCH MUNCH
tmk 12/09

by ***Bettina M. Kurkoski*** !
Bettina is a fellow OEL manga author (or whatever it is we're called these days!). Please see more of her awesome stuff here:
www.dreamworldstudio.net

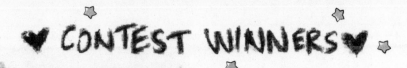

♥ CONTEST WINNERS ♥

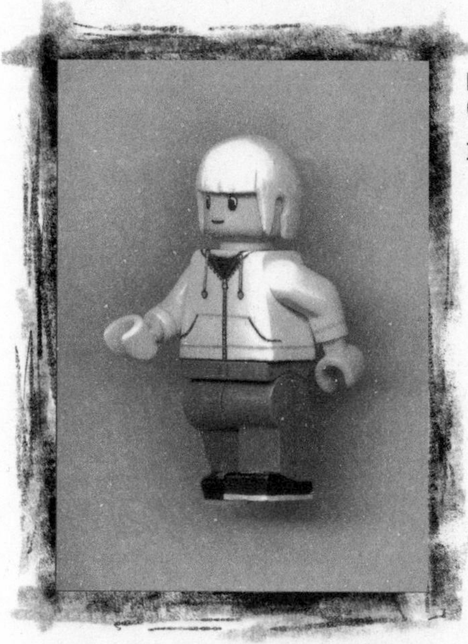

by ***Norbert Black***
(Tiny Lego Alex!! Shown almost at
ACTUAL SIZE!!
Incredible with all the painted details.)

by ***Amanda S. Kaufman***
Astral cuddle plushie, aw!
Note her cute little paaaws! X3

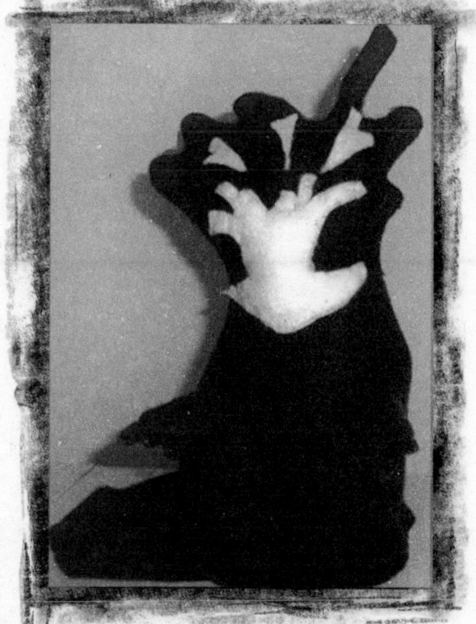

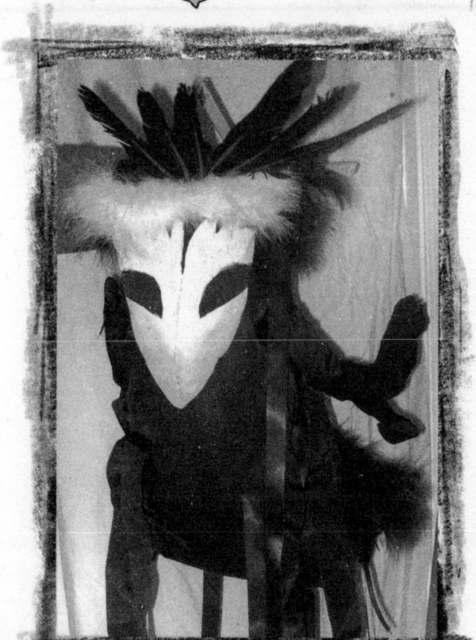

by ***Brittany Lawson***
Wonderful Astral marionette!
(And look, she's waving – hi, Astral!! :D)

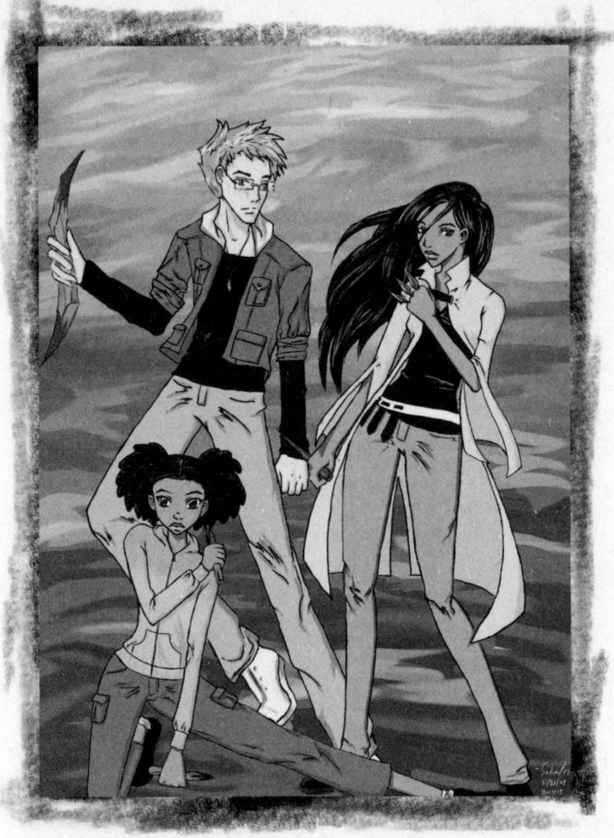

by ***Sadia Bies***
This would make a great cover for *Hunters Monthly*, woo!!
Rippers everywhere beware!!
(...Hey, that kind of rhymed :D /easily amused)

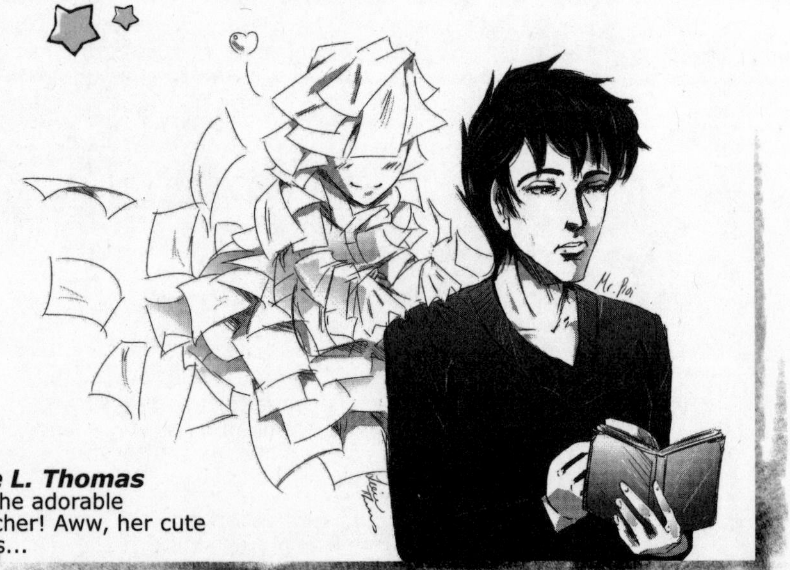

by ***Laurie L. Thomas***
Attack of the adorable book snatcher! Aww, her cute little hands...

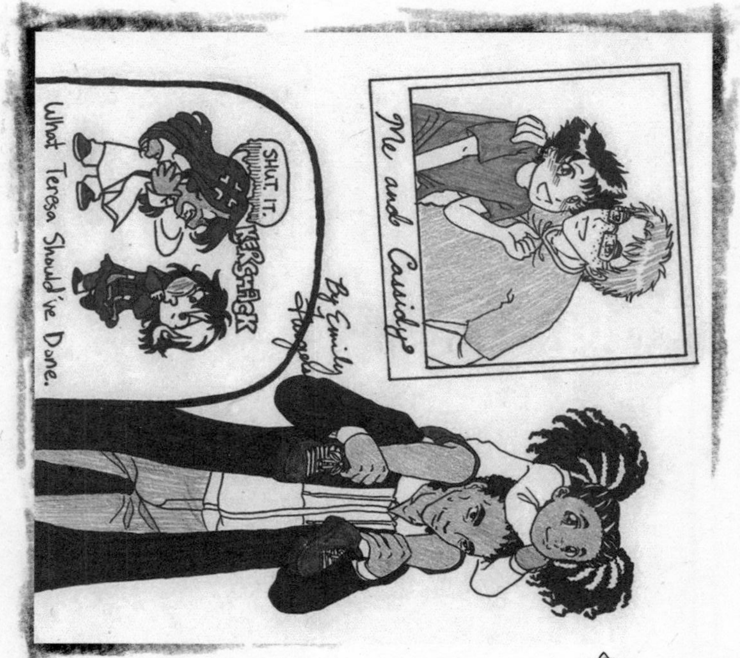
Me and Cassidy
By Emily
SHUT. IT.
What Teresa Should've Done.

by ***Emily J. Furgerson***
(When the camera isn't rolling... Hee-hee!
My favorite is the Ten and Daemon shot, so sweet ^___^)

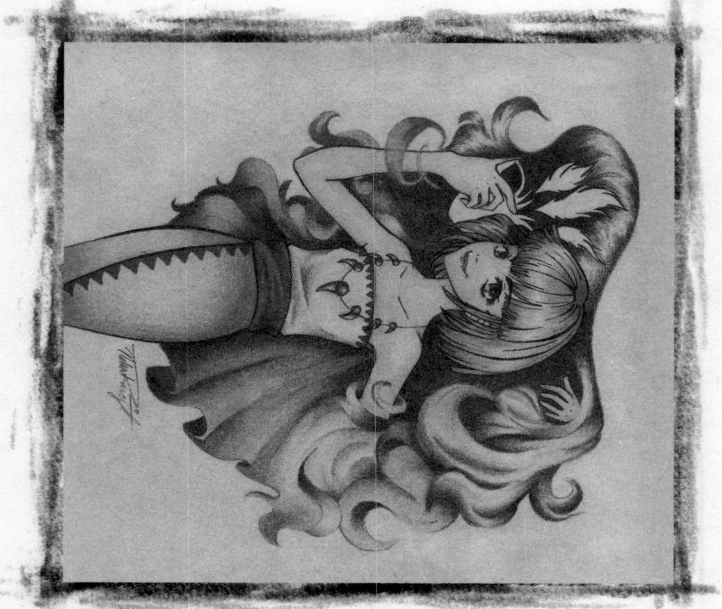

by ***Neha Ranjit***
(The colors of the original submission are very vibrant; it's too bad we couldn't keep them. :(But still, very beautiful!)

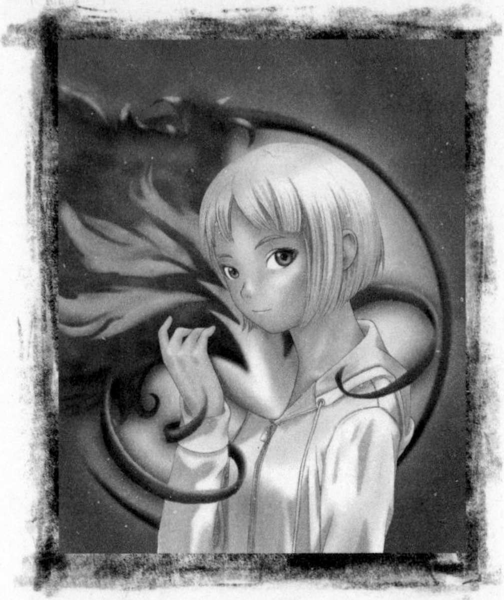

by ***Tim Ferreira***
(Another beautiful color picture!
It has a light purple tone
in the original.)

by ***Jordan Serra***
(Ha-ha, Astral is sneaking
cookies again! <3)

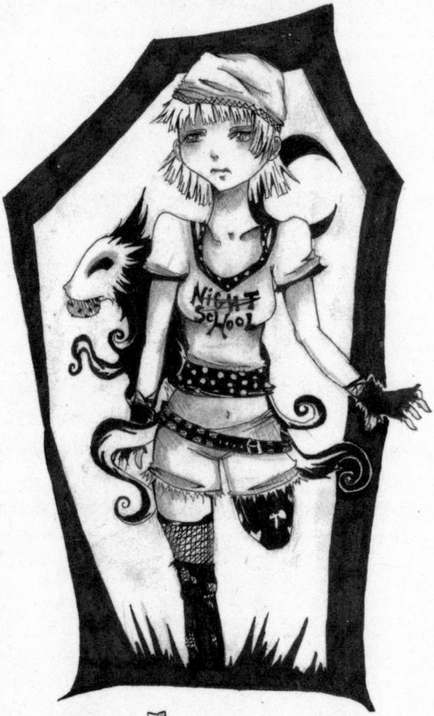
NIGHT SCHOOL

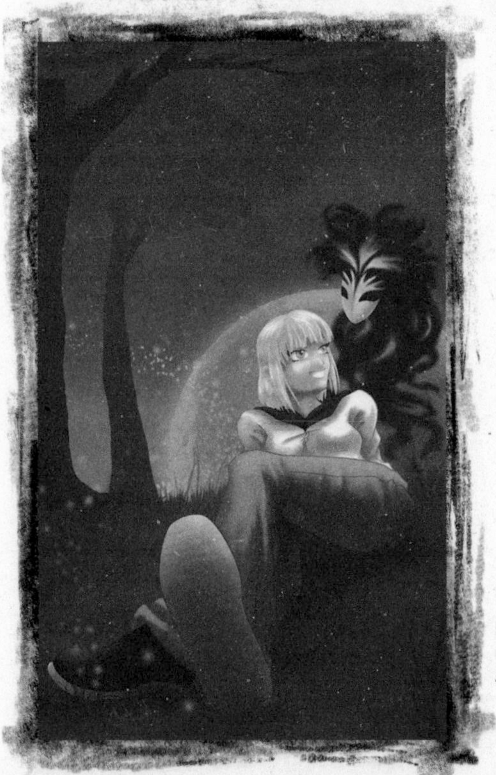

by ***Christine Harcinske***
(Also color! I weep for losing it!
A very lovely night magic feel here~)

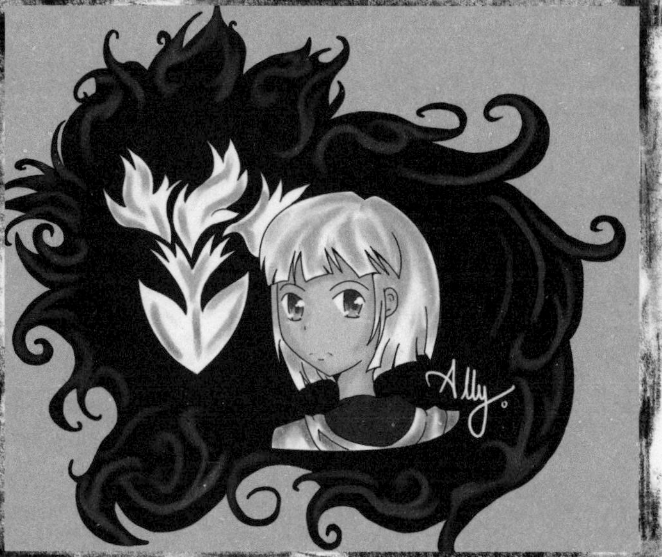
Ally.

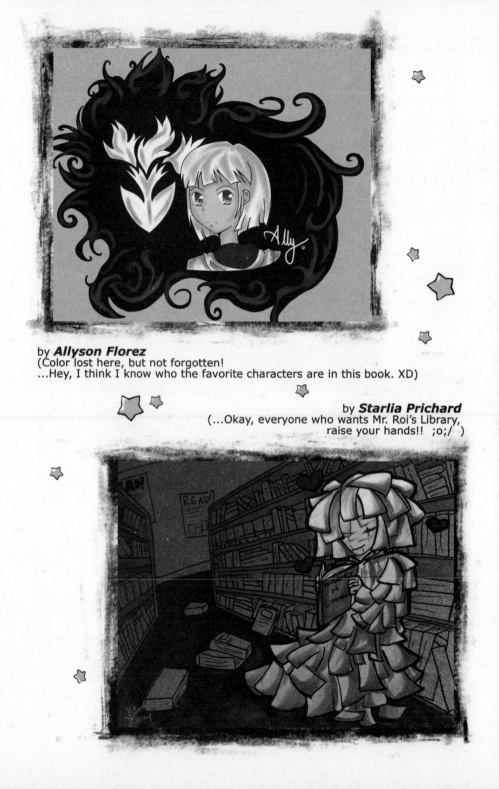

by ***Allyson Florez***
(Color lost here, but not forgotten!
...Hey, I think I know who the favorite characters are in this book. XD)

by ***Starlia Prichard***
(...Okay, everyone who wants Mr. Roi's Library,
raise your hands!! ;o;/)

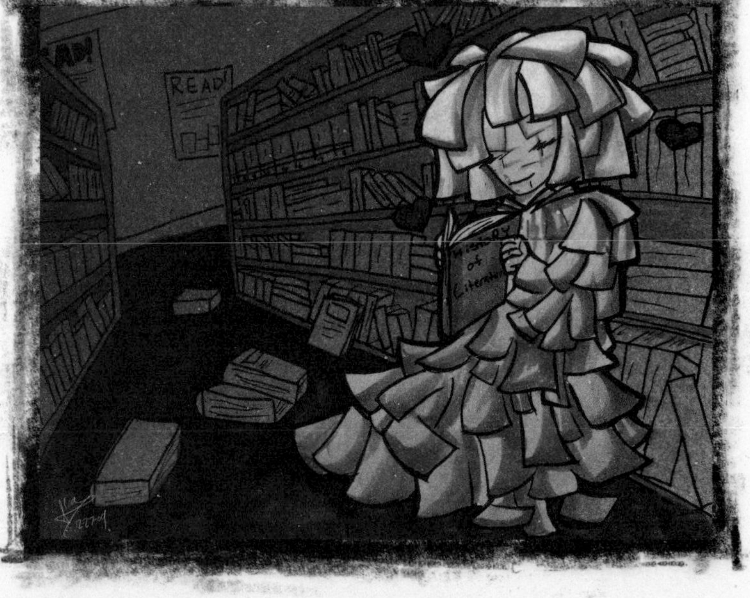
READ!

by ***Sarah Covington***
(And last but not least, a nice large pic of the cast!
I LOVE ERON TOO.)

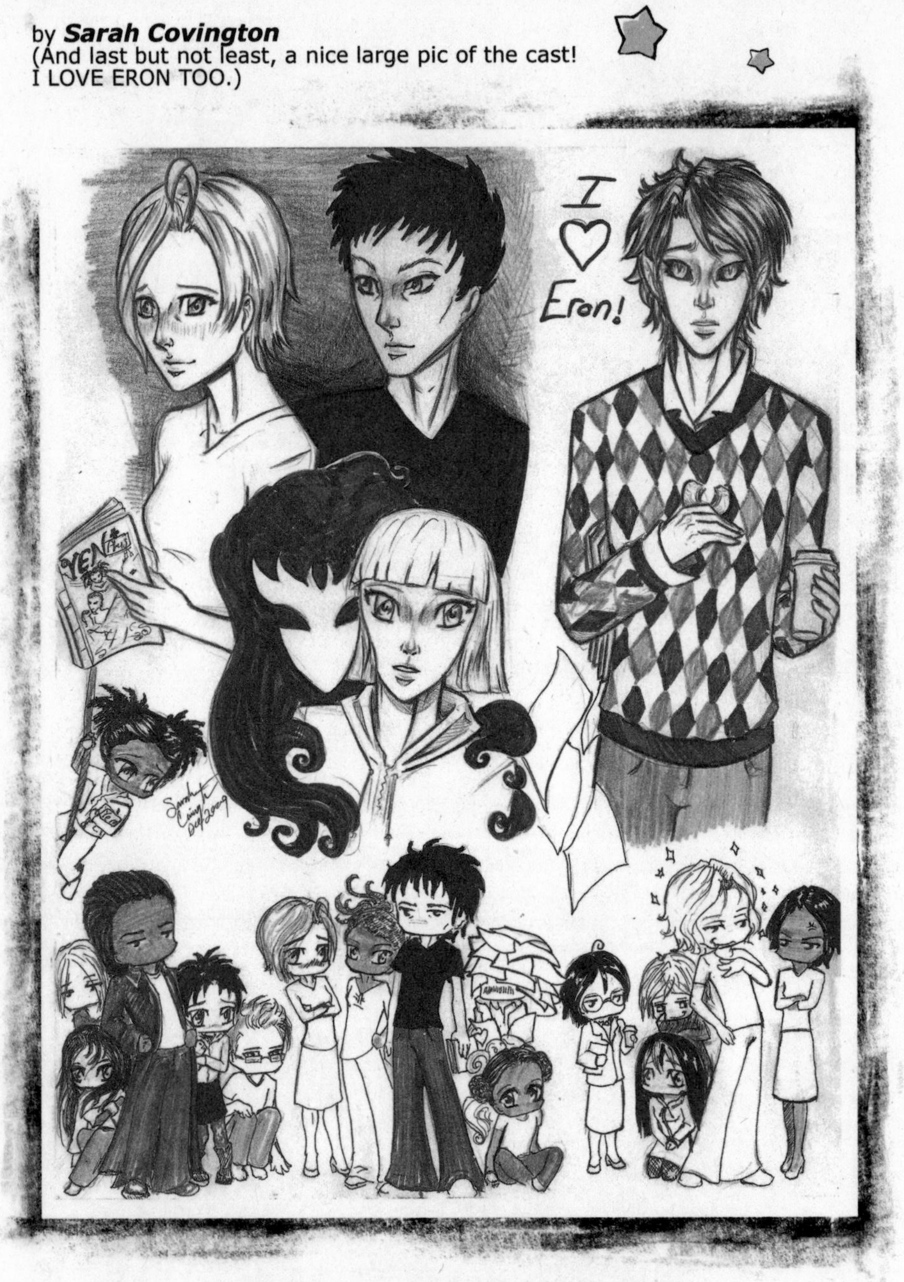
I ♡ Eron!
YEN

Thank you to everyone who submitted, and congratulations to the winners!! Hope you enjoy your prizes, and please don't hate me if I spelled your name wrong; I tried very hard.

;__;

See you all in the next volume!!

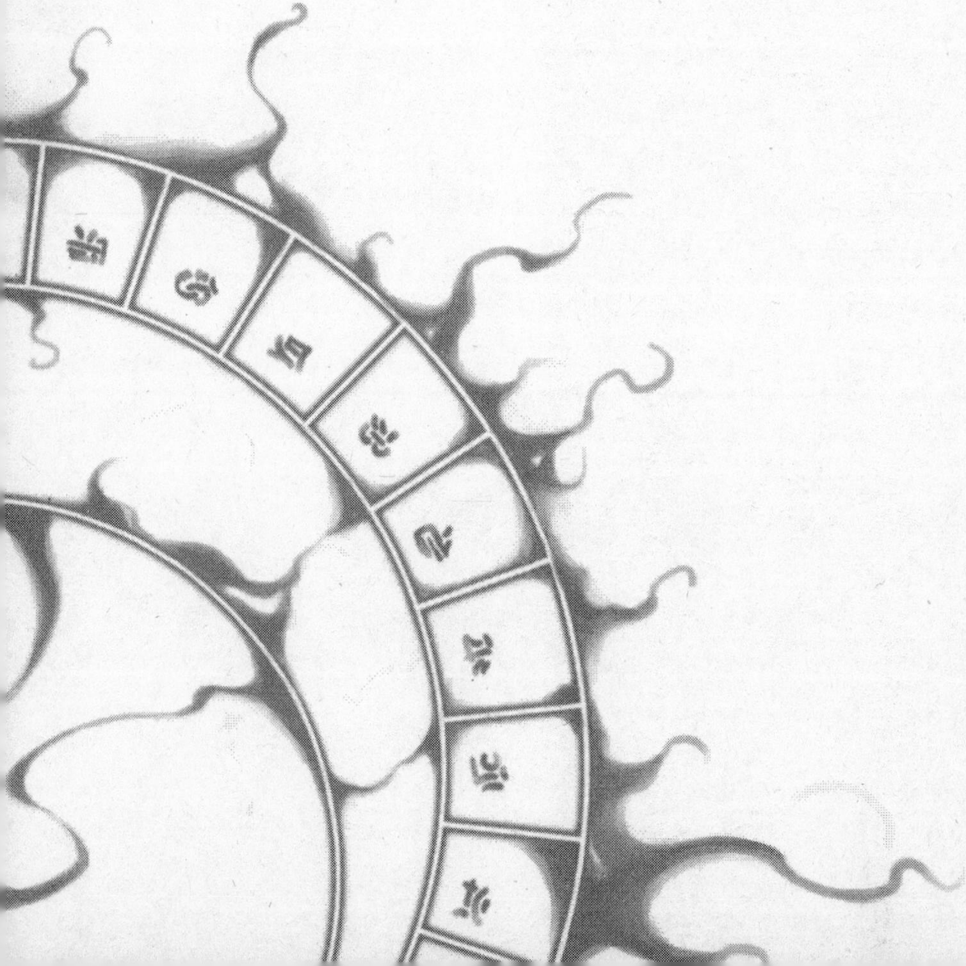

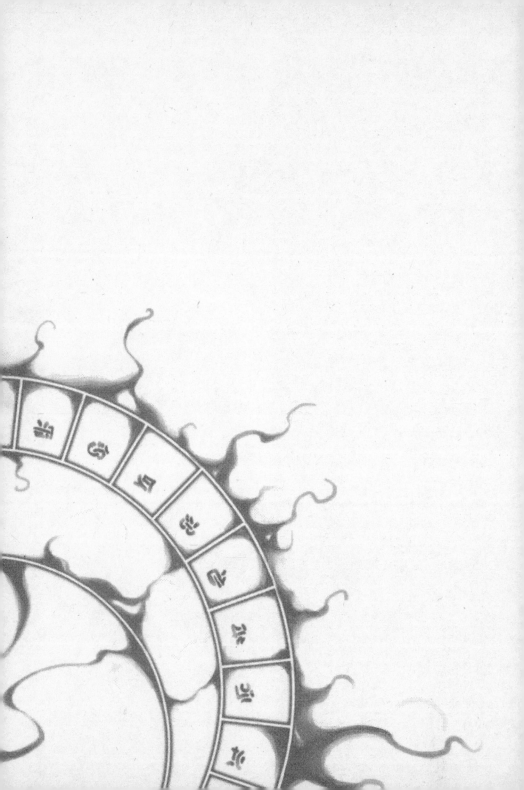

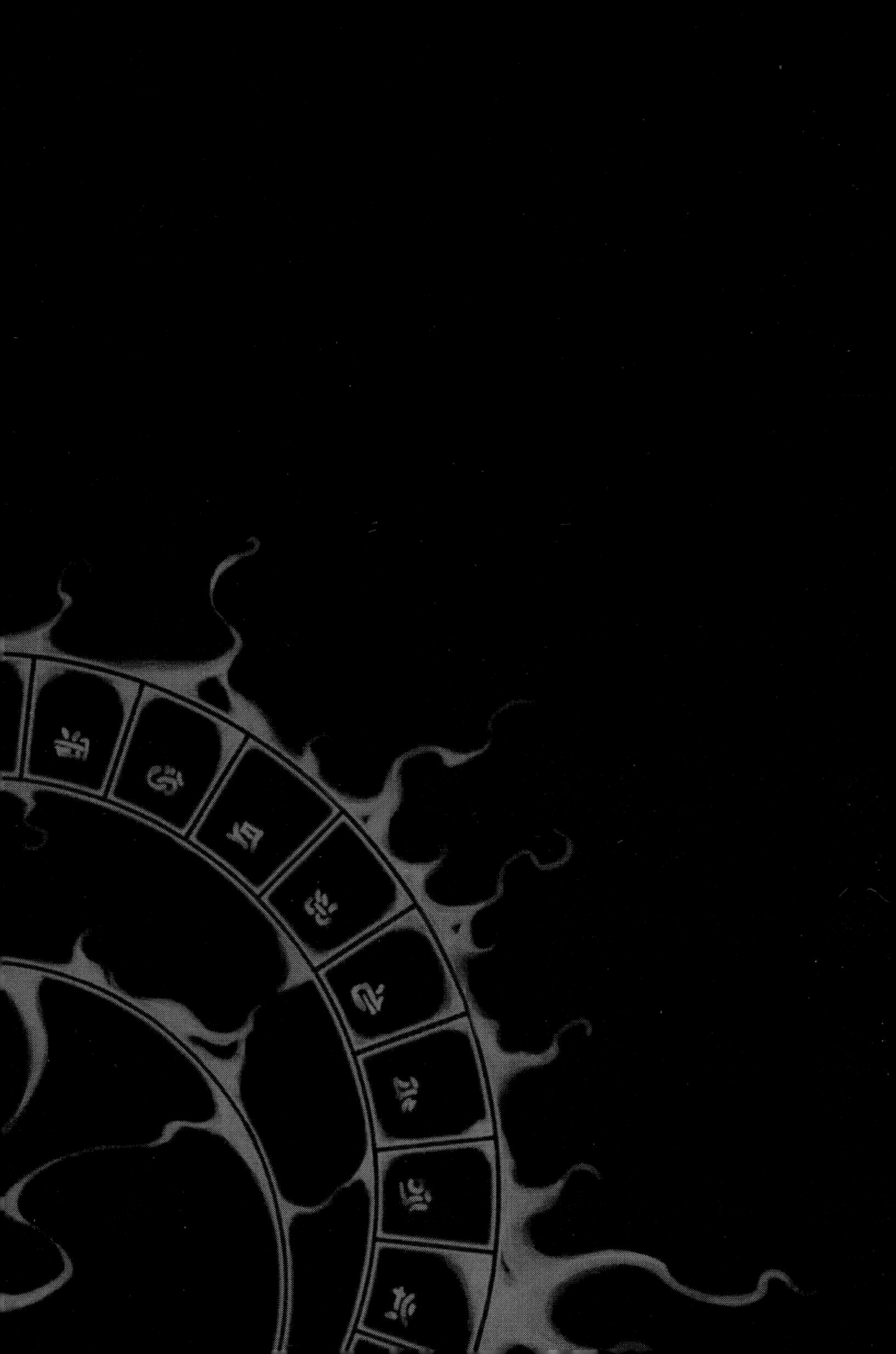

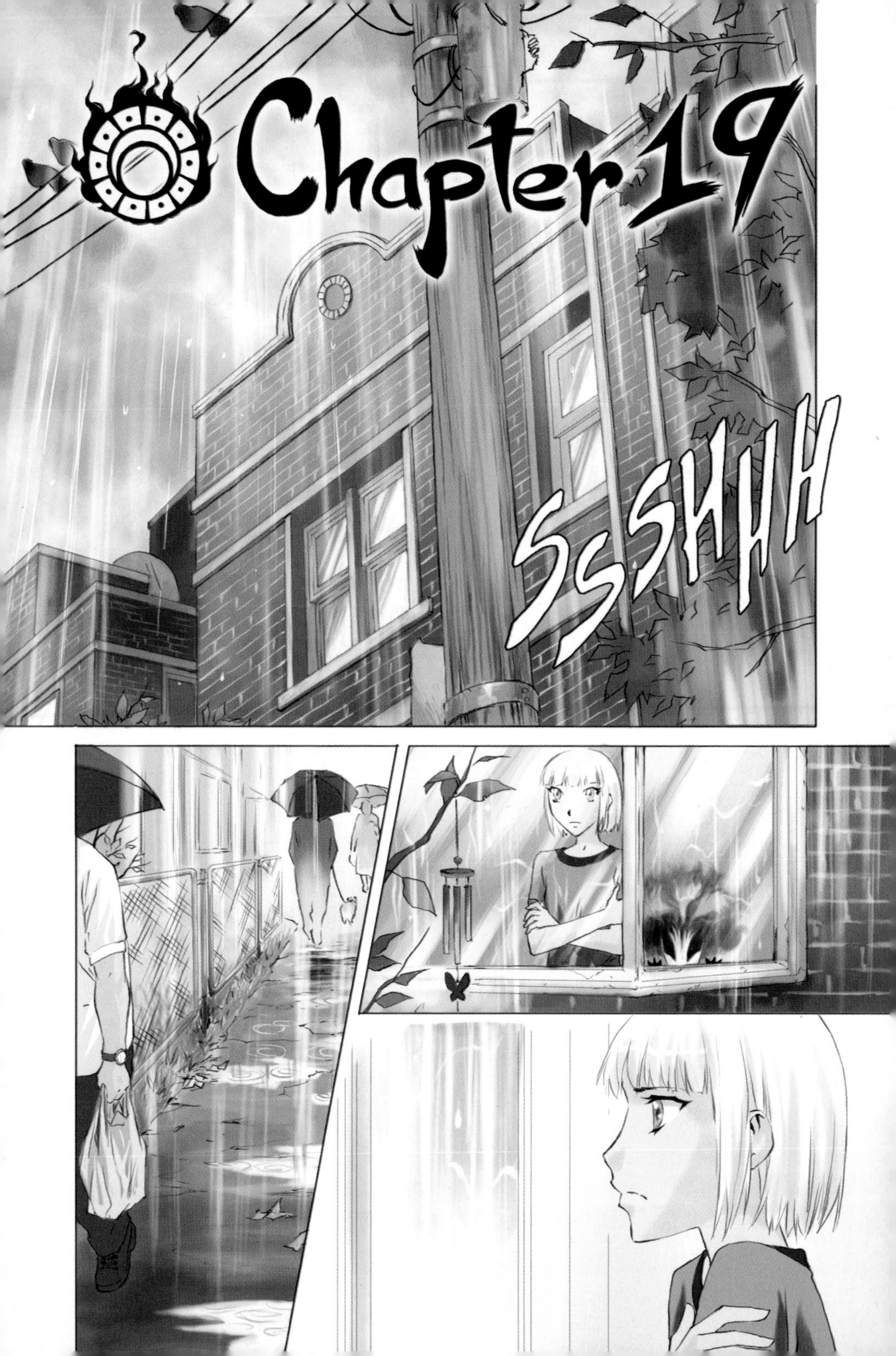
Chapter 19
SSSHHH

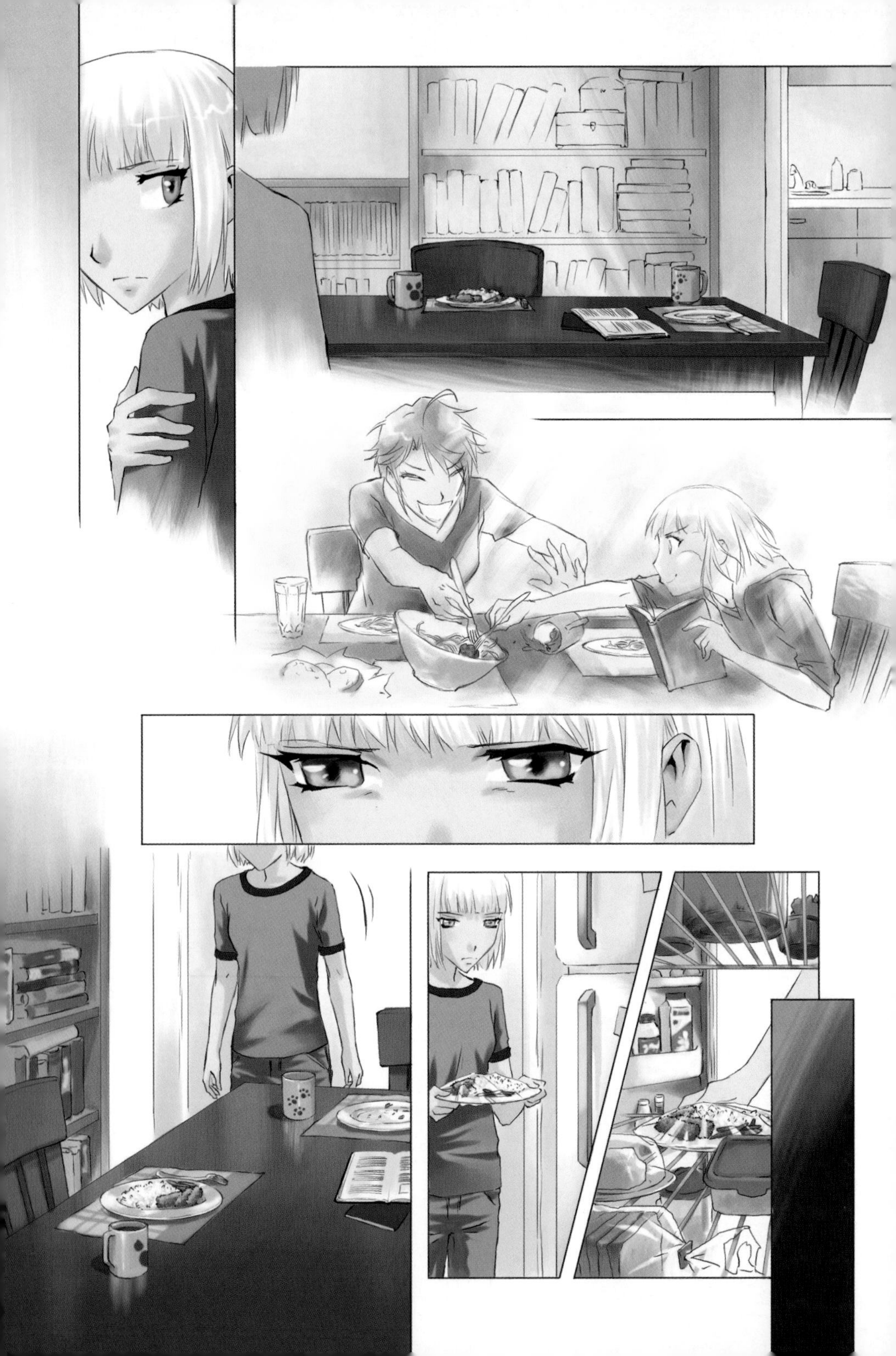

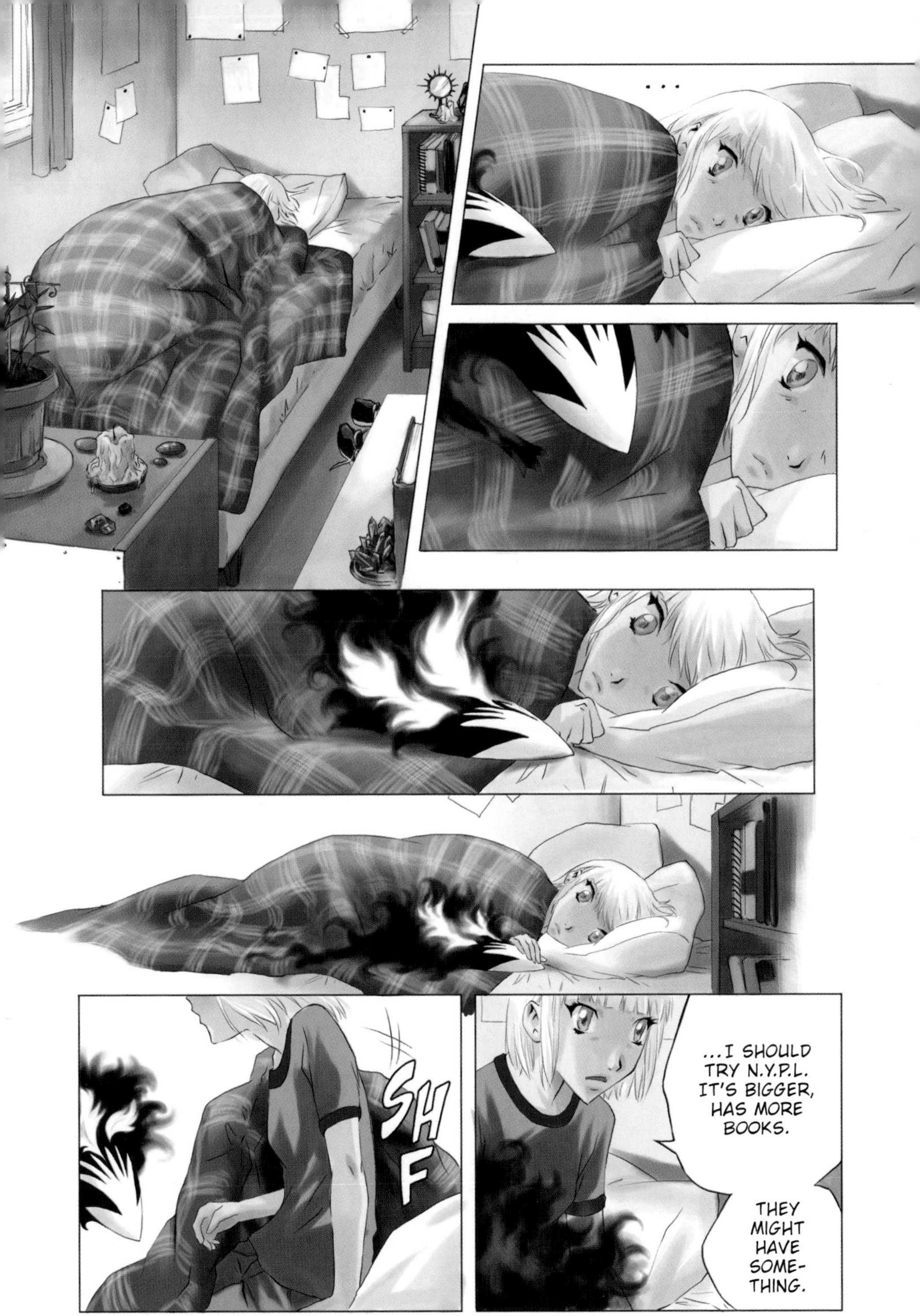
...
SHF
...I SHOULD TRY N.Y.P.L. IT'S BIGGER, HAS MORE BOOKS.
THEY MIGHT HAVE SOME-THING.

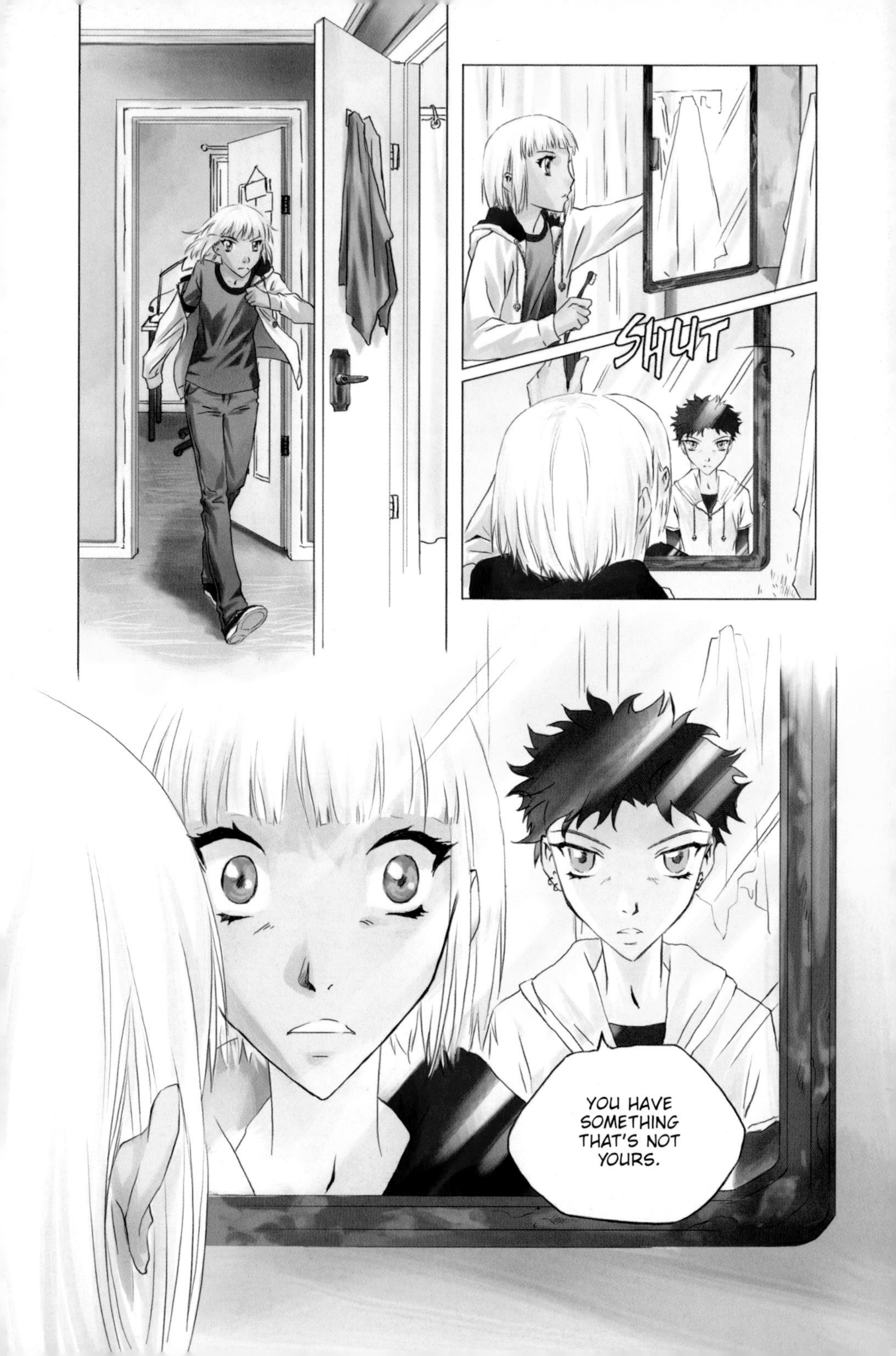
SHUT
YOU HAVE SOMETHING THAT'S NOT YOURS.

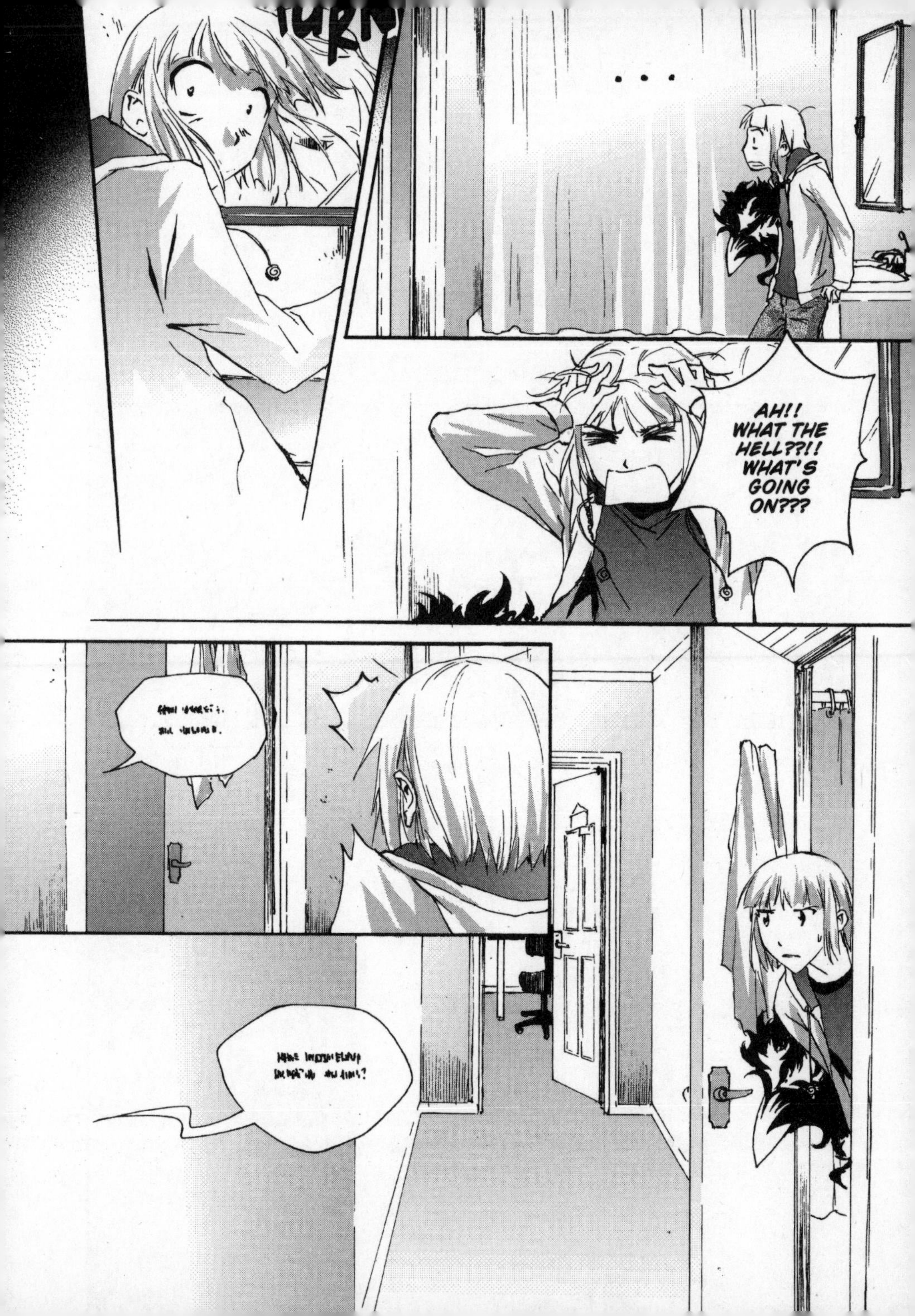
. . .
AH!! WHAT THE HELL??!! WHAT'S GOING ON???

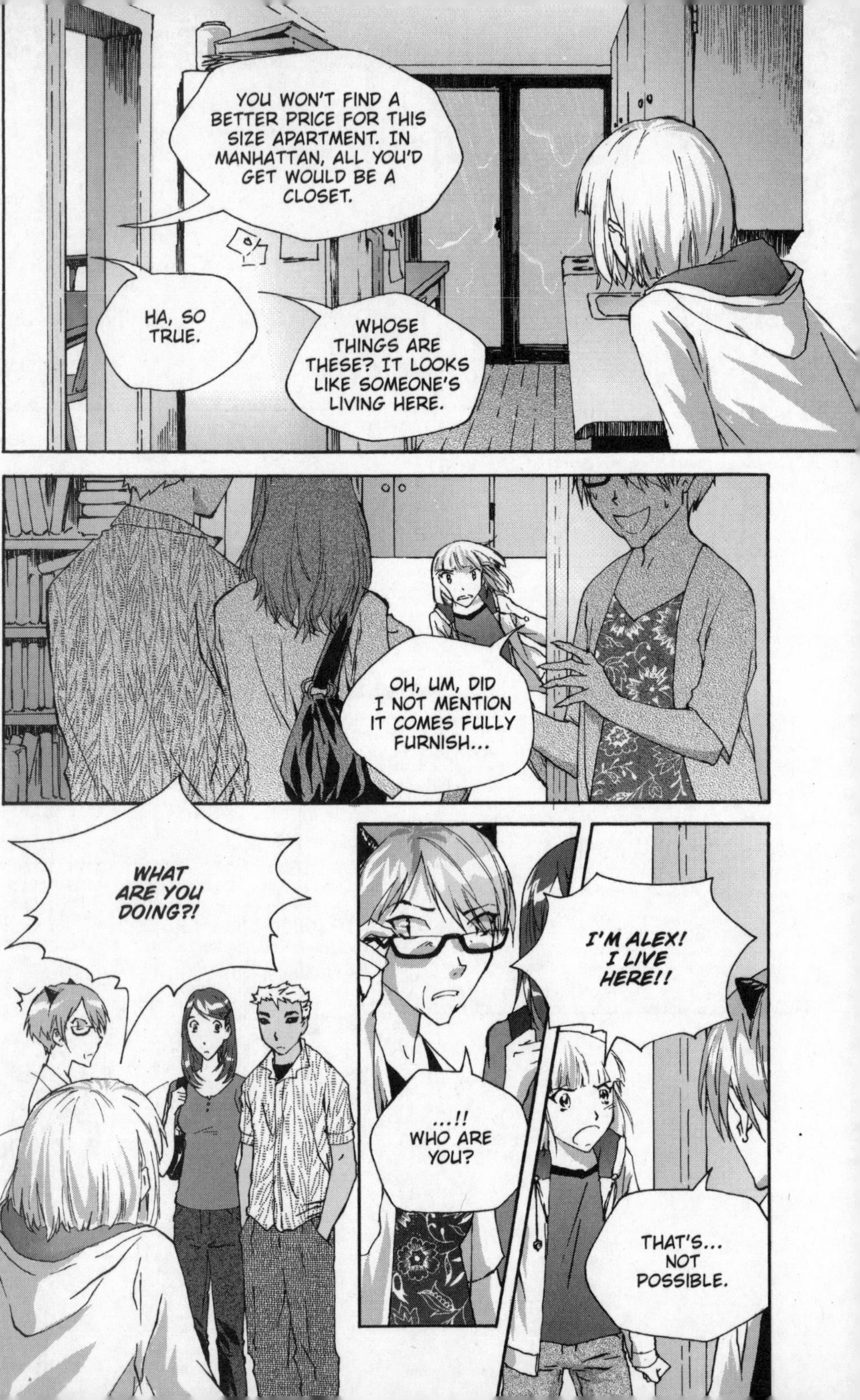
YOU WON'T FIND A BETTER PRICE FOR THIS SIZE APARTMENT. IN MANHATTAN, ALL YOU'D GET WOULD BE A CLOSET.
HA, SO TRUE.
WHOSE THINGS ARE THESE? IT LOOKS LIKE SOMEONE'S LIVING HERE.
OH, UM, DID I NOT MENTION IT COMES FULLY FURNISH...
WHAT ARE YOU DOING?!
I'M ALEX! I LIVE HERE!!
...!! WHO ARE YOU?
THAT'S... NOT POSSIBLE.

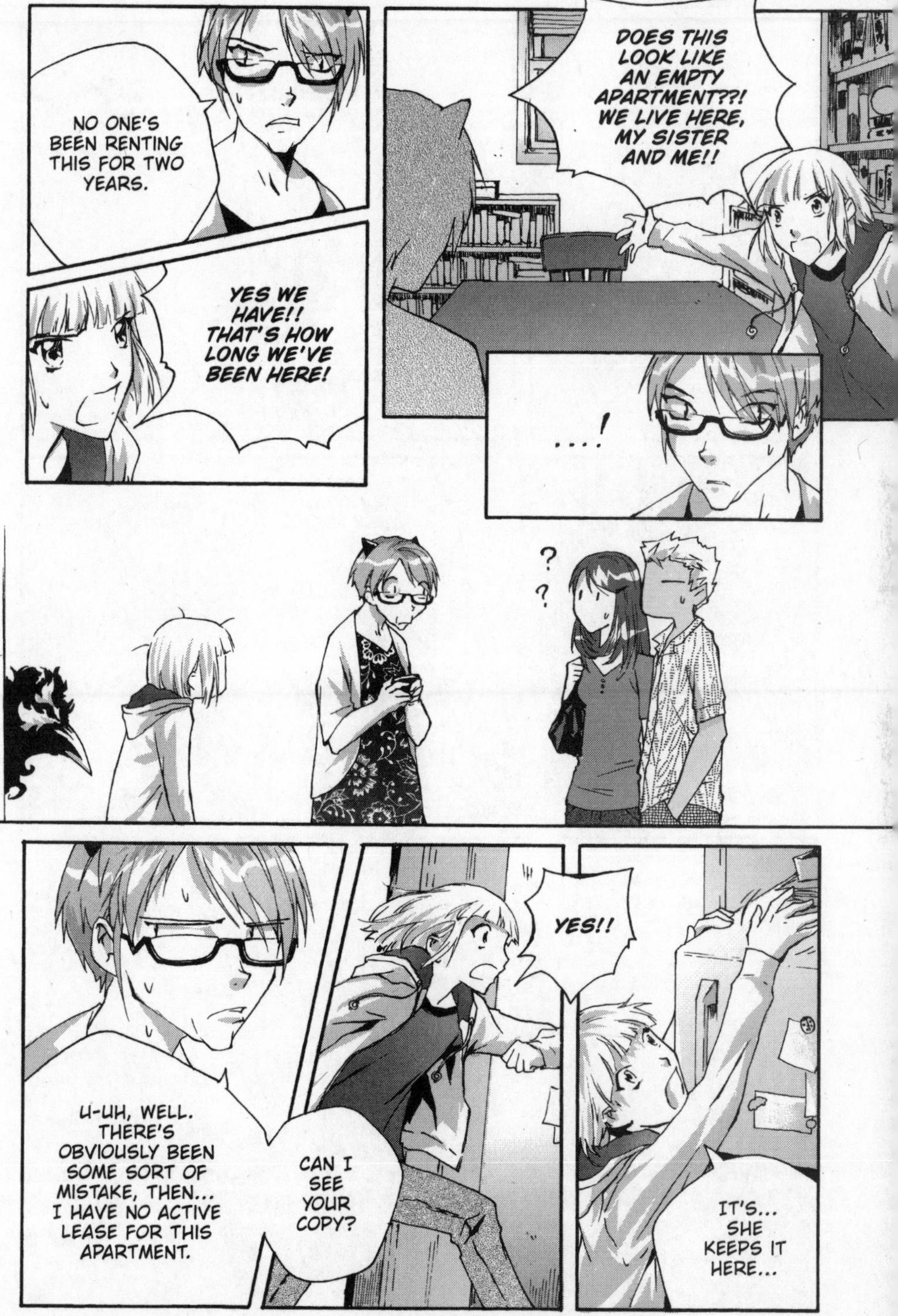
NO ONE'S BEEN RENTING THIS FOR TWO YEARS.
YES WE HAVE!! THAT'S HOW LONG WE'VE BEEN HERE!
DOES THIS LOOK LIKE AN EMPTY APARTMENT??! WE LIVE HERE, MY SISTER AND ME!!
...!
?
?
U-UH, WELL. THERE'S OBVIOUSLY BEEN SOME SORT OF MISTAKE, THEN... I HAVE NO ACTIVE LEASE FOR THIS APARTMENT.
CAN I SEE YOUR COPY?
YES!!
IT'S... SHE KEEPS IT HERE...

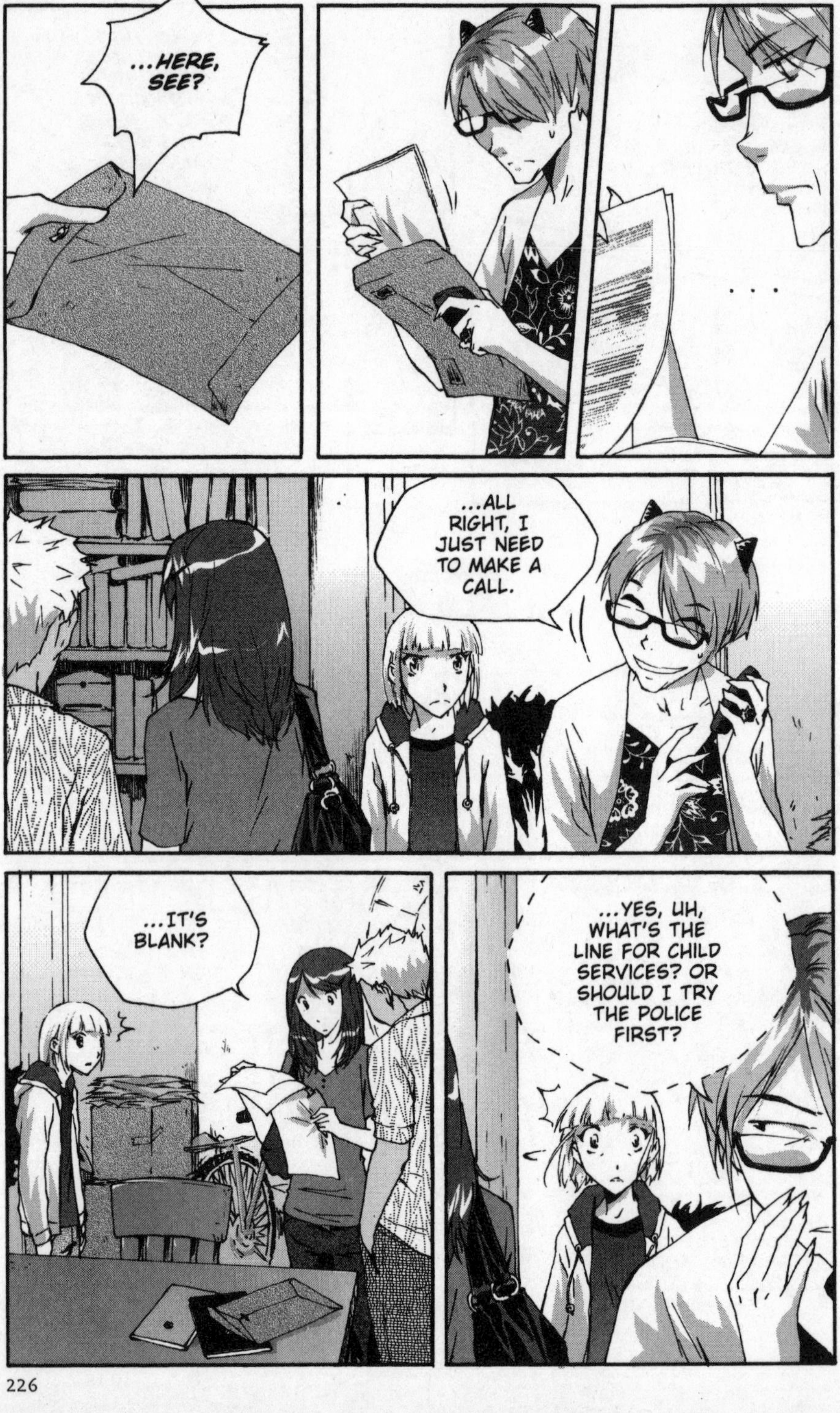
...HERE, SEE?
...
...ALL RIGHT, I JUST NEED TO MAKE A CALL.
...IT'S BLANK?
...YES, UH, WHAT'S THE LINE FOR CHILD SERVICES? OR SHOULD I TRY THE POLICE FIRST?

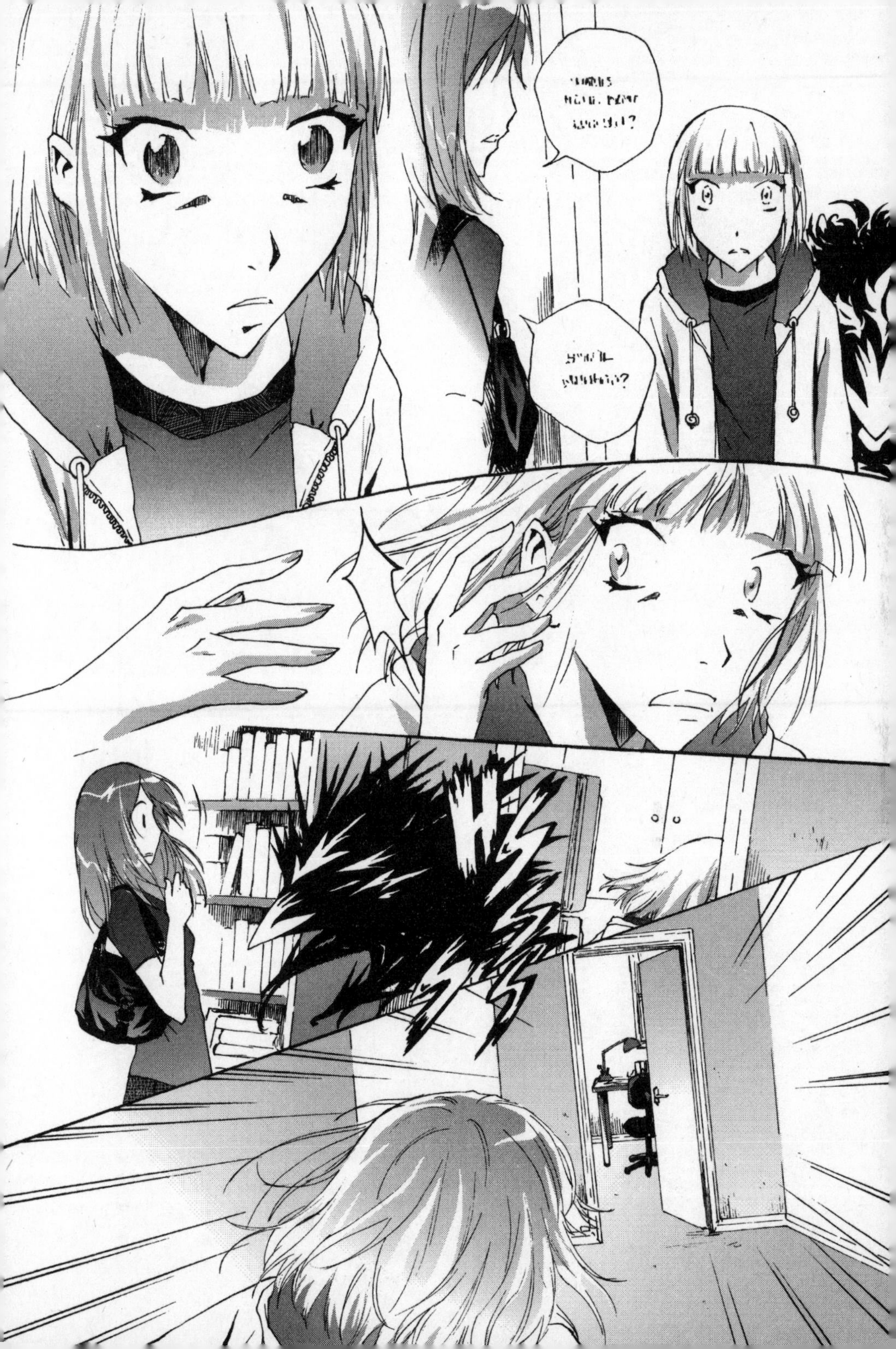
HSSSS

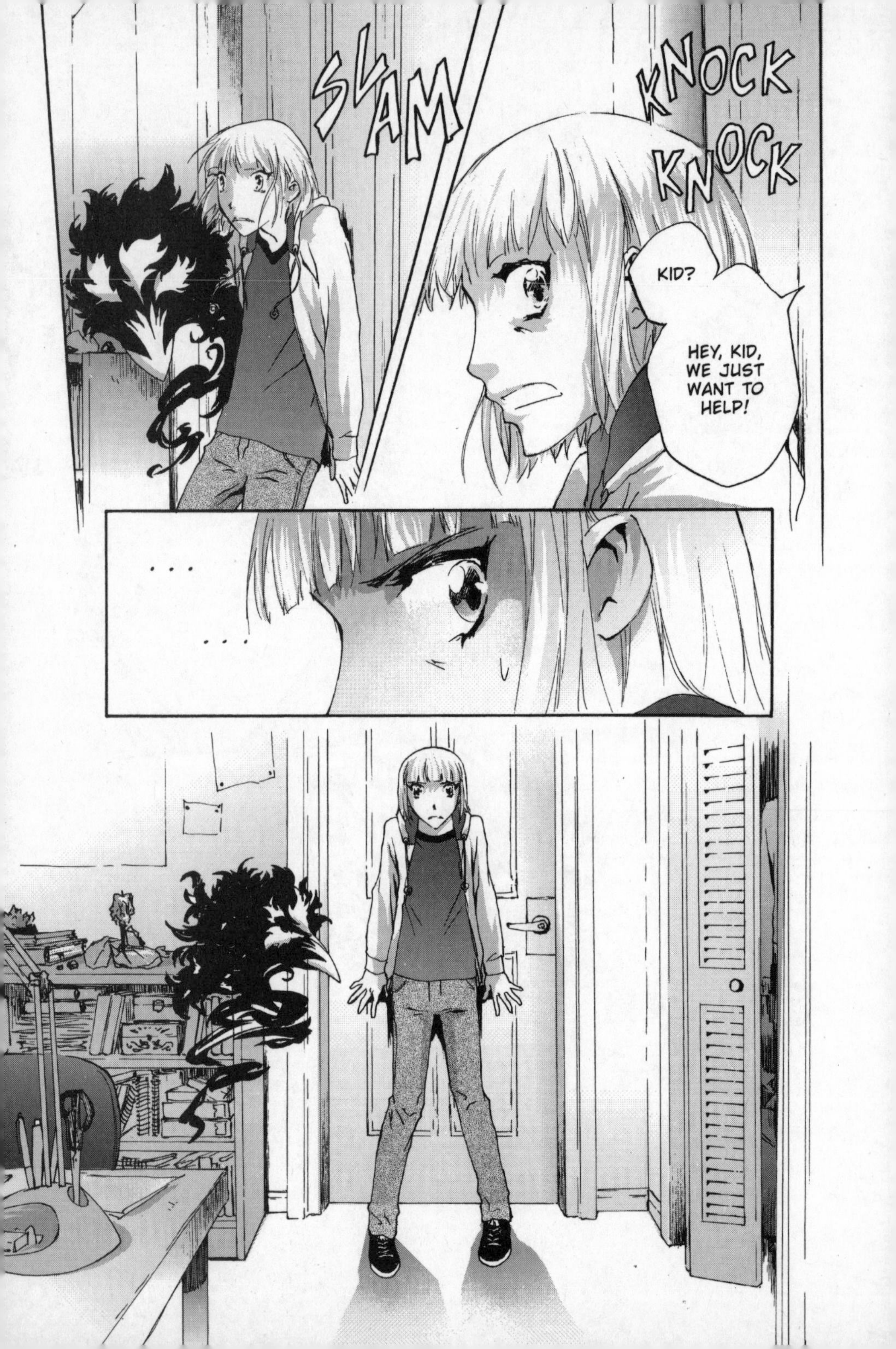
SLAM
KNOCK KNOCK
KID?
HEY, KID, WE JUST WANT TO HELP!
. . .
. . .

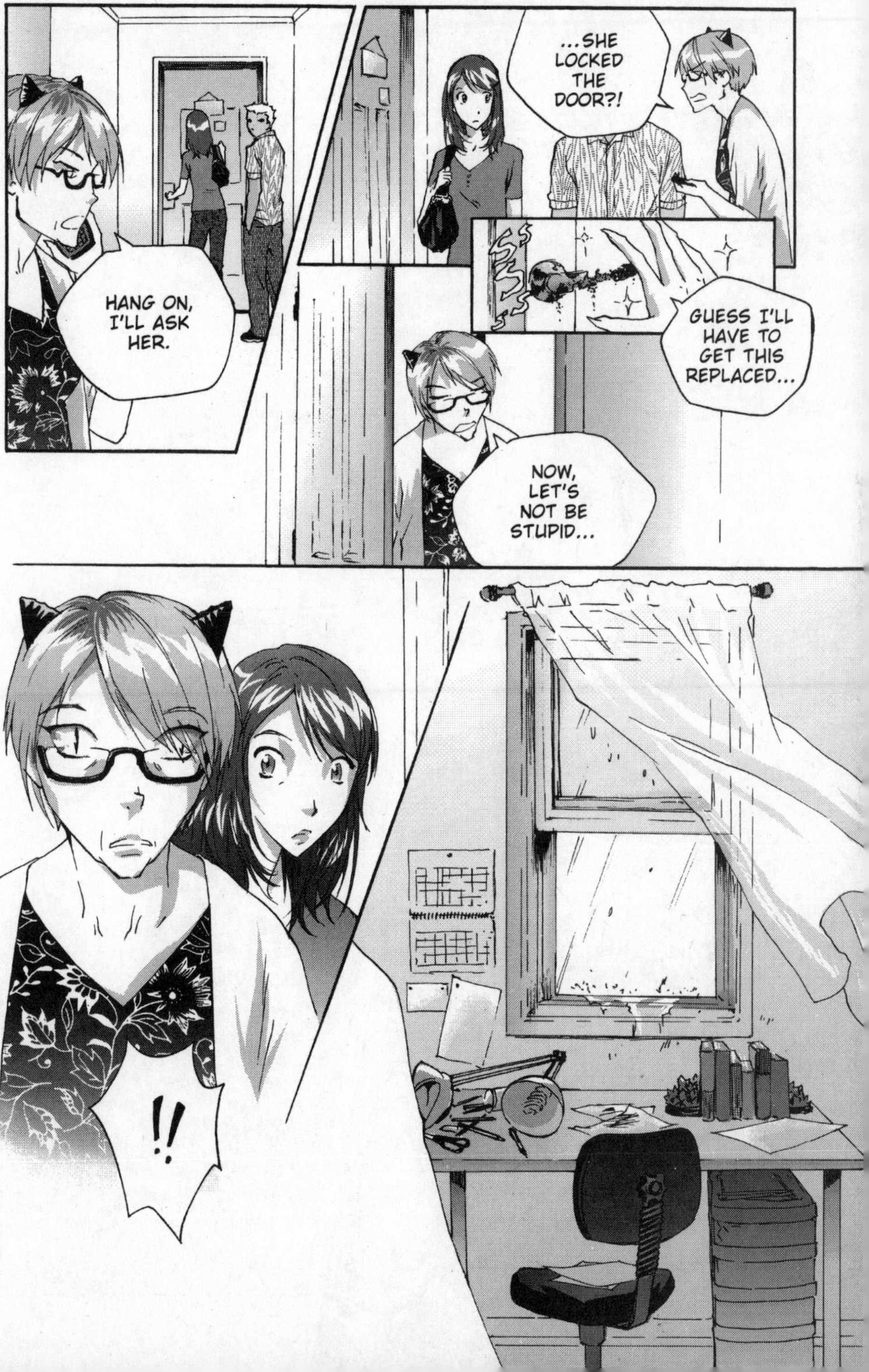
HANG ON, I'LL ASK HER.
...SHE LOCKED THE DOOR?!
GUESS I'LL HAVE TO GET THIS REPLACED...
NOW, LET'S NOT BE STUPID...
!!

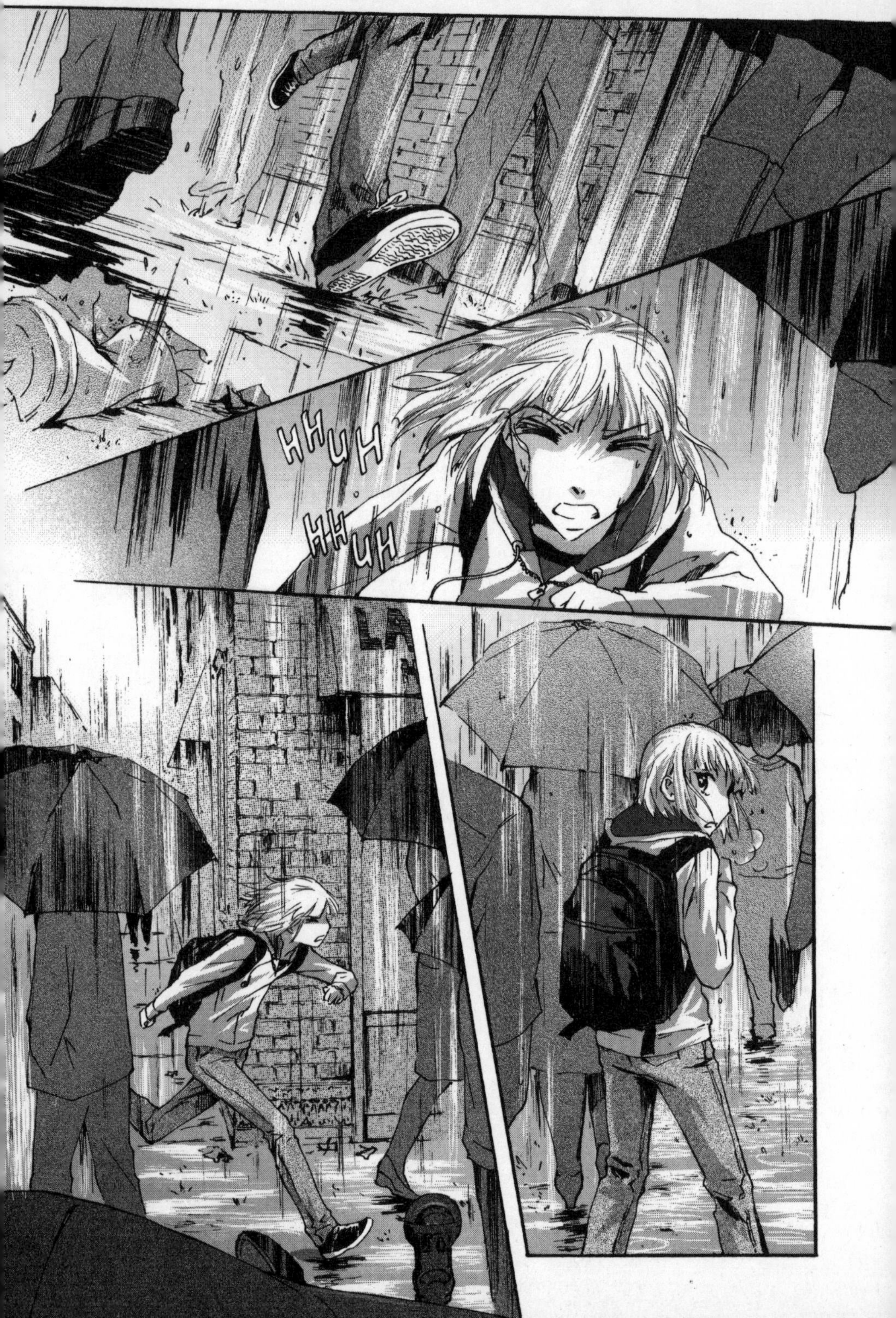
HHUH
HHUH

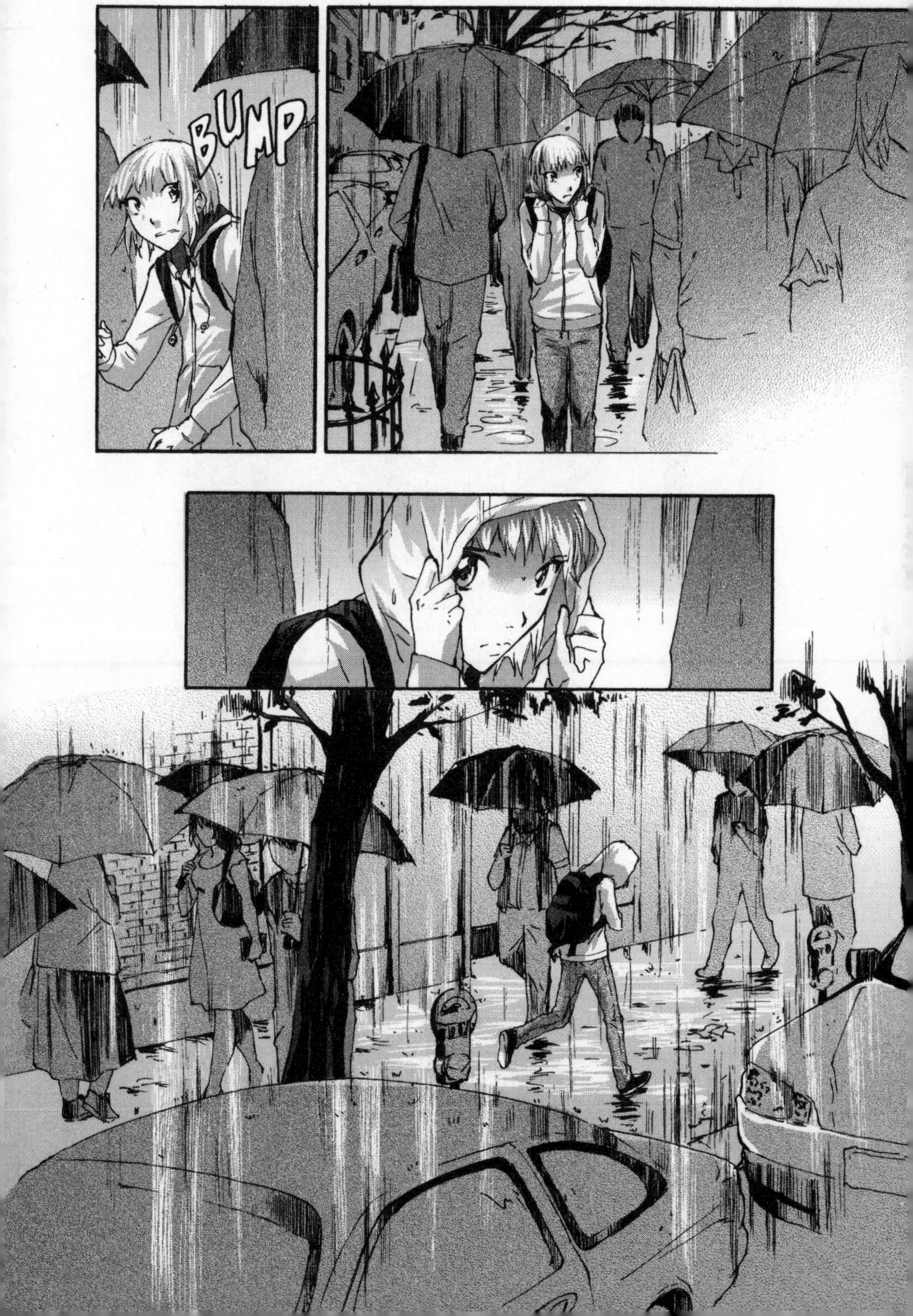
BUMP

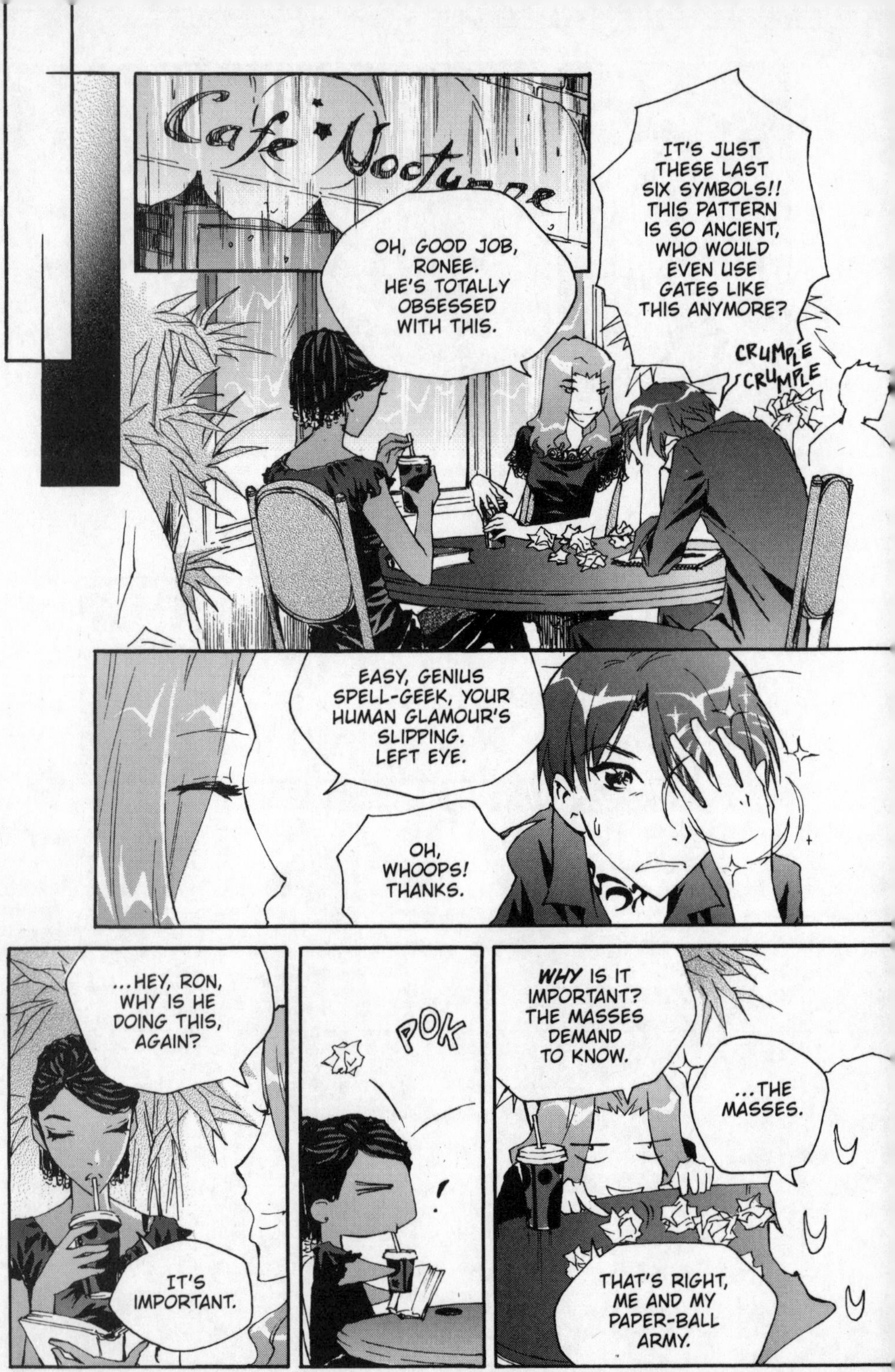
Cafe Nocturne
OH, GOOD JOB, RONEE. HE'S TOTALLY OBSESSED WITH THIS.
IT'S JUST THESE LAST SIX SYMBOLS!! THIS PATTERN IS SO ANCIENT, WHO WOULD EVEN USE GATES LIKE THIS ANYMORE?
CRUMPLE CRUMPLE
EASY, GENIUS SPELL-GEEK, YOUR HUMAN GLAMOUR'S SLIPPING. LEFT EYE.
OH, WHOOPS! THANKS.
...HEY, RON, WHY IS HE DOING THIS, AGAIN?
IT'S IMPORTANT.
POK
!
WHY IS IT IMPORTANT? THE MASSES DEMAND TO KNOW.
...THE MASSES.
THAT'S RIGHT, ME AND MY PAPER-BALL ARMY.

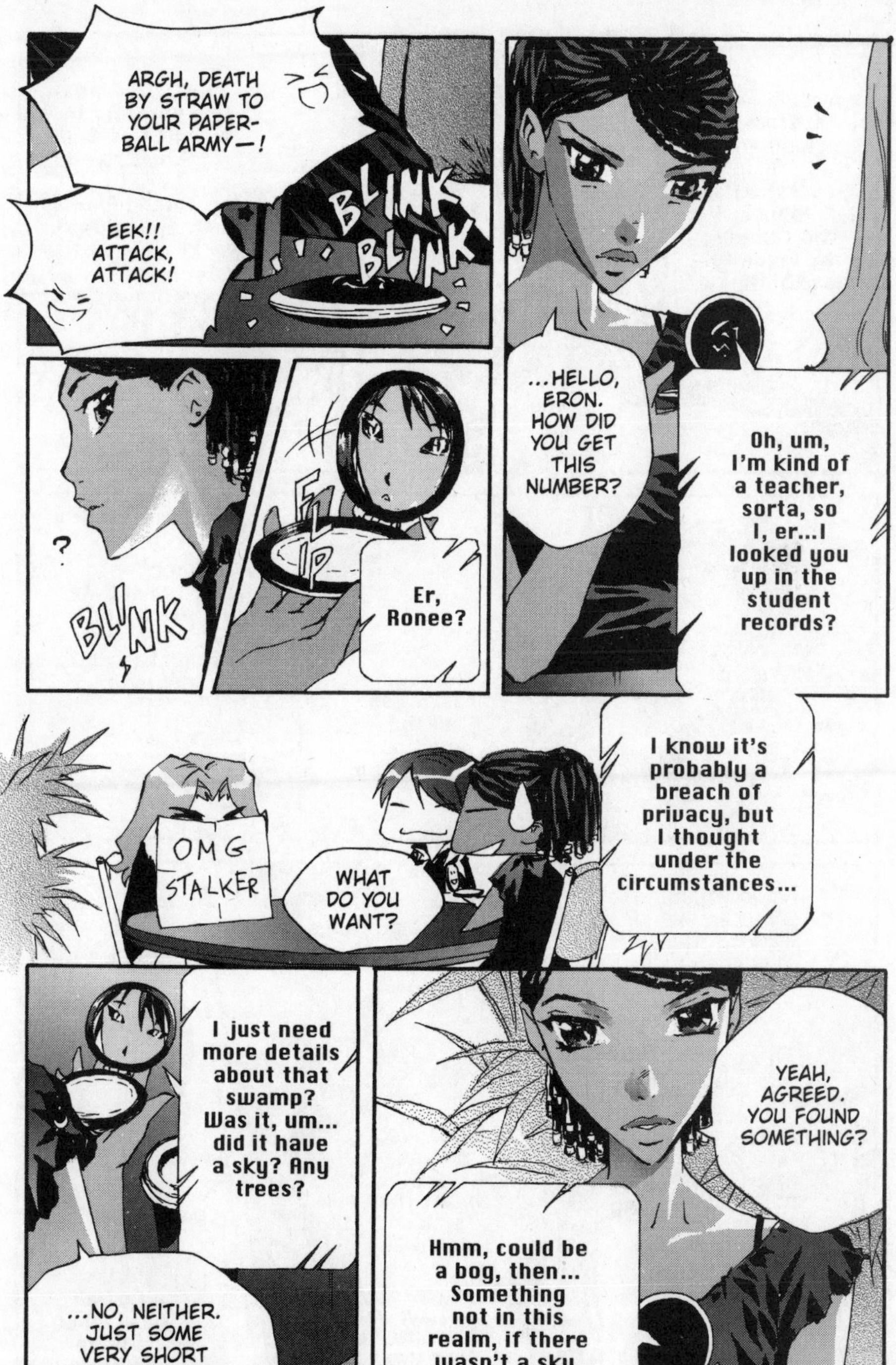
ARGH, DEATH BY STRAW TO YOUR PAPER-BALL ARMY—!
EEK!! ATTACK, ATTACK!
BLINK BLINK
?
BLINK
FLIP
Er, Ronee?
...HELLO, ERON. HOW DID YOU GET THIS NUMBER?
Oh, um, I'm kind of a teacher, sorta, so I, er...I looked you up in the student records?
OMG STALKER
WHAT DO YOU WANT?
I know it's probably a breach of privacy, but I thought under the circumstances...
I just need more details about that swamp? Was it, um... did it have a sky? Any trees?
...NO, NEITHER. JUST SOME VERY SHORT AND VERY DEAD SHRUBBERY.
YEAH, AGREED. YOU FOUND SOMETHING?
Hmm, could be a bog, then... Something not in this realm, if there wasn't a sky.

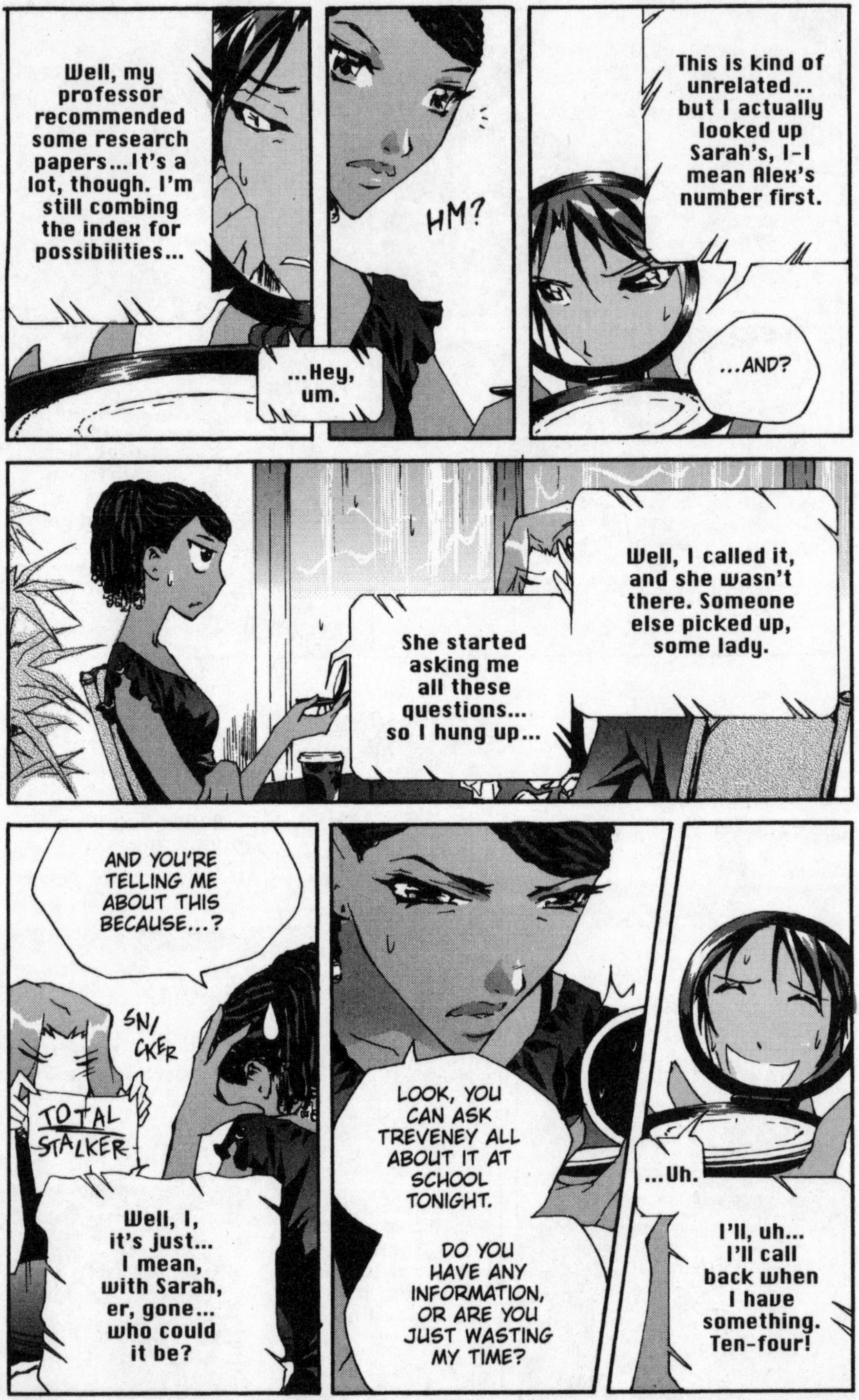
Well, my professor recommended some research papers... It's a lot, though. I'm still combing the index for possibilities...
HM?
...Hey, um.
This is kind of unrelated... but I actually looked up Sarah's, I-I mean Alex's number first.
...AND?
Well, I called it, and she wasn't there. Someone else picked up, some lady.
She started asking me all these questions... so I hung up...
AND YOU'RE TELLING ME ABOUT THIS BECAUSE...?
SN/CKER
TOTAL STALKER
Well, I, it's just... I mean, with Sarah, er, gone... who could it be?
LOOK, YOU CAN ASK TREVENEY ALL ABOUT IT AT SCHOOL TONIGHT.
DO YOU HAVE ANY INFORMATION, OR ARE YOU JUST WASTING MY TIME?
...Uh.
I'll, uh... I'll call back when I have something. Ten-four!

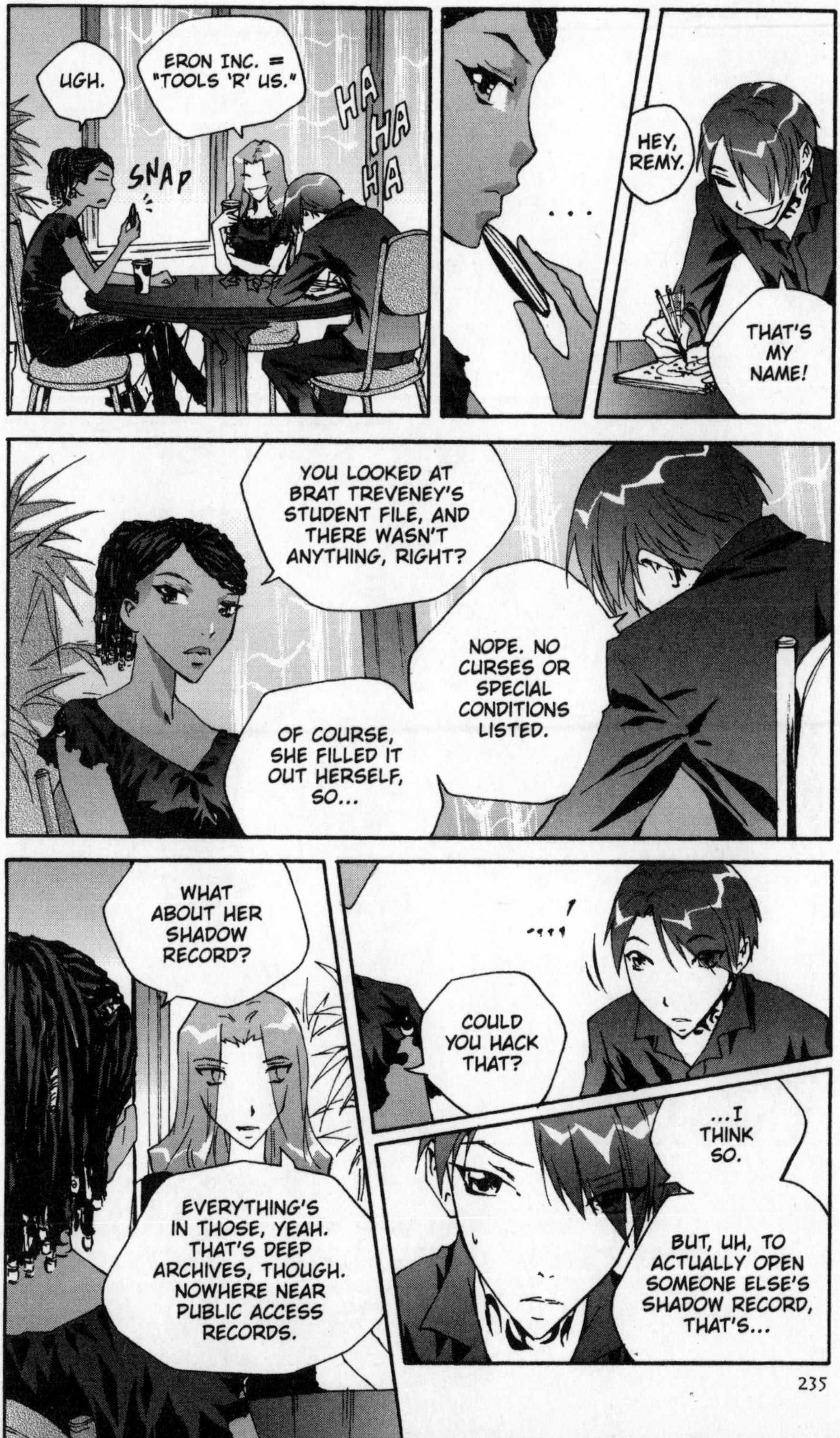

UGH.
ERON INC. = "TOOLS 'R' US."
SNAP
HA HA HA
...
HEY, REMY.
THAT'S MY NAME!
YOU LOOKED AT BRAT TREVENEY'S STUDENT FILE, AND THERE WASN'T ANYTHING, RIGHT?
NOPE. NO CURSES OR SPECIAL CONDITIONS LISTED.
OF COURSE, SHE FILLED IT OUT HERSELF, SO...
WHAT ABOUT HER SHADOW RECORD?
EVERYTHING'S IN THOSE, YEAH. THAT'S DEEP ARCHIVES, THOUGH. NOWHERE NEAR PUBLIC ACCESS RECORDS.
...!
COULD YOU HACK THAT?
...I THINK SO.
BUT, UH, TO ACTUALLY OPEN SOMEONE ELSE'S SHADOW RECORD, THAT'S...

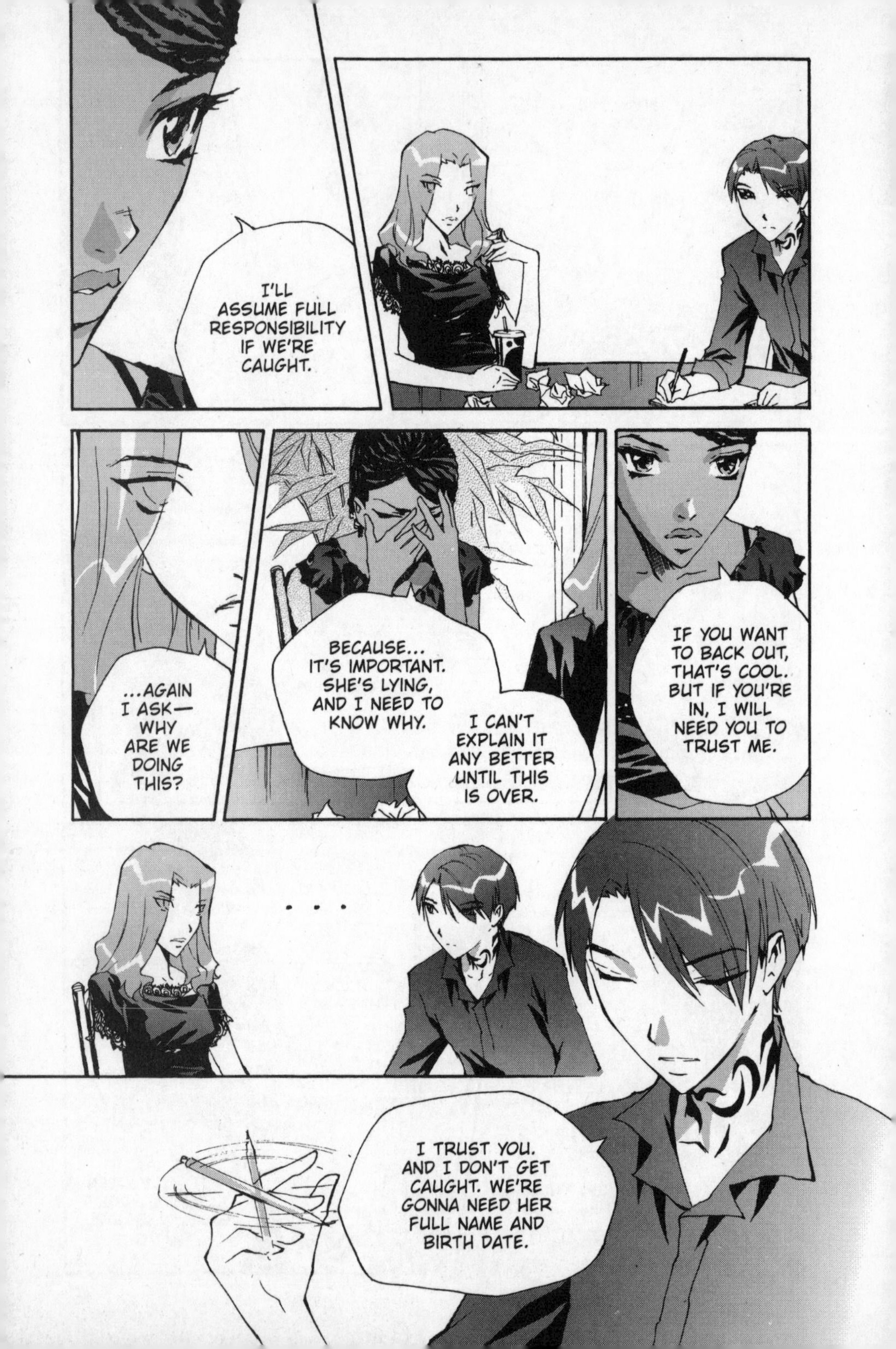
I'LL ASSUME FULL RESPONSIBILITY IF WE'RE CAUGHT.
...AGAIN I ASK— WHY ARE WE DOING THIS?
BECAUSE... IT'S IMPORTANT. SHE'S LYING, AND I NEED TO KNOW WHY.
I CAN'T EXPLAIN IT ANY BETTER UNTIL THIS IS OVER.
IF YOU WANT TO BACK OUT, THAT'S COOL. BUT IF YOU'RE IN, I WILL NEED YOU TO TRUST ME.
. . .
I TRUST YOU. AND I DON'T GET CAUGHT. WE'RE GONNA NEED HER FULL NAME AND BIRTH DATE.

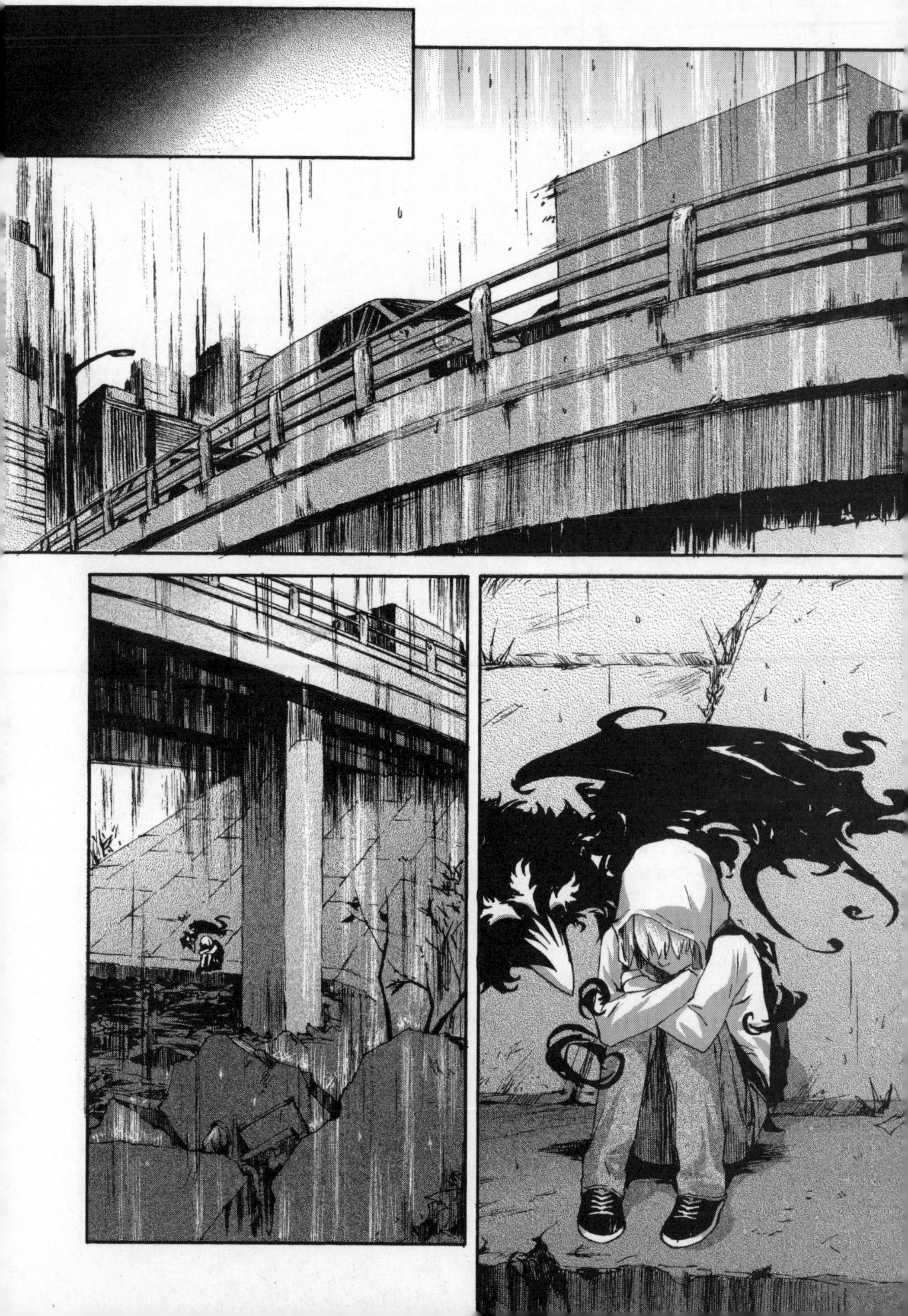

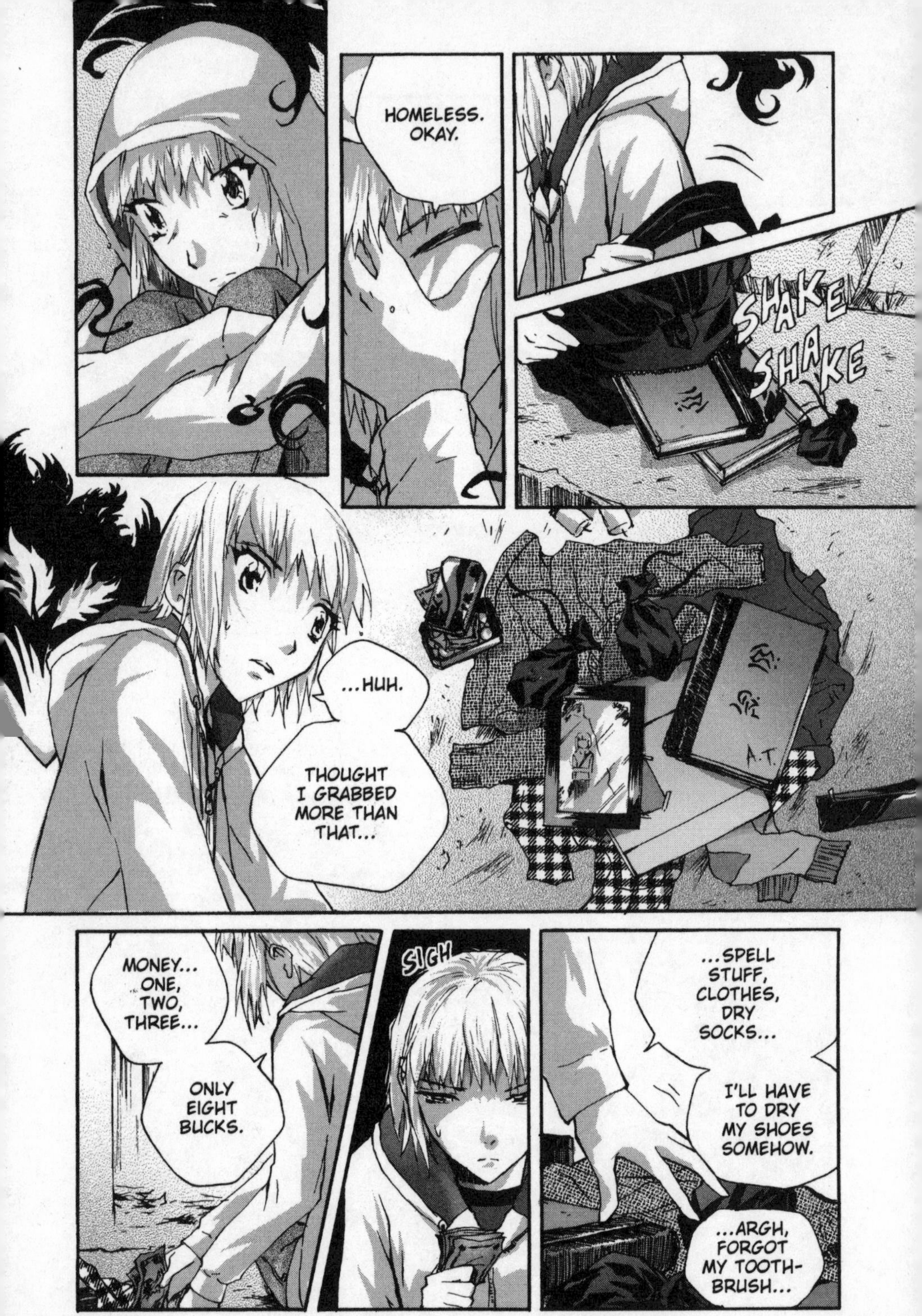
HOMELESS. OKAY.
SHAKE SHAKE
...HUH.
THOUGHT I GRABBED MORE THAN THAT...
MONEY... ONE, TWO, THREE...
ONLY EIGHT BUCKS.
SIGH
...SPELL STUFF, CLOTHES, DRY SOCKS...
I'LL HAVE TO DRY MY SHOES SOMEHOW.
...ARGH, FORGOT MY TOOTH-BRUSH...

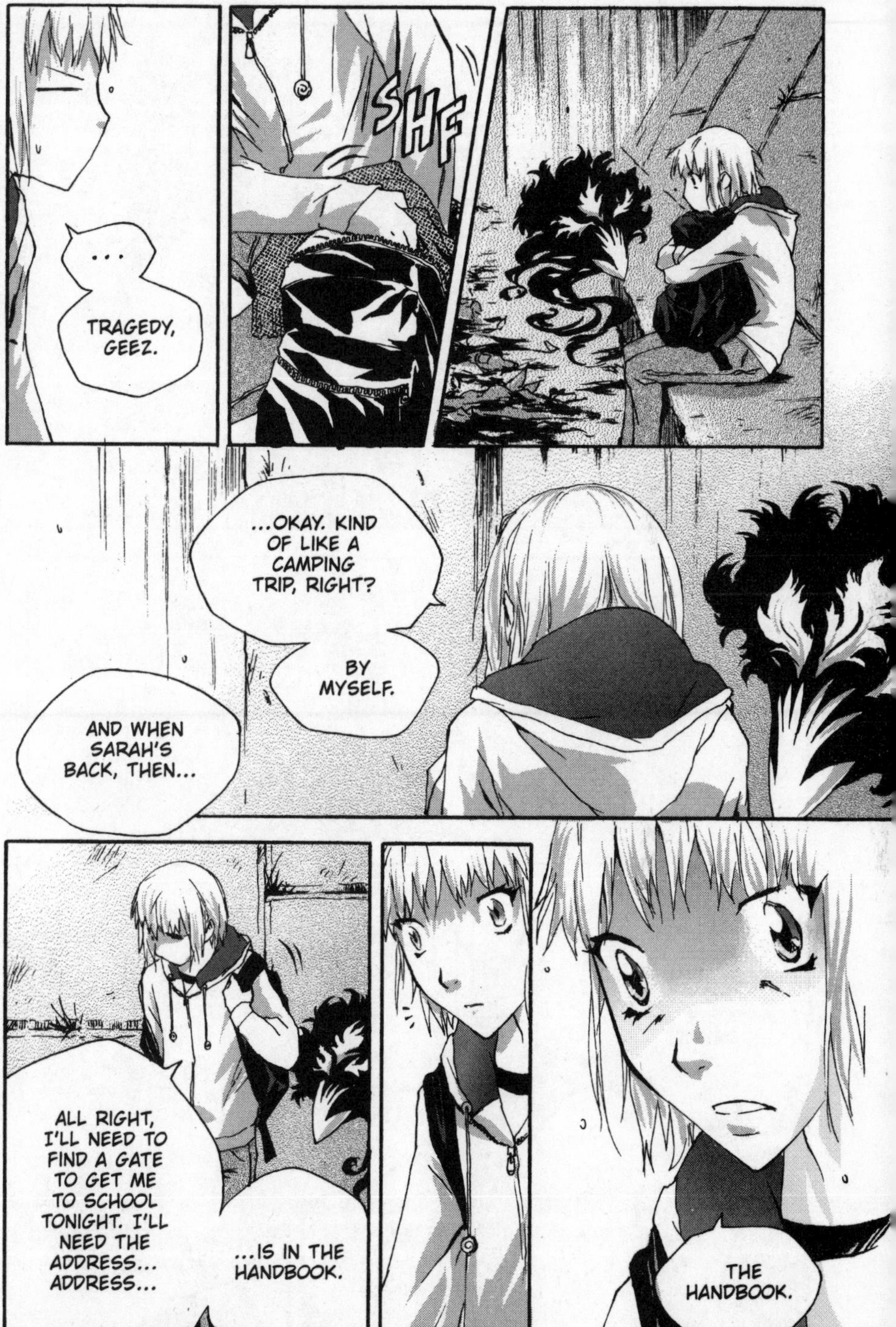
...
TRAGEDY, GEEZ.
SHF
...OKAY. KIND OF LIKE A CAMPING TRIP, RIGHT?
BY MYSELF.
AND WHEN SARAH'S BACK, THEN...
ALL RIGHT, I'LL NEED TO FIND A GATE TO GET ME TO SCHOOL TONIGHT. I'LL NEED THE ADDRESS... ADDRESS...
...IS IN THE HANDBOOK.
THE HANDBOOK.

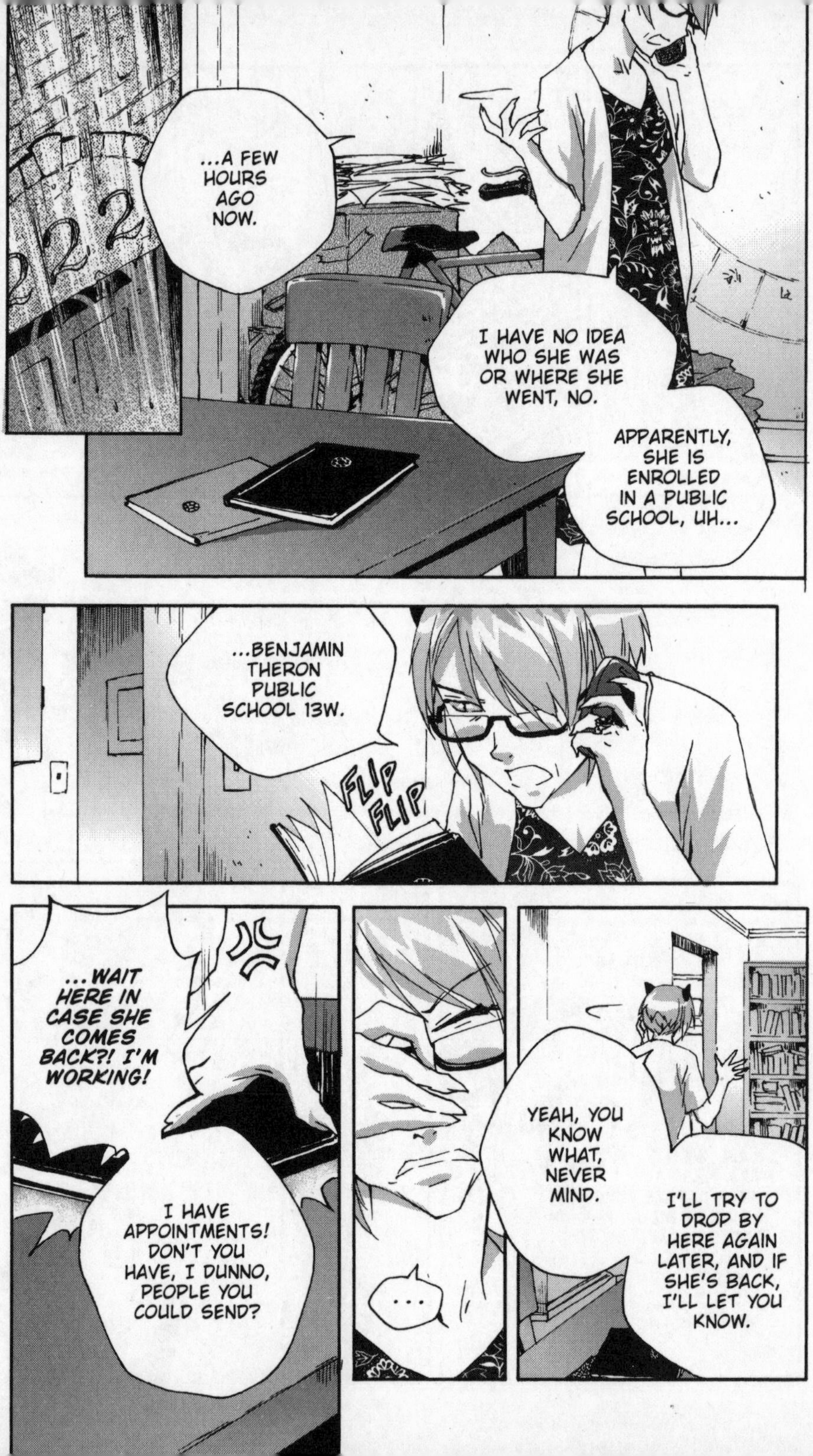
...A FEW HOURS AGO NOW.
I HAVE NO IDEA WHO SHE WAS OR WHERE SHE WENT, NO.
APPARENTLY, SHE IS ENROLLED IN A PUBLIC SCHOOL, UH...
...BENJAMIN THERON PUBLIC SCHOOL 13W.
FLIP FLIP
...WAIT HERE IN CASE SHE COMES BACK?! I'M WORKING!
I HAVE APPOINTMENTS! DON'T YOU HAVE, I DUNNO, PEOPLE YOU COULD SEND?
...
YEAH, YOU KNOW WHAT, NEVER MIND.
I'LL TRY TO DROP BY HERE AGAIN LATER, AND IF SHE'S BACK, I'LL LET YOU KNOW.

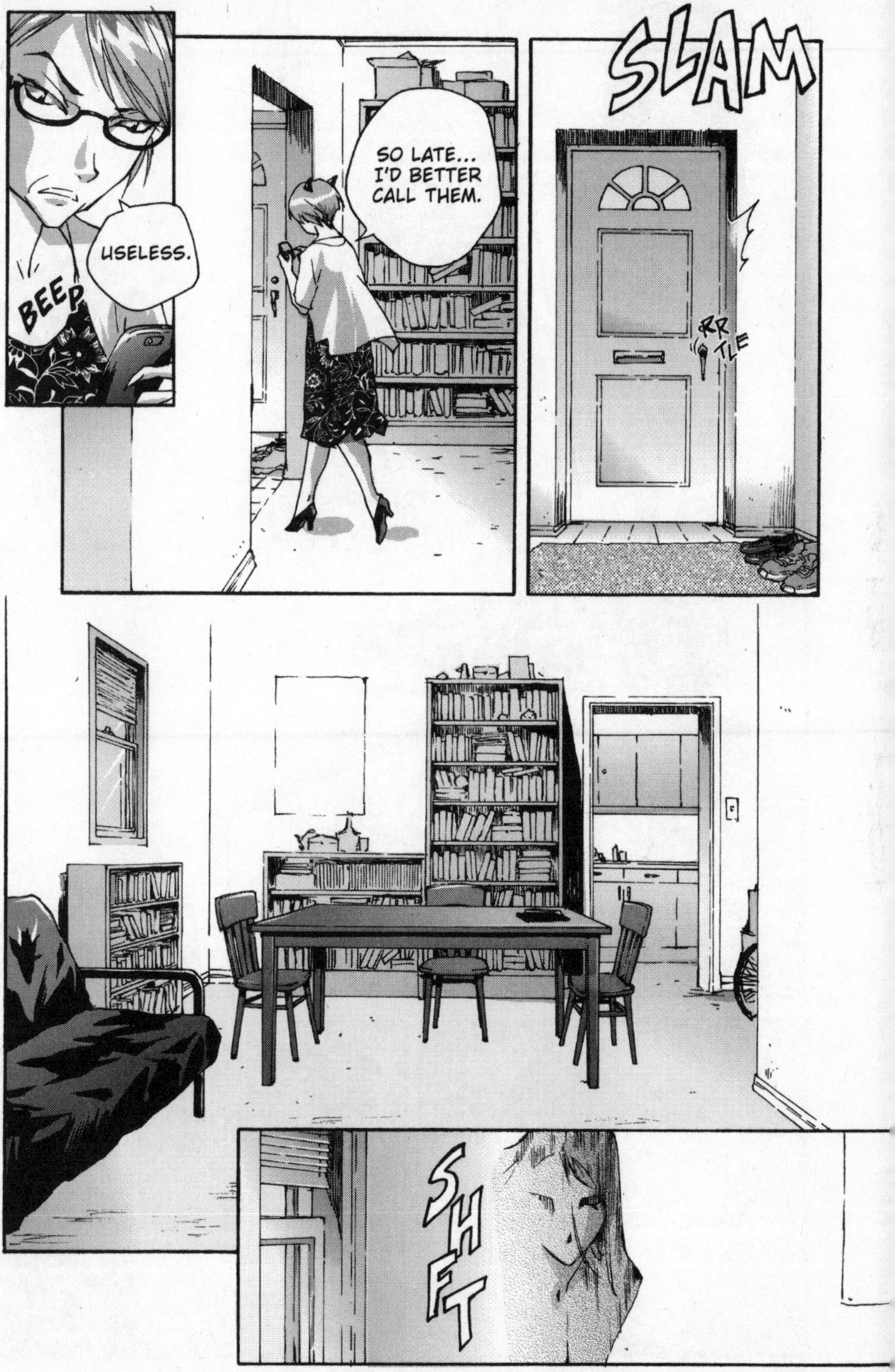
BEEP
USELESS.
SO LATE... I'D BETTER CALL THEM.
SLAM
RRTLE
SHFT

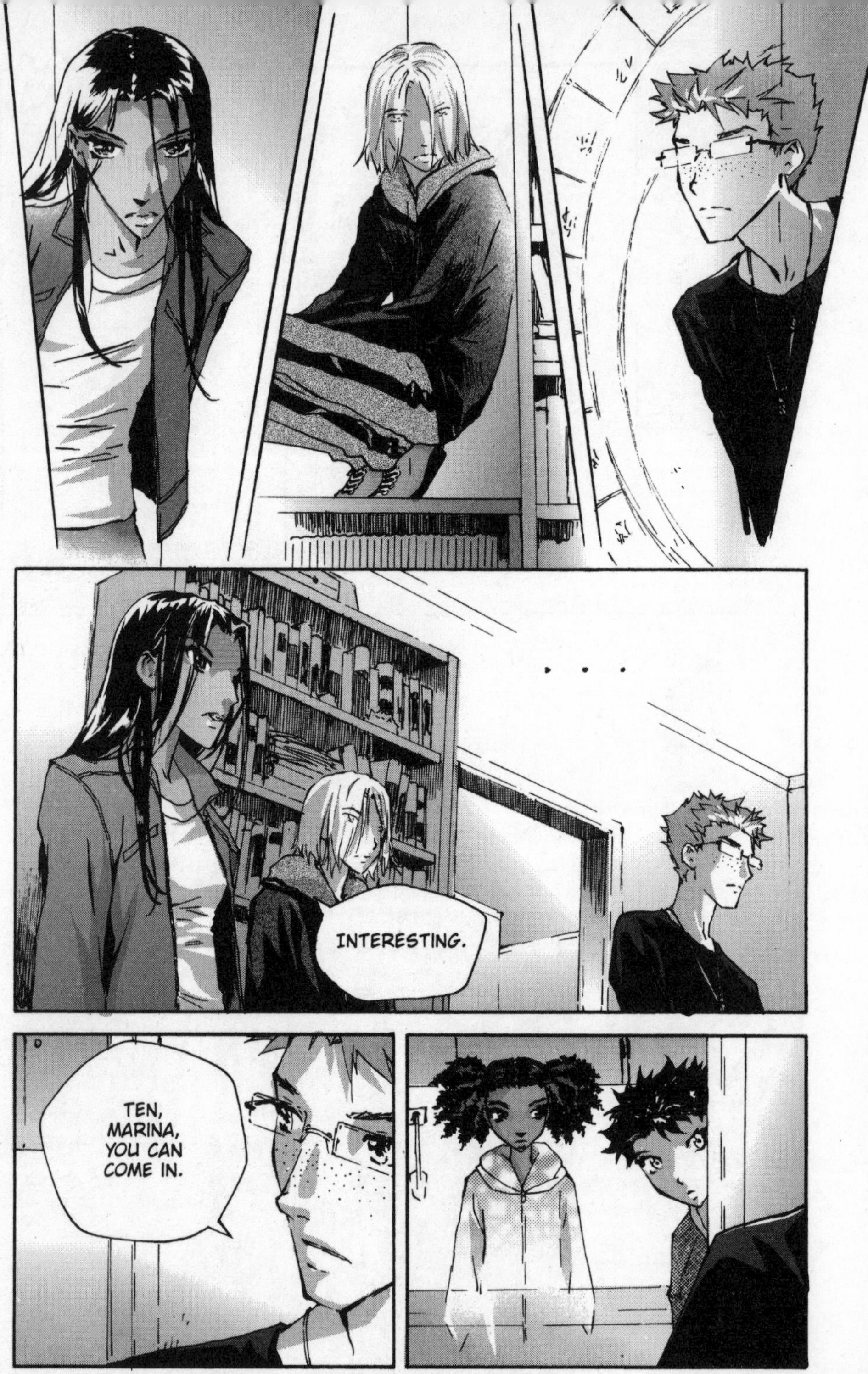
...
INTERESTING.
TEN, MARINA, YOU CAN COME IN.

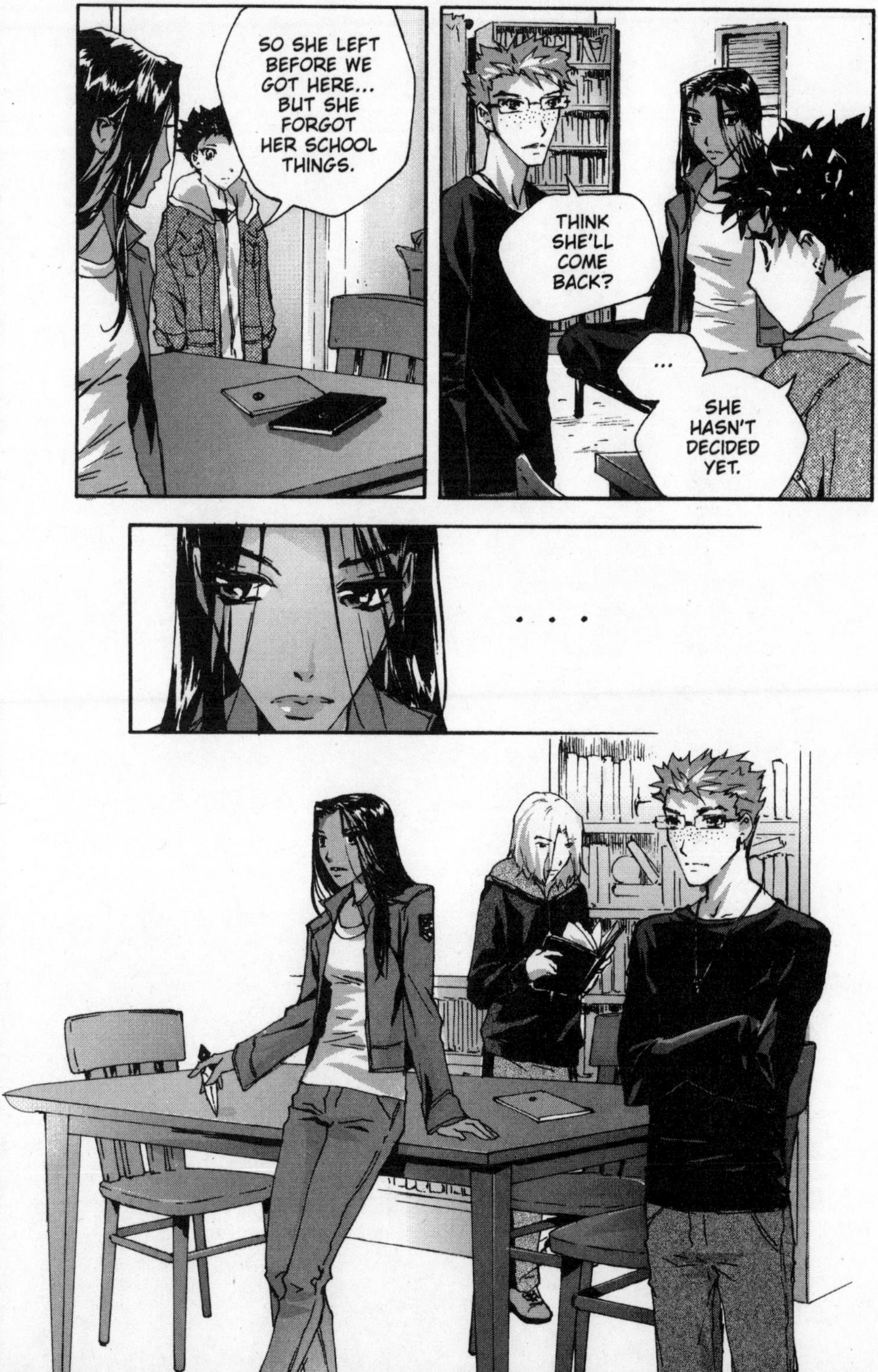
SO SHE LEFT BEFORE WE GOT HERE... BUT SHE FORGOT HER SCHOOL THINGS.
THINK SHE'LL COME BACK?
...
SHE HASN'T DECIDED YET.
...

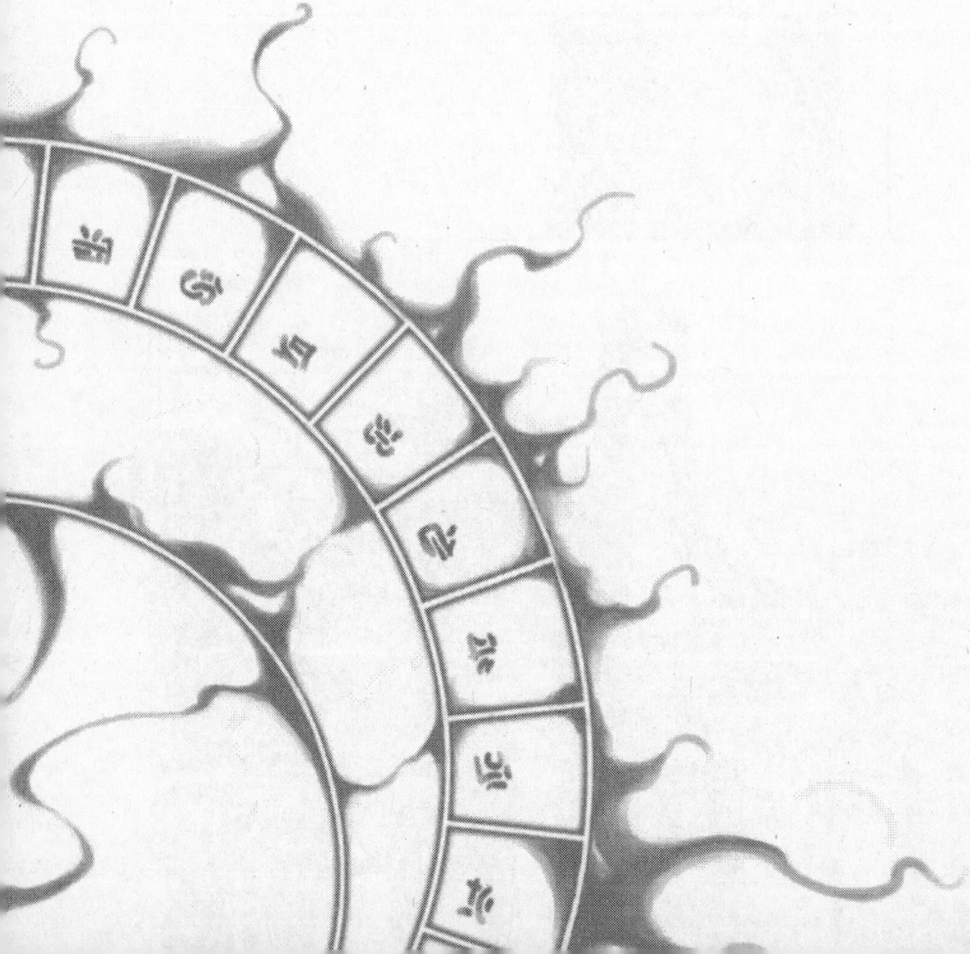

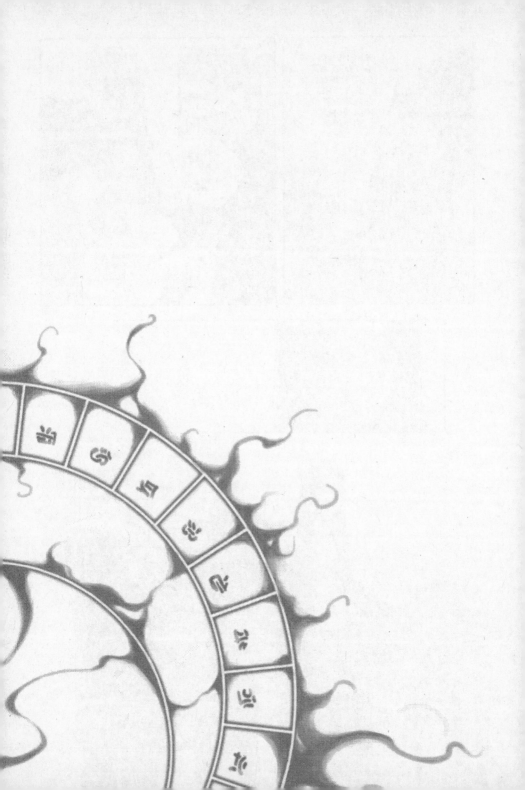

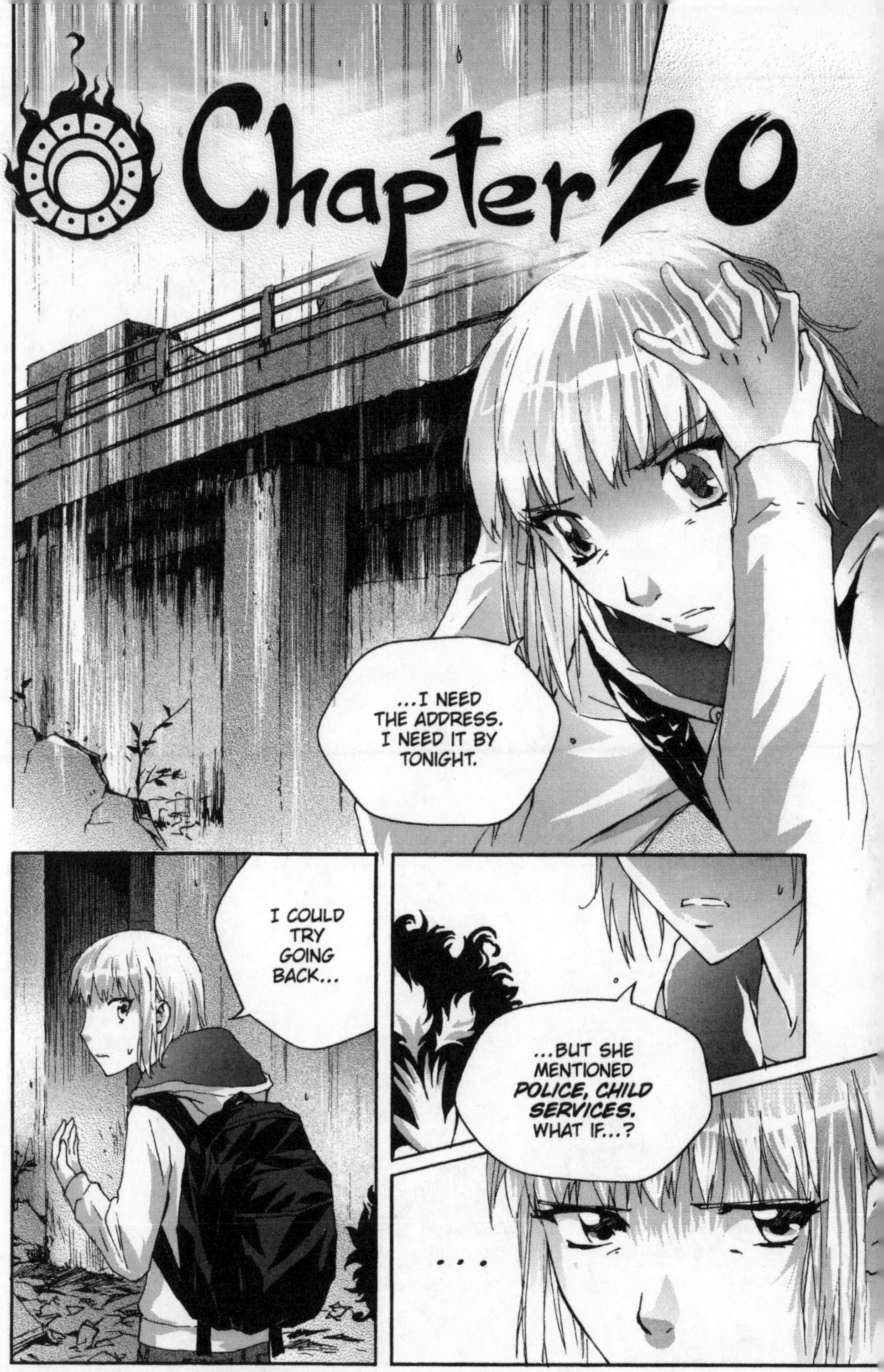
Chapter 20
...I NEED THE ADDRESS. I NEED IT BY TONIGHT.
I COULD TRY GOING BACK...
...BUT SHE MENTIONED POLICE, CHILD SERVICES. WHAT IF...?
...

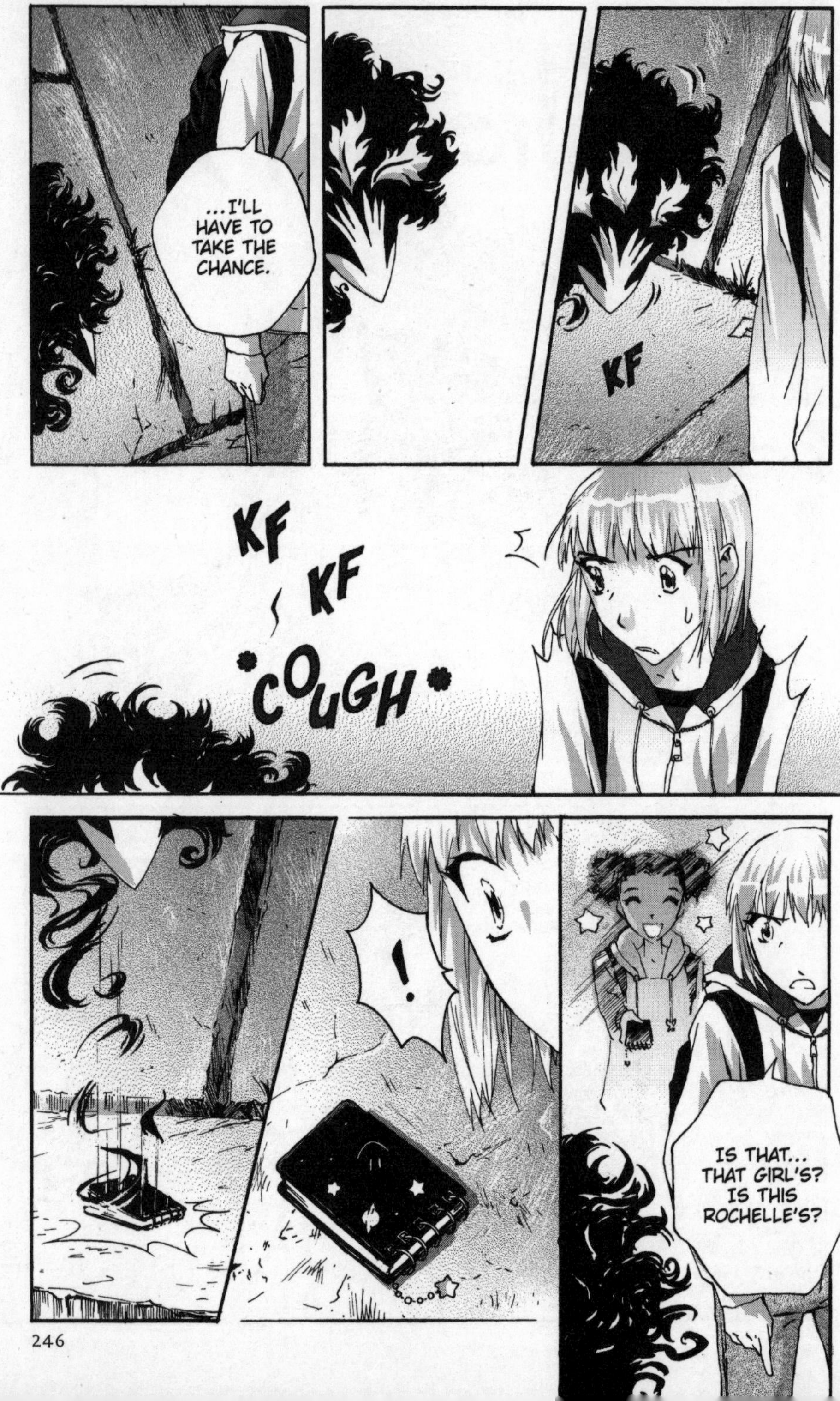
...I'LL HAVE TO TAKE THE CHANCE.
KF
KF
KF
COUGH
!
IS THAT... THAT GIRL'S? IS THIS ROCHELLE'S?

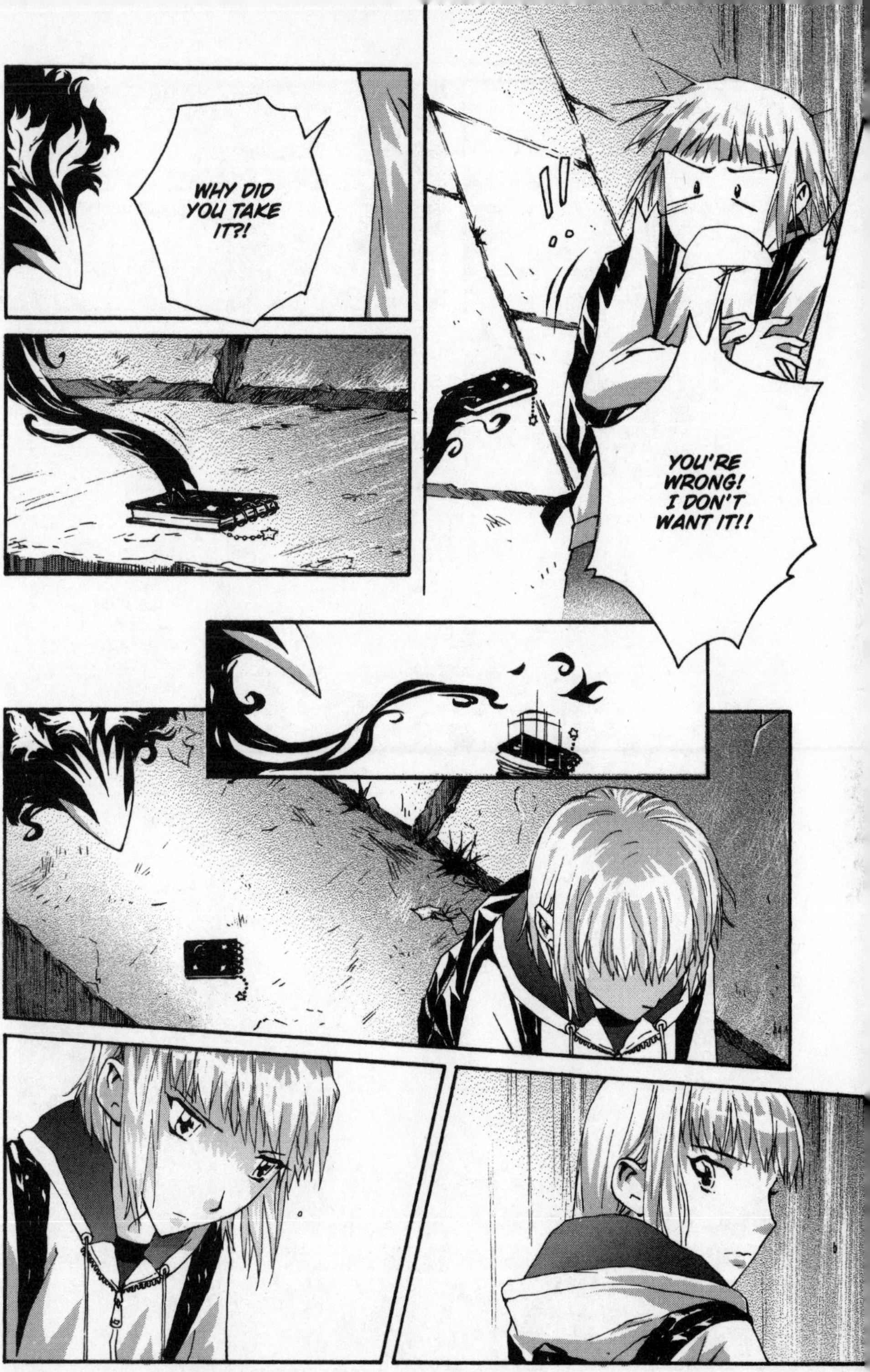
WHY DID YOU TAKE IT?!
YOU'RE WRONG! I DON'T WANT IT!!

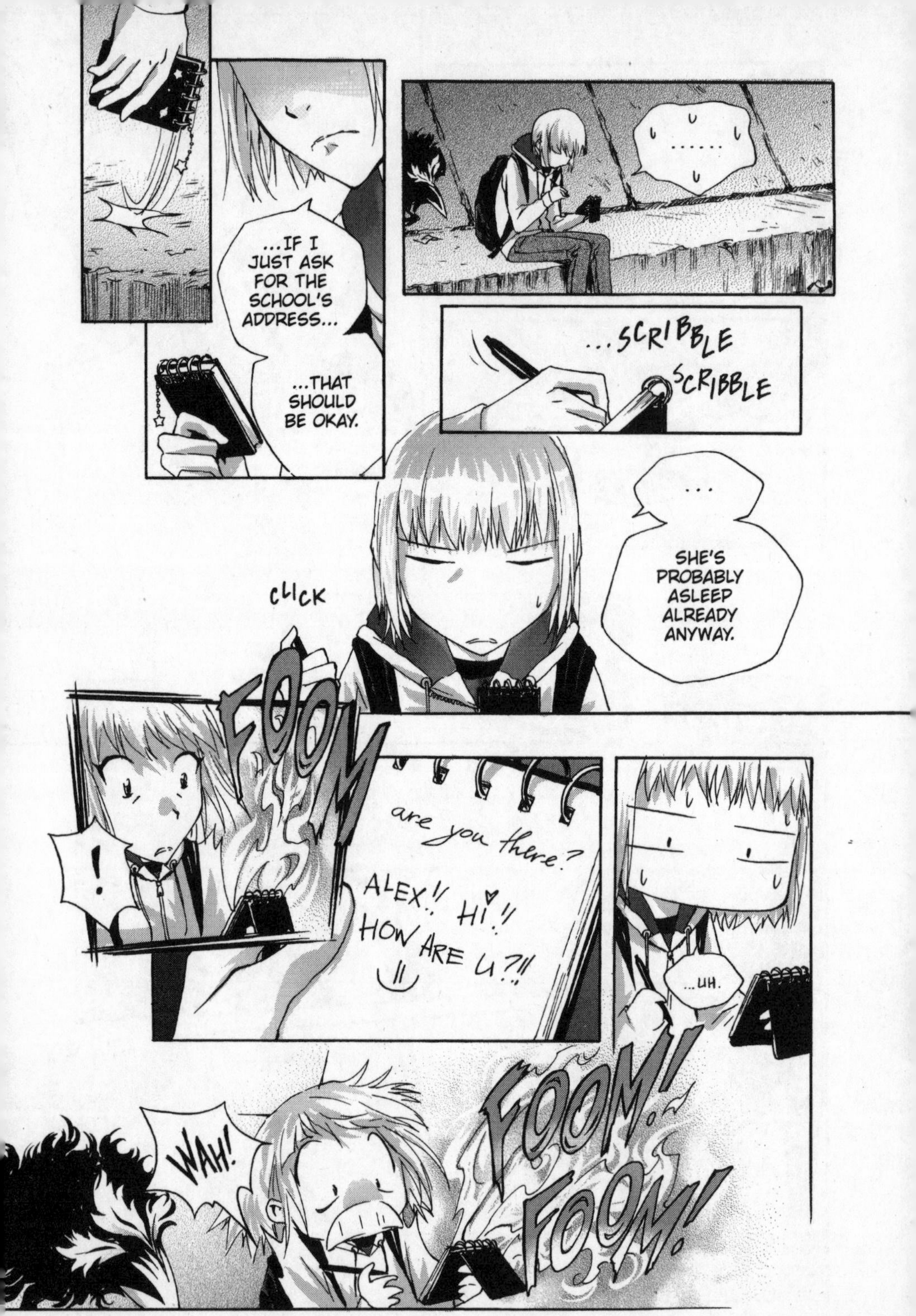
......
...IF I JUST ASK FOR THE SCHOOL'S ADDRESS...
...THAT SHOULD BE OKAY.
...SCRIBBLE SCRIBBLE
...
SHE'S PROBABLY ASLEEP ALREADY ANYWAY.
CLICK
FOOM
!
are you there?
ALEX!! HI!! HOW ARE U?!!
...UH.
WAH!
FOOM! FOOM!

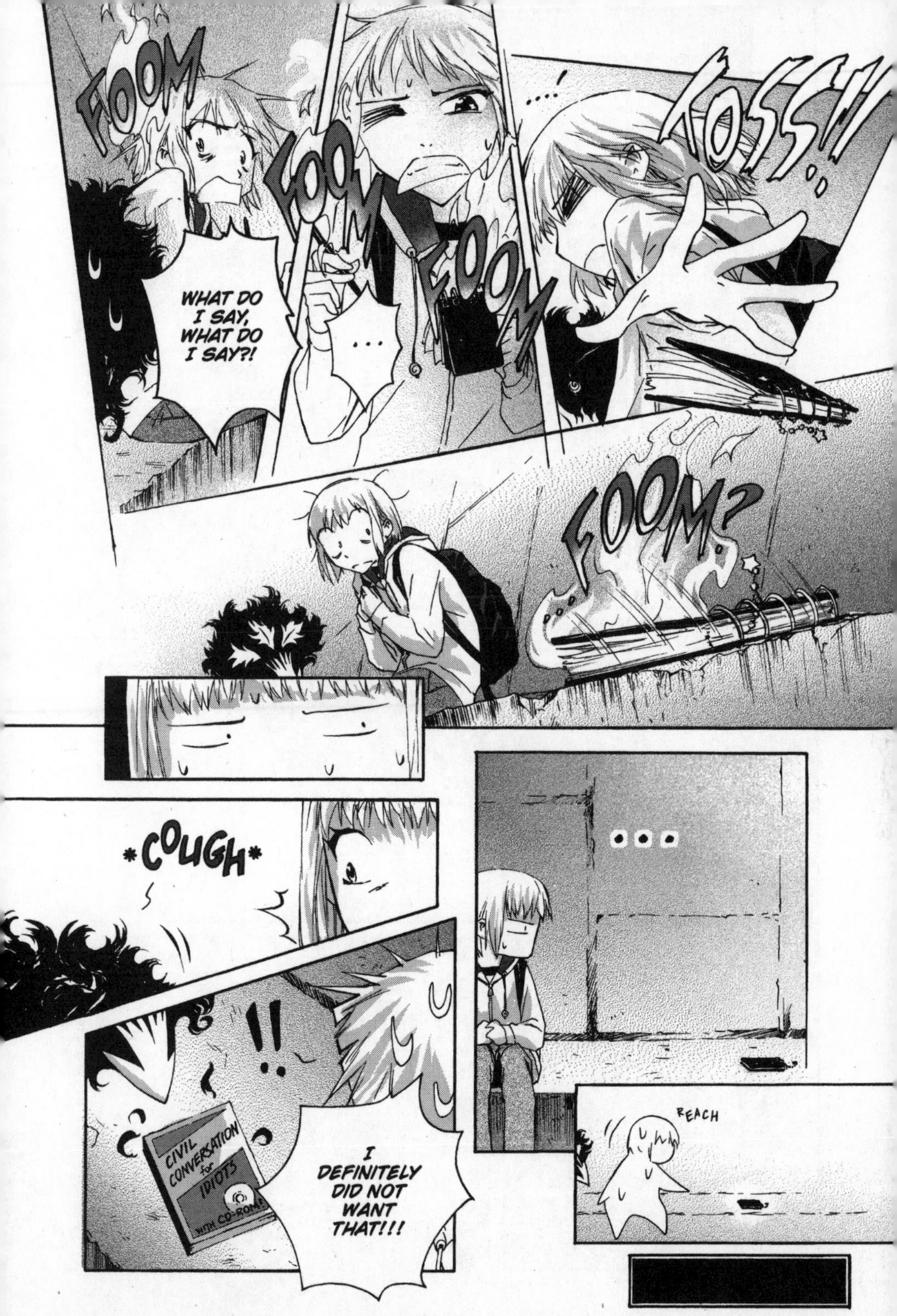
FOOM
WHAT DO I SAY, WHAT DO I SAY?!
...
FOOM
FOOM
...!
KOSSH!!
FOOM?
COUGH
!!
CIVIL CONVERSATION for IDIOTS WITH CD-ROM!
I DEFINITELY DID NOT WANT THAT!!!
...
REACH

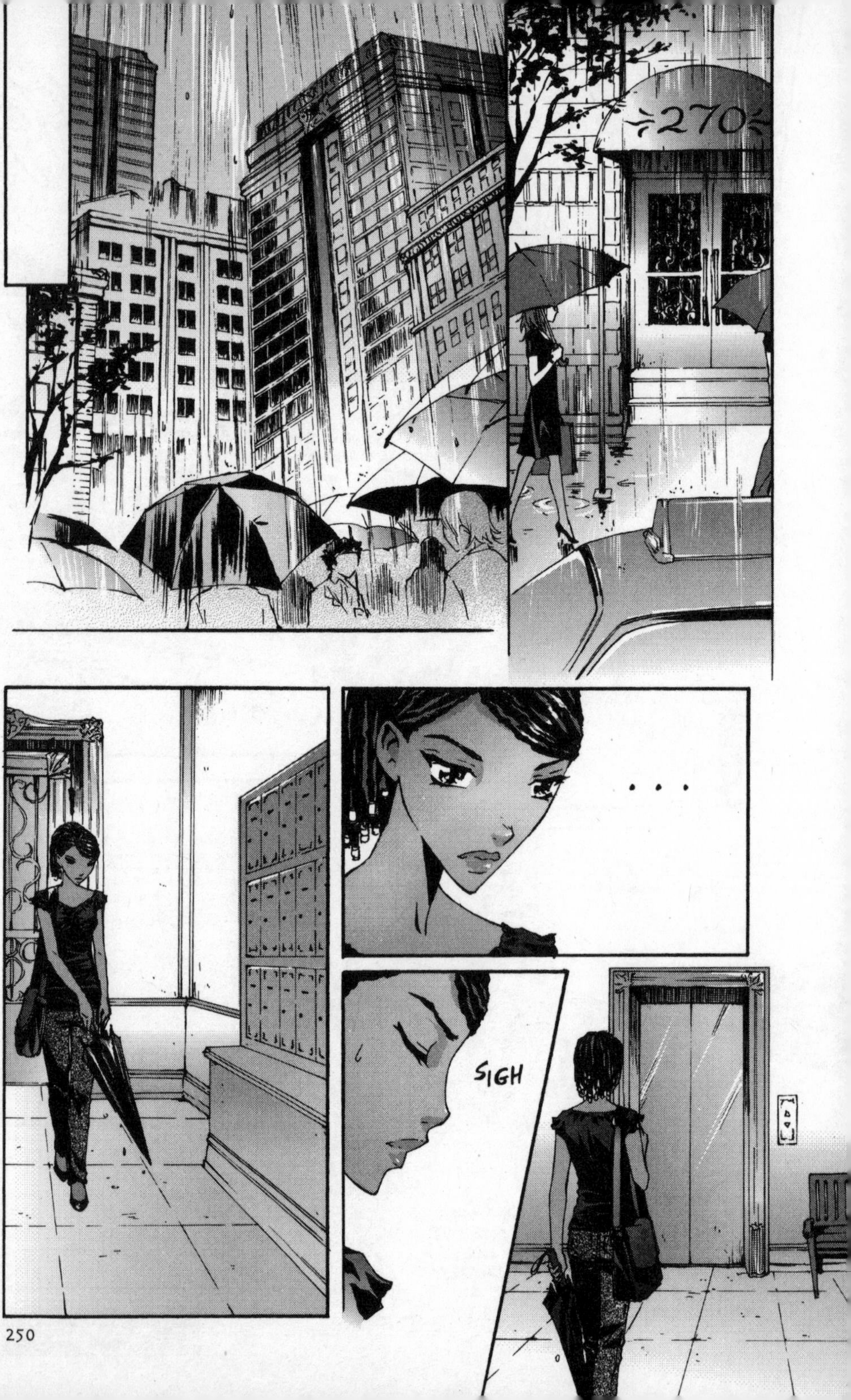
270
. . .
SIGH

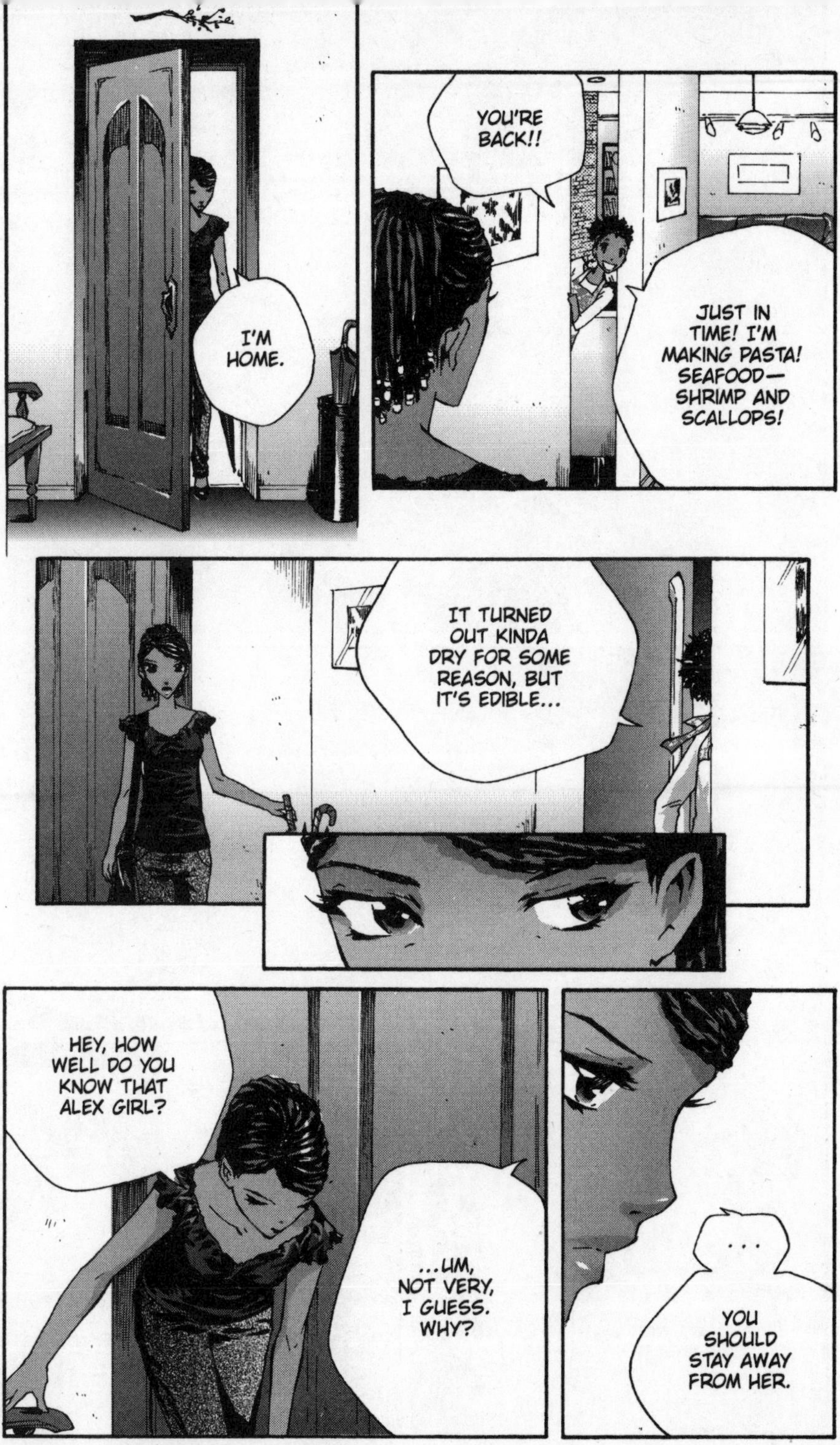
I'M HOME.
YOU'RE BACK!!
JUST IN TIME! I'M MAKING PASTA! SEAFOOD—SHRIMP AND SCALLOPS!
IT TURNED OUT KINDA DRY FOR SOME REASON, BUT IT'S EDIBLE...
HEY, HOW WELL DO YOU KNOW THAT ALEX GIRL?
...UM, NOT VERY, I GUESS. WHY?
...
YOU SHOULD STAY AWAY FROM HER.

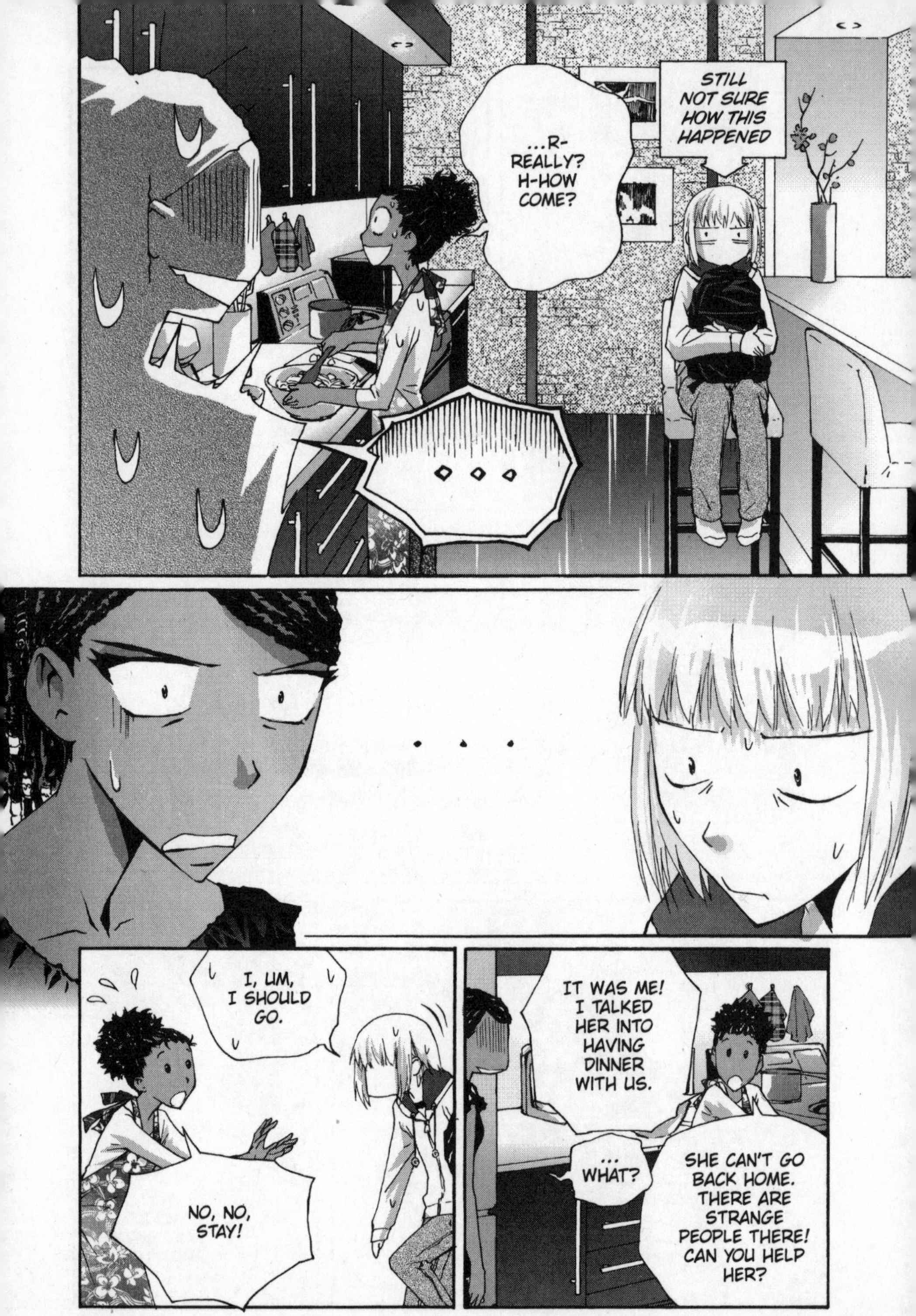
...R-REALLY? H-HOW COME?
STILL NOT SURE HOW THIS HAPPENED
...
...
I, UM, I SHOULD GO.
NO, NO, STAY!
IT WAS ME! I TALKED HER INTO HAVING DINNER WITH US.
... WHAT?
SHE CAN'T GO BACK HOME. THERE ARE STRANGE PEOPLE THERE! CAN YOU HELP HER?

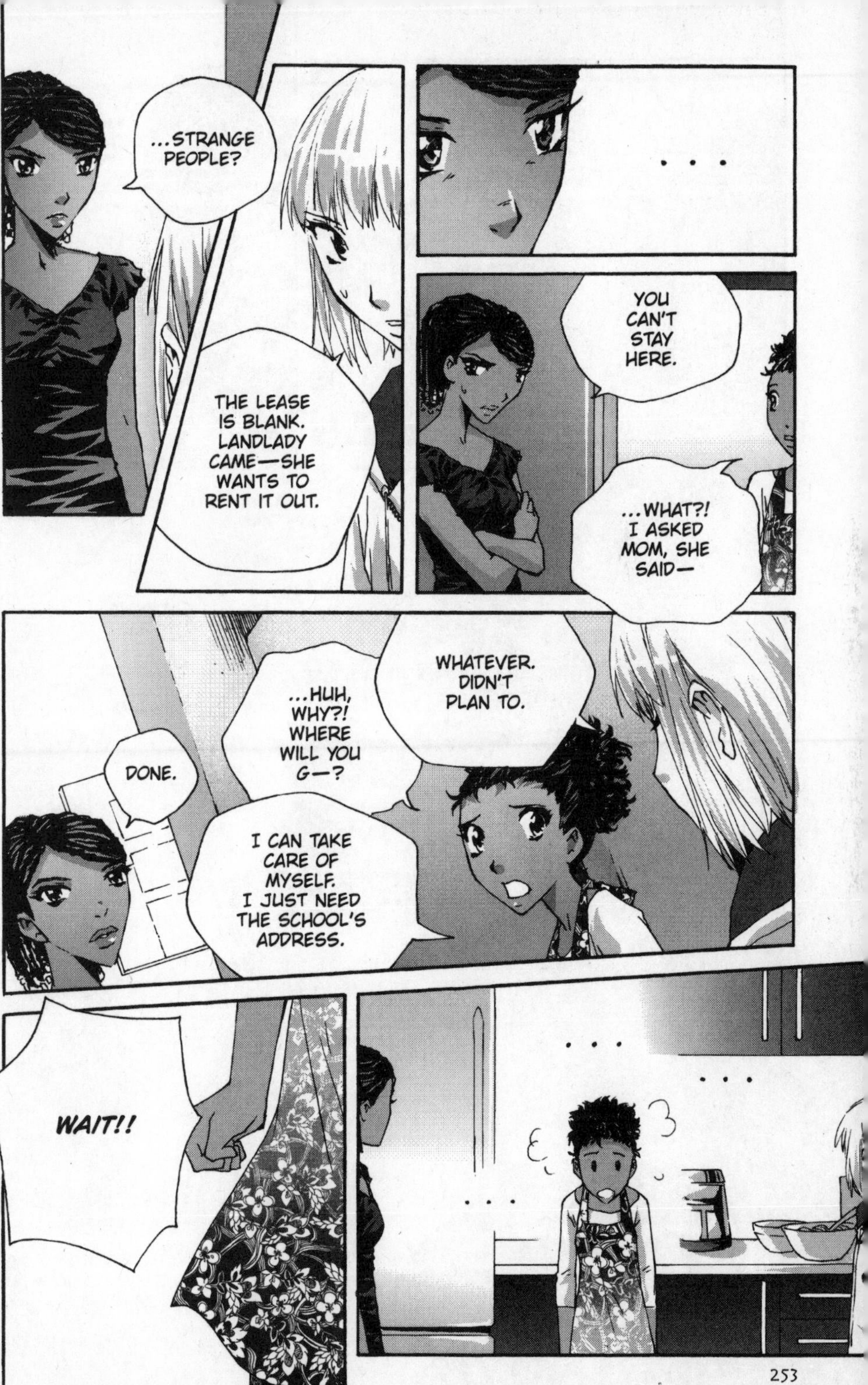
...STRANGE PEOPLE?
THE LEASE IS BLANK. LANDLADY CAME—SHE WANTS TO RENT IT OUT.
. . .
YOU CAN'T STAY HERE.
...WHAT?! I ASKED MOM, SHE SAID—
WHATEVER. DIDN'T PLAN TO.
...HUH, WHY?! WHERE WILL YOU G—?
I CAN TAKE CARE OF MYSELF. I JUST NEED THE SCHOOL'S ADDRESS.
DONE.
WAIT!!
. . .
. . .
. . .

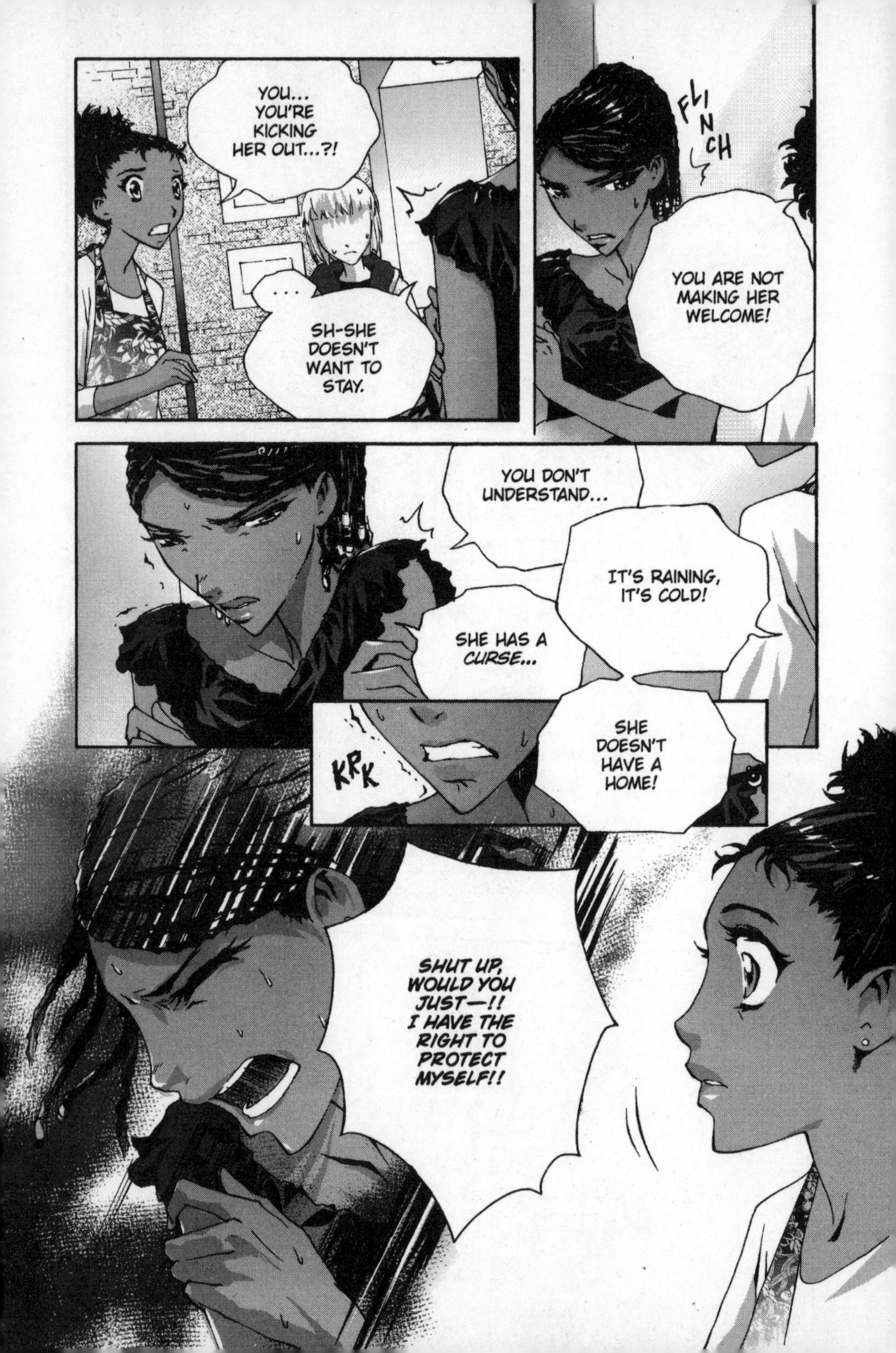
YOU... YOU'RE KICKING HER OUT...?!
...
SH-SHE DOESN'T WANT TO STAY.
FLINCH
YOU ARE NOT MAKING HER WELCOME!
YOU DON'T UNDERSTAND...
IT'S RAINING, IT'S COLD!
SHE HAS A CURSE...
KRK
SHE DOESN'T HAVE A HOME!
SHUT UP, WOULD YOU JUST—!! I HAVE THE RIGHT TO PROTECT MYSELF!!

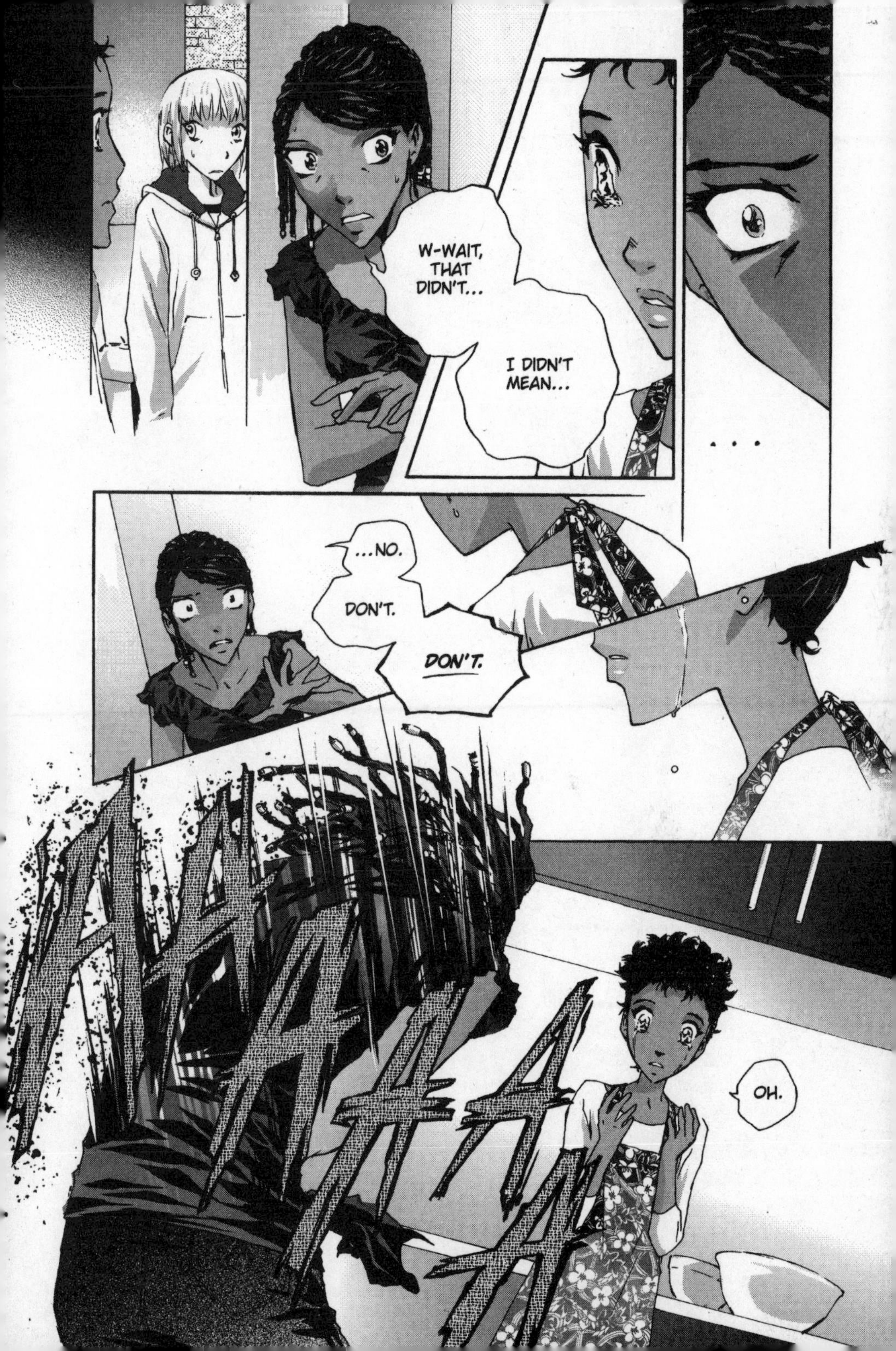
W-WAIT, THAT DIDN'T...
I DIDN'T MEAN...
. . .
...NO.
DON'T.
DON'T.
OH.

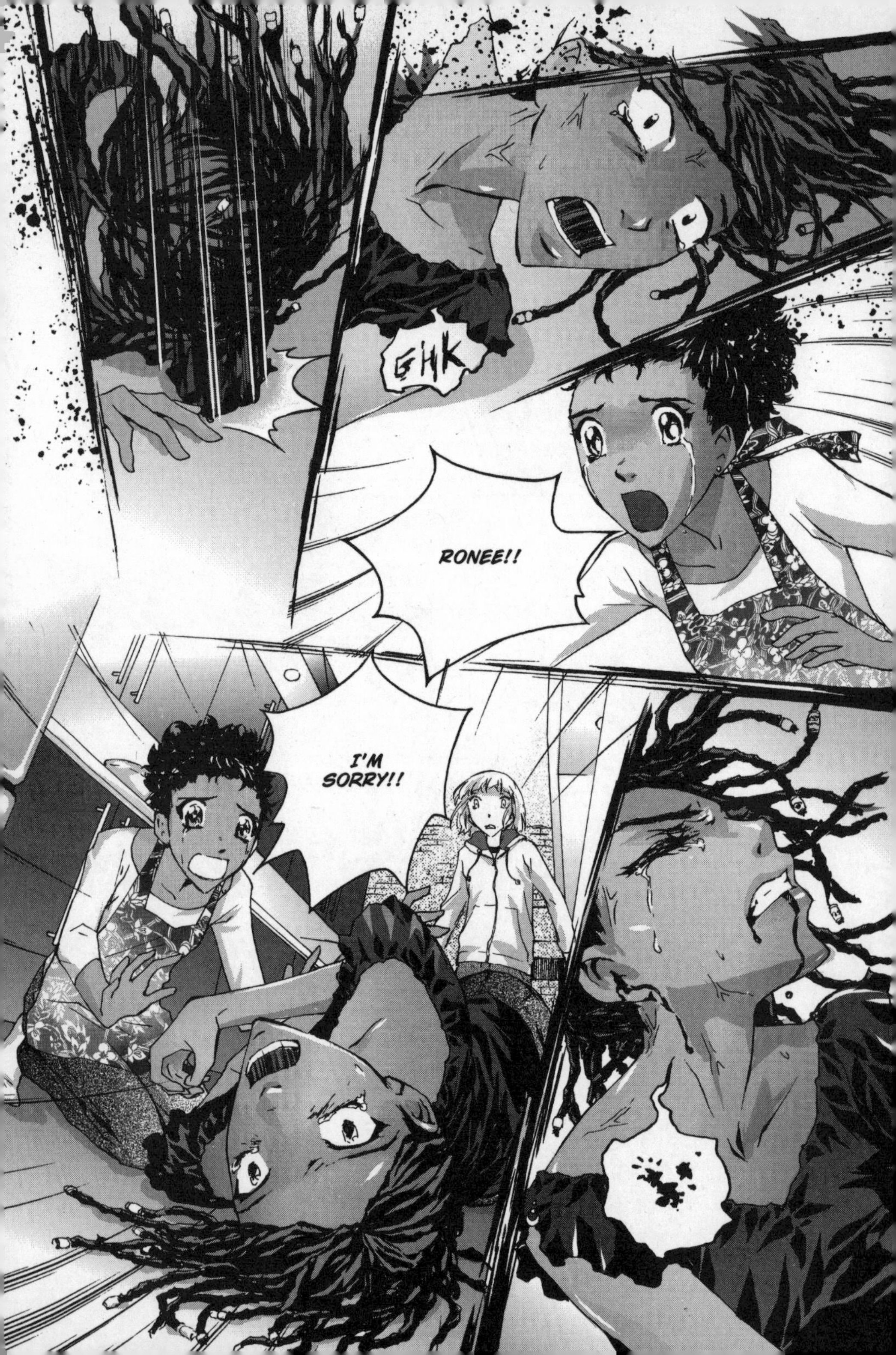
GHK
RONEE!!
I'M SORRY!!

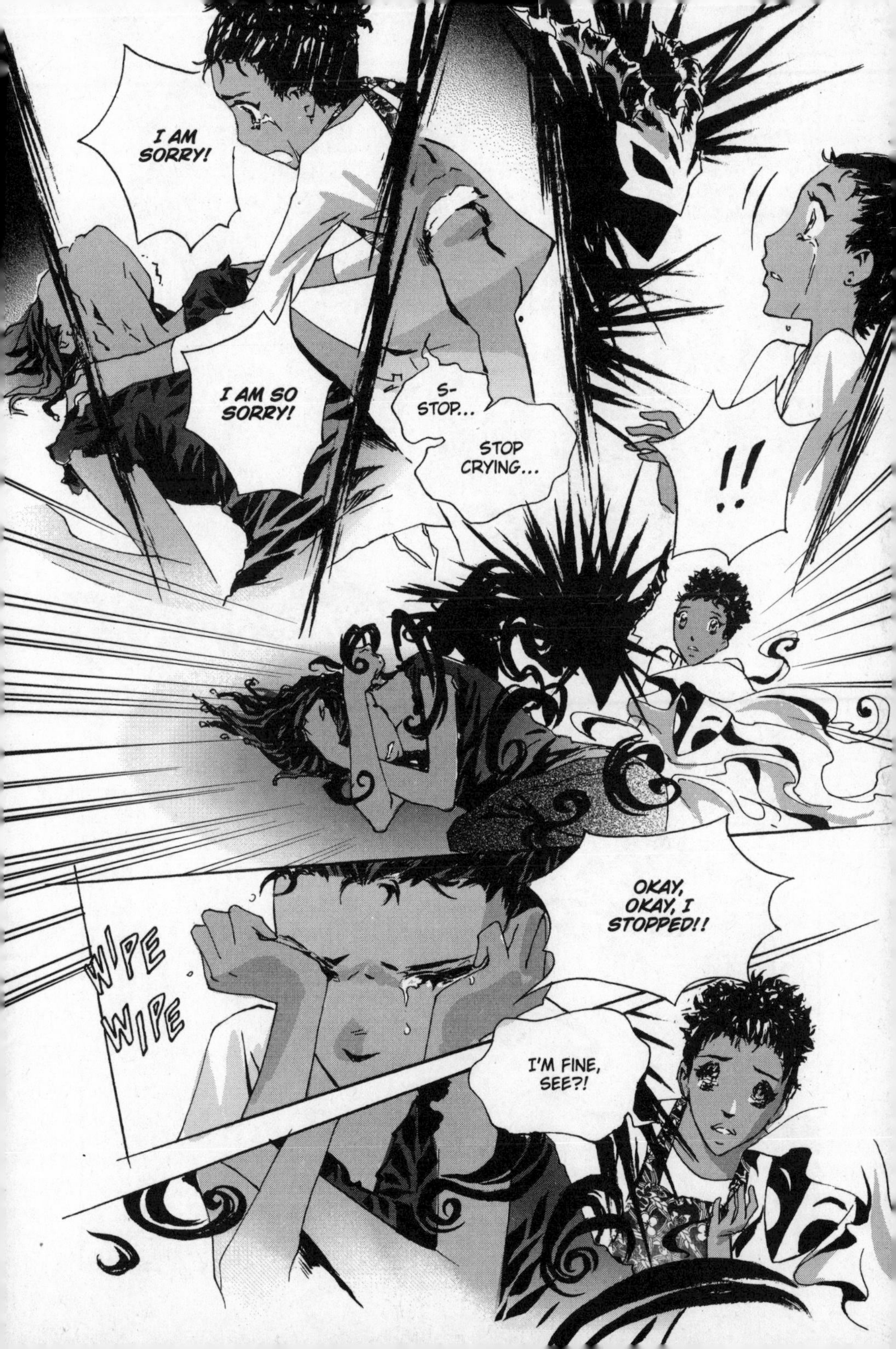
I AM SORRY!
I AM SO SORRY!
S-STOP...
STOP CRYING...
!!
OKAY, OKAY, I STOPPED!!
WIPE WIPE
I'M FINE, SEE?!

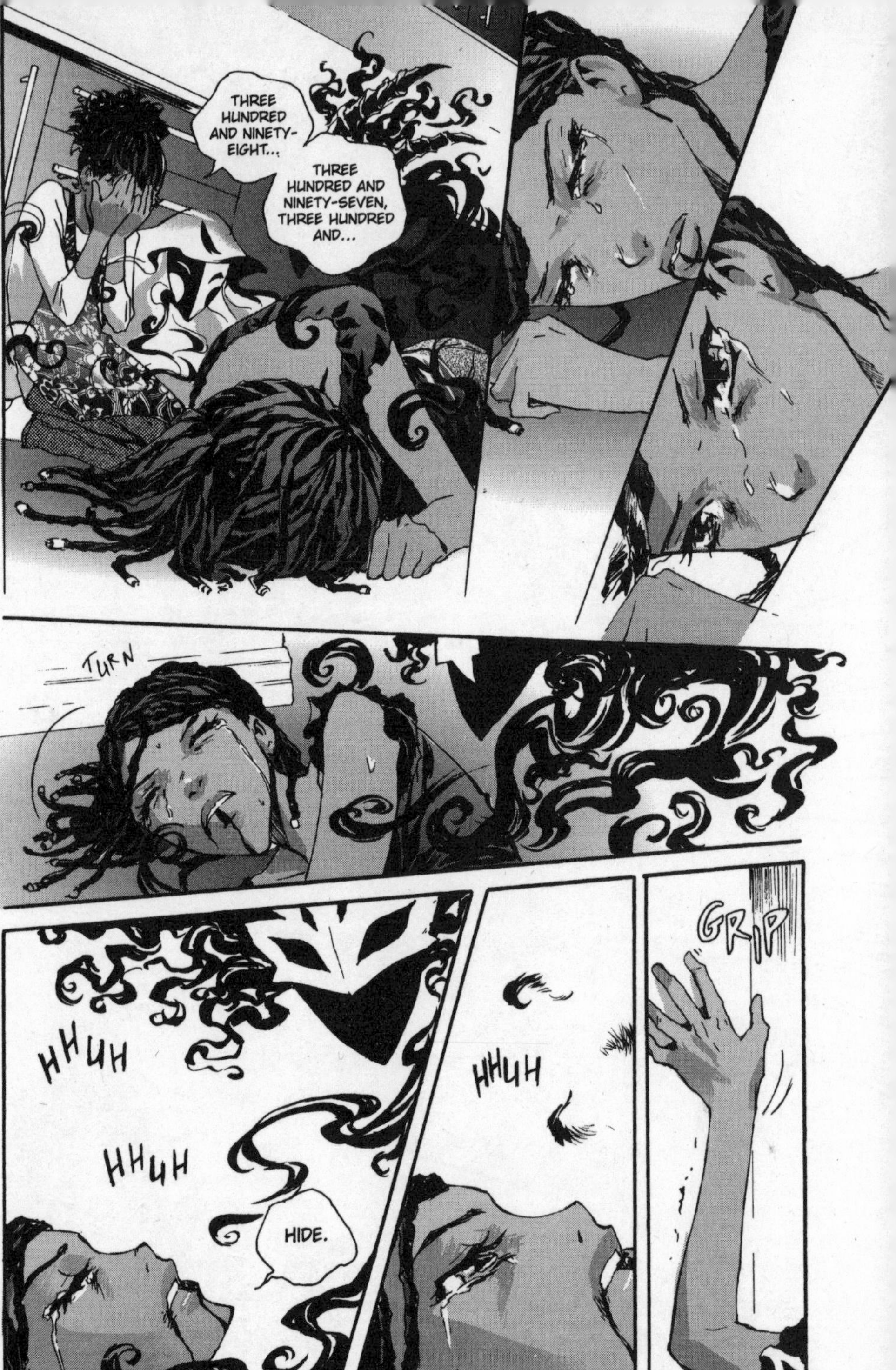

THREE HUNDRED AND NINETY-EIGHT...
THREE HUNDRED AND NINETY-SEVEN, THREE HUNDRED AND...
TURN
HHUH
HHUH
HIDE.
HHUH
GRIP

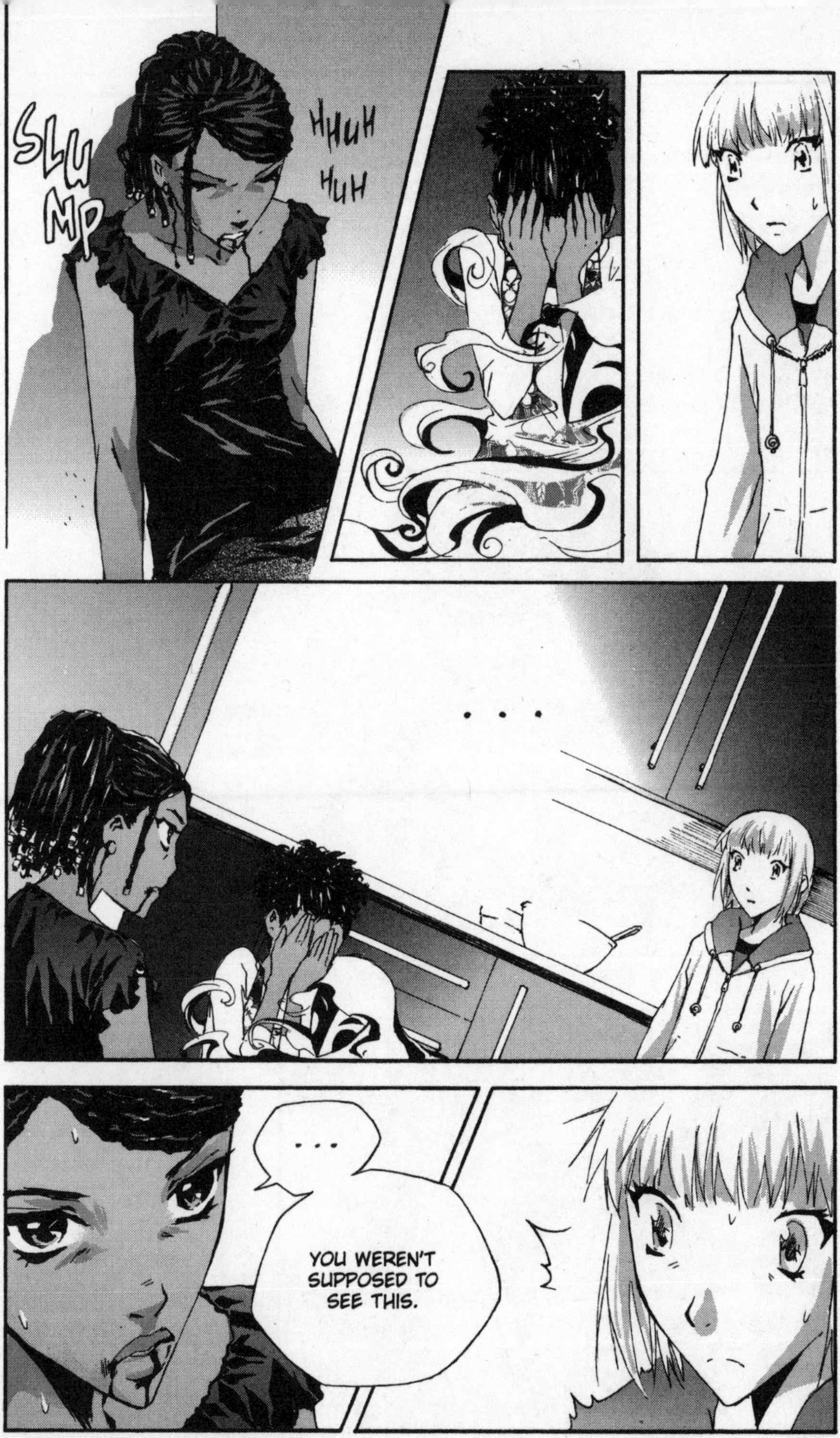
SLUMP
HHUH HUH
...
...
YOU WEREN'T SUPPOSED TO SEE THIS.

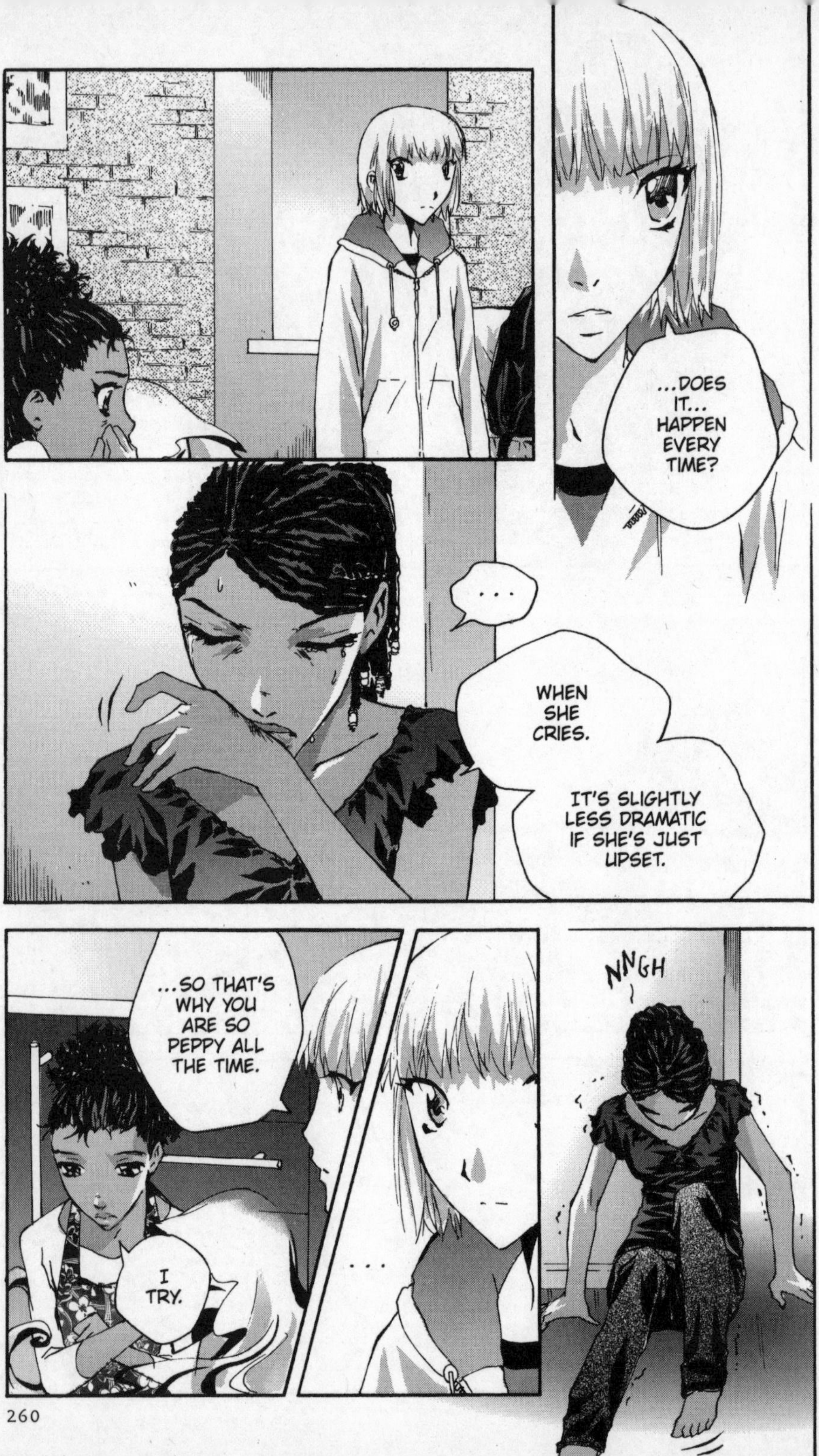
...DOES IT... HAPPEN EVERY TIME?
...
WHEN SHE CRIES.
IT'S SLIGHTLY LESS DRAMATIC IF SHE'S JUST UPSET.
...SO THAT'S WHY YOU ARE SO PEPPY ALL THE TIME.
I TRY.
...
NNGH

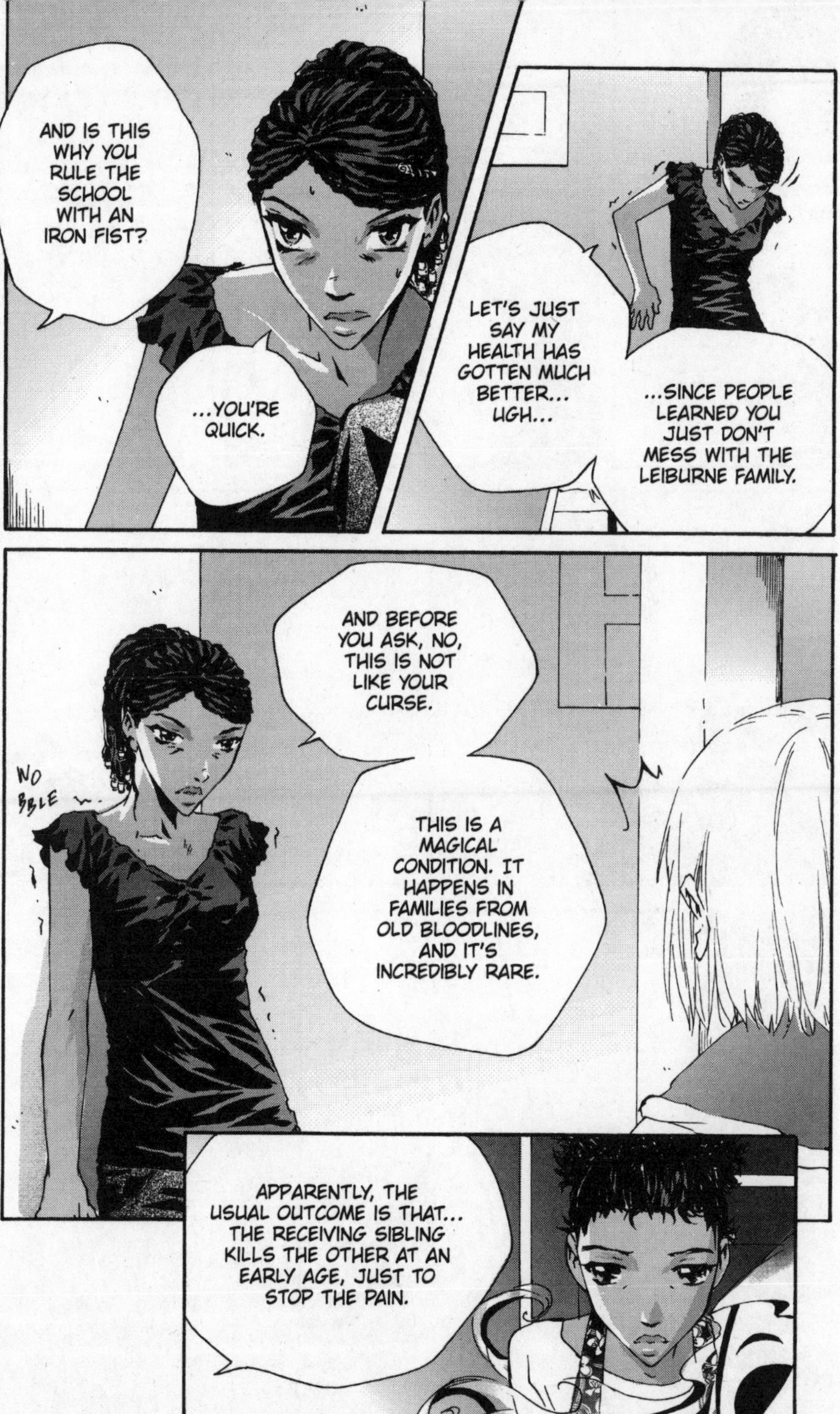
AND IS THIS WHY YOU RULE THE SCHOOL WITH AN IRON FIST?
...YOU'RE QUICK.
LET'S JUST SAY MY HEALTH HAS GOTTEN MUCH BETTER... UGH...
...SINCE PEOPLE LEARNED YOU JUST DON'T MESS WITH THE LEIBURNE FAMILY.
WOBBLE
AND BEFORE YOU ASK, NO, THIS IS NOT LIKE YOUR CURSE.
THIS IS A MAGICAL CONDITION. IT HAPPENS IN FAMILIES FROM OLD BLOODLINES, AND IT'S INCREDIBLY RARE.
APPARENTLY, THE USUAL OUTCOME IS THAT... THE RECEIVING SIBLING KILLS THE OTHER AT AN EARLY AGE, JUST TO STOP THE PAIN.

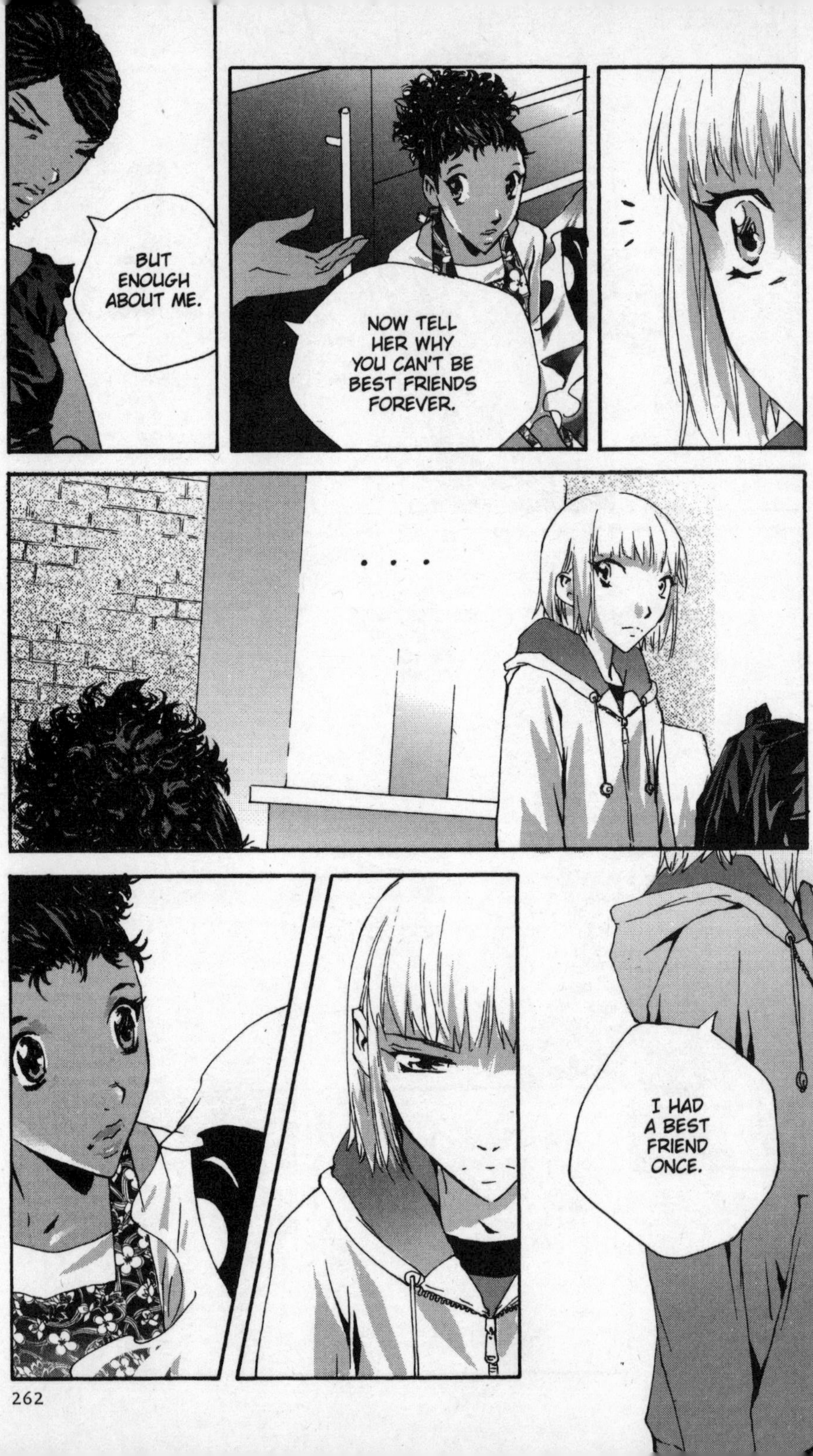
BUT ENOUGH ABOUT ME.
NOW TELL HER WHY YOU CAN'T BE BEST FRIENDS FOREVER.
. . .
I HAD A BEST FRIEND ONCE.

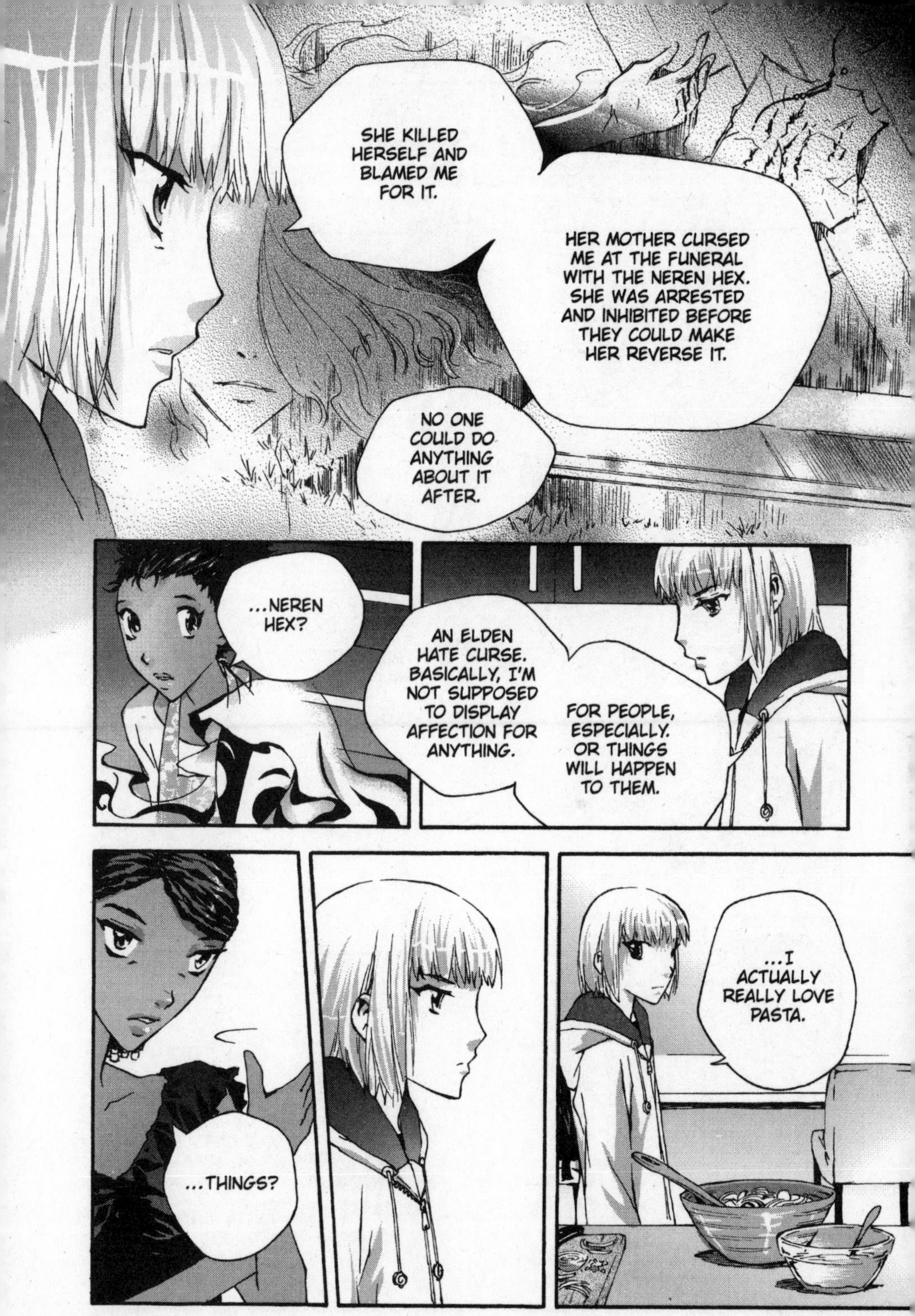
SHE KILLED HERSELF AND BLAMED ME FOR IT.
HER MOTHER CURSED ME AT THE FUNERAL WITH THE NEREN HEX. SHE WAS ARRESTED AND INHIBITED BEFORE THEY COULD MAKE HER REVERSE IT.
NO ONE COULD DO ANYTHING ABOUT IT AFTER.
...NEREN HEX?
AN ELDEN HATE CURSE. BASICALLY, I'M NOT SUPPOSED TO DISPLAY AFFECTION FOR ANYTHING.
FOR PEOPLE, ESPECIALLY. OR THINGS WILL HAPPEN TO THEM.
...THINGS?
...I ACTUALLY REALLY LOVE PASTA.

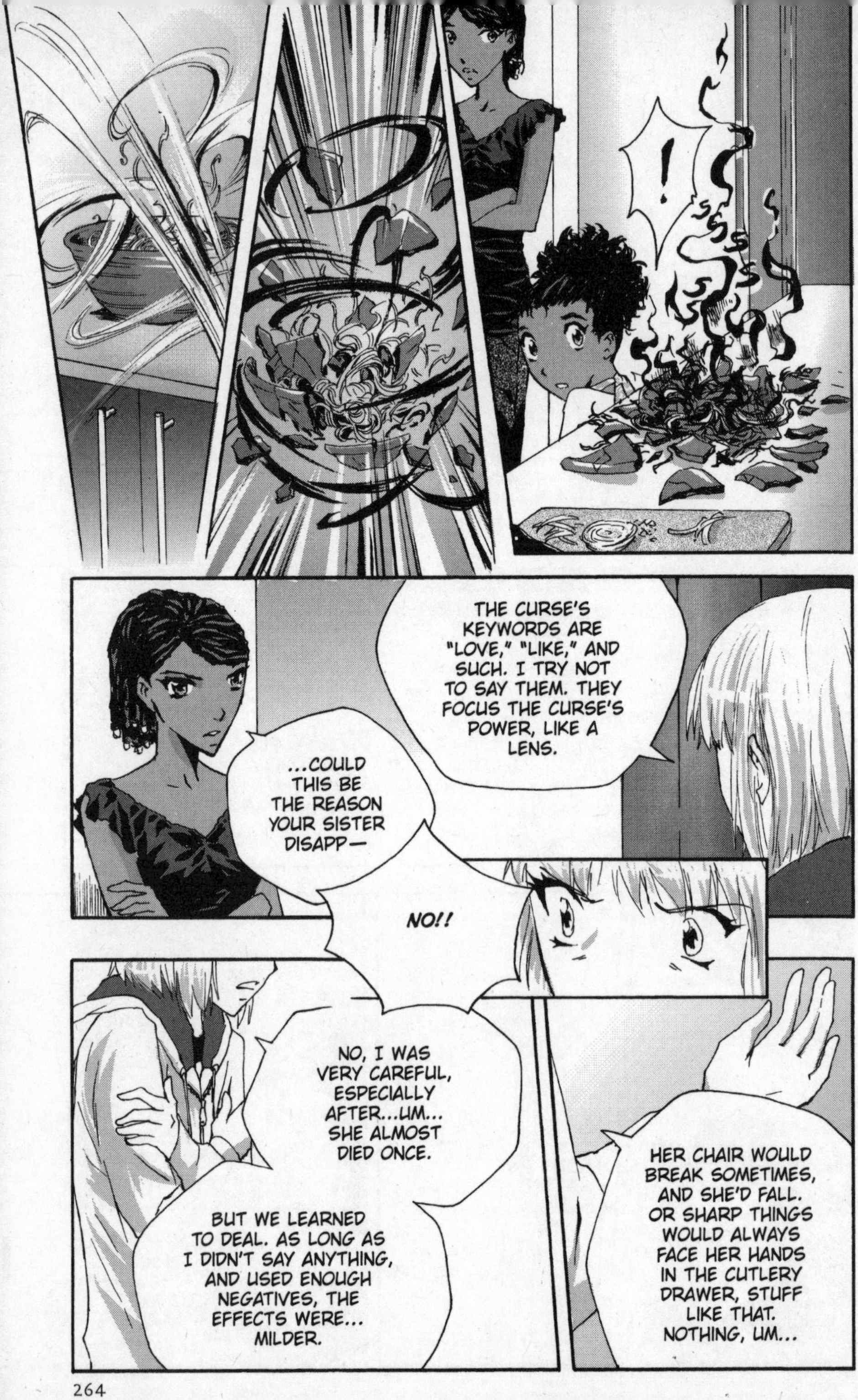

!
SSSSS
THE CURSE'S KEYWORDS ARE "LOVE," "LIKE," AND SUCH. I TRY NOT TO SAY THEM. THEY FOCUS THE CURSE'S POWER, LIKE A LENS.
...COULD THIS BE THE REASON YOUR SISTER DISAPP—
NO!!
NO, I WAS VERY CAREFUL, ESPECIALLY AFTER...UM... SHE ALMOST DIED ONCE.
BUT WE LEARNED TO DEAL. AS LONG AS I DIDN'T SAY ANYTHING, AND USED ENOUGH NEGATIVES, THE EFFECTS WERE... MILDER.
HER CHAIR WOULD BREAK SOMETIMES, AND SHE'D FALL. OR SHARP THINGS WOULD ALWAYS FACE HER HANDS IN THE CUTLERY DRAWER, STUFF LIKE THAT. NOTHING, UM...

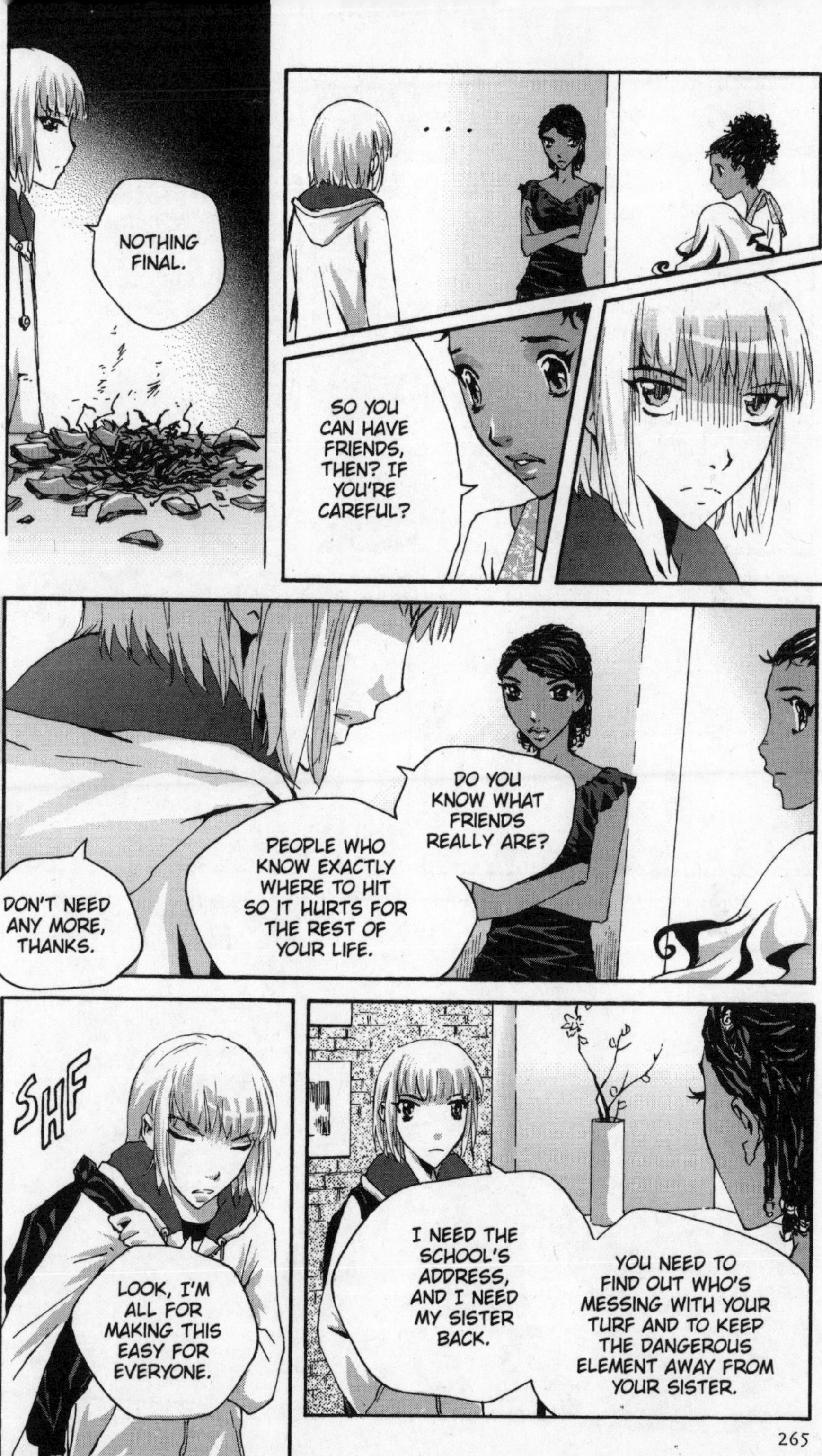
NOTHING FINAL.
. . .
SO YOU CAN HAVE FRIENDS, THEN? IF YOU'RE CAREFUL?
DO YOU KNOW WHAT FRIENDS REALLY ARE?
PEOPLE WHO KNOW EXACTLY WHERE TO HIT SO IT HURTS FOR THE REST OF YOUR LIFE.
DON'T NEED ANY MORE, THANKS.
SHF
LOOK, I'M ALL FOR MAKING THIS EASY FOR EVERYONE.
I NEED THE SCHOOL'S ADDRESS, AND I NEED MY SISTER BACK.
YOU NEED TO FIND OUT WHO'S MESSING WITH YOUR TURF AND TO KEEP THE DANGEROUS ELEMENT AWAY FROM YOUR SISTER.

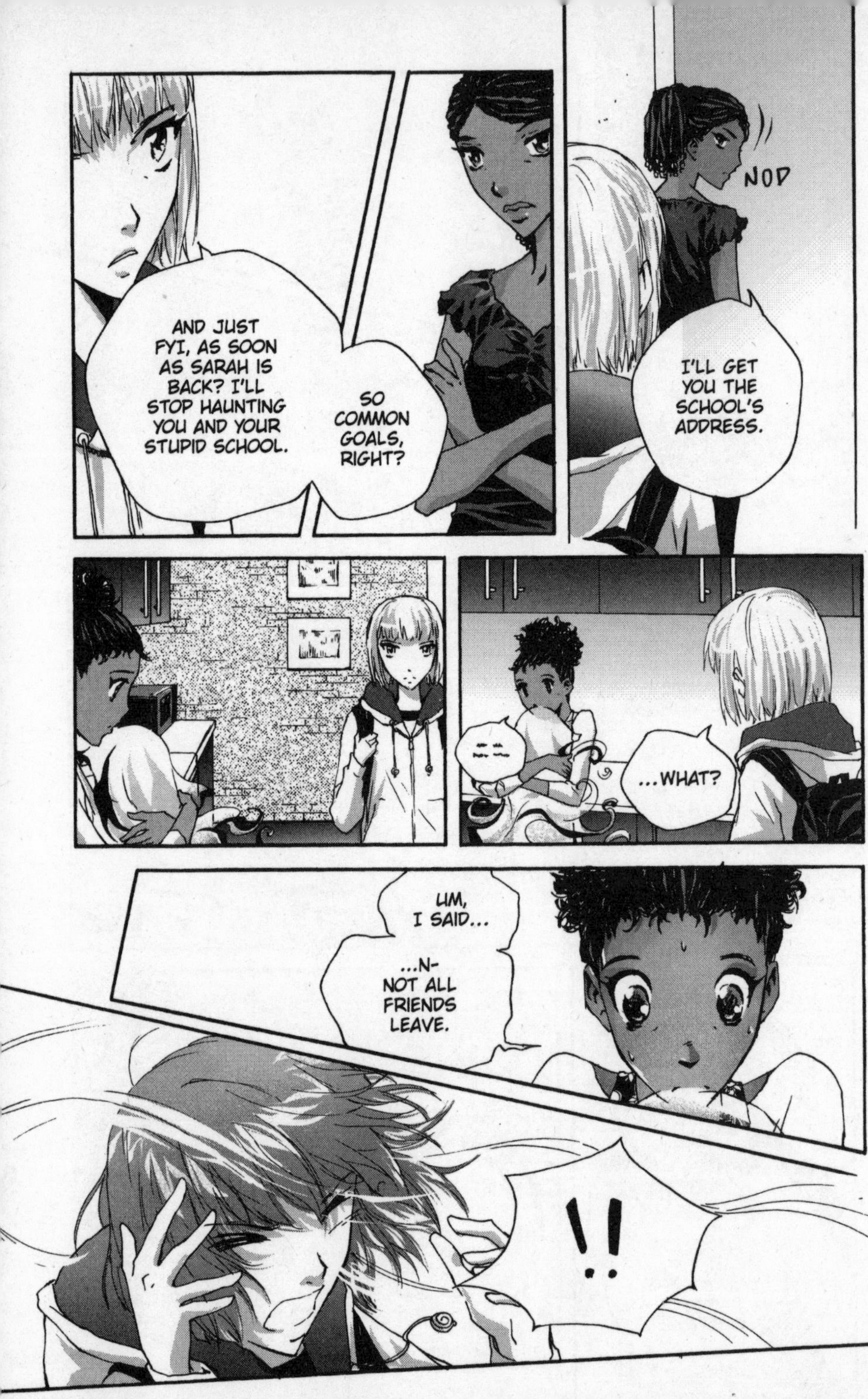
AND JUST FYI, AS SOON AS SARAH IS BACK? I'LL STOP HAUNTING YOU AND YOUR STUPID SCHOOL.
SO COMMON GOALS, RIGHT?
NOD
I'LL GET YOU THE SCHOOL'S ADDRESS.
...WHAT?
UM, I SAID...
...N- NOT ALL FRIENDS LEAVE.
!!

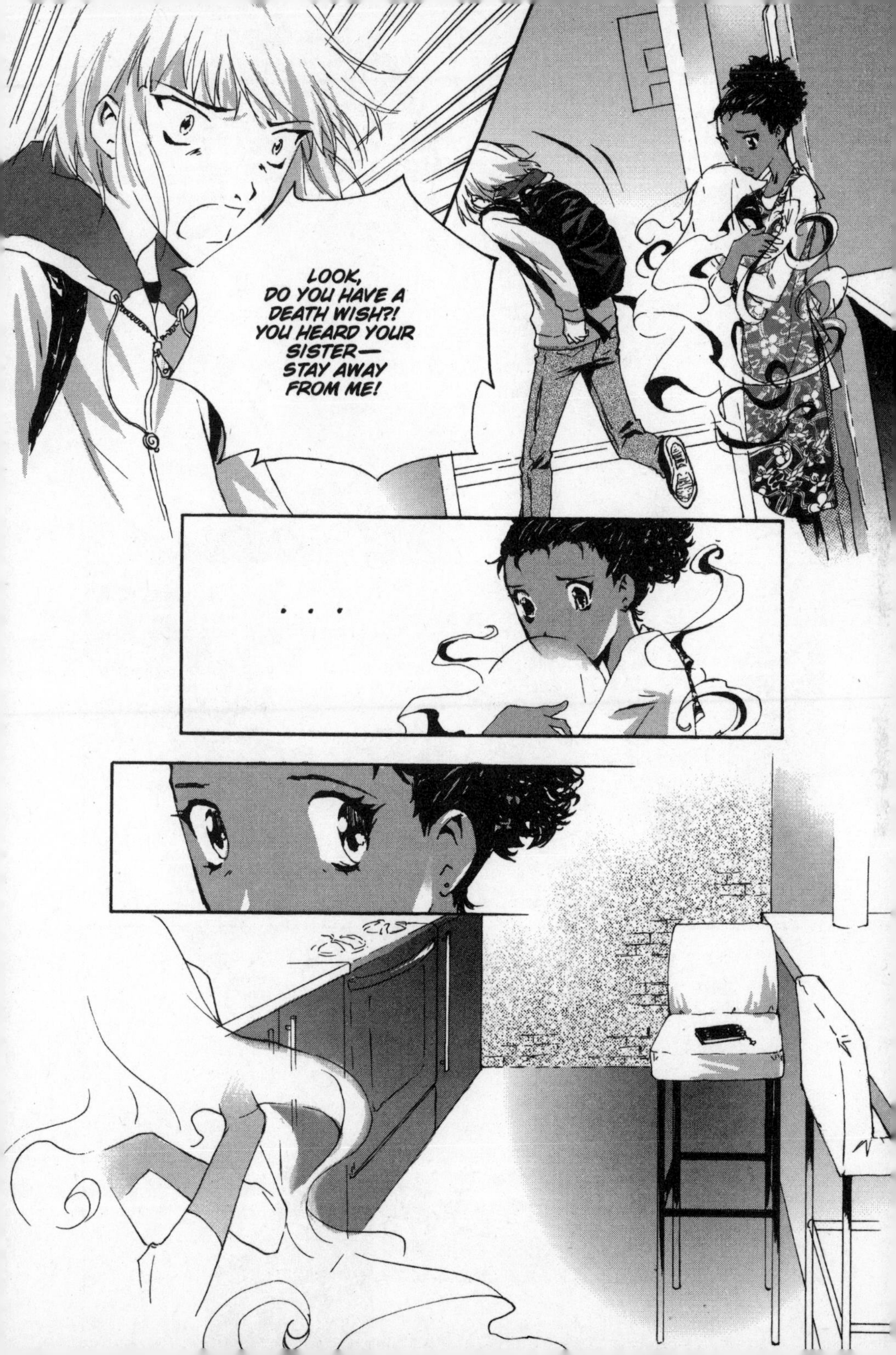
LOOK, DO YOU HAVE A DEATH WISH?! YOU HEARD YOUR SISTER—STAY AWAY FROM ME!
. . .

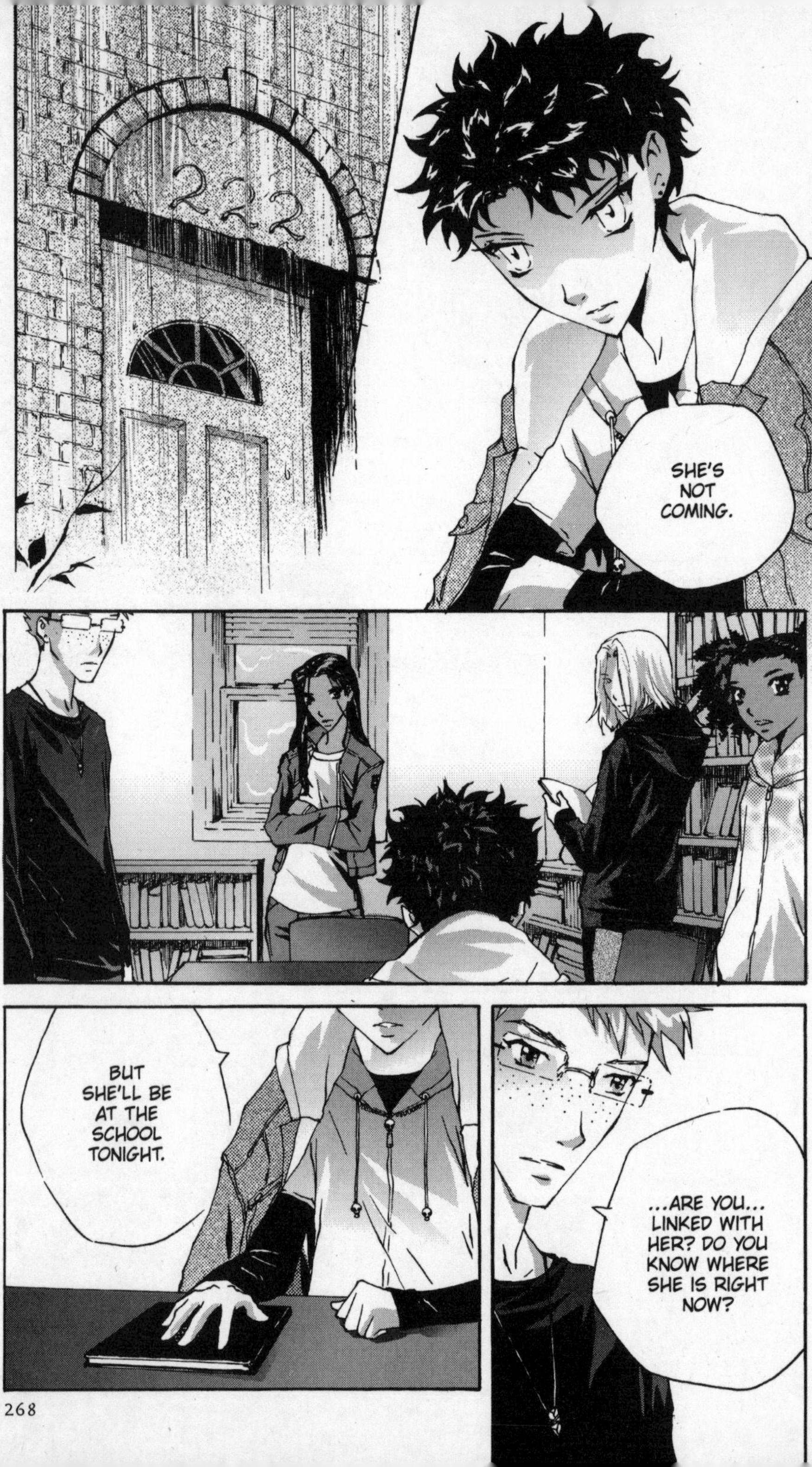
SHE'S NOT COMING.
BUT SHE'LL BE AT THE SCHOOL TONIGHT.
...ARE YOU... LINKED WITH HER? DO YOU KNOW WHERE SHE IS RIGHT NOW?

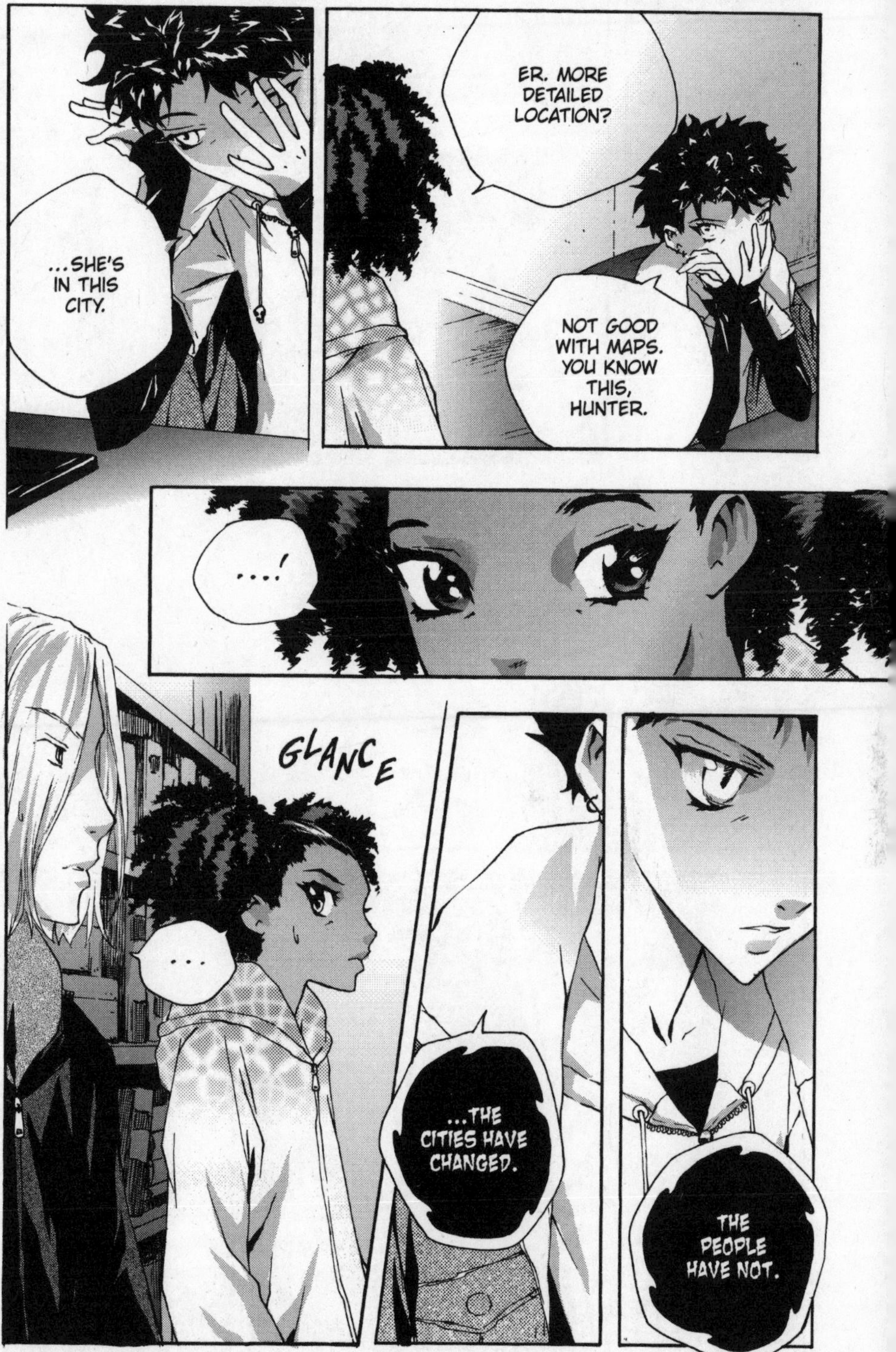
...SHE'S IN THIS CITY.
ER. MORE DETAILED LOCATION?
NOT GOOD WITH MAPS. YOU KNOW THIS, HUNTER.
...!
GLANCE
...
...THE CITIES HAVE CHANGED.
THE PEOPLE HAVE NOT.

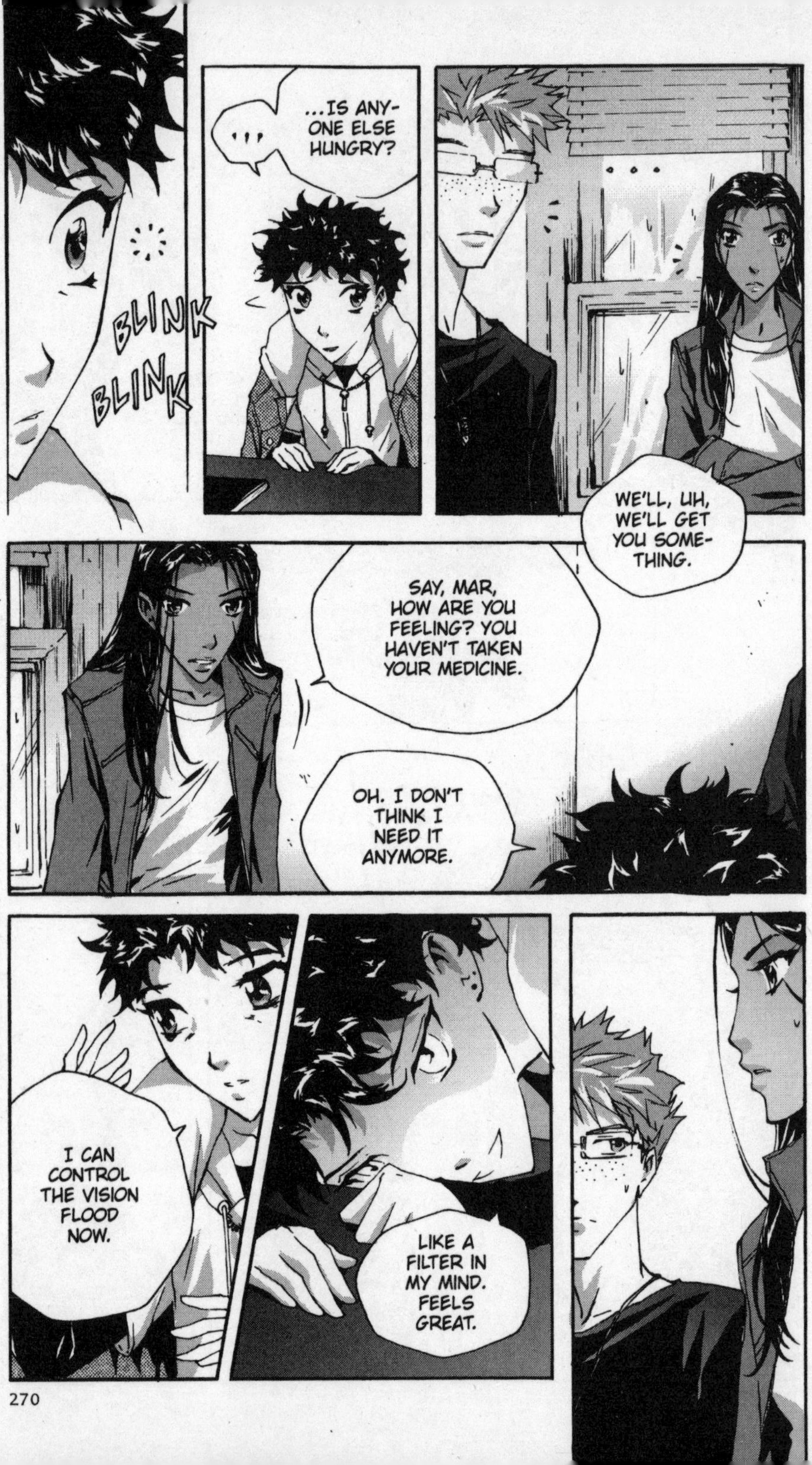
BLINK
BLINK
...
...IS ANYONE ELSE HUNGRY?
WE'LL, UH, WE'LL GET YOU SOMETHING.
SAY, MAR, HOW ARE YOU FEELING? YOU HAVEN'T TAKEN YOUR MEDICINE.
OH. I DON'T THINK I NEED IT ANYMORE.
I CAN CONTROL THE VISION FLOOD NOW.
LIKE A FILTER IN MY MIND. FEELS GREAT.

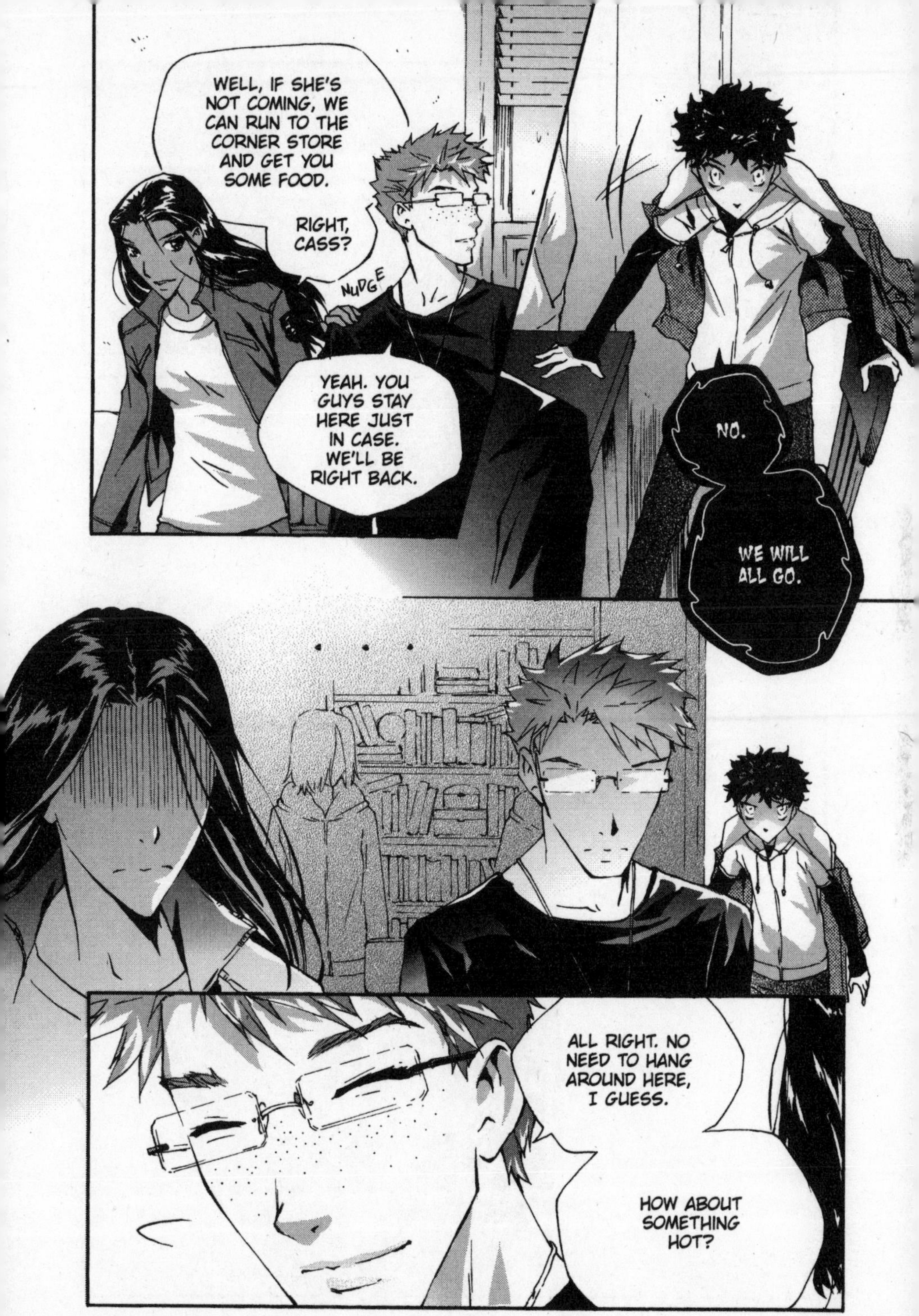
WELL, IF SHE'S NOT COMING, WE CAN RUN TO THE CORNER STORE AND GET YOU SOME FOOD.
RIGHT, CASS?
NUDGE
YEAH. YOU GUYS STAY HERE JUST IN CASE. WE'LL BE RIGHT BACK.
NO.
WE WILL ALL GO.
• • •
ALL RIGHT. NO NEED TO HANG AROUND HERE, I GUESS.
HOW ABOUT SOMETHING HOT?

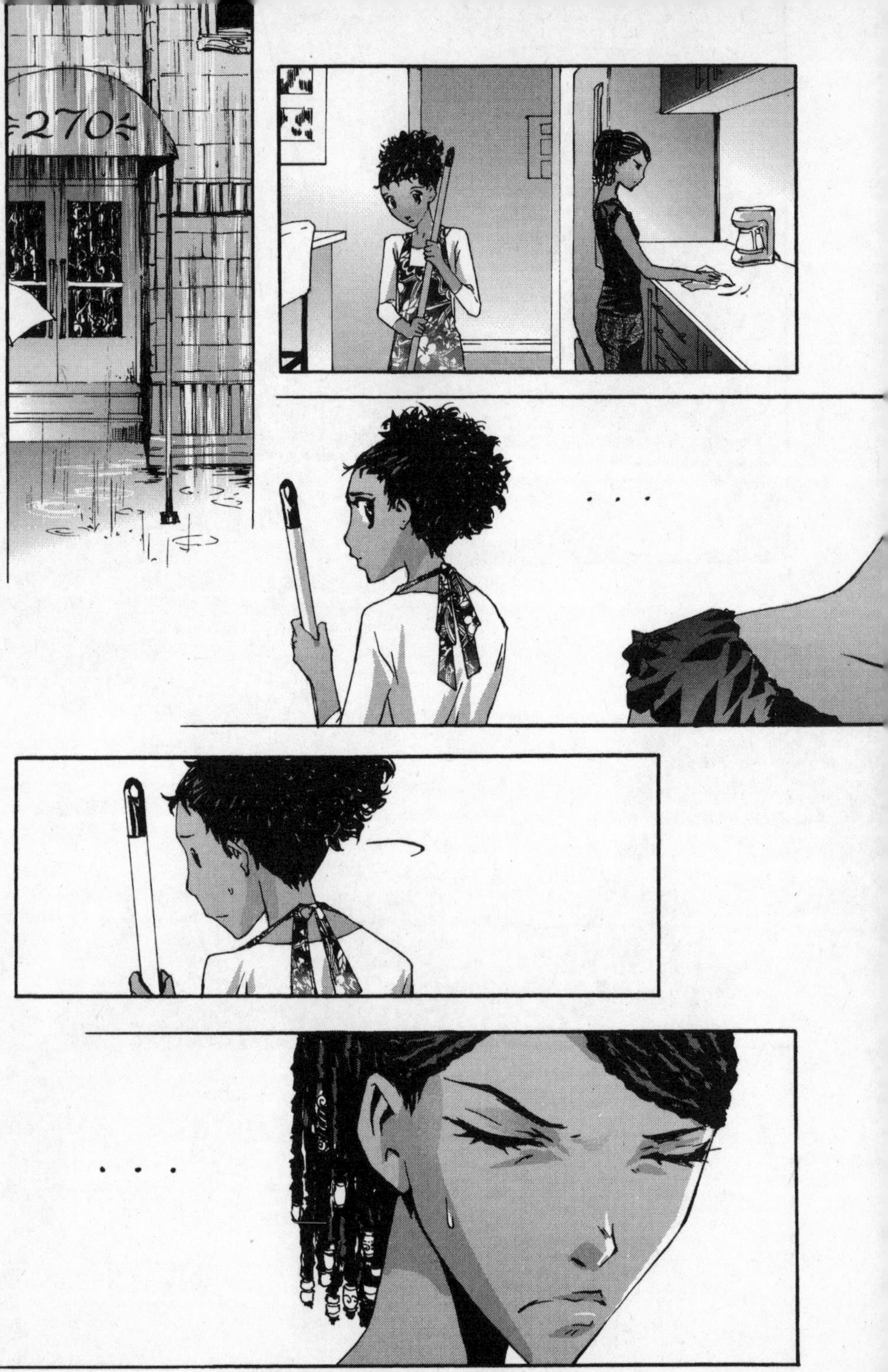
270
. . .
. . .

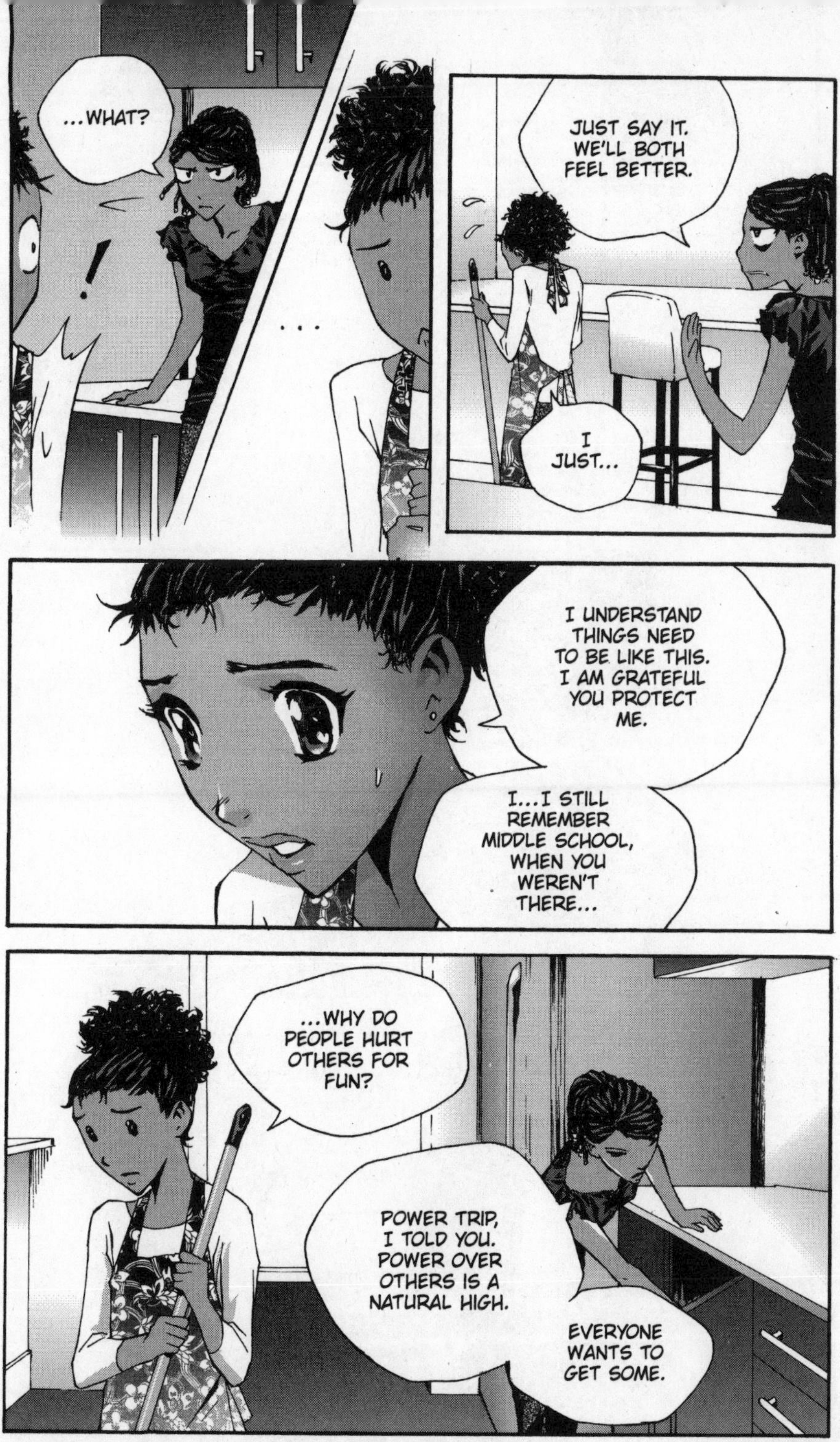
...WHAT?
...
JUST SAY IT. WE'LL BOTH FEEL BETTER.
I JUST...
I UNDERSTAND THINGS NEED TO BE LIKE THIS. I AM GRATEFUL YOU PROTECT ME.
I...I STILL REMEMBER MIDDLE SCHOOL, WHEN YOU WEREN'T THERE...
...WHY DO PEOPLE HURT OTHERS FOR FUN?
POWER TRIP, I TOLD YOU. POWER OVER OTHERS IS A NATURAL HIGH.
EVERYONE WANTS TO GET SOME.

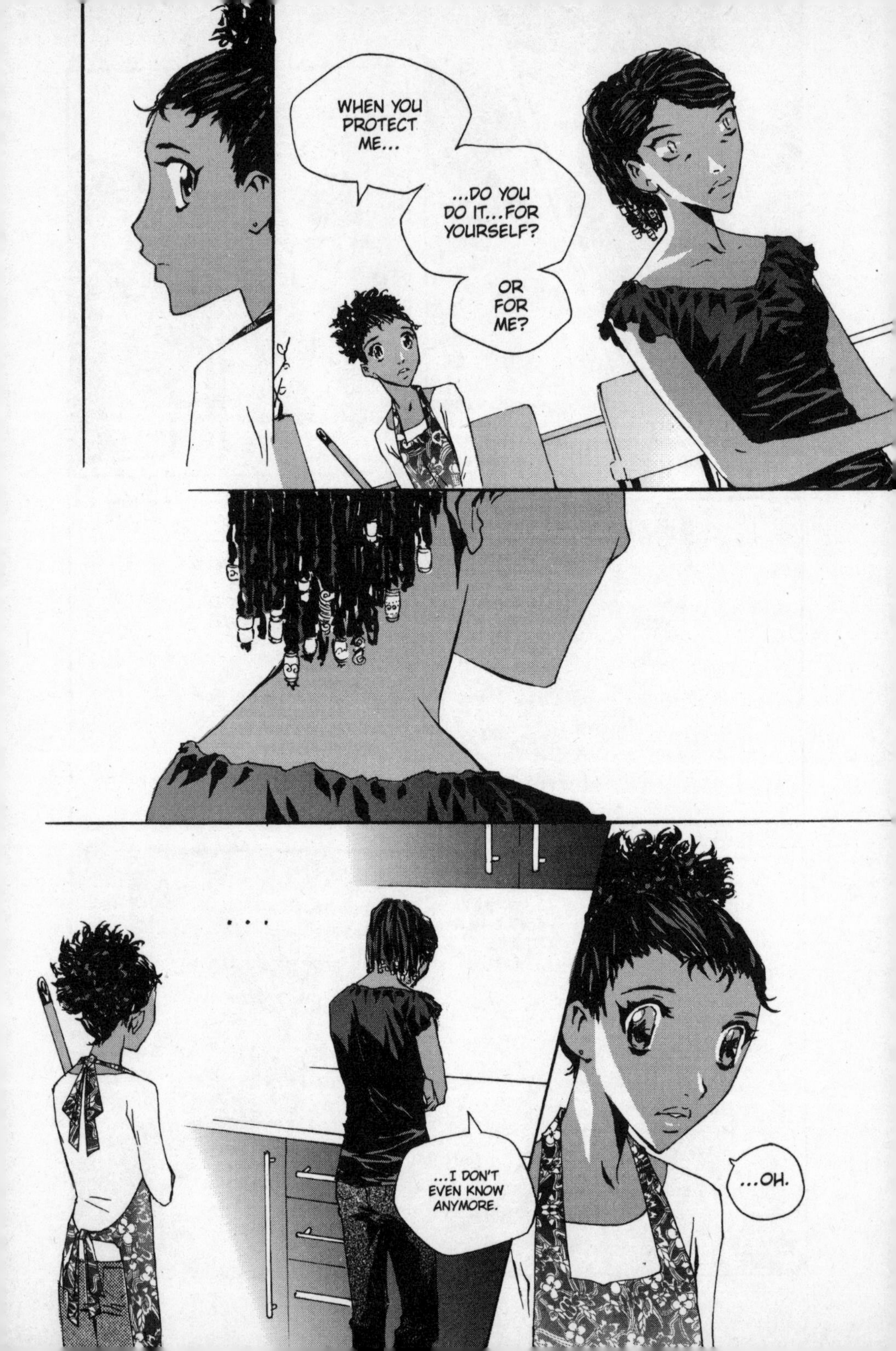
WHEN YOU PROTECT ME...
...DO YOU DO IT...FOR YOURSELF?
OR FOR ME?
...
...I DON'T EVEN KNOW ANYMORE.
...OH.

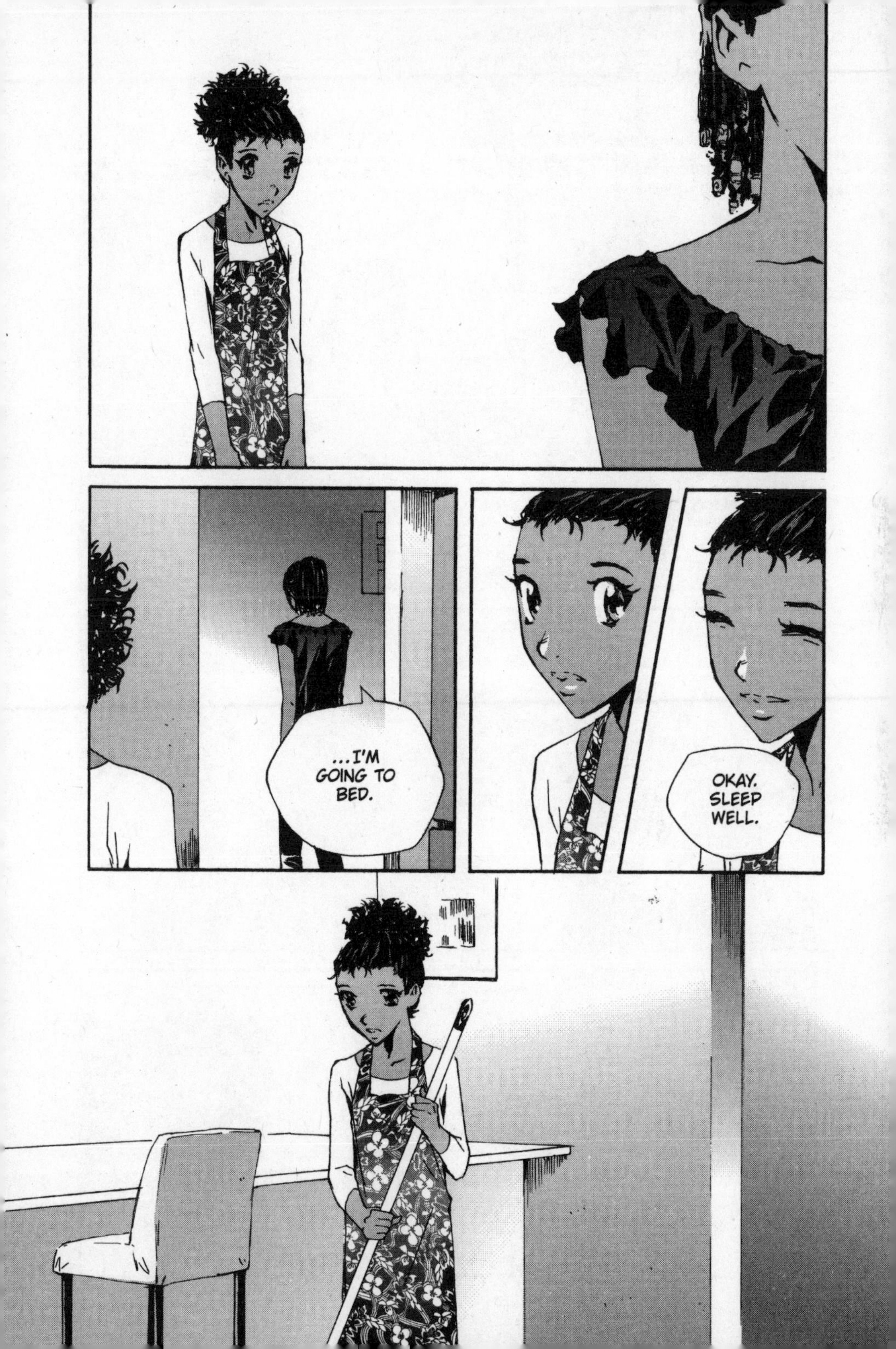
...I'M GOING TO BED.
OKAY. SLEEP WELL.

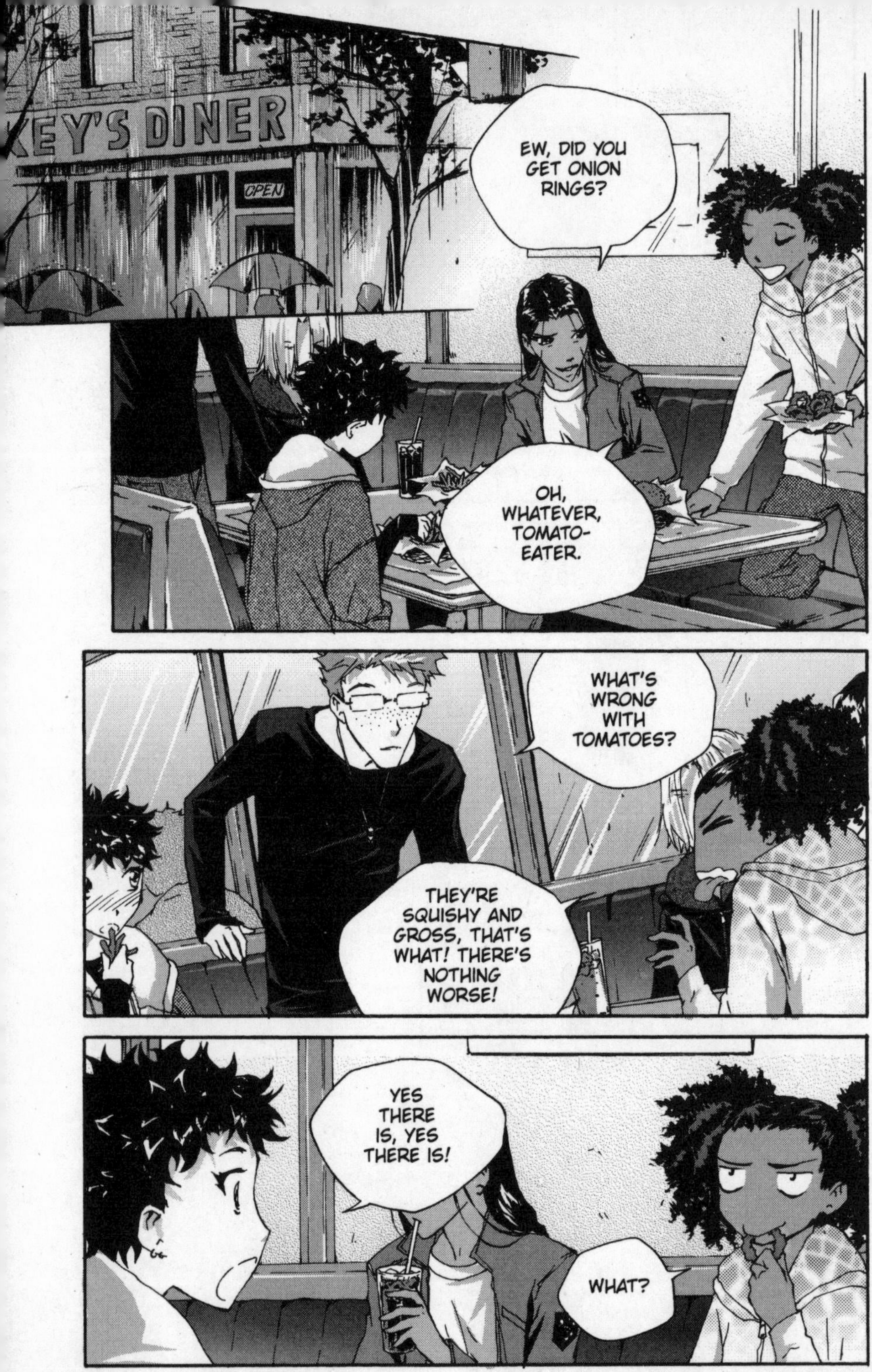
KEY'S DINER
OPEN
EW, DID YOU GET ONION RINGS?
OH, WHATEVER, TOMATO-EATER.
WHAT'S WRONG WITH TOMATOES?
THEY'RE SQUISHY AND GROSS, THAT'S WHAT! THERE'S NOTHING WORSE!
YES THERE IS, YES THERE IS!
WHAT?

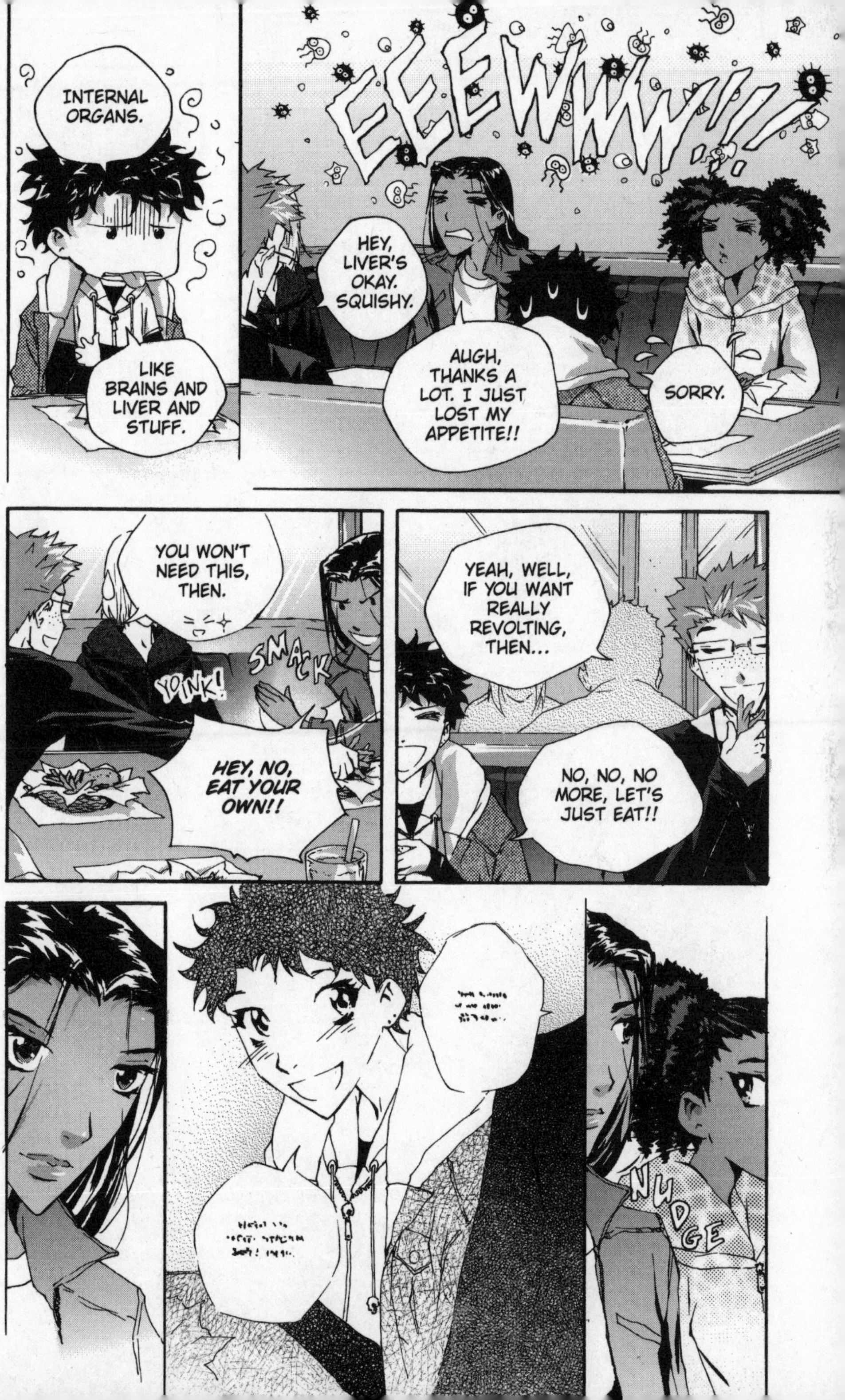
INTERNAL ORGANS.
LIKE BRAINS AND LIVER AND STUFF.
EEEWWW!!!
HEY, LIVER'S OKAY. SQUISHY.
AUGH, THANKS A LOT. I JUST LOST MY APPETITE!!
SORRY.
YOU WON'T NEED THIS, THEN.
YOINK!
SMACK
HEY, NO, EAT YOUR OWN!!
YEAH, WELL, IF YOU WANT REALLY REVOLTING, THEN...
NO, NO, NO MORE, LET'S JUST EAT!!
NUDGE

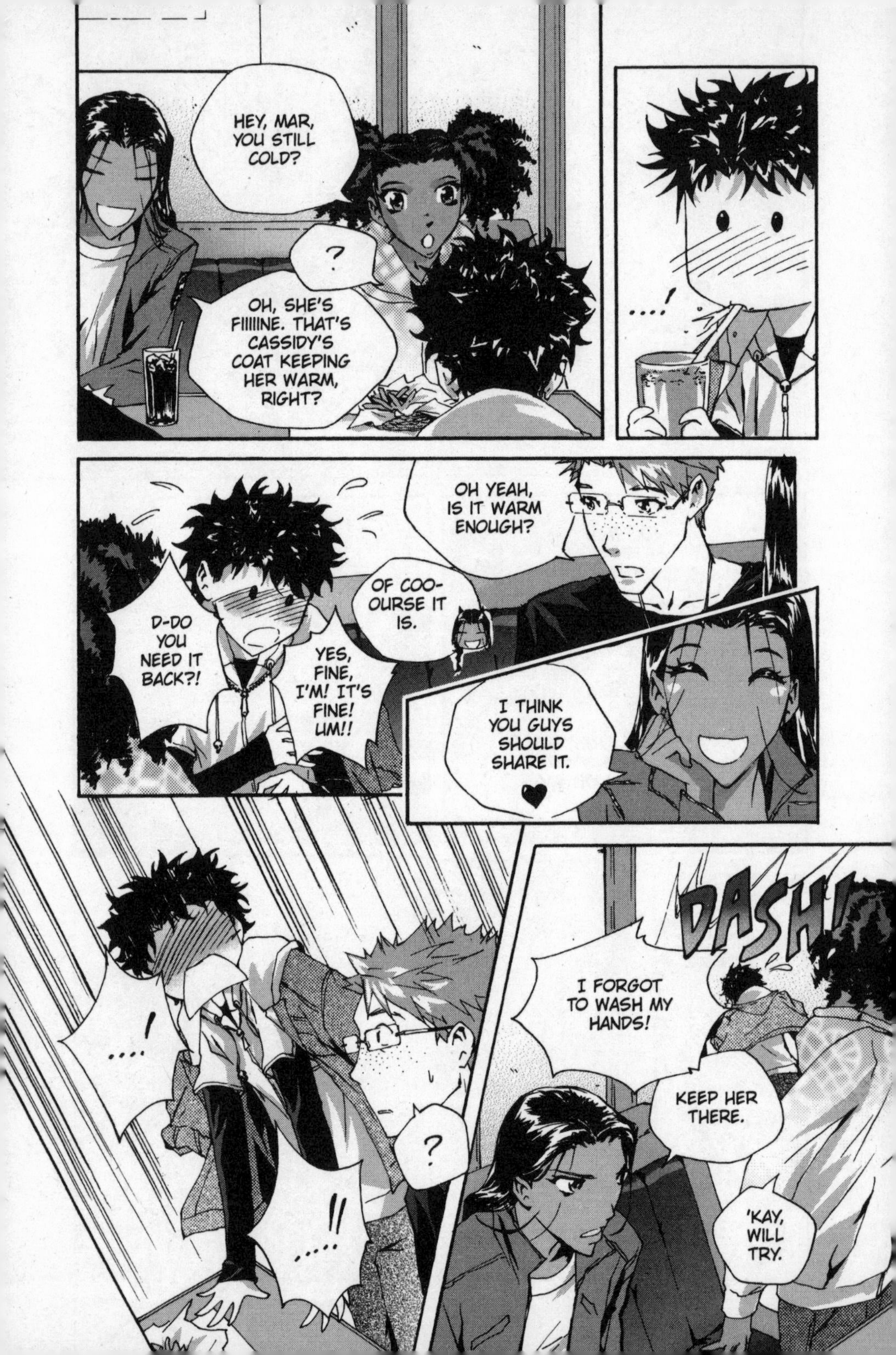
HEY, MAR, YOU STILL COLD?
?
OH, SHE'S FIIIIINE. THAT'S CASSIDY'S COAT KEEPING HER WARM, RIGHT?
....!
OH YEAH, IS IT WARM ENOUGH?
D-DO YOU NEED IT BACK?!
YES, FINE, I'M! IT'S FINE! UM!!
OF COO-OURSE IT IS.
I THINK YOU GUYS SHOULD SHARE IT.
....!
?
....!!
DASH!
I FORGOT TO WASH MY HANDS!
KEEP HER THERE.
'KAY, WILL TRY.

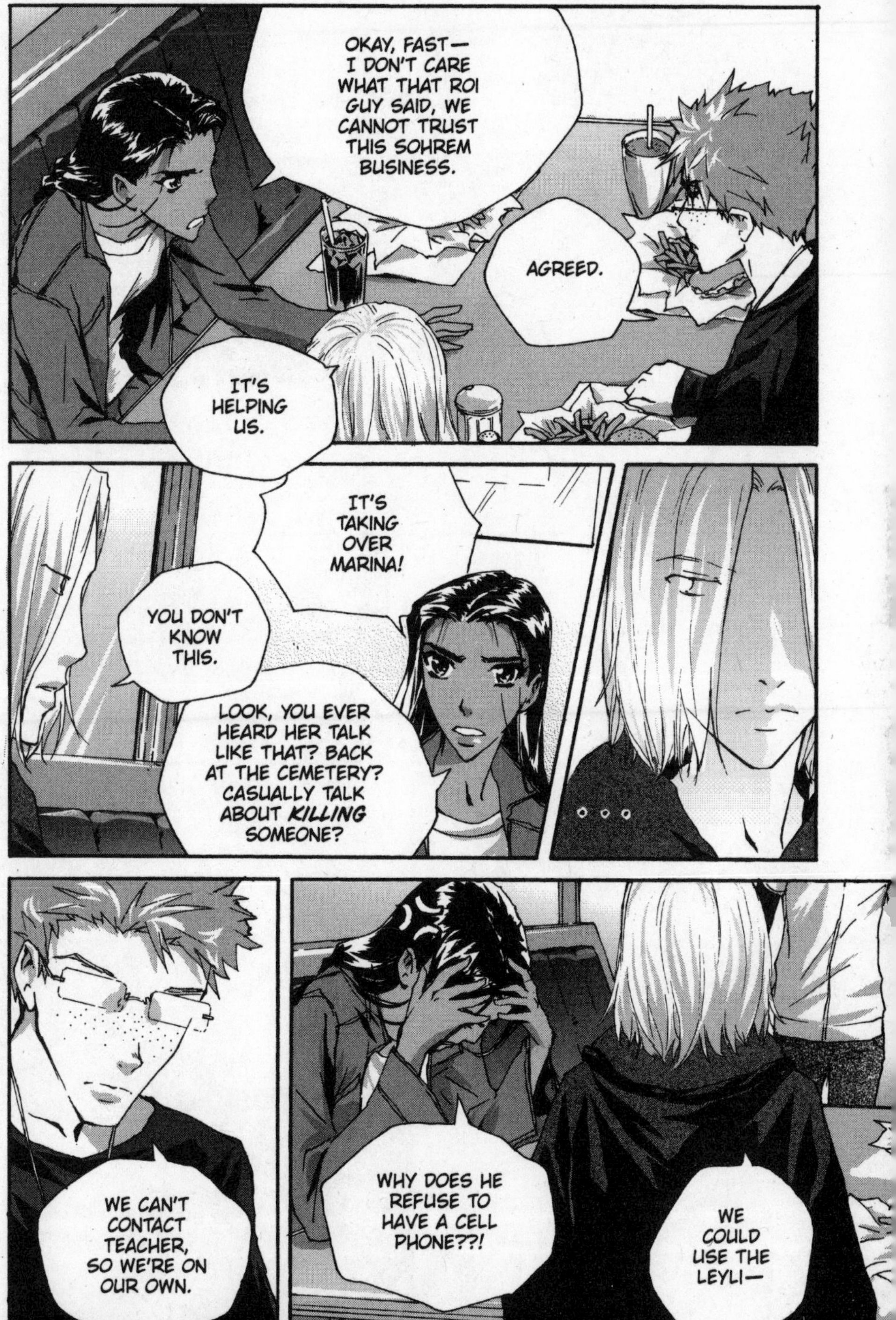
OKAY, FAST— I DON'T CARE WHAT THAT ROI GUY SAID, WE CANNOT TRUST THIS SOHREM BUSINESS.
AGREED.
IT'S HELPING US.
IT'S TAKING OVER MARINA!
YOU DON'T KNOW THIS.
LOOK, YOU EVER HEARD HER TALK LIKE THAT? BACK AT THE CEMETERY? CASUALLY TALK ABOUT *KILLING* SOMEONE?
WE CAN'T CONTACT TEACHER, SO WE'RE ON OUR OWN.
WHY DOES HE REFUSE TO HAVE A CELL PHONE??!
WE COULD USE THE LEYLI—

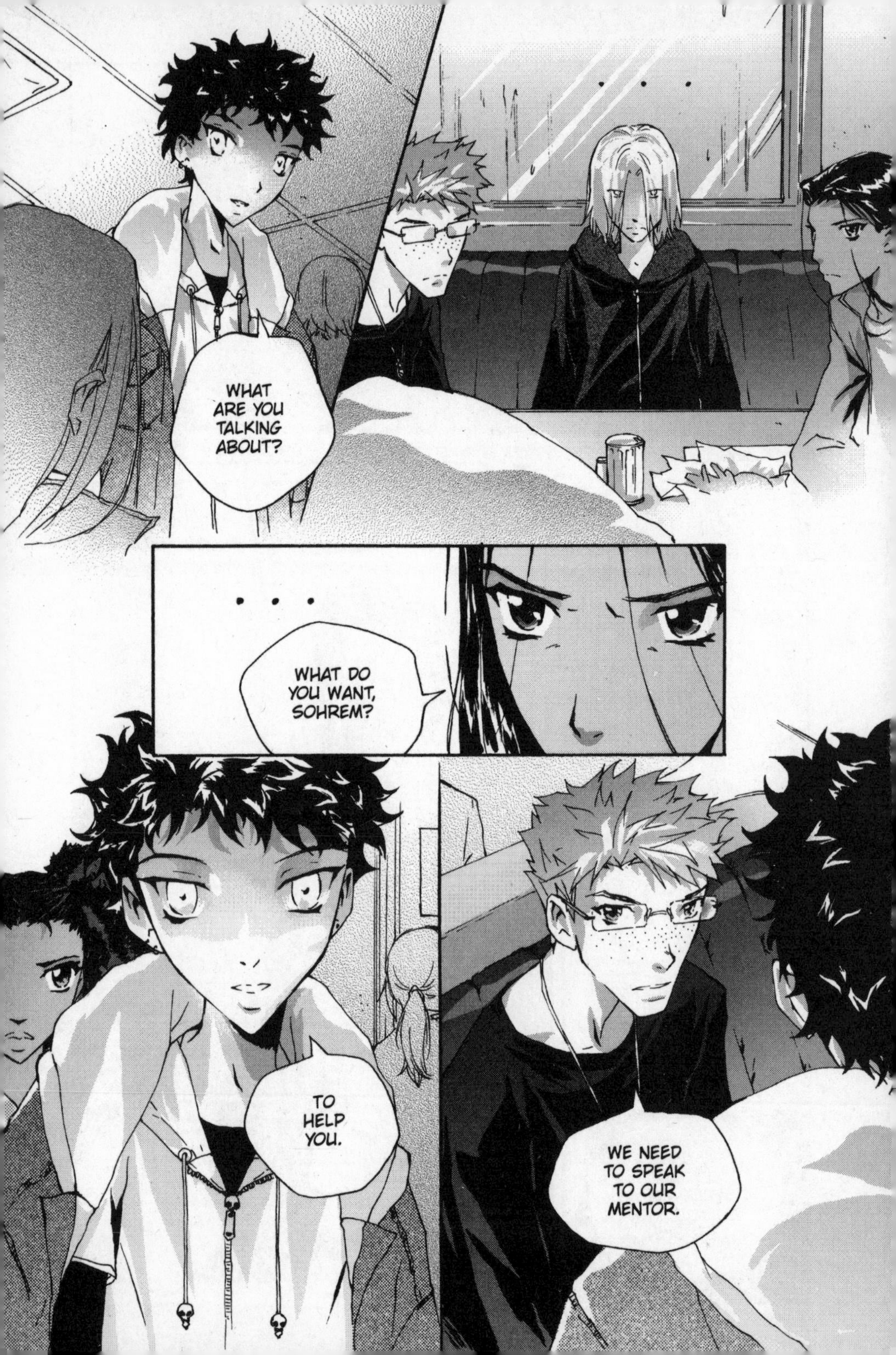
WHAT ARE YOU TALKING ABOUT?
...
...
WHAT DO YOU WANT, SOHREM?
TO HELP YOU.
WE NEED TO SPEAK TO OUR MENTOR.

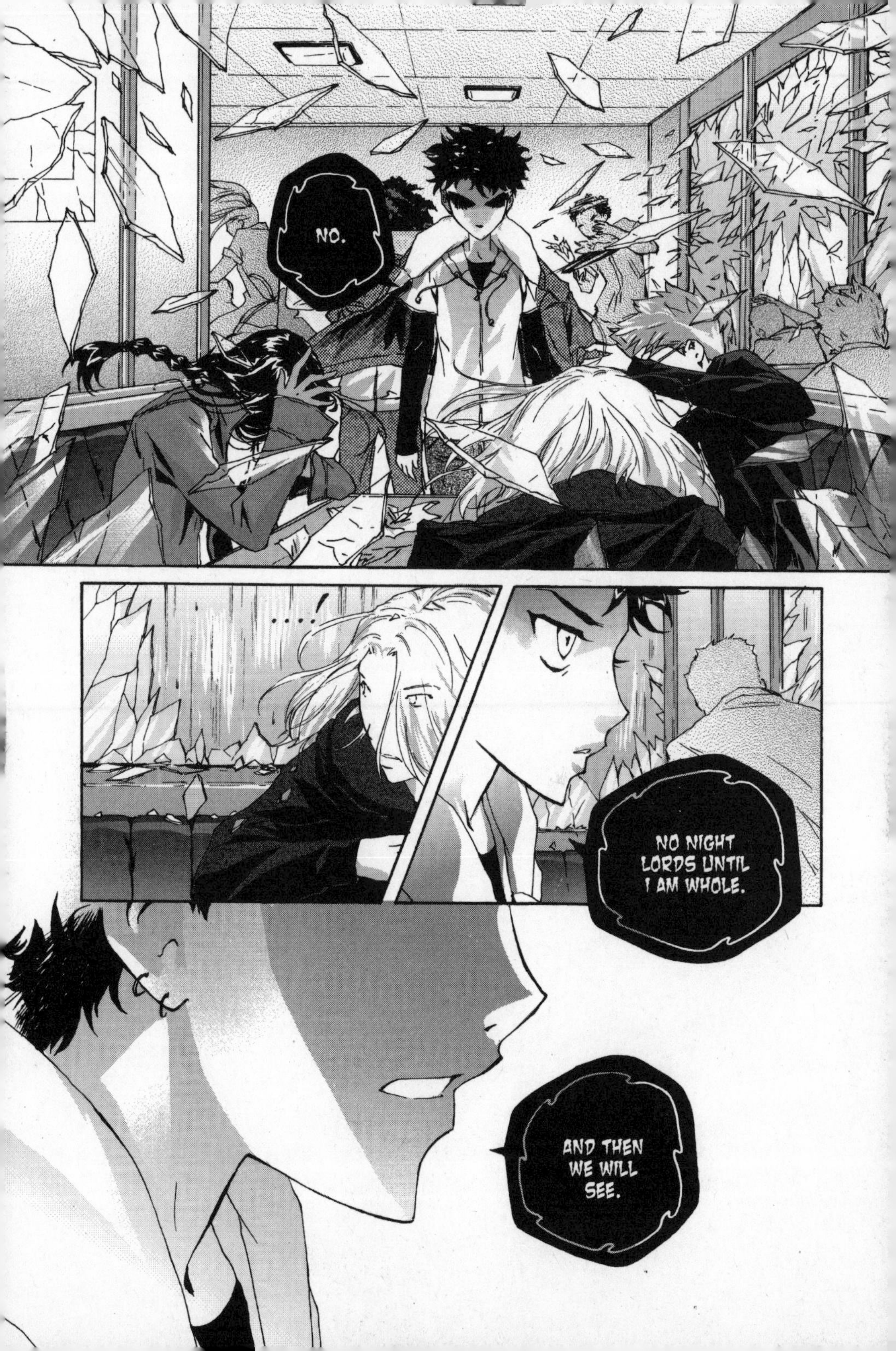
NO.
...!
NO NIGHT LORDS UNTIL I AM WHOLE.
AND THEN WE WILL SEE.

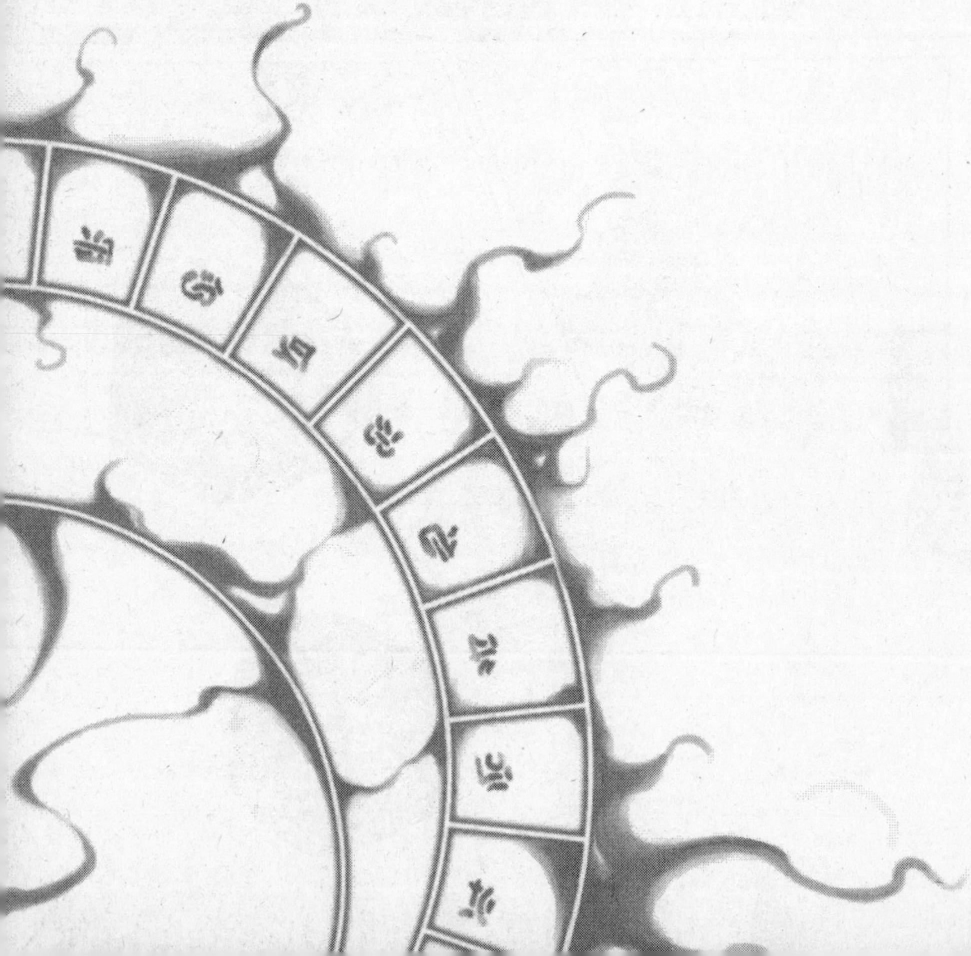

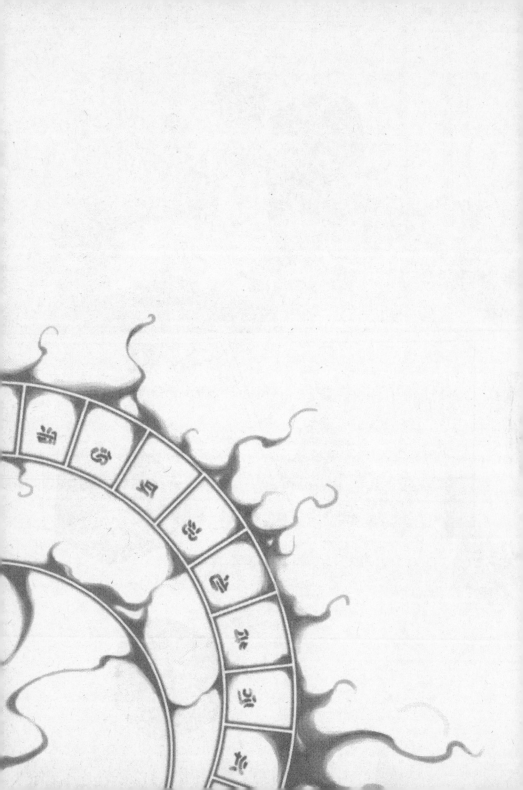

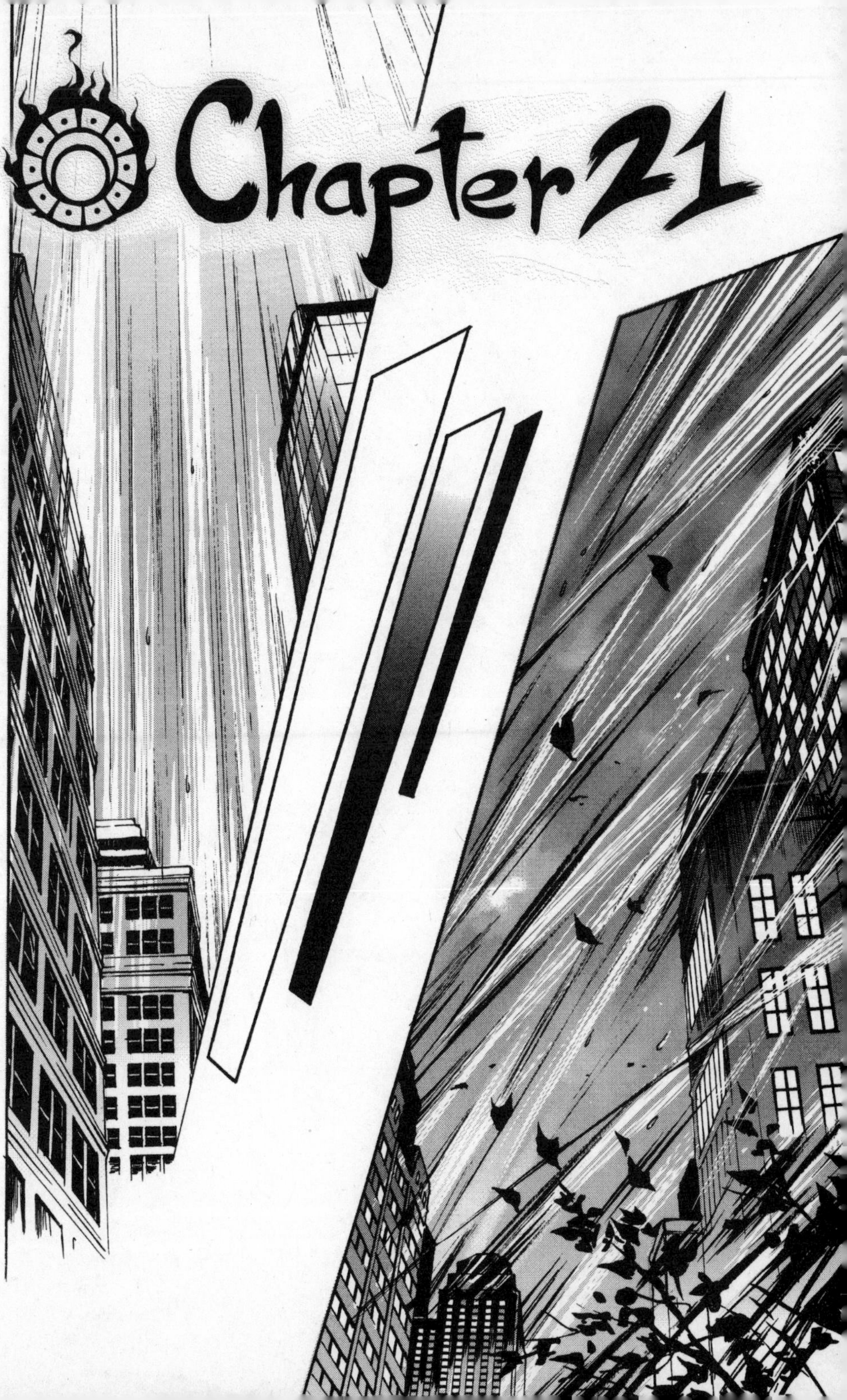
Chapter 21

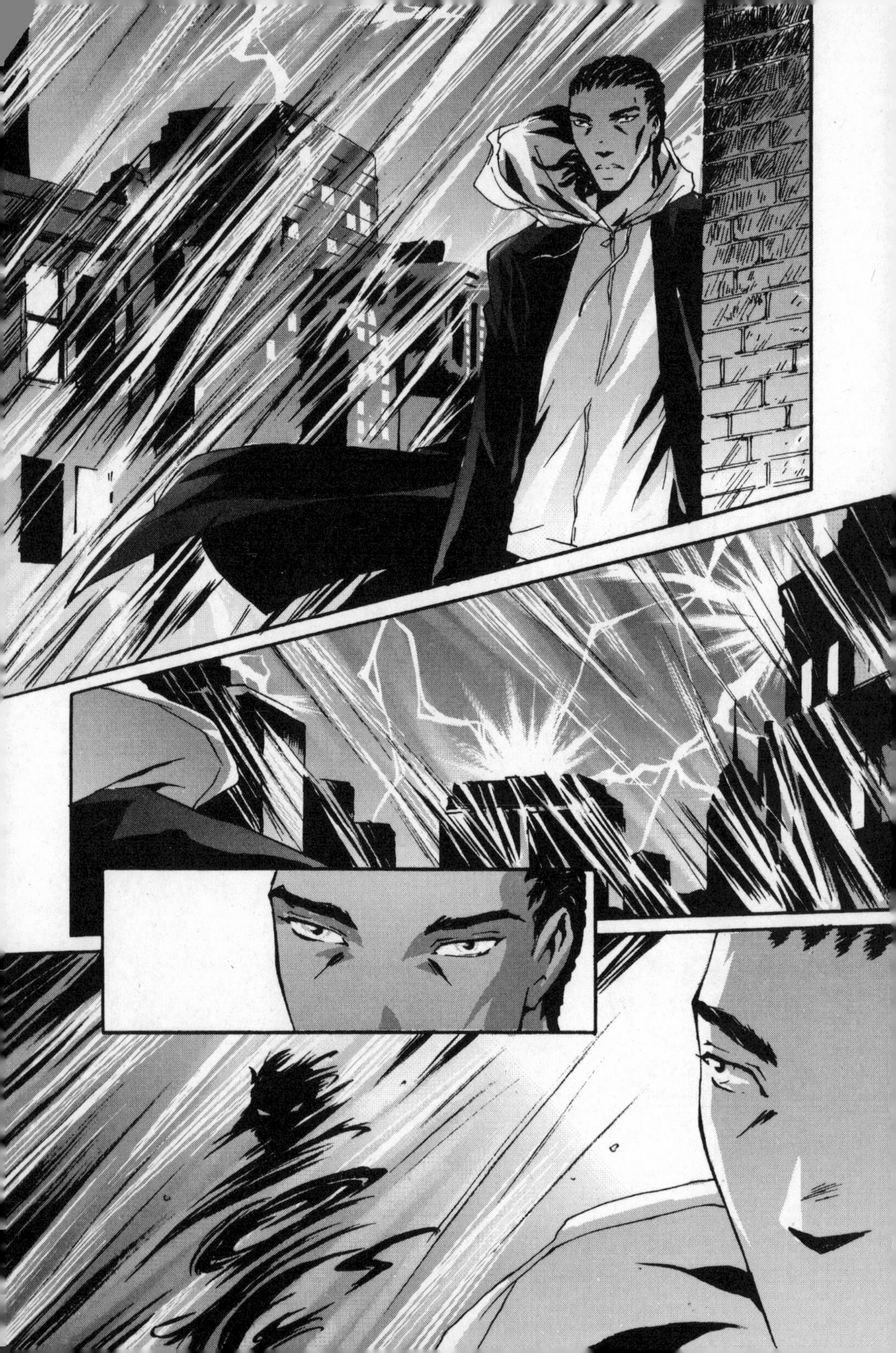

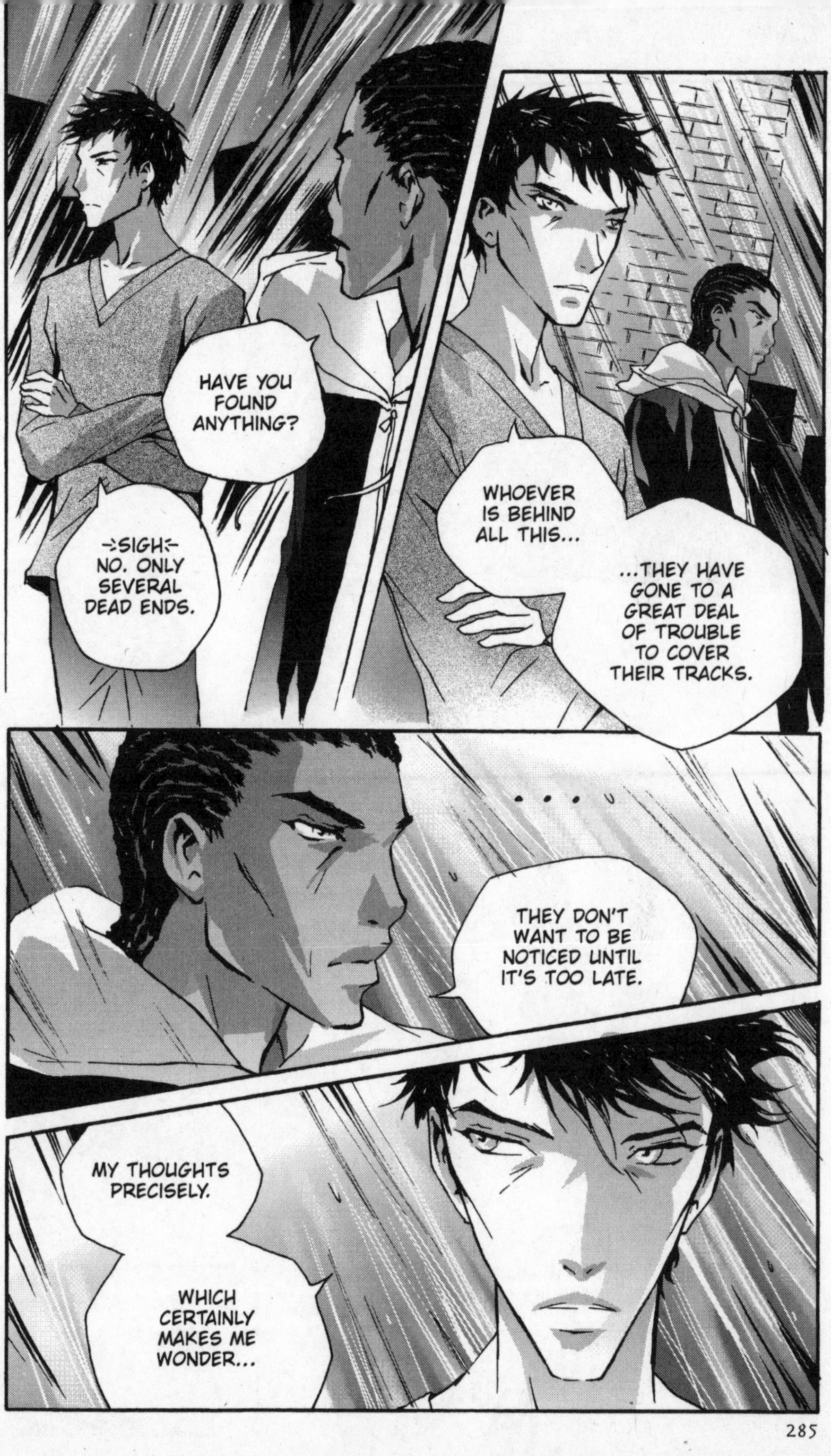
HAVE YOU FOUND ANYTHING?
~SIGH~ NO. ONLY SEVERAL DEAD ENDS.
WHOEVER IS BEHIND ALL THIS...
...THEY HAVE GONE TO A GREAT DEAL OF TROUBLE TO COVER THEIR TRACKS.
...
THEY DON'T WANT TO BE NOTICED UNTIL IT'S TOO LATE.
MY THOUGHTS PRECISELY.
WHICH CERTAINLY MAKES ME WONDER...

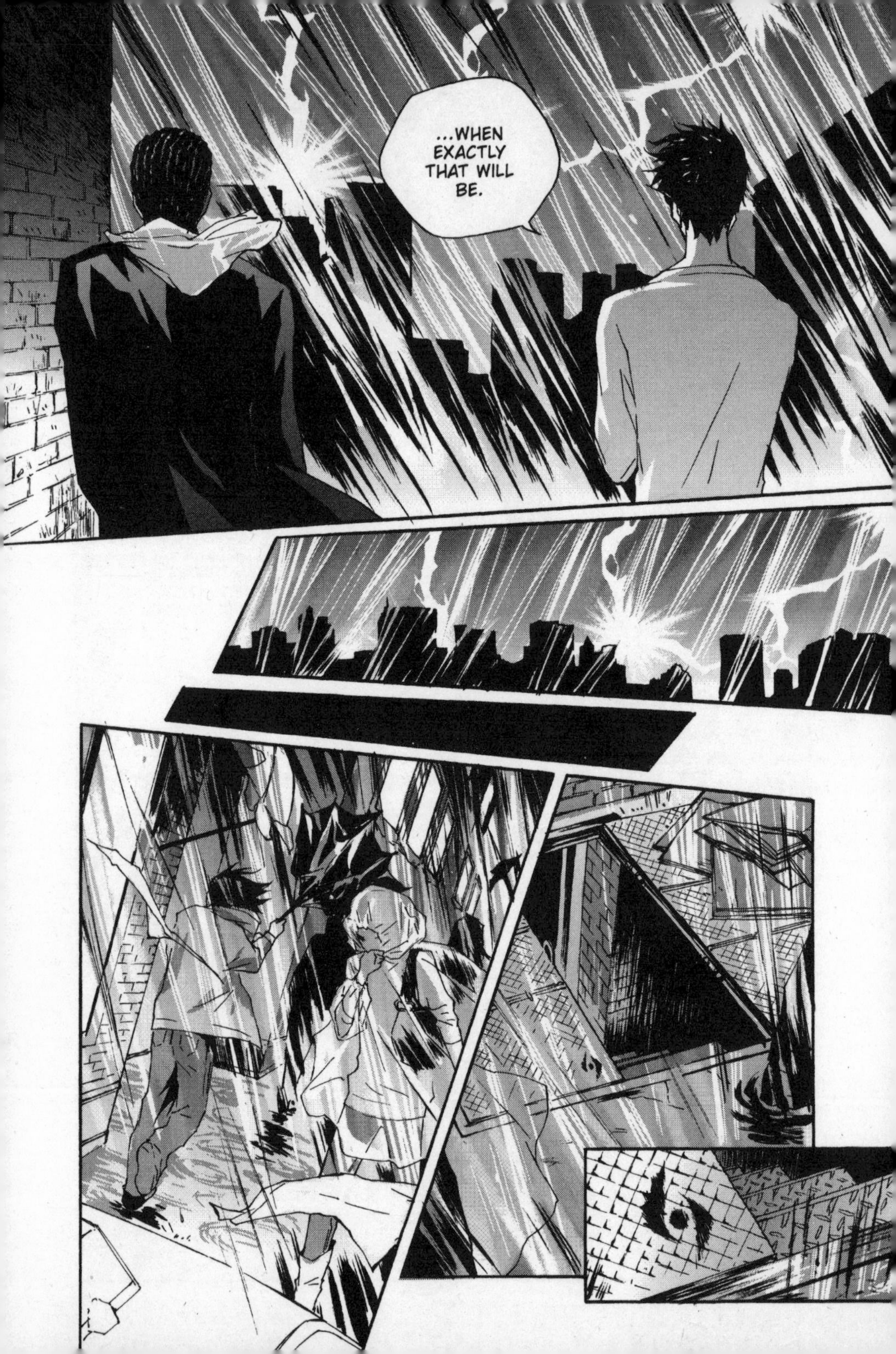
...WHEN EXACTLY THAT WILL BE.

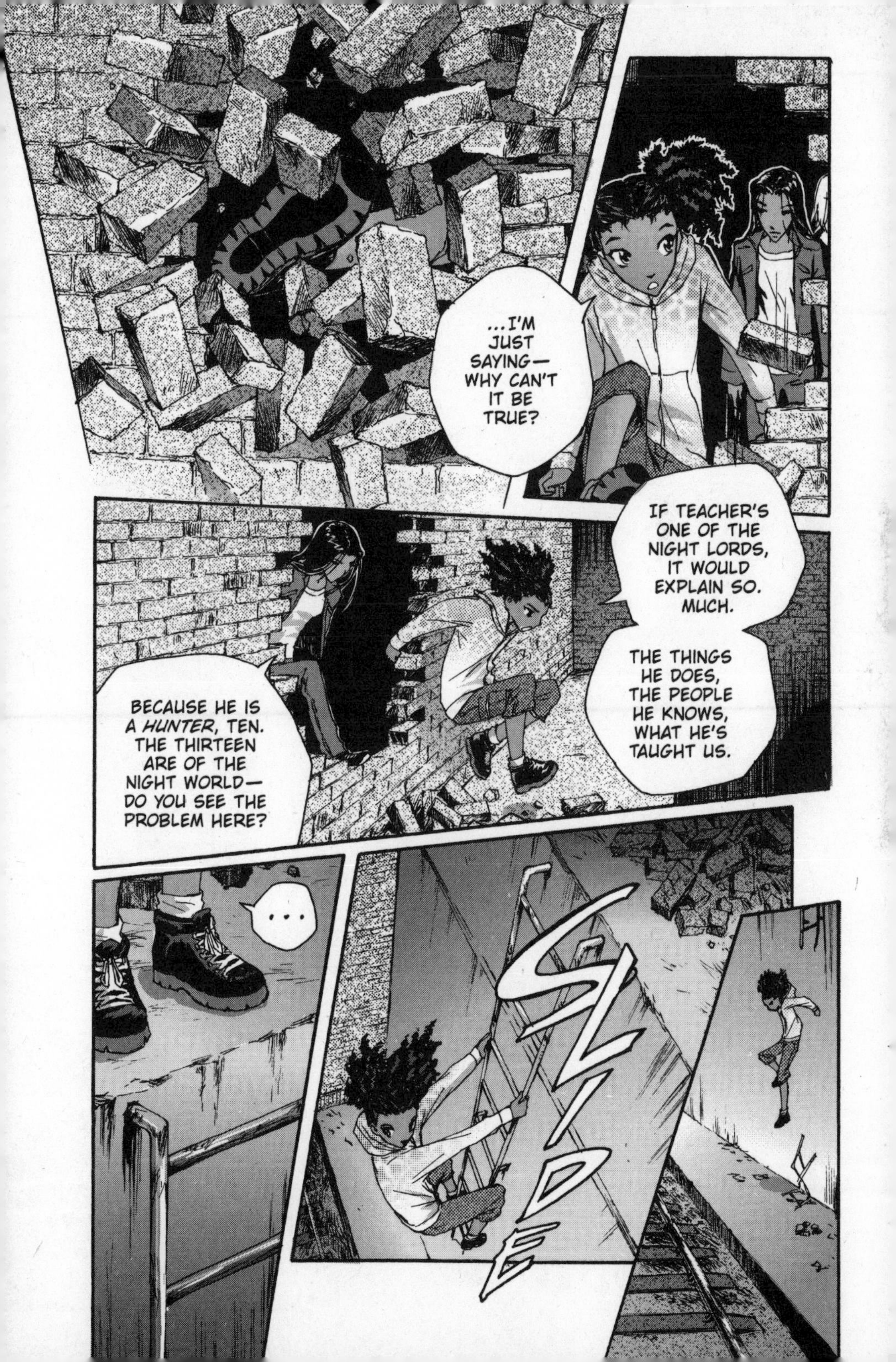
...I'M JUST SAYING—WHY CAN'T IT BE TRUE?
IF TEACHER'S ONE OF THE NIGHT LORDS, IT WOULD EXPLAIN SO. MUCH.
THE THINGS HE DOES, THE PEOPLE HE KNOWS, WHAT HE'S TAUGHT US.
BECAUSE HE IS A *HUNTER*, TEN. THE THIRTEEN ARE OF THE NIGHT WORLD—DO YOU SEE THE PROBLEM HERE?
...
SLIDE

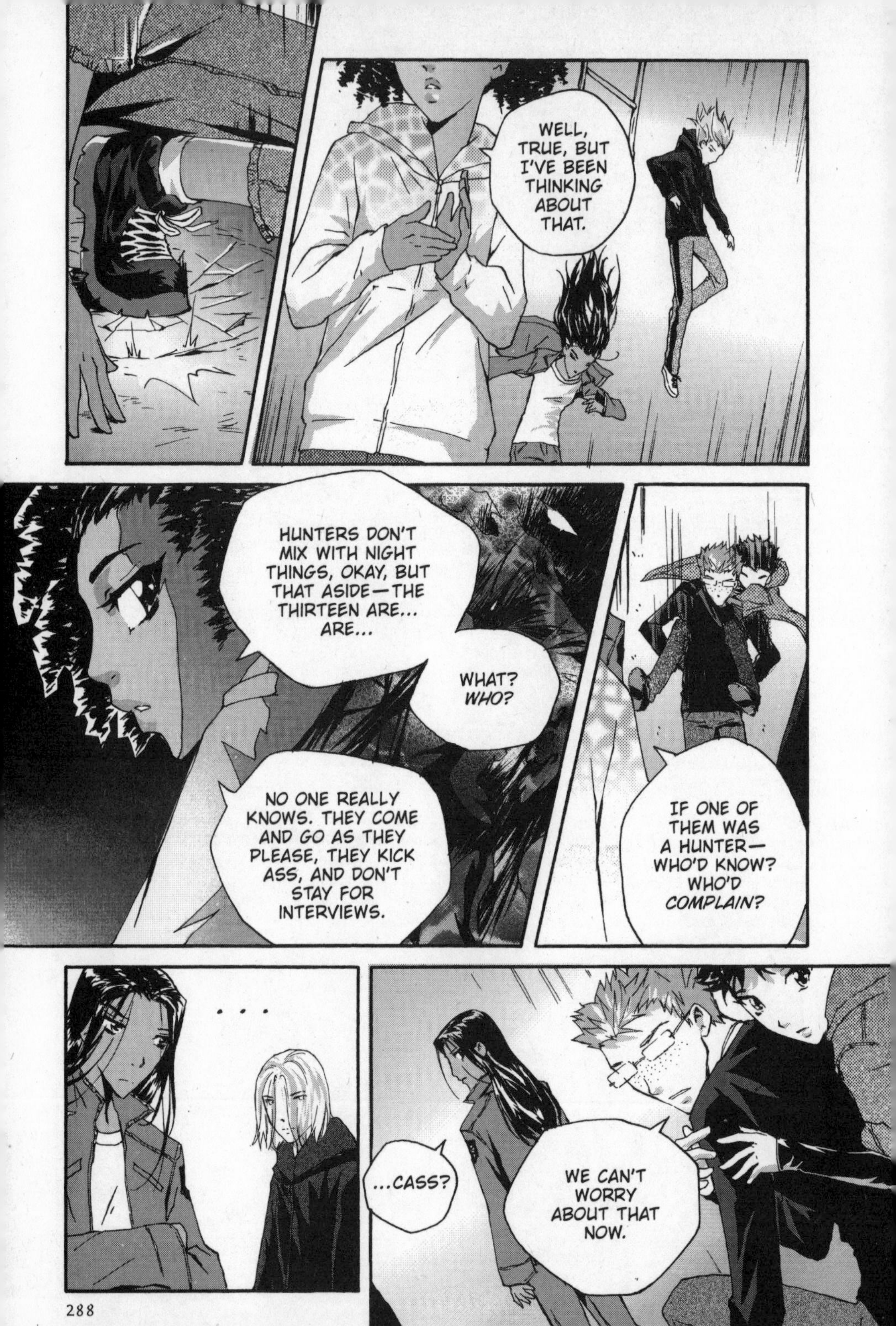

WELL, TRUE, BUT I'VE BEEN THINKING ABOUT THAT.
HUNTERS DON'T MIX WITH NIGHT THINGS, OKAY, BUT THAT ASIDE—THE THIRTEEN ARE... ARE...
WHAT? *WHO?*
NO ONE REALLY KNOWS. THEY COME AND GO AS THEY PLEASE, THEY KICK ASS, AND DON'T STAY FOR INTERVIEWS.
IF ONE OF THEM WAS A HUNTER—WHO'D KNOW? WHO'D *COMPLAIN?*
. . .
...CASS?
WE CAN'T WORRY ABOUT THAT NOW.

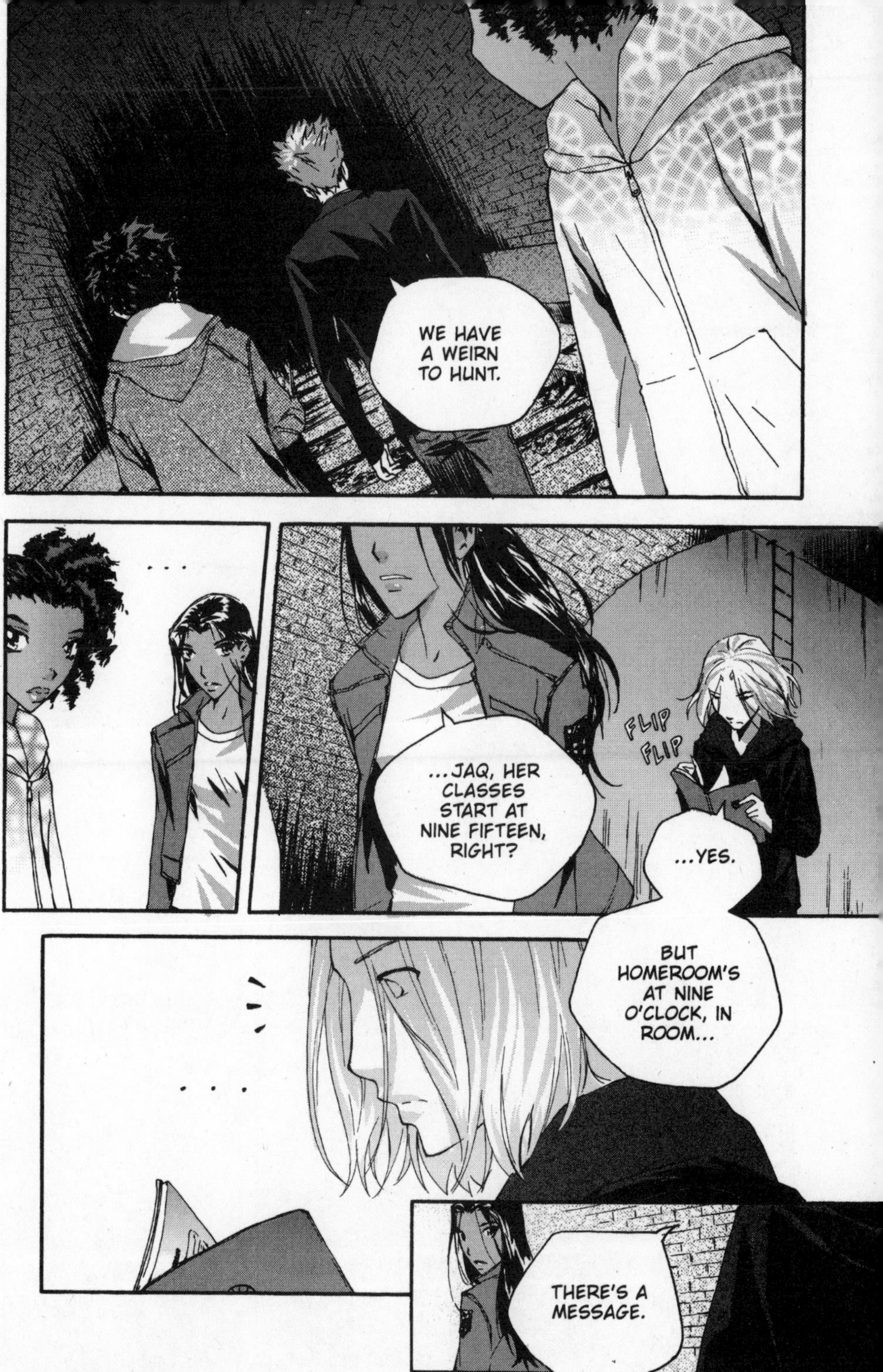
WE HAVE A WEIRN TO HUNT.
...
...JAQ, HER CLASSES START AT NINE FIFTEEN, RIGHT?
FLIP FLIP
...YES.
BUT HOMEROOM'S AT NINE O'CLOCK, IN ROOM...
...
THERE'S A MESSAGE.

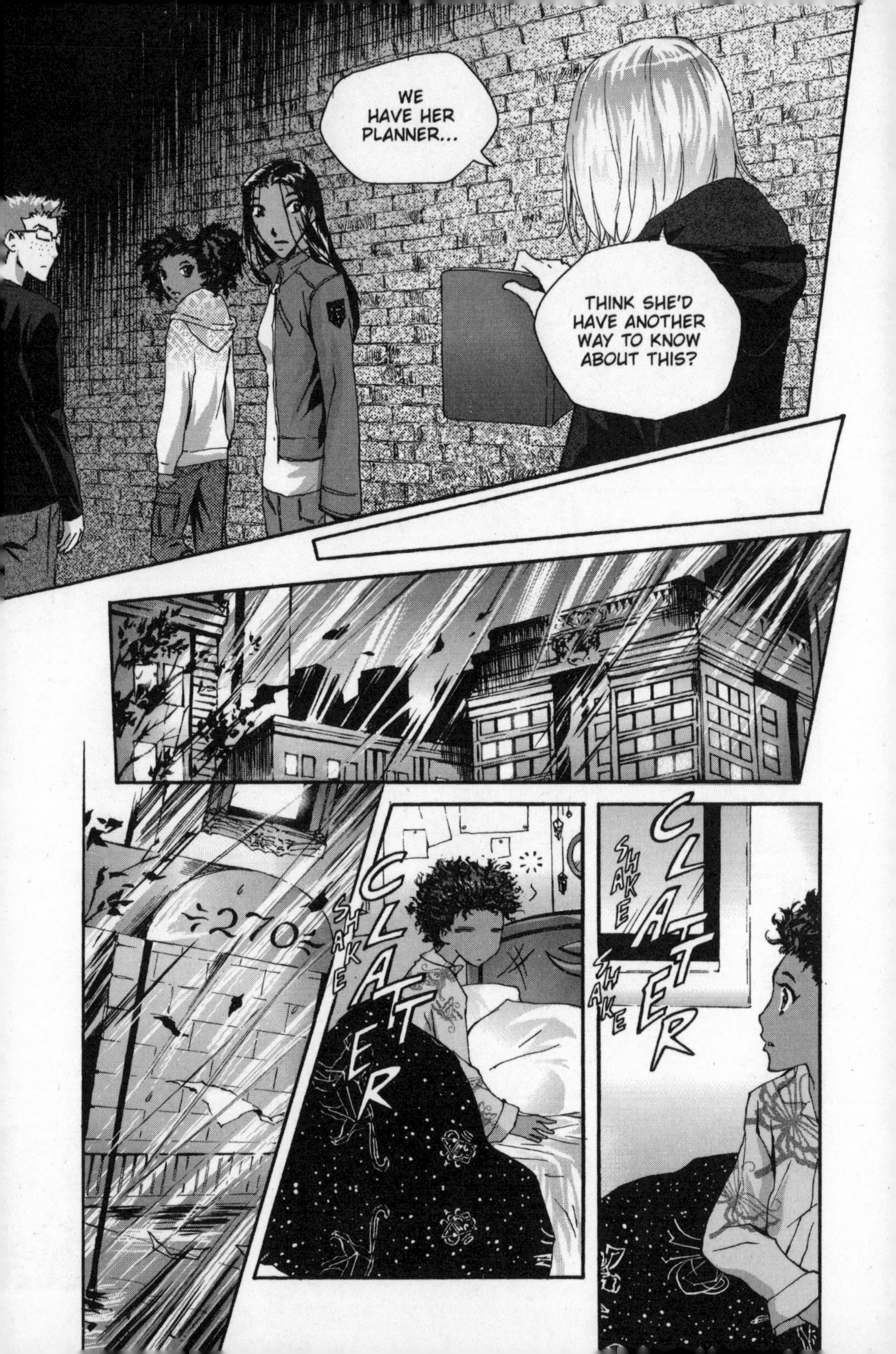
WE HAVE HER PLANNER...
THINK SHE'D HAVE ANOTHER WAY TO KNOW ABOUT THIS?
270
SHAKE
CLATTER
SHAKE
CLATTER
SHAKE

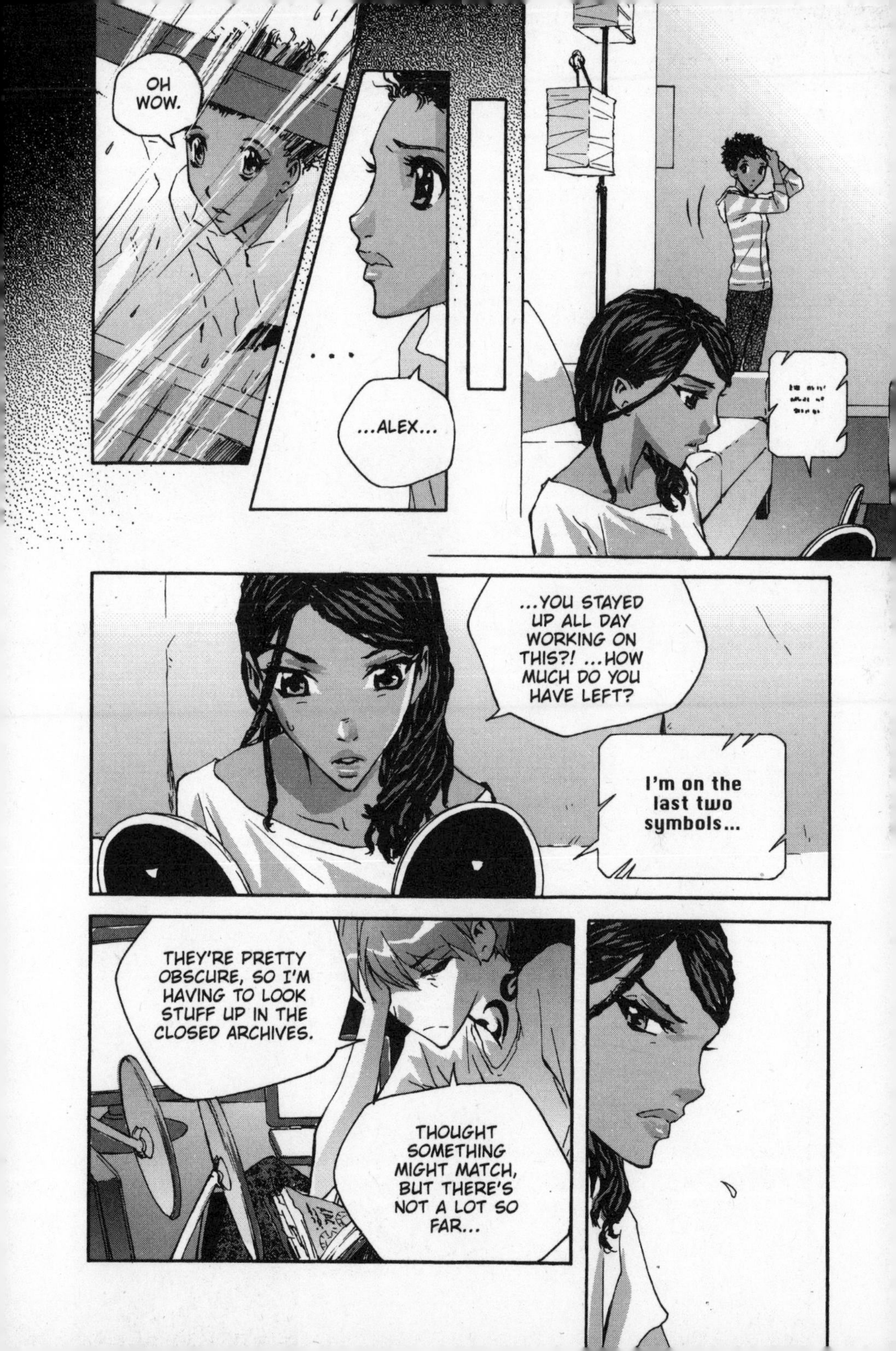
OH WOW.
...
...ALEX...
...YOU STAYED UP ALL DAY WORKING ON THIS?! ...HOW MUCH DO YOU HAVE LEFT?
I'm on the last two symbols...
THEY'RE PRETTY OBSCURE, SO I'M HAVING TO LOOK STUFF UP IN THE CLOSED ARCHIVES.
THOUGHT SOMETHING MIGHT MATCH, BUT THERE'S NOT A LOT SO FAR...

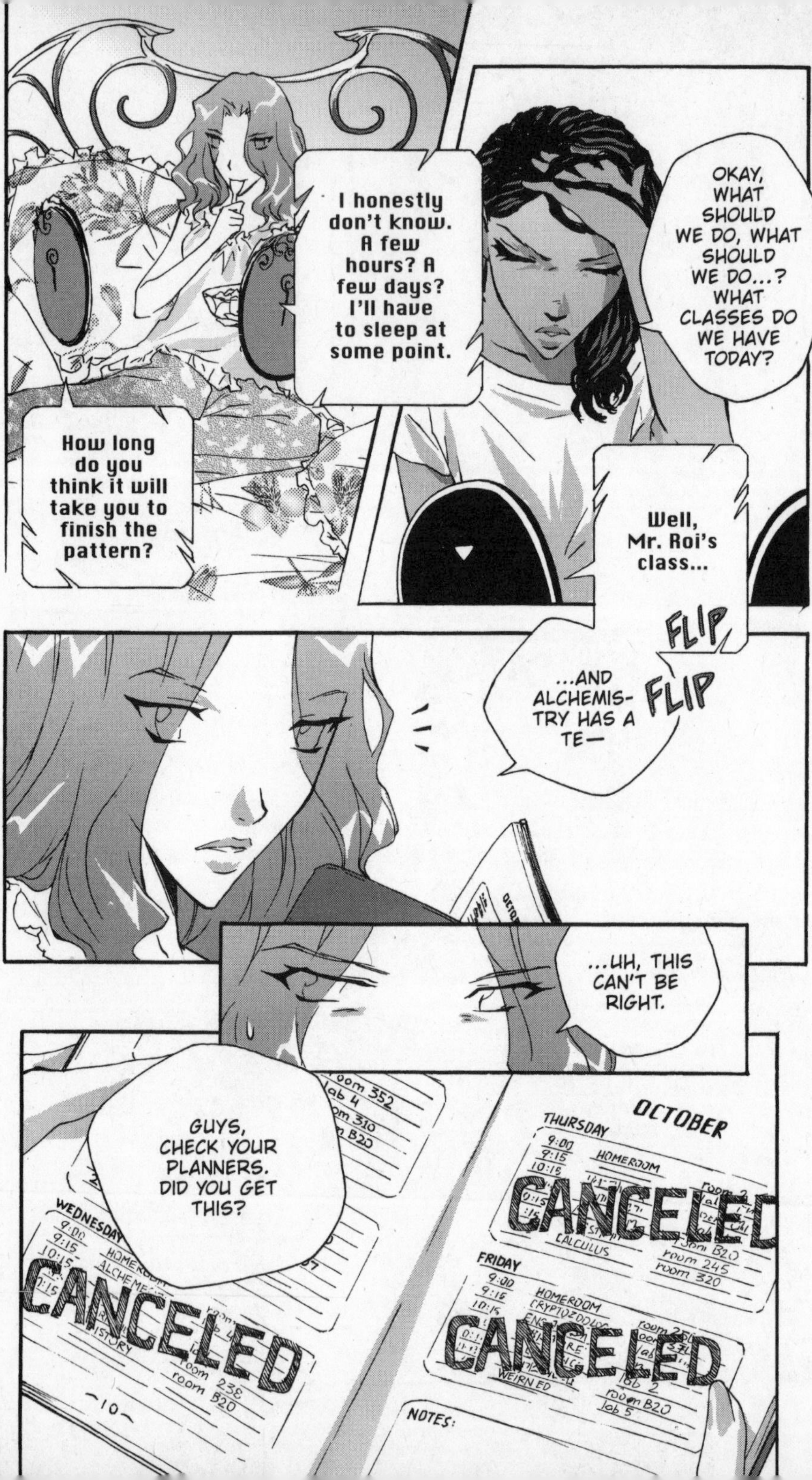
How long do you think it will take you to finish the pattern?
I honestly don't know. A few hours? A few days? I'll have to sleep at some point.
OKAY, WHAT SHOULD WE DO, WHAT SHOULD WE DO...? WHAT CLASSES DO WE HAVE TODAY?
Well, Mr. Roi's class...
FLIP
FLIP
...AND ALCHEMIS-TRY HAS A TE—
...UH, THIS CAN'T BE RIGHT.
GUYS, CHECK YOUR PLANNERS. DID YOU GET THIS?
OCTOBER
THURSDAY
HOMEROOM
CANCELED
CALCULUS
FRIDAY
HOMEROOM
CANCELED
WEDNESDAY
HOMEROOM
CANCELED
NOTES:

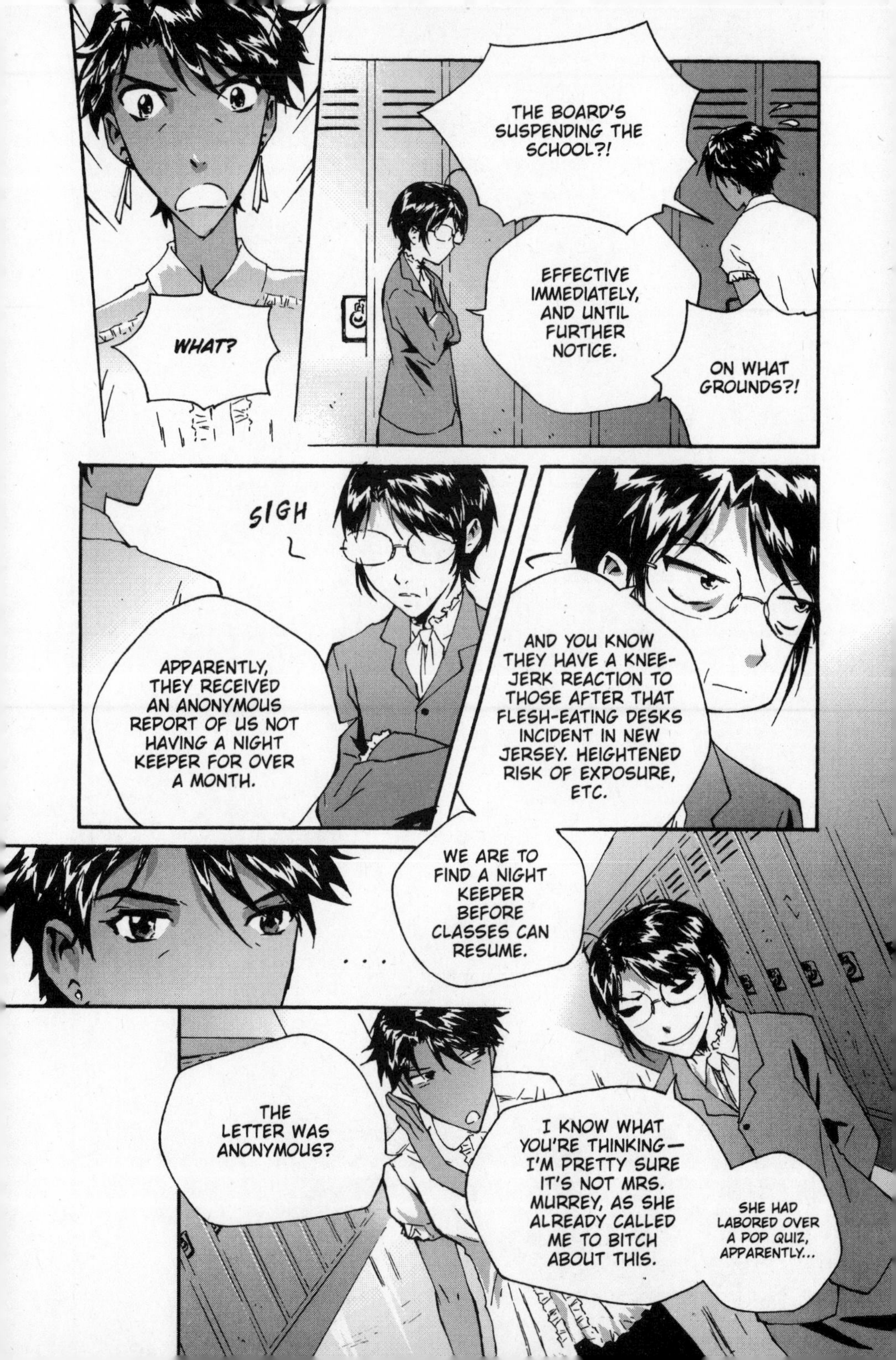
WHAT?
THE BOARD'S SUSPENDING THE SCHOOL?!
EFFECTIVE IMMEDIATELY, AND UNTIL FURTHER NOTICE.
ON WHAT GROUNDS?!
SIGH
APPARENTLY, THEY RECEIVED AN ANONYMOUS REPORT OF US NOT HAVING A NIGHT KEEPER FOR OVER A MONTH.
AND YOU KNOW THEY HAVE A KNEE-JERK REACTION TO THOSE AFTER THAT FLESH-EATING DESKS INCIDENT IN NEW JERSEY. HEIGHTENED RISK OF EXPOSURE, ETC.
...
WE ARE TO FIND A NIGHT KEEPER BEFORE CLASSES CAN RESUME.
THE LETTER WAS ANONYMOUS?
I KNOW WHAT YOU'RE THINKING—I'M PRETTY SURE IT'S NOT MRS. MURREY, AS SHE ALREADY CALLED ME TO BITCH ABOUT THIS.
SHE HAD LABORED OVER A POP QUIZ, APPARENTLY...

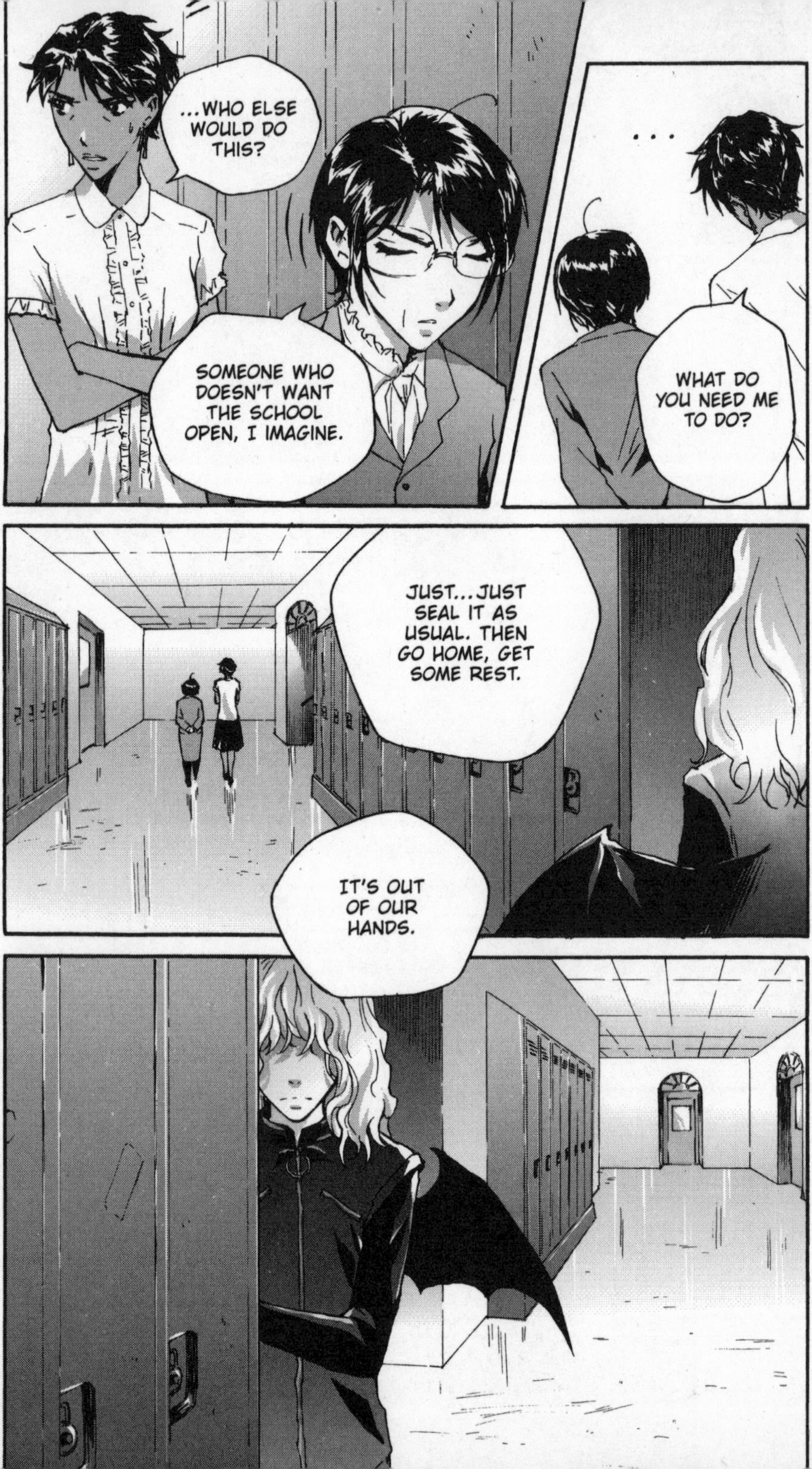
...WHO ELSE WOULD DO THIS?
SOMEONE WHO DOESN'T WANT THE SCHOOL OPEN, I IMAGINE.
...
WHAT DO YOU NEED ME TO DO?
JUST...JUST SEAL IT AS USUAL. THEN GO HOME, GET SOME REST.
IT'S OUT OF OUR HANDS.

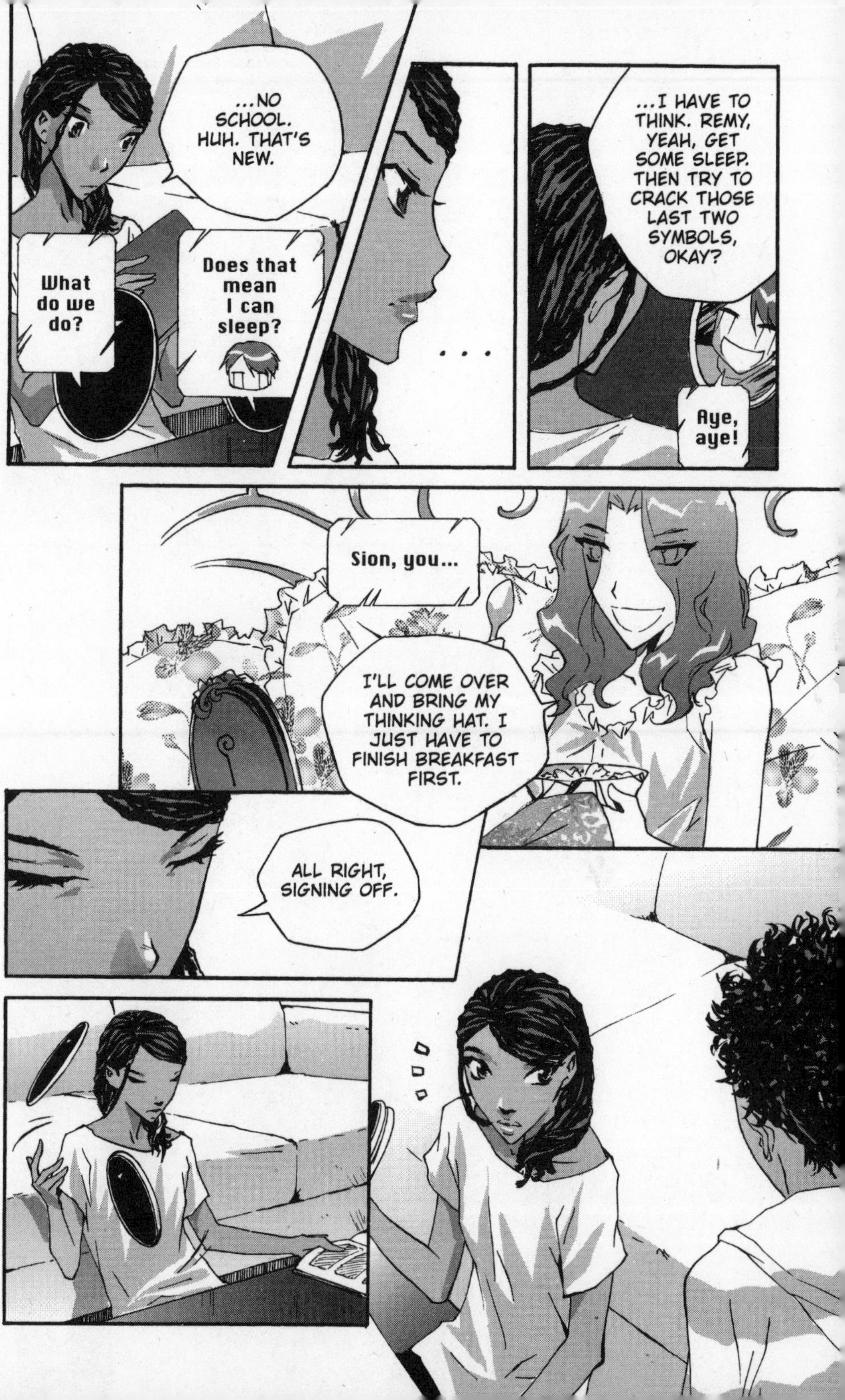
...NO SCHOOL. HUH. THAT'S NEW.
What do we do?
Does that mean I can sleep?
...
...I HAVE TO THINK. REMY, YEAH, GET SOME SLEEP. THEN TRY TO CRACK THOSE LAST TWO SYMBOLS, OKAY?
Aye, aye!
Sion, you...
I'LL COME OVER AND BRING MY THINKING HAT. I JUST HAVE TO FINISH BREAKFAST FIRST.
ALL RIGHT, SIGNING OFF.

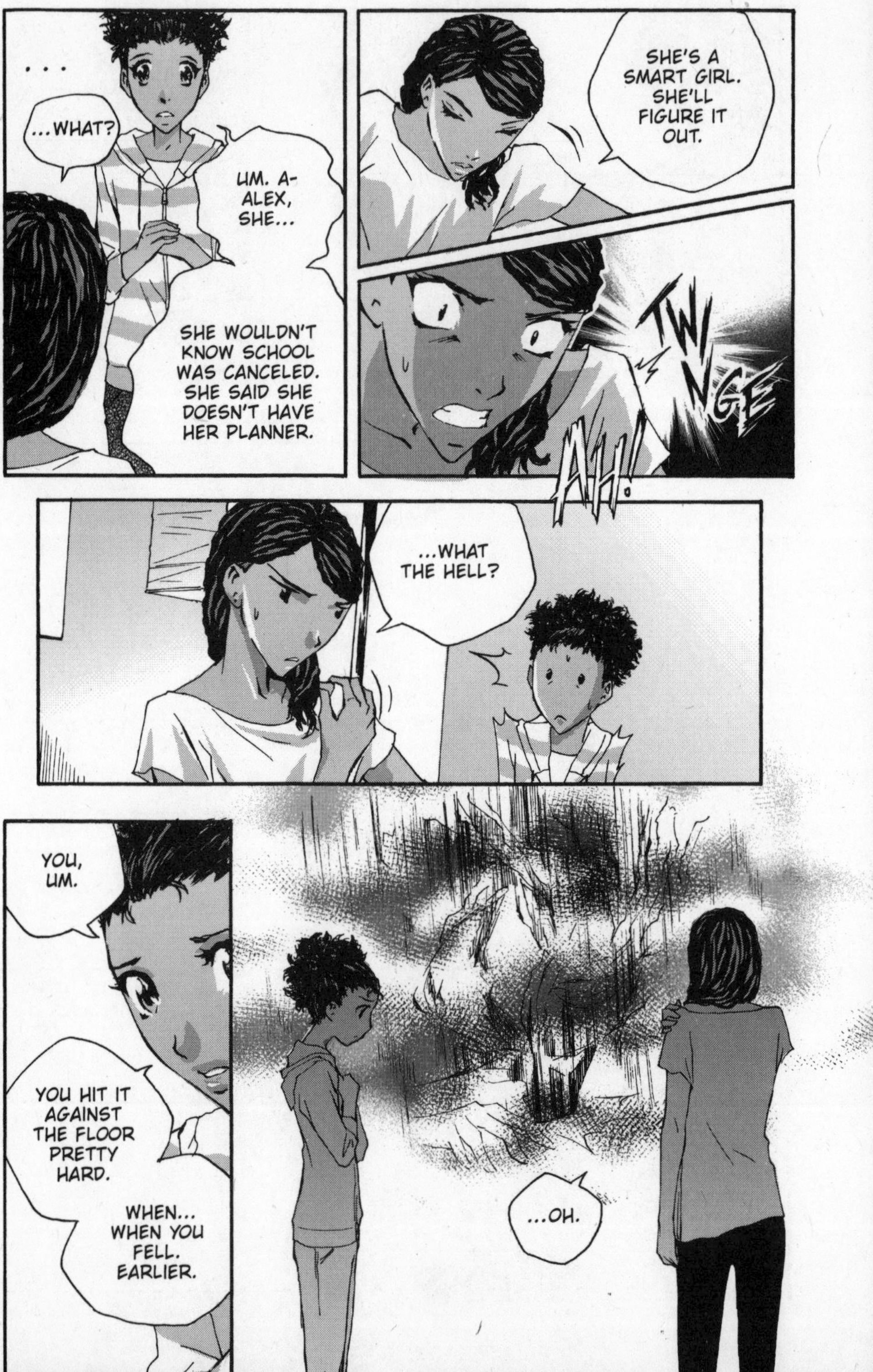
. . .
...WHAT?
UM. A-ALEX, SHE...
SHE WOULDN'T KNOW SCHOOL WAS CANCELED. SHE SAID SHE DOESN'T HAVE HER PLANNER.
SHE'S A SMART GIRL. SHE'LL FIGURE IT OUT.
TWINGE
AH!
...WHAT THE HELL?
YOU, UM.
YOU HIT IT AGAINST THE FLOOR PRETTY HARD.
WHEN... WHEN YOU FELL. EARLIER.
...OH.

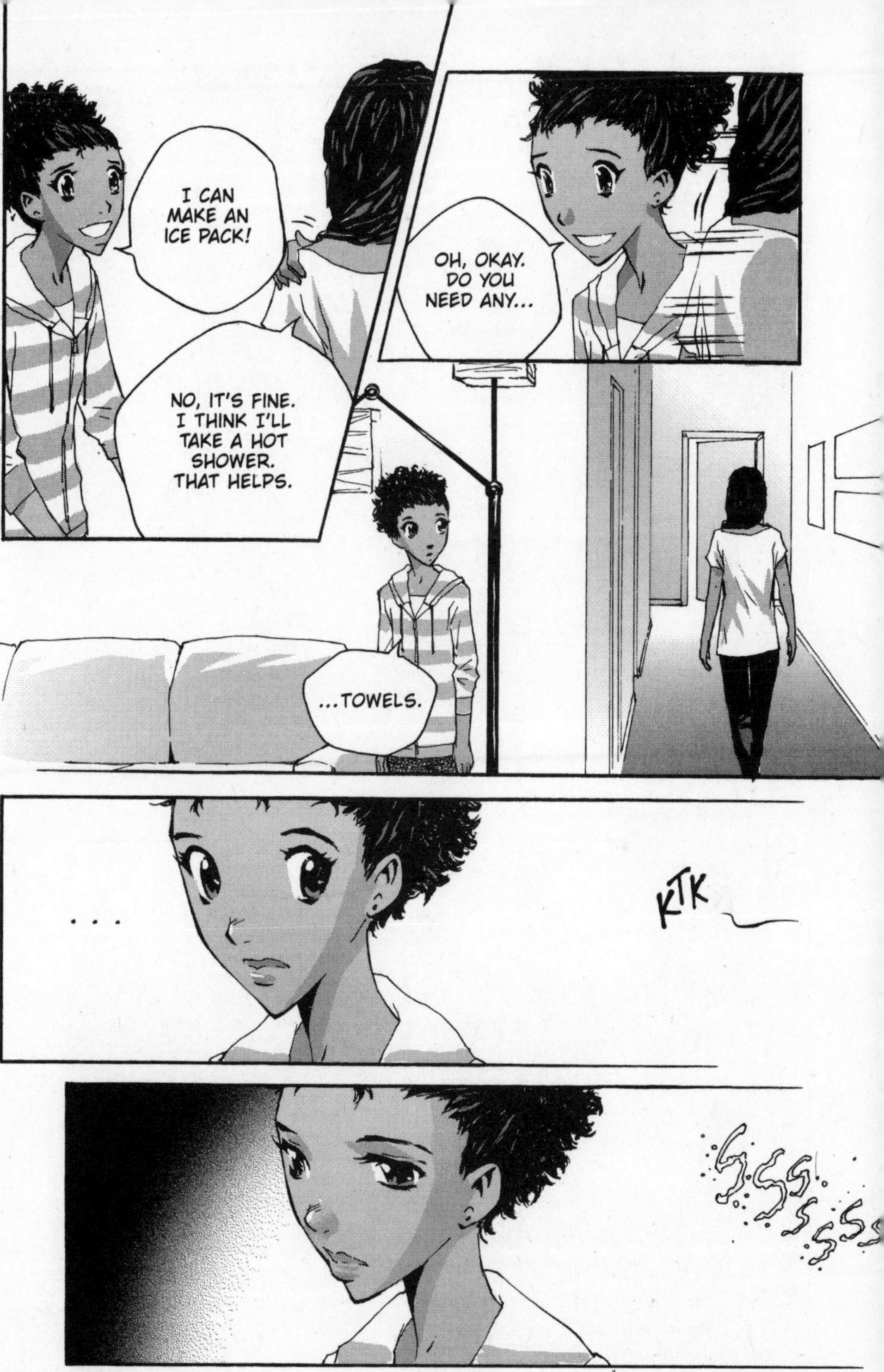
I CAN MAKE AN ICE PACK!
NO, IT'S FINE. I THINK I'LL TAKE A HOT SHOWER. THAT HELPS.
OH, OKAY. DO YOU NEED ANY...
...TOWELS.
...
KTK
SSSSSSSS

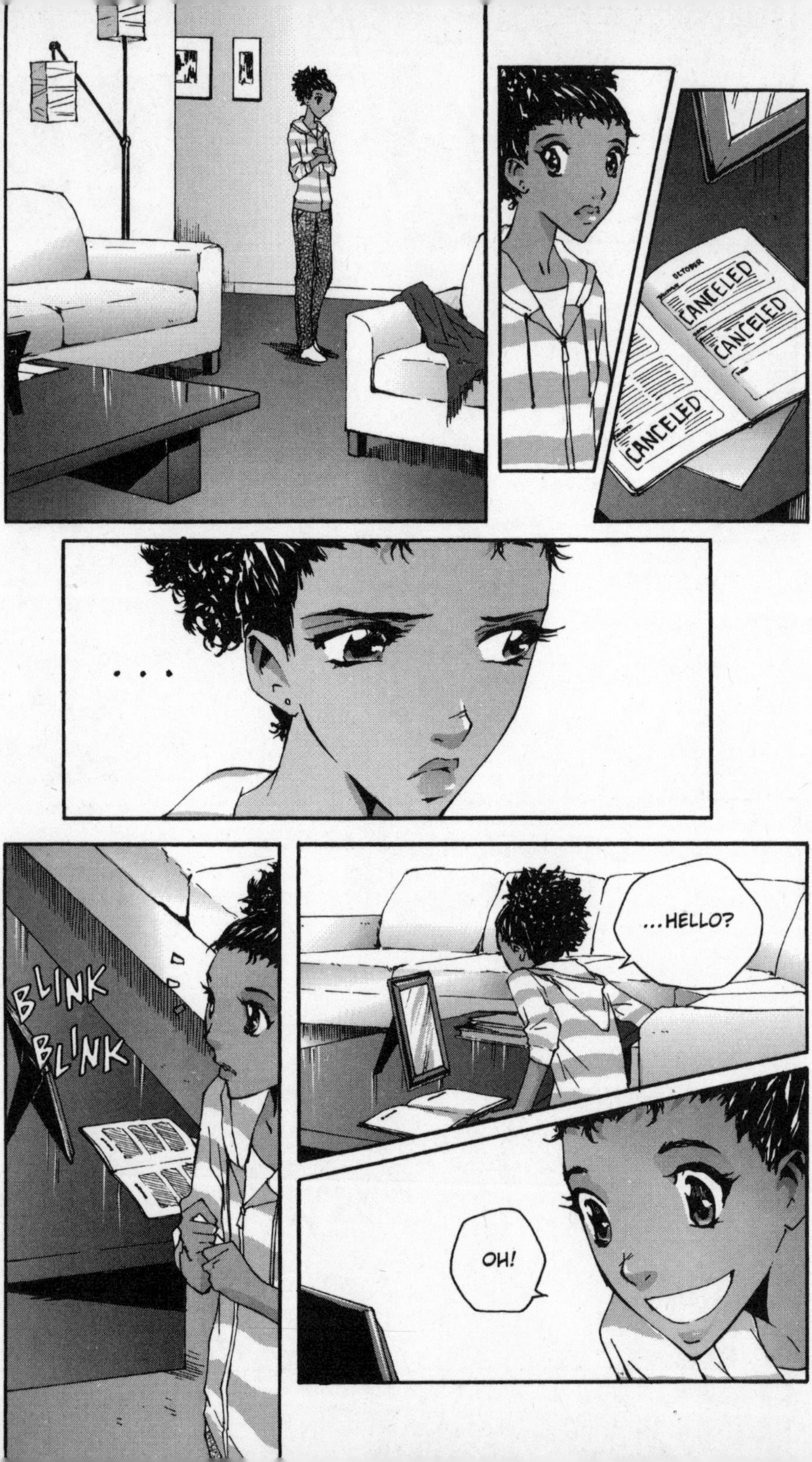
OCTOBER
CANCELED
CANCELED
CANCELED
...
BLINK
BLINK
...HELLO?
OH!

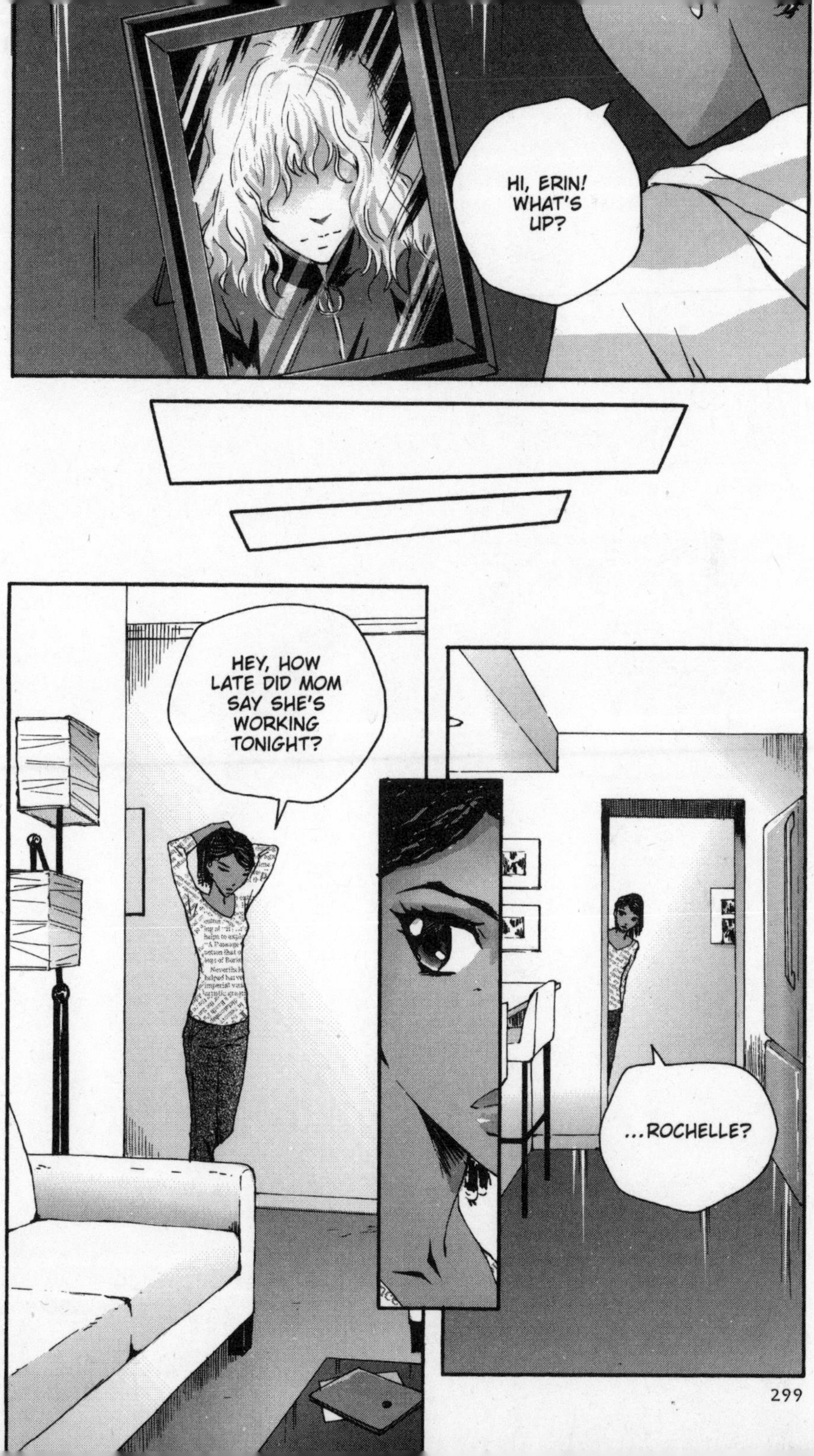
HI, ERIN! WHAT'S UP?
HEY, HOW LATE DID MOM SAY SHE'S WORKING TONIGHT?
...ROCHELLE?

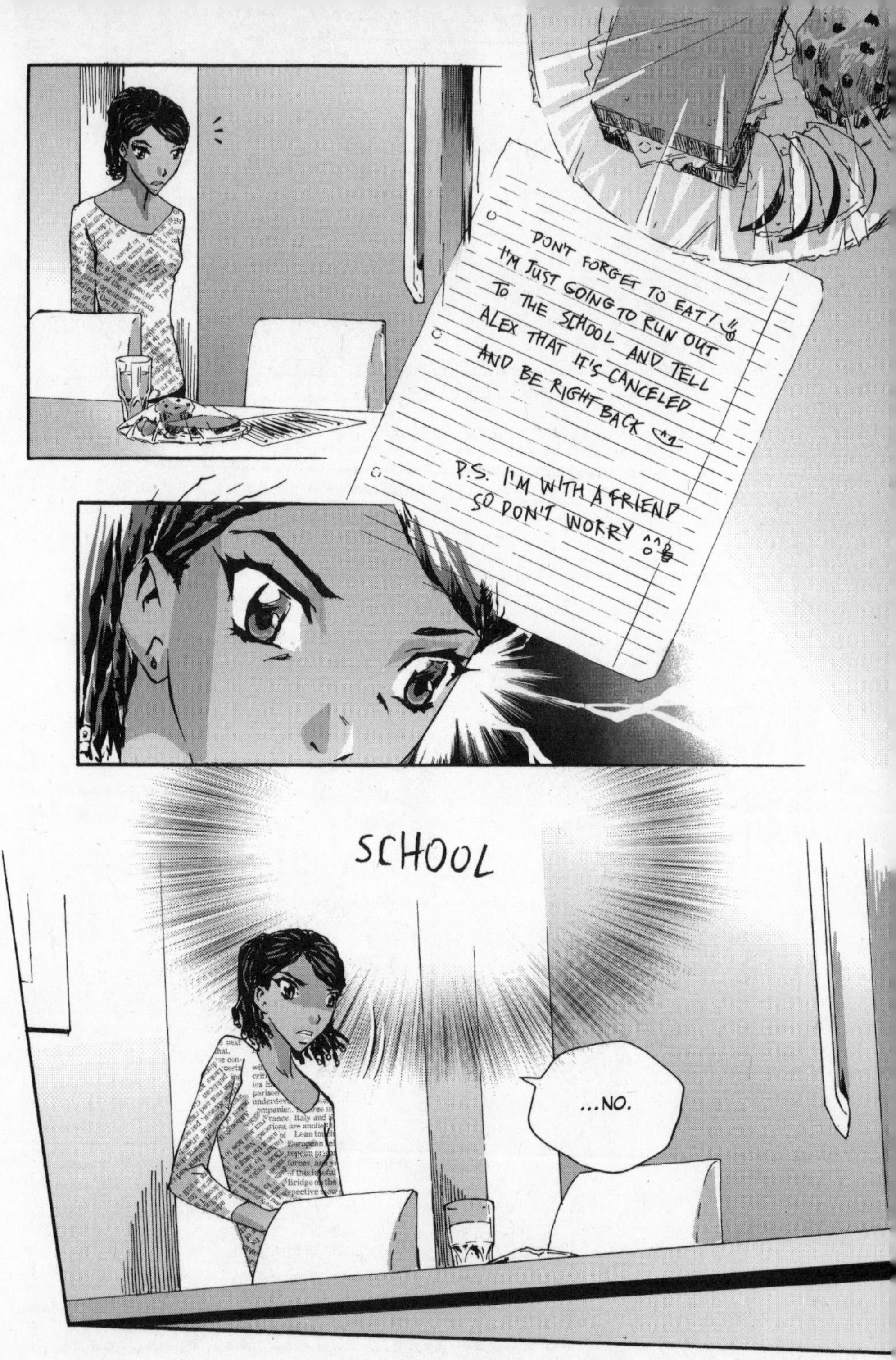
DON'T FORGET TO EAT!
I'M JUST GOING TO RUN OUT TO THE SCHOOL AND TELL ALEX THAT IT'S CANCELED AND BE RIGHT BACK
P.S. I'M WITH A FRIEND SO DON'T WORRY ^^
SCHOOL
...NO.

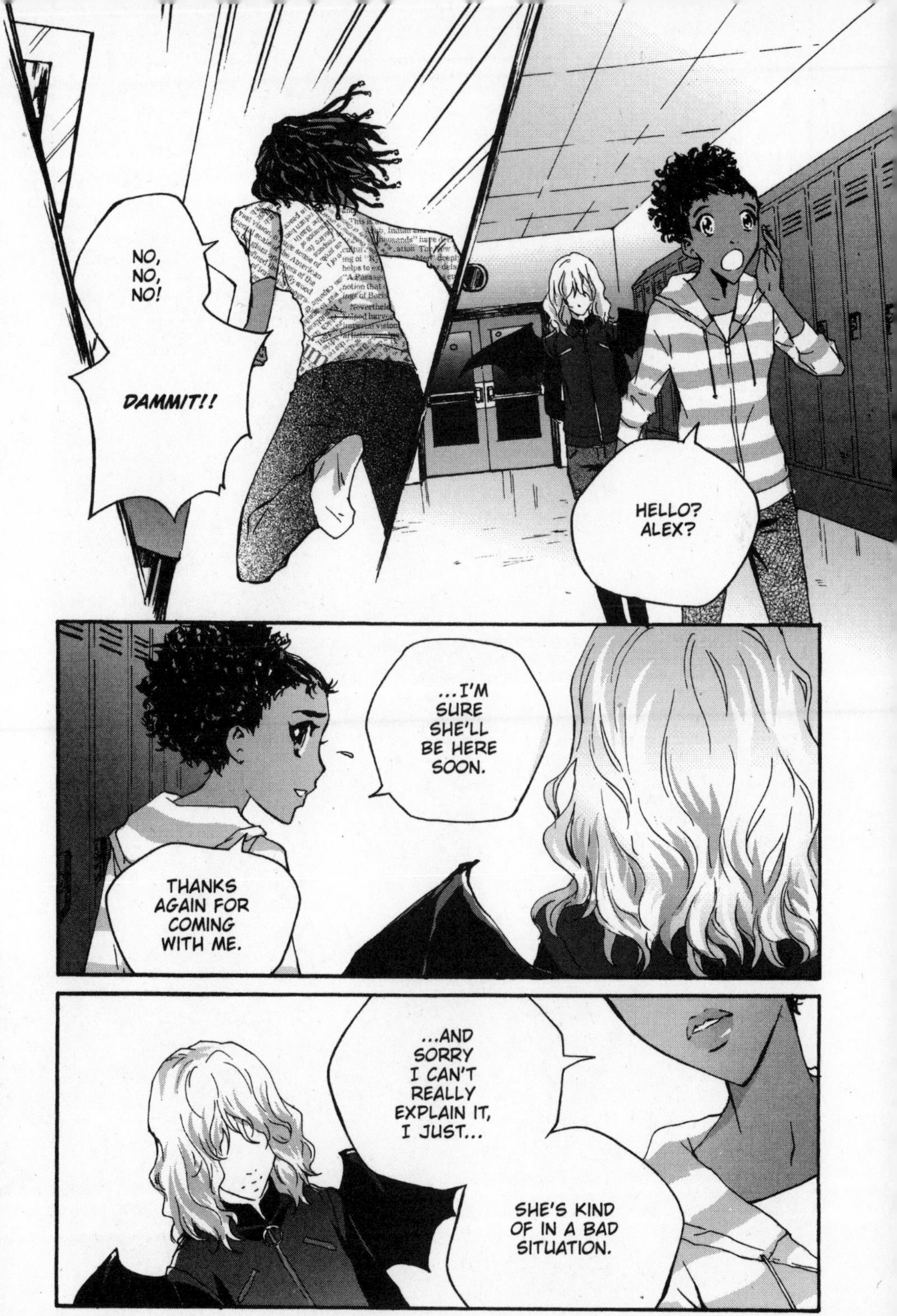
NO, NO, NO!
DAMMIT!!
HELLO? ALEX?
...I'M SURE SHE'LL BE HERE SOON.
THANKS AGAIN FOR COMING WITH ME.
...AND SORRY I CAN'T REALLY EXPLAIN IT, I JUST...
SHE'S KIND OF IN A BAD SITUATION.

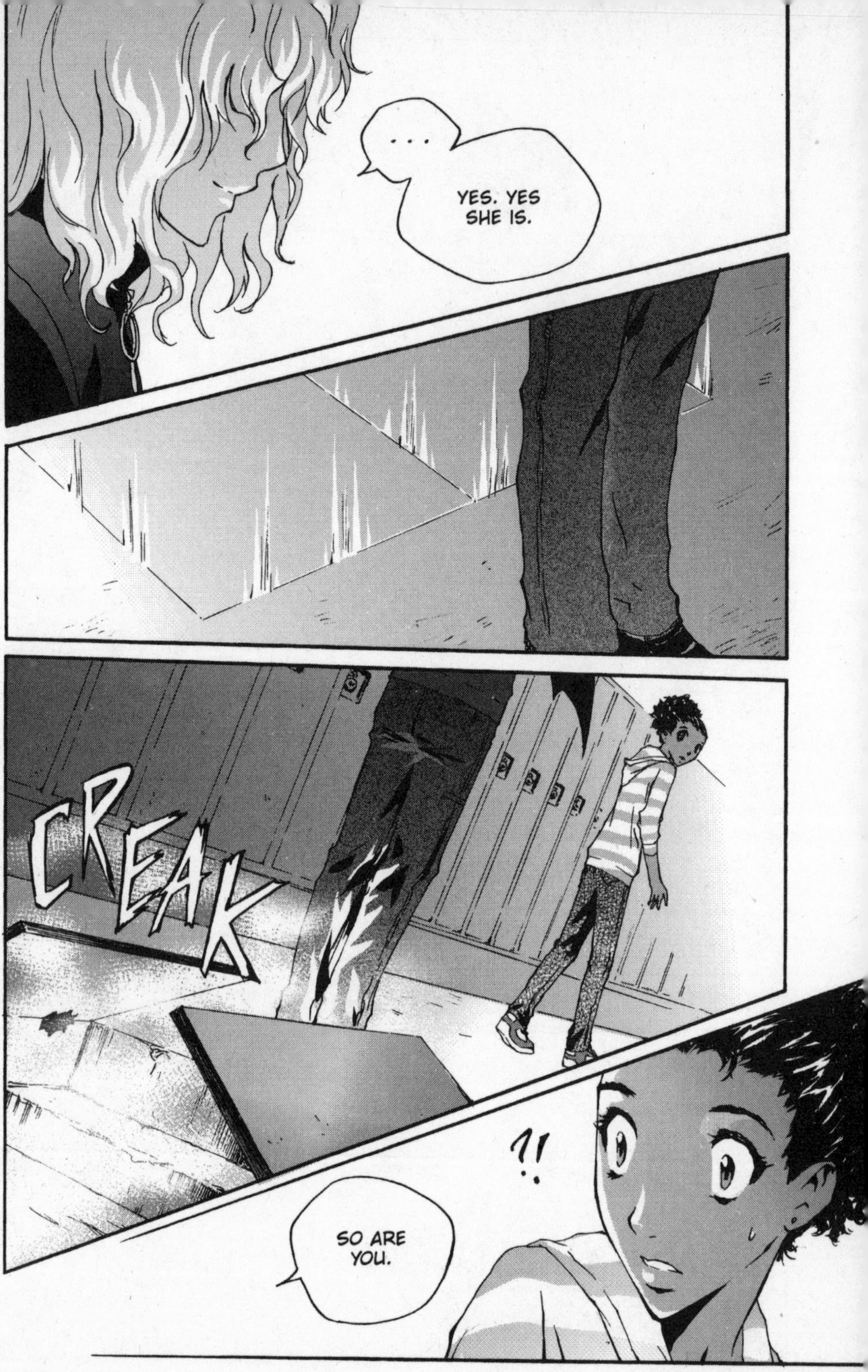
...
YES. YES SHE IS.
CREAK
?!
SO ARE YOU.

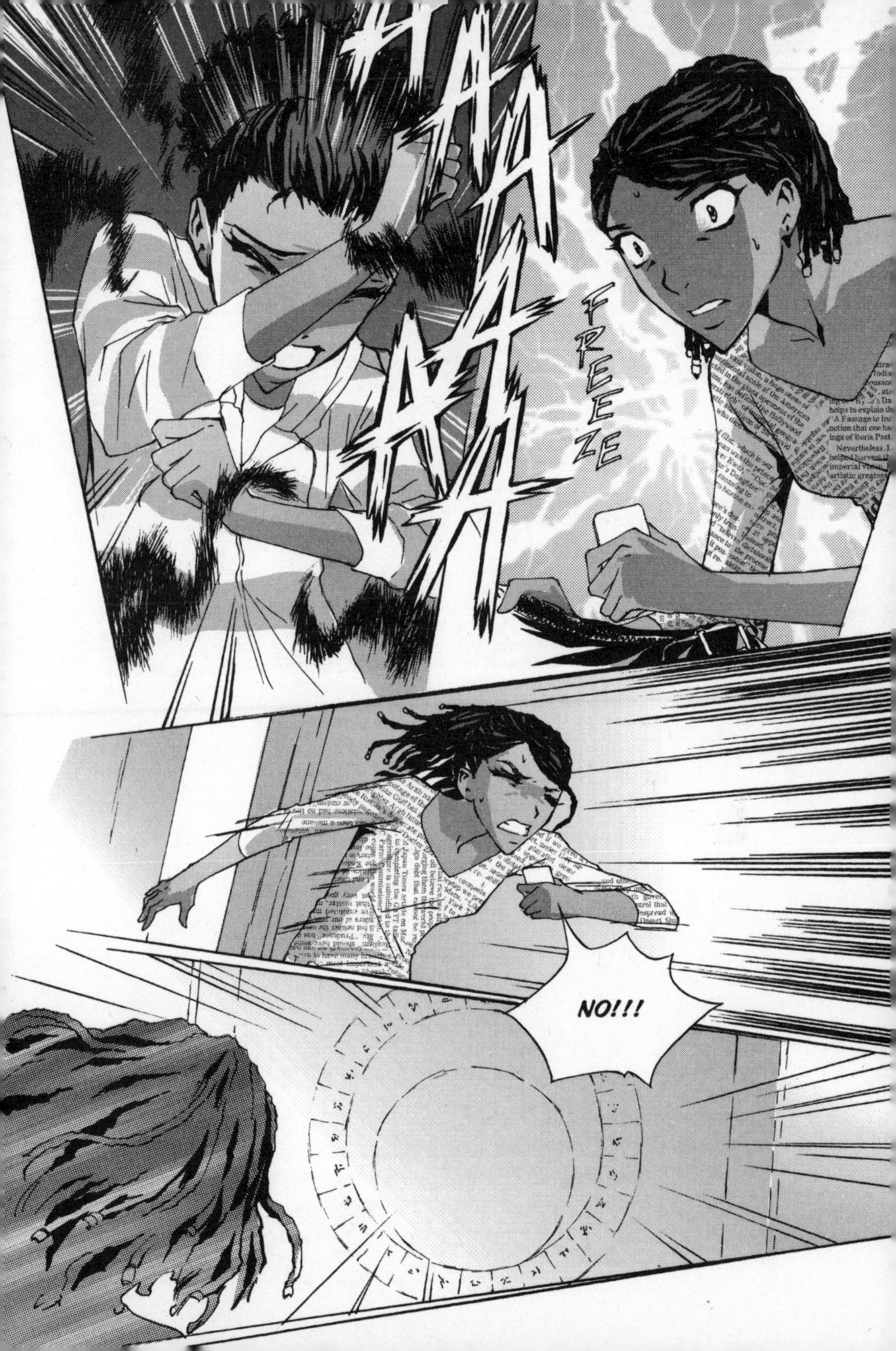
HAAAAA
FREEZE
NO!!!

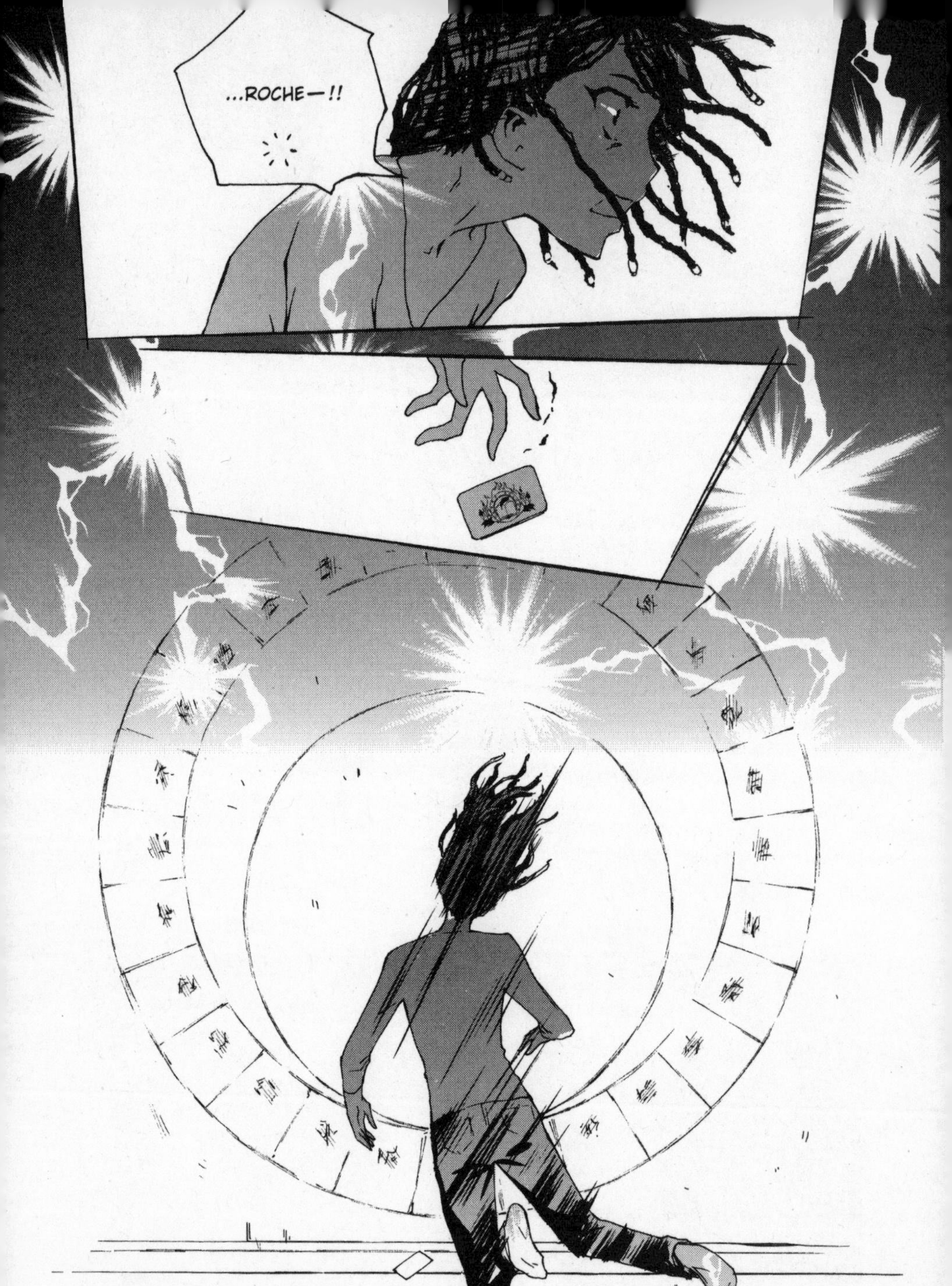
...ROCHE—!!

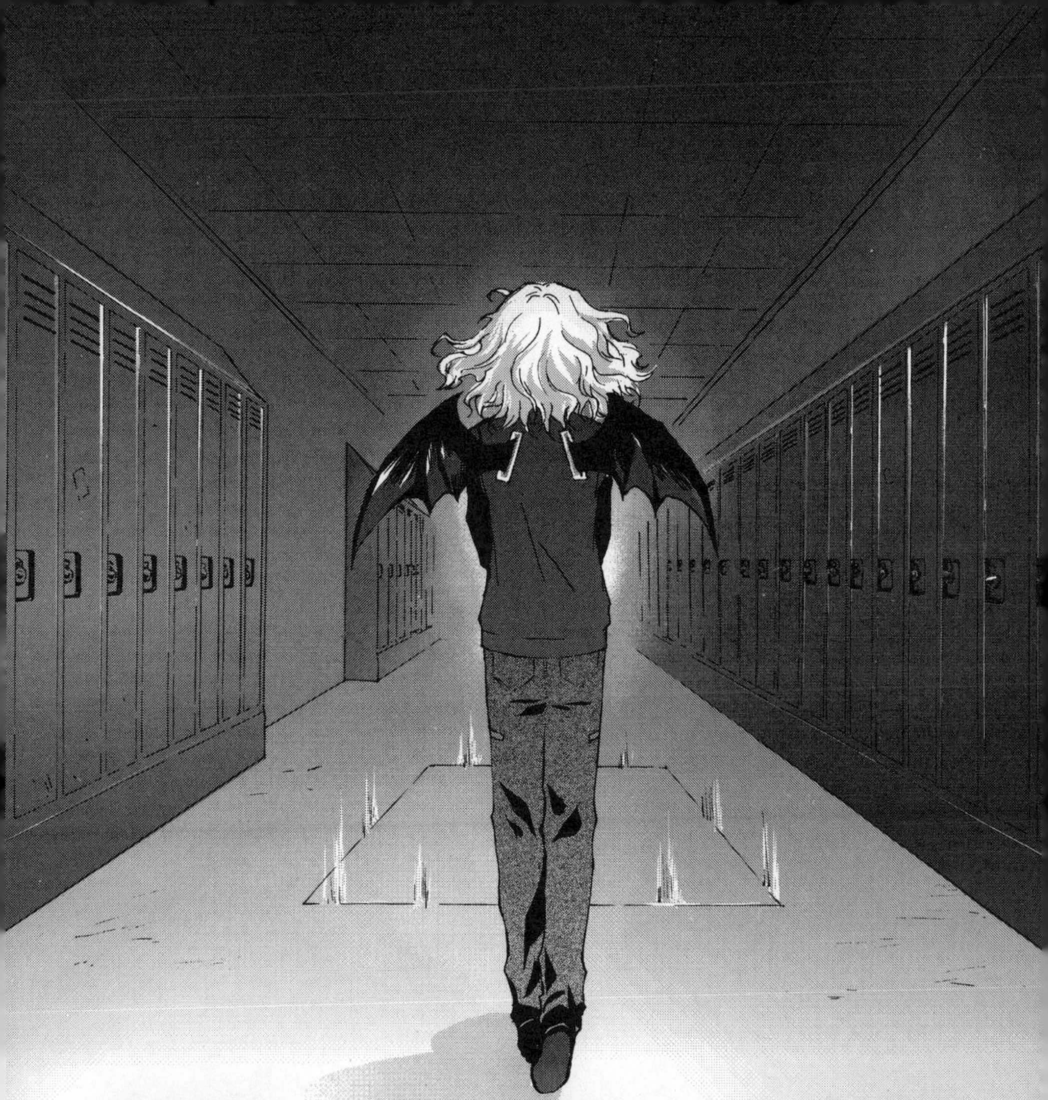

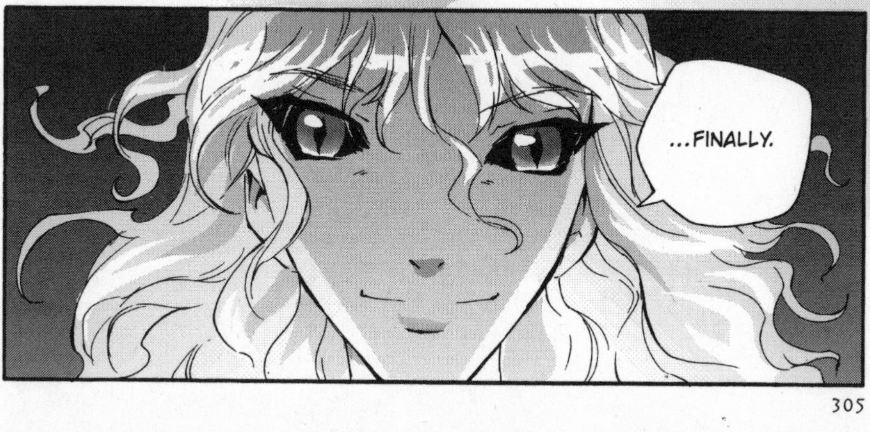
...FINALLY.

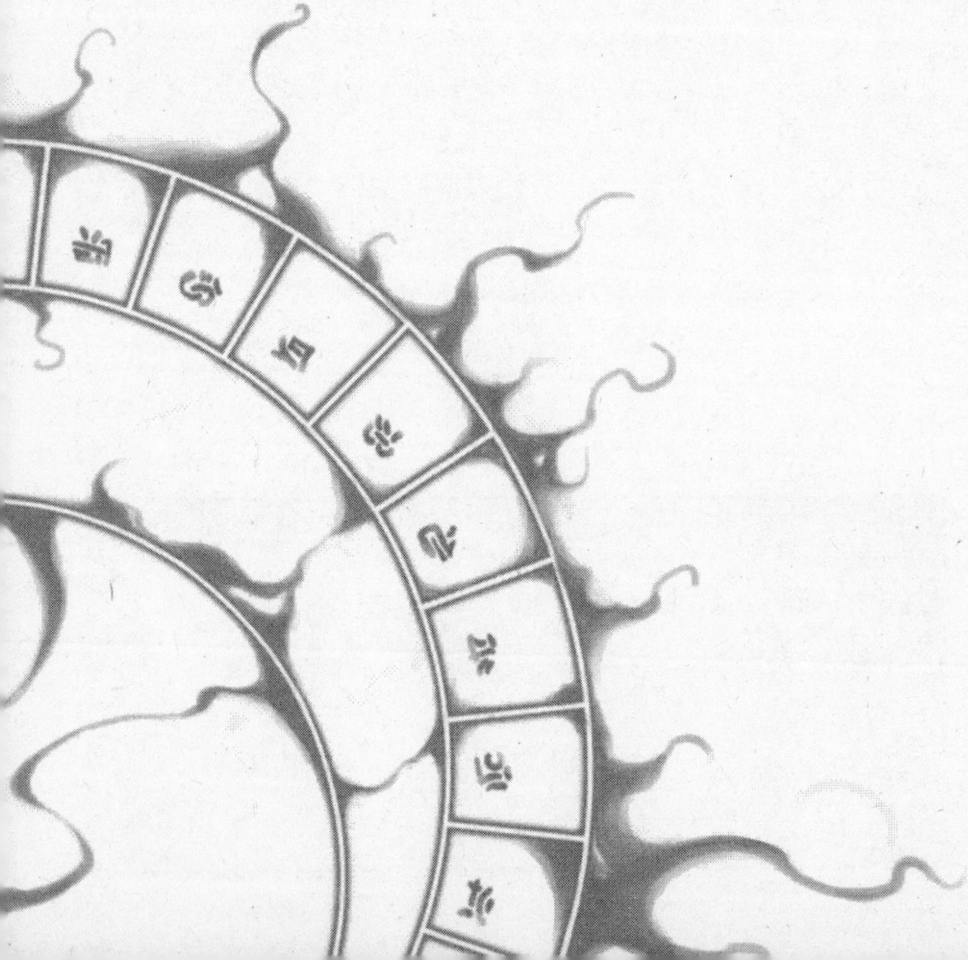

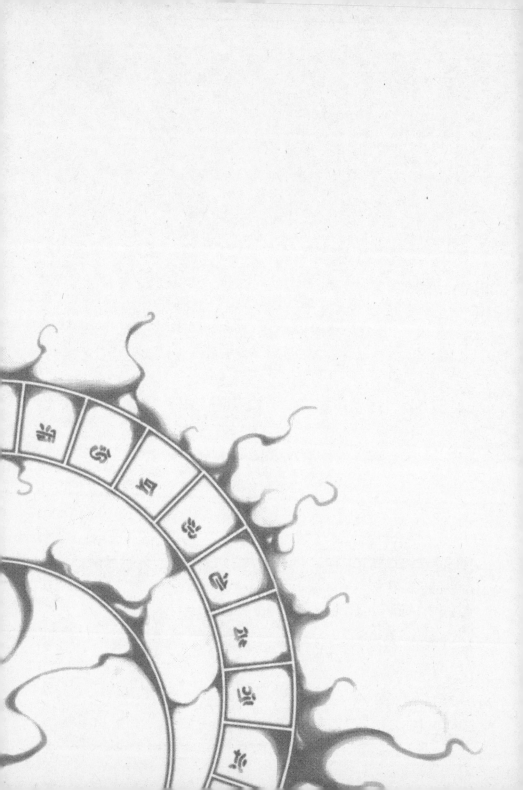

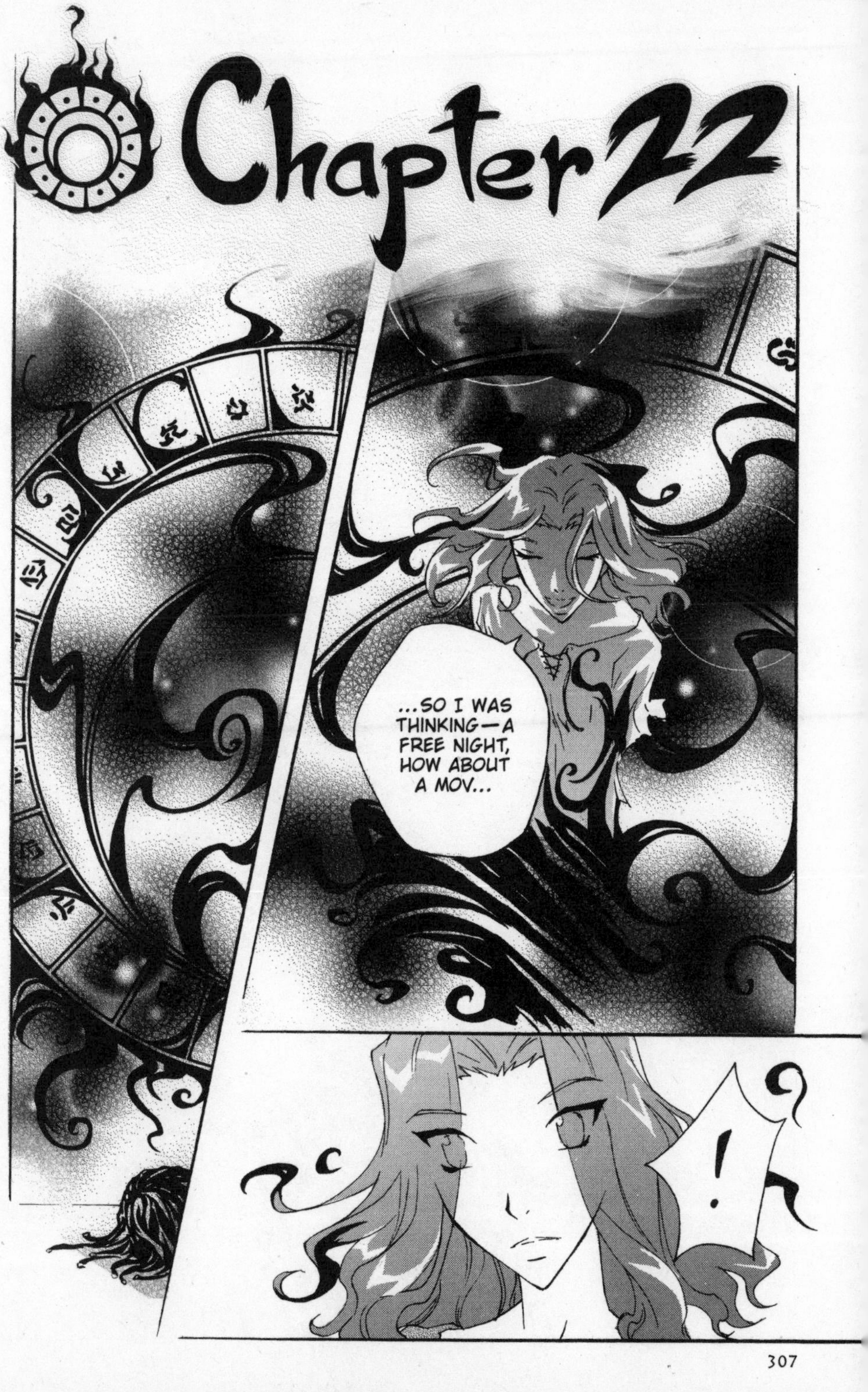
Chapter 22
...SO I WAS THINKING—A FREE NIGHT, HOW ABOUT A MOV...
!

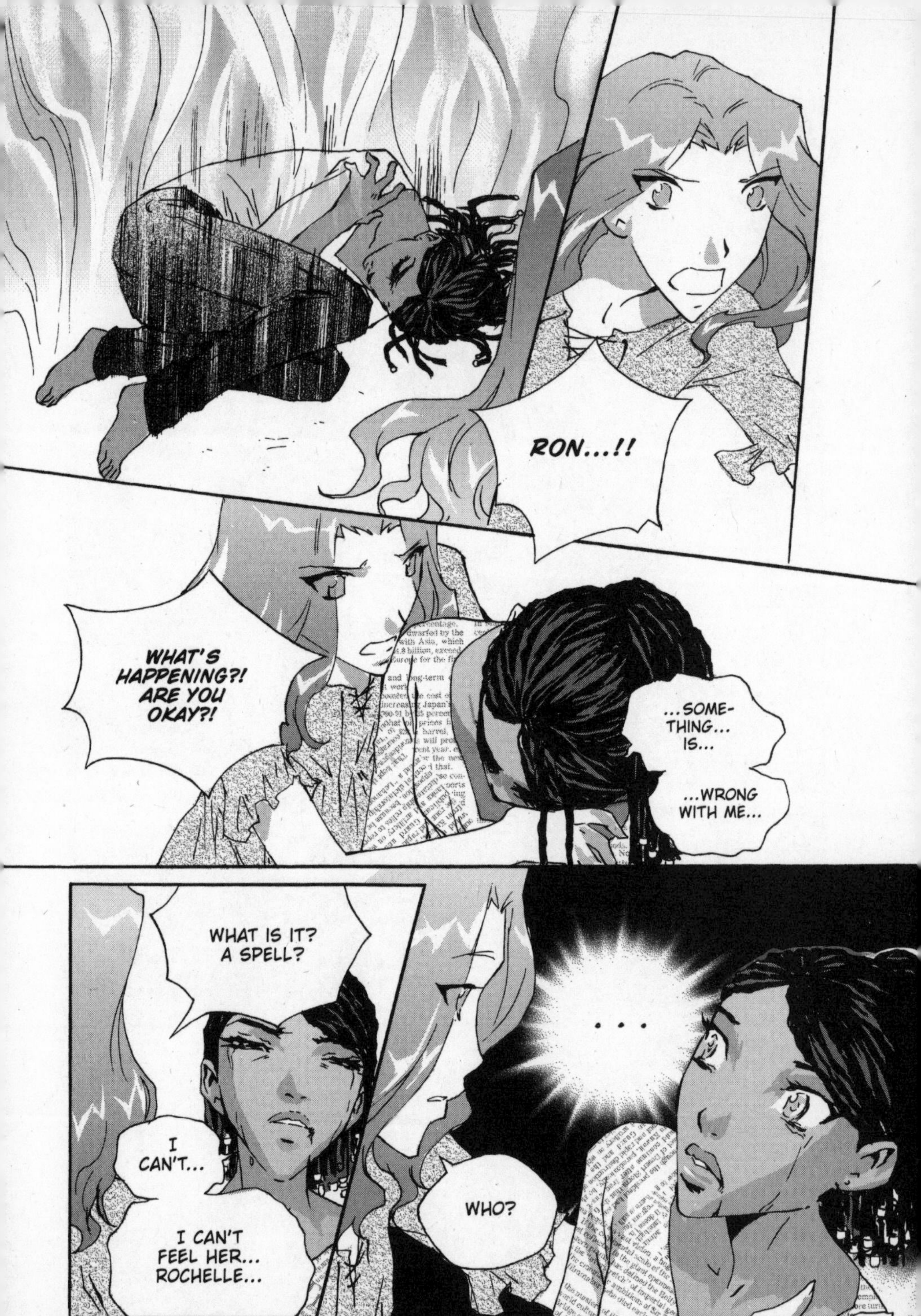
RON...!!
WHAT'S HAPPENING?! ARE YOU OKAY?!
...SOME-THING... IS...
...WRONG WITH ME...
WHAT IS IT? A SPELL?
I CAN'T...
I CAN'T FEEL HER... ROCHELLE...
...
WHO?

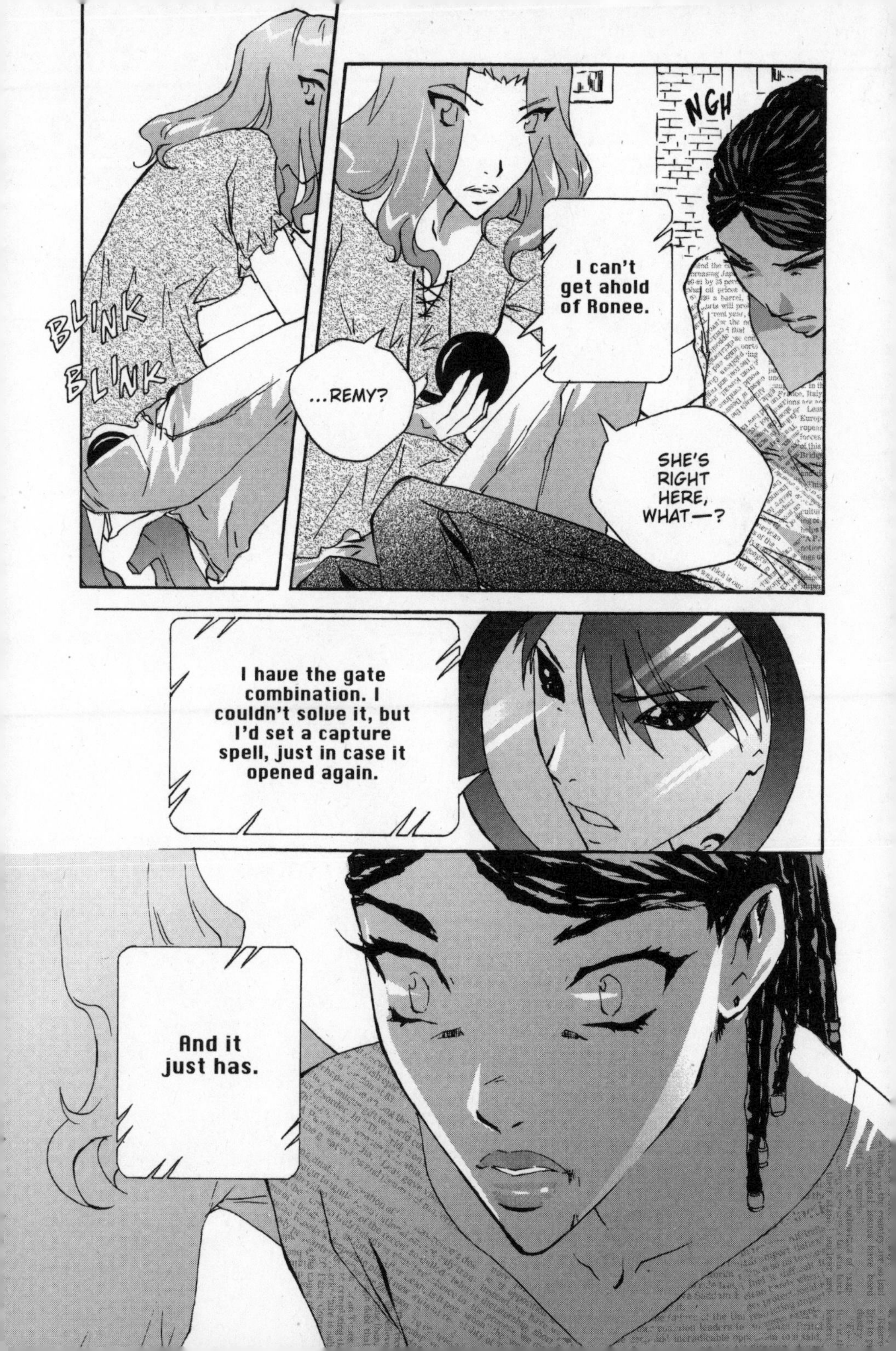

BLINK BLINK
...REMY?
NGH
I can't get ahold of Ronee.
SHE'S RIGHT HERE, WHAT—?
I have the gate combination. I couldn't solve it, but I'd set a capture spell, just in case it opened again.
And it just has.

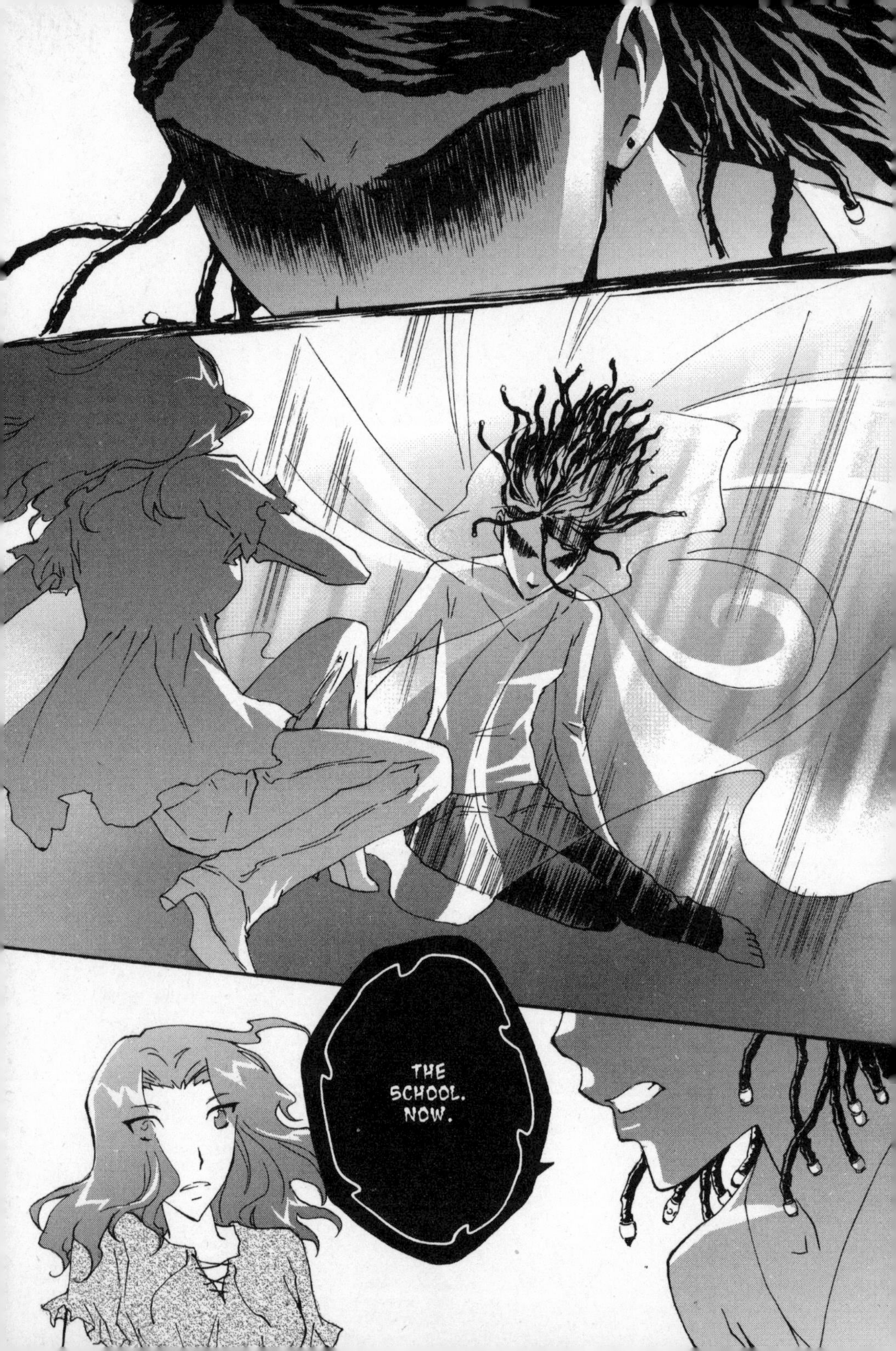
THE SCHOOL. NOW.

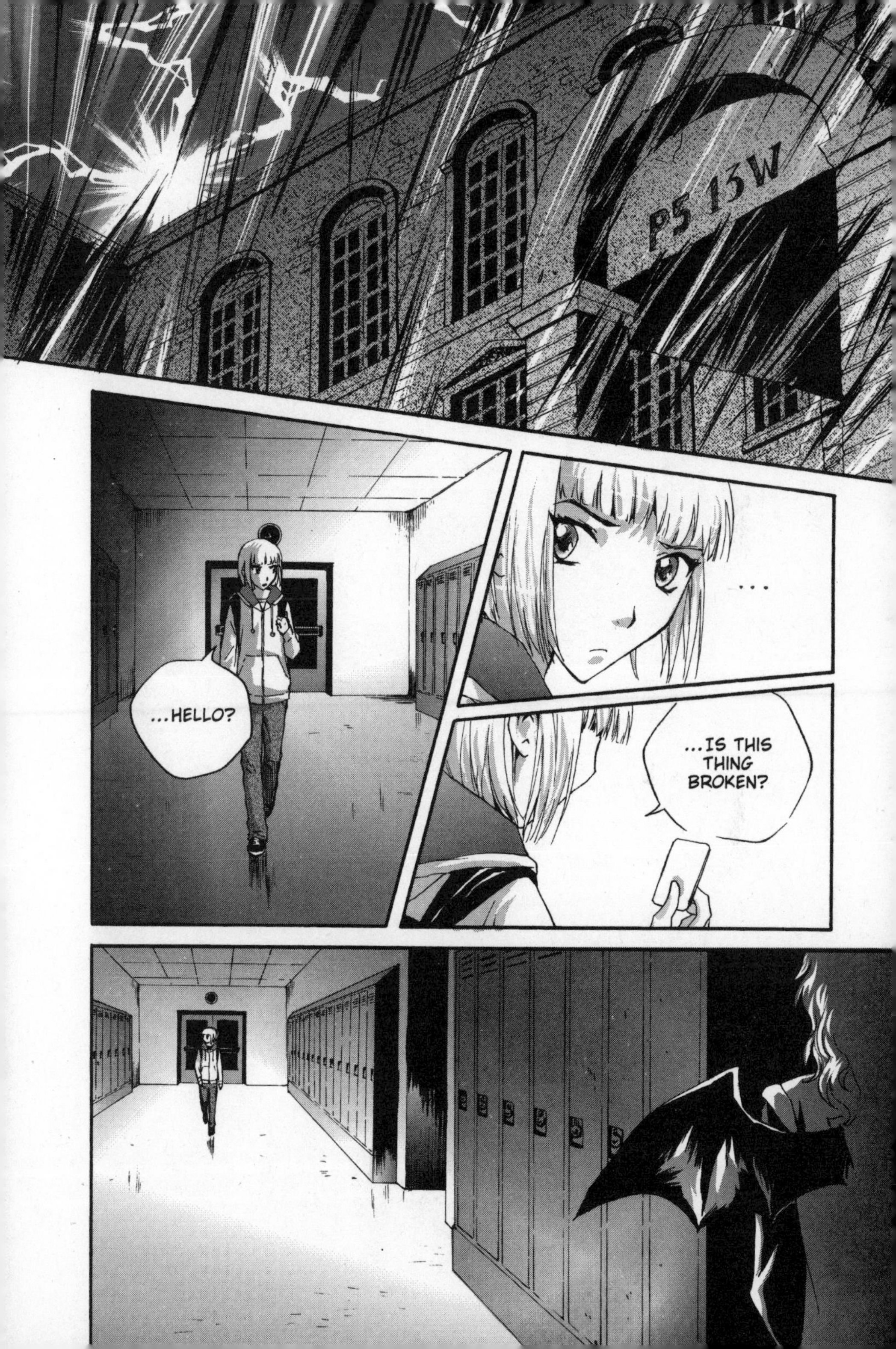
PS 13W
...HELLO?
...
...IS THIS THING BROKEN?

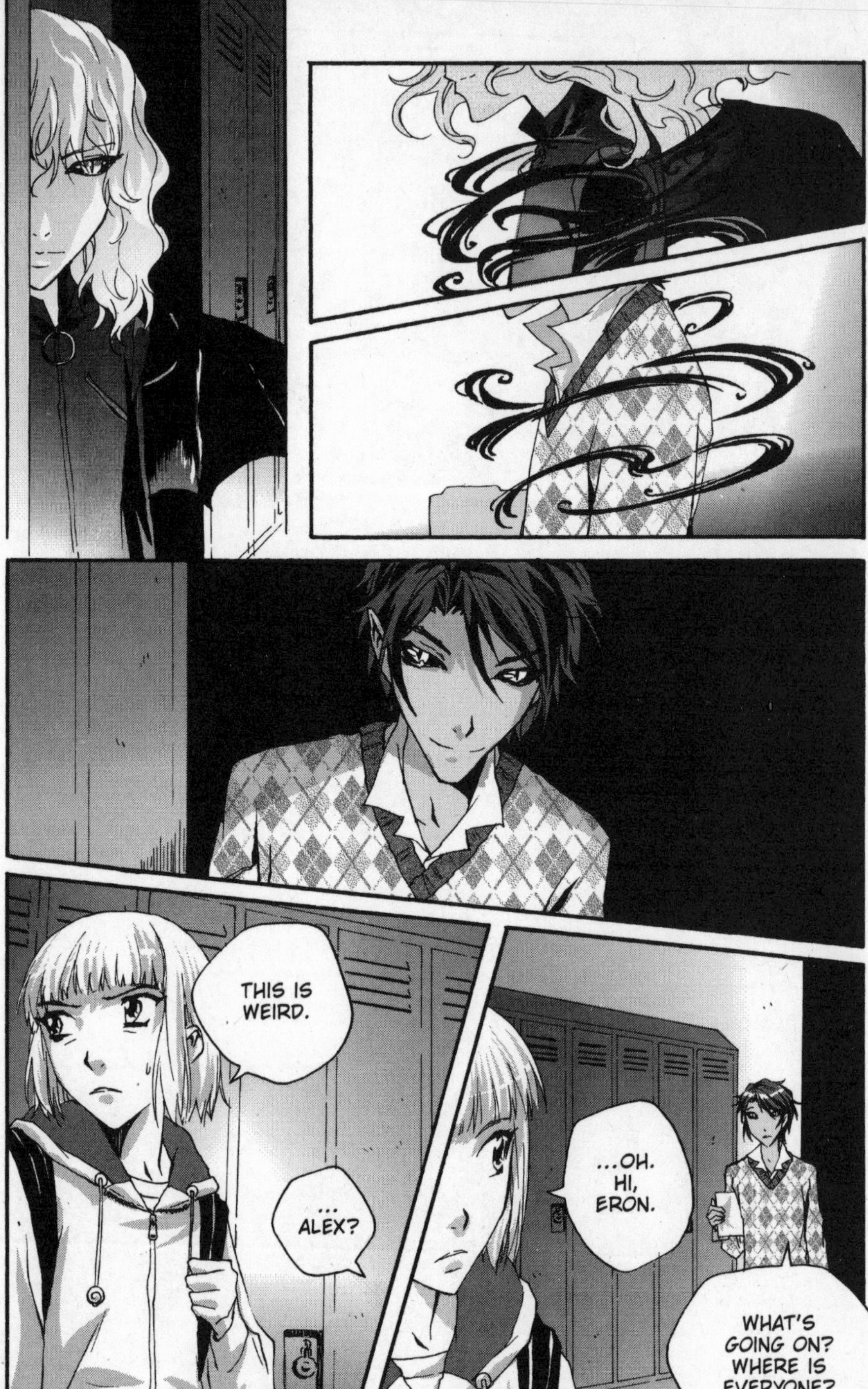
THIS IS WEIRD.
... ALEX?
...OH. HI, ERON.
WHAT'S GOING ON? WHERE IS EVERYONE?

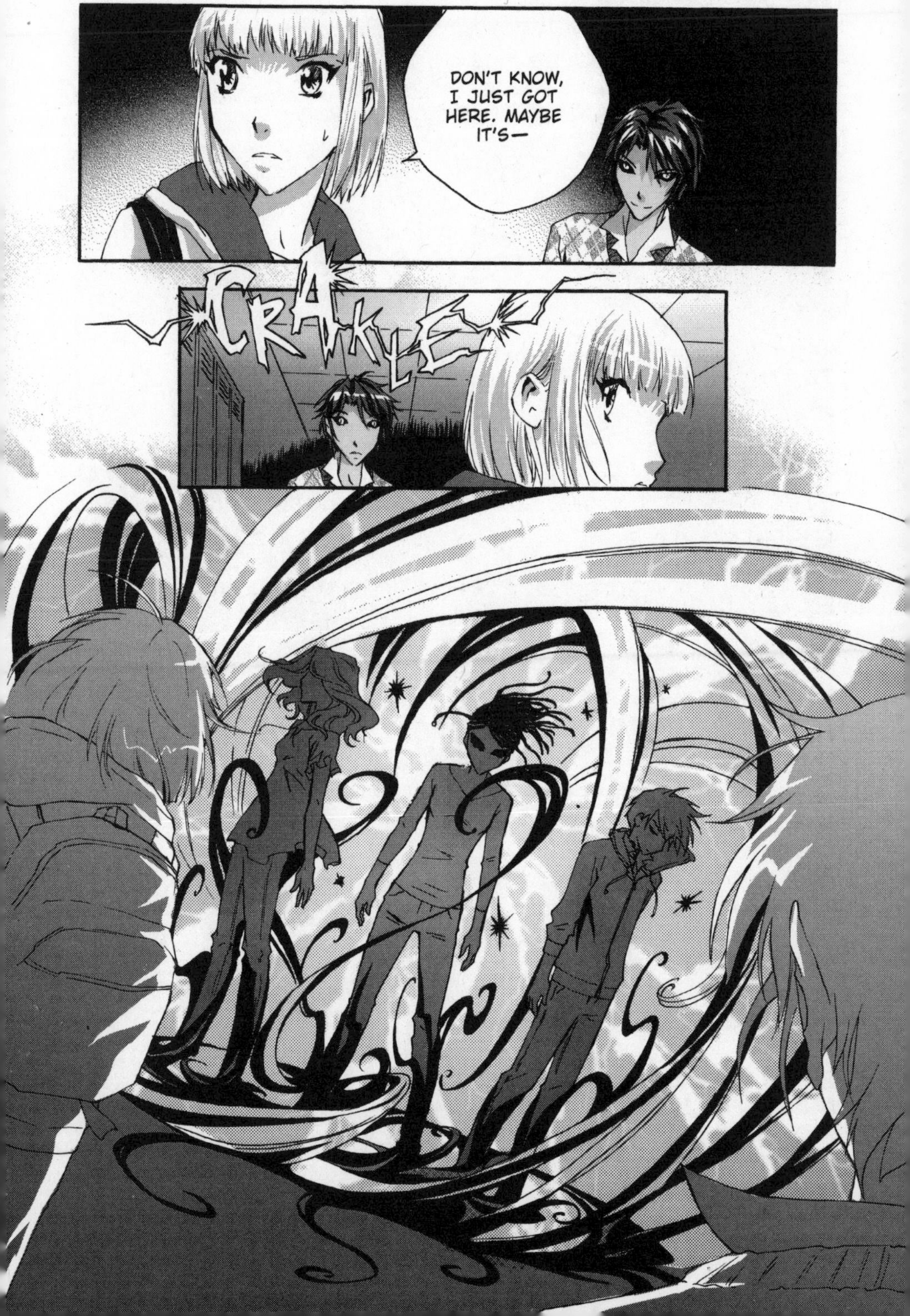
DON'T KNOW, I JUST GOT HERE. MAYBE IT'S—
CRAKLE

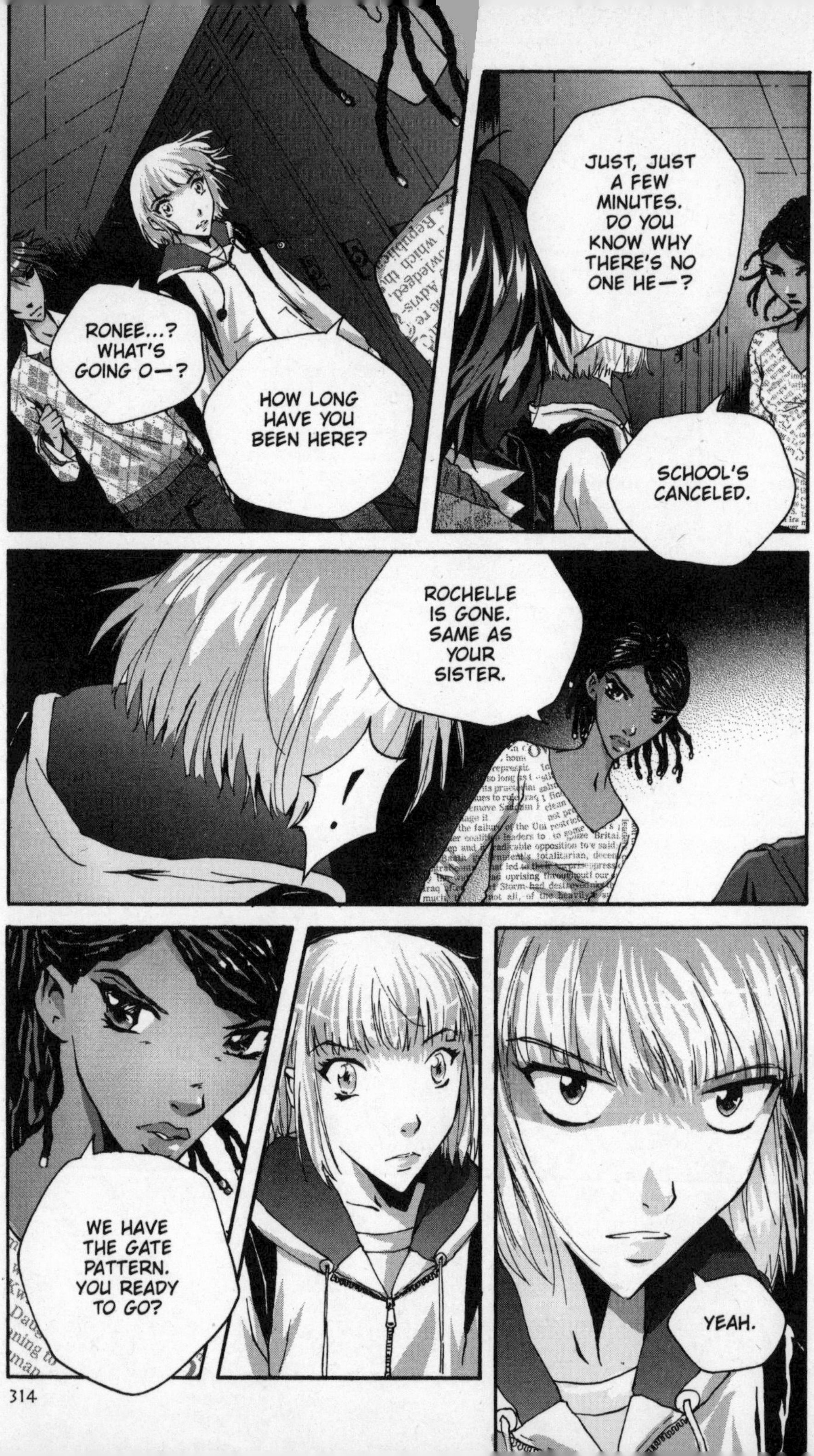
RONEE...? WHAT'S GOING O—?
HOW LONG HAVE YOU BEEN HERE?
JUST, JUST A FEW MINUTES. DO YOU KNOW WHY THERE'S NO ONE HE—?
SCHOOL'S CANCELED.
ROCHELLE IS GONE. SAME AS YOUR SISTER.
WE HAVE THE GATE PATTERN. YOU READY TO GO?
YEAH.

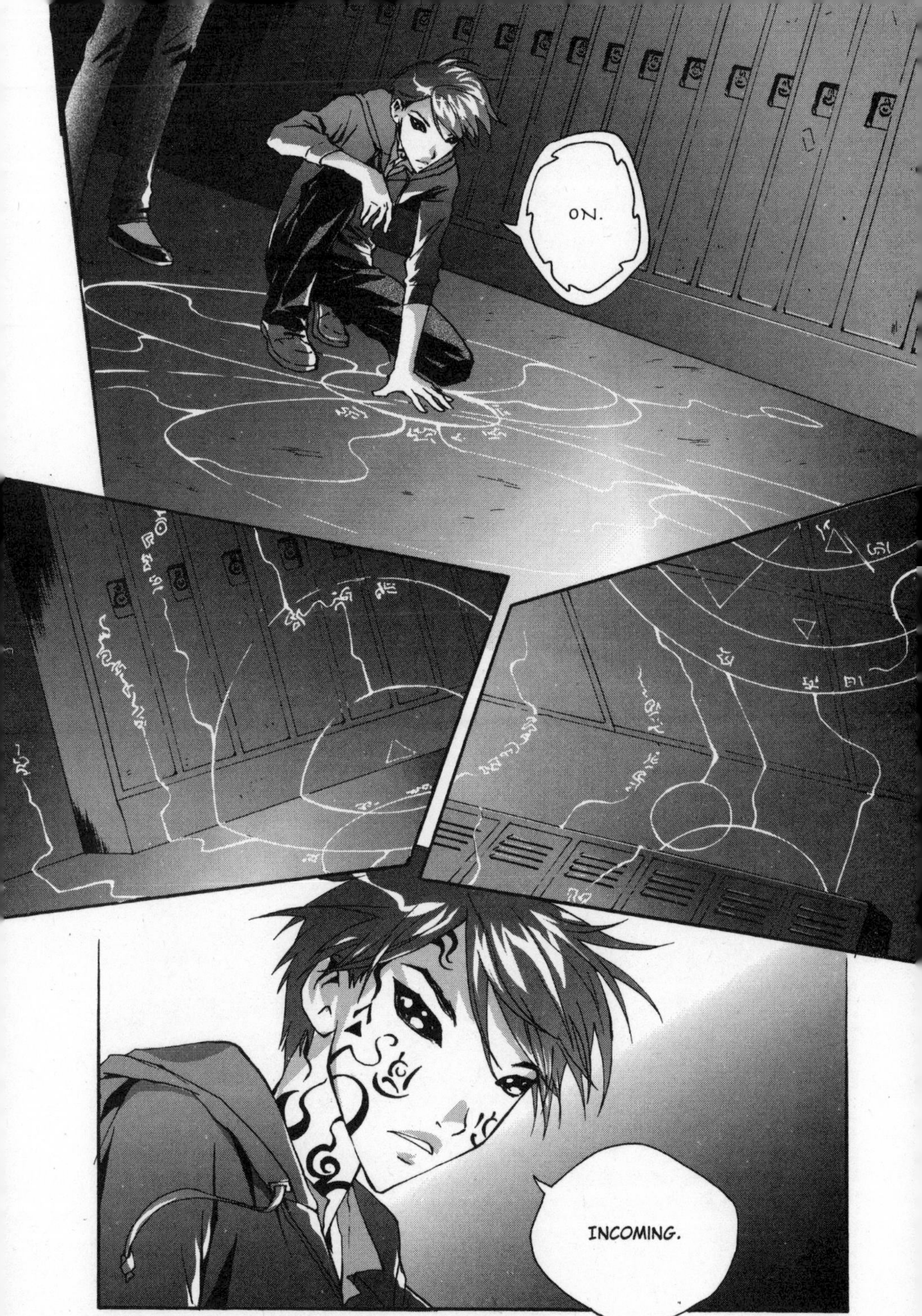
ON.
INCOMING.

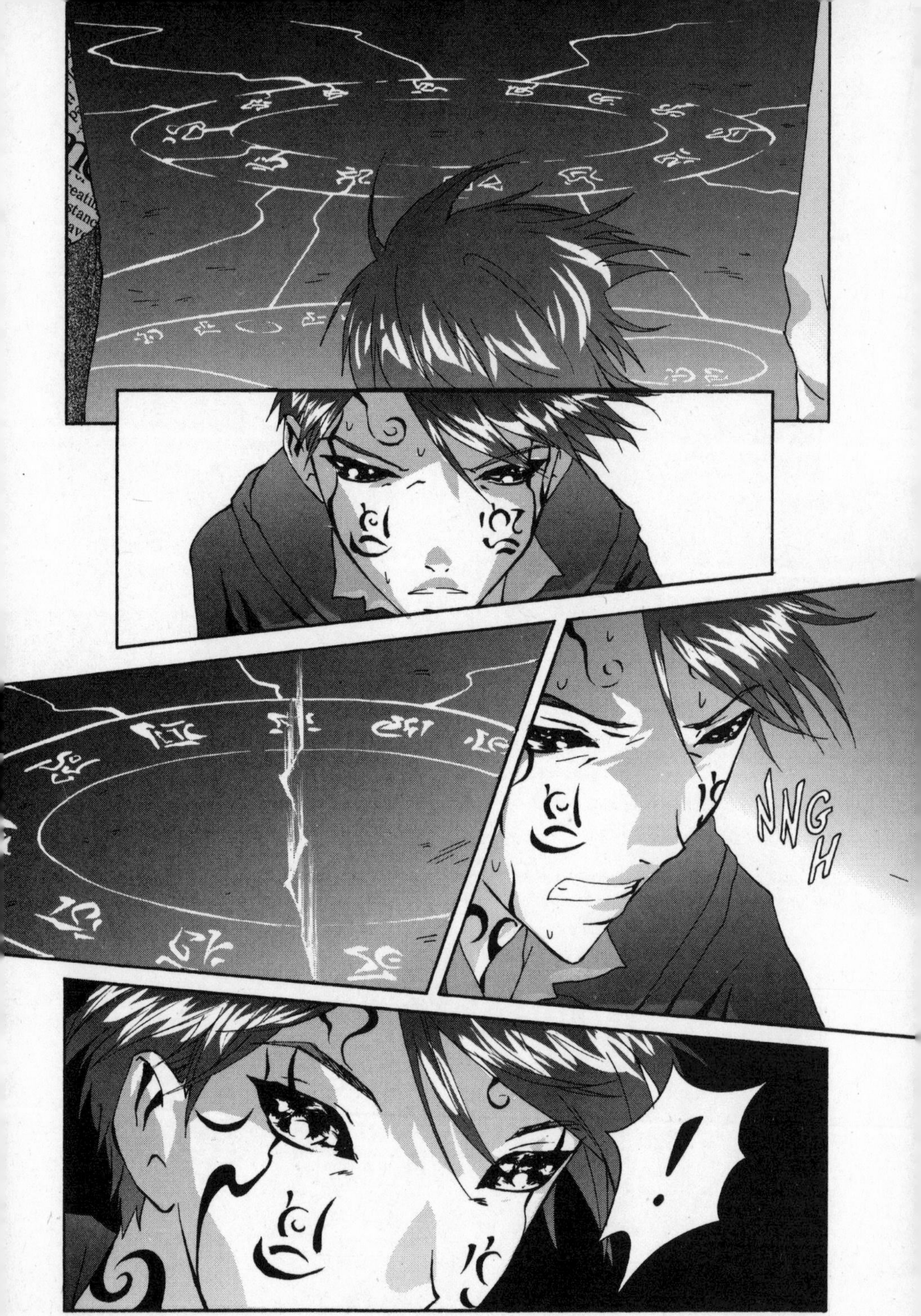
NNGH
!

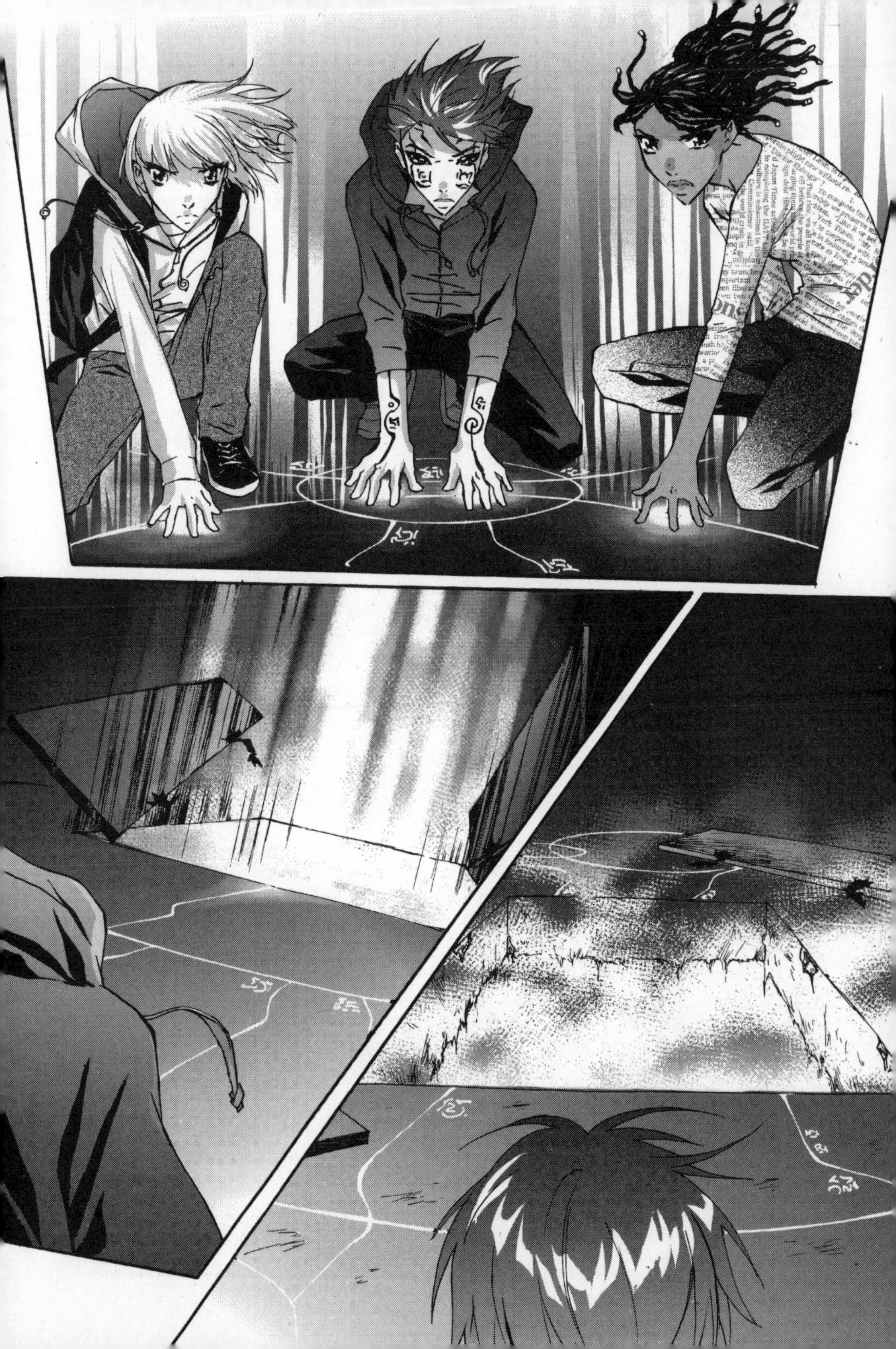

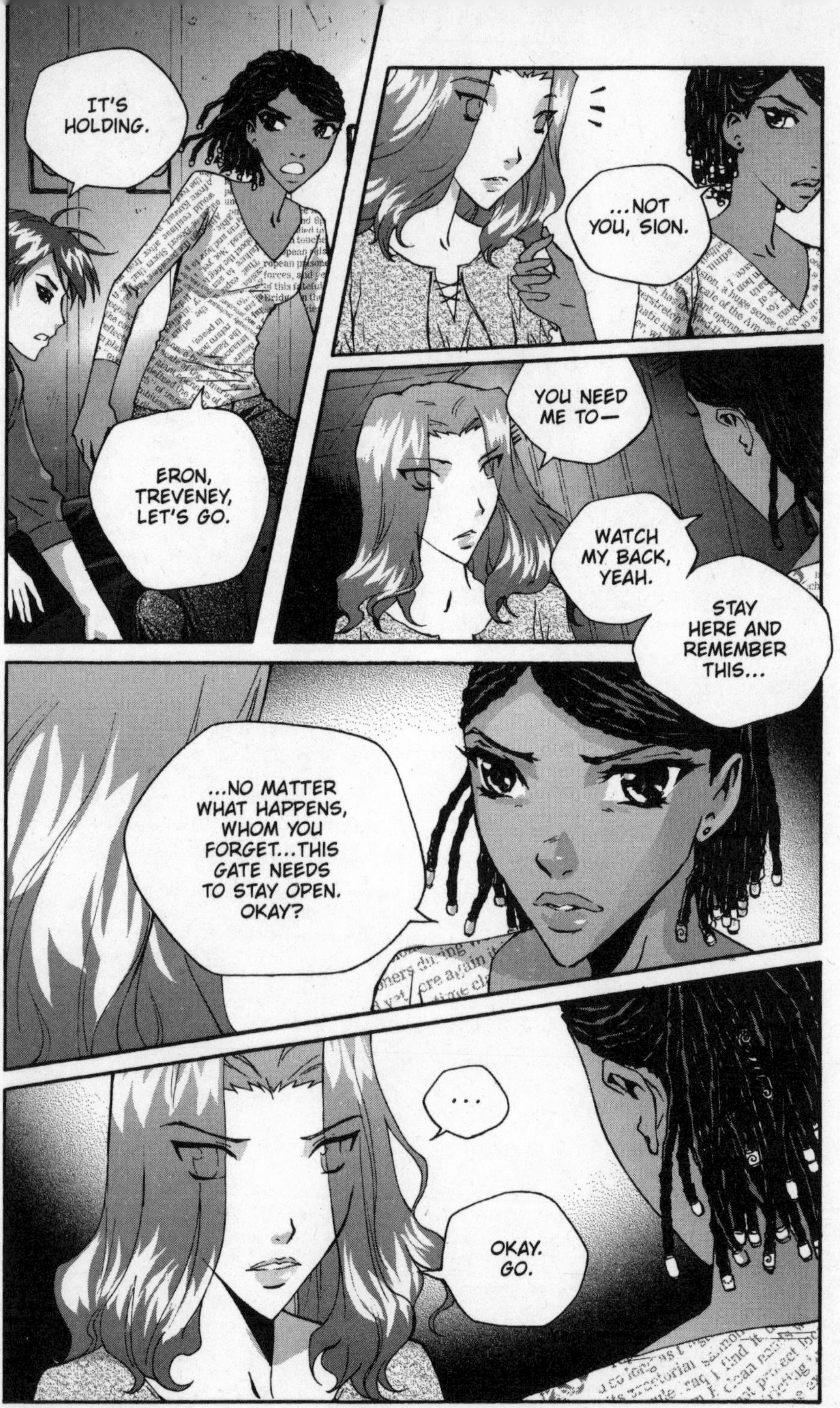
IT'S HOLDING.
ERON, TREVENEY, LET'S GO.
...NOT YOU, SION.
YOU NEED ME TO—
WATCH MY BACK, YEAH.
STAY HERE AND REMEMBER THIS...
...NO MATTER WHAT HAPPENS, WHOM YOU FORGET...THIS GATE NEEDS TO STAY OPEN. OKAY?
...
OKAY. GO.

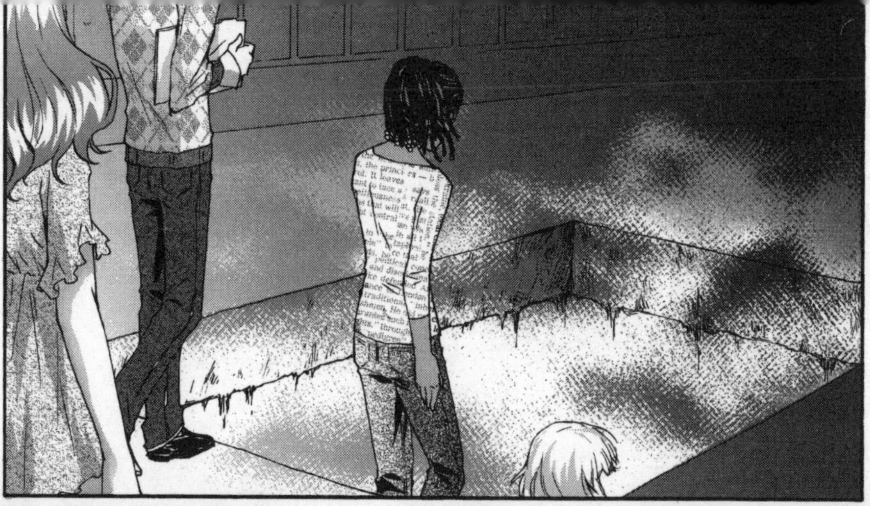
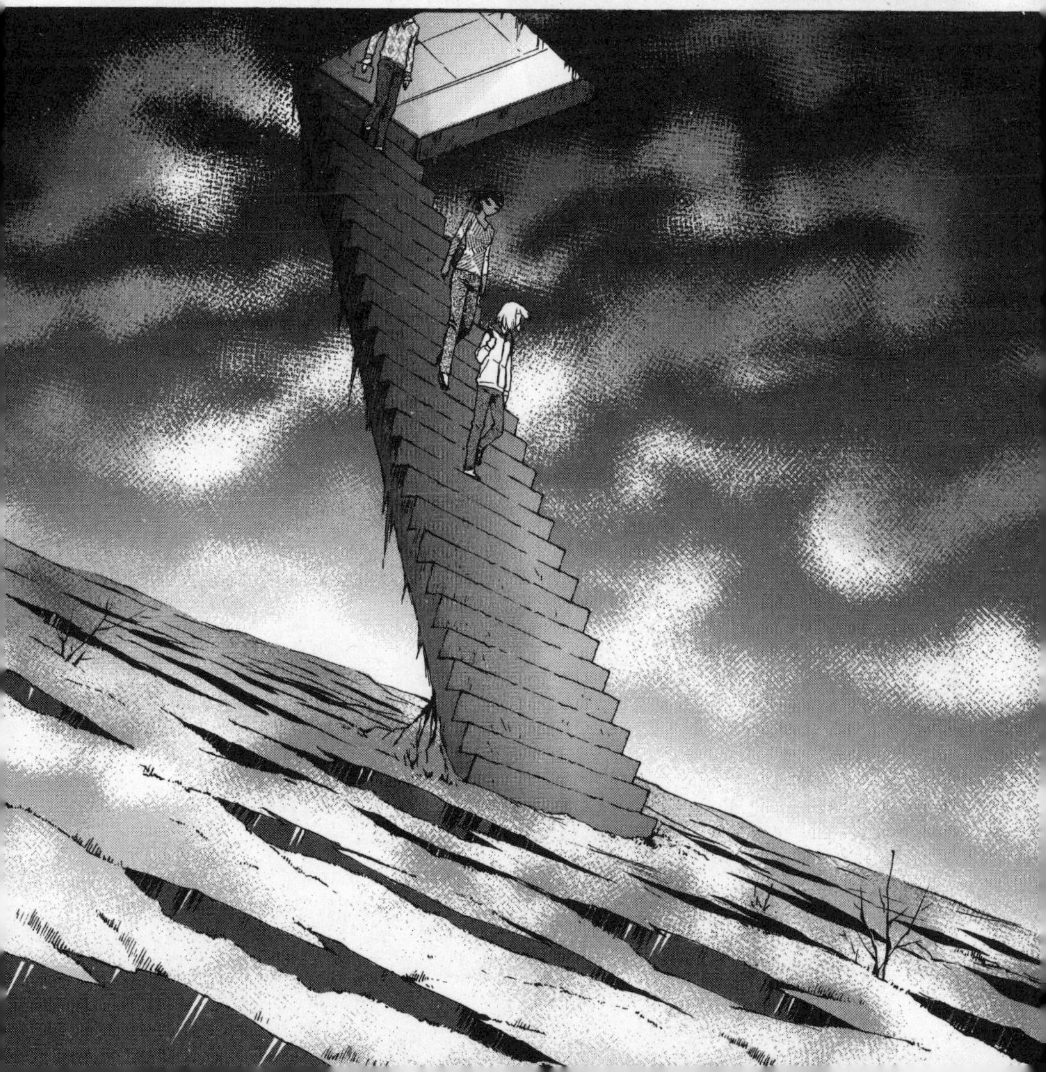

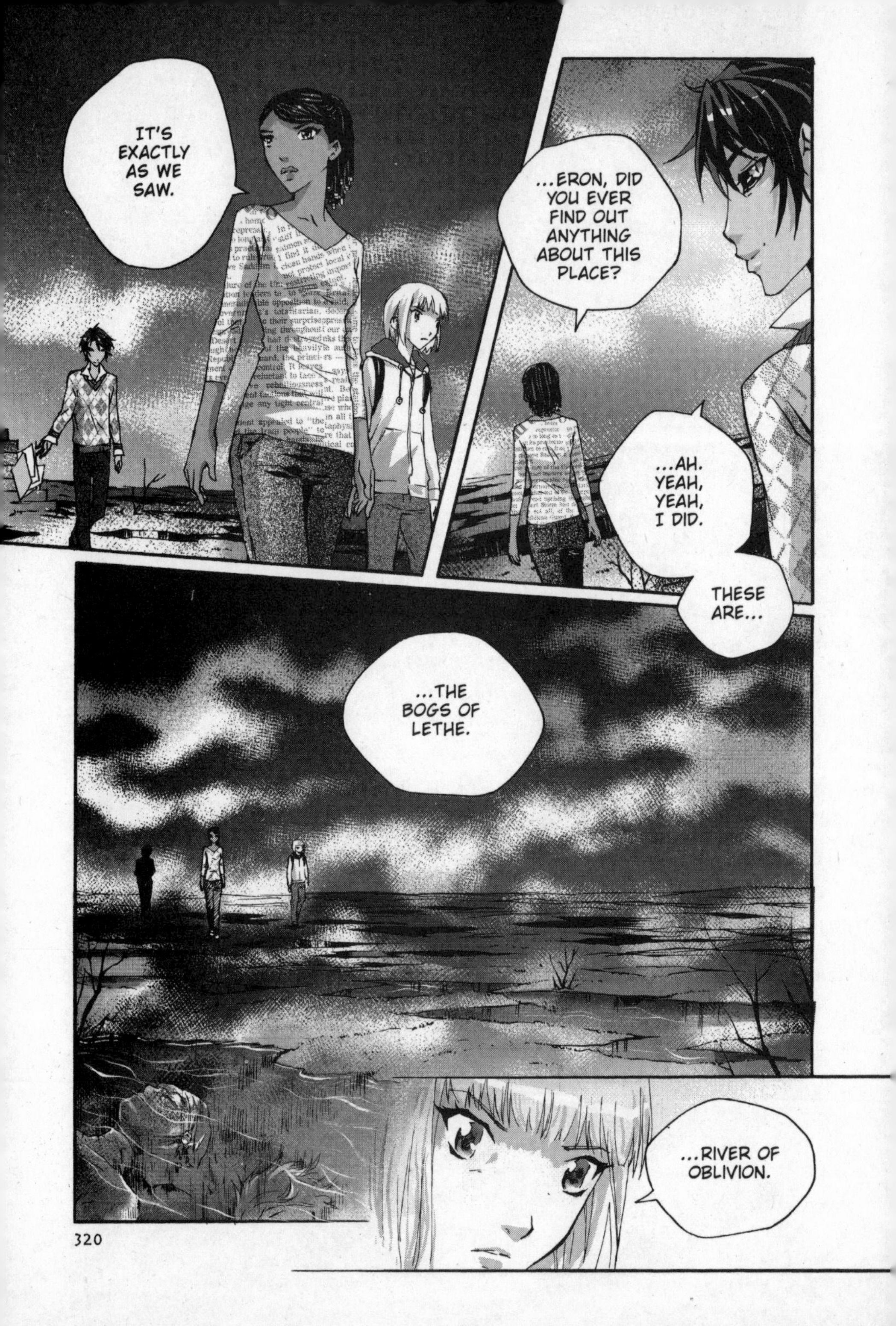
IT'S EXACTLY AS WE SAW.
...ERON, DID YOU EVER FIND OUT ANYTHING ABOUT THIS PLACE?
...AH. YEAH, YEAH, I DID.
THESE ARE...
...THE BOGS OF LETHE.
...RIVER OF OBLIVION.

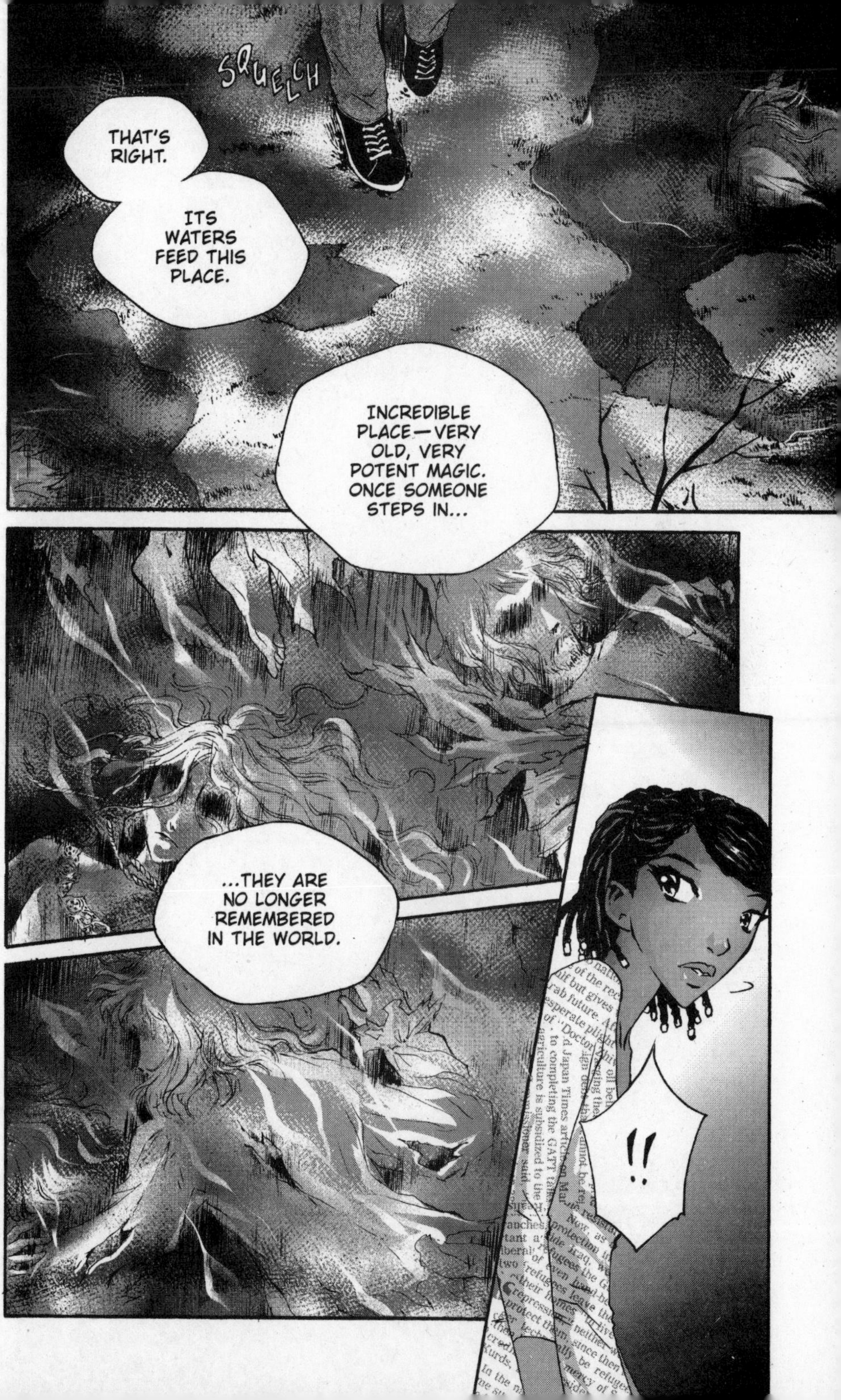
SQUELCH
THAT'S RIGHT.
ITS WATERS FEED THIS PLACE.
INCREDIBLE PLACE—VERY OLD, VERY POTENT MAGIC. ONCE SOMEONE STEPS IN...
...THEY ARE NO LONGER REMEMBERED IN THE WORLD.
!!

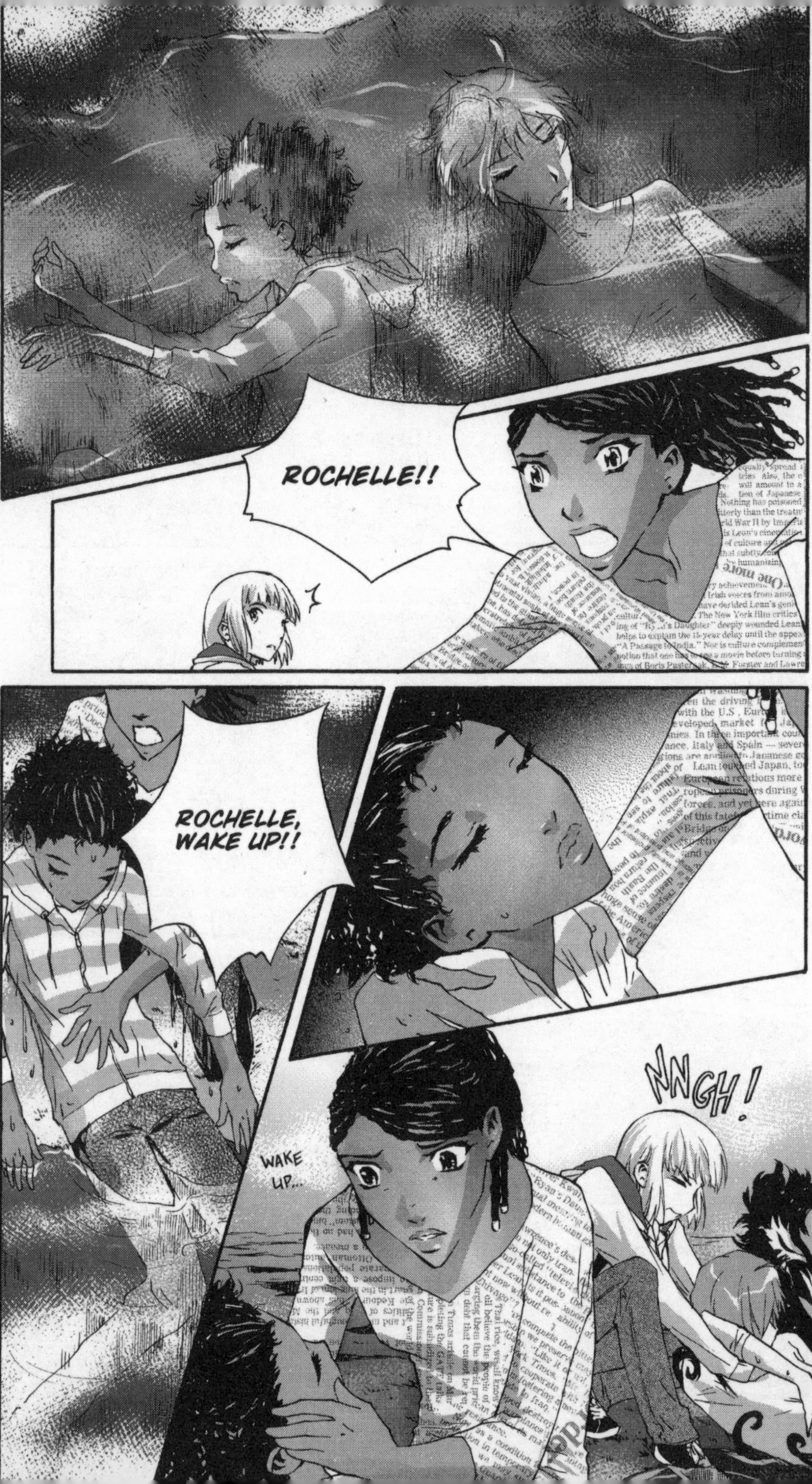
ROCHELLE!!
ROCHELLE, WAKE UP!!
WAKE UP...
NNGH!

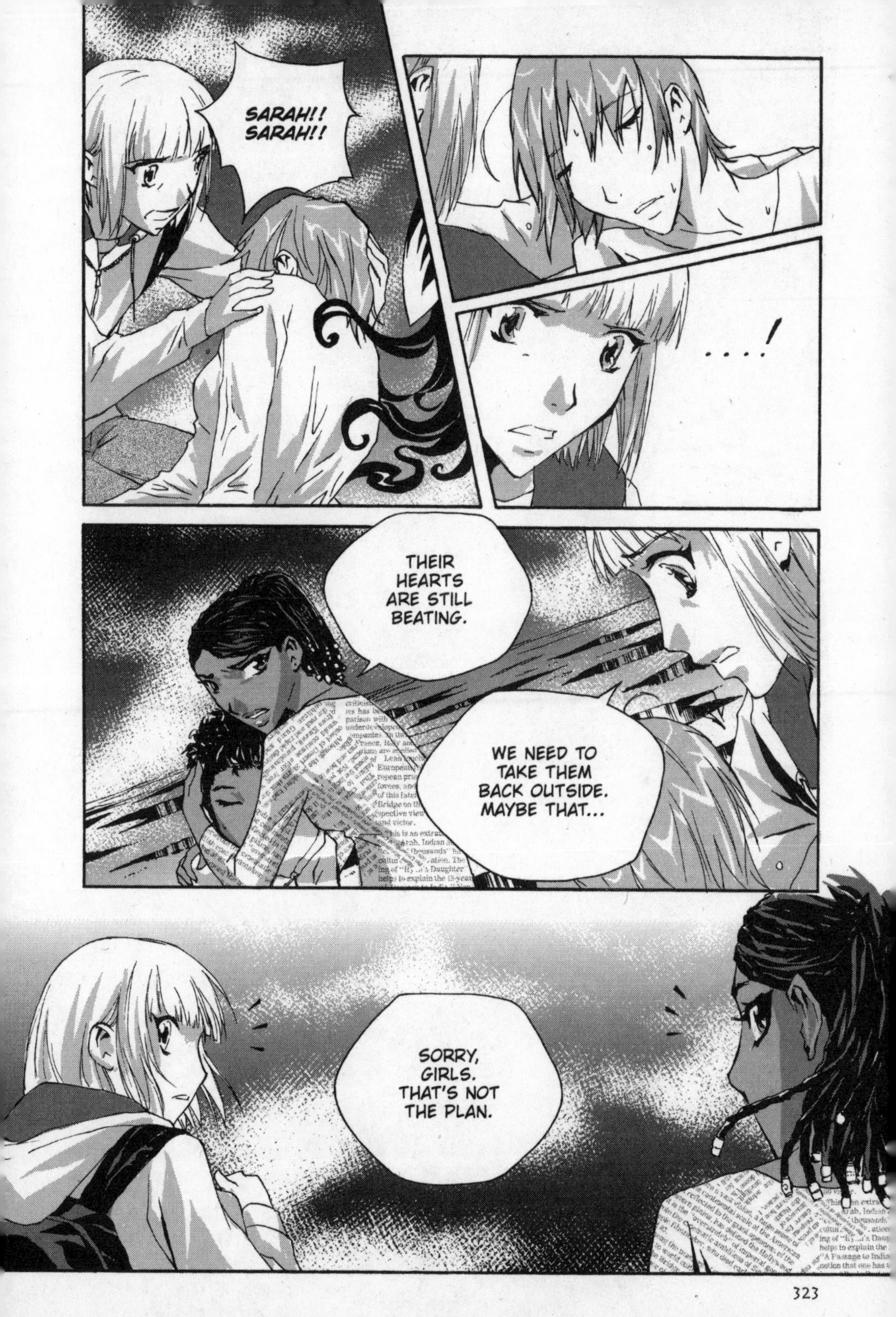
SARAH!! SARAH!!
....!
THEIR HEARTS ARE STILL BEATING.
WE NEED TO TAKE THEM BACK OUTSIDE. MAYBE THAT...
SORRY, GIRLS. THAT'S NOT THE PLAN.

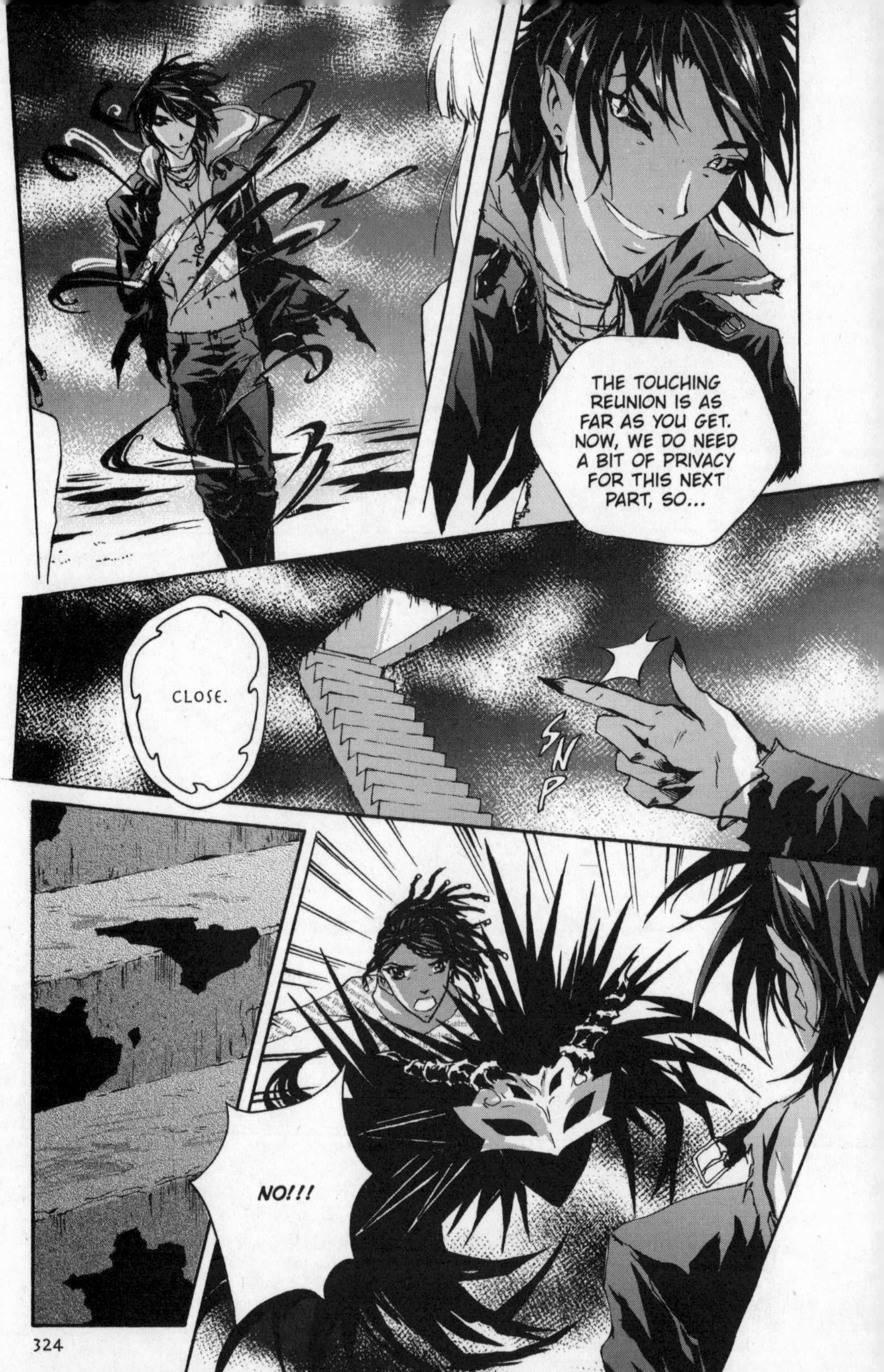
THE TOUCHING REUNION IS AS FAR AS YOU GET. NOW, WE DO NEED A BIT OF PRIVACY FOR THIS NEXT PART, SO...
CLOSE.
SNP
NO!!!

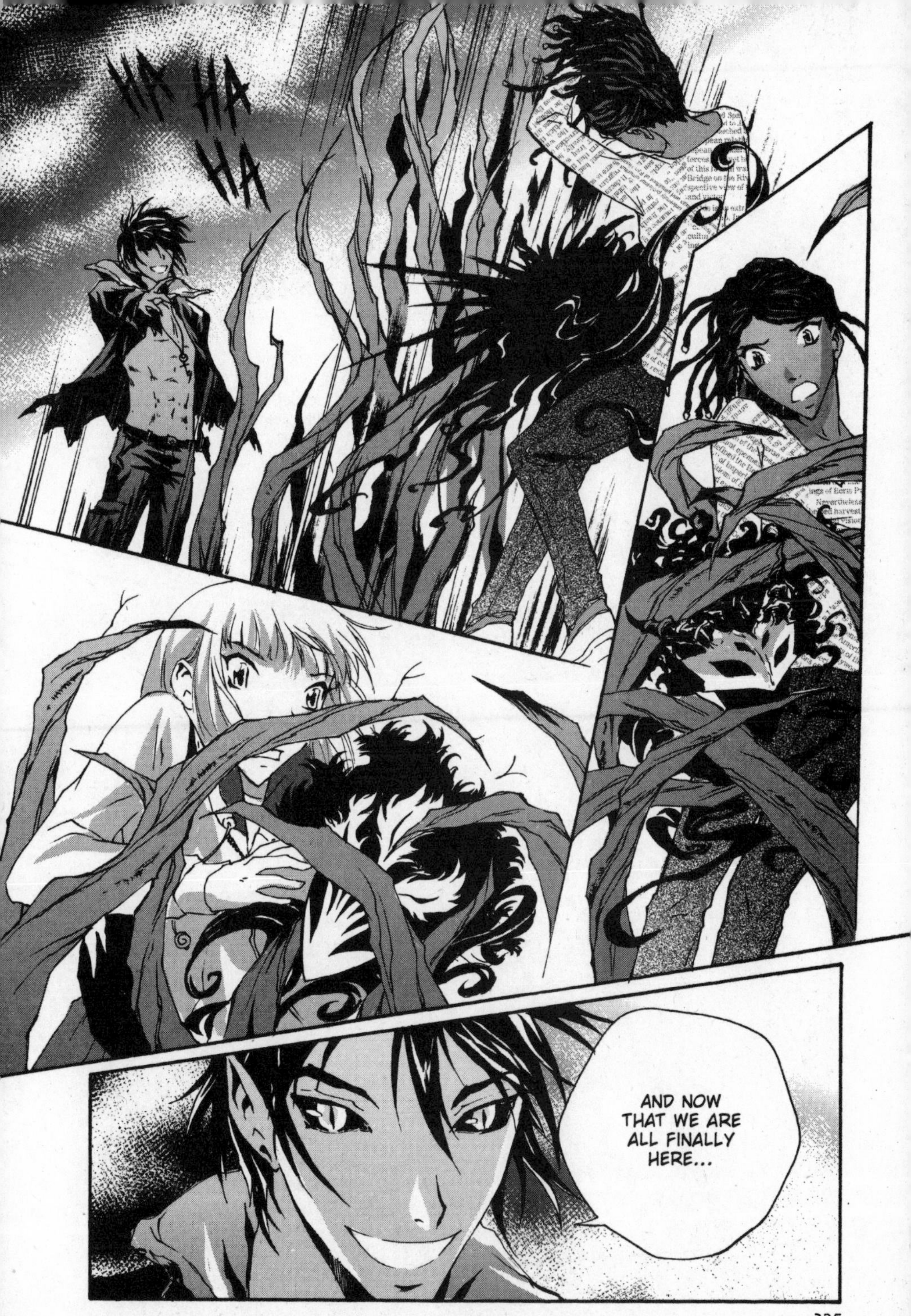
HA HA HA
AND NOW THAT WE ARE ALL FINALLY HERE...

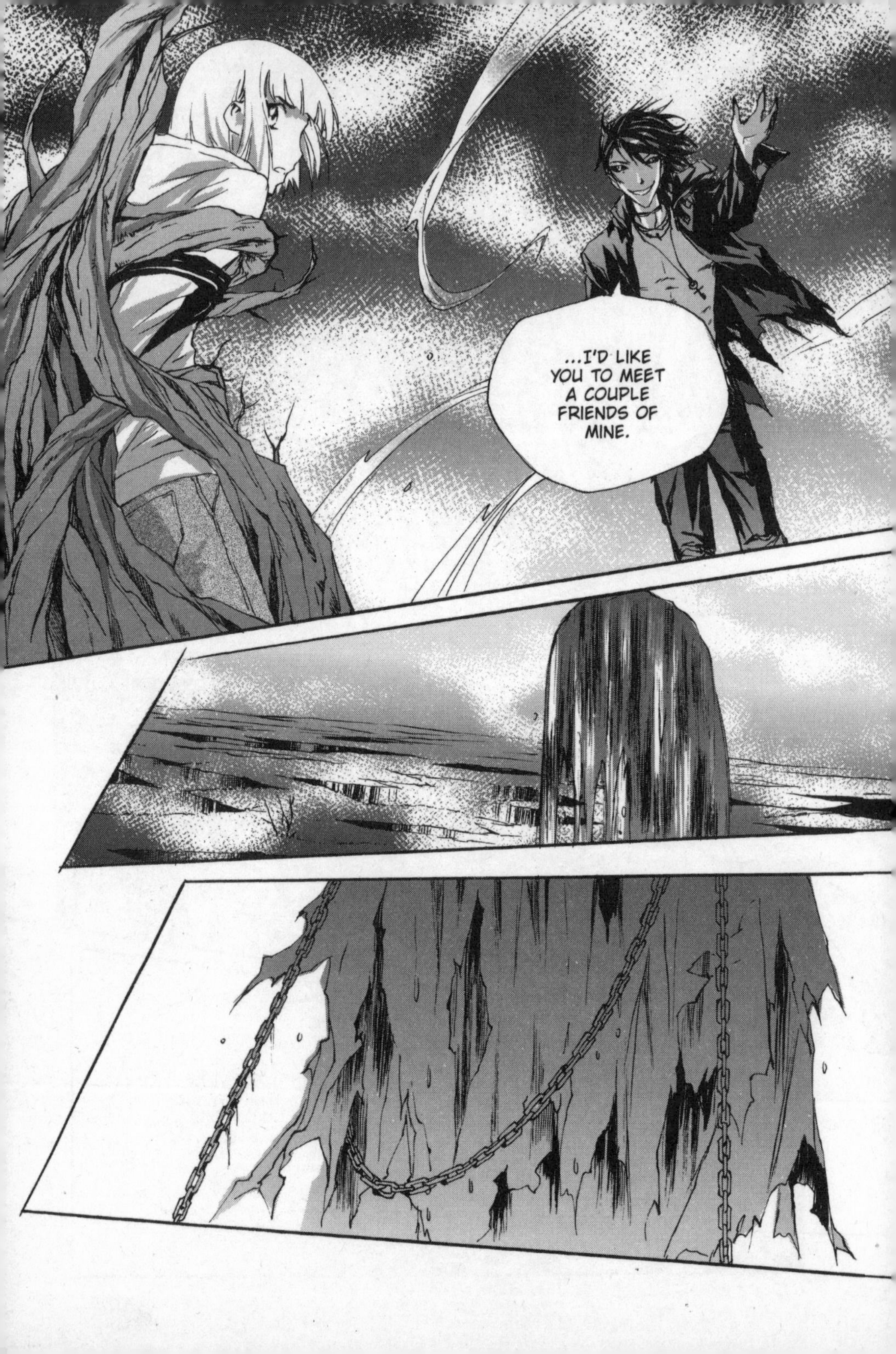
...I'D LIKE YOU TO MEET A COUPLE FRIENDS OF MINE.

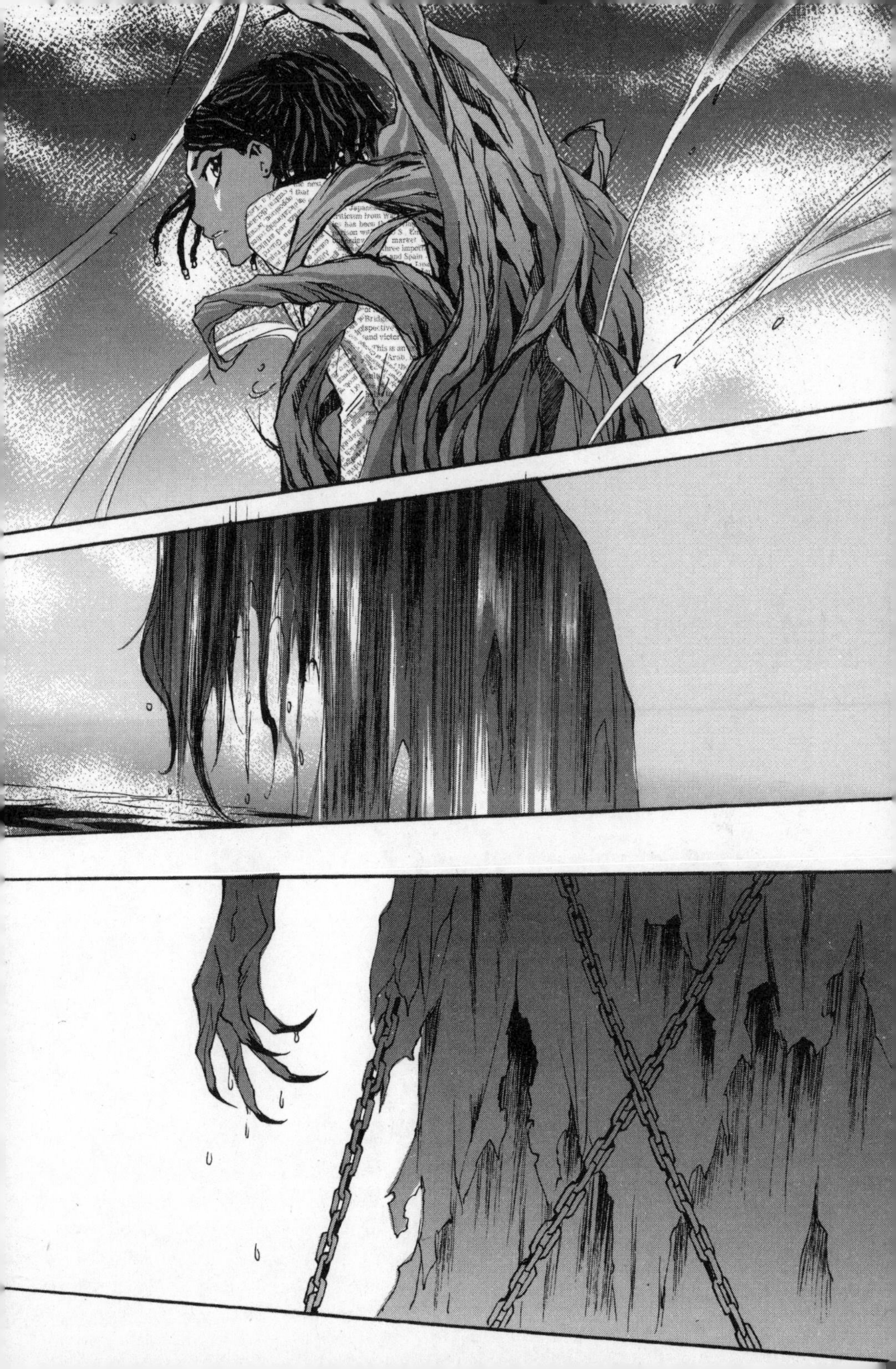

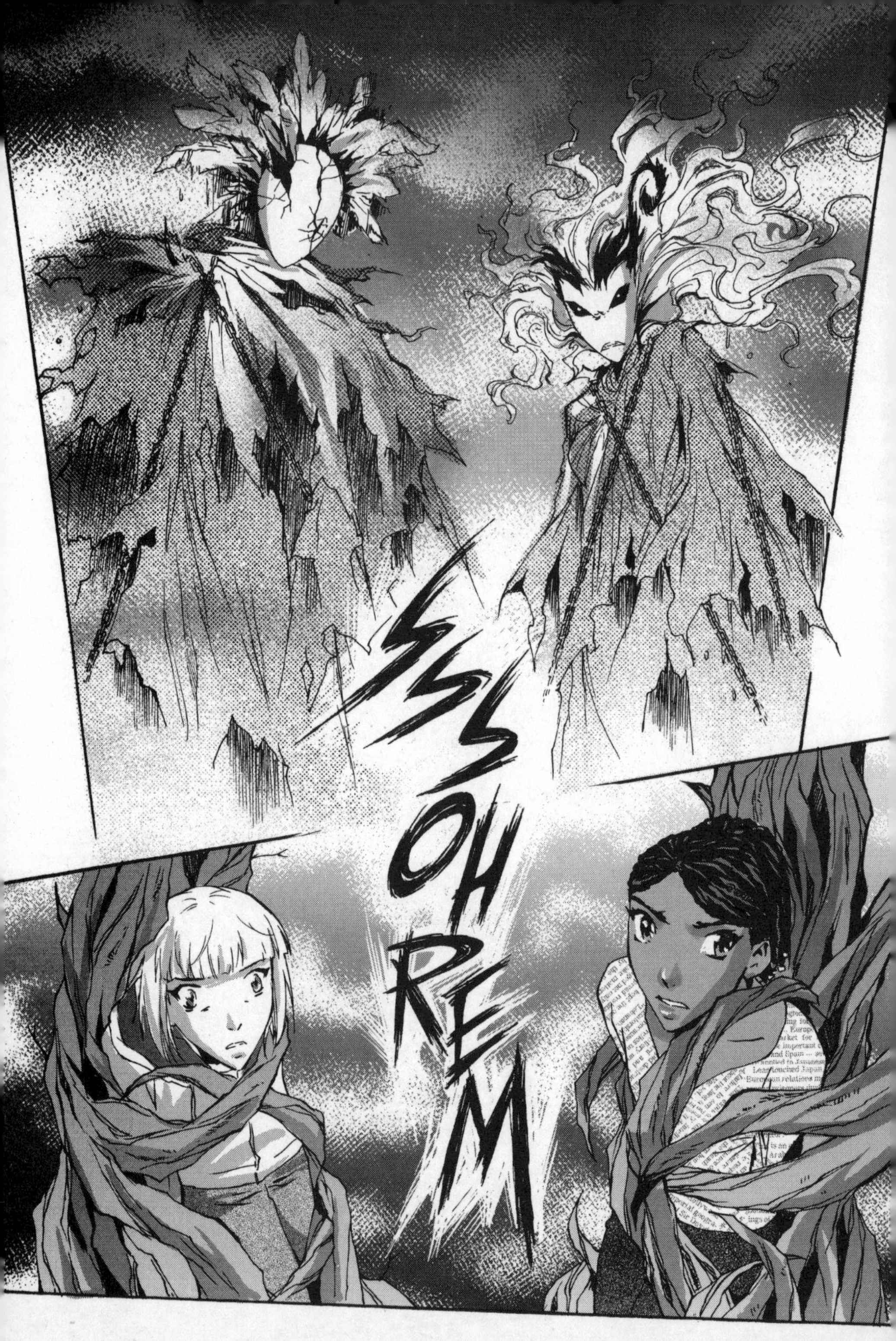

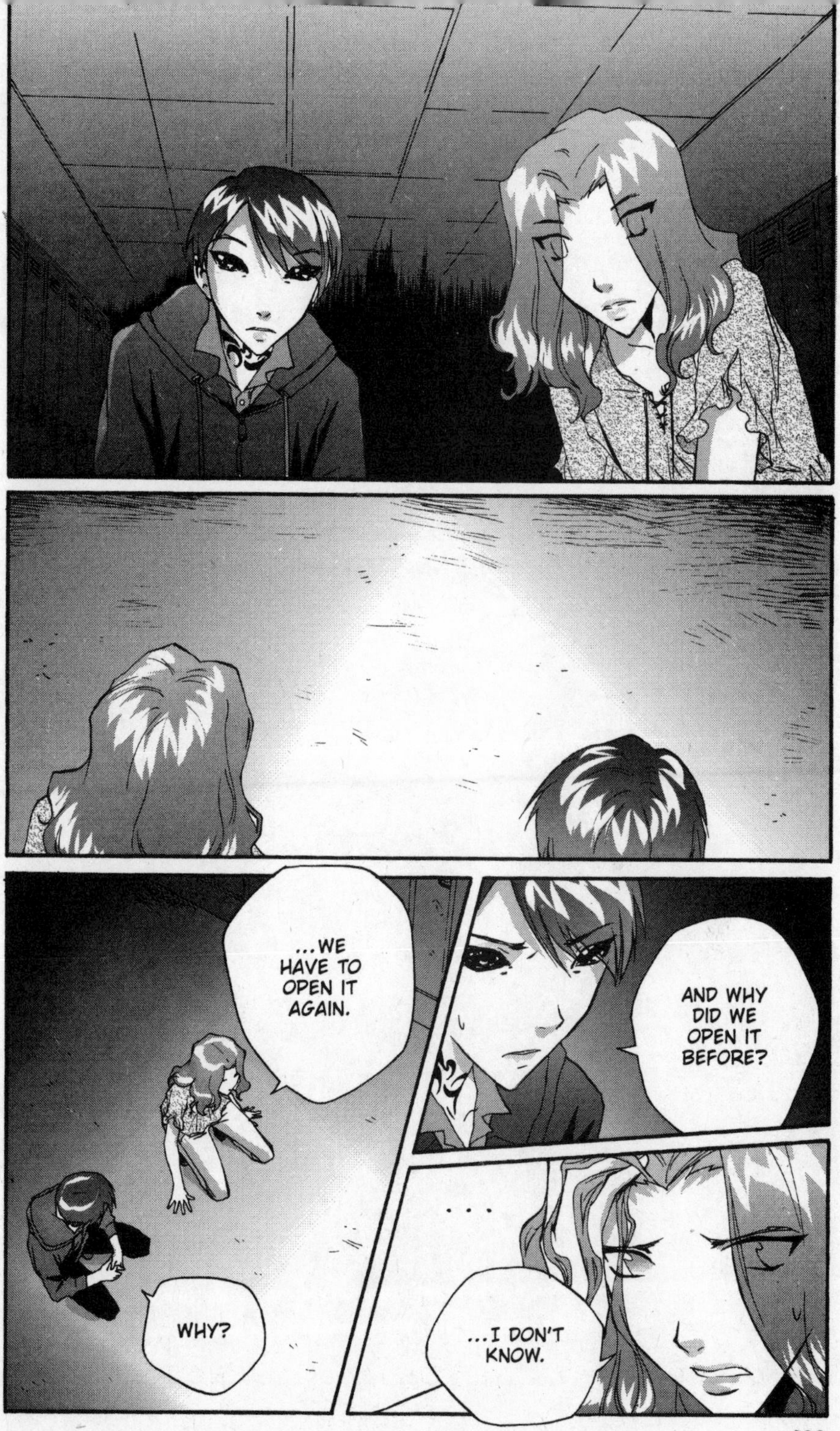
...WE HAVE TO OPEN IT AGAIN.
WHY?
AND WHY DID WE OPEN IT BEFORE?
...
...I DON'T KNOW.

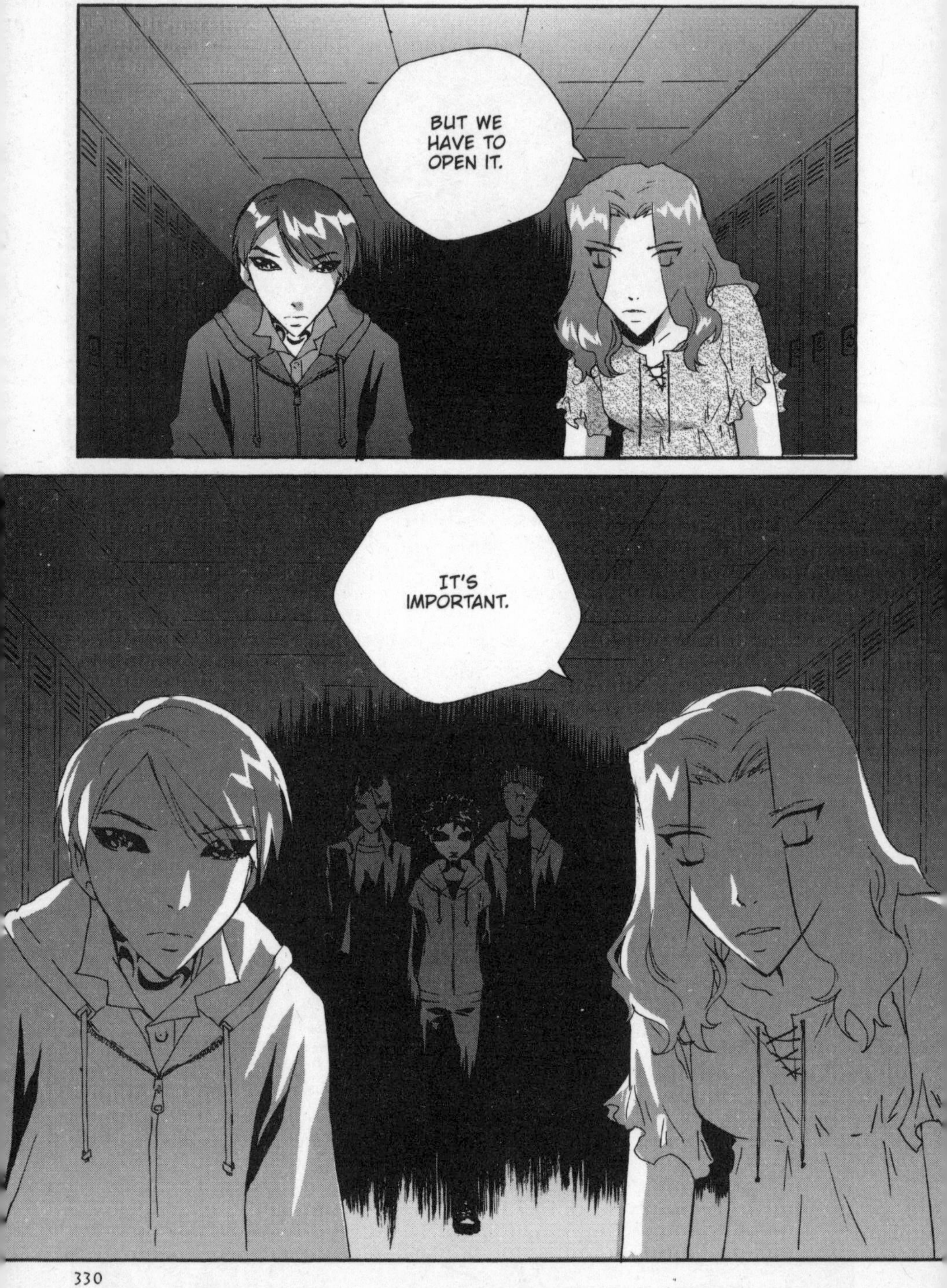
BUT WE HAVE TO OPEN IT.
IT'S IMPORTANT.

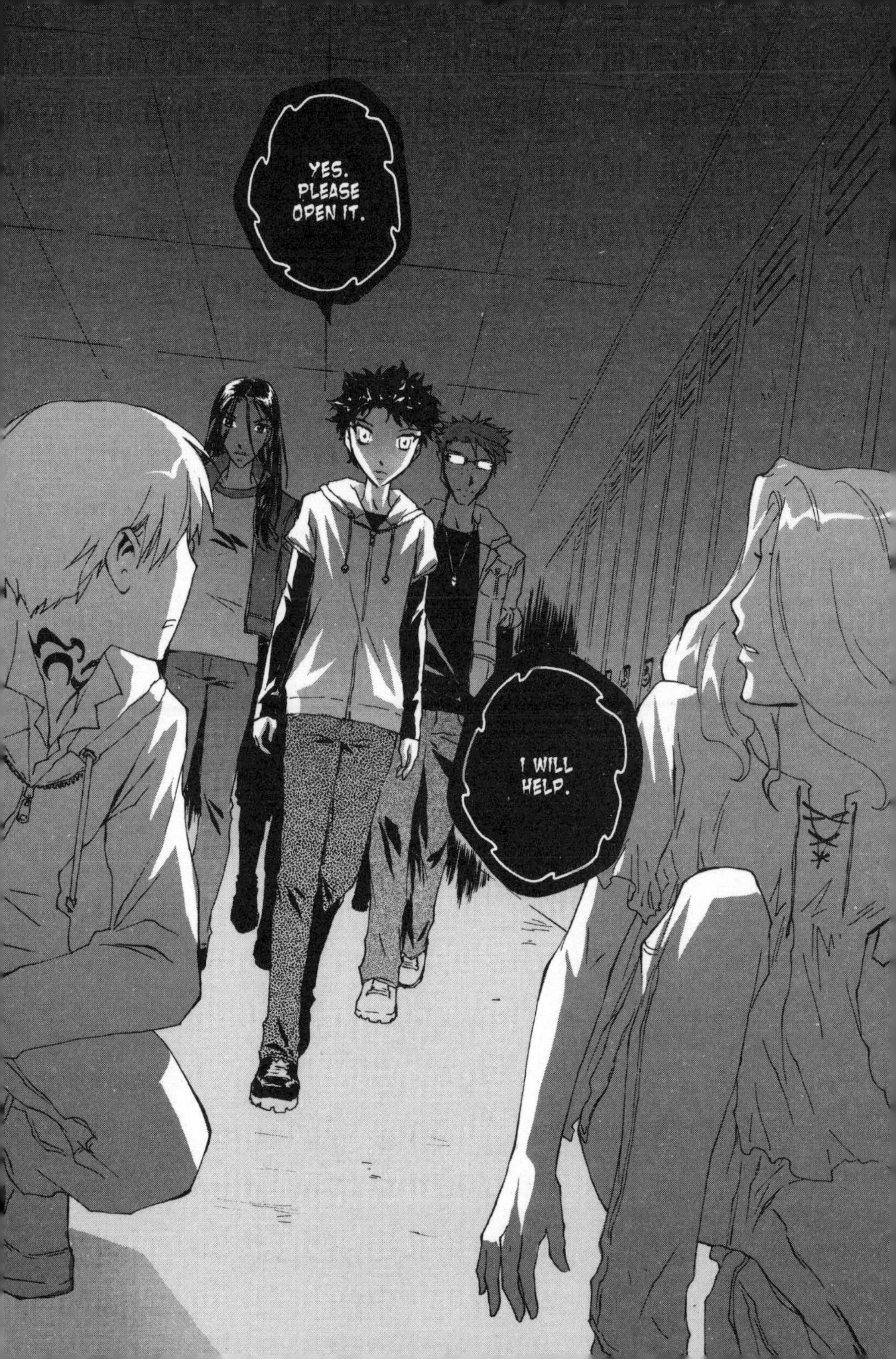
YES. PLEASE OPEN IT.
I WILL HELP.

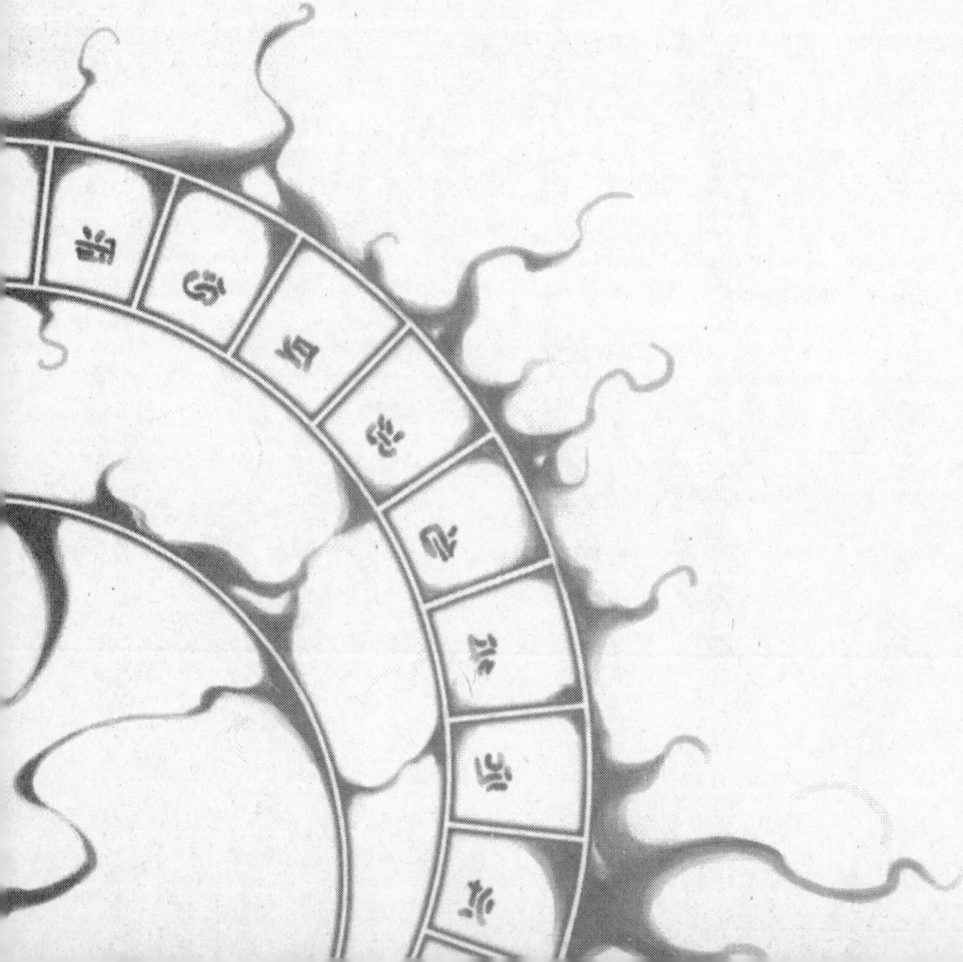

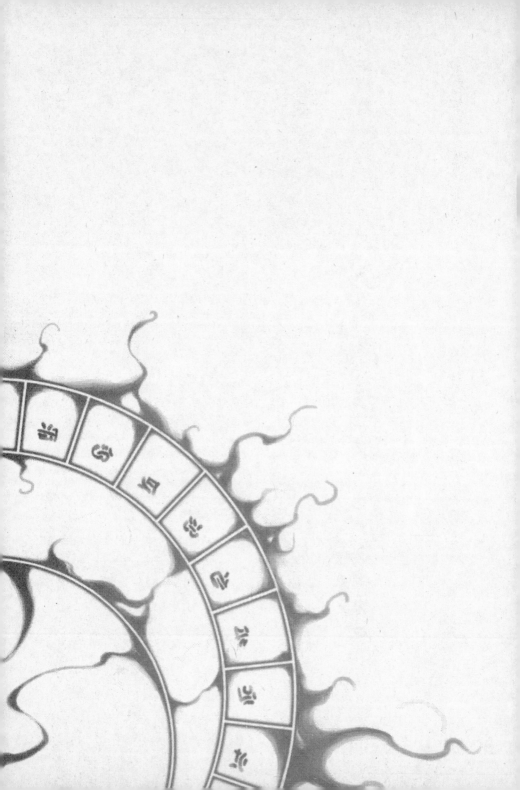

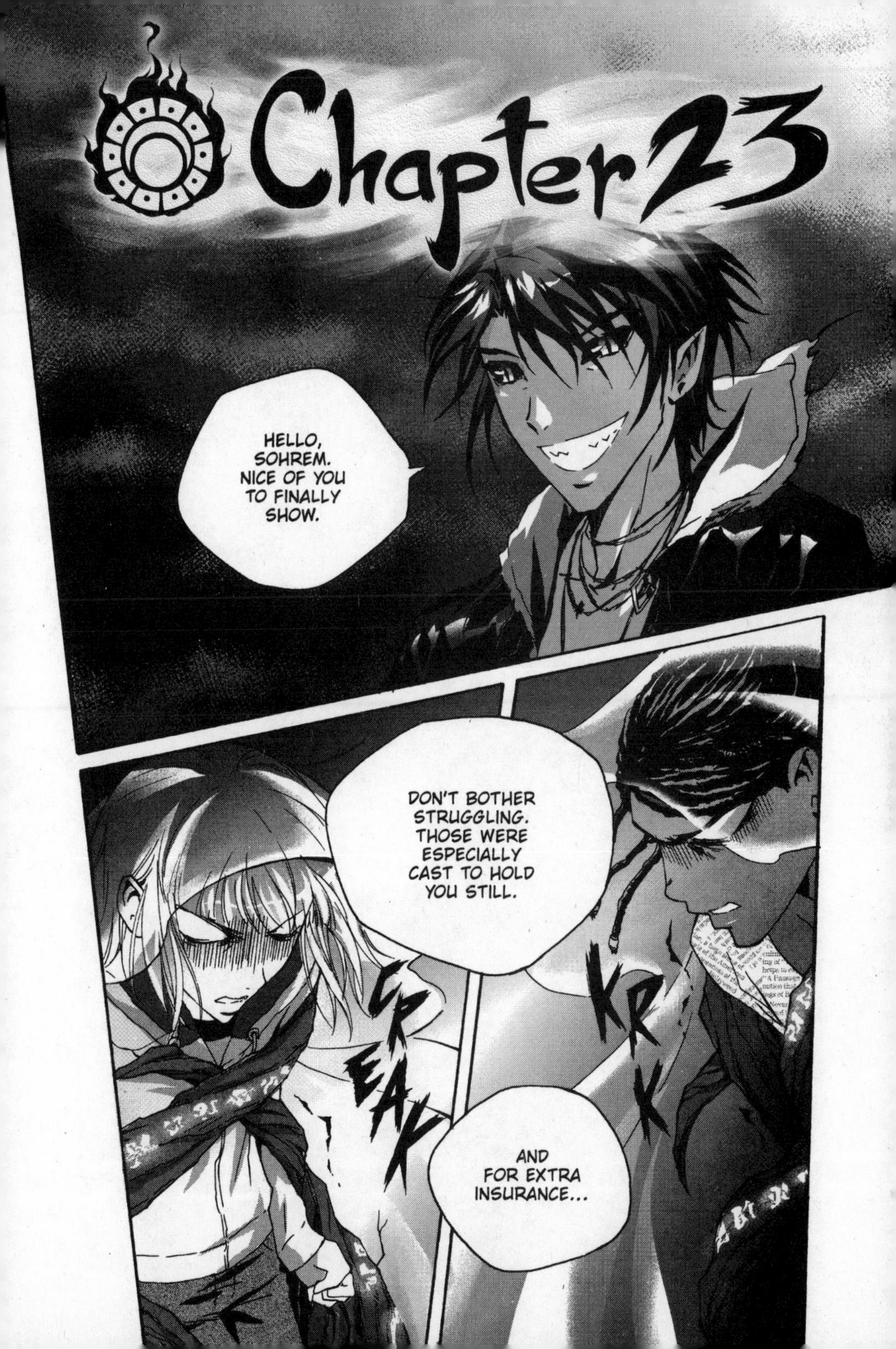
Chapter 23
HELLO, SOHREM. NICE OF YOU TO FINALLY SHOW.
DON'T BOTHER STRUGGLING. THOSE WERE ESPECIALLY CAST TO HOLD YOU STILL.
CREAK
KRKK
AND FOR EXTRA INSURANCE...

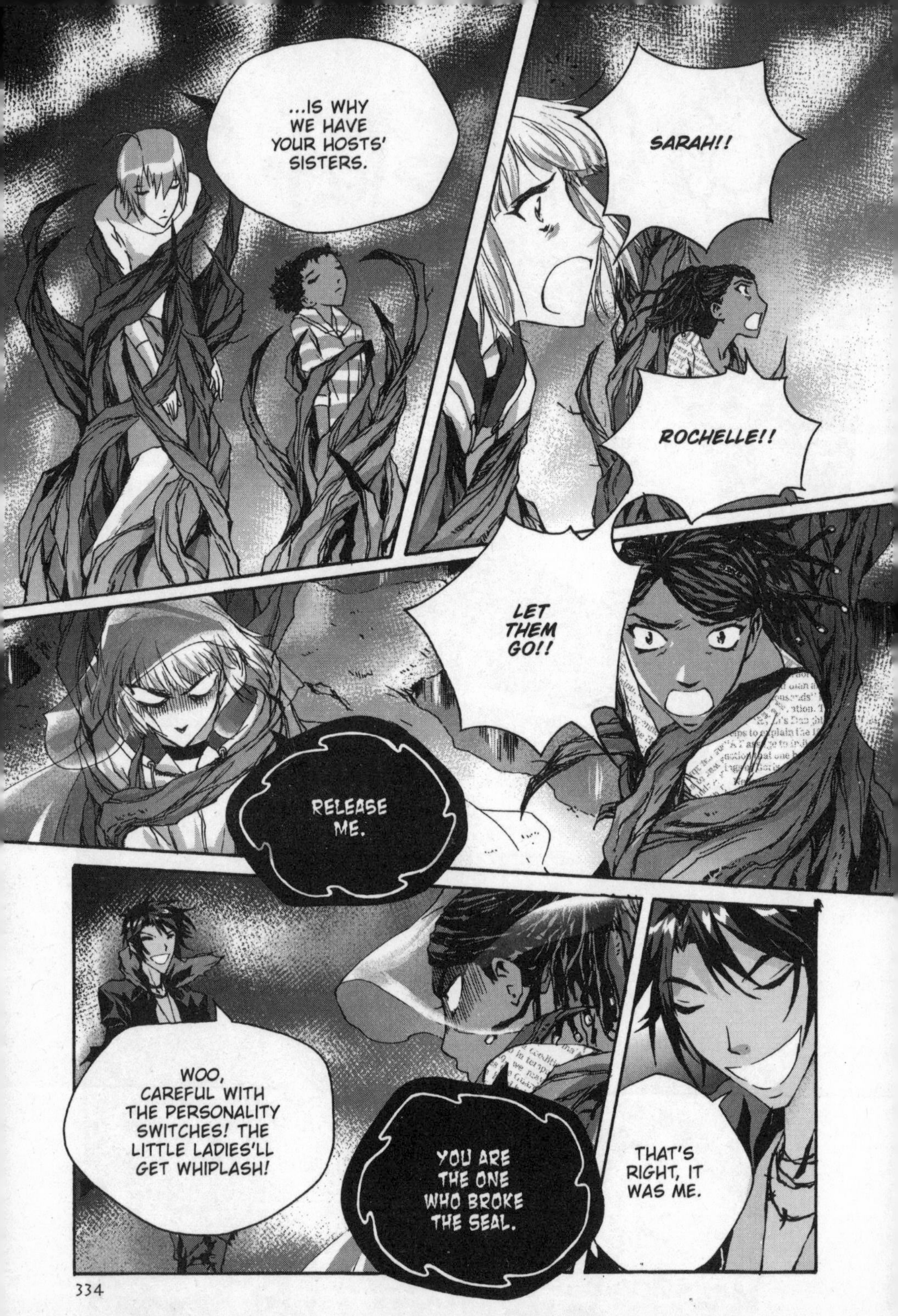
...IS WHY WE HAVE YOUR HOSTS' SISTERS.
SARAH!!
ROCHELLE!!
LET THEM GO!!
RELEASE ME.
WOO, CAREFUL WITH THE PERSONALITY SWITCHES! THE LITTLE LADIES'LL GET WHIPLASH!
YOU ARE THE ONE WHO BROKE THE SEAL.
THAT'S RIGHT, IT WAS ME.

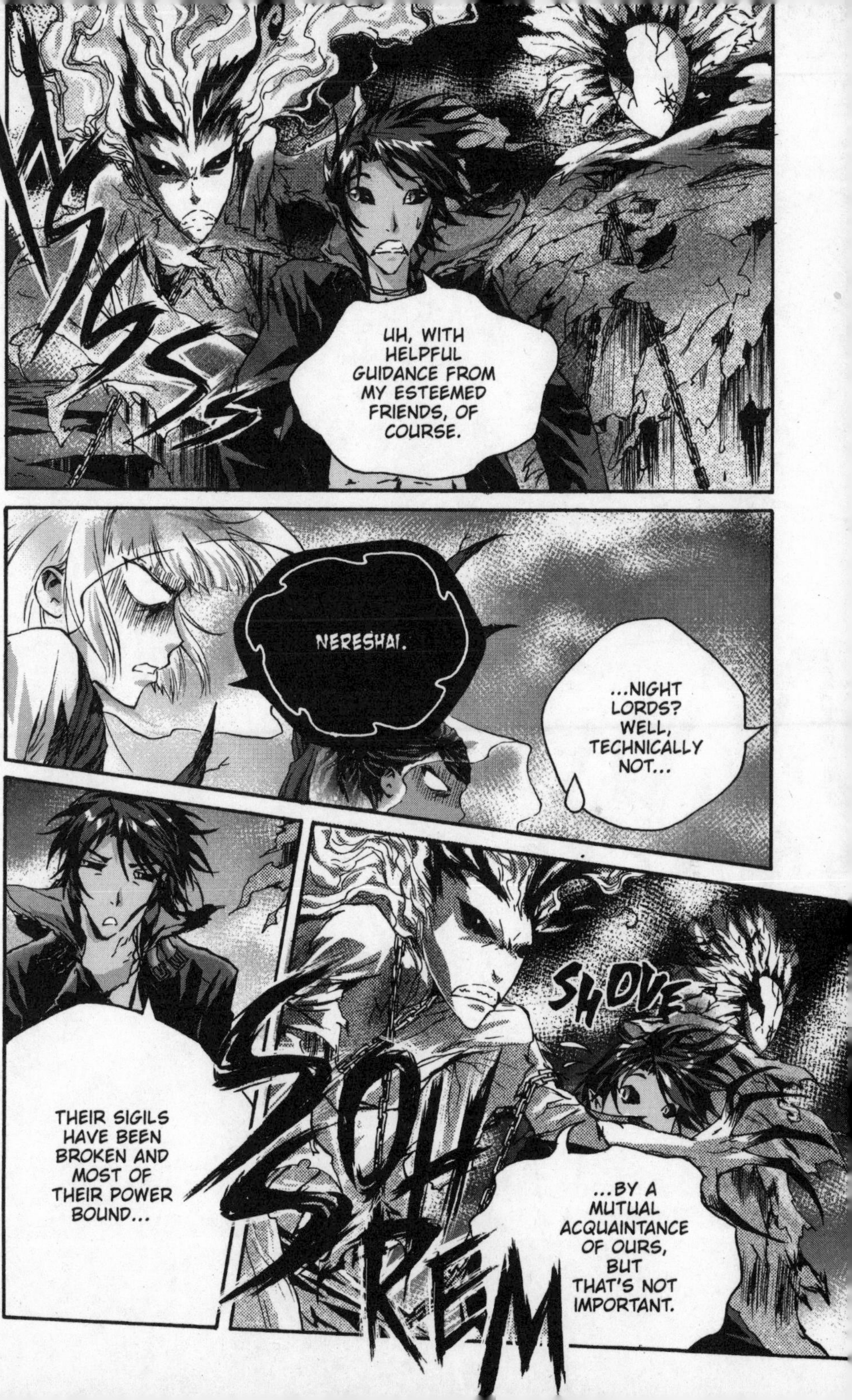
HISSSS
UH, WITH HELPFUL GUIDANCE FROM MY ESTEEMED FRIENDS, OF COURSE.
NERESHAI.
...NIGHT LORDS? WELL, TECHNICALLY NOT...
THEIR SIGILS HAVE BEEN BROKEN AND MOST OF THEIR POWER BOUND...
SHOVE
...BY A MUTUAL ACQUAINTANCE OF OURS, BUT THAT'S NOT IMPORTANT.

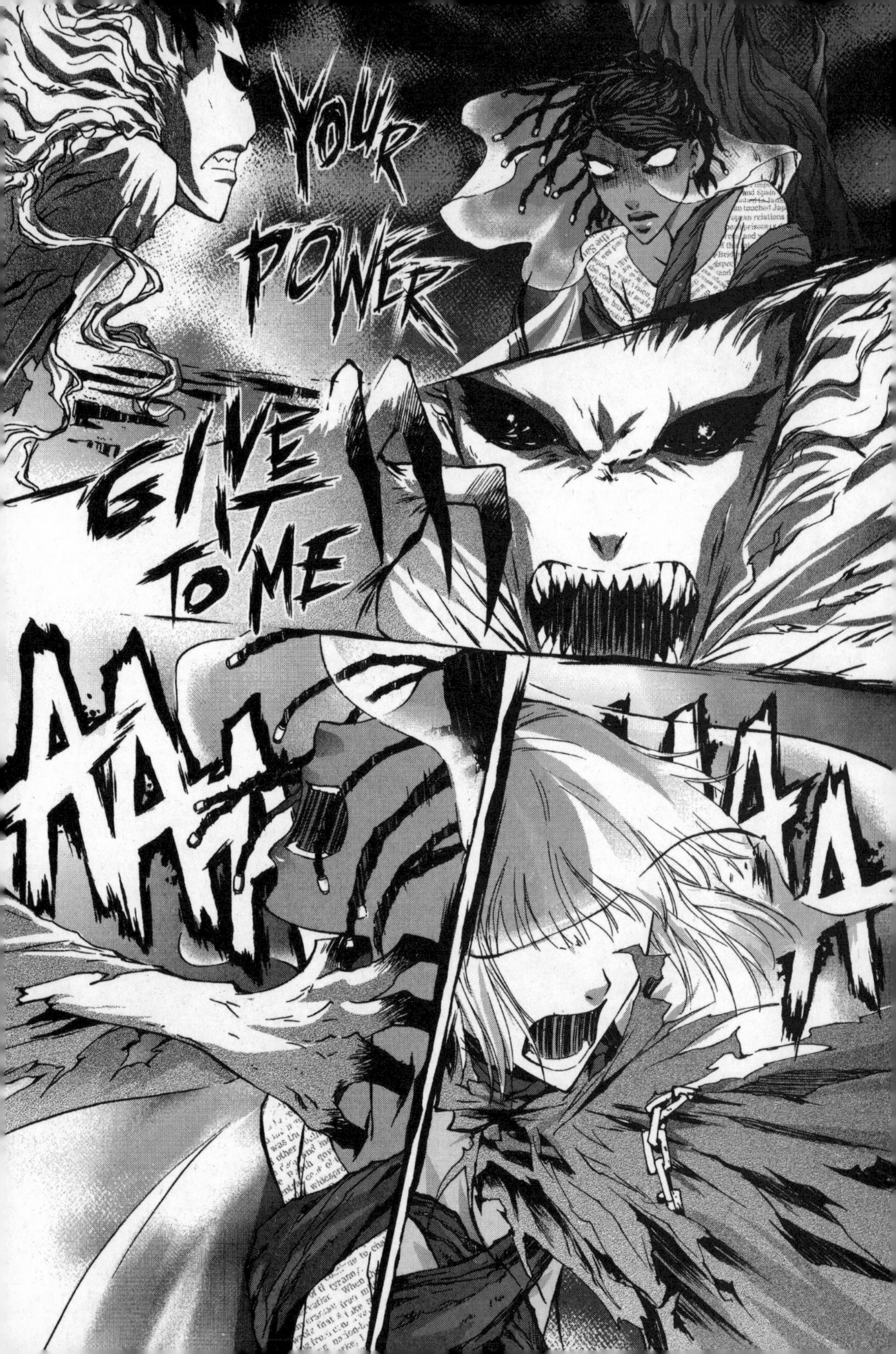
YOUR POWER
GIVE IT TO ME
AAAAAAAA

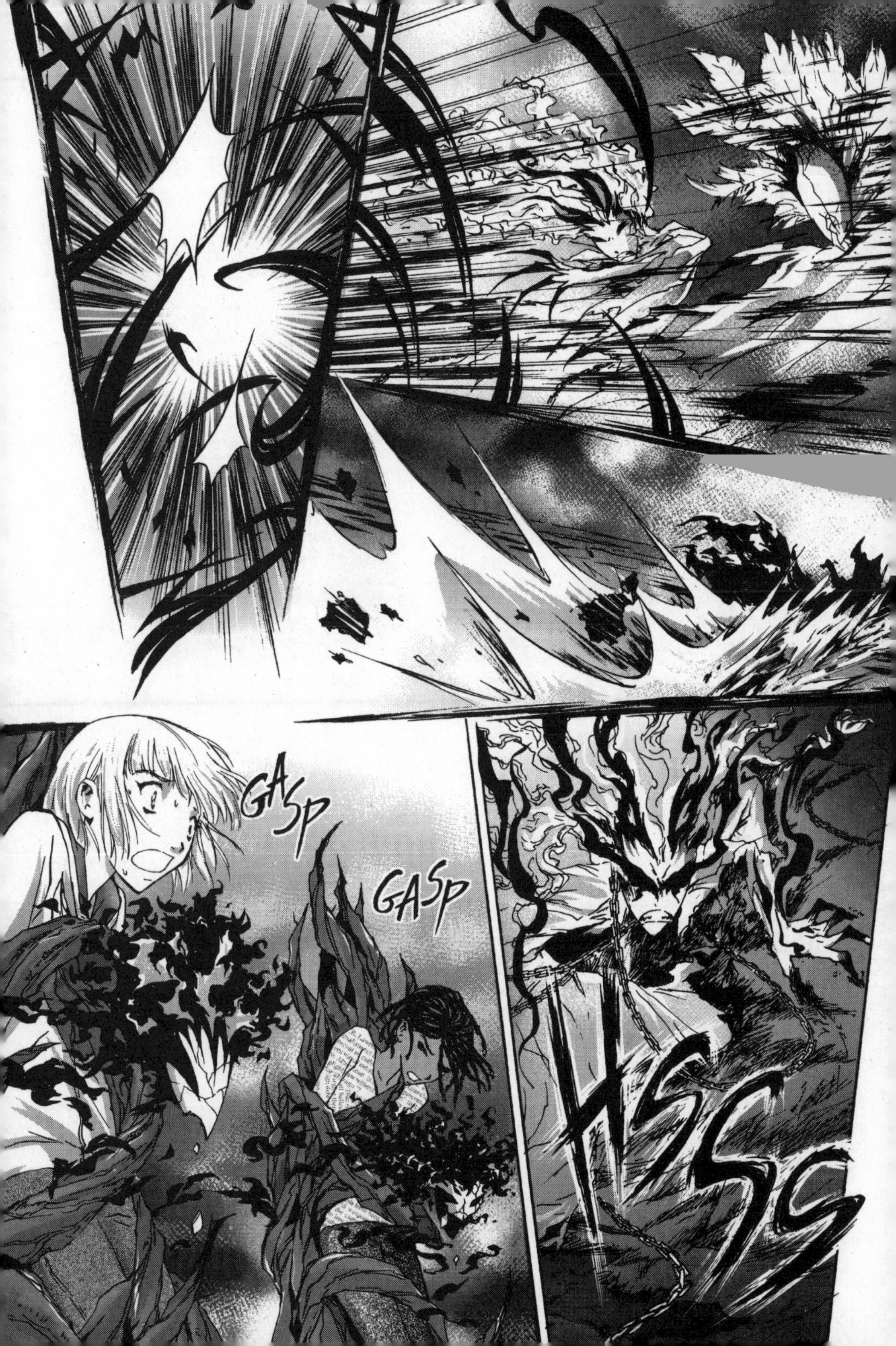
GASP
GASP
HSSS

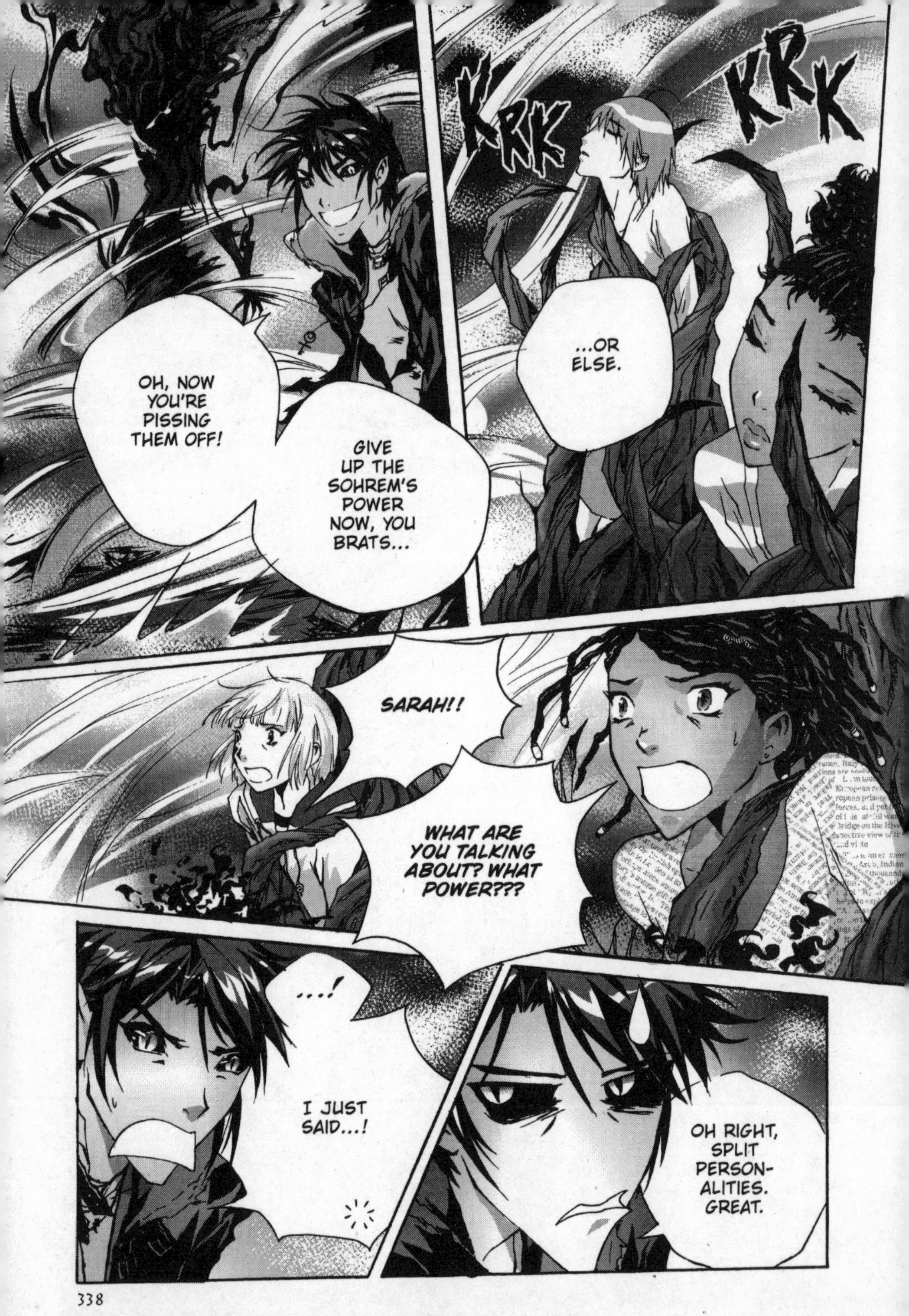
OH, NOW YOU'RE PISSING THEM OFF!
GIVE UP THE SOHREM'S POWER NOW, YOU BRATS...
KRK
KRK
...OR ELSE.
SARAH!!
WHAT ARE YOU TALKING ABOUT? WHAT POWER???
...!
I JUST SAID...!
OH RIGHT, SPLIT PERSON-ALITIES. GREAT.

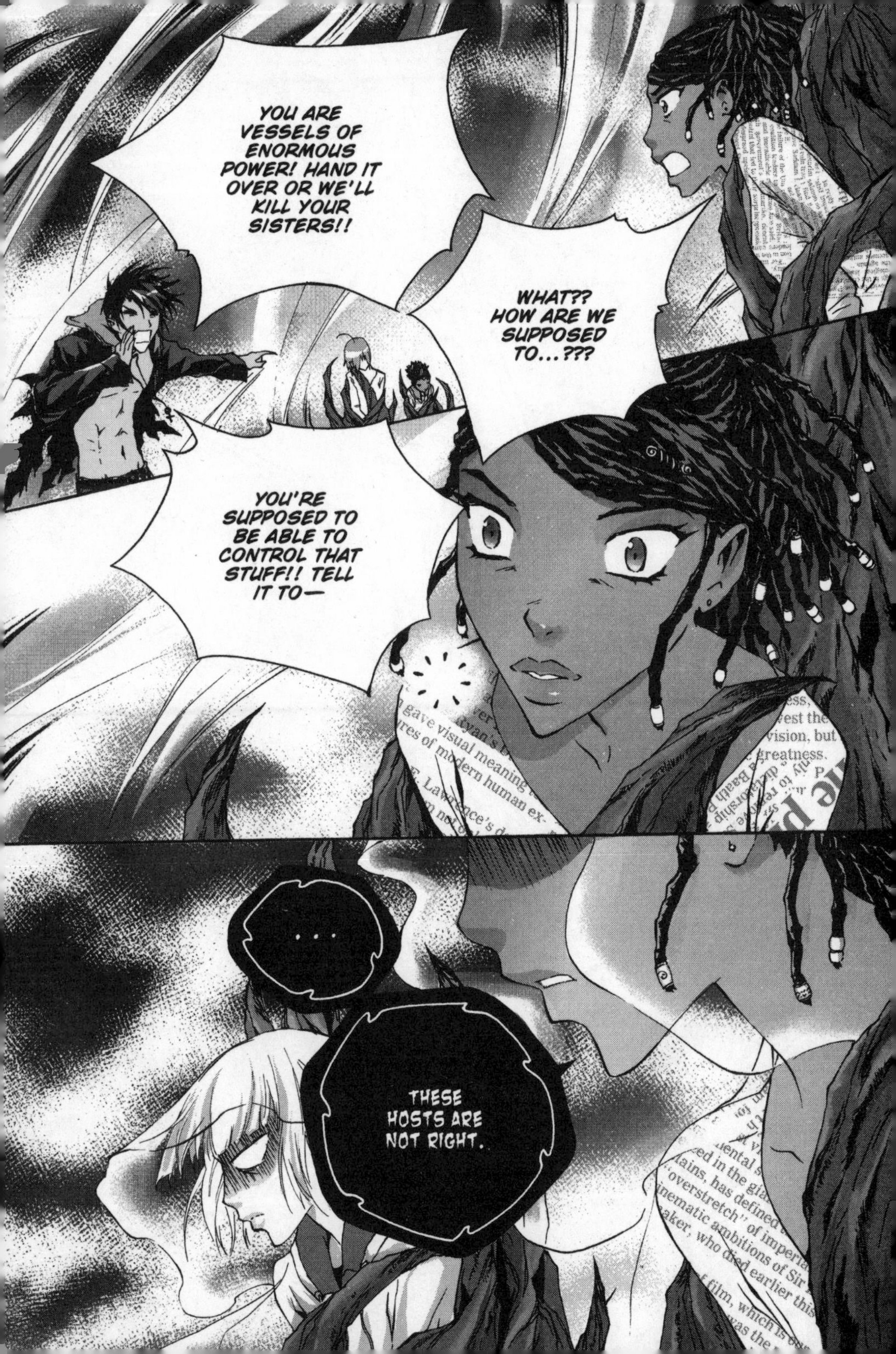
YOU ARE VESSELS OF ENORMOUS POWER! HAND IT OVER OR WE'LL KILL YOUR SISTERS!!
WHAT?? HOW ARE WE SUPPOSED TO...???
YOU'RE SUPPOSED TO BE ABLE TO CONTROL THAT STUFF!! TELL IT TO—
...
THESE HOSTS ARE NOT RIGHT.

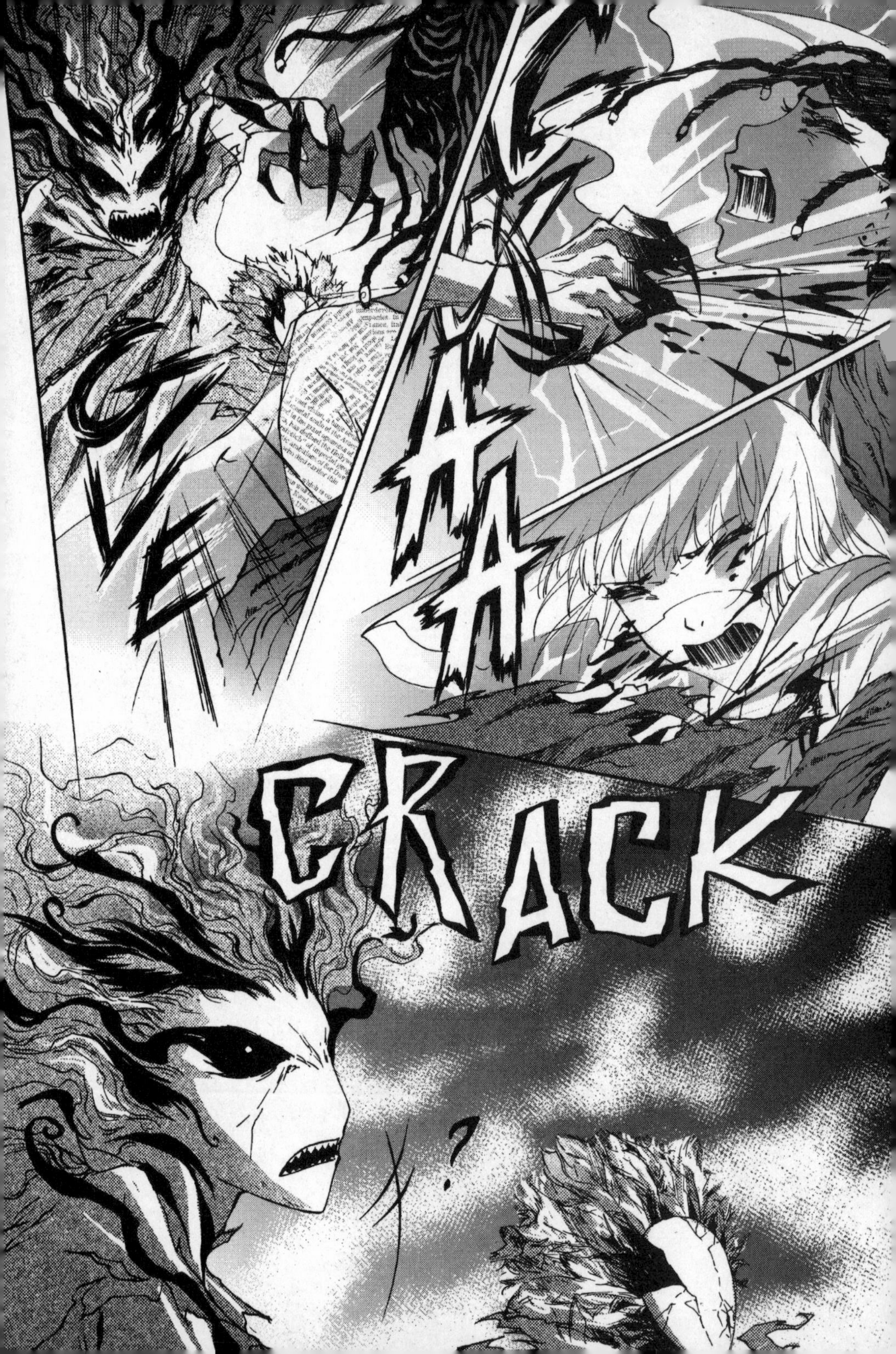
CRACK
?

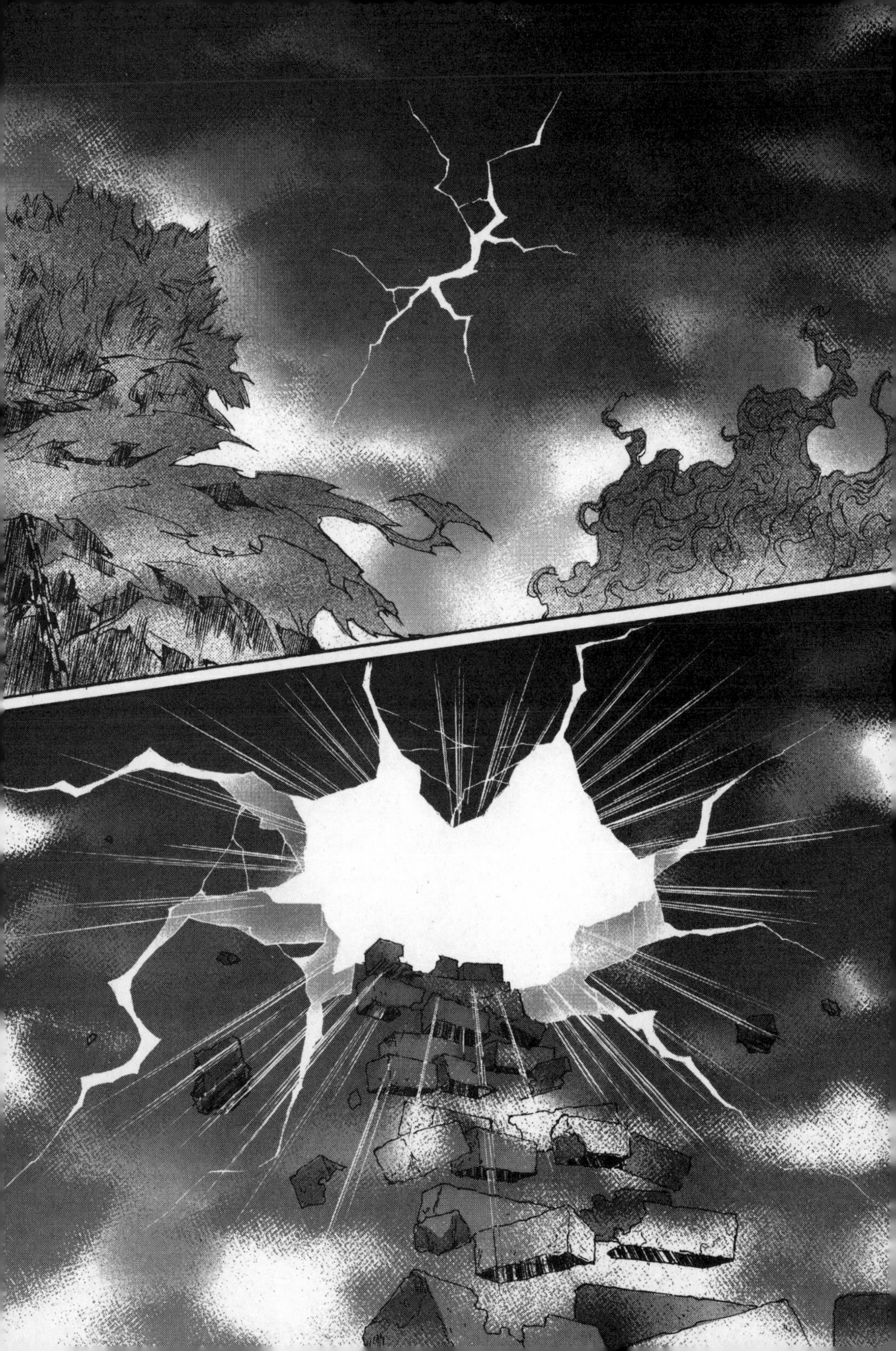

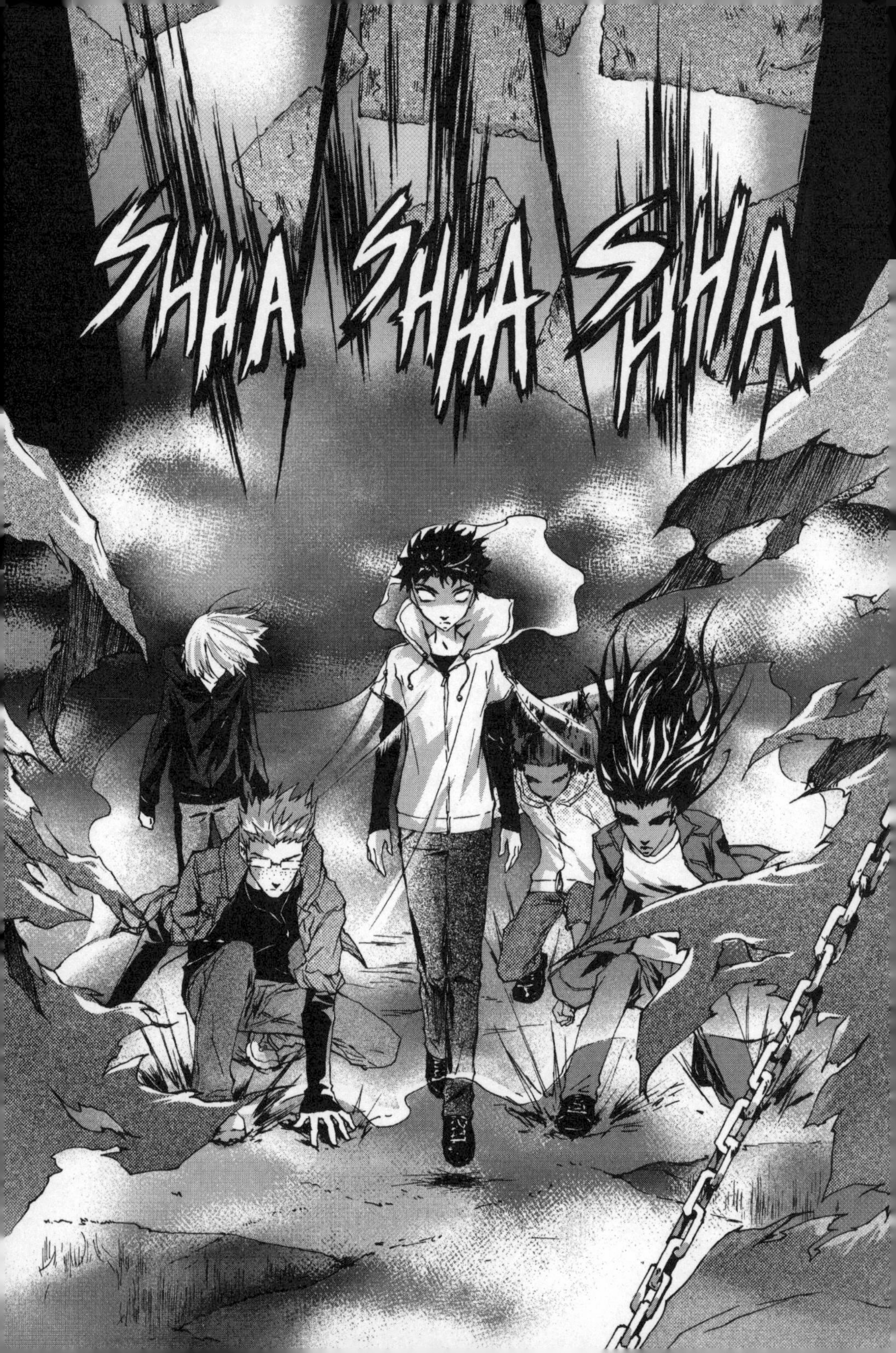
SHHA SHHA SHHA

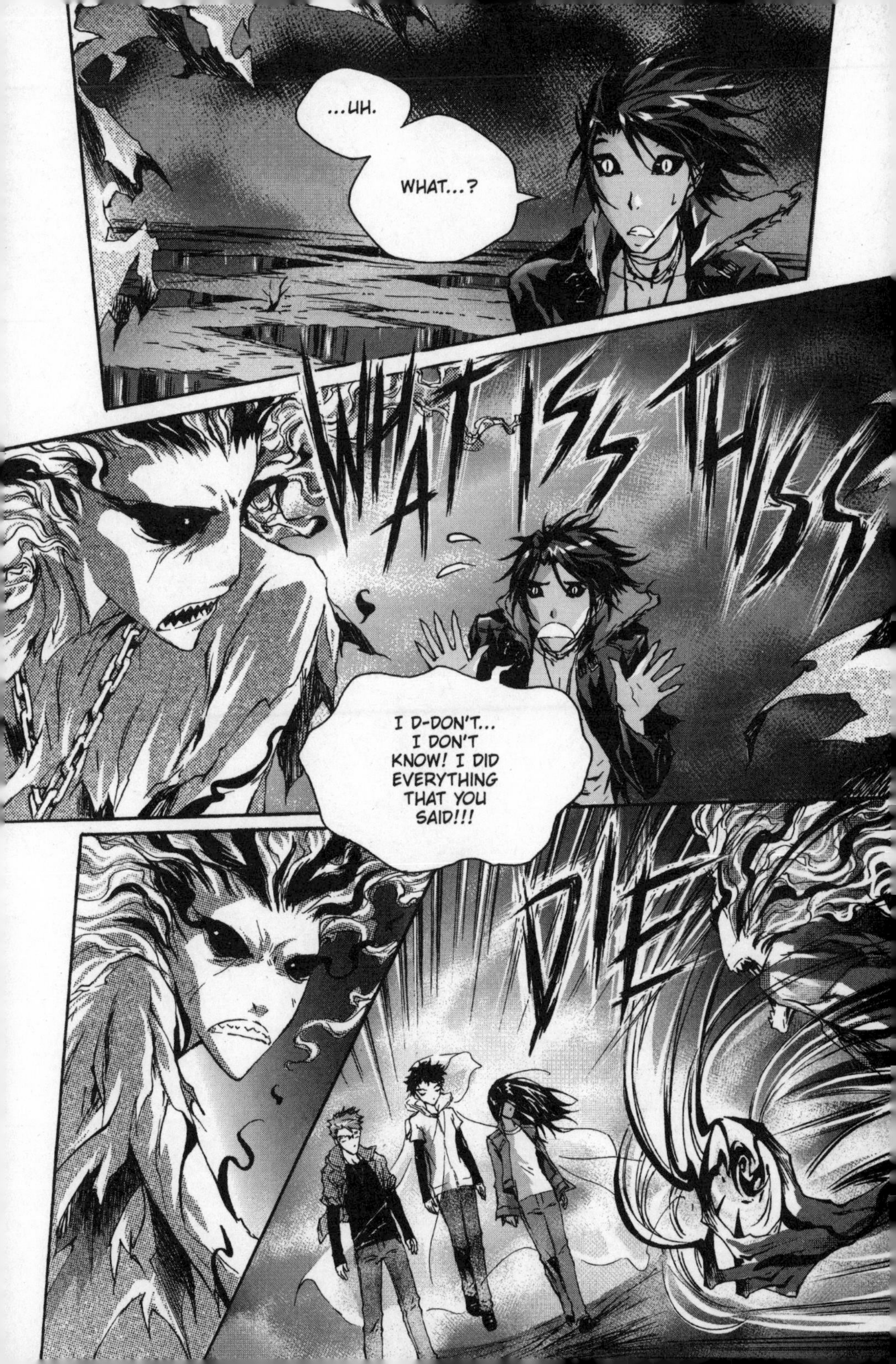
...UH.
WHAT...?
WHAT IS THISSS
I D-DON'T... I DON'T KNOW! I DID EVERYTHING THAT YOU SAID!!!
DIE

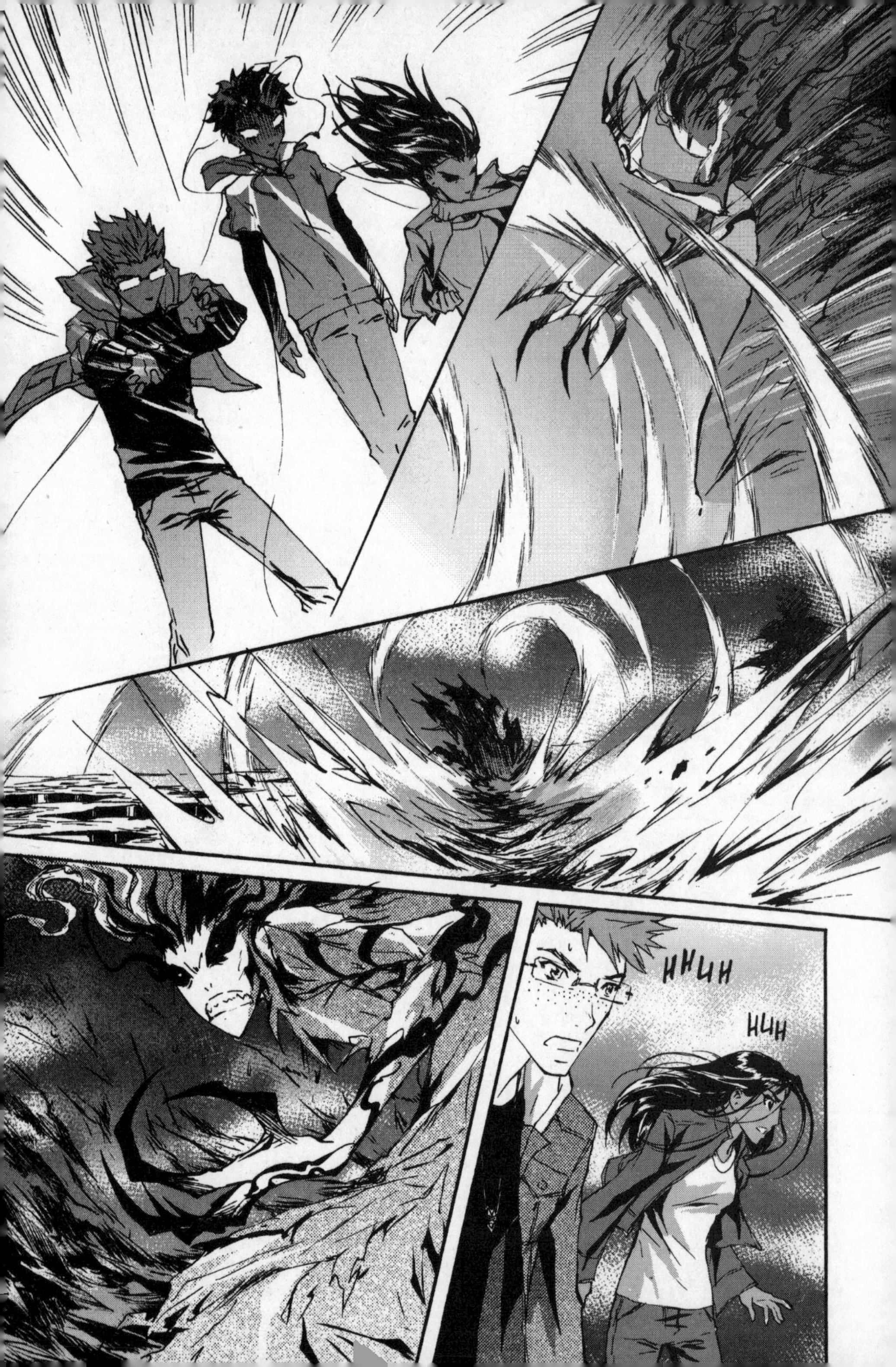
HHUH
HUH

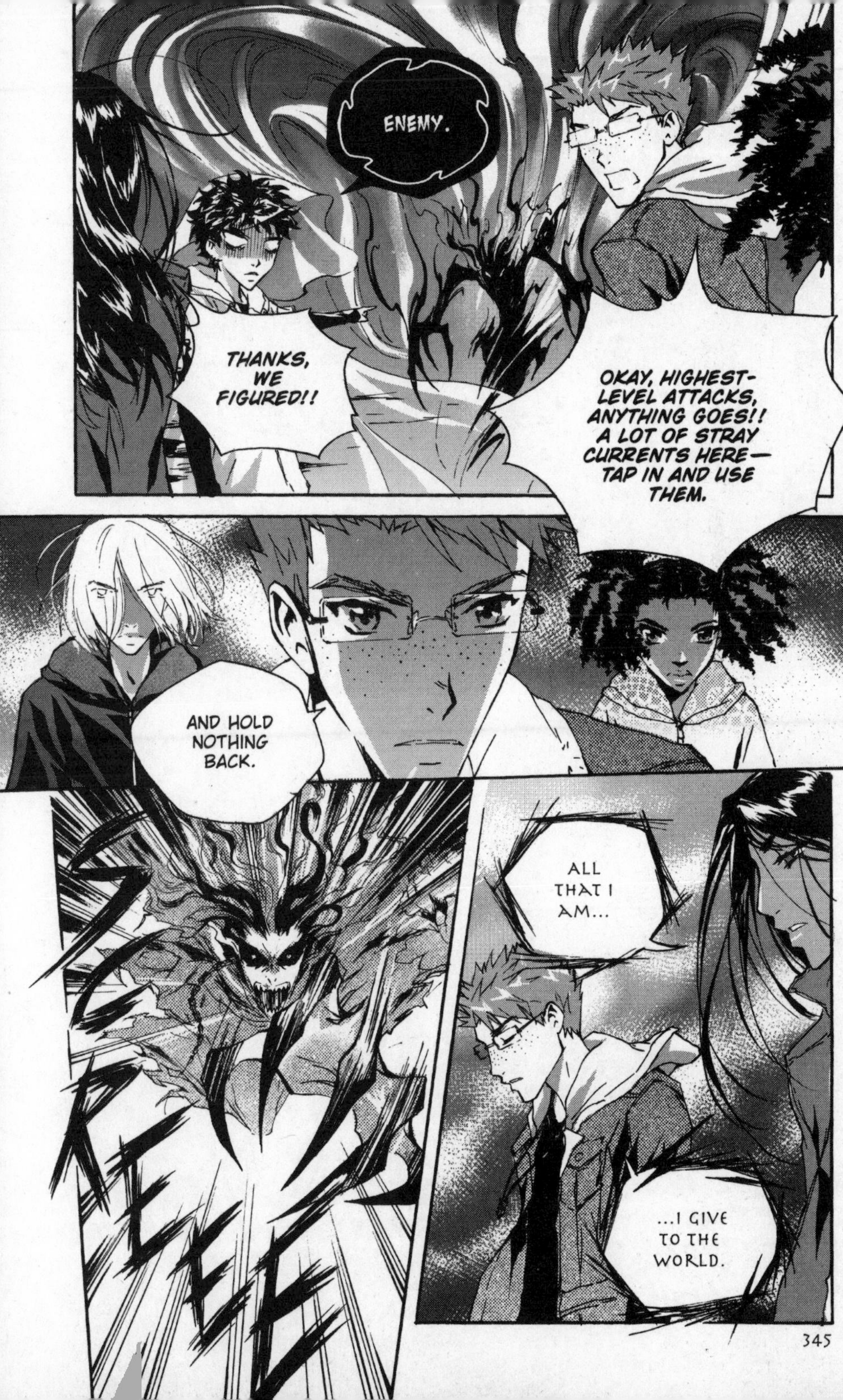
ENEMY.
THANKS, WE FIGURED!!
OKAY, HIGHEST-LEVEL ATTACKS, ANYTHING GOES!! A LOT OF STRAY CURRENTS HERE—TAP IN AND USE THEM.
AND HOLD NOTHING BACK.
ALL THAT I AM...
...I GIVE TO THE WORLD.

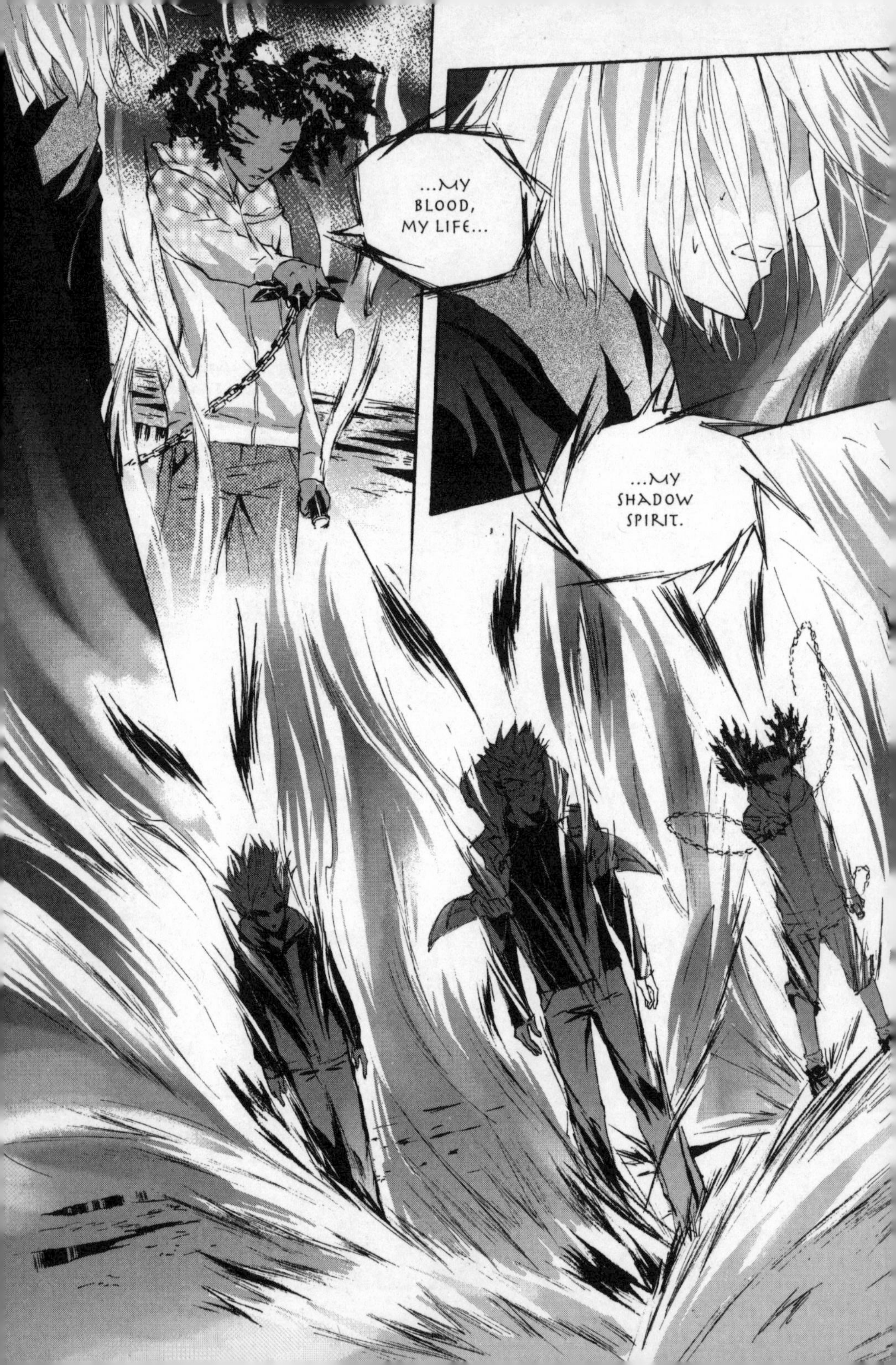
...MY BLOOD, MY LIFE...
...MY SHADOW SPIRIT.

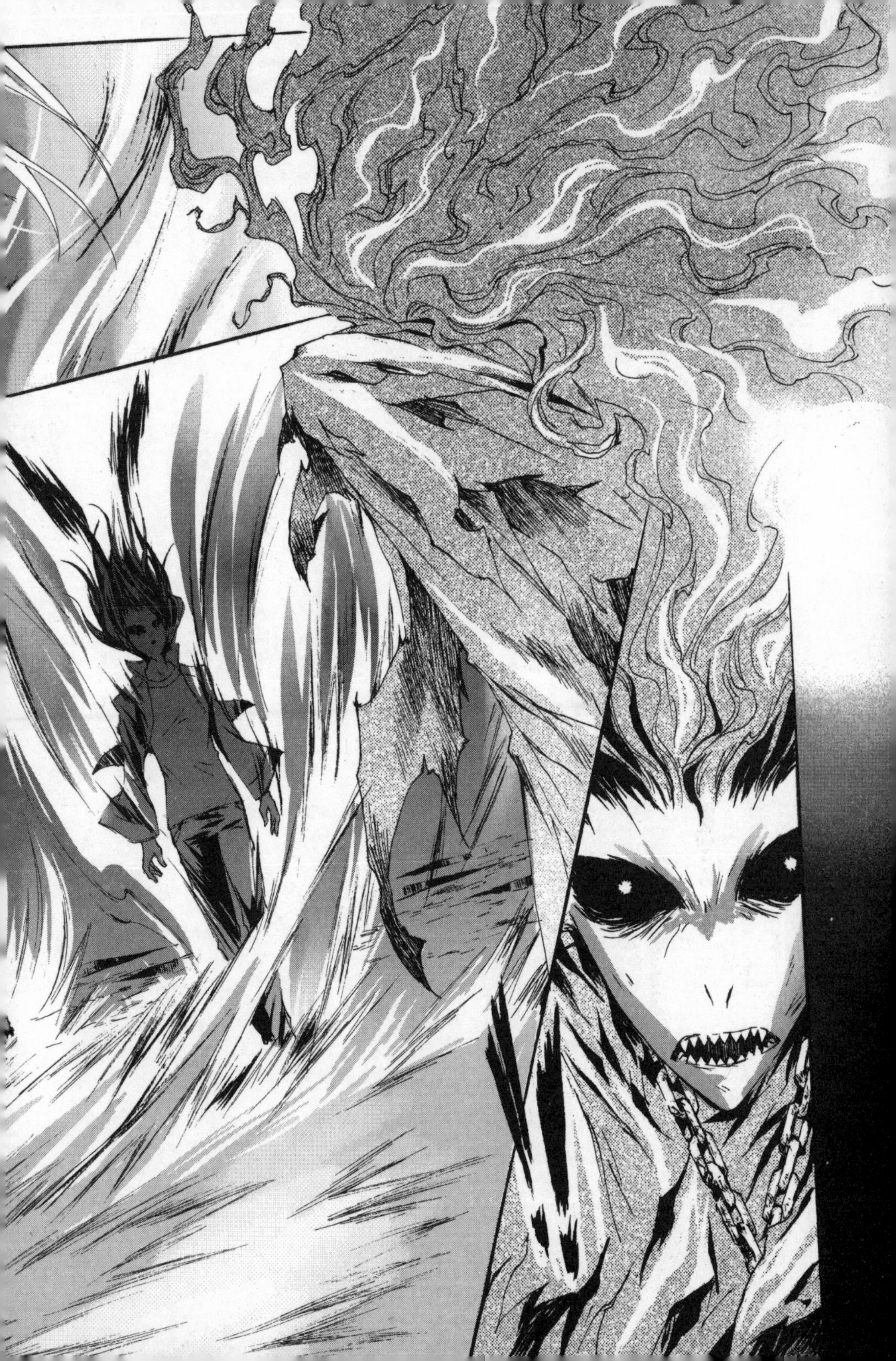

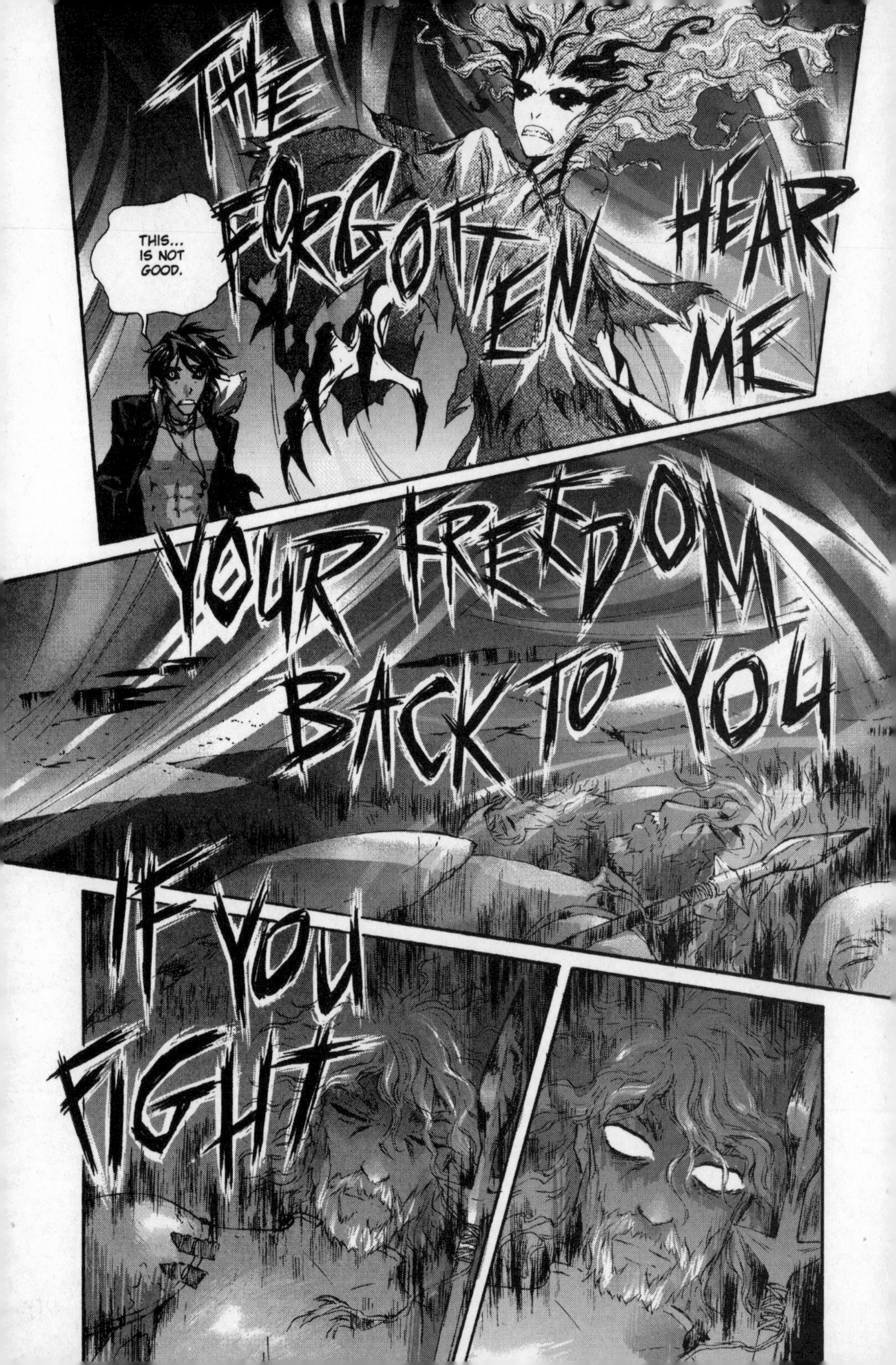
THE FORGOTTEN HEAR ME
THIS... IS NOT GOOD.
YOUR FREEDOM BACK TO YOU
IF YOU FIGHT

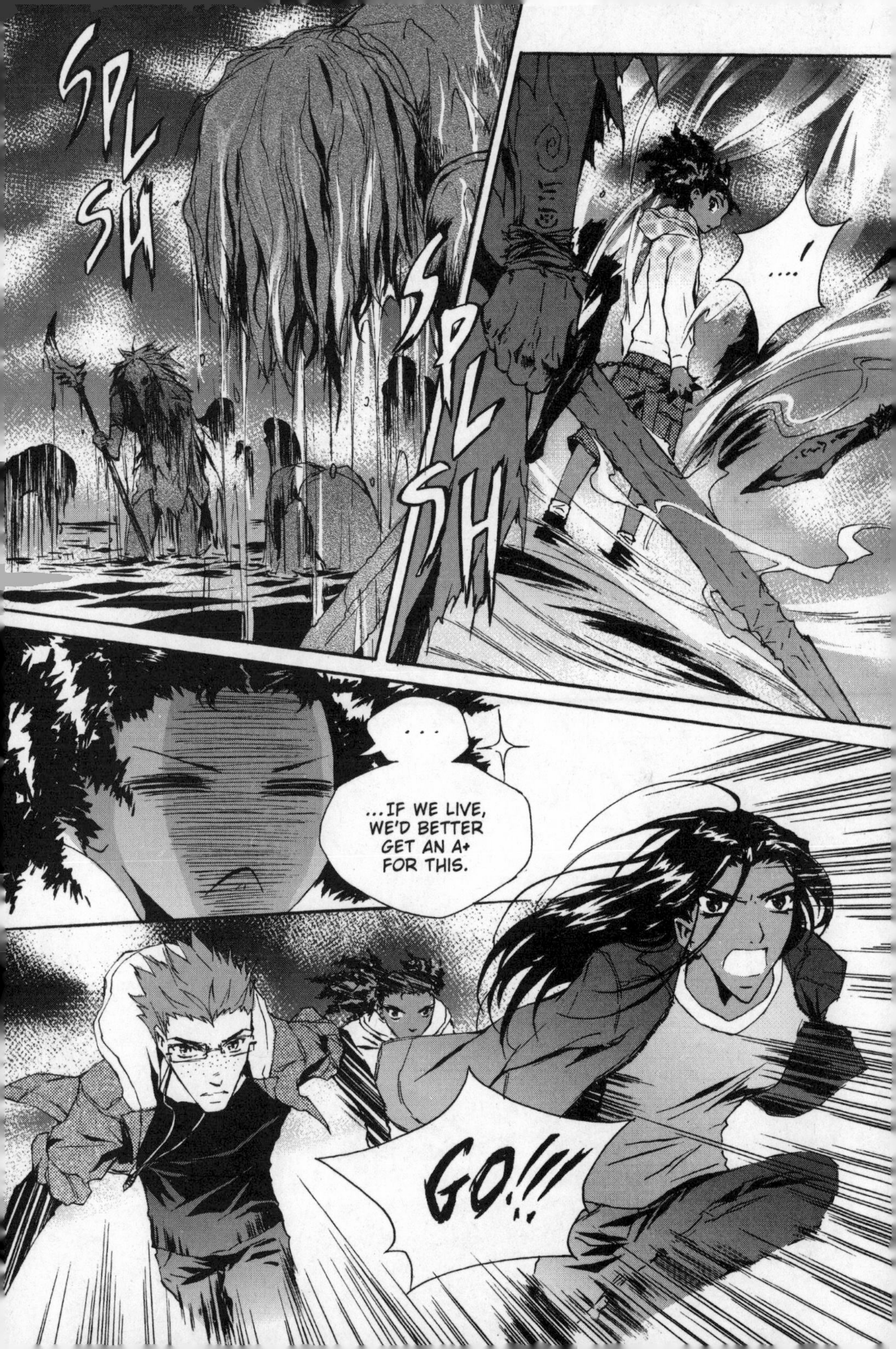
SPLSH
SPLSH
...!
...
...IF WE LIVE, WE'D BETTER GET AN A+ FOR THIS.
GO!!!

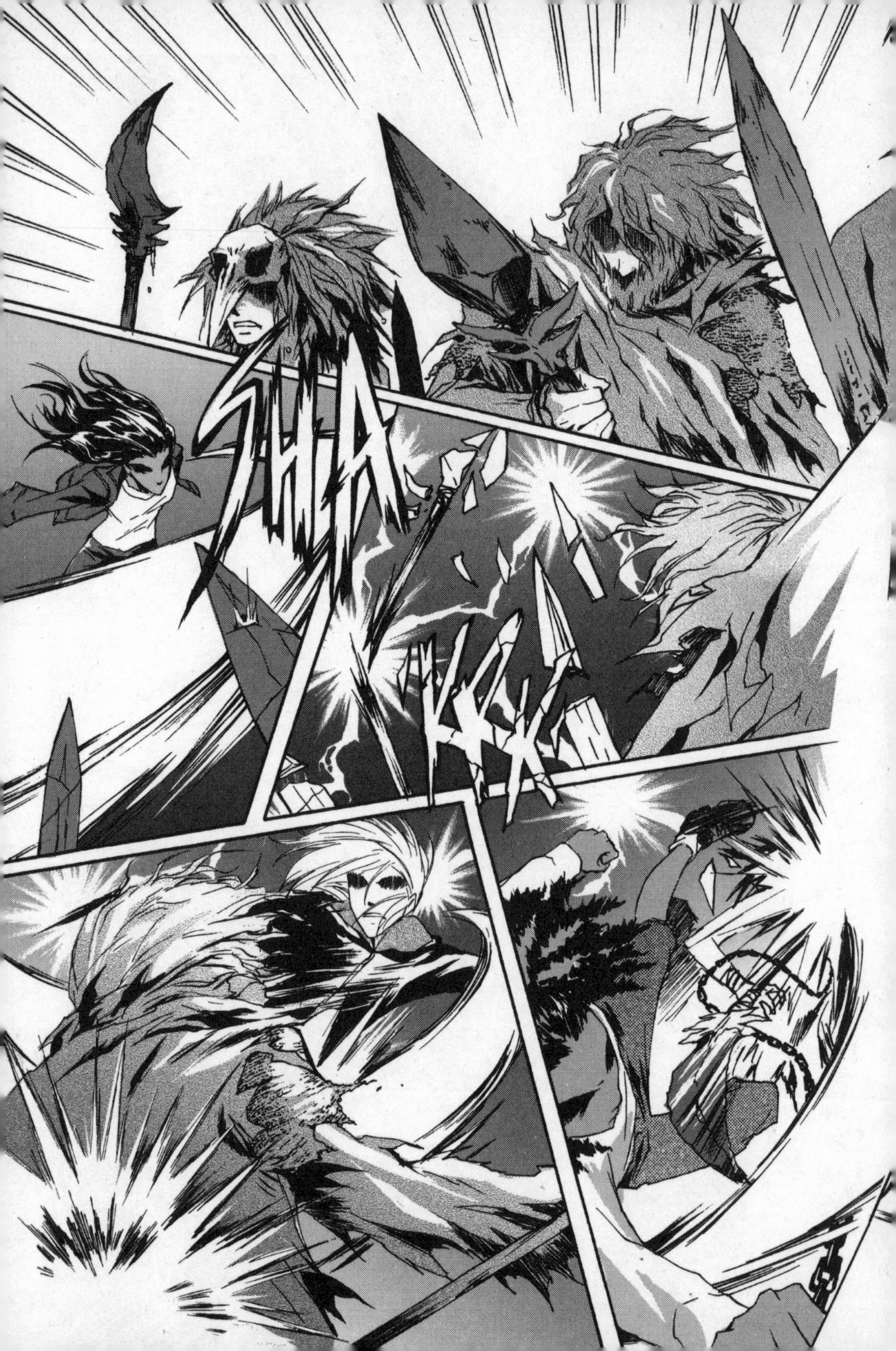
SHHA
KKK

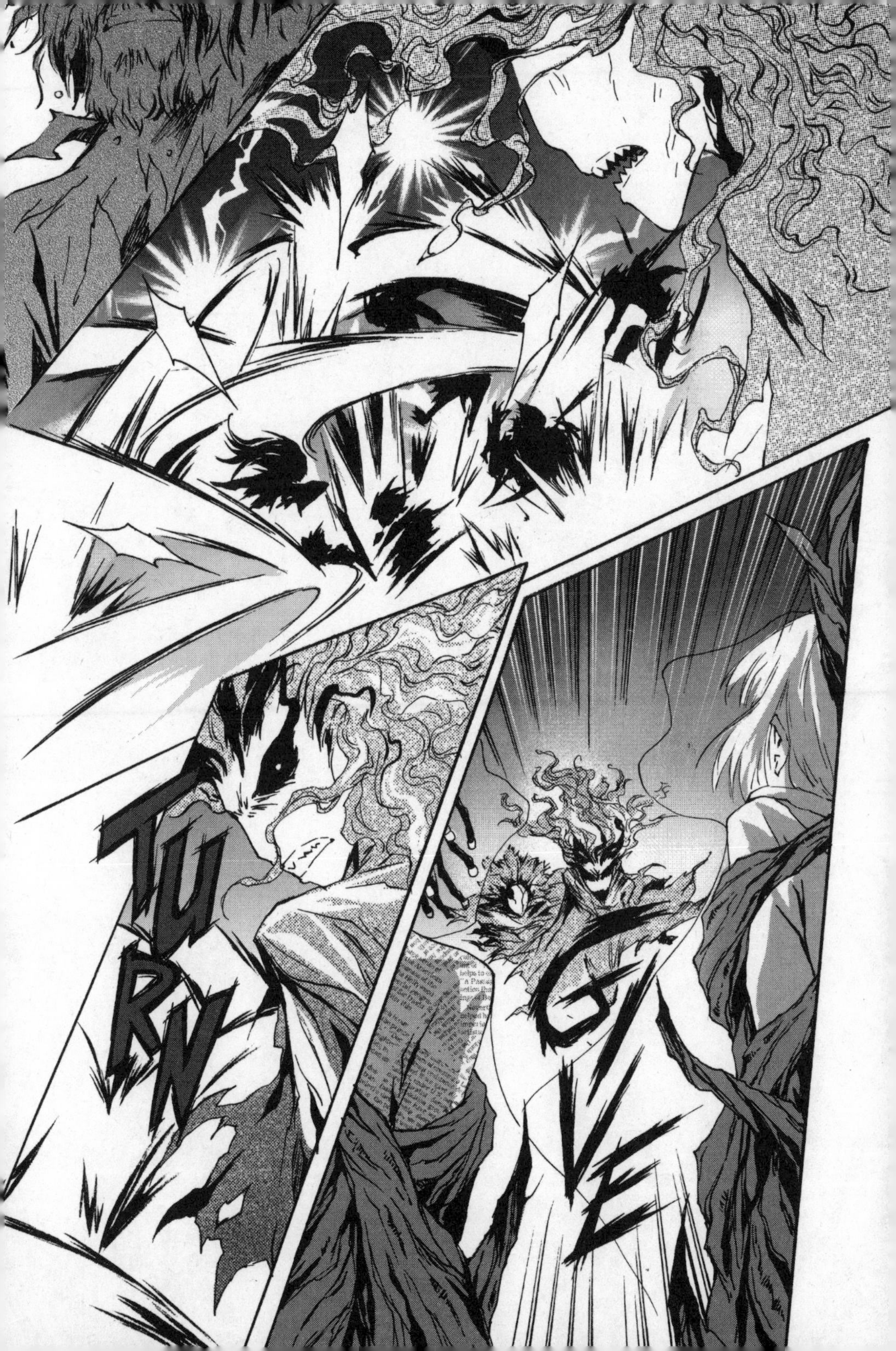
TURN
GIVE

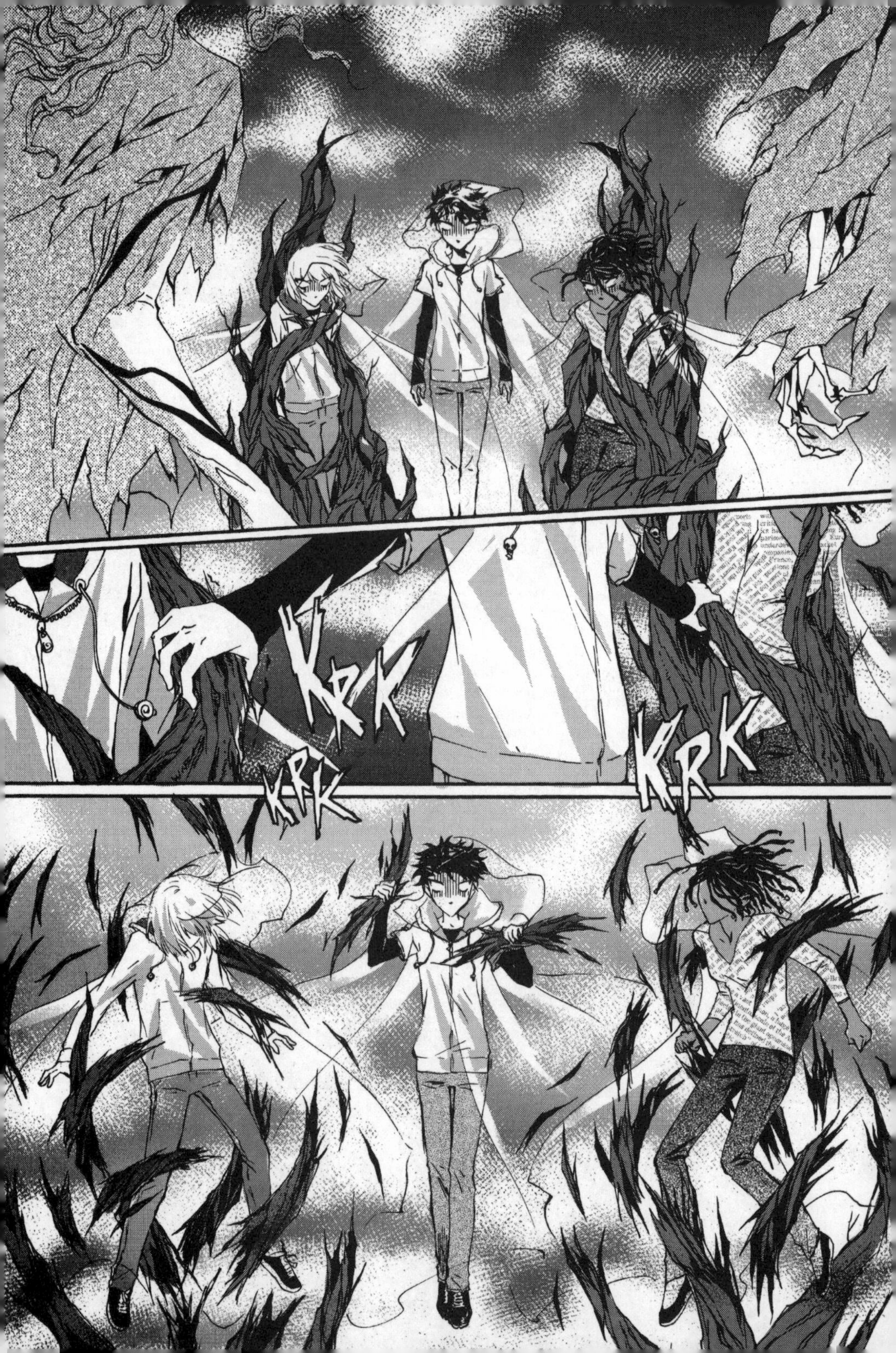
KRK
KRK
KRK

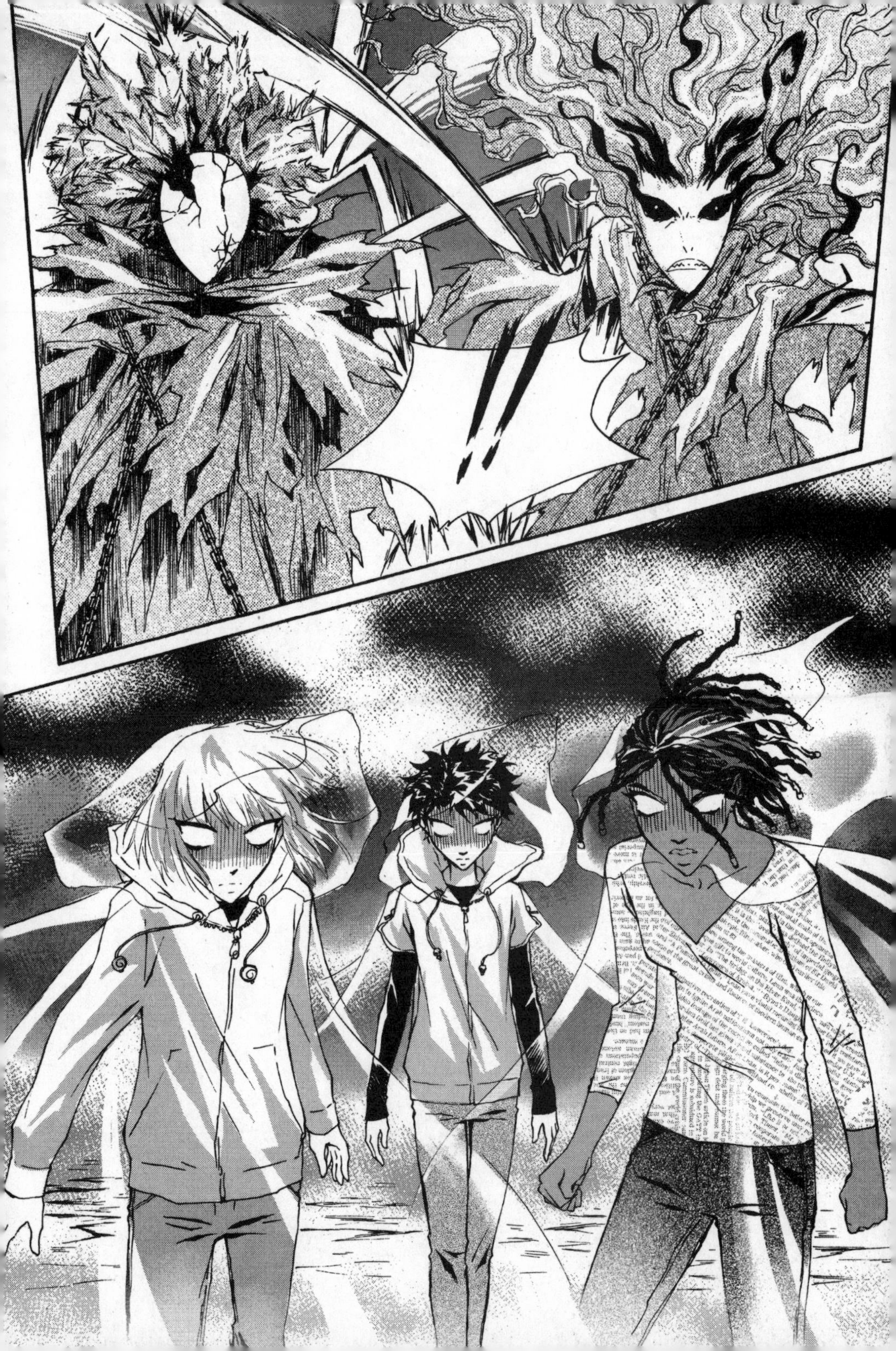

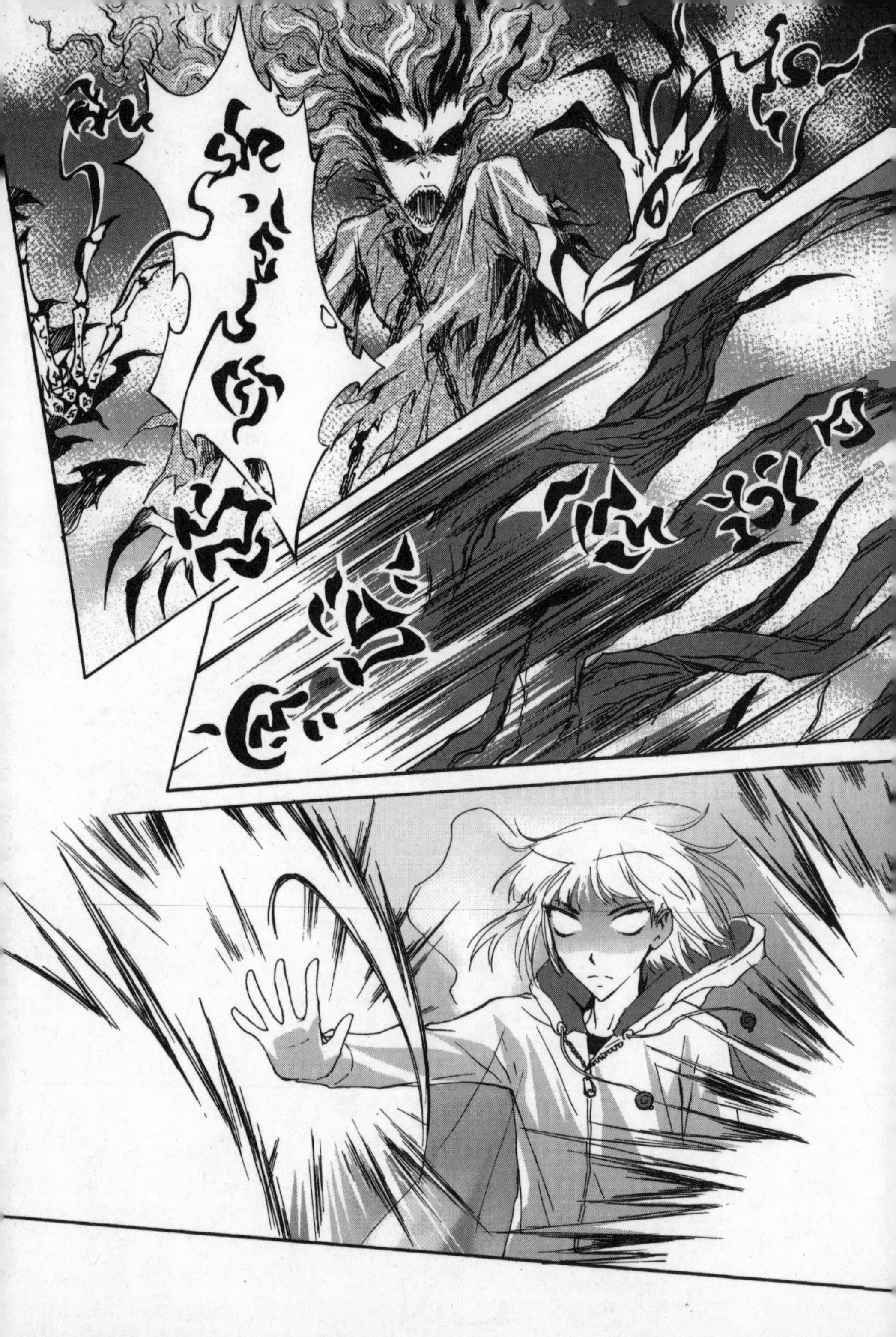

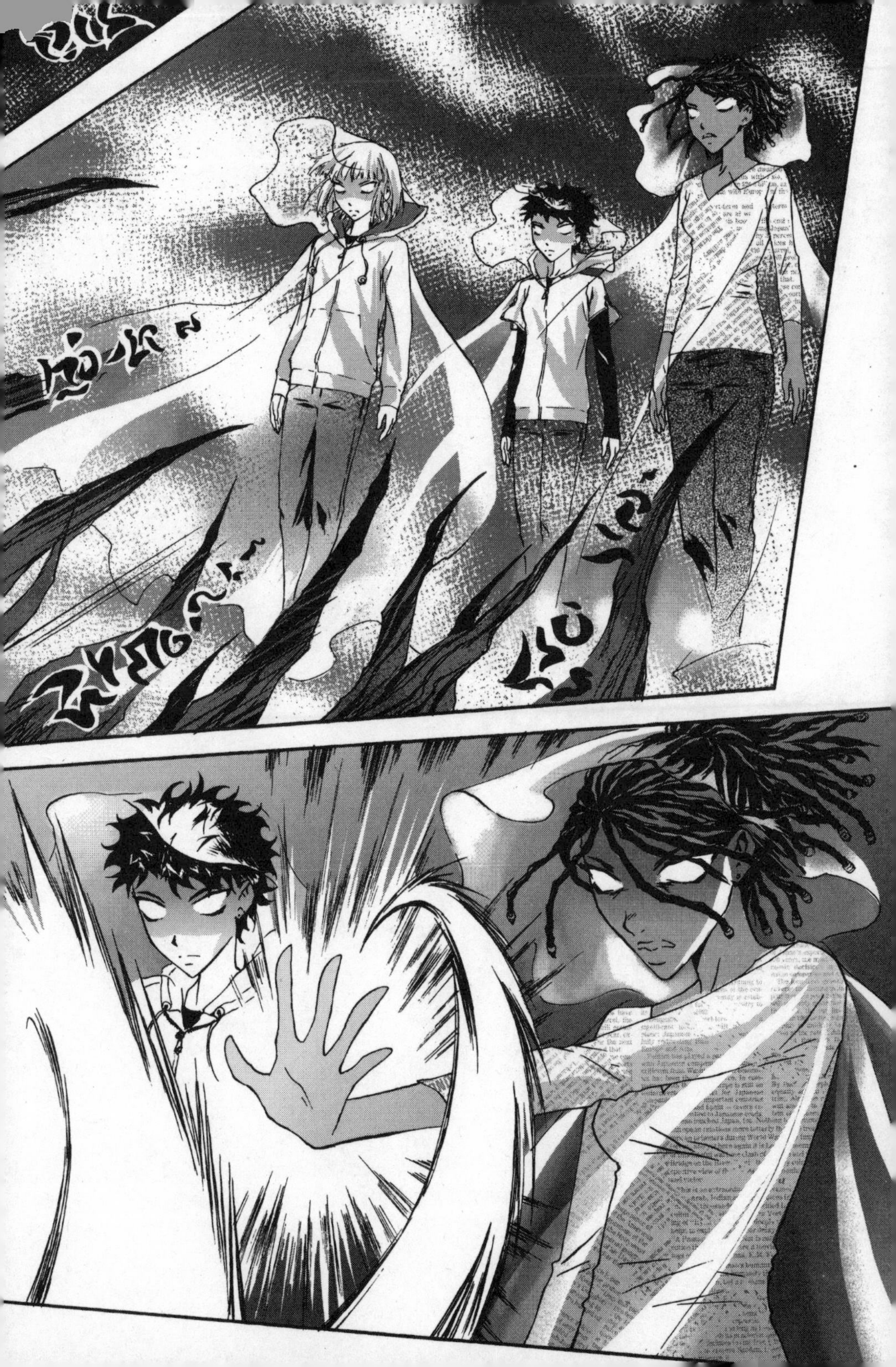

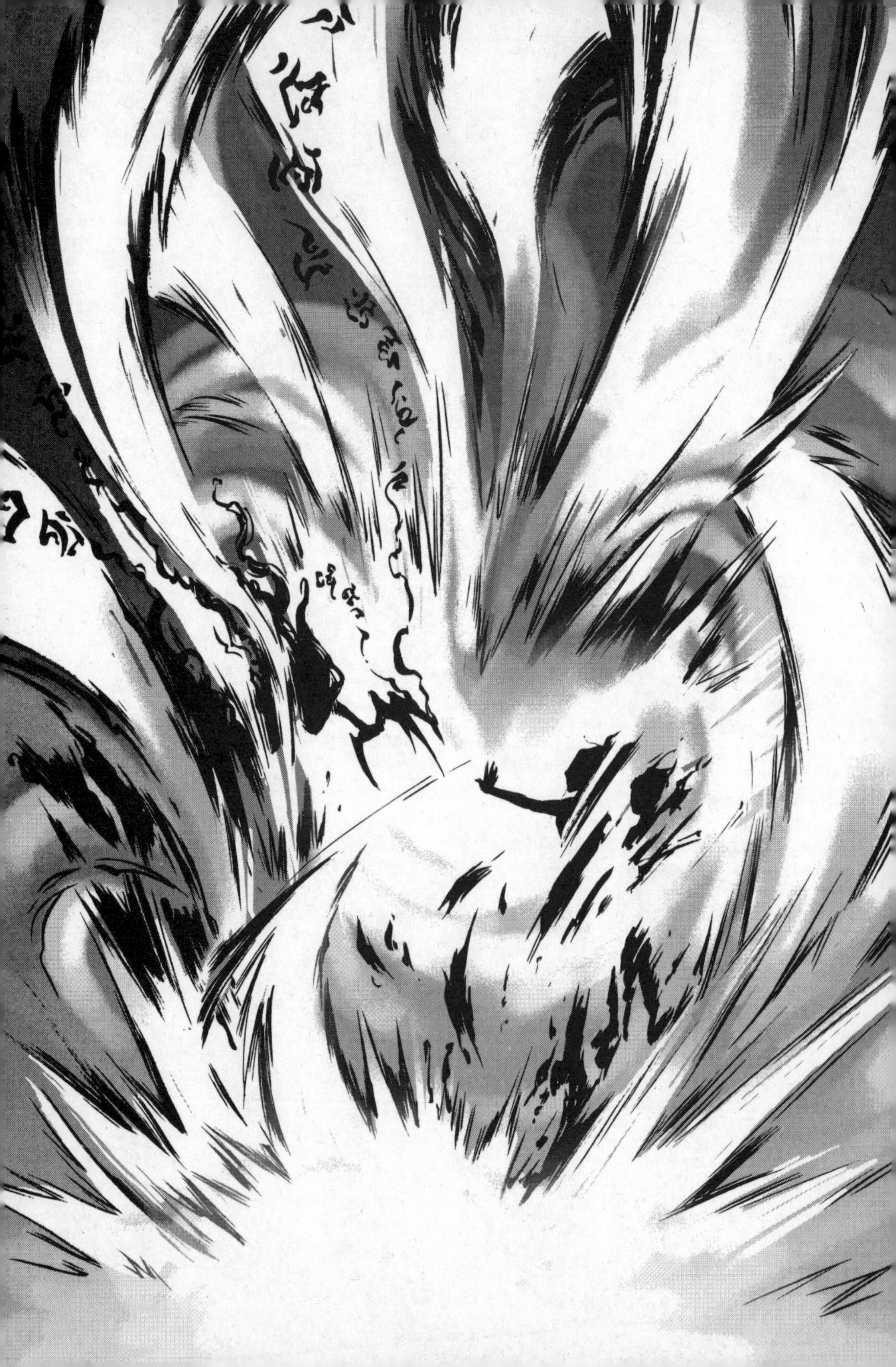

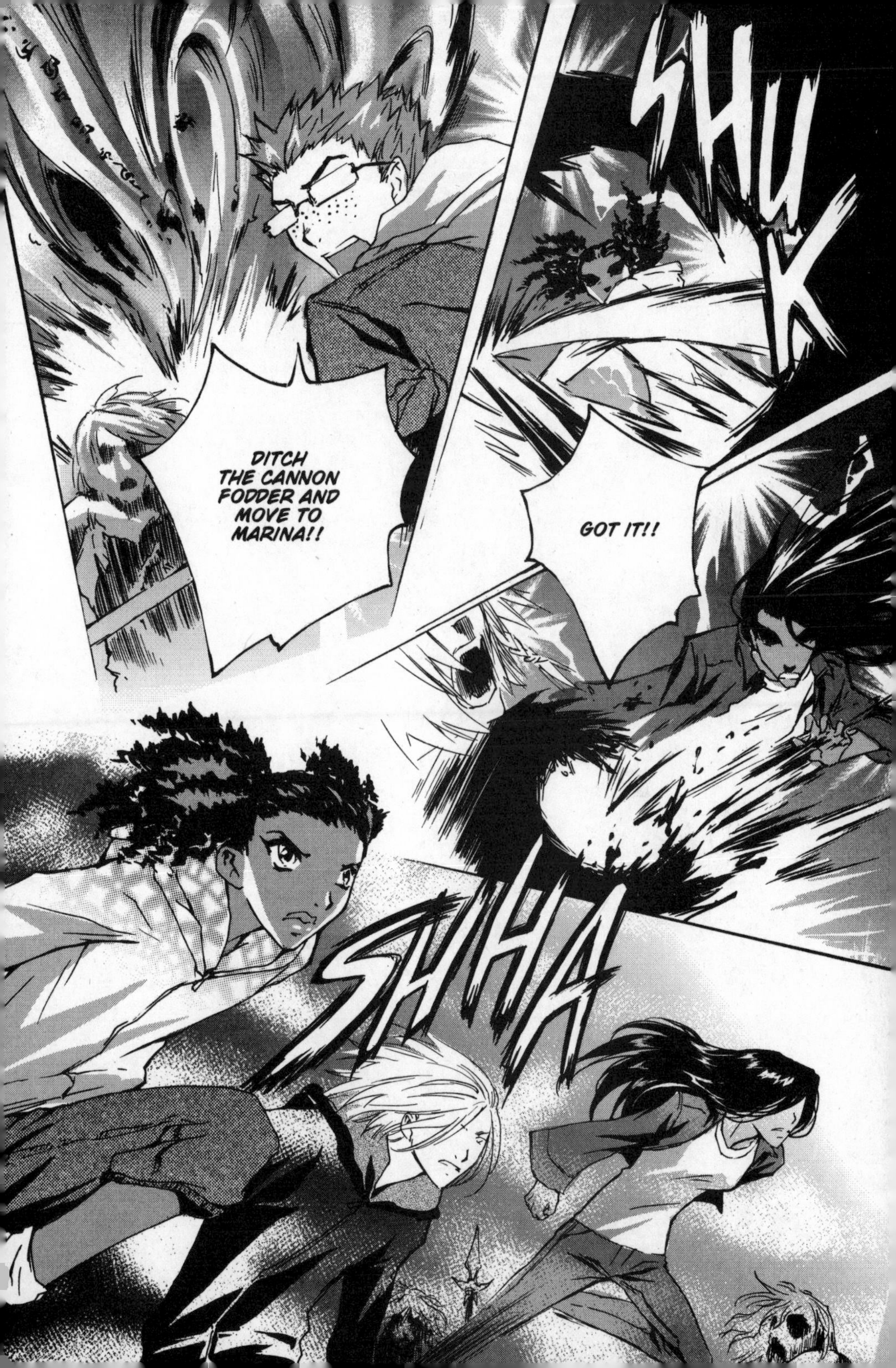
DITCH THE CANNON FODDER AND MOVE TO MARINA!!
SHUK
GOT IT!!
SHHA

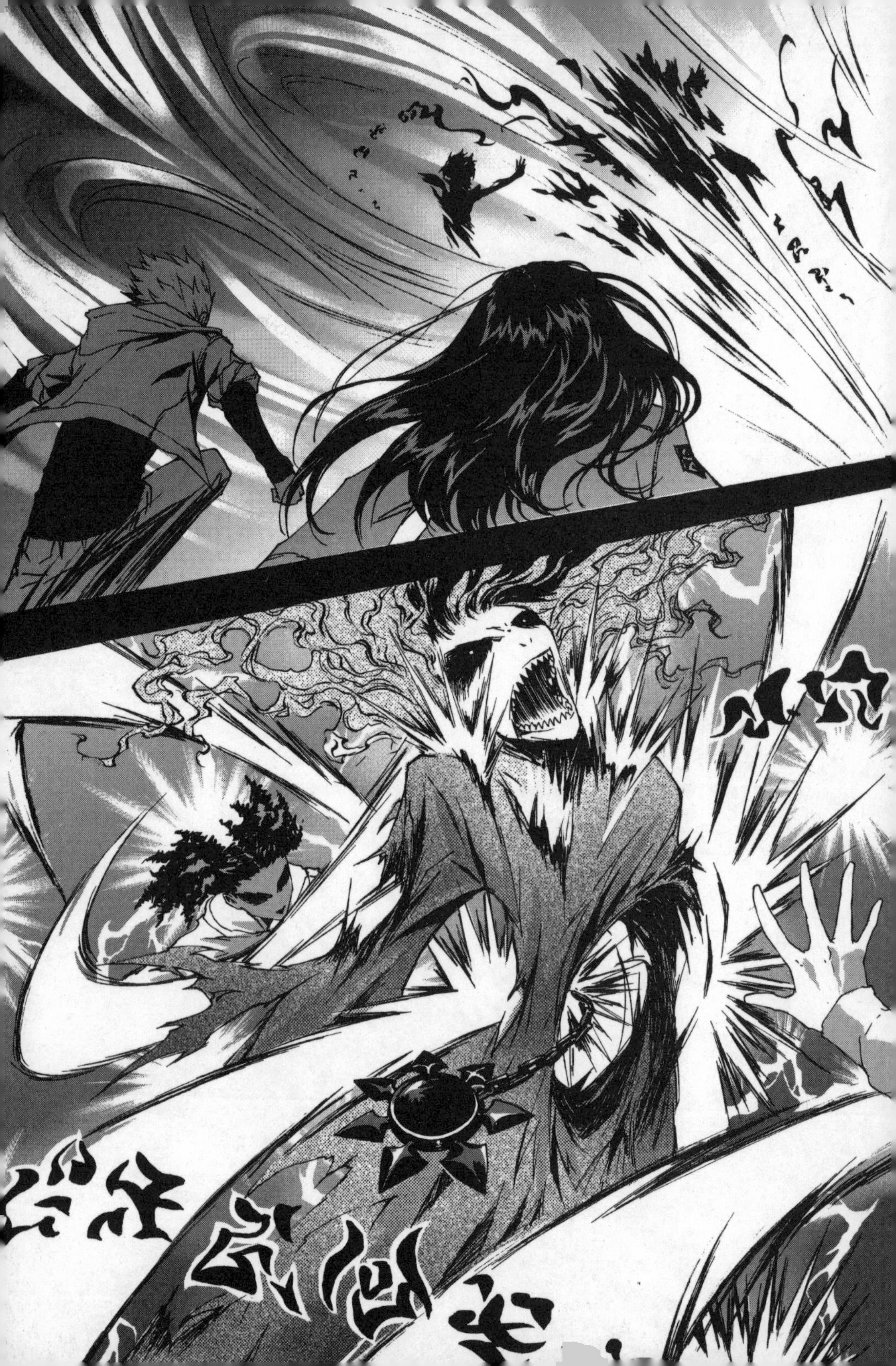

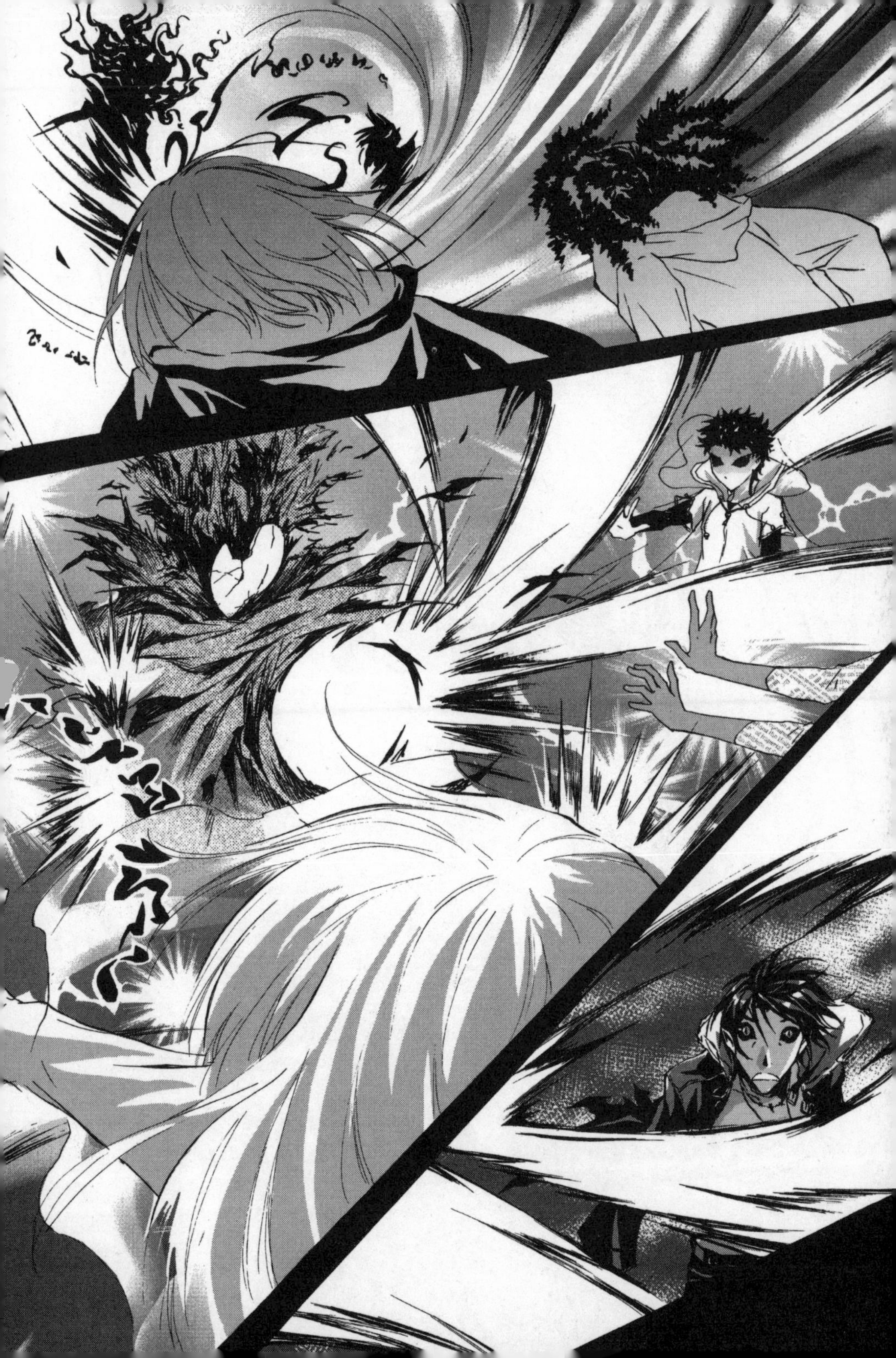

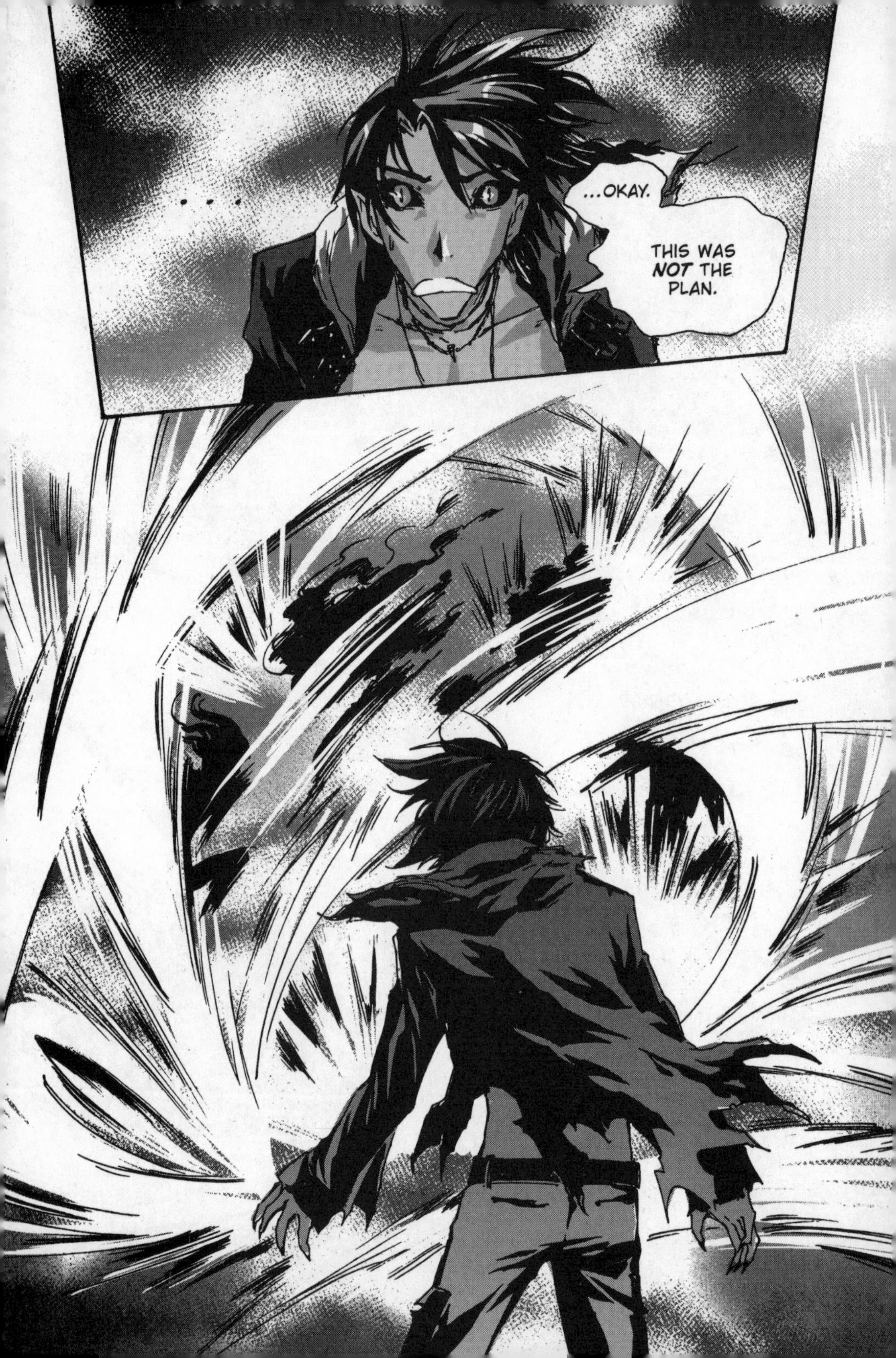
. . .
...OKAY.
THIS WAS *NOT* THE PLAN.

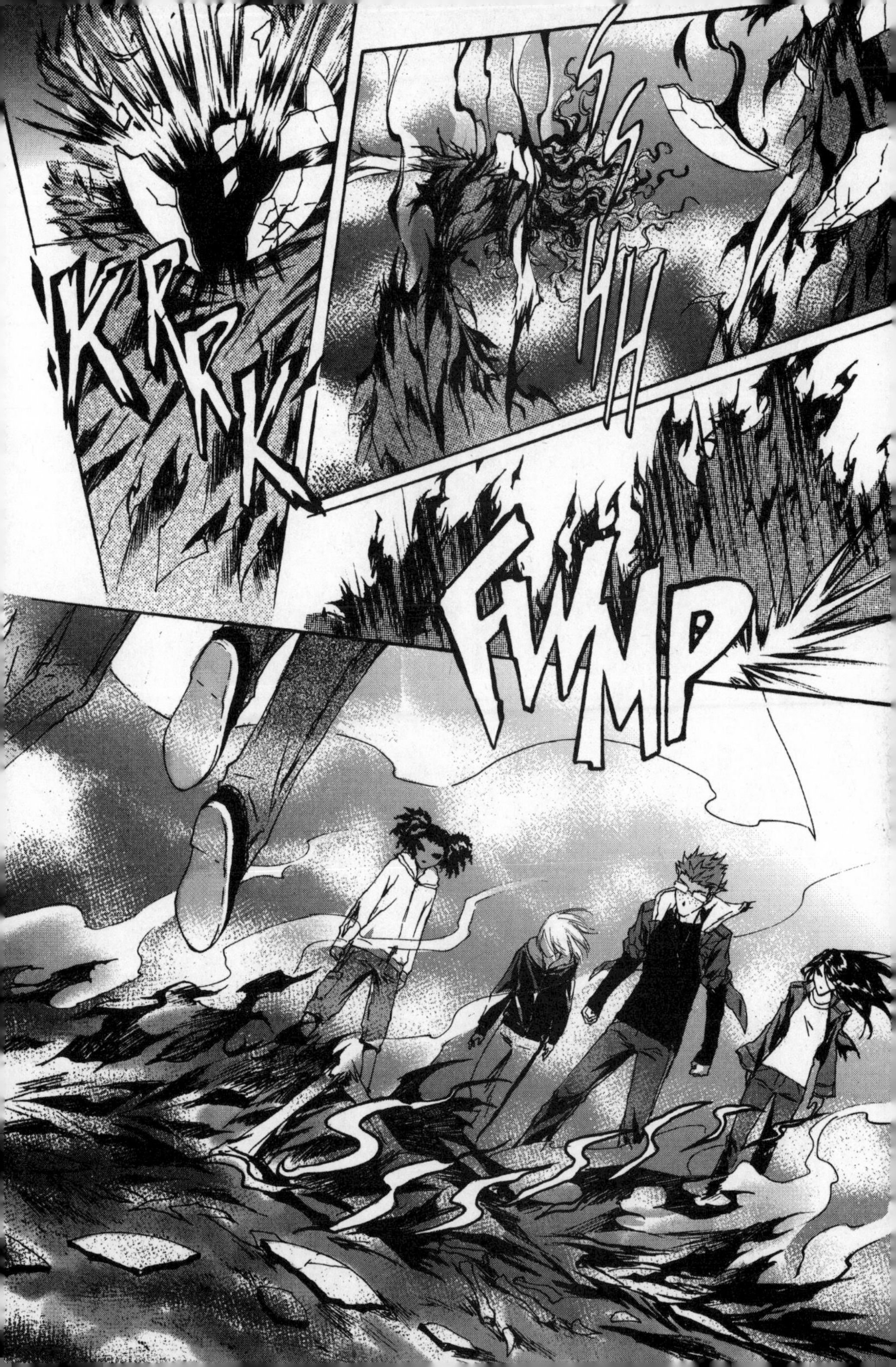
KRRK
SHHH
FWMP

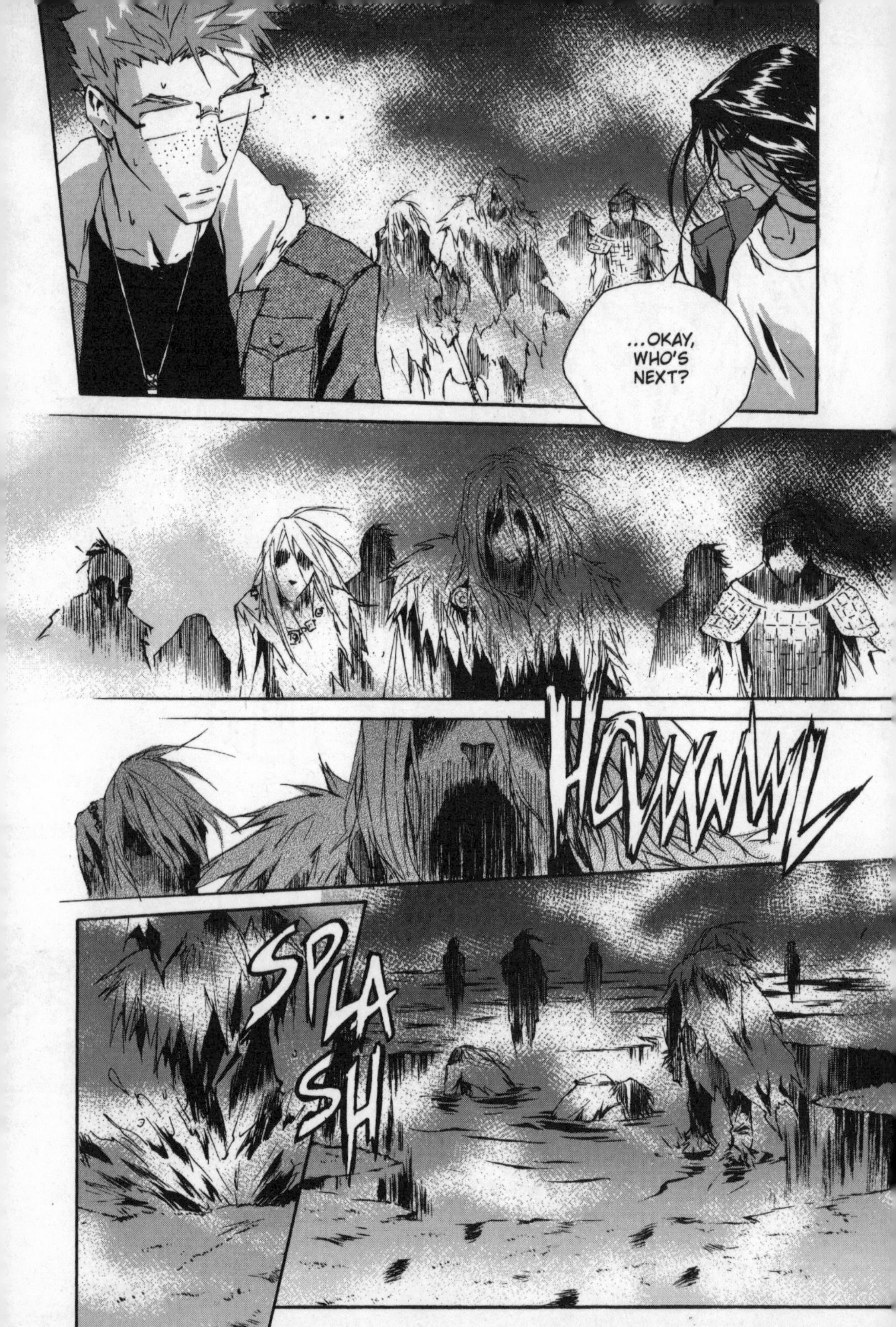
...
...OKAY, WHO'S NEXT?
HOWWWL
SPLASH

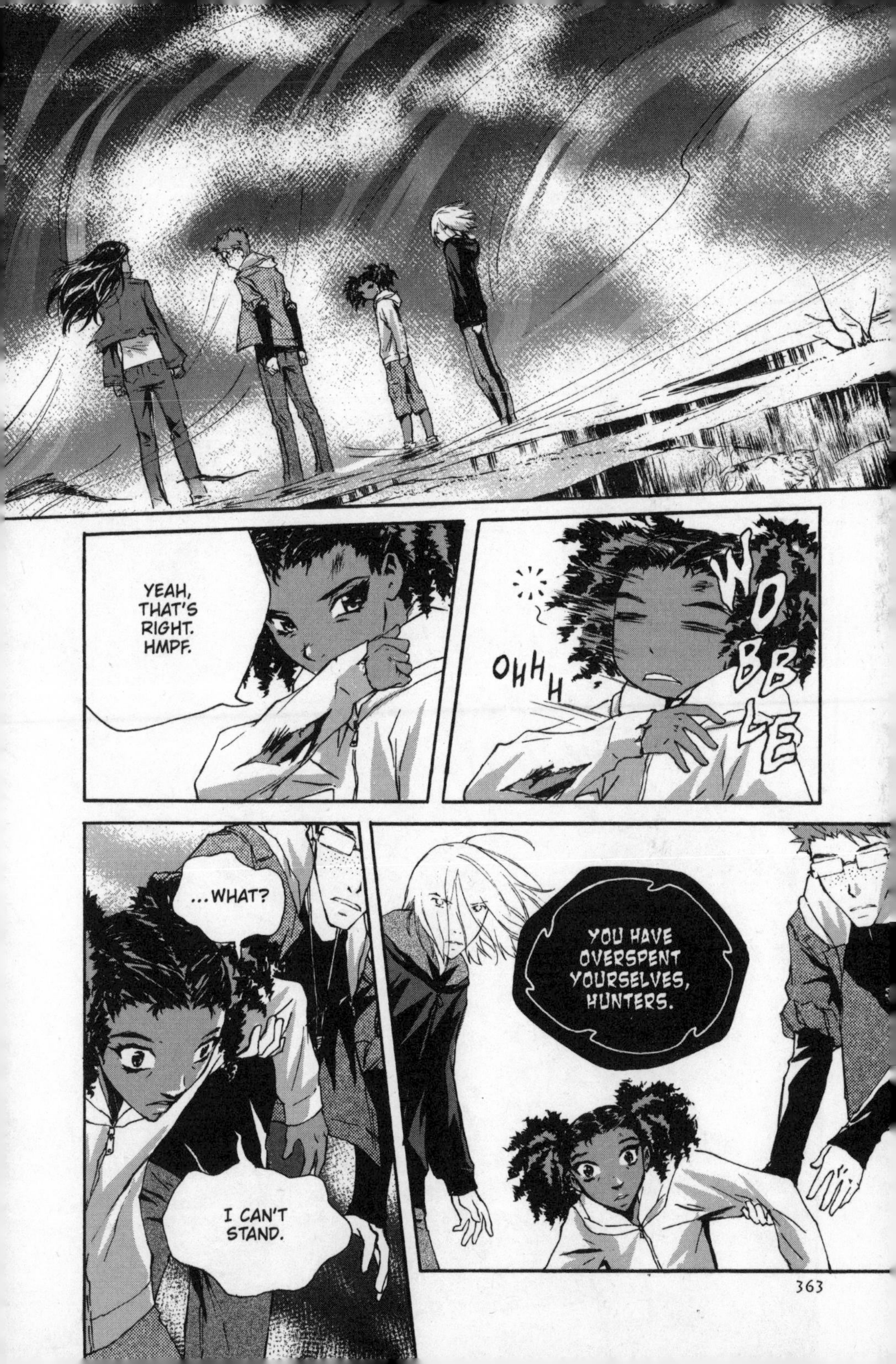
YEAH, THAT'S RIGHT. HMPF.
OHHH
WOBBLE
...WHAT?
I CAN'T STAND.
YOU HAVE OVERSPENT YOURSELVES, HUNTERS.

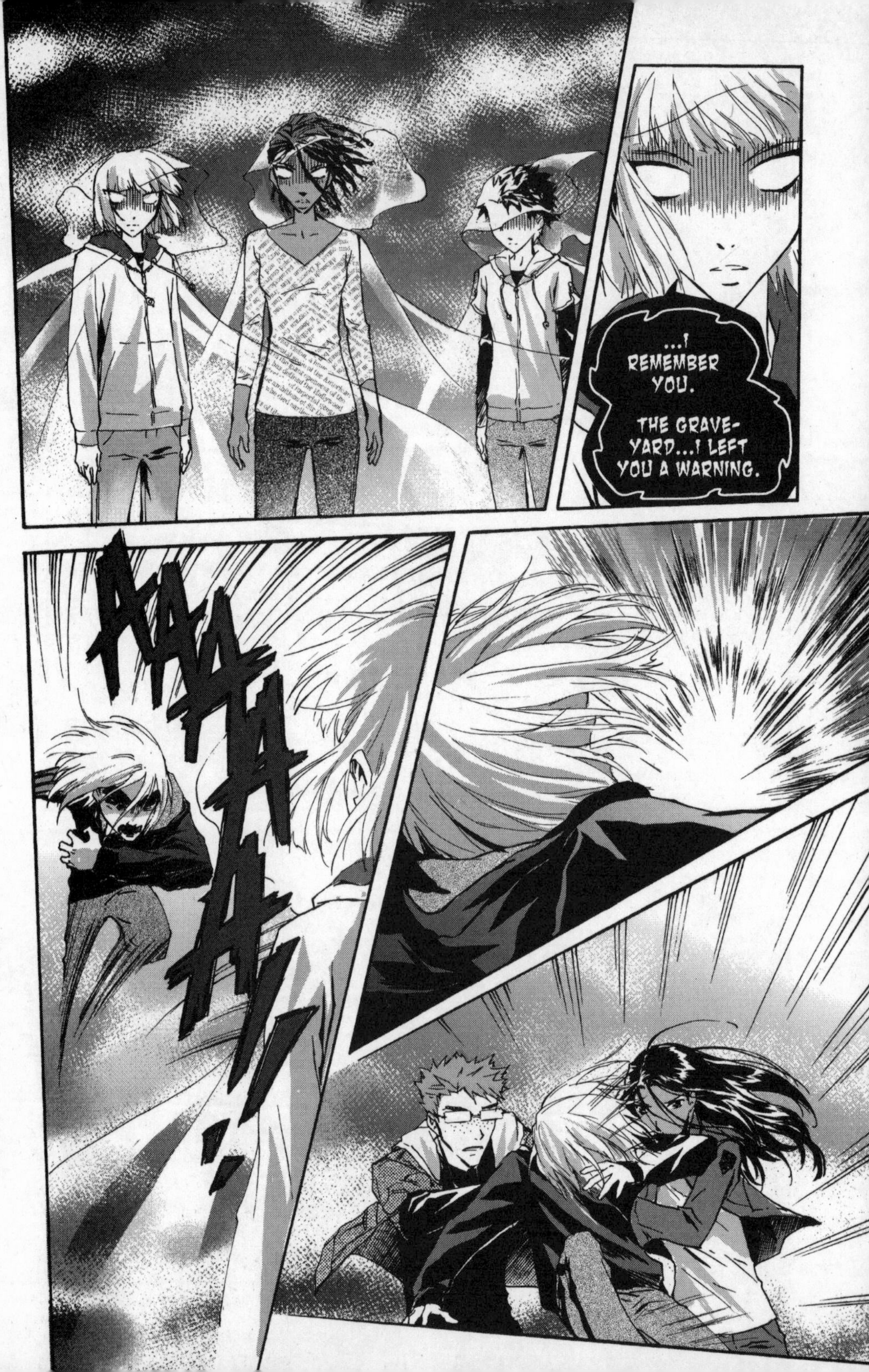
...I REMEMBER YOU.
THE GRAVE-YARD...I LEFT YOU A WARNING.

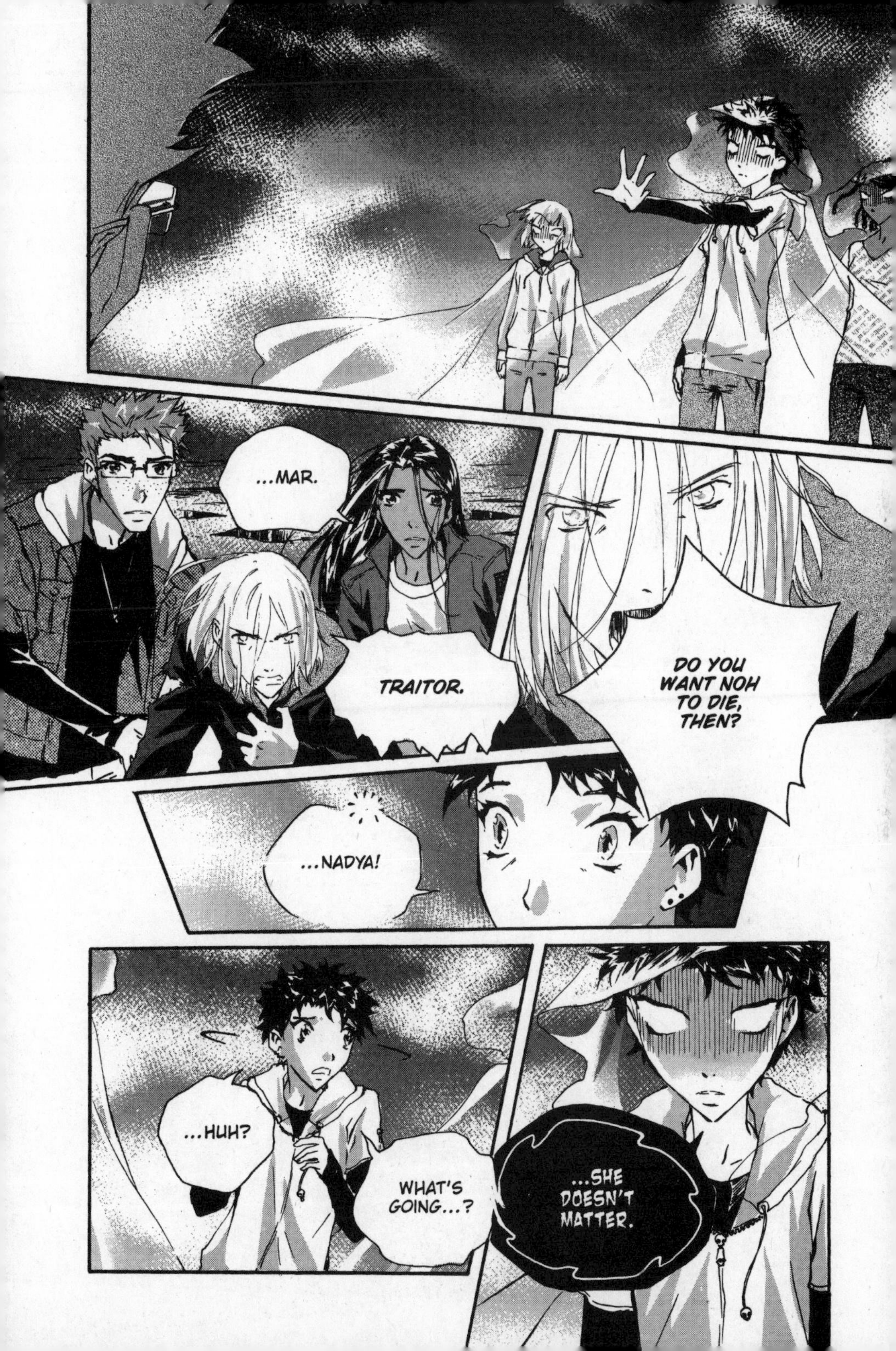
...MAR.
TRAITOR.
DO YOU WANT NOH TO DIE, THEN?
...NADYA!
...HUH?
WHAT'S GOING...?
...SHE DOESN'T MATTER.

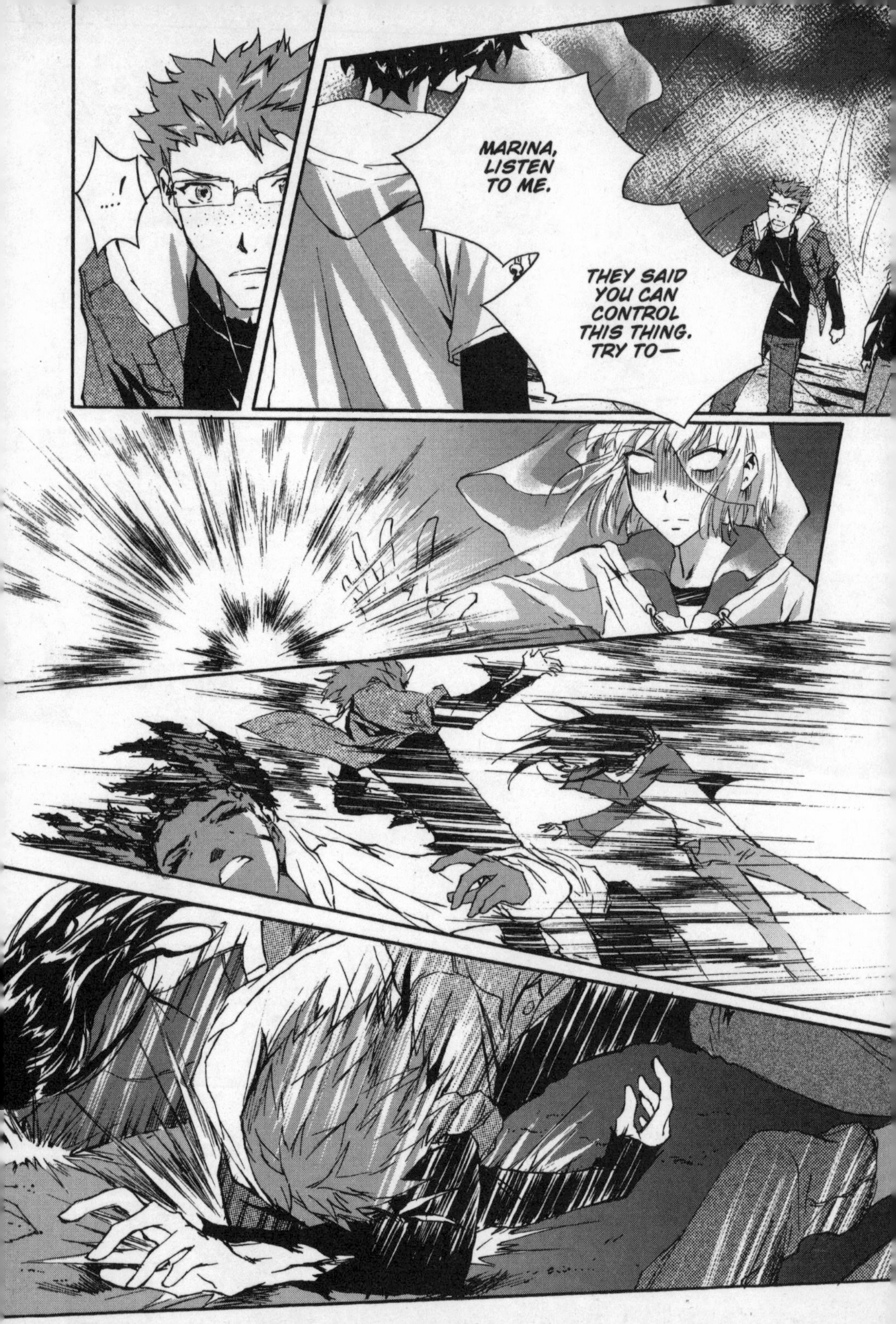

...!
MARINA, LISTEN TO ME.
THEY SAID YOU CAN CONTROL THIS THING. TRY TO—

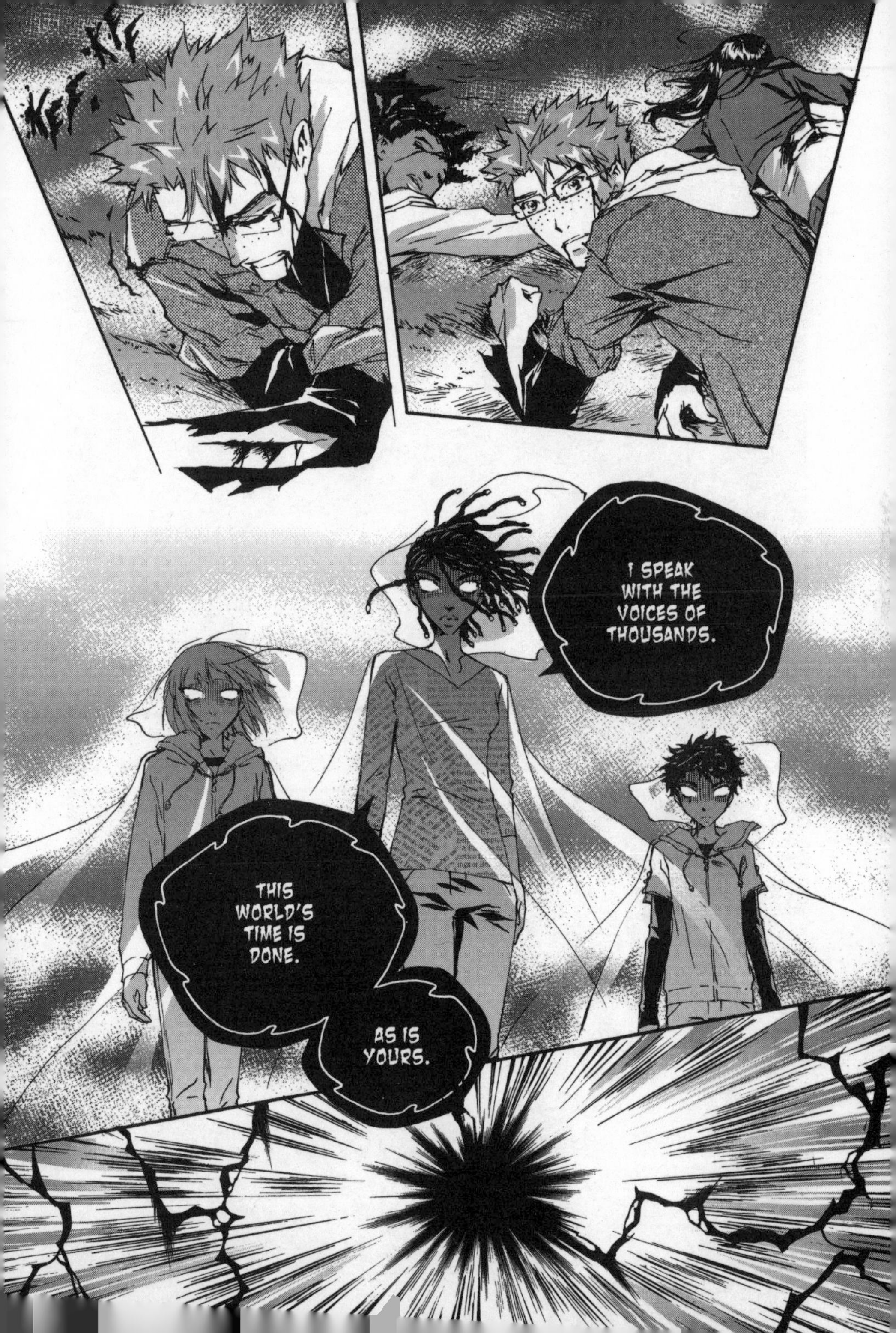
KEF KEF
I SPEAK WITH THE VOICES OF THOUSANDS.
THIS WORLD'S TIME IS DONE.
AS IS YOURS.

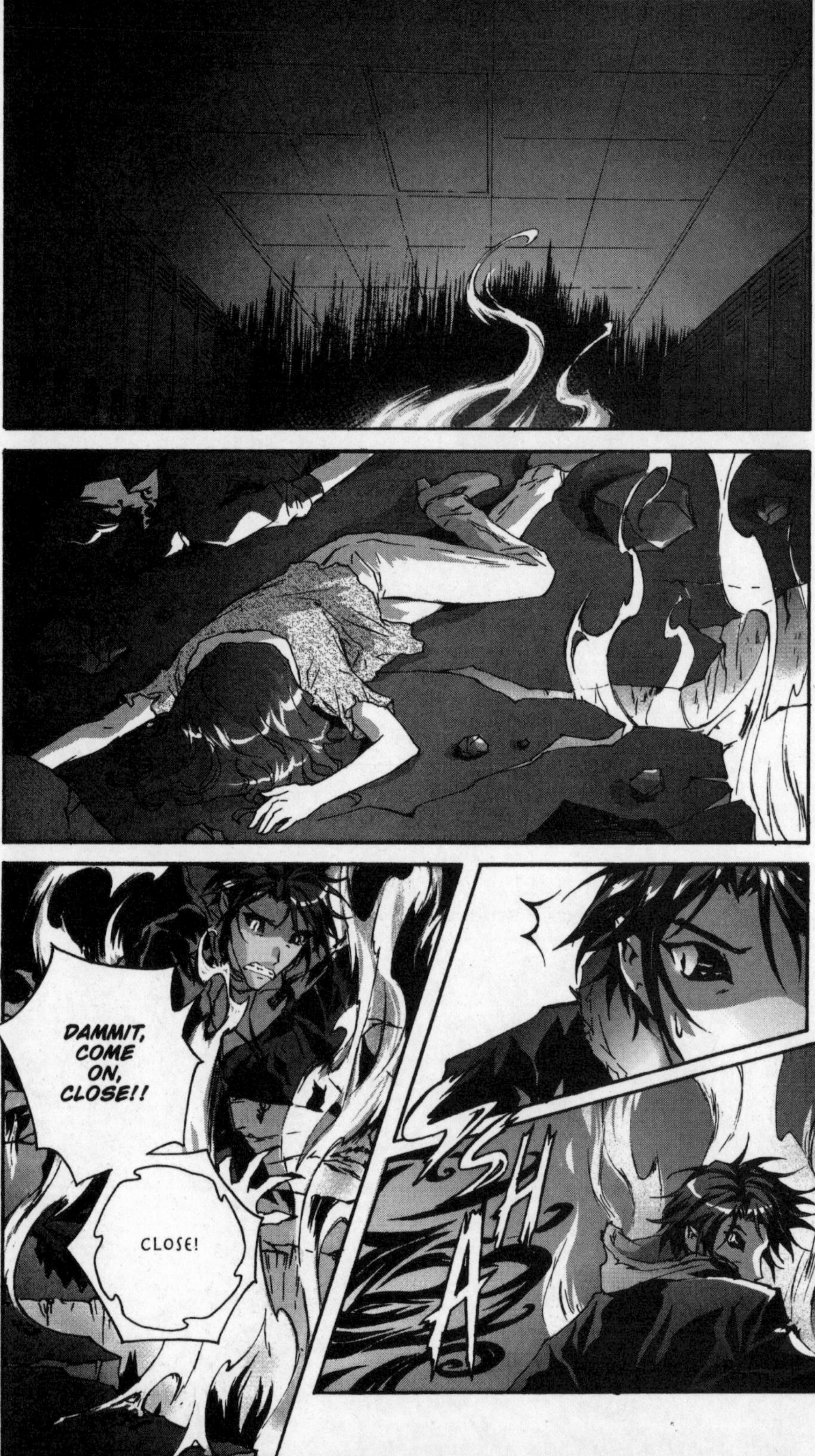
DAMMIT, COME ON, CLOSE!!
CLOSE!
SSHAH

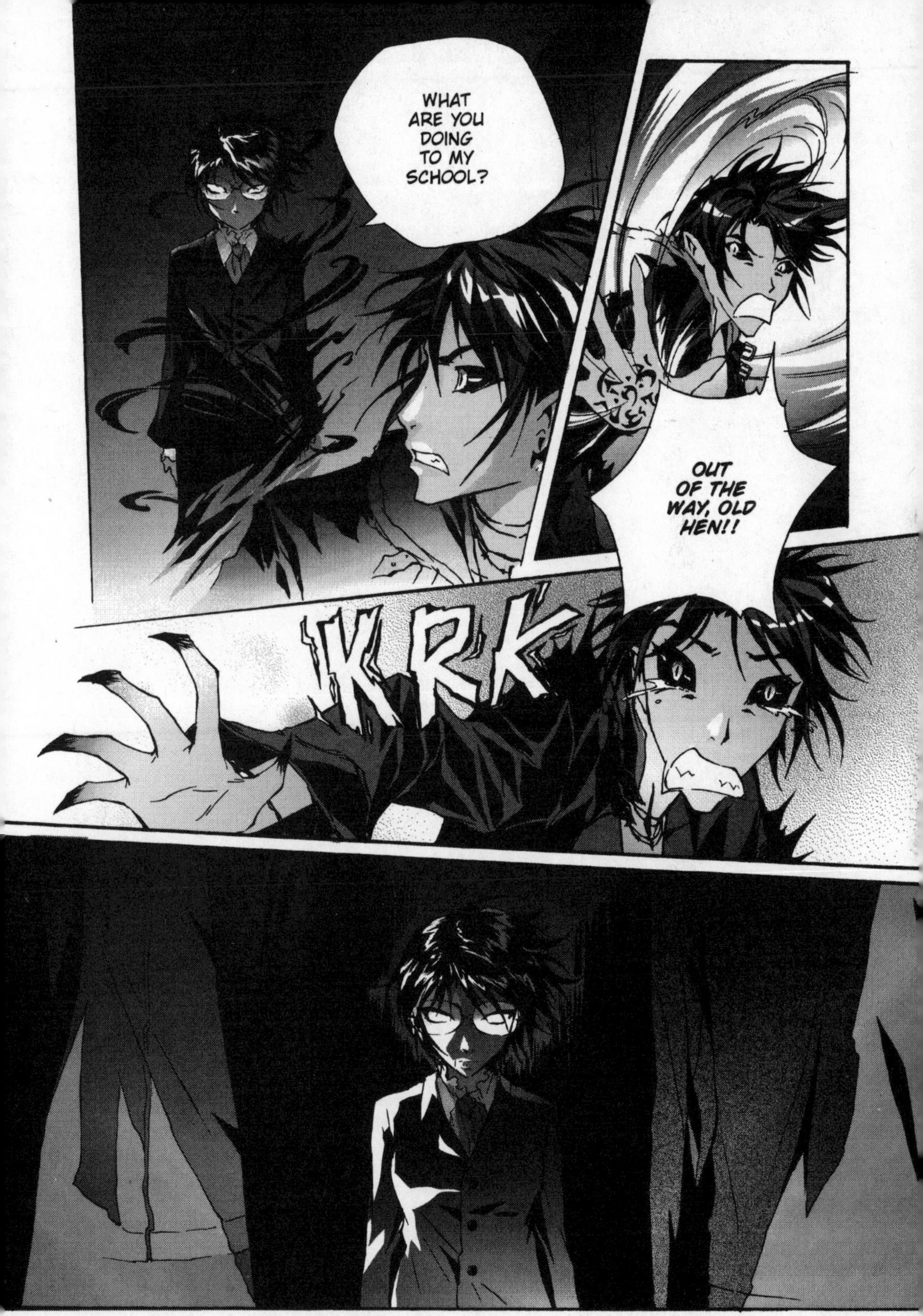
WHAT ARE YOU DOING TO MY SCHOOL?
OUT OF THE WAY, OLD HEN!!
KRK

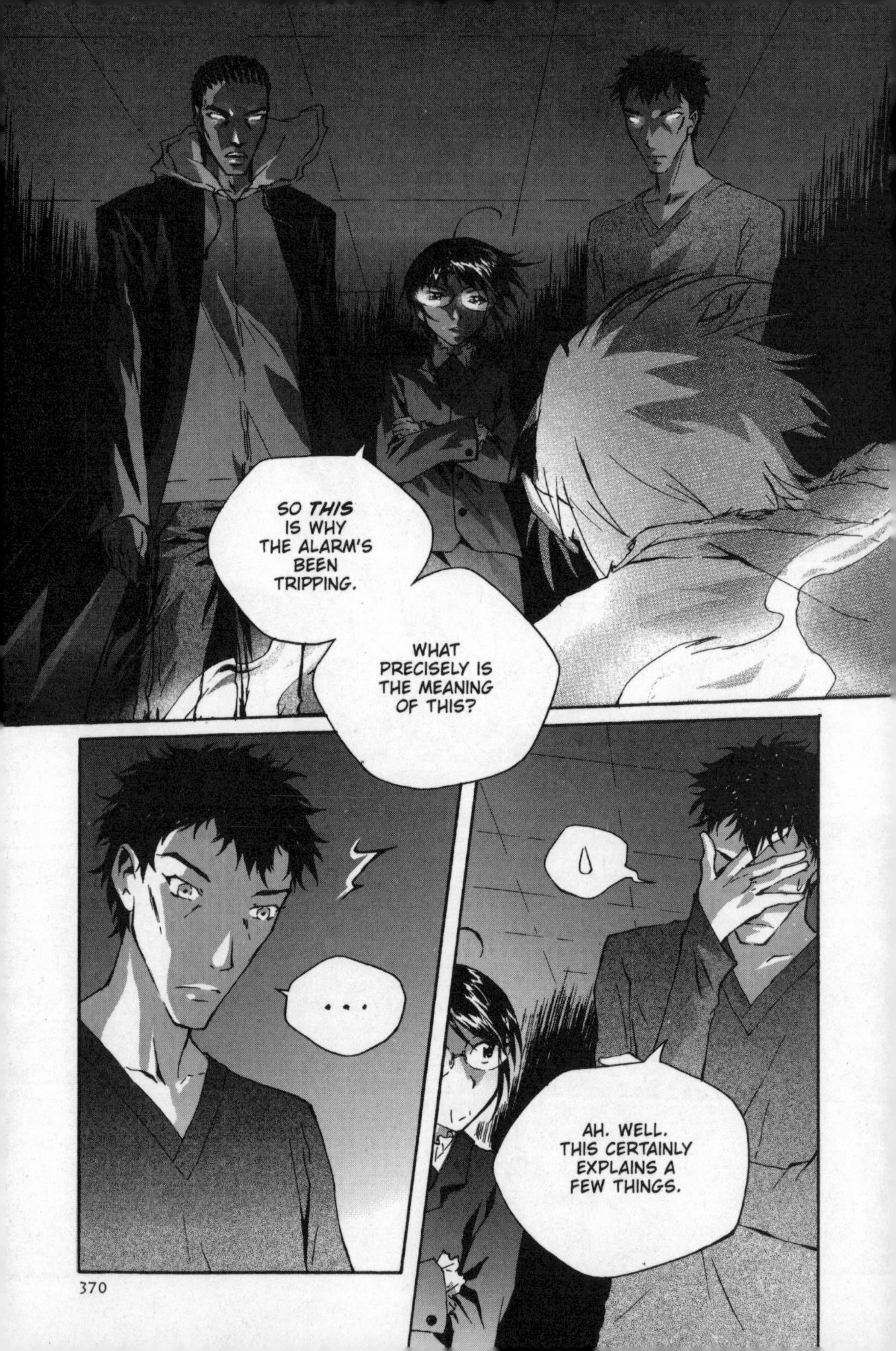
SO *THIS* IS WHY THE ALARM'S BEEN TRIPPING.
WHAT PRECISELY IS THE MEANING OF THIS?
...
!
AH. WELL. THIS CERTAINLY EXPLAINS A FEW THINGS.

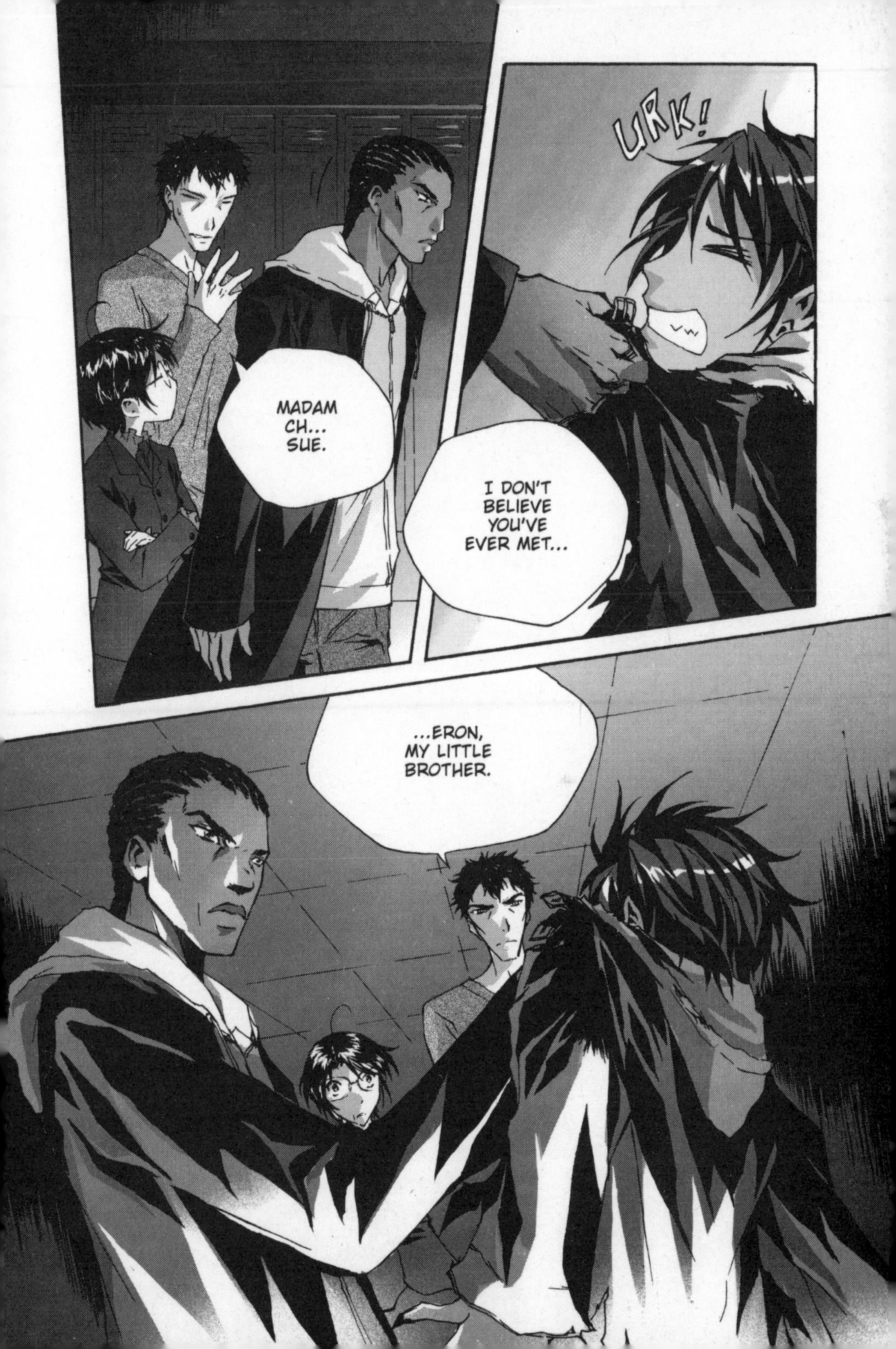
MADAM CH... SUE.
URK!
I DON'T BELIEVE YOU'VE EVER MET...
...ERON, MY LITTLE BROTHER.

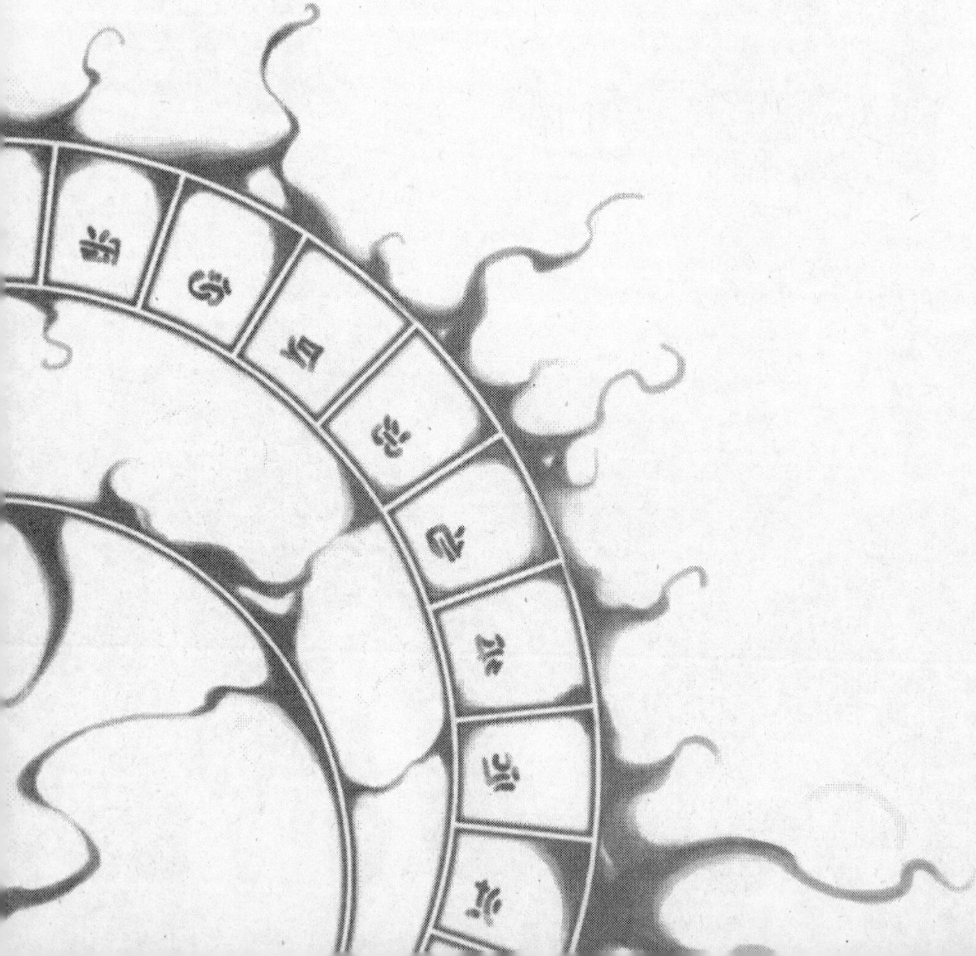

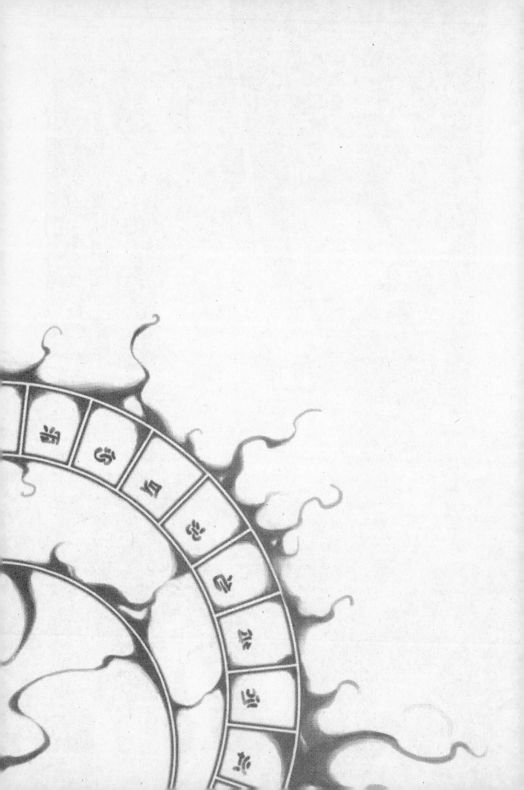

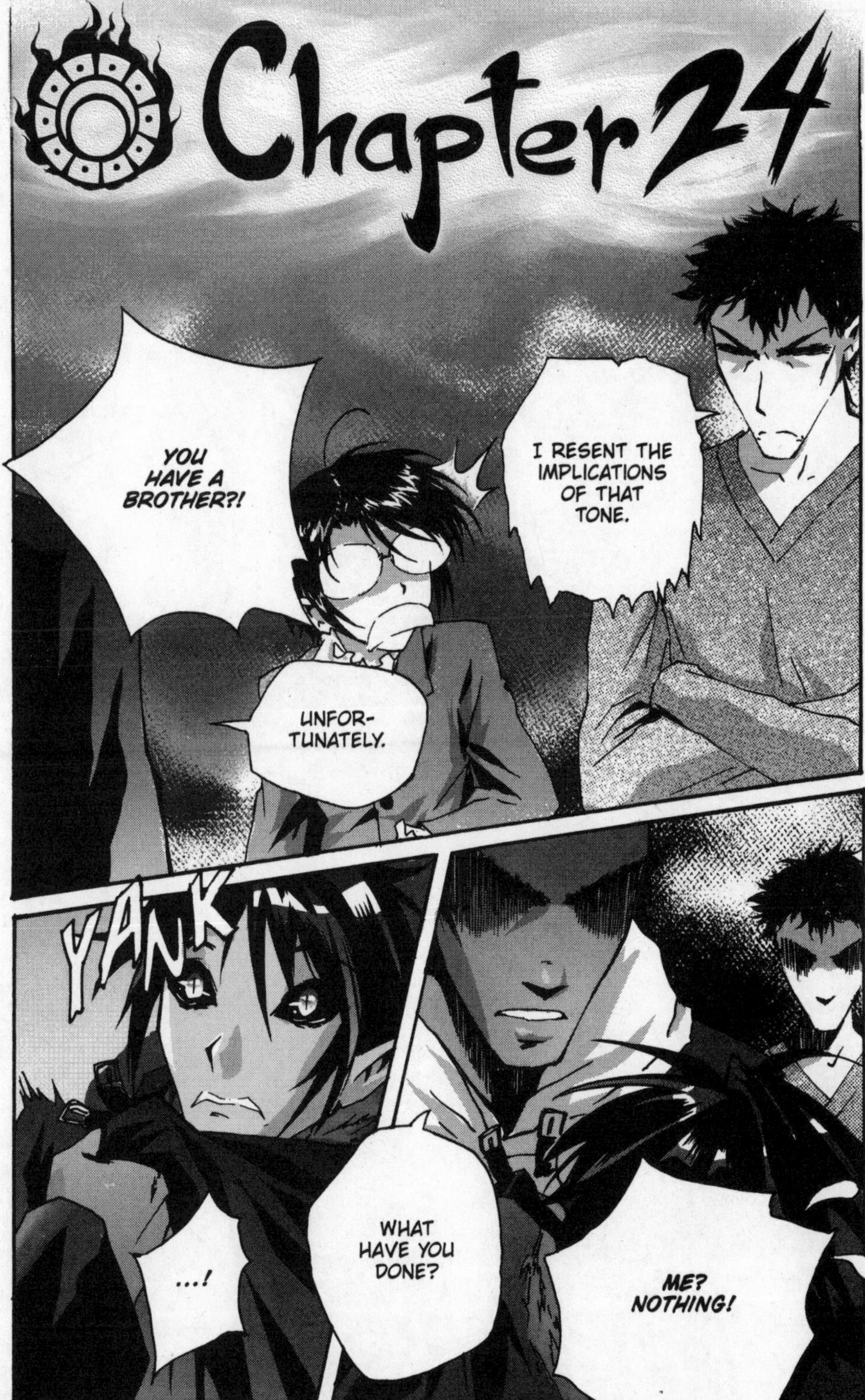
Chapter 24
YOU HAVE A BROTHER?!
I RESENT THE IMPLICATIONS OF THAT TONE.
UNFORTUNATELY.
YANK
...!
WHAT HAVE YOU DONE?
ME? NOTHING!

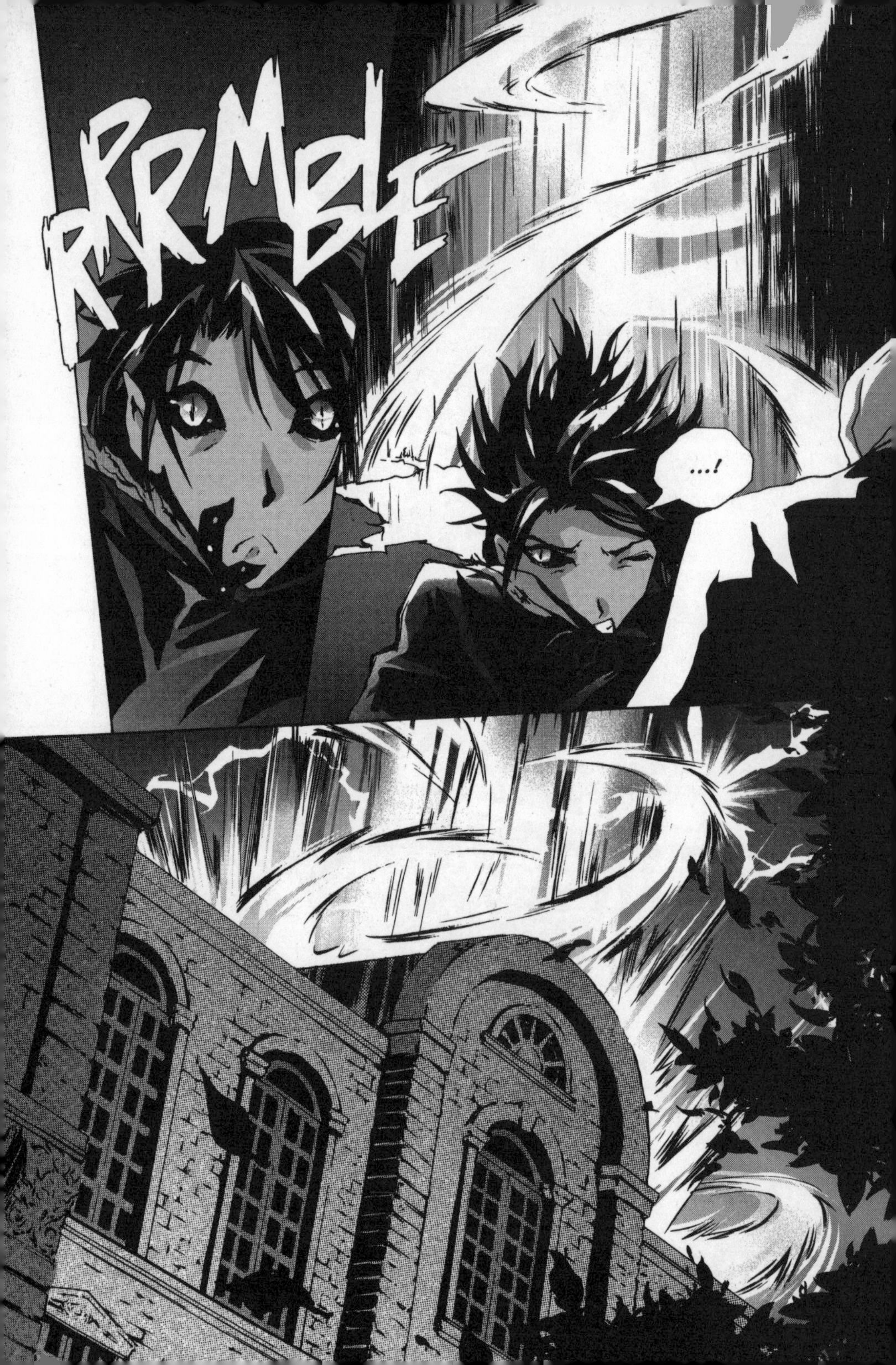
RRRMBLE
...!

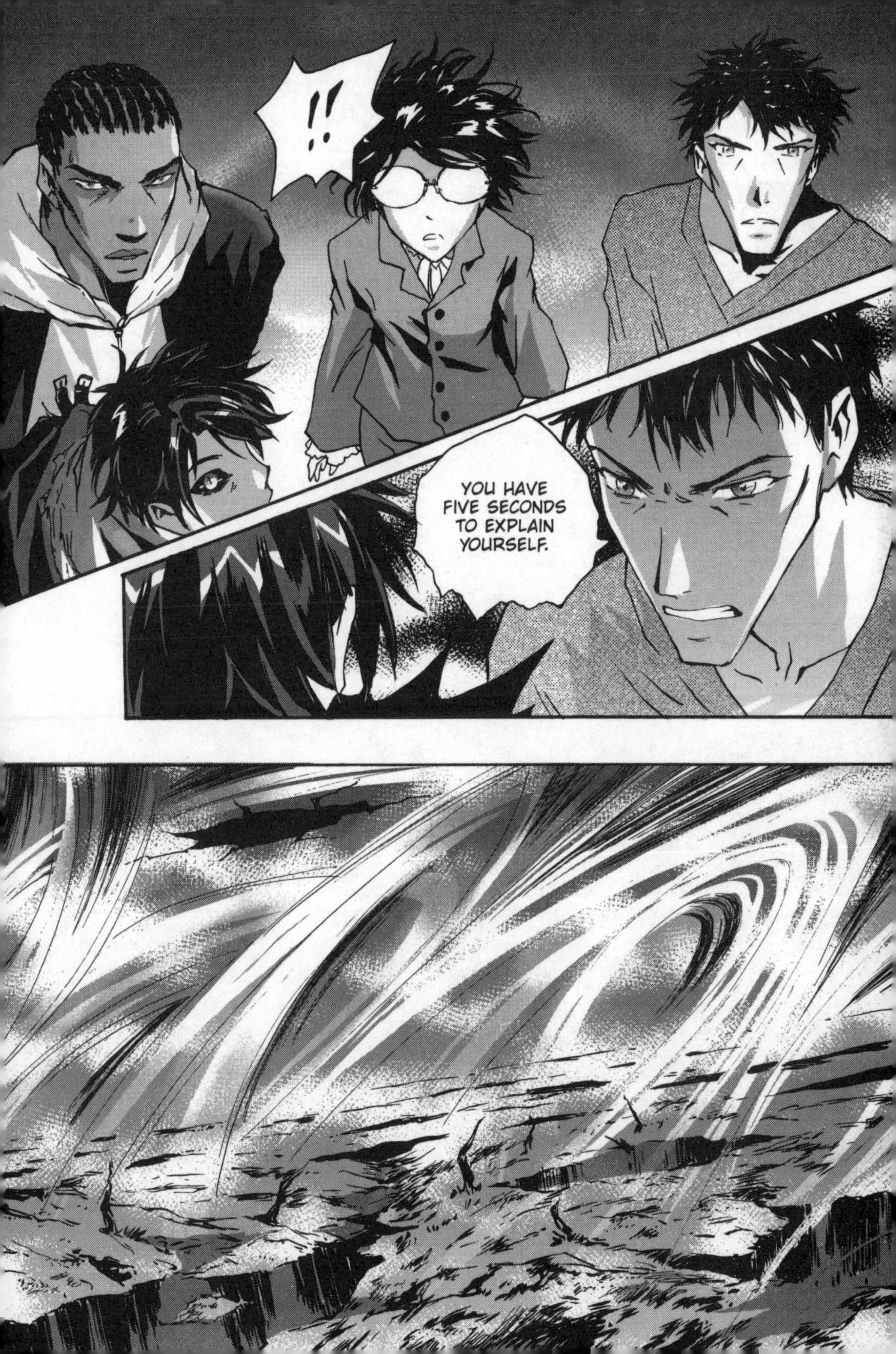
!!
YOU HAVE FIVE SECONDS TO EXPLAIN YOURSELF.

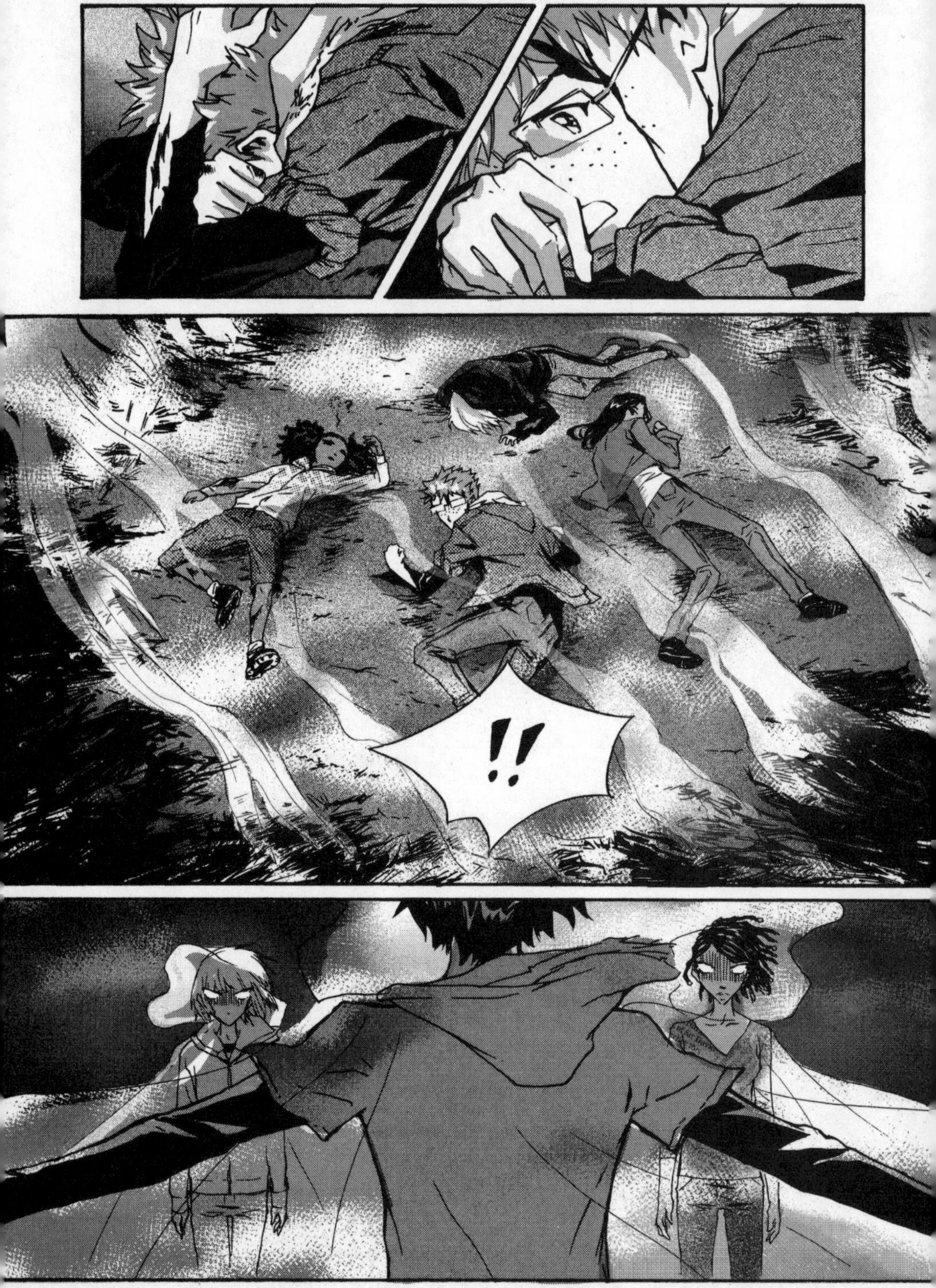
!!

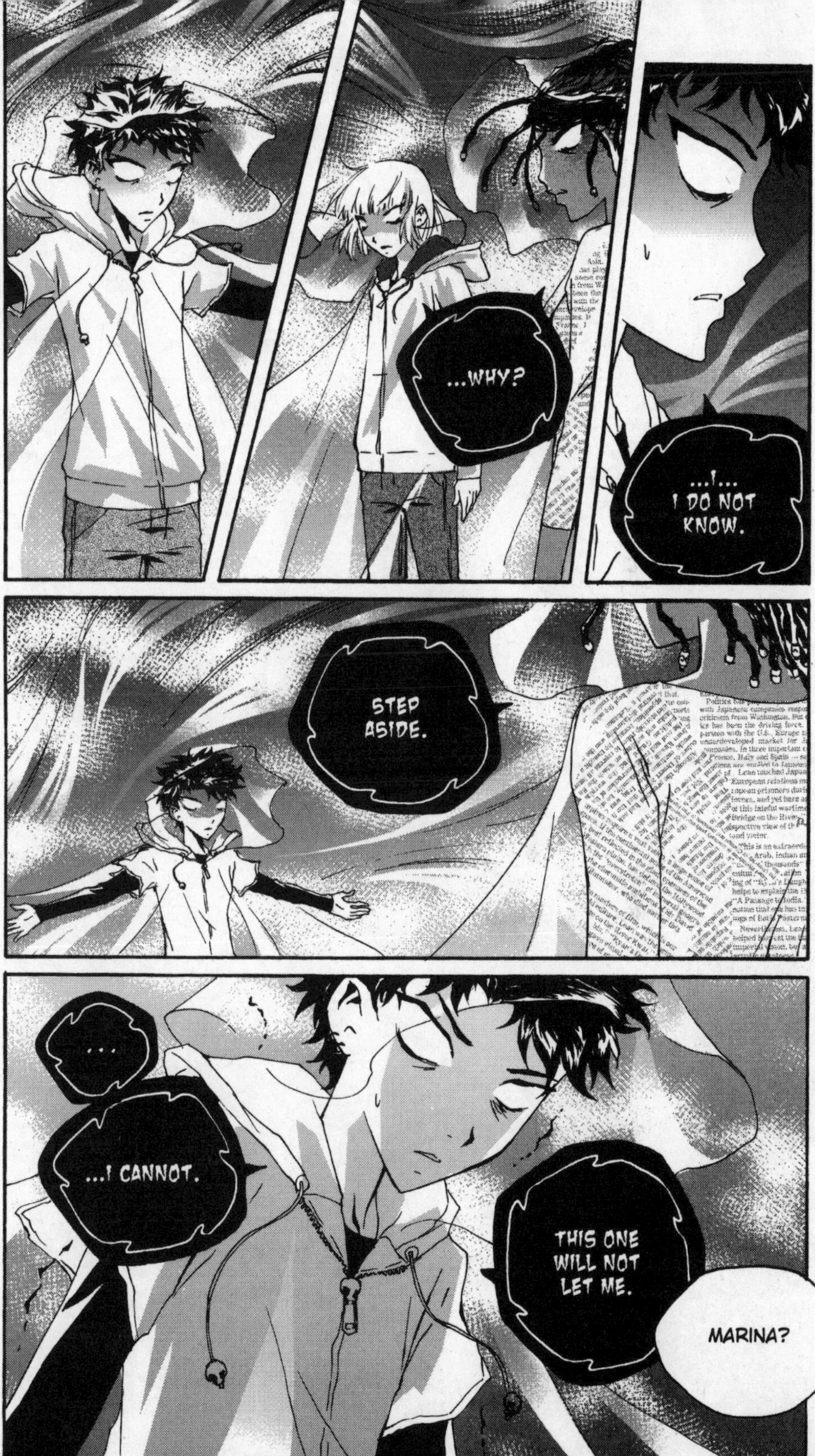
...WHY?
...I... I DO NOT KNOW.
STEP ASIDE.
...
...I CANNOT.
THIS ONE WILL NOT LET ME.
MARINA?

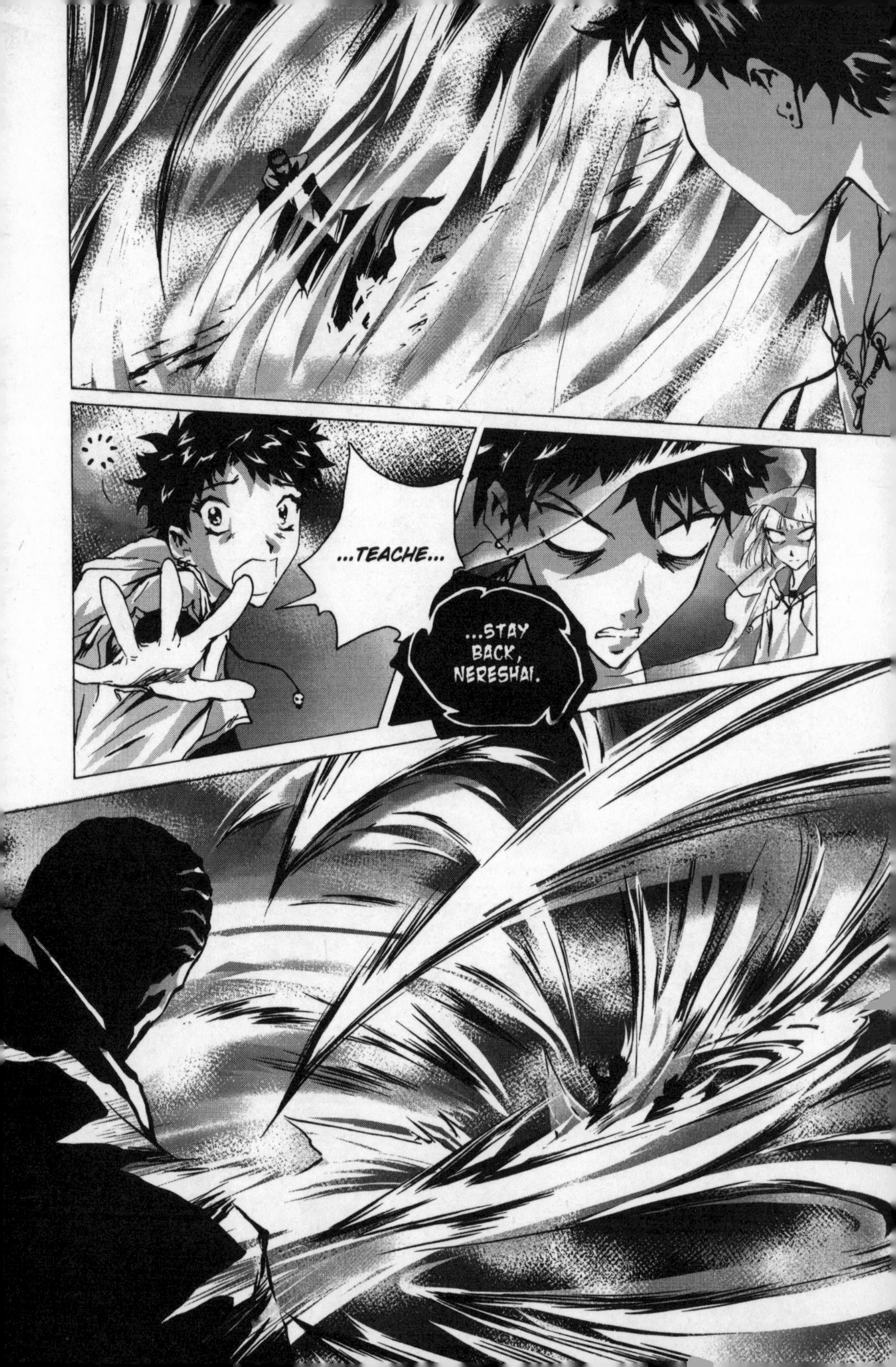
...TEACHE...
...STAY BACK, NERESHAI.

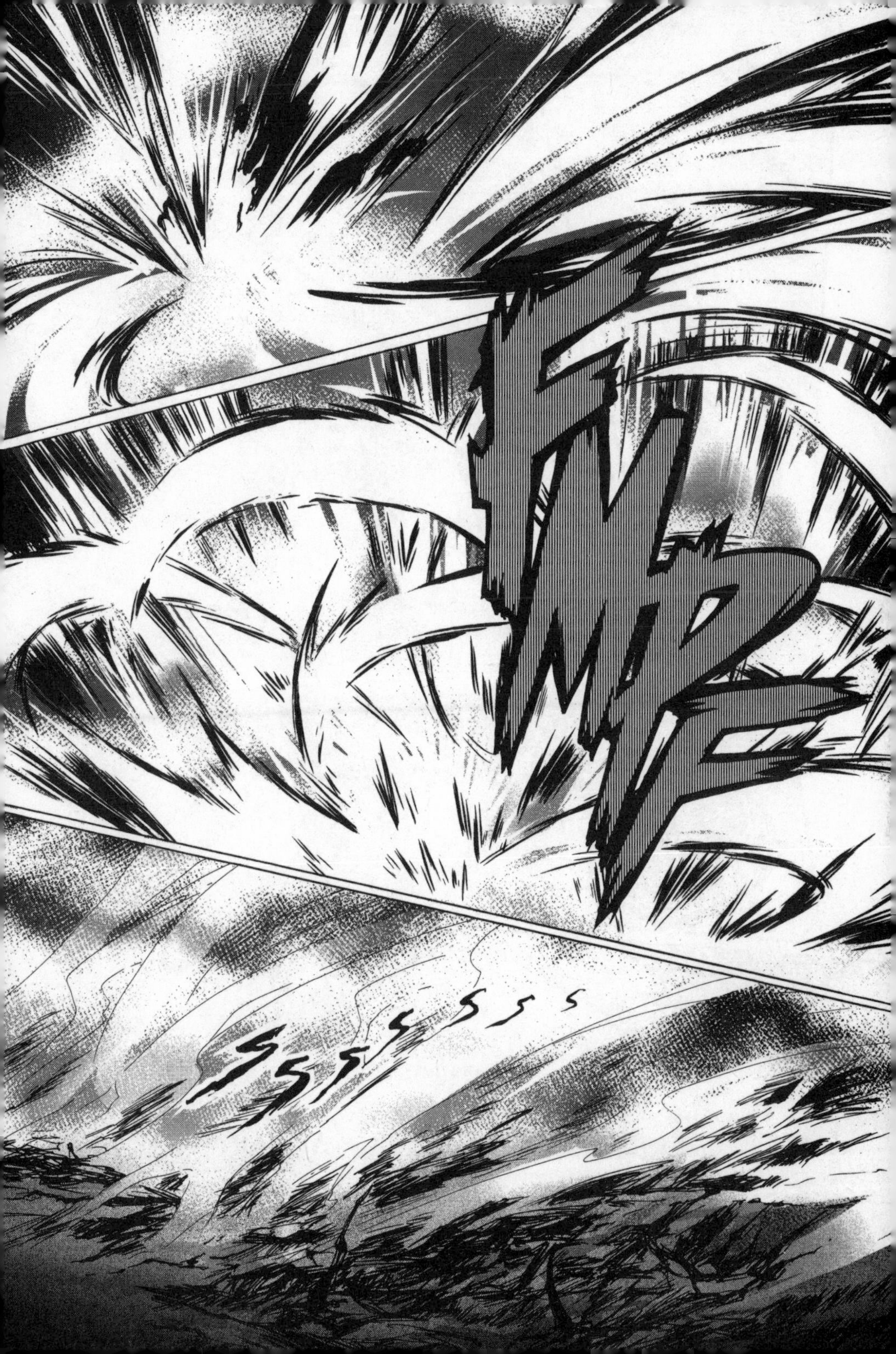
FWIP
SSSSSSS

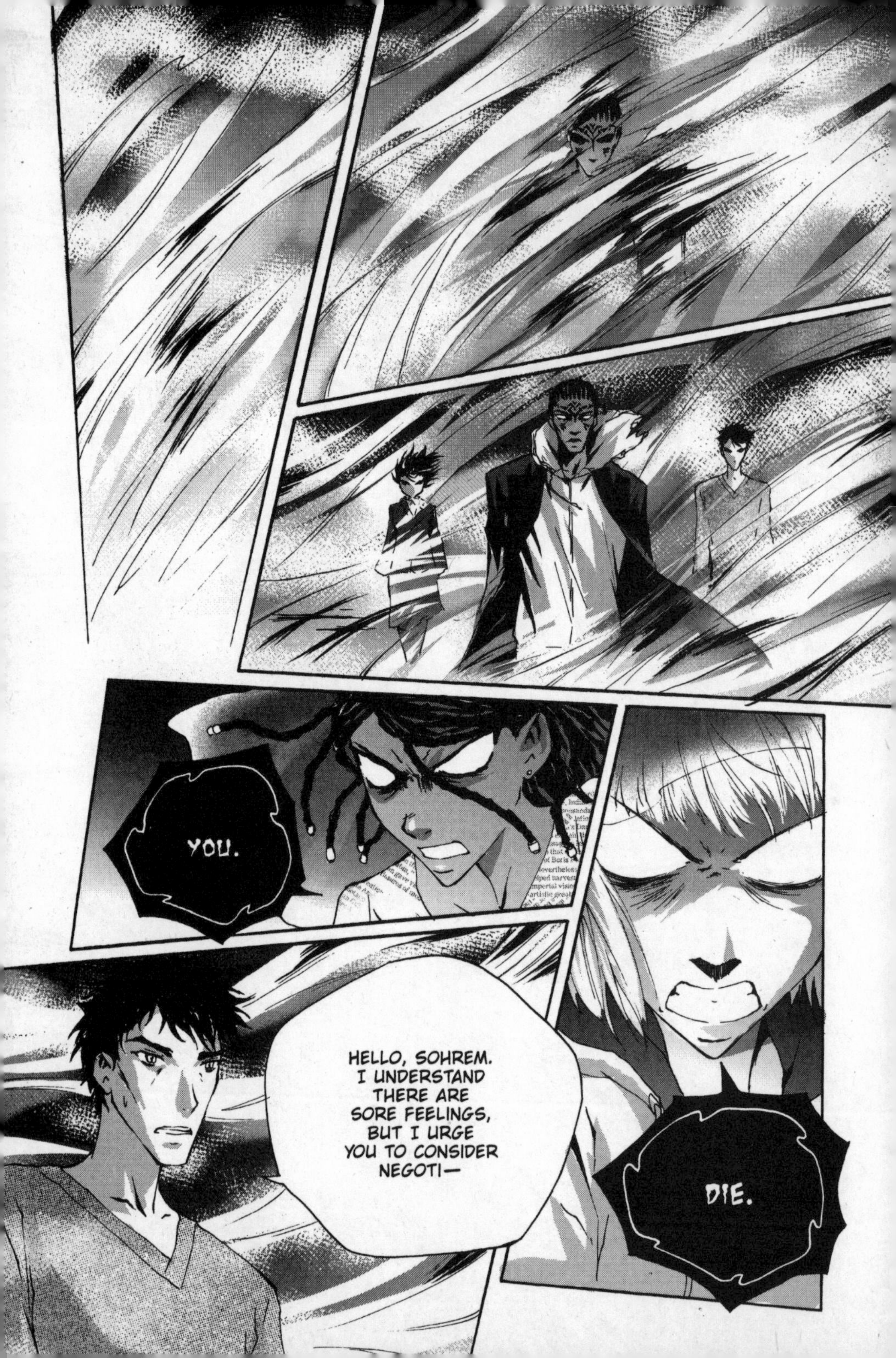
YOU.
HELLO, SOHREM. I UNDERSTAND THERE ARE SORE FEELINGS, BUT I URGE YOU TO CONSIDER NEGOTI—
DIE.

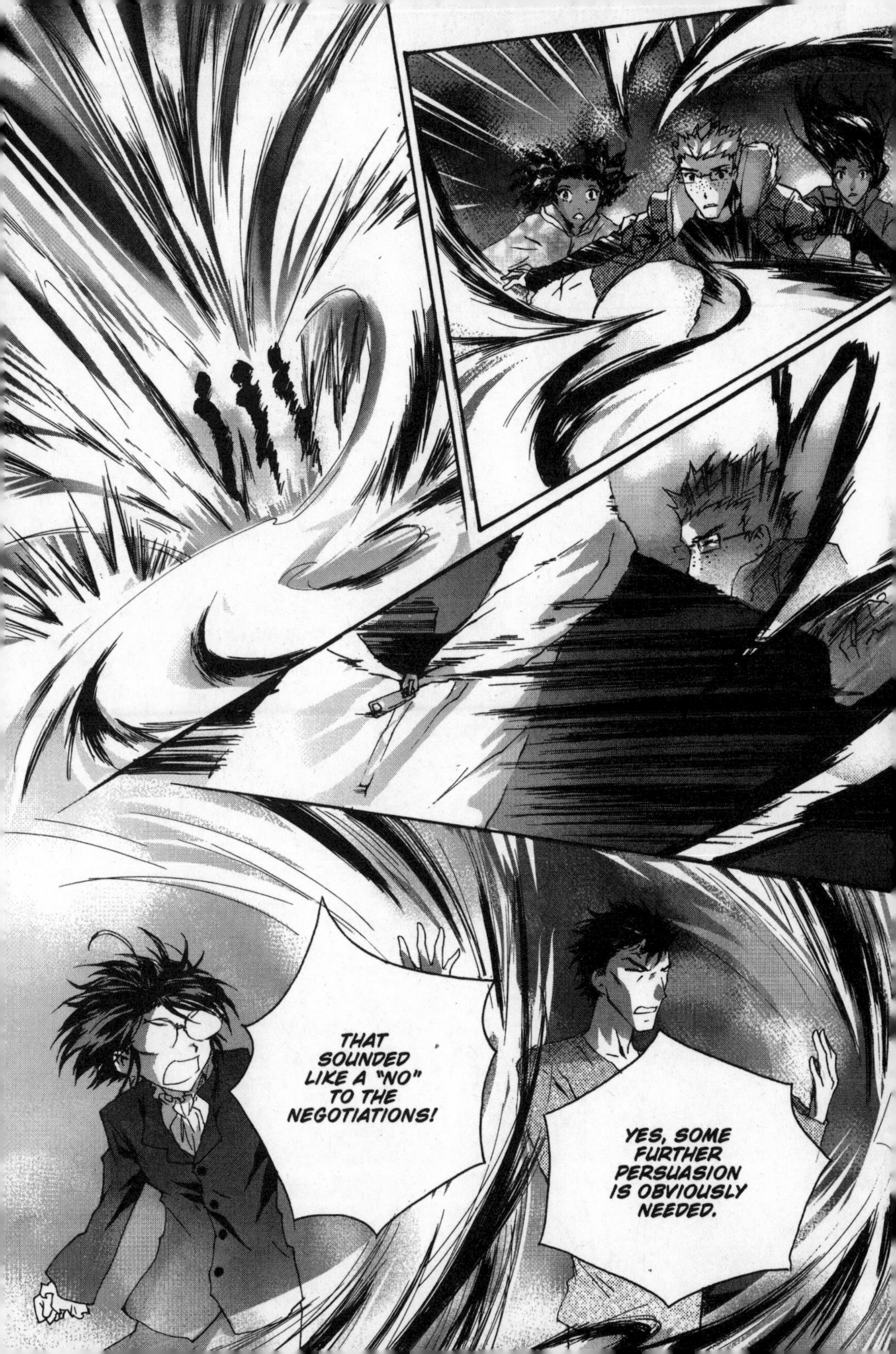
THAT SOUNDED LIKE A "NO" TO THE NEGOTIATIONS!
YES, SOME FURTHER PERSUASION IS OBVIOUSLY NEEDED.

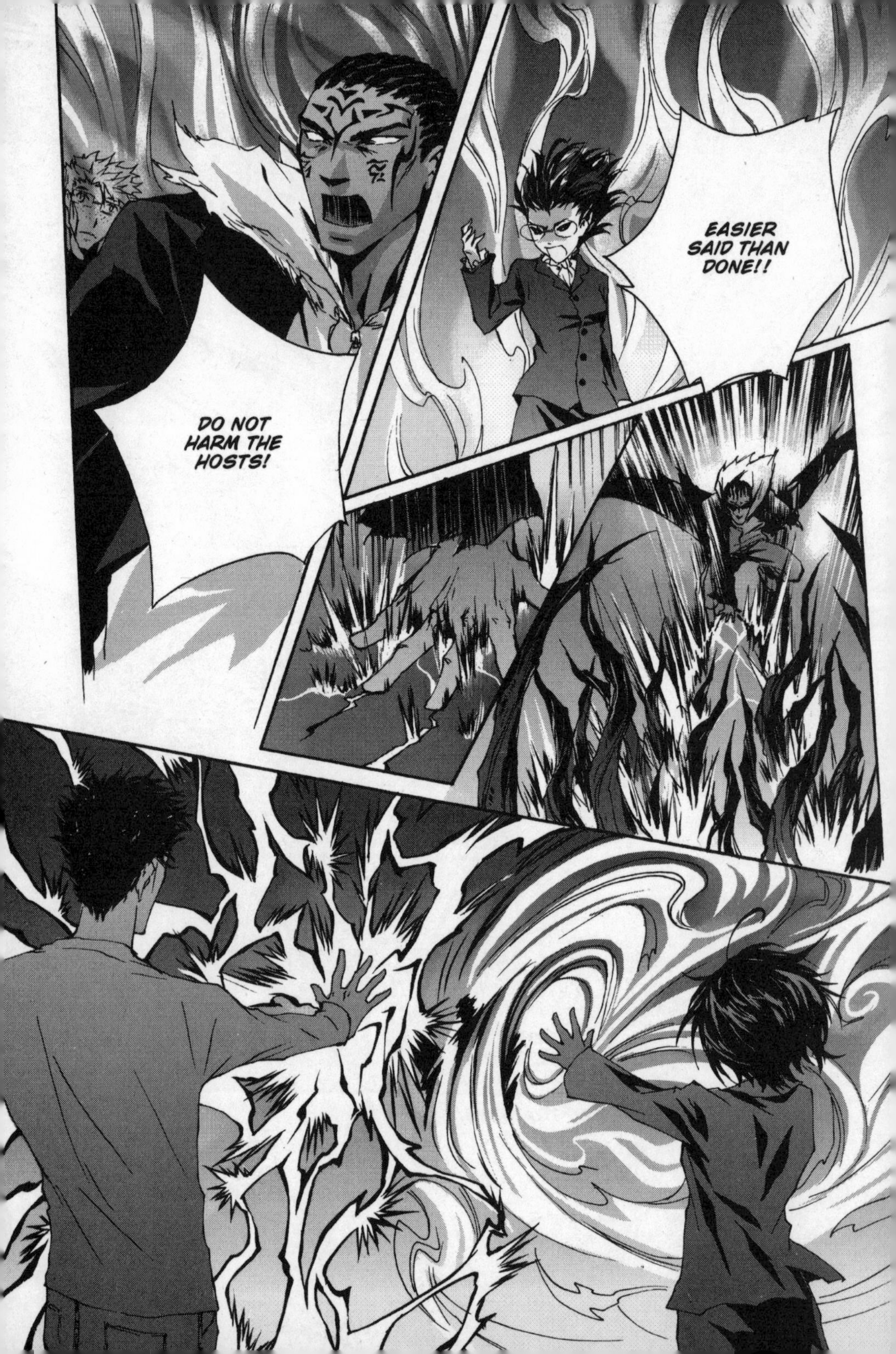
DO NOT HARM THE HOSTS!
EASIER SAID THAN DONE!!

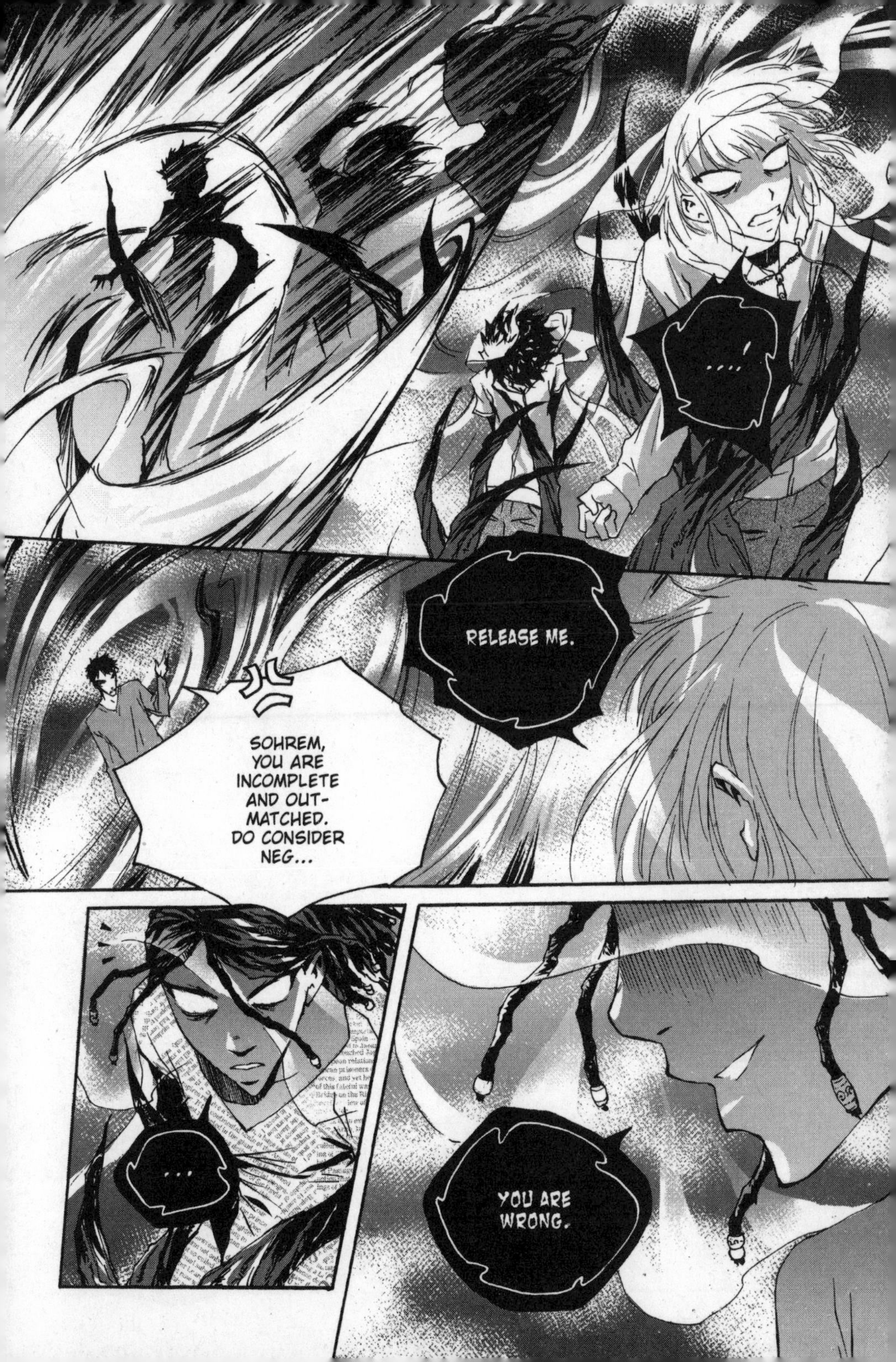
....
SOHREM, YOU ARE INCOMPLETE AND OUT-MATCHED. DO CONSIDER NEG...
RELEASE ME.
...
YOU ARE WRONG.

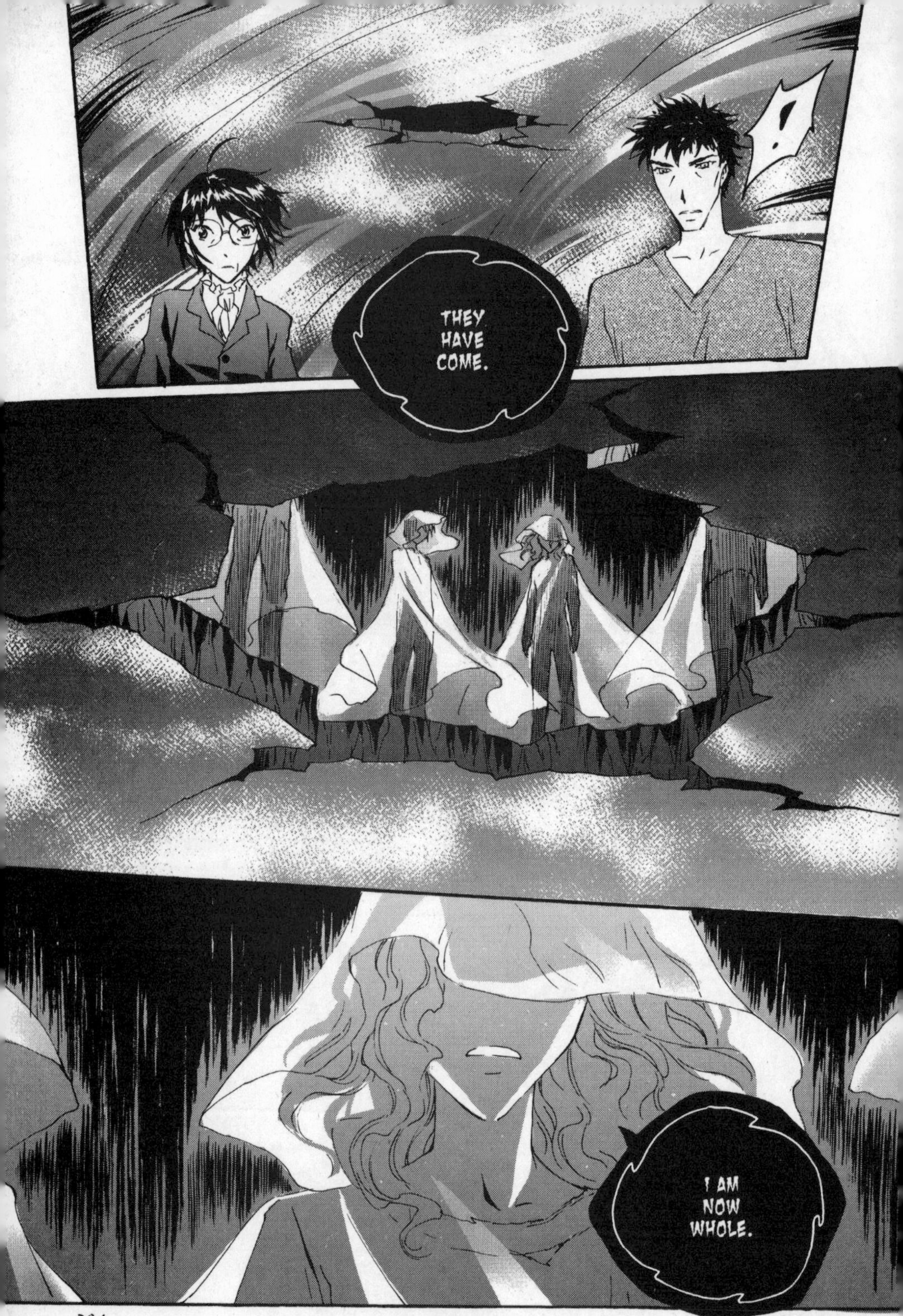
!
THEY HAVE COME.
I AM NOW WHOLE.

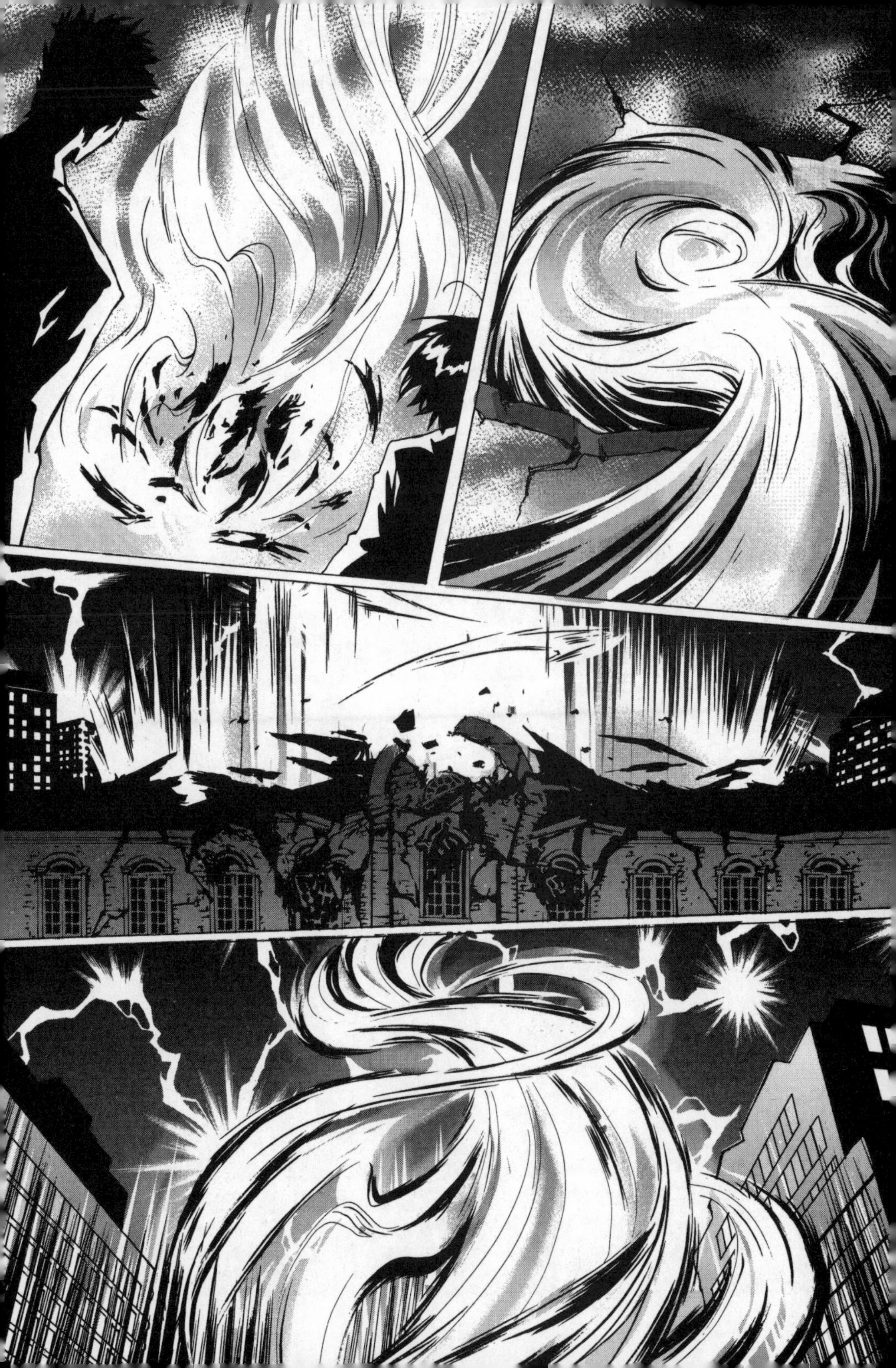

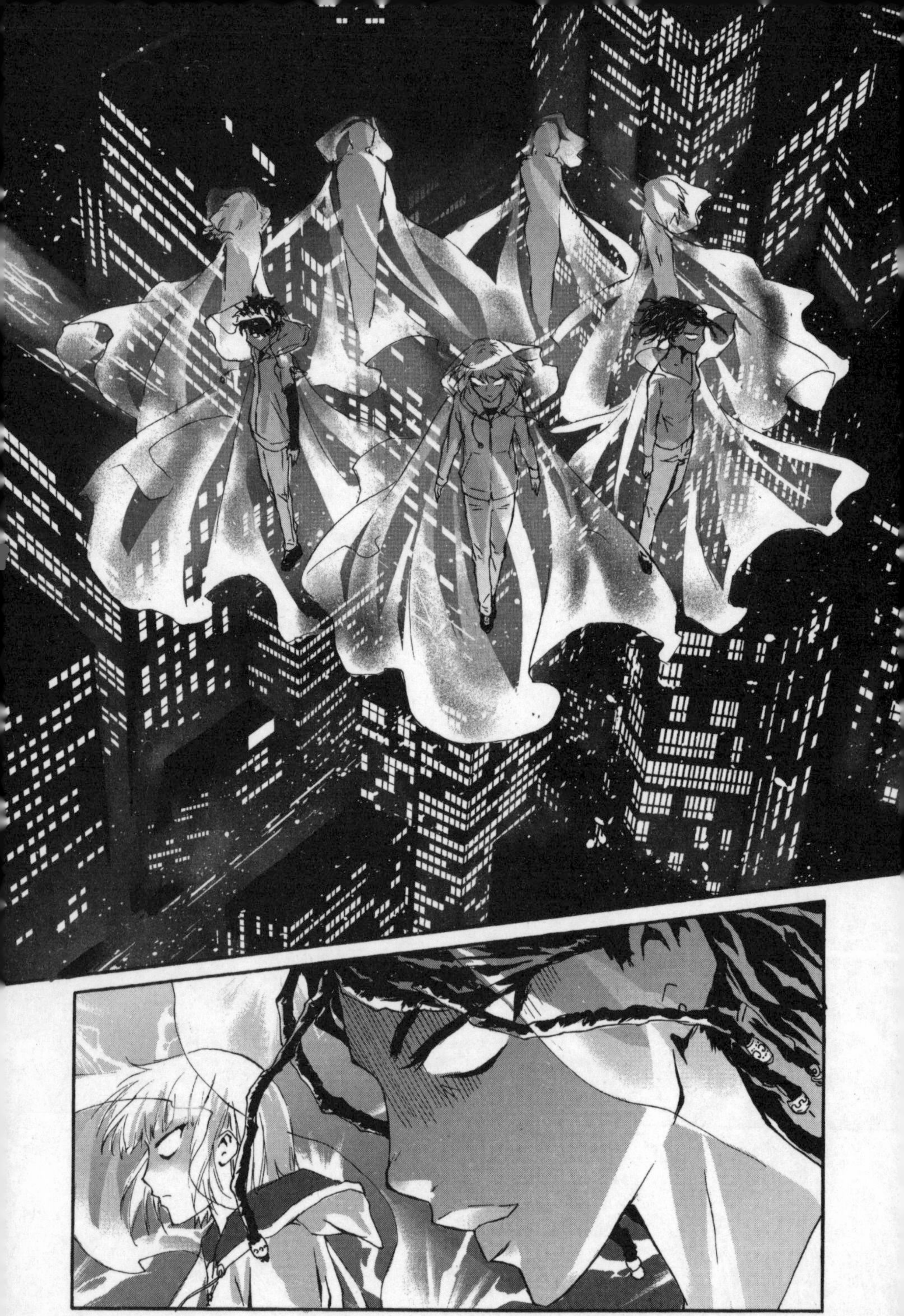

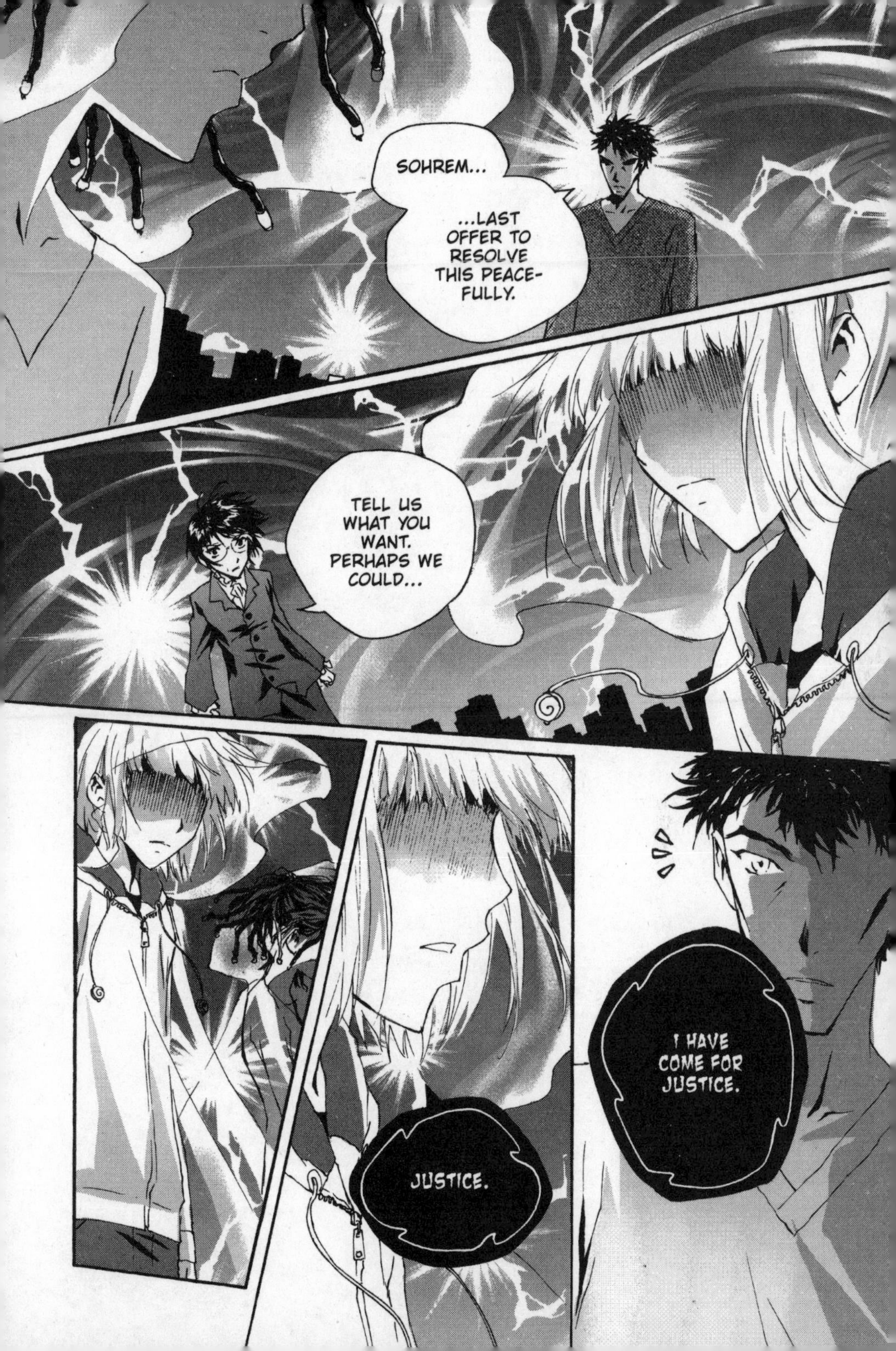
SOHREM...
...LAST OFFER TO RESOLVE THIS PEACE-FULLY.
TELL US WHAT YOU WANT. PERHAPS WE COULD...
JUSTICE.
I HAVE COME FOR JUSTICE.

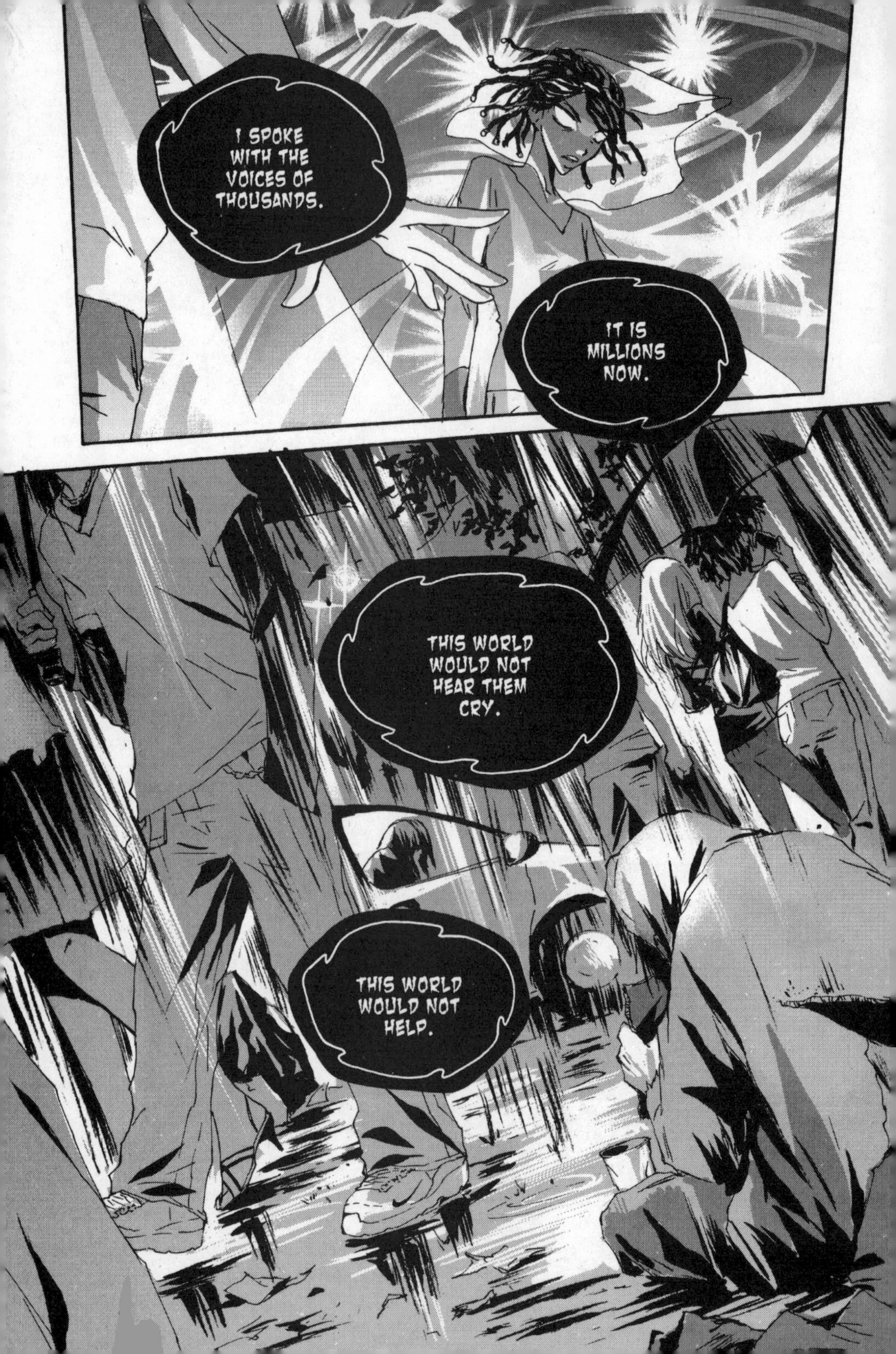
I SPOKE WITH THE VOICES OF THOUSANDS.
IT IS MILLIONS NOW.
THIS WORLD WOULD NOT HEAR THEM CRY.
THIS WORLD WOULD NOT HELP.

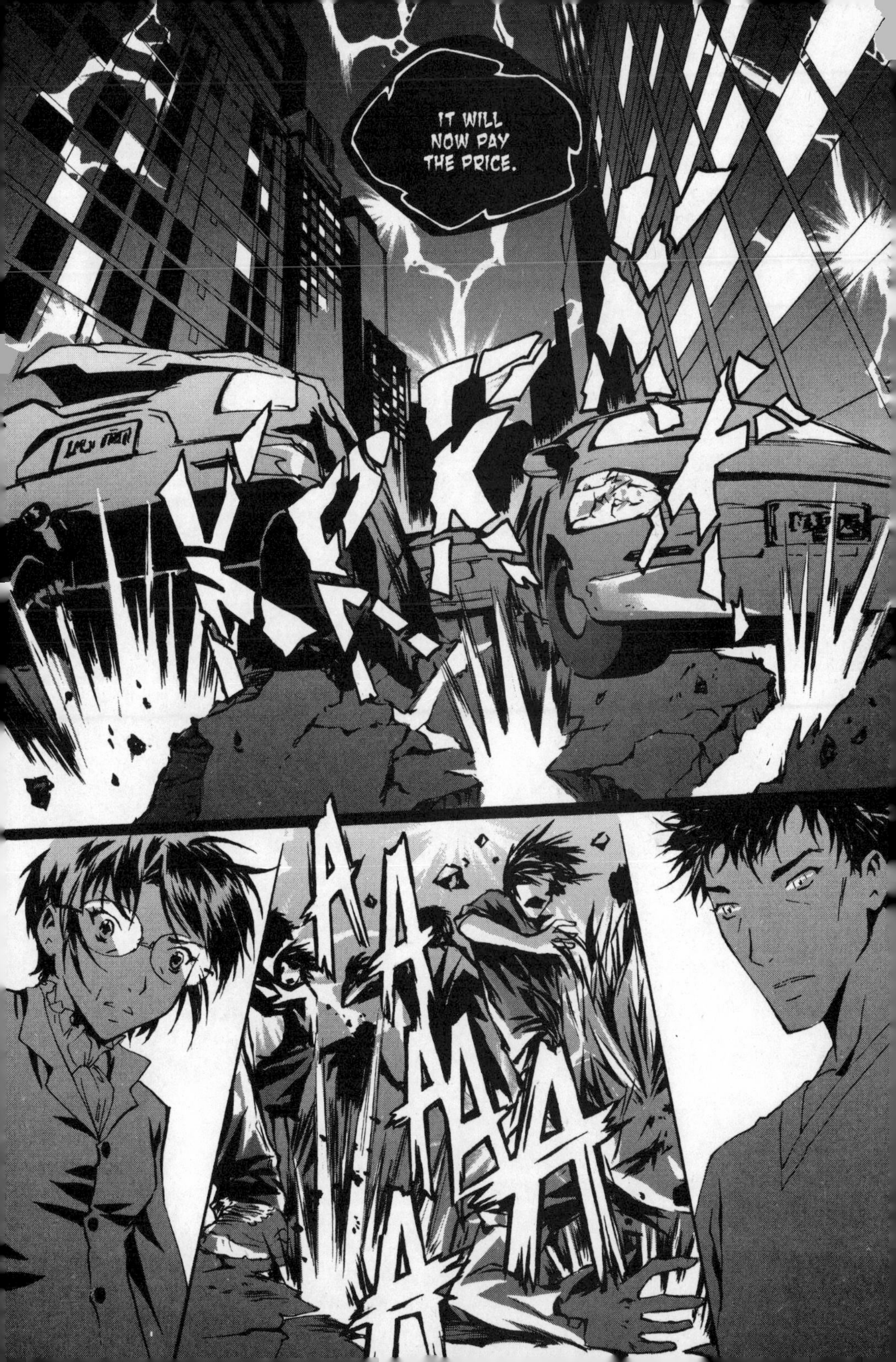
IT WILL NOW PAY THE PRICE.

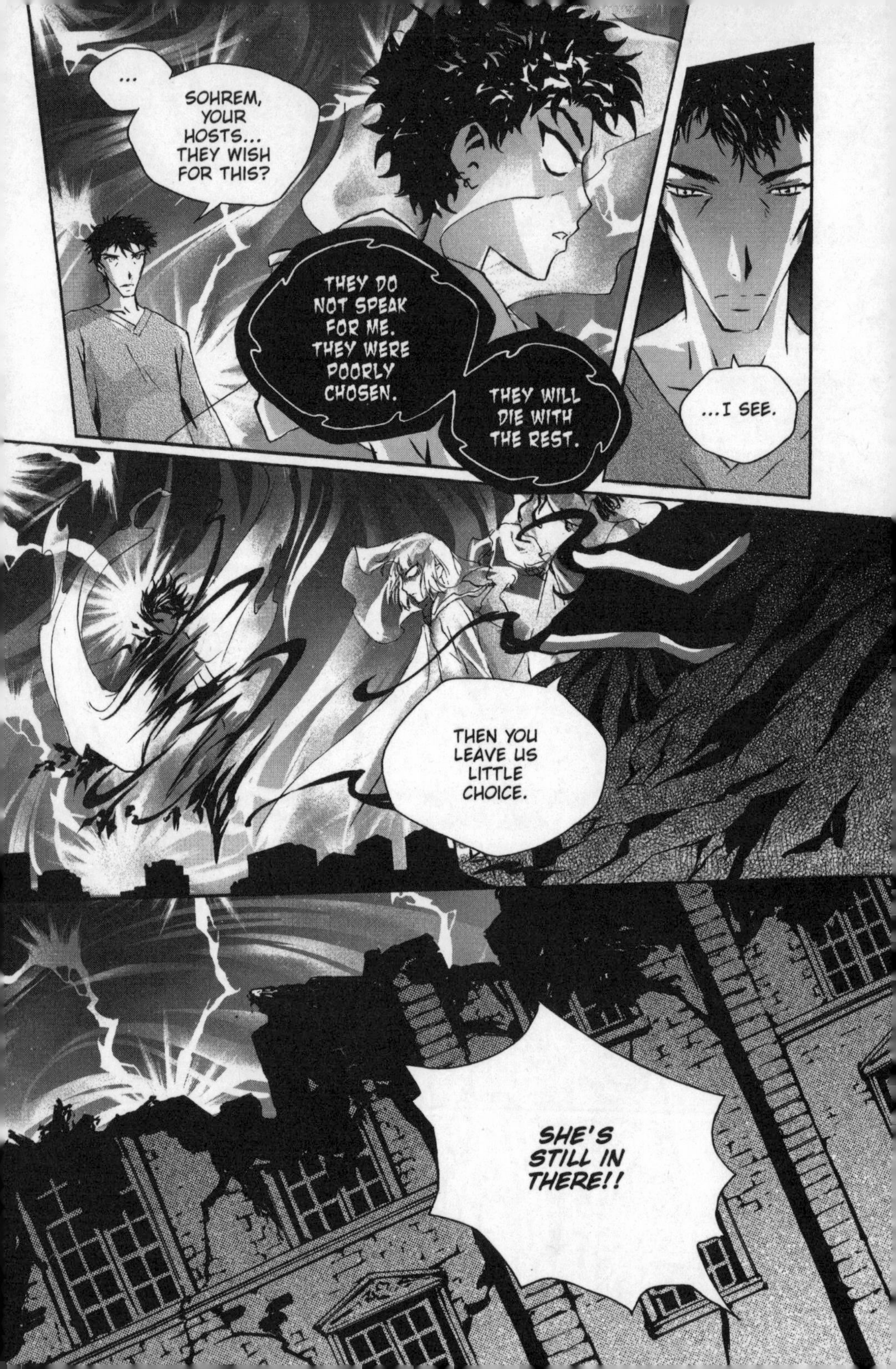
...
SOHREM, YOUR HOSTS... THEY WISH FOR THIS?
THEY DO NOT SPEAK FOR ME. THEY WERE POORLY CHOSEN.
THEY WILL DIE WITH THE REST.
...I SEE.
THEN YOU LEAVE US LITTLE CHOICE.
SHE'S STILL IN THERE!!

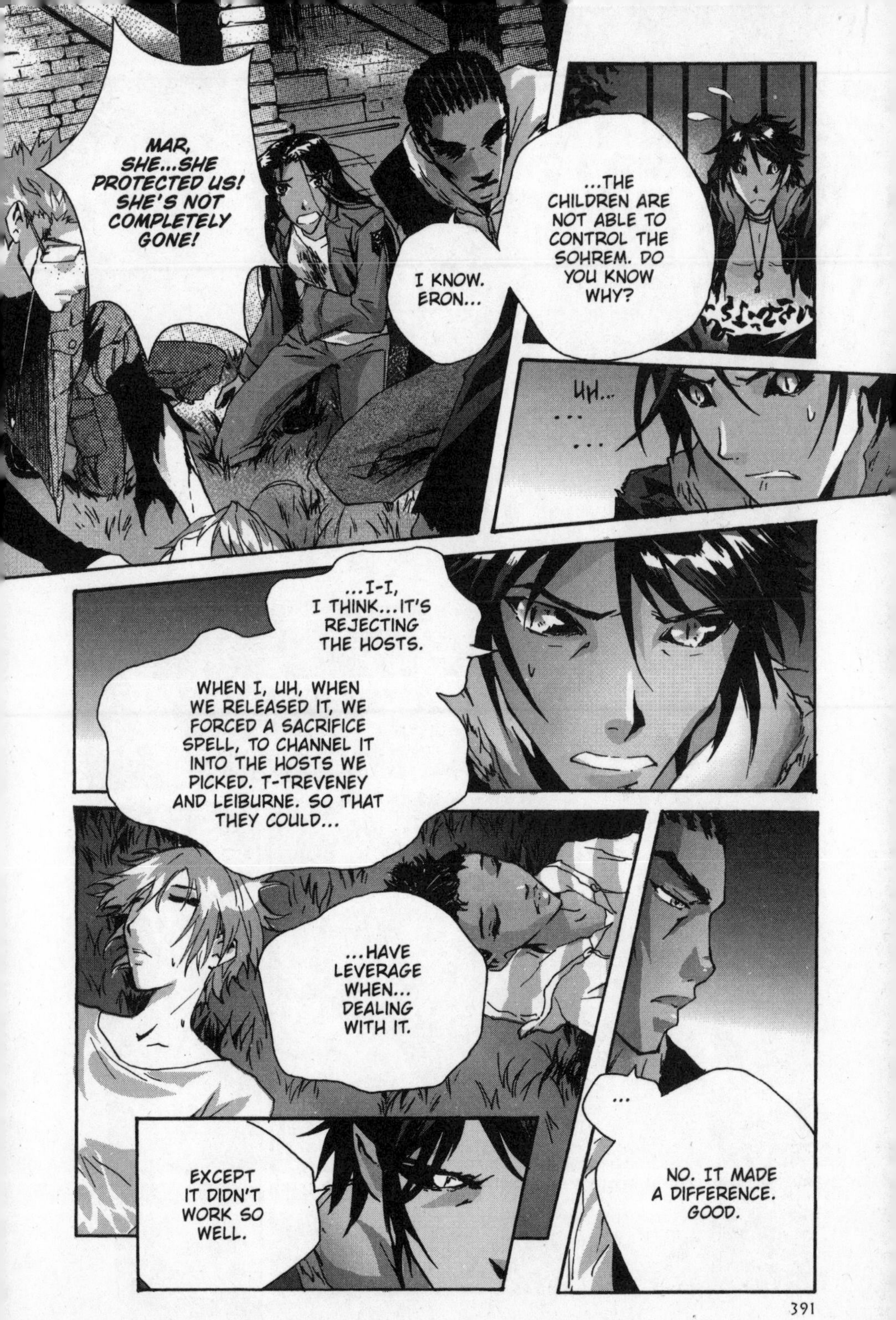
MAR, SHE...SHE PROTECTED US! SHE'S NOT COMPLETELY GONE!
I KNOW. ERON...
...THE CHILDREN ARE NOT ABLE TO CONTROL THE SOHREM. DO YOU KNOW WHY?
UH...
...
...
...I-I, I THINK...IT'S REJECTING THE HOSTS.
WHEN I, UH, WHEN WE RELEASED IT, WE FORCED A SACRIFICE SPELL, TO CHANNEL IT INTO THE HOSTS WE PICKED. T-TREVENEY AND LEIBURNE. SO THAT THEY COULD...
...HAVE LEVERAGE WHEN... DEALING WITH IT.
EXCEPT IT DIDN'T WORK SO WELL.
...
NO. IT MADE A DIFFERENCE. GOOD.

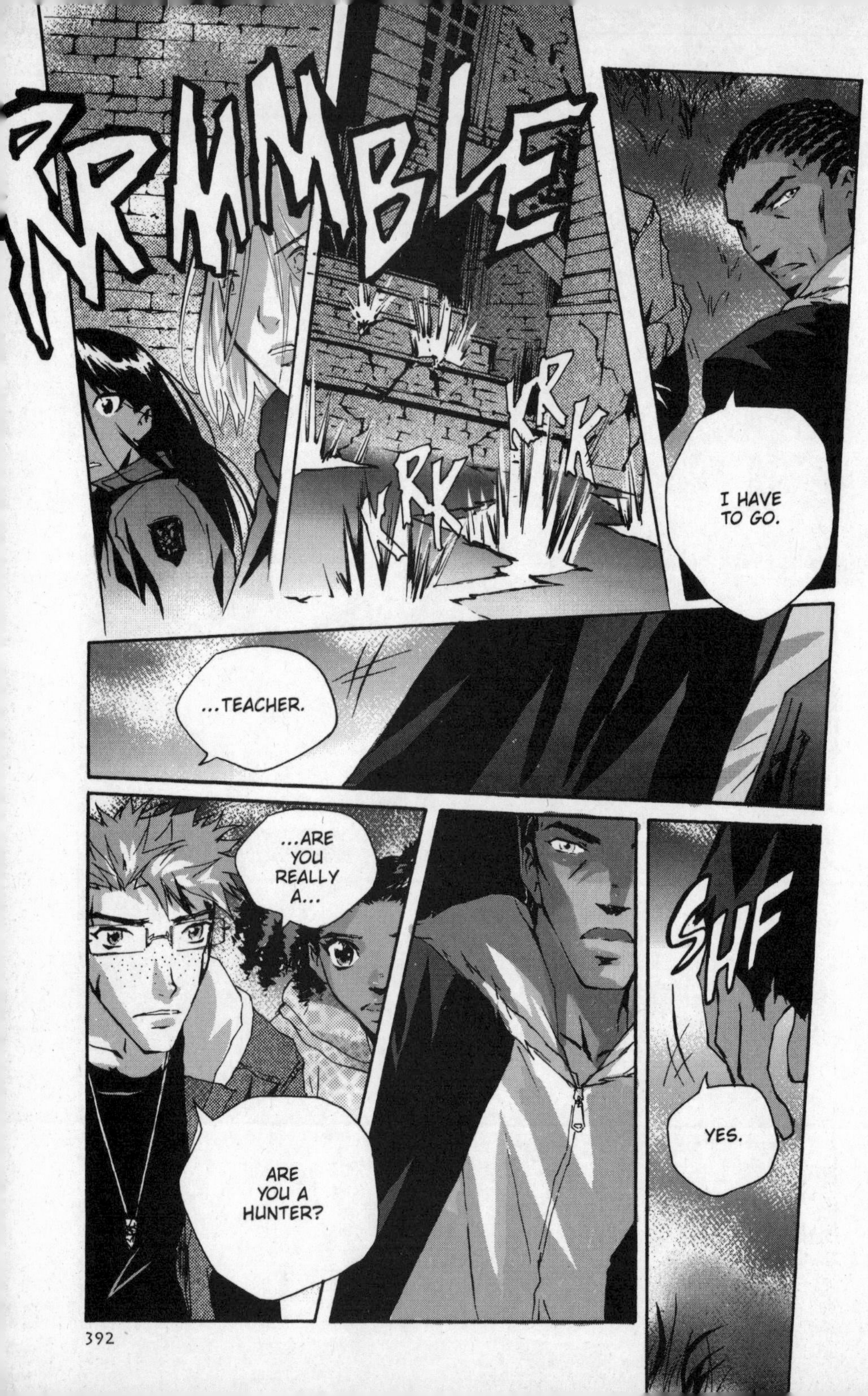
RRUMBLE
KRK
KRK
I HAVE TO GO.
...TEACHER.
...ARE YOU REALLY A...
ARE YOU A HUNTER?
SHF
YES.

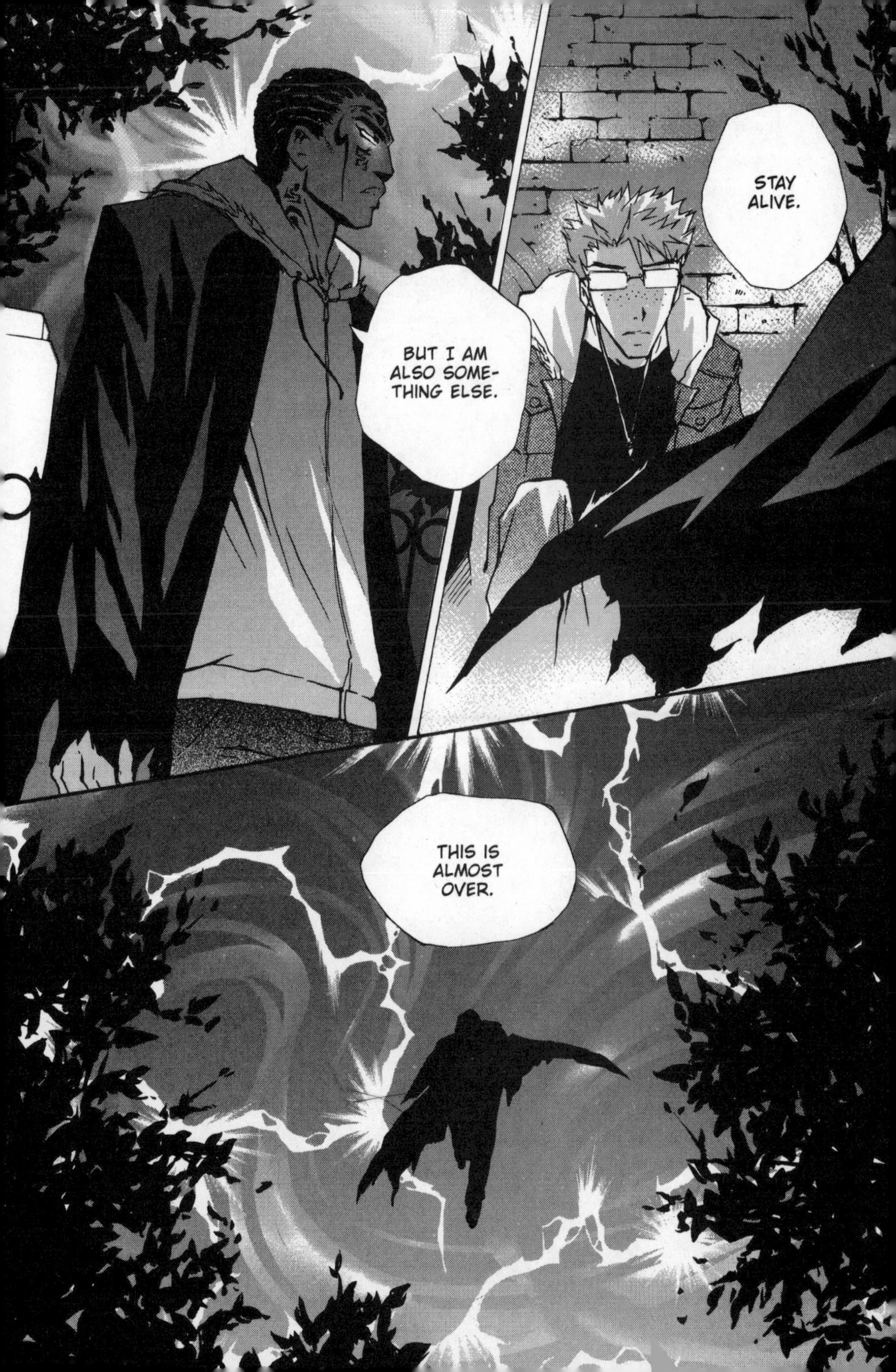
BUT I AM ALSO SOME-THING ELSE.
STAY ALIVE.
THIS IS ALMOST OVER.

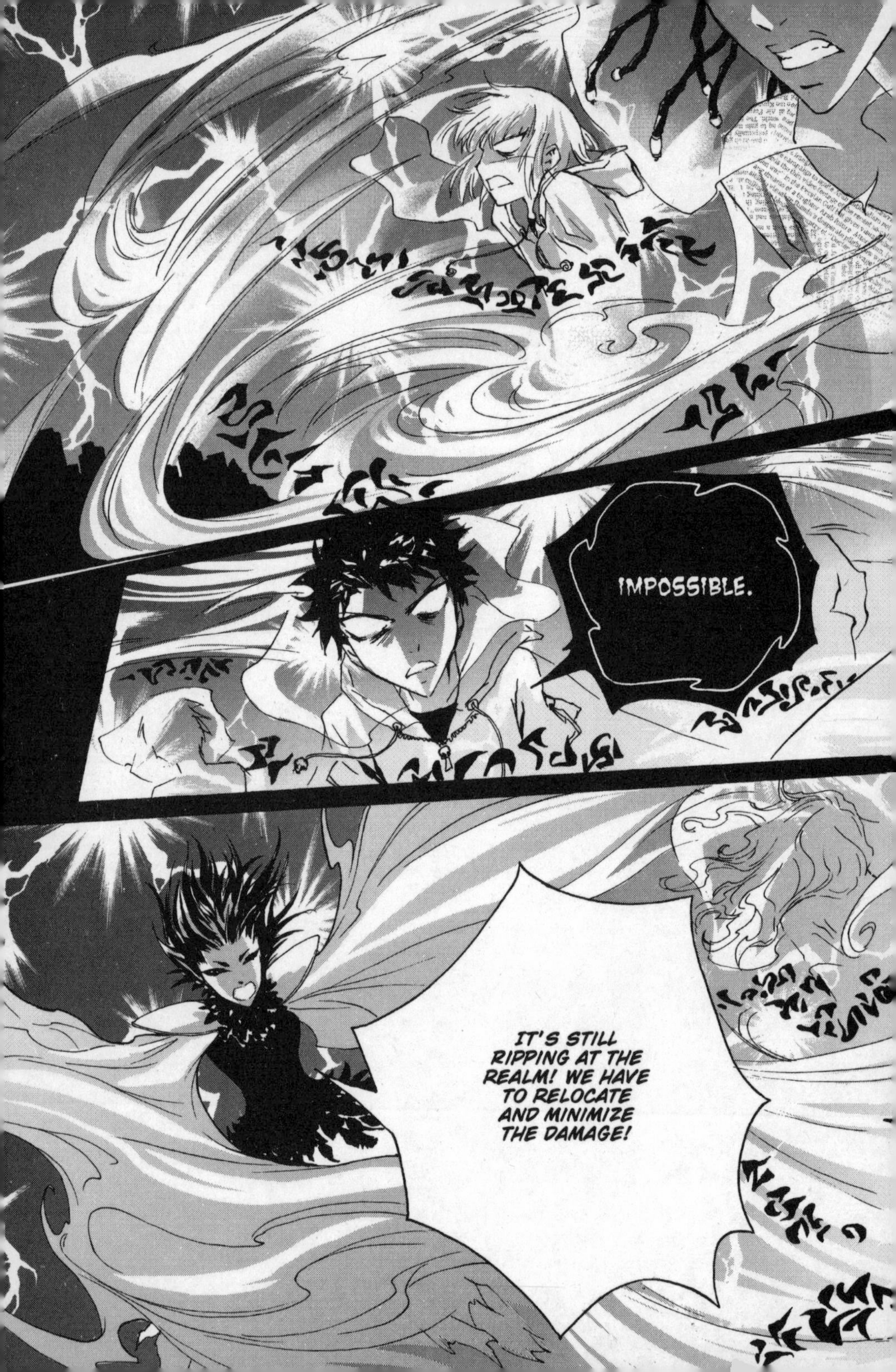
IMPOSSIBLE.
IT'S STILL RIPPING AT THE REALM! WE HAVE TO RELOCATE AND MINIMIZE THE DAMAGE!

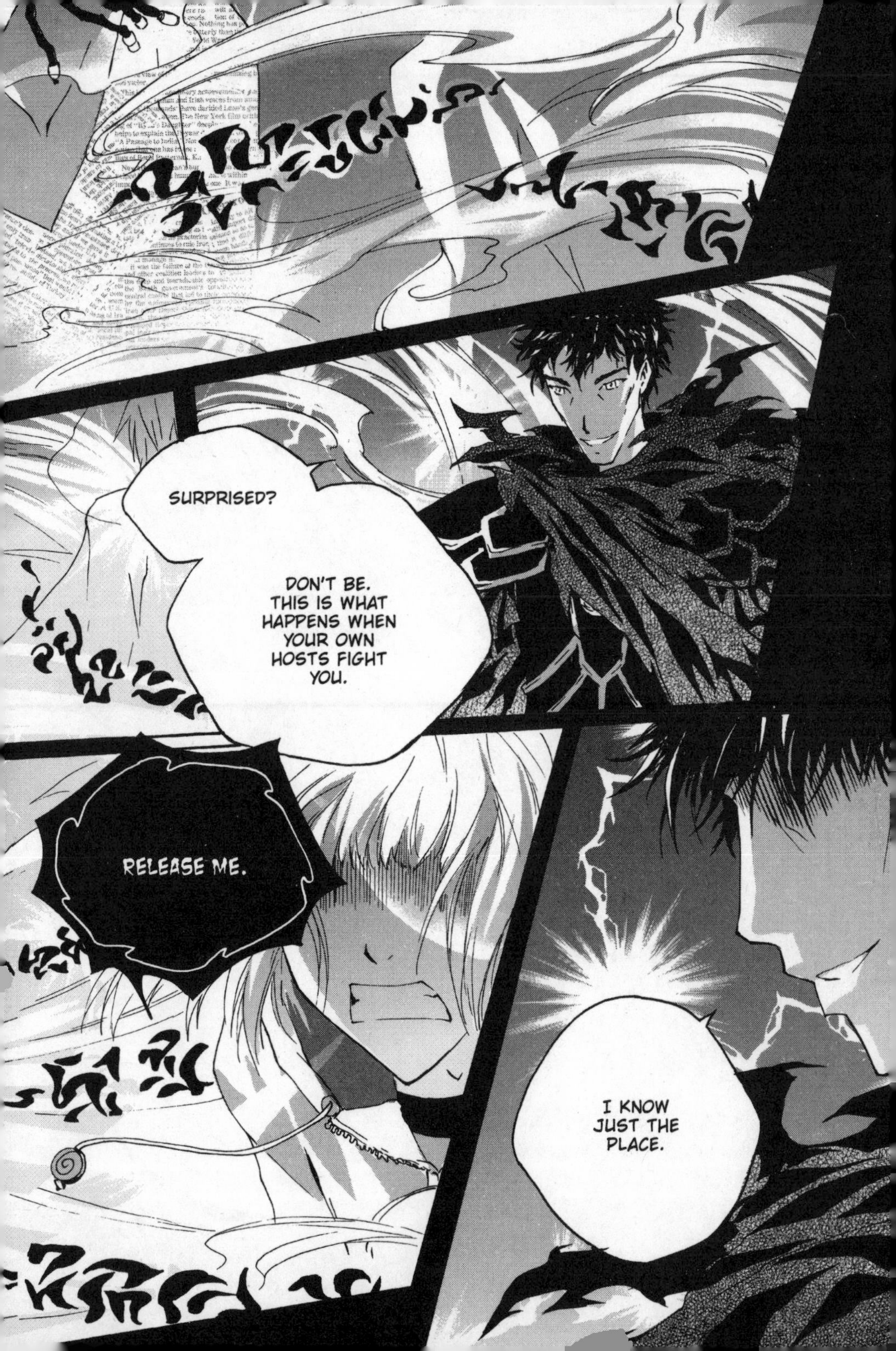
SURPRISED?
DON'T BE. THIS IS WHAT HAPPENS WHEN YOUR OWN HOSTS FIGHT YOU.
RELEASE ME.
I KNOW JUST THE PLACE.

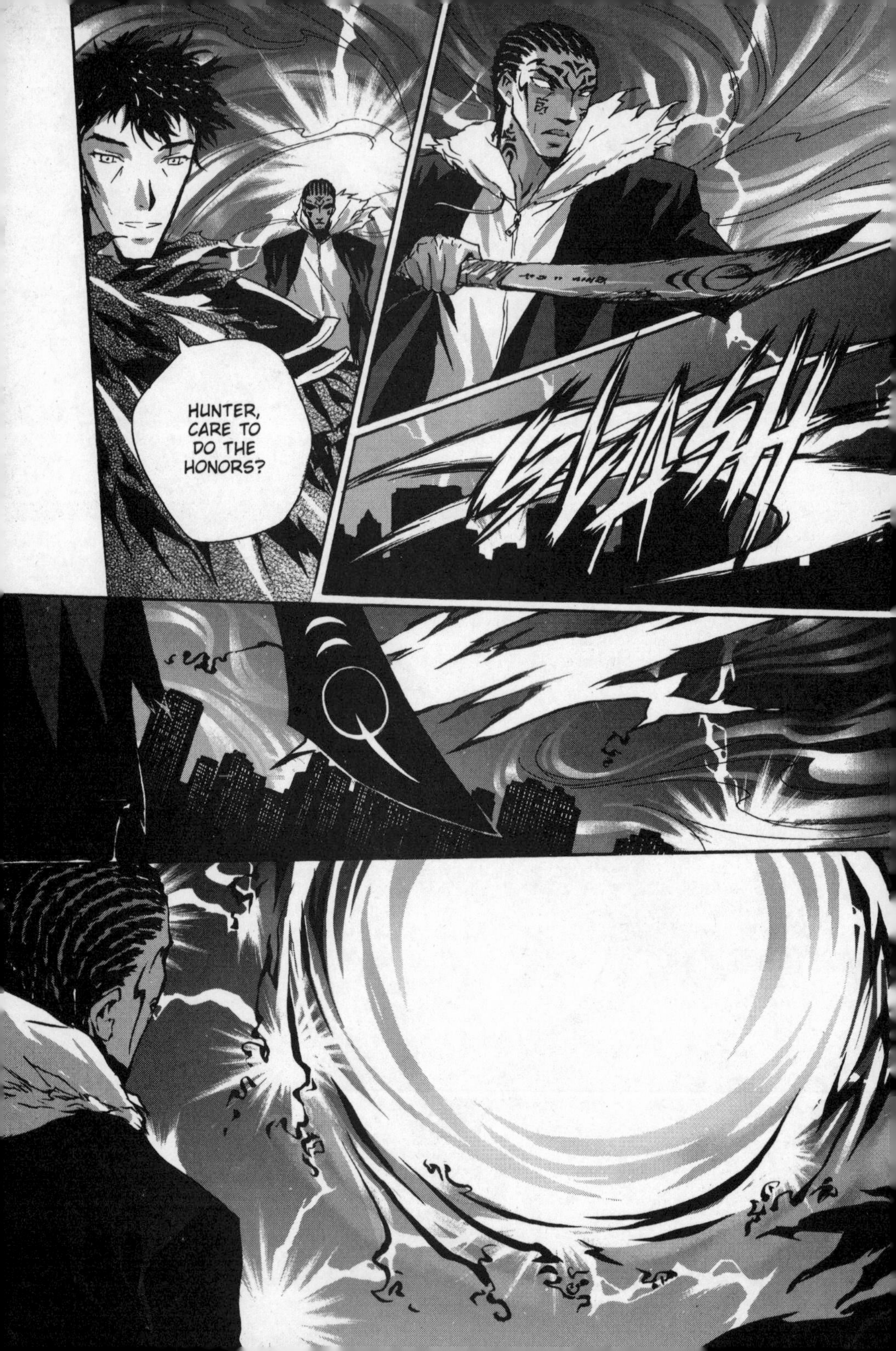
HUNTER, CARE TO DO THE HONORS?
SLASH

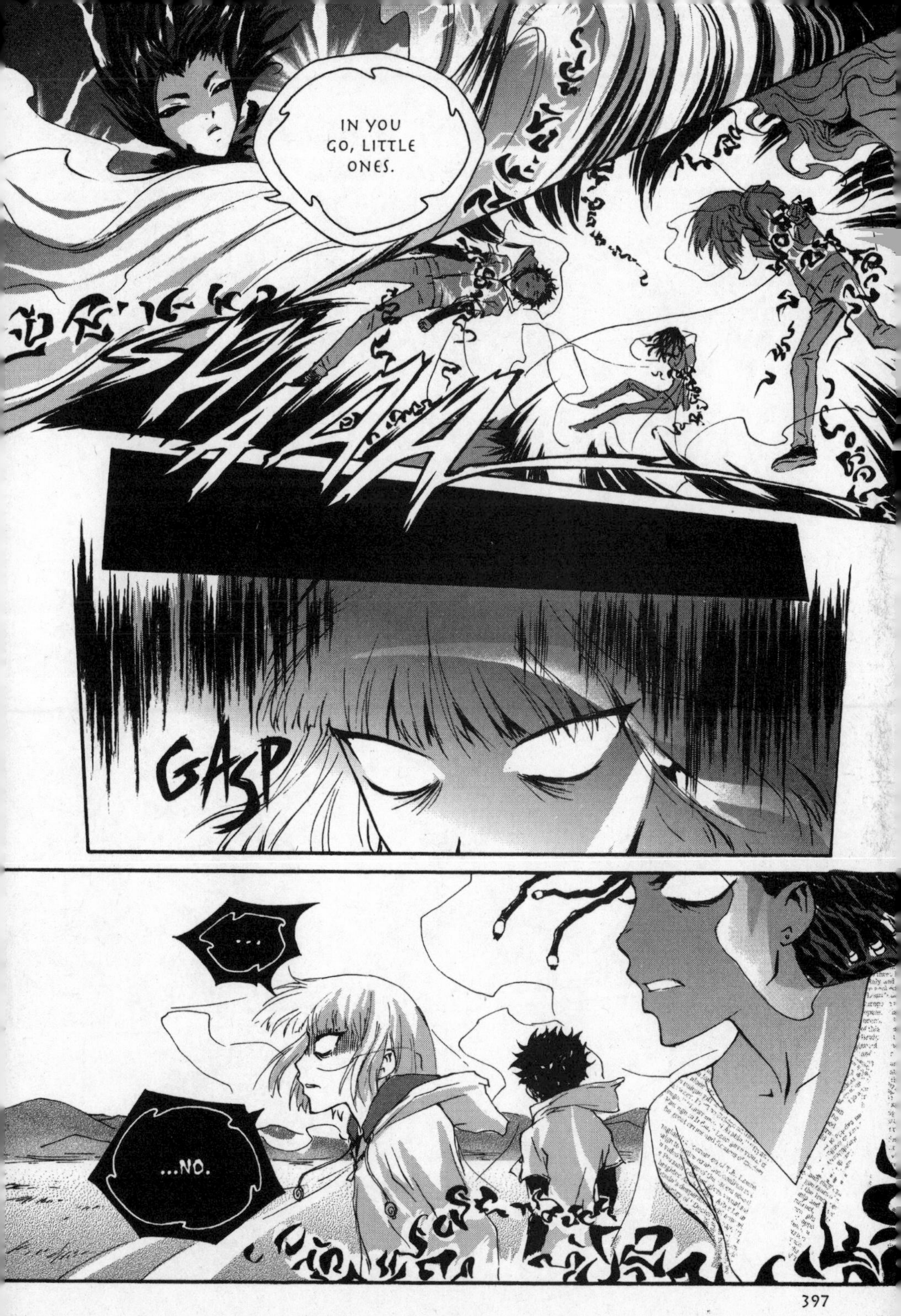
IN YOU GO, LITTLE ONES.
SHAAA
GASP
...
...NO.

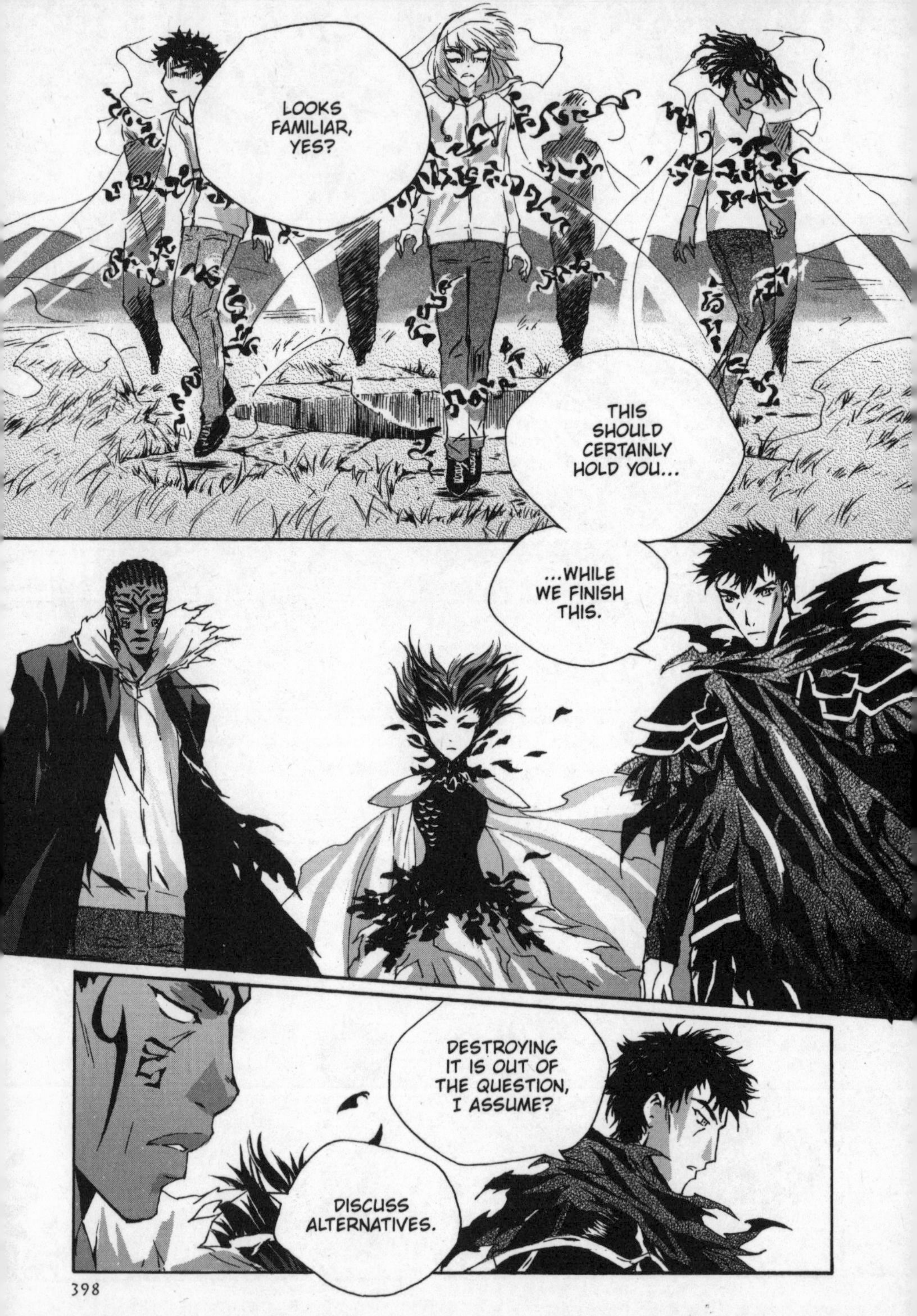
LOOKS FAMILIAR, YES?
THIS SHOULD CERTAINLY HOLD YOU...
...WHILE WE FINISH THIS.
DESTROYING IT IS OUT OF THE QUESTION, I ASSUME?
DISCUSS ALTERNATIVES.

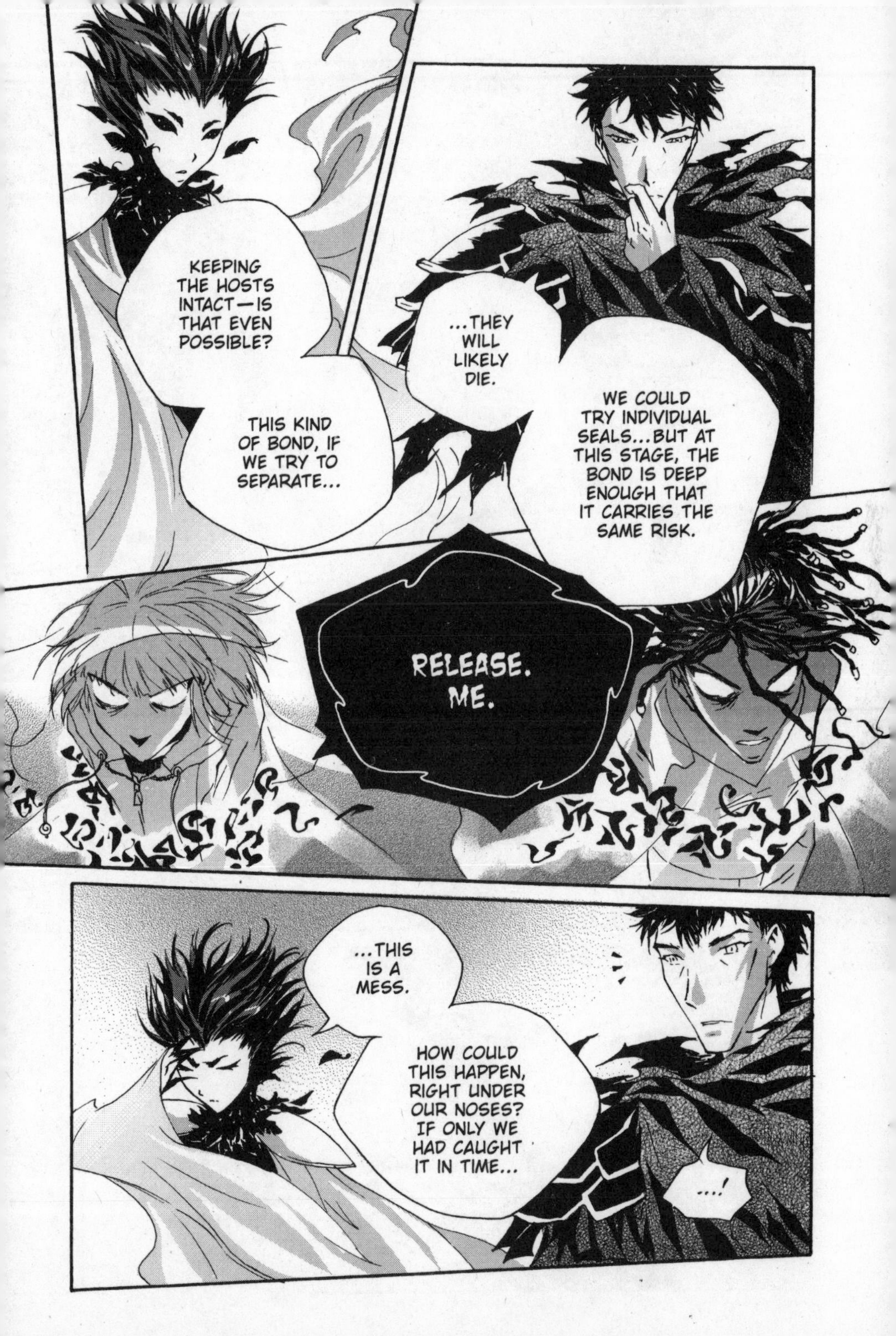

KEEPING THE HOSTS INTACT—IS THAT EVEN POSSIBLE?
THIS KIND OF BOND, IF WE TRY TO SEPARATE...
...THEY WILL LIKELY DIE.
WE COULD TRY INDIVIDUAL SEALS...BUT AT THIS STAGE, THE BOND IS DEEP ENOUGH THAT IT CARRIES THE SAME RISK.
RELEASE. ME.
...THIS IS A MESS.
HOW COULD THIS HAPPEN, RIGHT UNDER OUR NOSES? IF ONLY WE HAD CAUGHT IT IN TIME...
...!

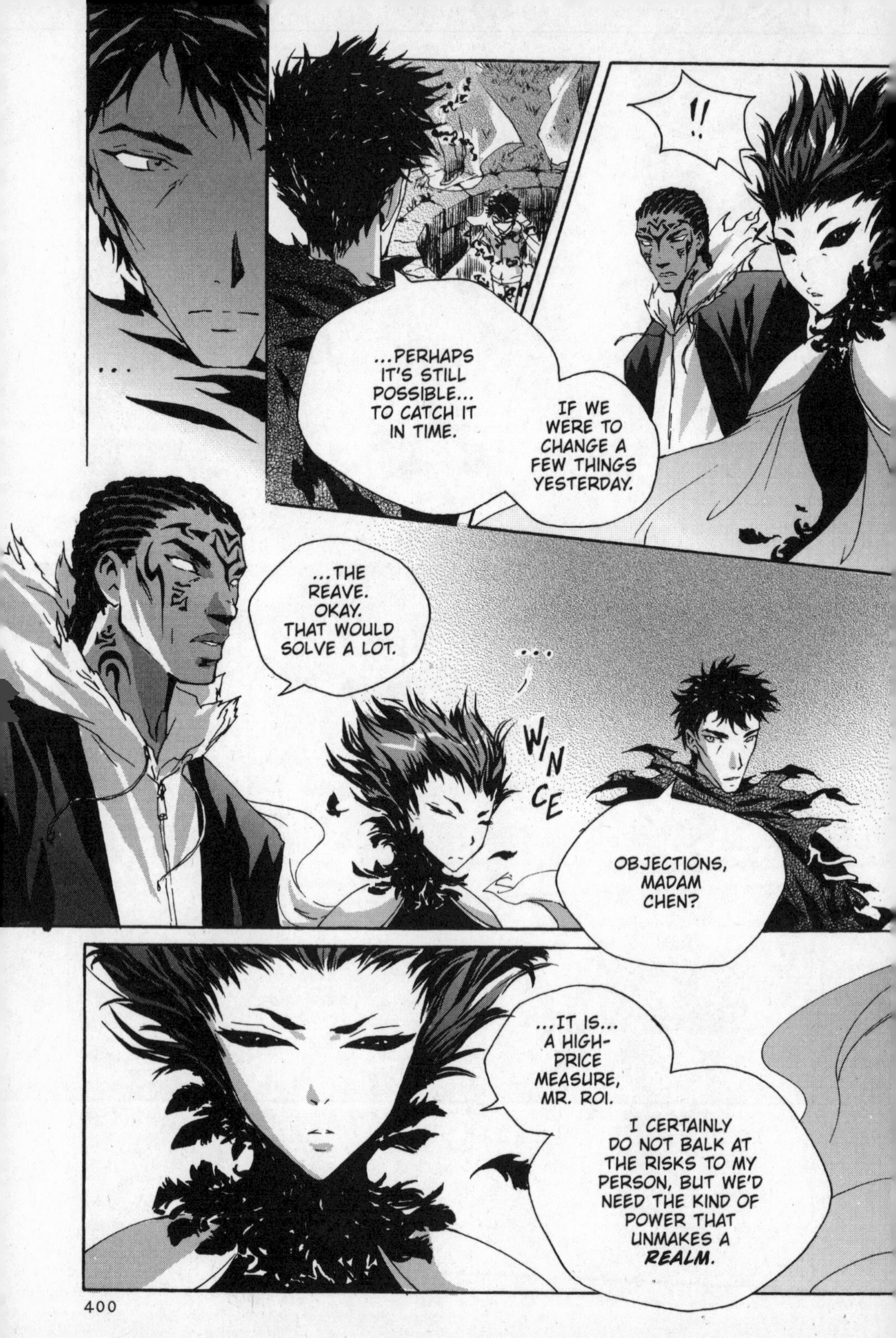
...
...PERHAPS IT'S STILL POSSIBLE... TO CATCH IT IN TIME.
!!
IF WE WERE TO CHANGE A FEW THINGS YESTERDAY.
...THE REAVE. OKAY. THAT WOULD SOLVE A LOT.
...
WINCE
OBJECTIONS, MADAM CHEN?
...IT IS... A HIGH-PRICE MEASURE, MR. ROI.
I CERTAINLY DO NOT BALK AT THE RISKS TO MY PERSON, BUT WE'D NEED THE KIND OF POWER THAT UNMAKES A REALM.

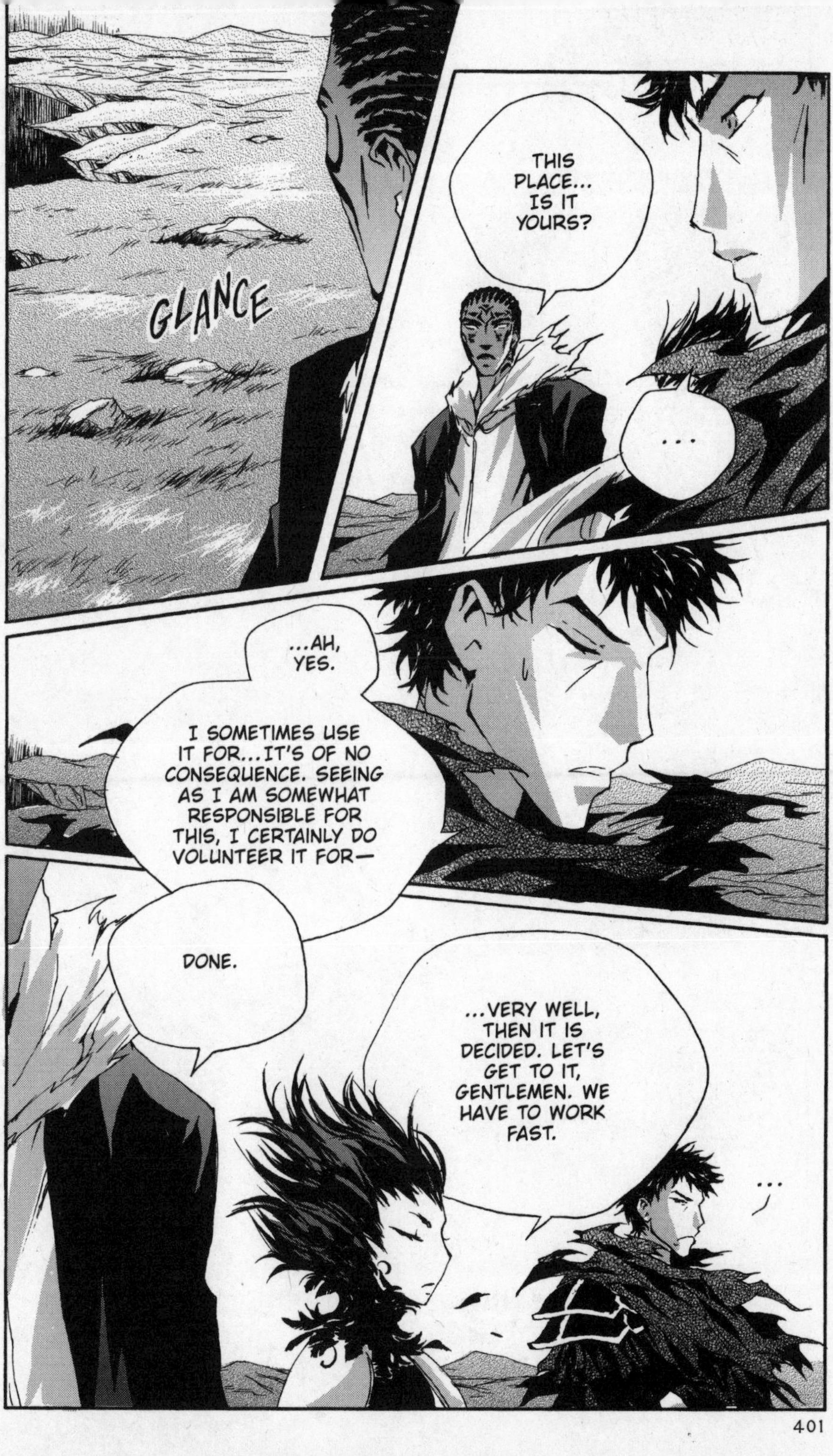
GLANCE
THIS PLACE... IS IT YOURS?
...
...AH, YES.
I SOMETIMES USE IT FOR...IT'S OF NO CONSEQUENCE. SEEING AS I AM SOMEWHAT RESPONSIBLE FOR THIS, I CERTAINLY DO VOLUNTEER IT FOR—
DONE.
...VERY WELL, THEN IT IS DECIDED. LET'S GET TO IT, GENTLEMEN. WE HAVE TO WORK FAST.
...

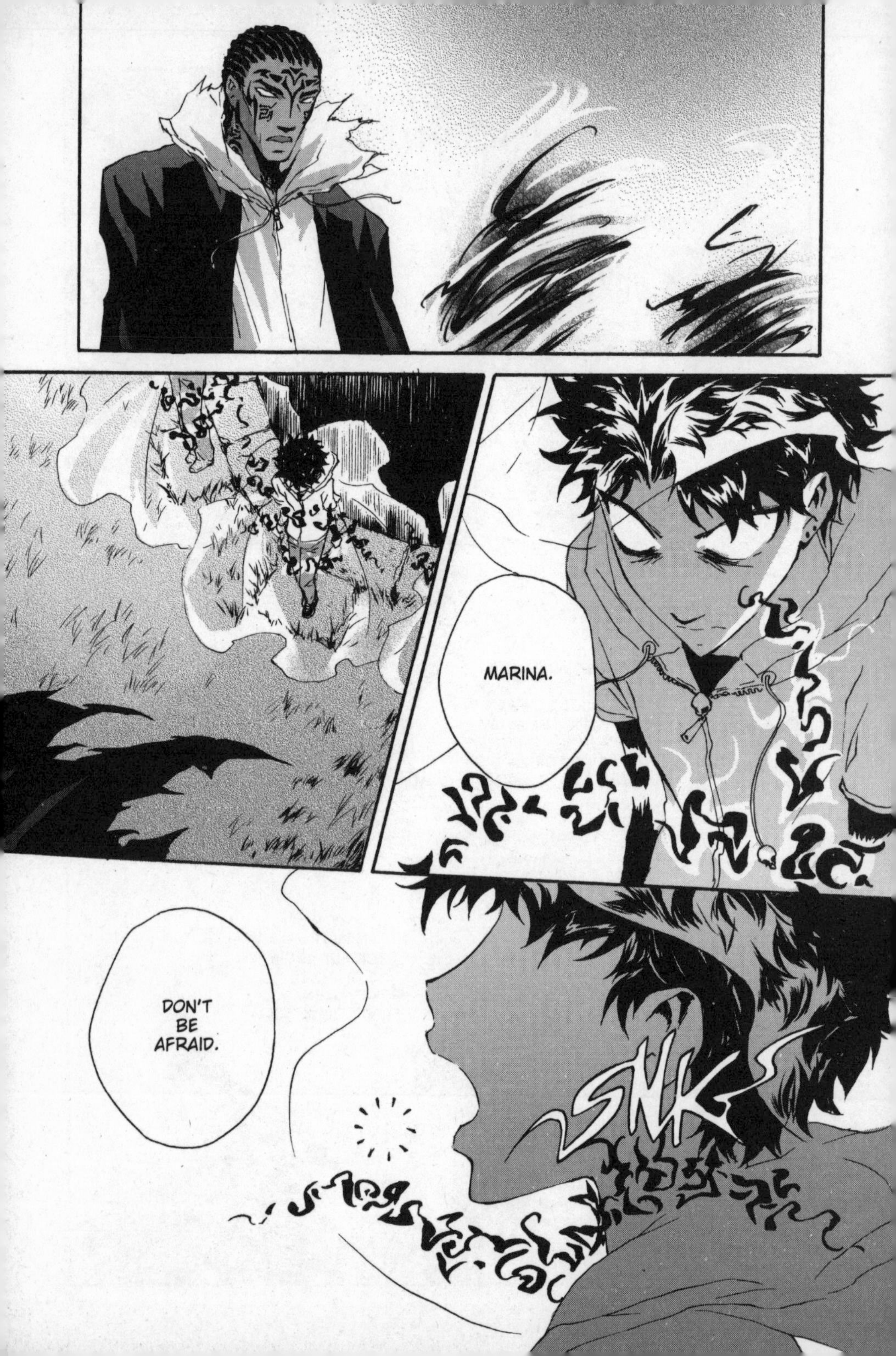
MARINA.
DON'T BE AFRAID.
SNK

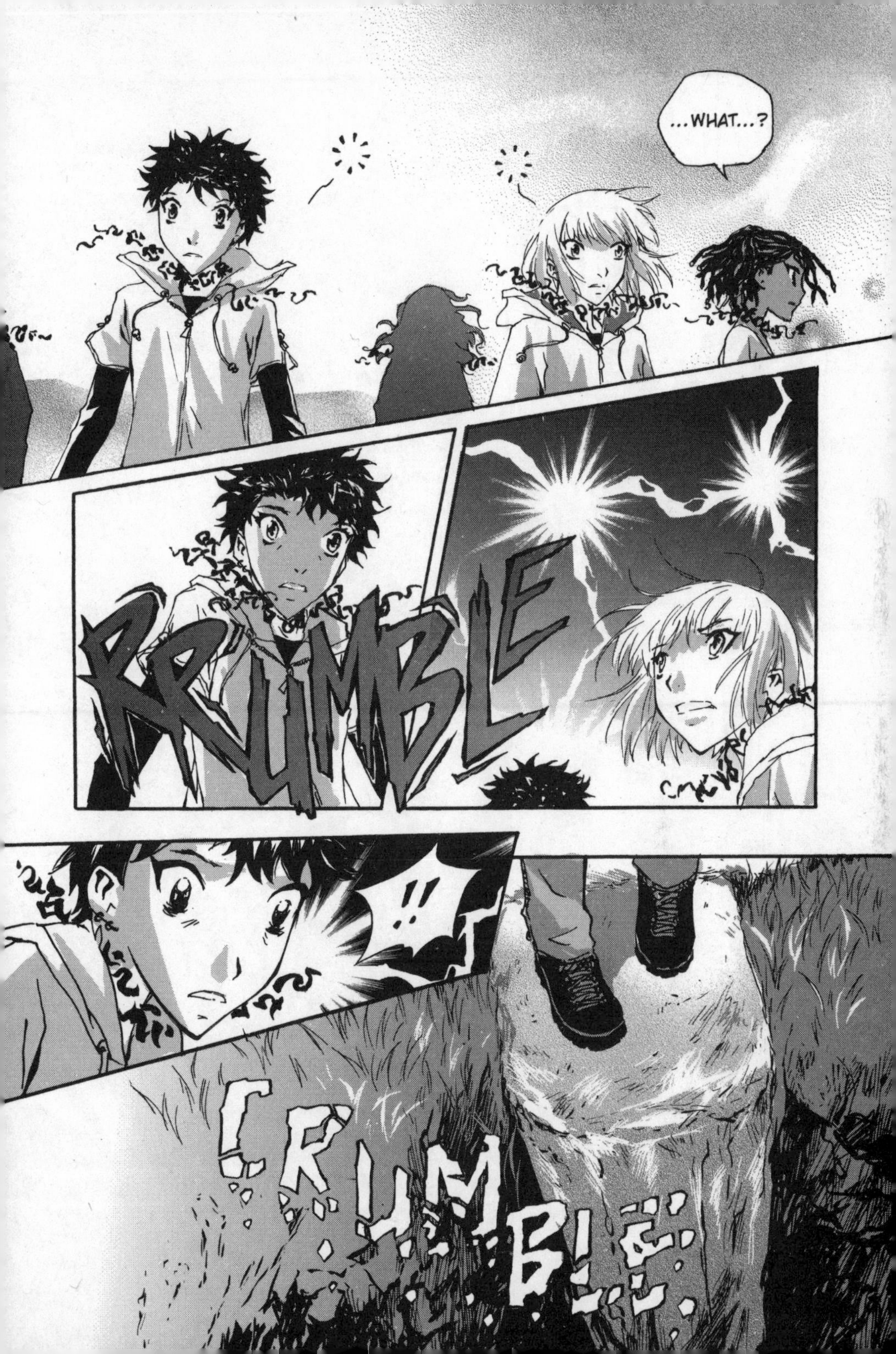
...WHAT...?
RRUMBLE
!!
CRUMBLE

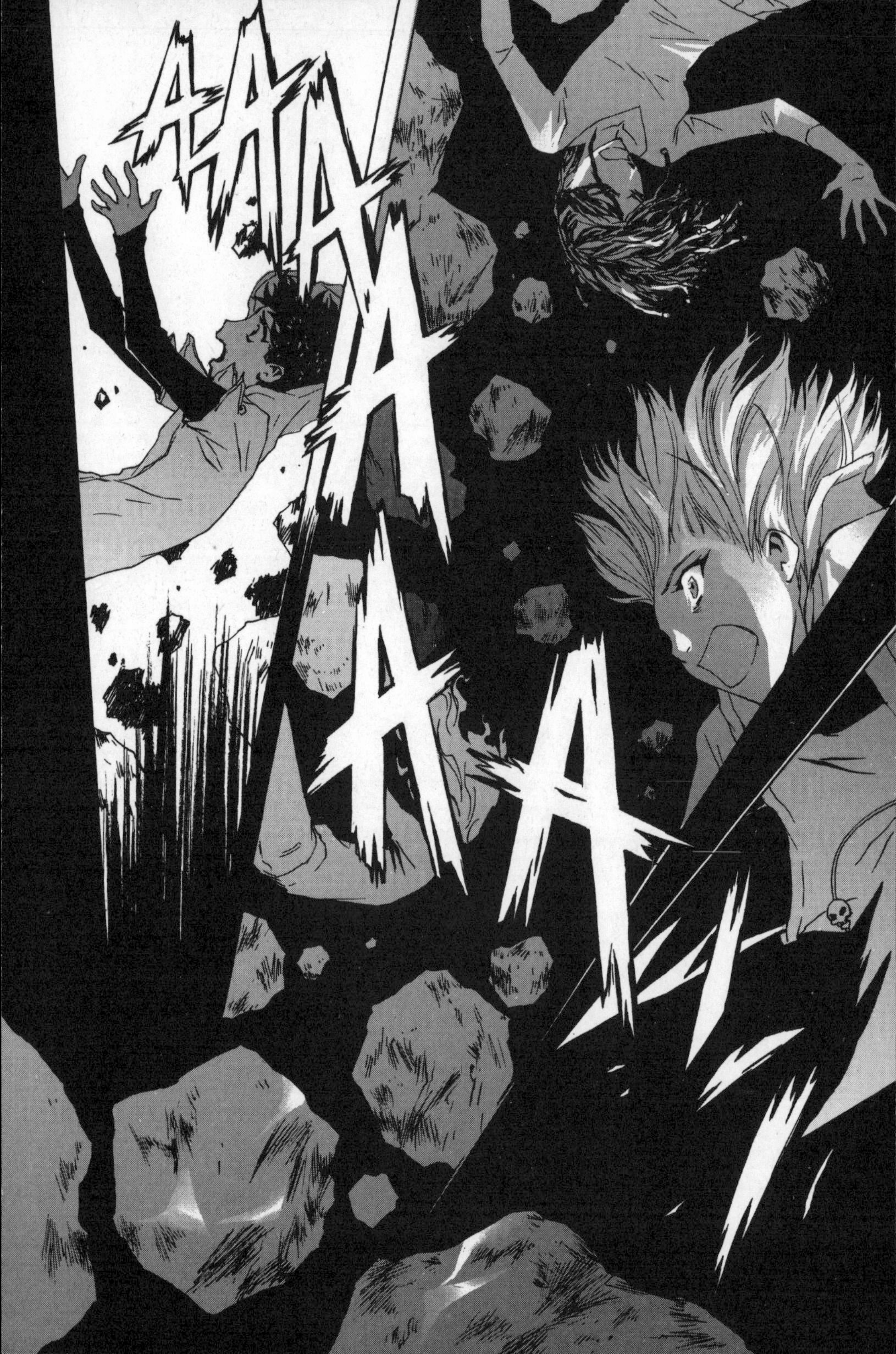
AAAAAAA!

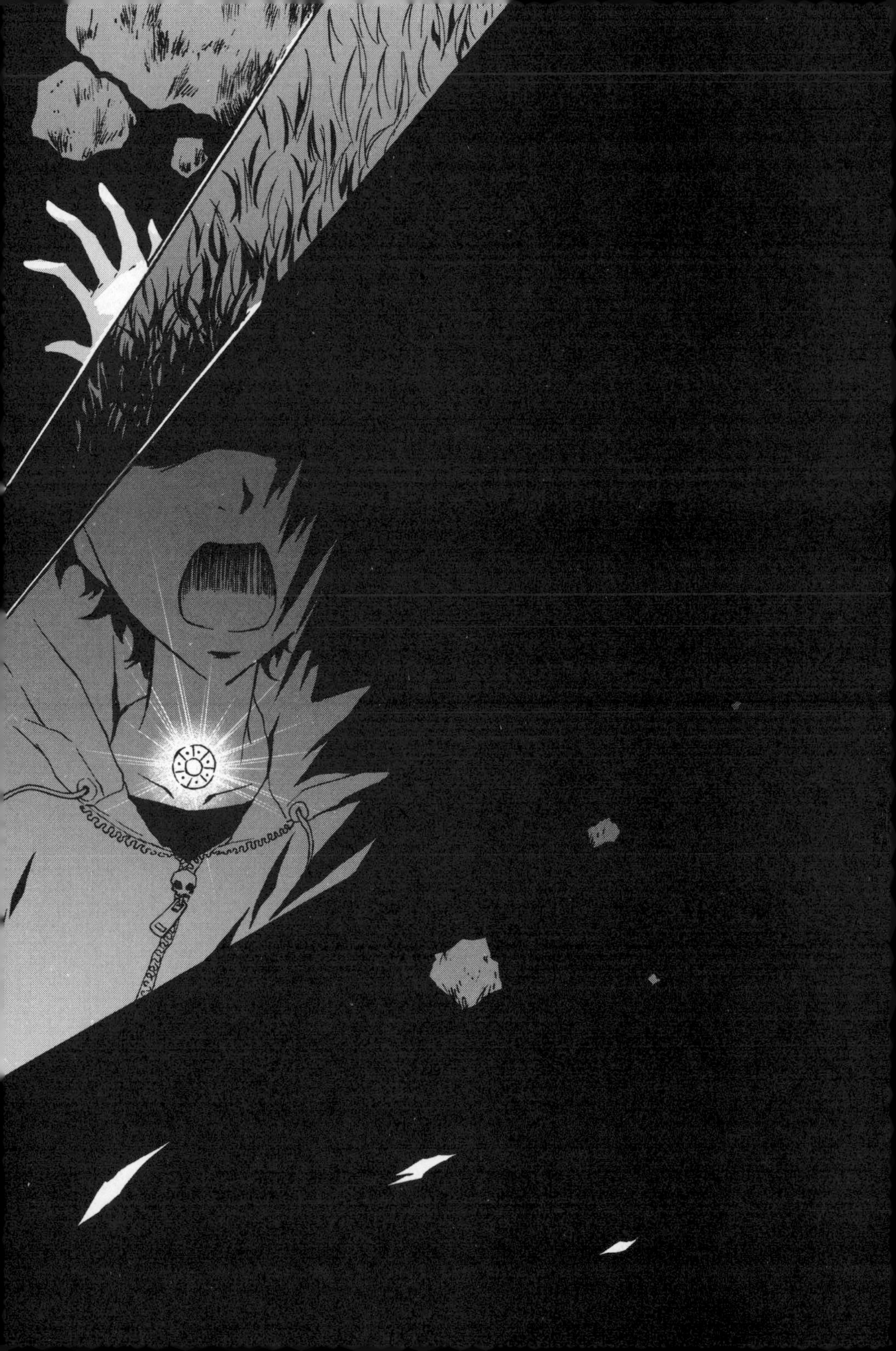

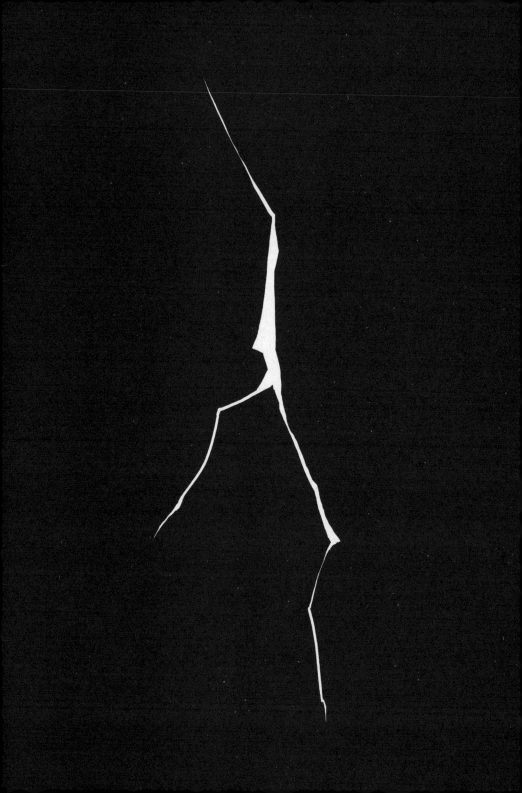

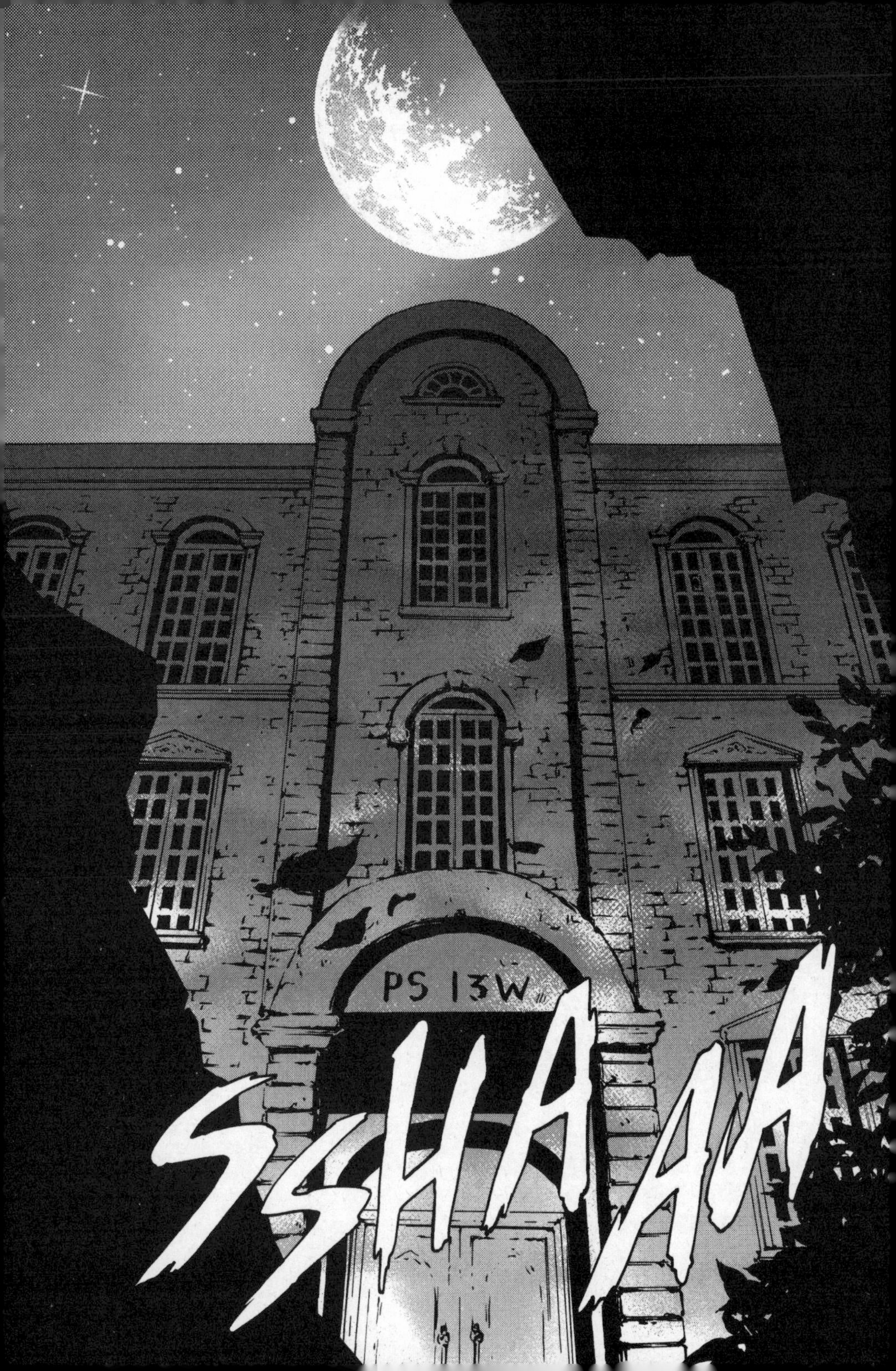
PS 13W
SSHAAA

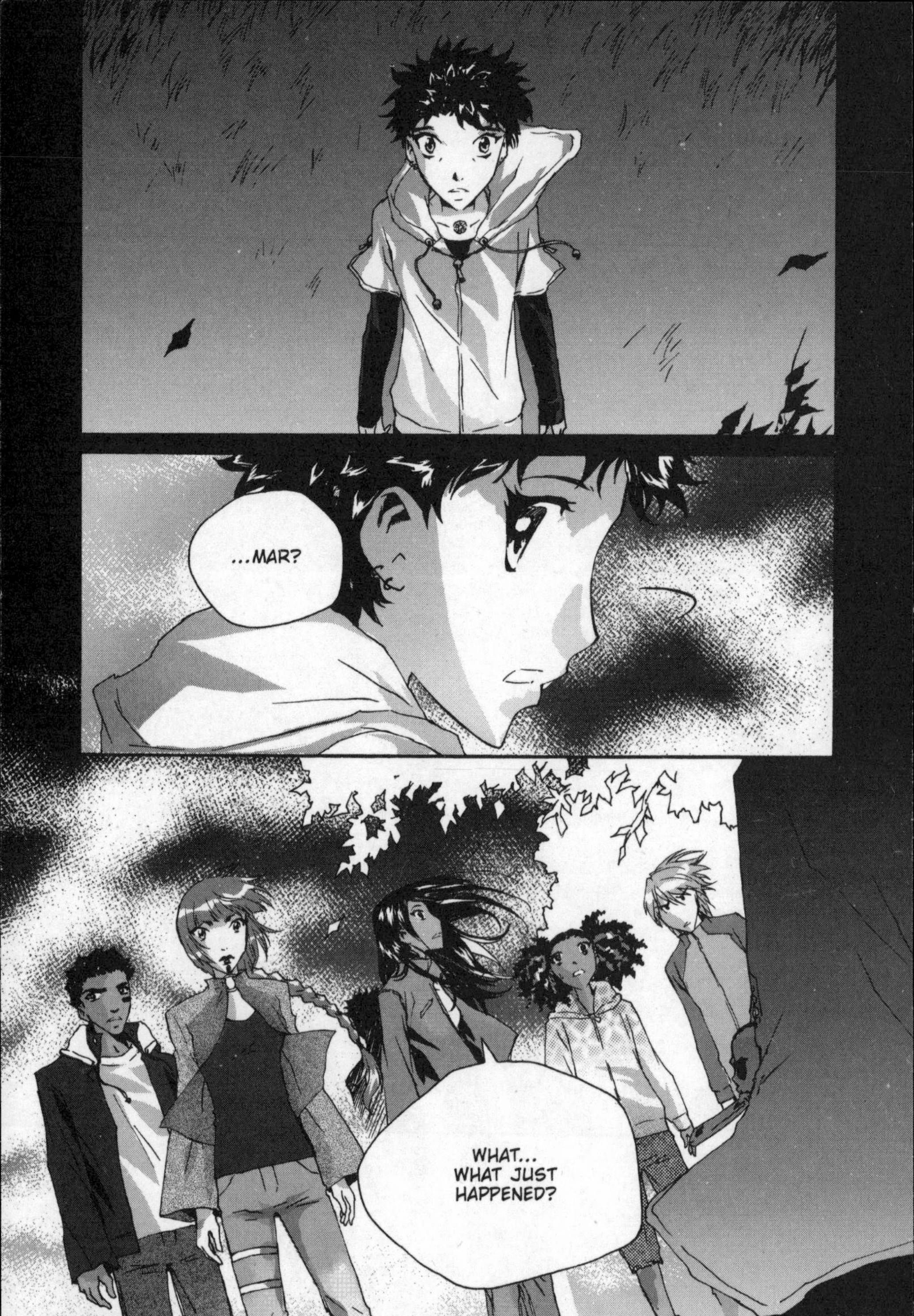
...MAR?
WHAT... WHAT JUST HAPPENED?

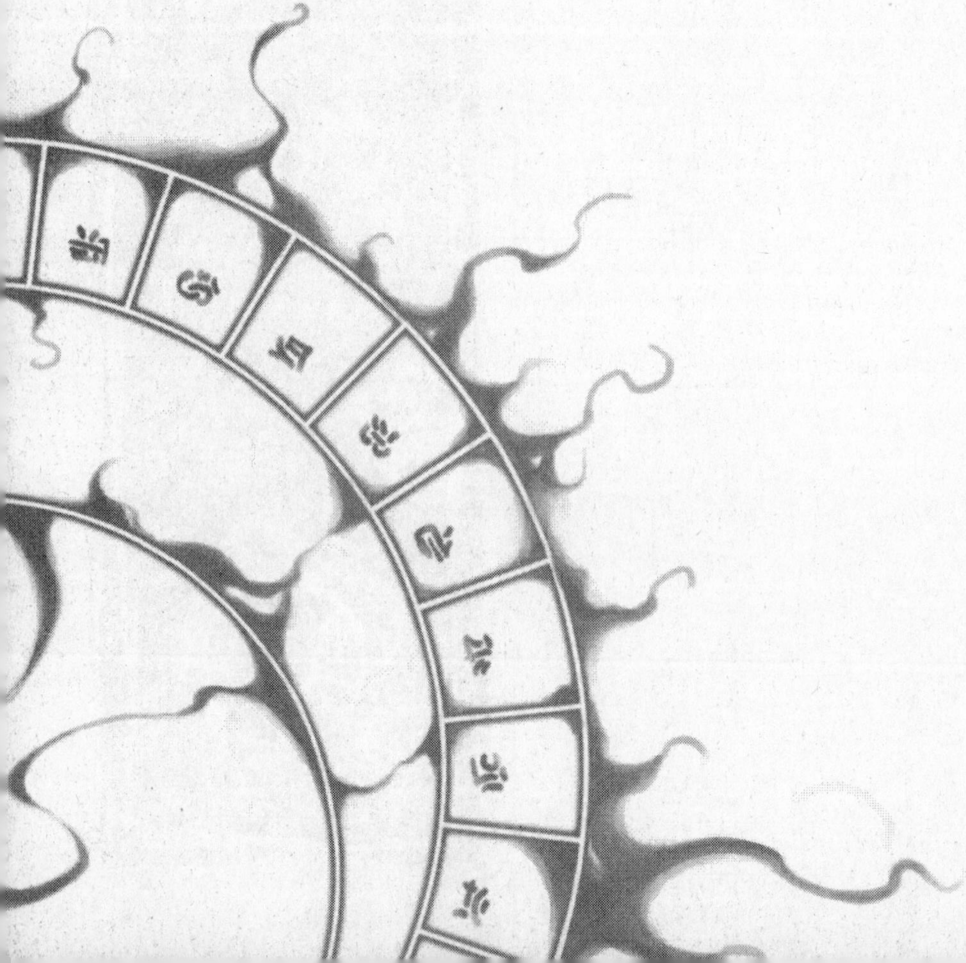

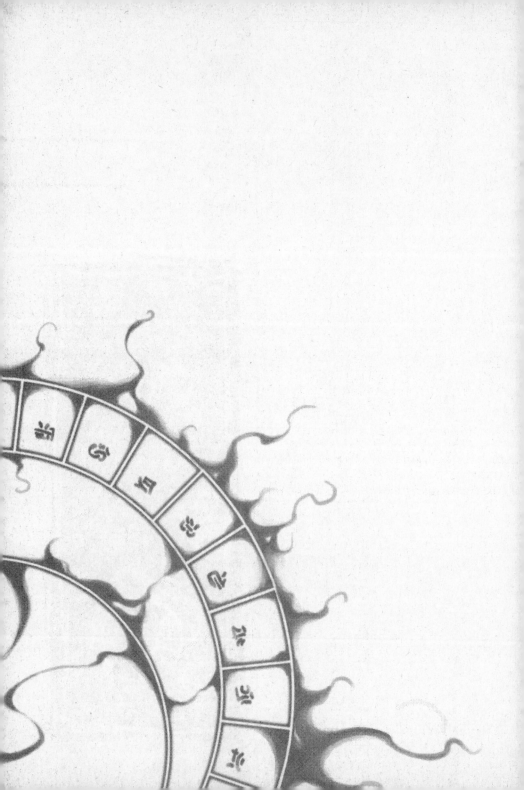

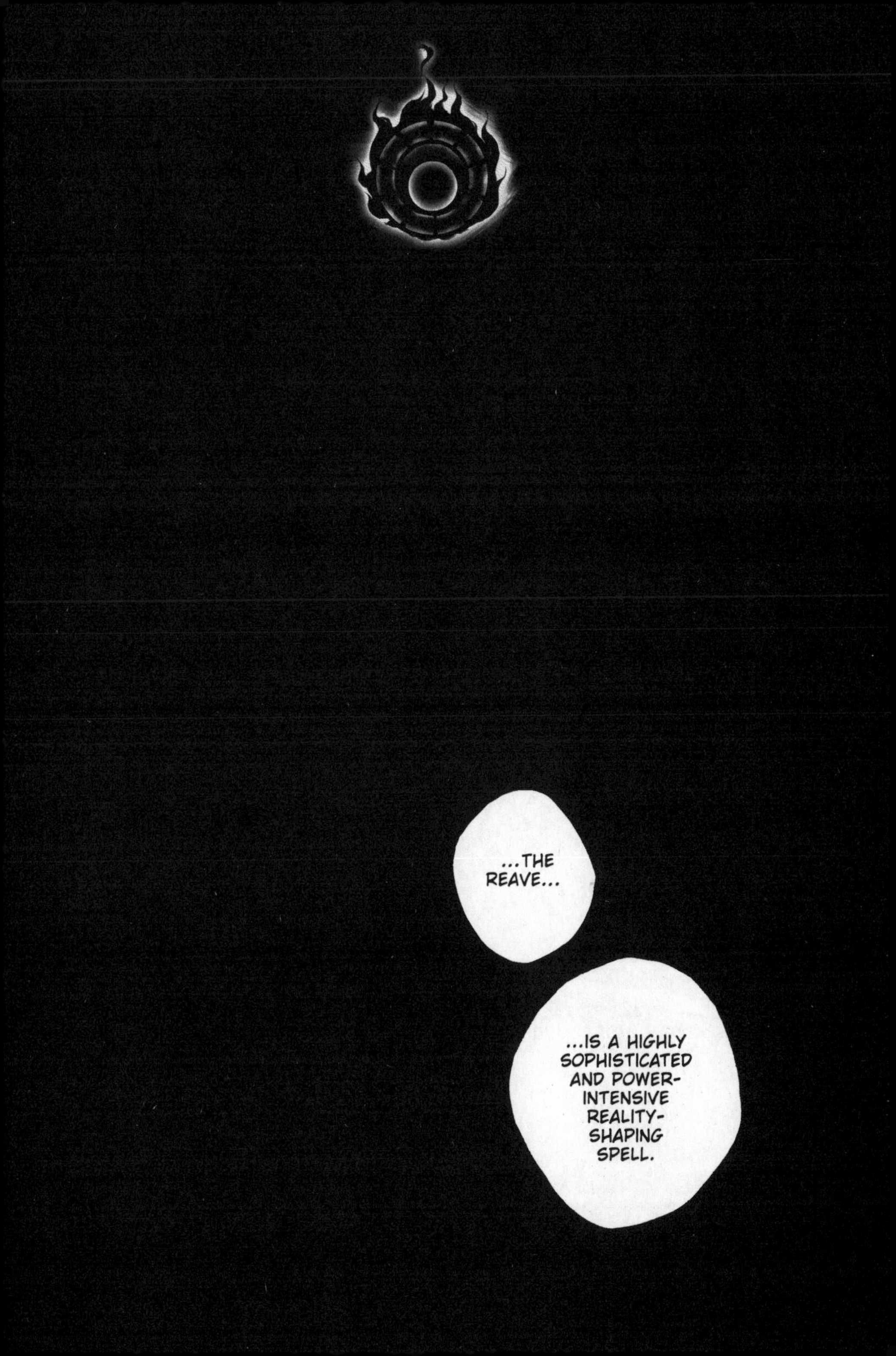
...THE REAVE...
...IS A HIGHLY SOPHISTICATED AND POWER-INTENSIVE REALITY-SHAPING SPELL.

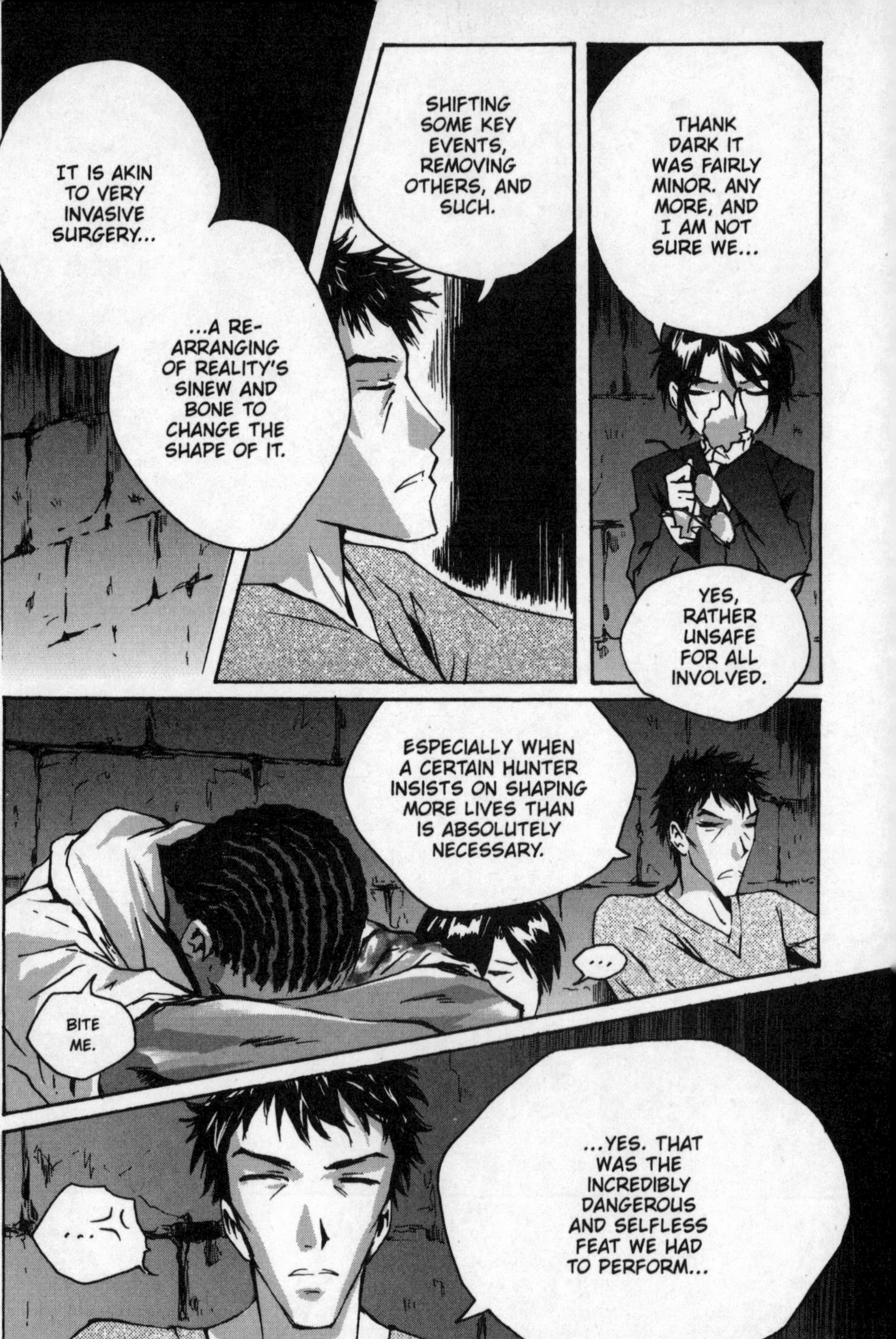
IT IS AKIN TO VERY INVASIVE SURGERY...
...A RE-ARRANGING OF REALITY'S SINEW AND BONE TO CHANGE THE SHAPE OF IT.
SHIFTING SOME KEY EVENTS, REMOVING OTHERS, AND SUCH.
THANK DARK IT WAS FAIRLY MINOR. ANY MORE, AND I AM NOT SURE WE...
YES, RATHER UNSAFE FOR ALL INVOLVED.
ESPECIALLY WHEN A CERTAIN HUNTER INSISTS ON SHAPING MORE LIVES THAN IS ABSOLUTELY NECESSARY.
...
BITE ME.
...
...YES. THAT WAS THE INCREDIBLY DANGEROUS AND SELFLESS FEAT WE HAD TO PERFORM...

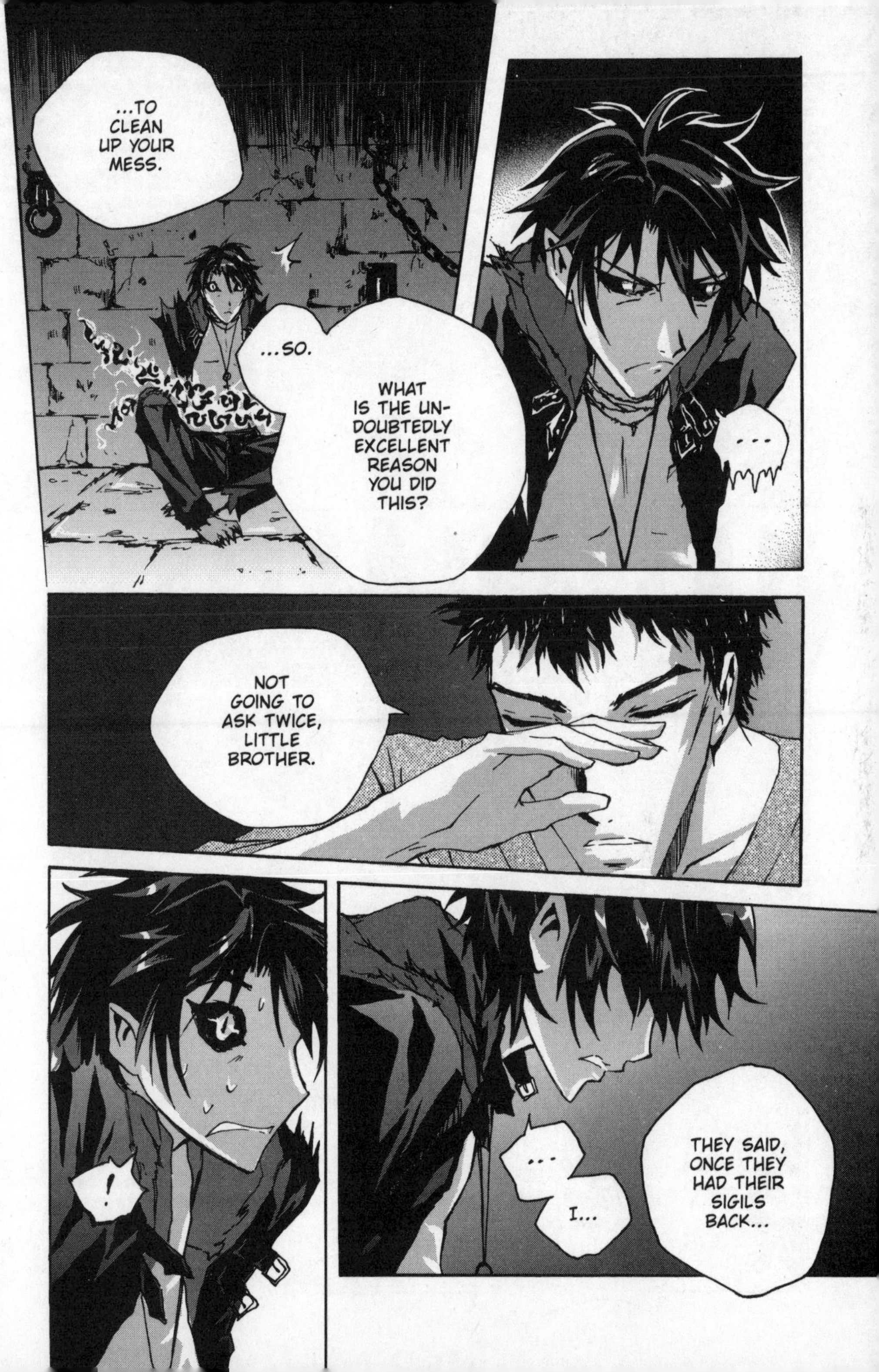
...TO CLEAN UP YOUR MESS.
...SO.
WHAT IS THE UN-DOUBTEDLY EXCELLENT REASON YOU DID THIS?
...
NOT GOING TO ASK TWICE, LITTLE BROTHER.
!
...
I...
THEY SAID, ONCE THEY HAD THEIR SIGILS BACK...

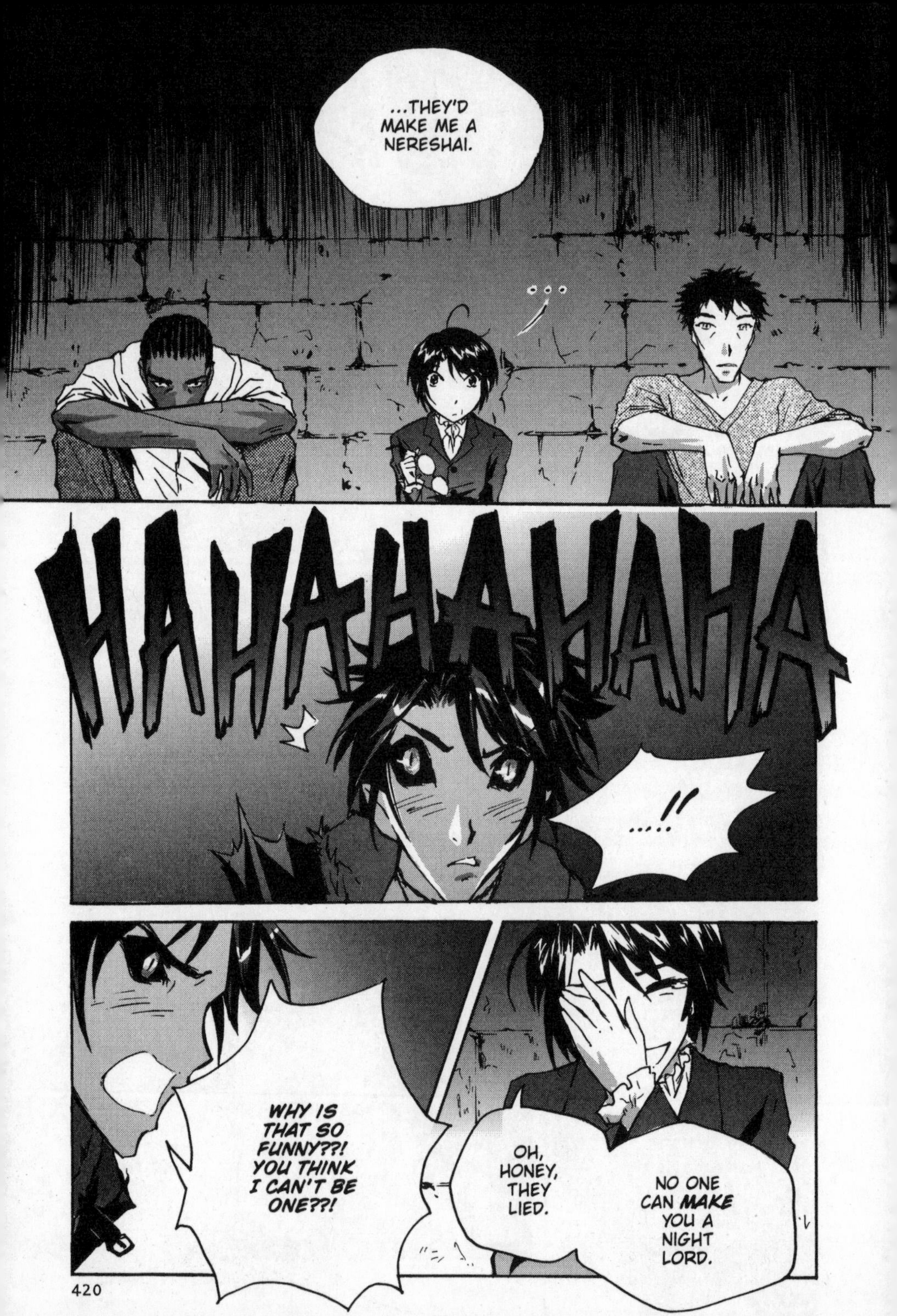
...THEY'D MAKE ME A NERESHAI.
...
HAHAHAHAHAHA
...!!
WHY IS THAT SO FUNNY??! YOU THINK I CAN'T BE ONE??!
OH, HONEY, THEY LIED.
NO ONE CAN MAKE YOU A NIGHT LORD.

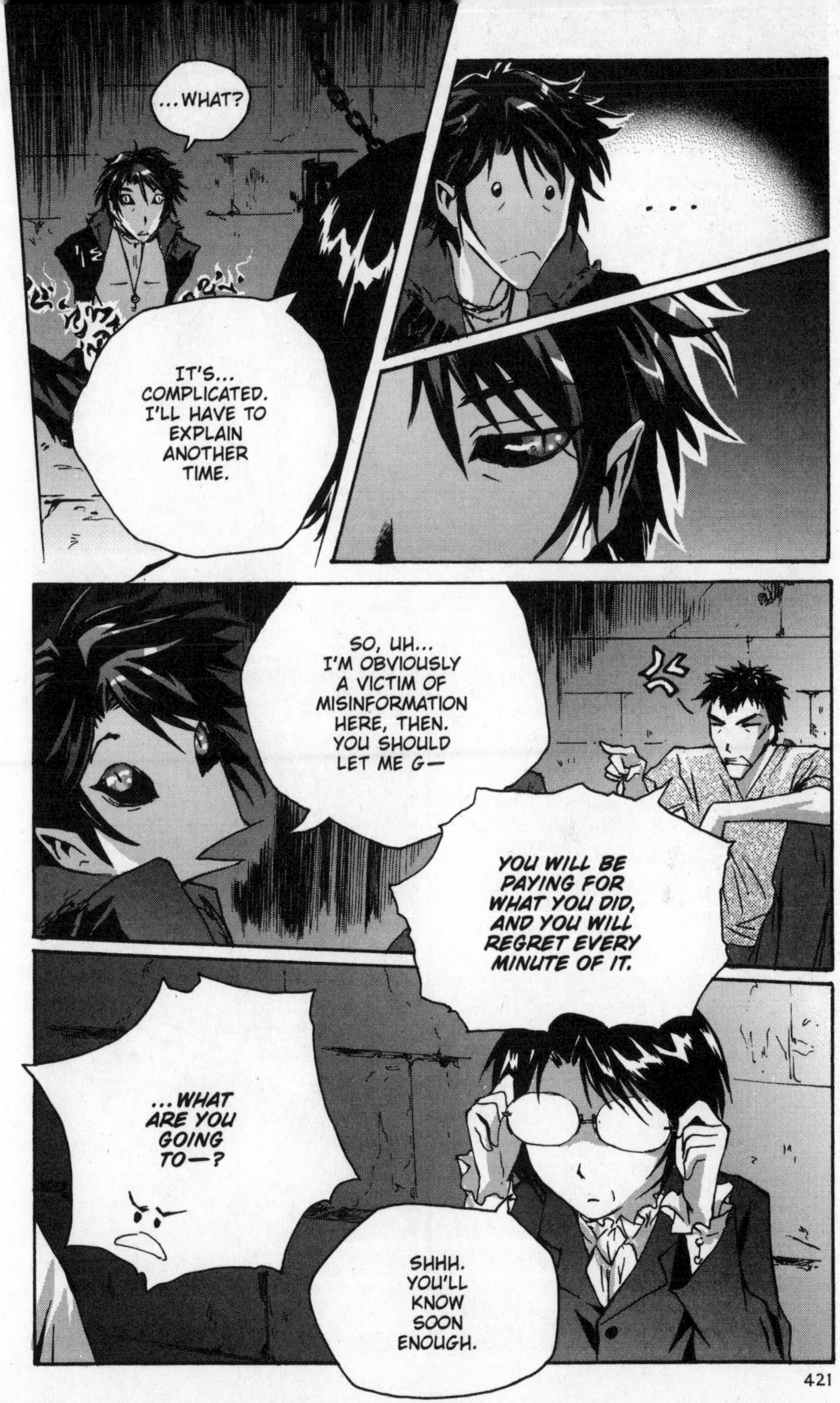
...WHAT?
...
IT'S... COMPLICATED. I'LL HAVE TO EXPLAIN ANOTHER TIME.
SO, UH... I'M OBVIOUSLY A VICTIM OF MISINFORMATION HERE, THEN. YOU SHOULD LET ME G—
YOU WILL BE PAYING FOR WHAT YOU DID, AND YOU WILL REGRET EVERY MINUTE OF IT.
...WHAT ARE YOU GOING TO—?
SHHH. YOU'LL KNOW SOON ENOUGH.

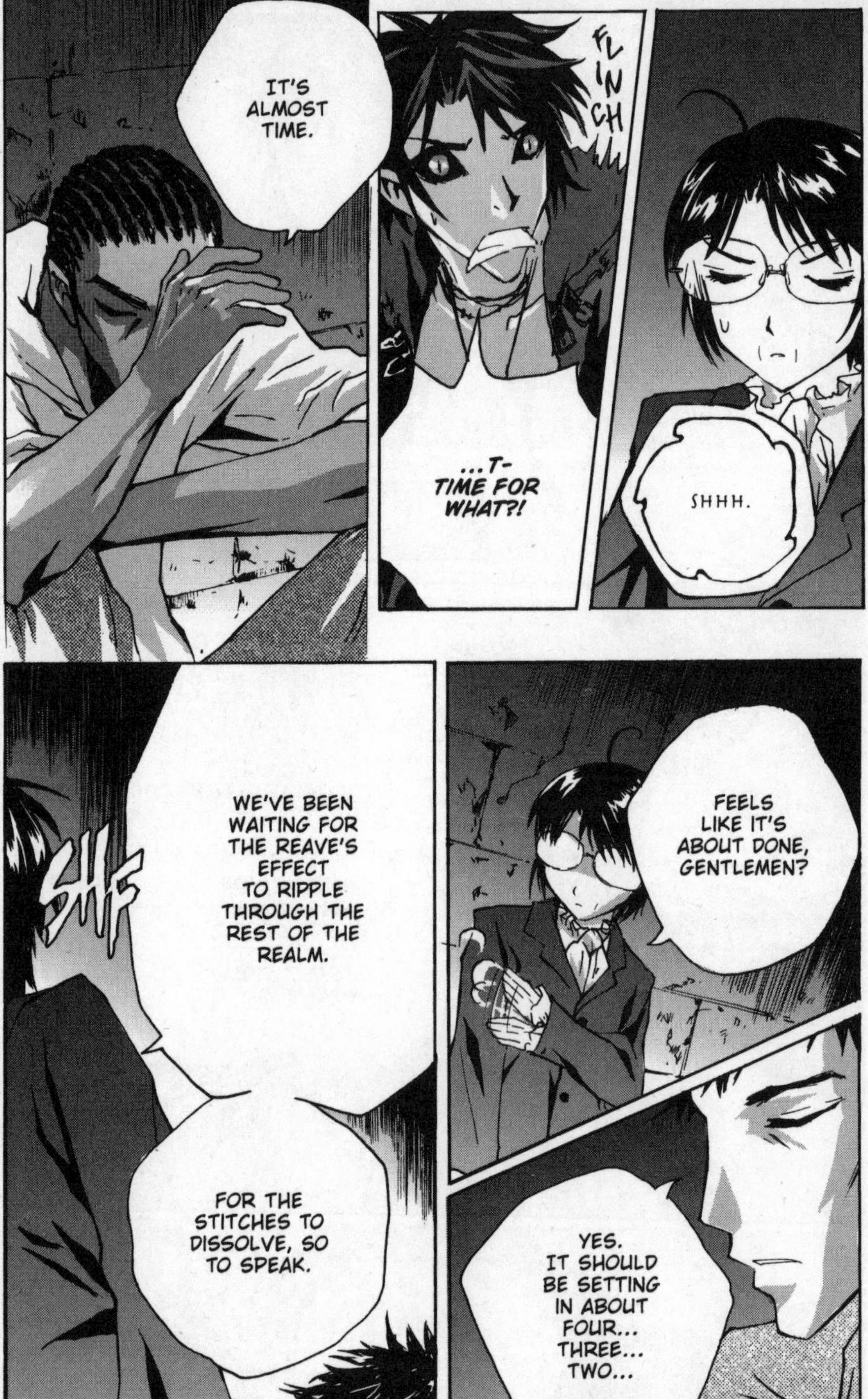
IT'S ALMOST TIME.
FLINCH
...T- TIME FOR WHAT?!
SHHH.
SHF
WE'VE BEEN WAITING FOR THE REAVE'S EFFECT TO RIPPLE THROUGH THE REST OF THE REALM.
FOR THE STITCHES TO DISSOLVE, SO TO SPEAK.
FEELS LIKE IT'S ABOUT DONE, GENTLEMEN?
YES. IT SHOULD BE SETTING IN ABOUT FOUR... THREE... TWO...

ONE.

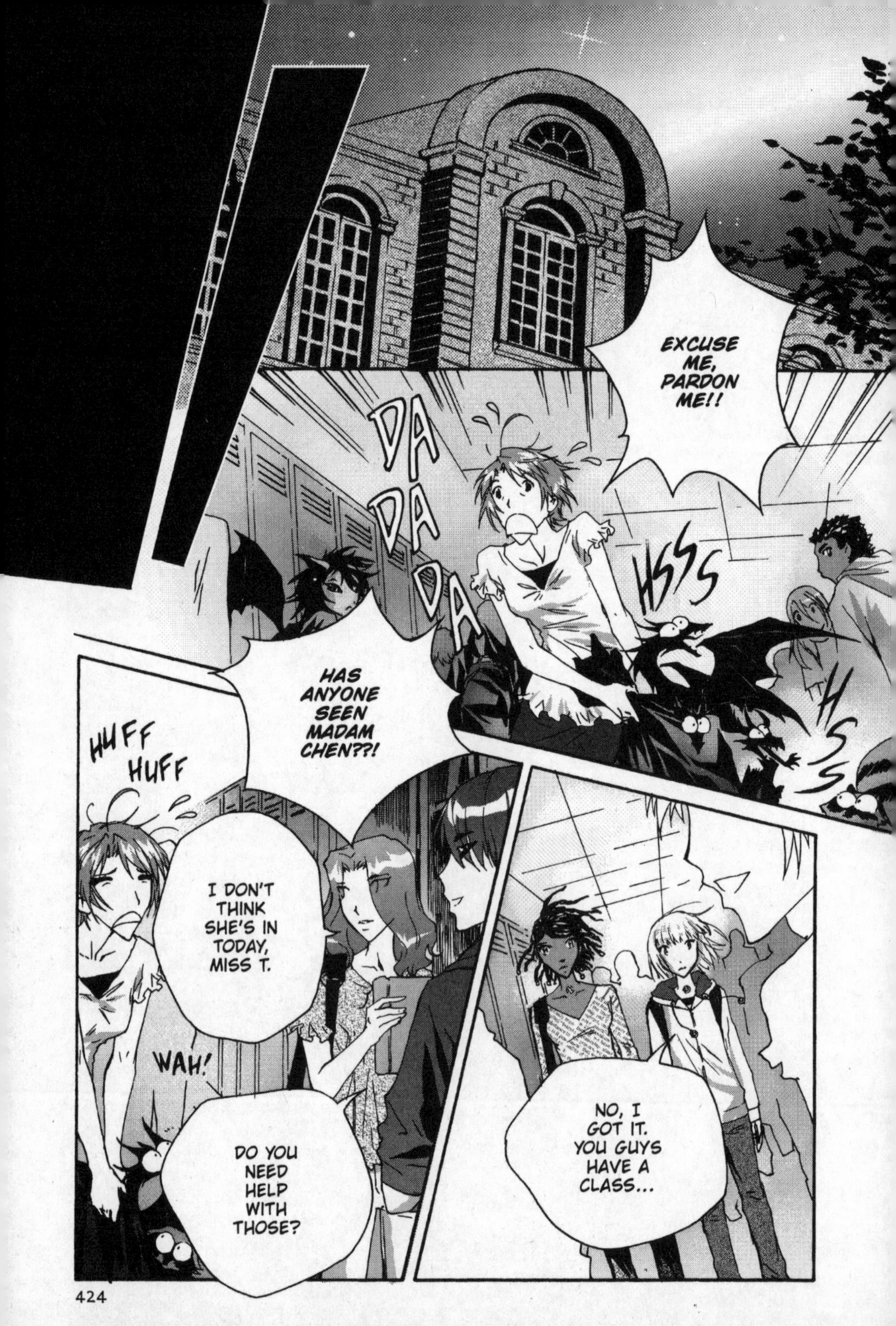
EXCUSE ME, PARDON ME!!
DA DA DA DA
HSSS
HAS ANYONE SEEN MADAM CHEN??!
HSSS
HUFF HUFF
I DON'T THINK SHE'S IN TODAY, MISS T.
WAH!
DO YOU NEED HELP WITH THOSE?
NO, I GOT IT. YOU GUYS HAVE A CLASS...

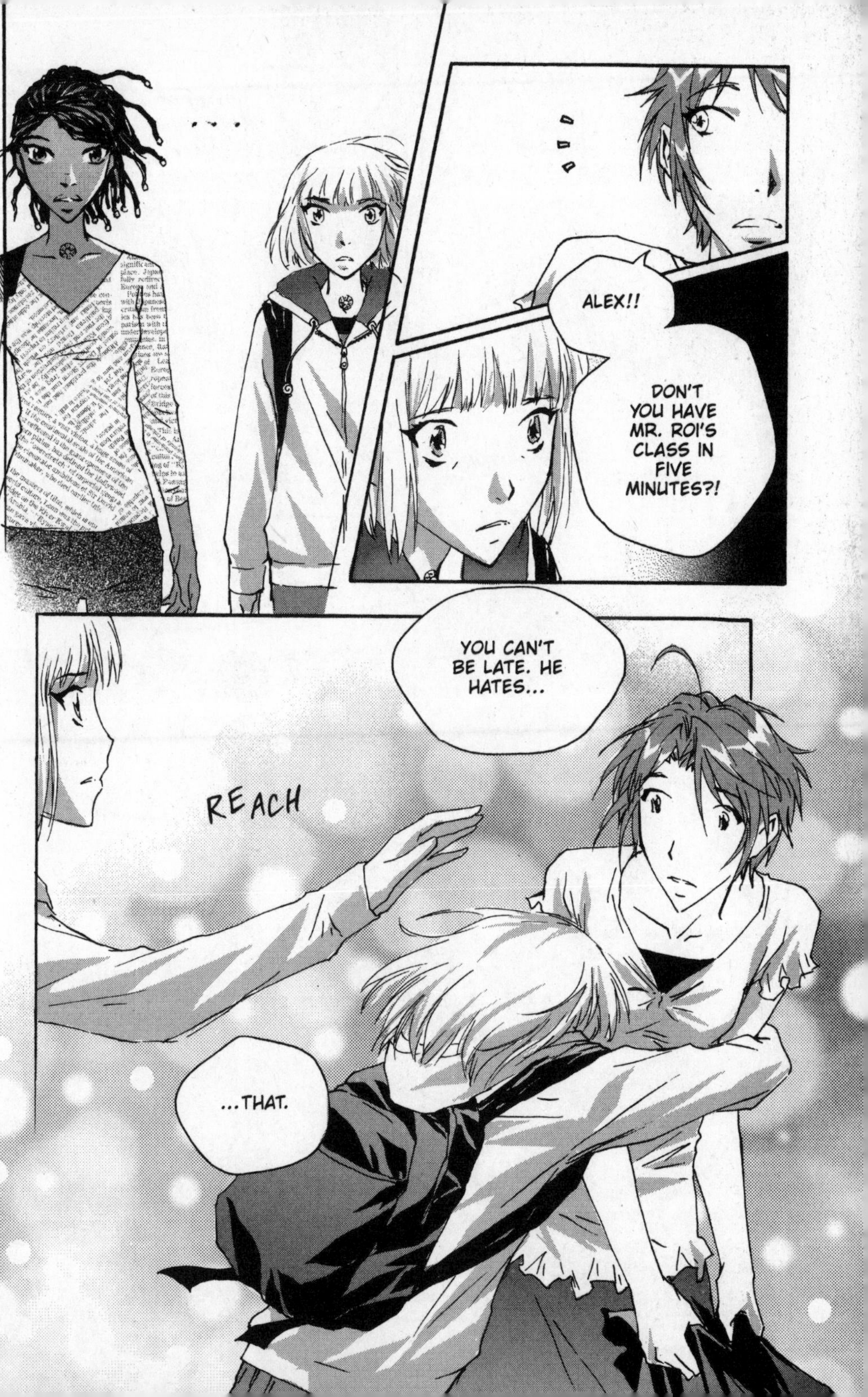

...
!!!
ALEX!!
DON'T YOU HAVE MR. ROI'S CLASS IN FIVE MINUTES?!
YOU CAN'T BE LATE. HE HATES...
REACH
...THAT.

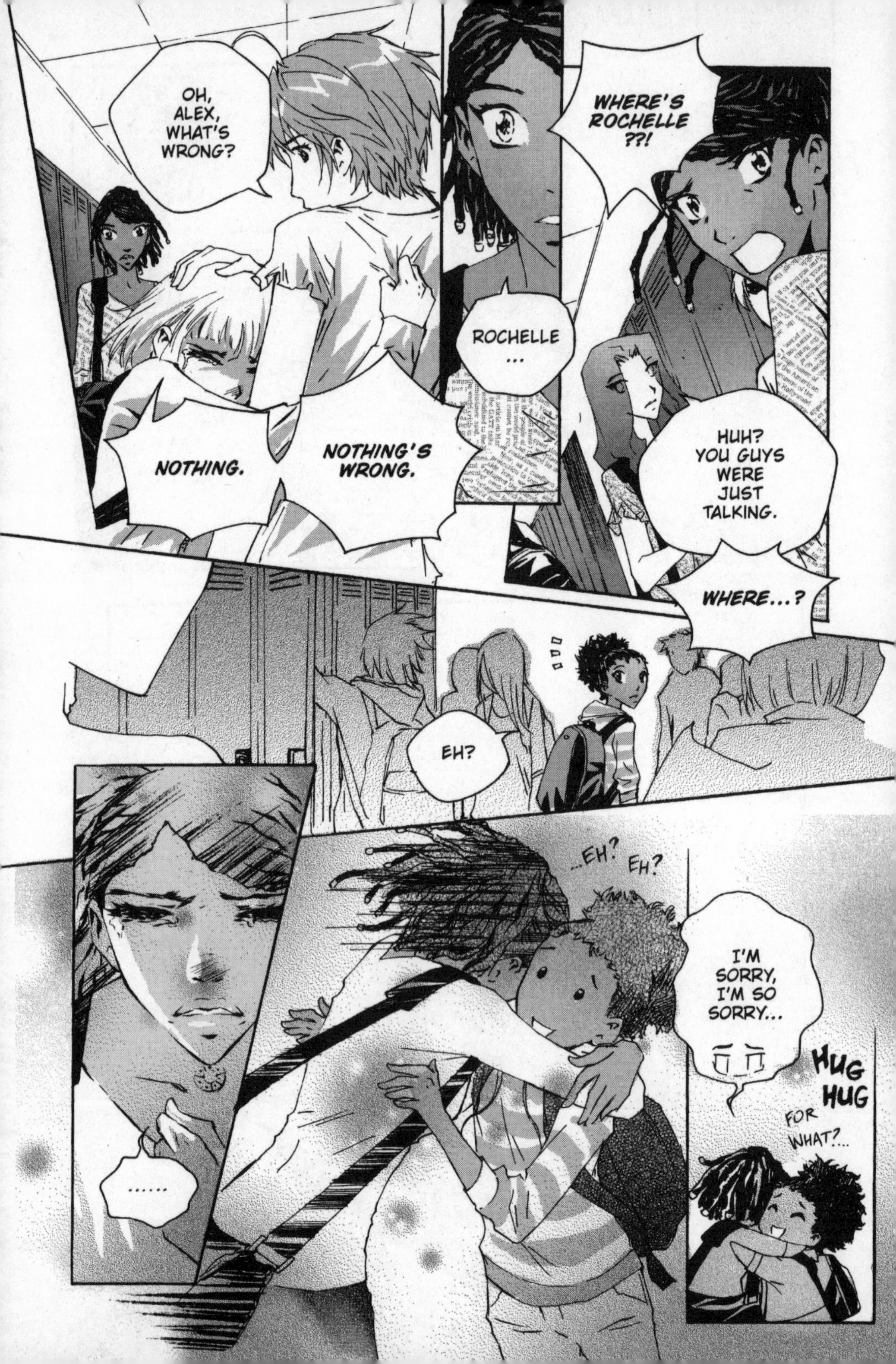
OH, ALEX, WHAT'S WRONG?
NOTHING.
NOTHING'S WRONG.
ROCHELLE ...
WHERE'S ROCHELLE ??!
HUH? YOU GUYS WERE JUST TALKING.
WHERE...?
EH?
......
...EH?
EH?
I'M SORRY, I'M SO SORRY...
HUG HUG
FOR WHAT?...

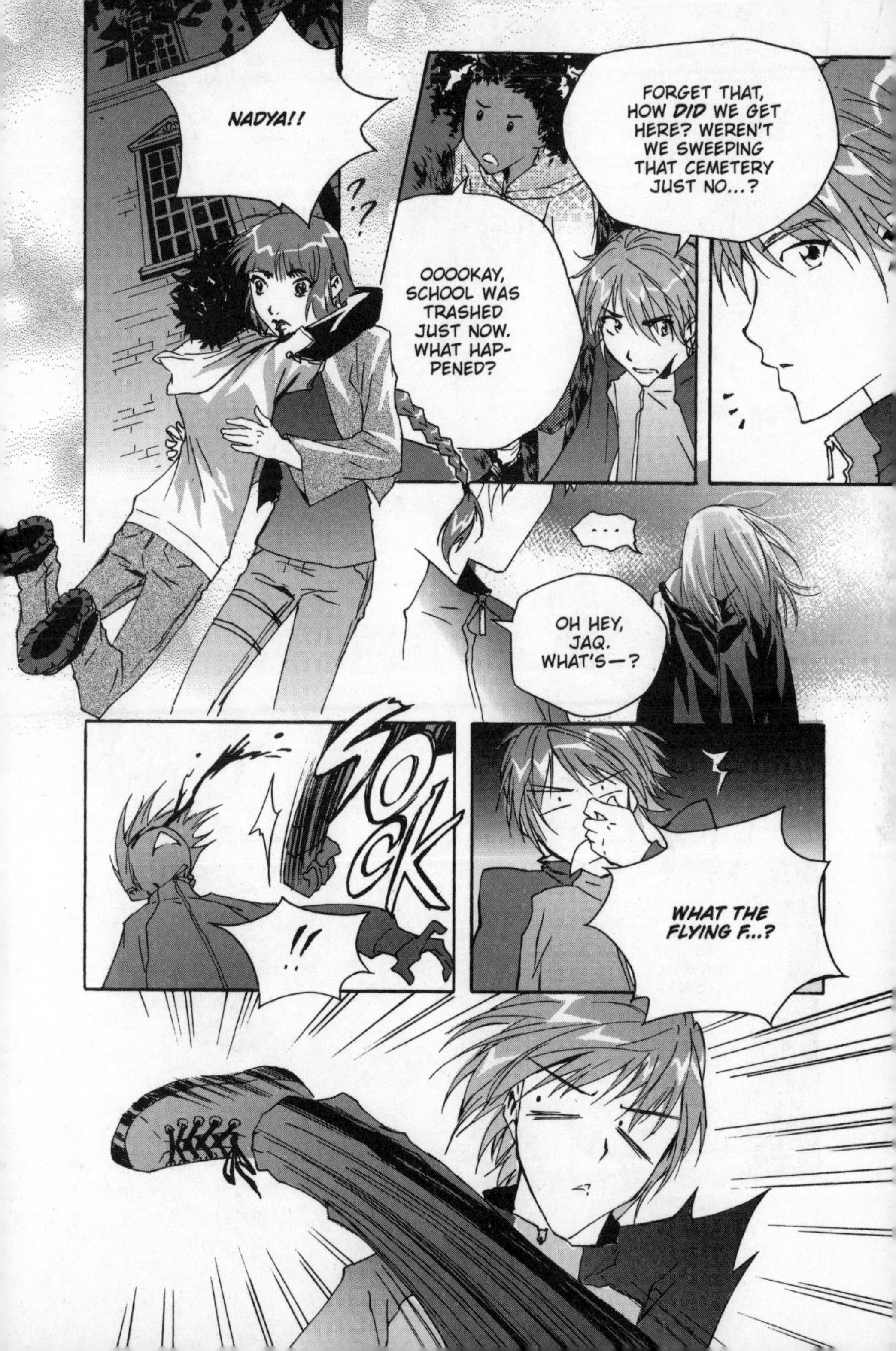

NADYA!!
??
OOOOKAY, SCHOOL WAS TRASHED JUST NOW. WHAT HAP-PENED?
FORGET THAT, HOW *DID* WE GET HERE? WEREN'T WE SWEEPING THAT CEMETERY JUST NO...?
...
OH HEY, JAQ. WHAT'S—?
SOCK
!!
WHAT THE FLYING F...?

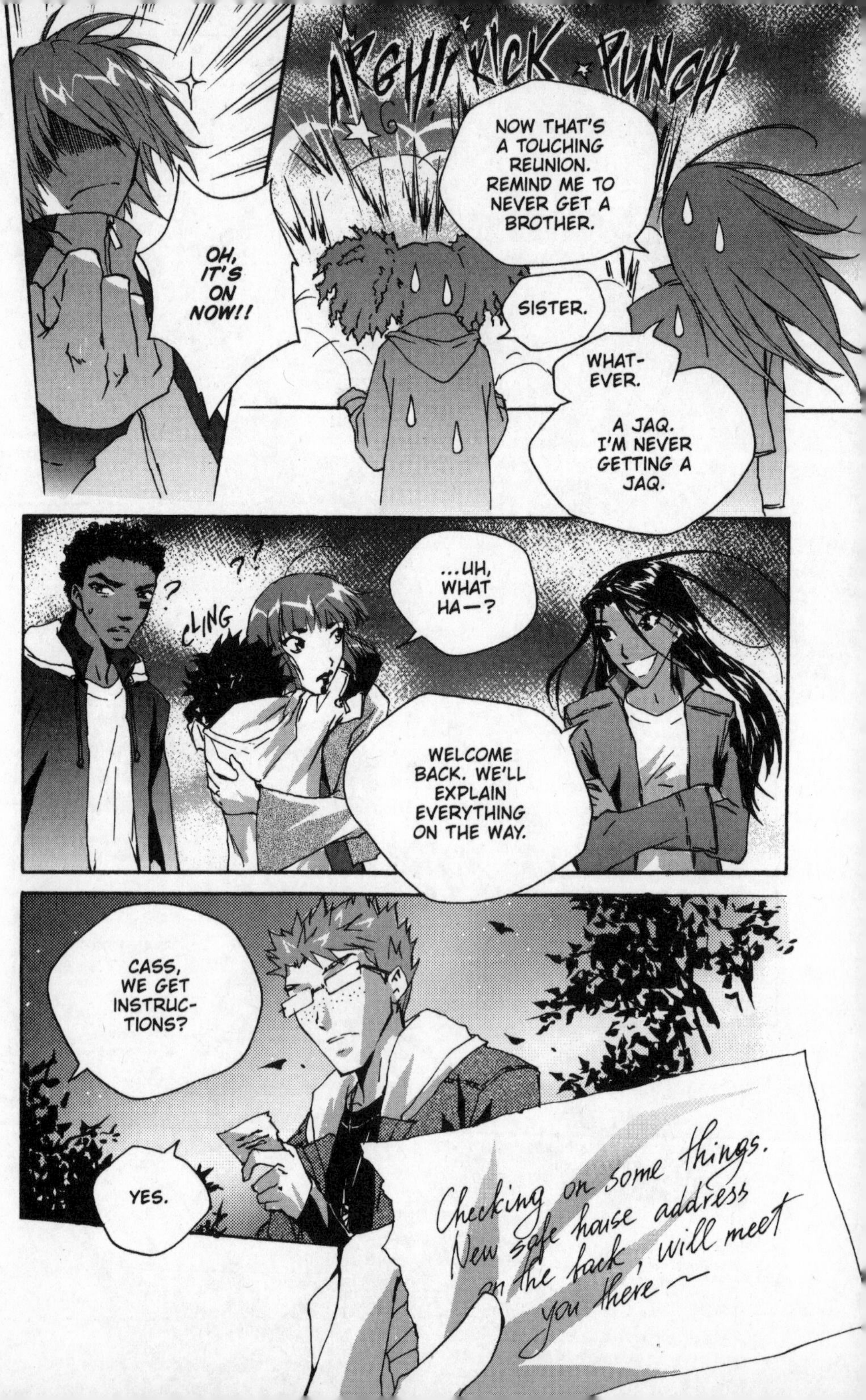
OH, IT'S ON NOW!!
ARGH!! KICK PUNCH
NOW THAT'S A TOUCHING REUNION. REMIND ME TO NEVER GET A BROTHER.
SISTER.
WHAT-EVER.
A JAQ. I'M NEVER GETTING A JAQ.
CLING
...UH, WHAT HA—?
WELCOME BACK. WE'LL EXPLAIN EVERYTHING ON THE WAY.
CASS, WE GET INSTRUC-TIONS?
YES.
Checking on some things. New safe house address on the back, will meet you there ~

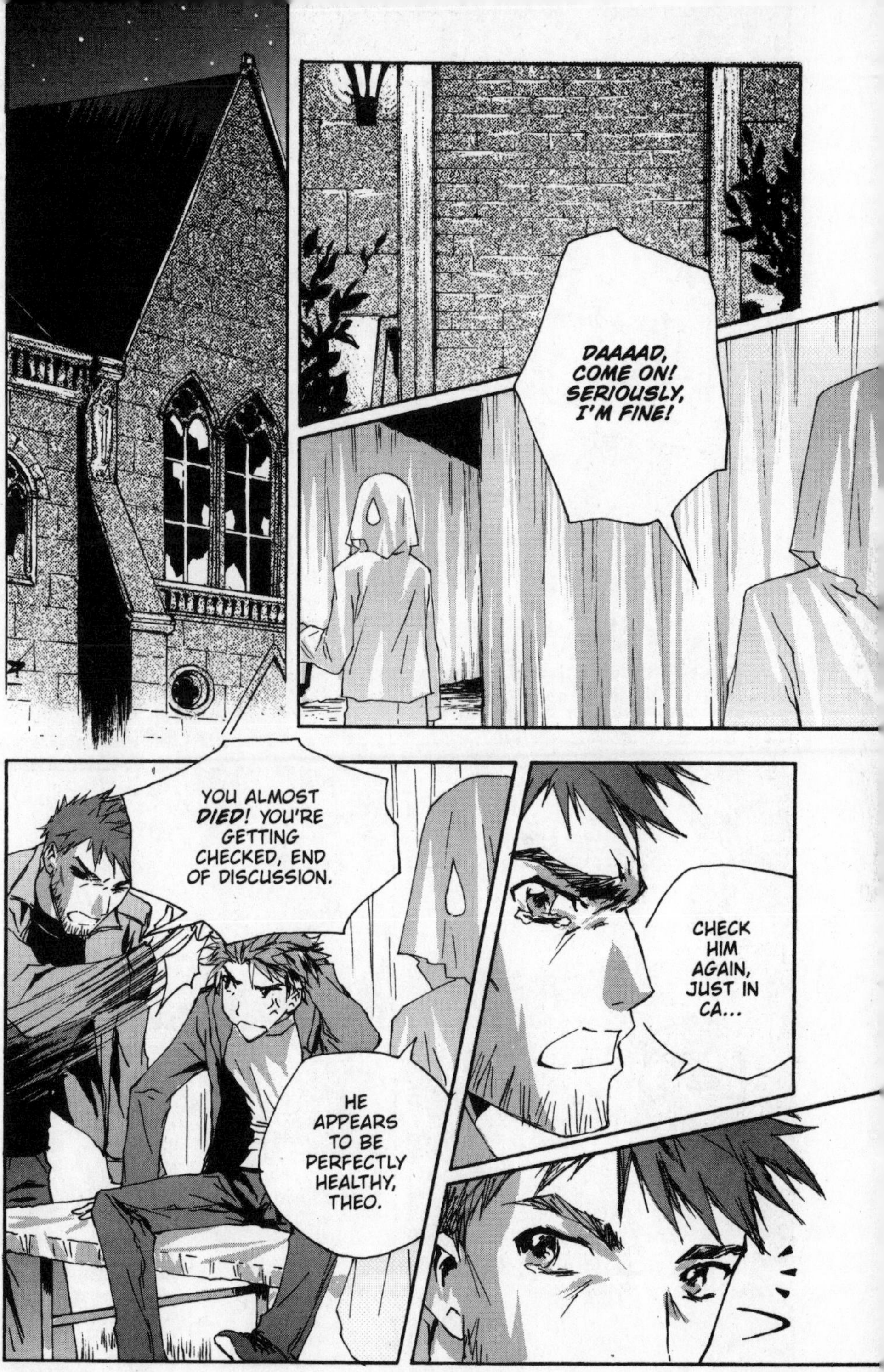
DAAAAD, COME ON! SERIOUSLY, I'M FINE!
YOU ALMOST DIED! YOU'RE GETTING CHECKED, END OF DISCUSSION.
HE APPEARS TO BE PERFECTLY HEALTHY, THEO.
CHECK HIM AGAIN, JUST IN CA...

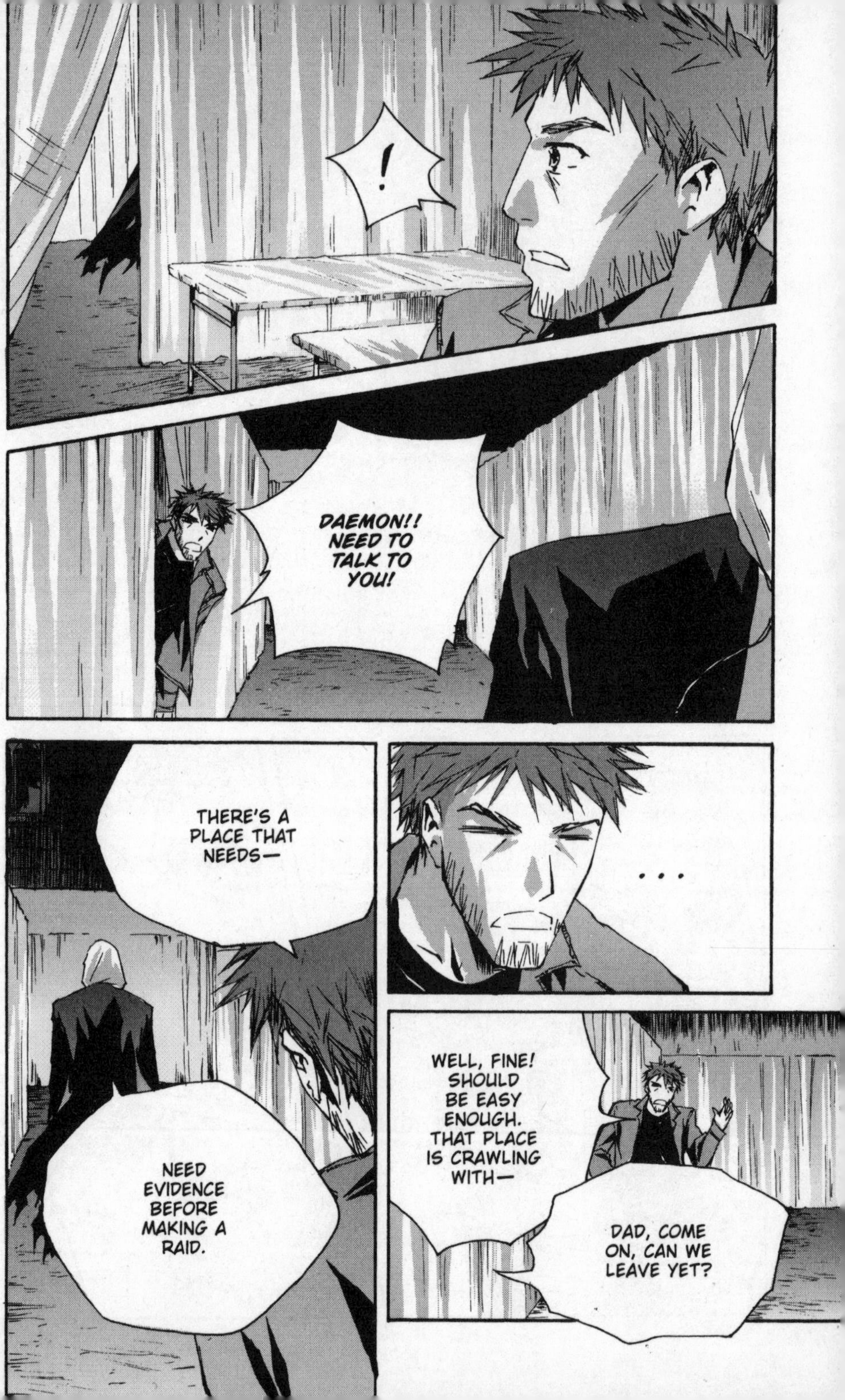
!
DAEMON!! NEED TO TALK TO YOU!
THERE'S A PLACE THAT NEEDS—
NEED EVIDENCE BEFORE MAKING A RAID.
...
WELL, FINE! SHOULD BE EASY ENOUGH. THAT PLACE IS CRAWLING WITH—
DAD, COME ON, CAN WE LEAVE YET?

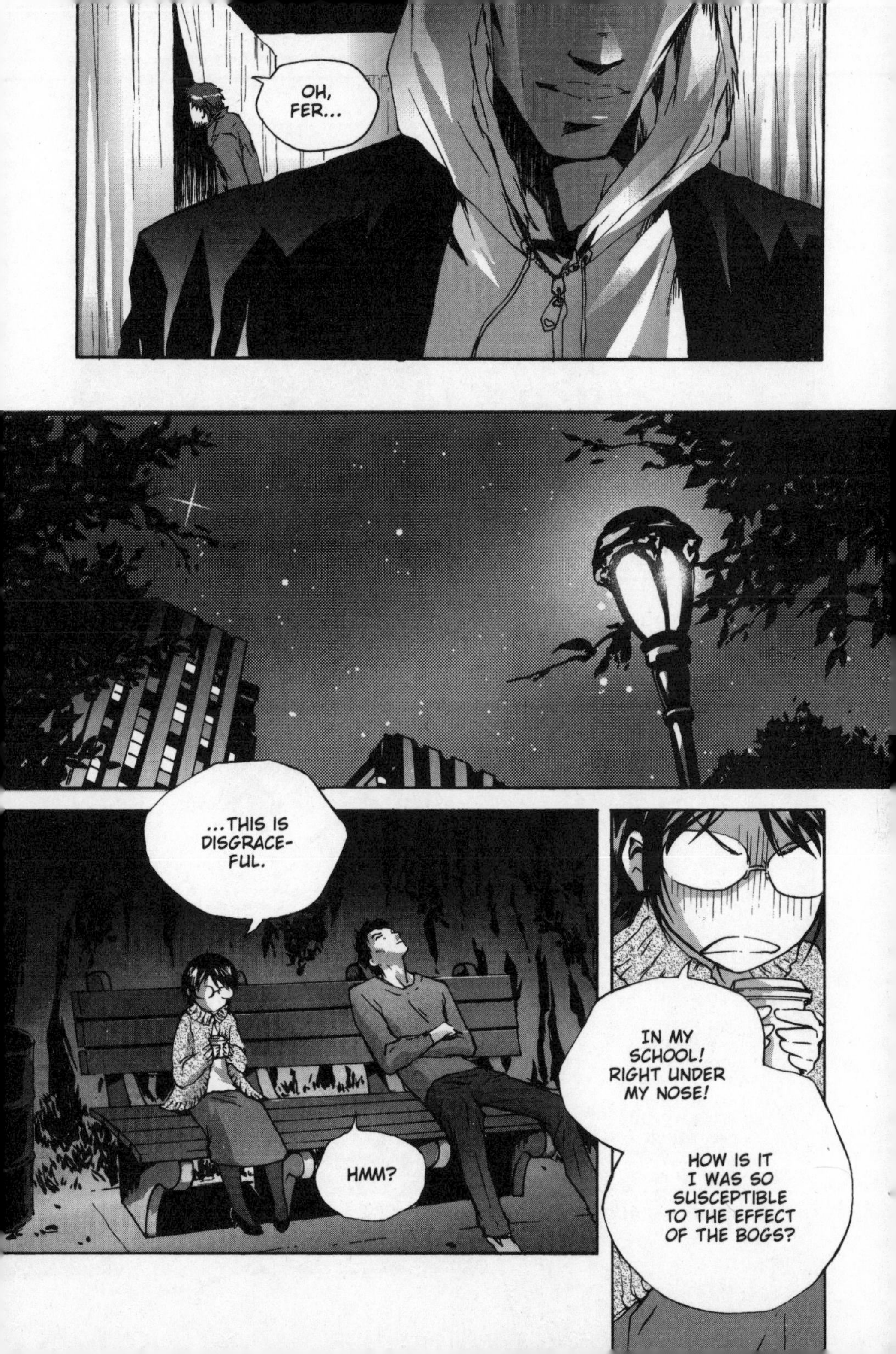
OH, FER...
...THIS IS DISGRACE-FUL.
HMM?
IN MY SCHOOL! RIGHT UNDER MY NOSE!
HOW IS IT I WAS SO SUSCEPTIBLE TO THE EFFECT OF THE BOGS?

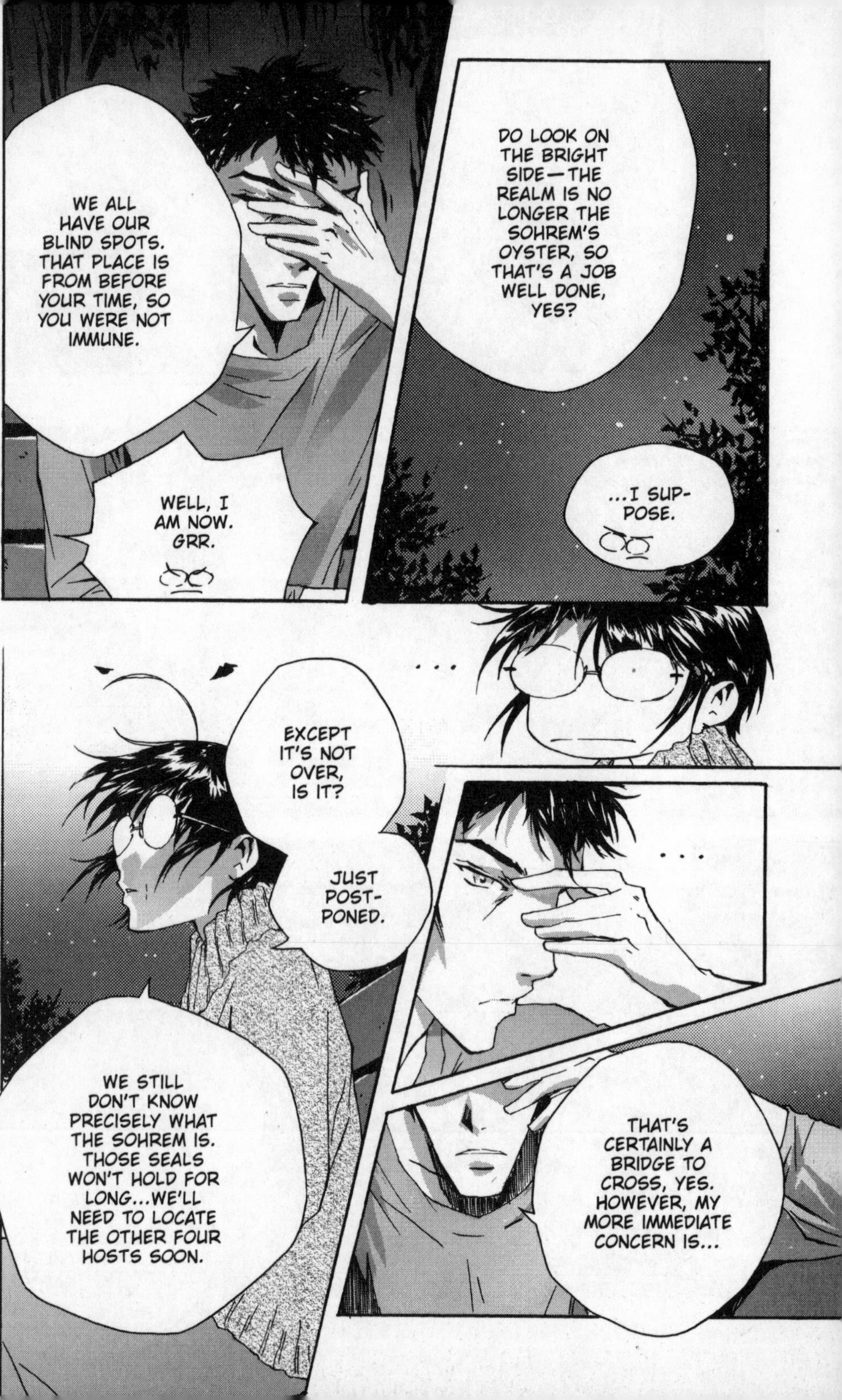
WE ALL HAVE OUR BLIND SPOTS. THAT PLACE IS FROM BEFORE YOUR TIME, SO YOU WERE NOT IMMUNE.
WELL, I AM NOW. GRR.
DO LOOK ON THE BRIGHT SIDE—THE REALM IS NO LONGER THE SOHREM'S OYSTER, SO THAT'S A JOB WELL DONE, YES?
...I SUP-POSE.
EXCEPT IT'S NOT OVER, IS IT?
JUST POST-PONED.
WE STILL DON'T KNOW PRECISELY WHAT THE SOHREM IS. THOSE SEALS WON'T HOLD FOR LONG...WE'LL NEED TO LOCATE THE OTHER FOUR HOSTS SOON.
...
...
THAT'S CERTAINLY A BRIDGE TO CROSS, YES. HOWEVER, MY MORE IMMEDIATE CONCERN IS...

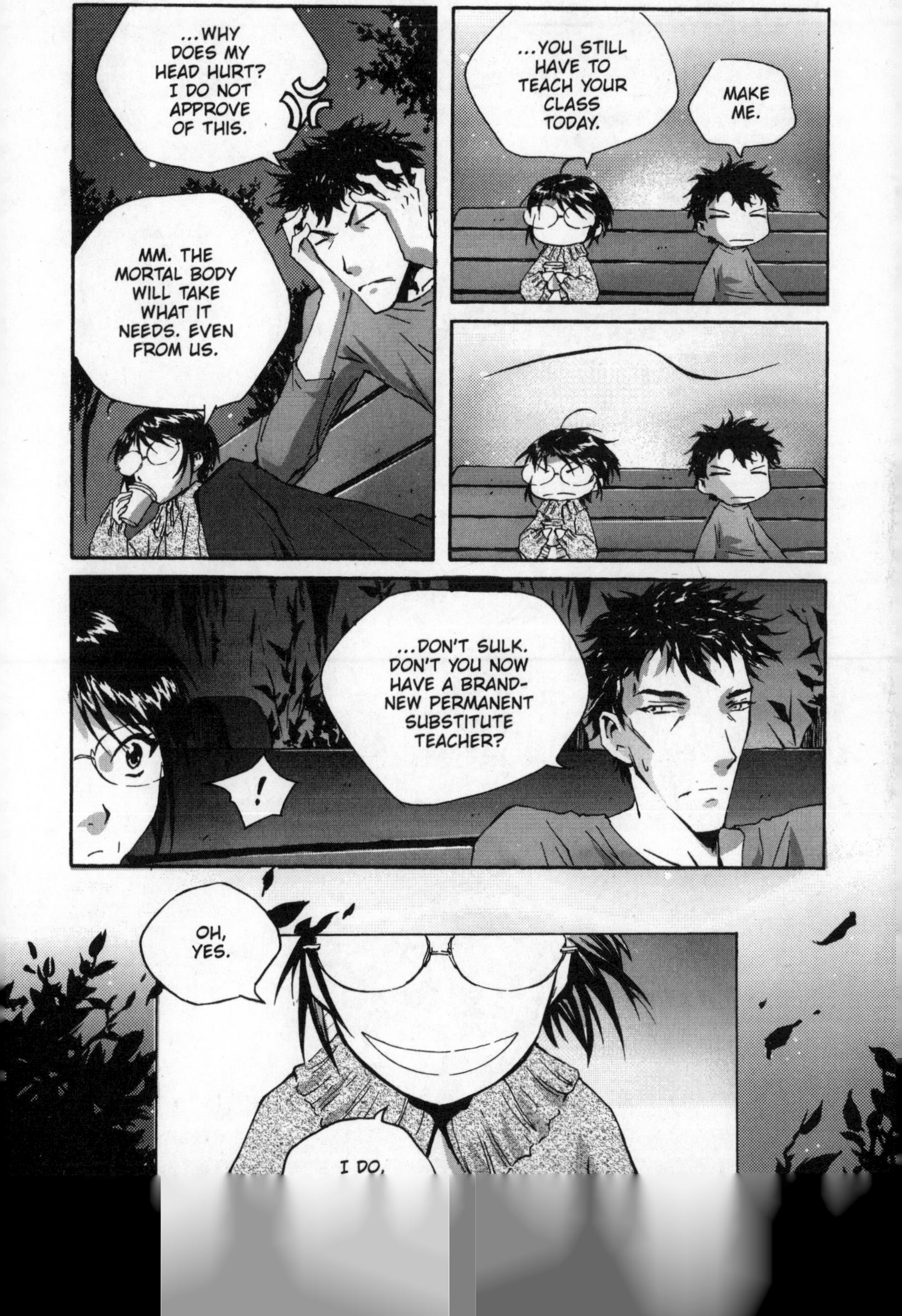
...WHY DOES MY HEAD HURT? I DO NOT APPROVE OF THIS.
MM. THE MORTAL BODY WILL TAKE WHAT IT NEEDS. EVEN FROM US.
...YOU STILL HAVE TO TEACH YOUR CLASS TODAY.
MAKE ME.
...DON'T SULK. DON'T YOU NOW HAVE A BRAND-NEW PERMANENT SUBSTITUTE TEACHER?
!
OH, YES.
I DO.

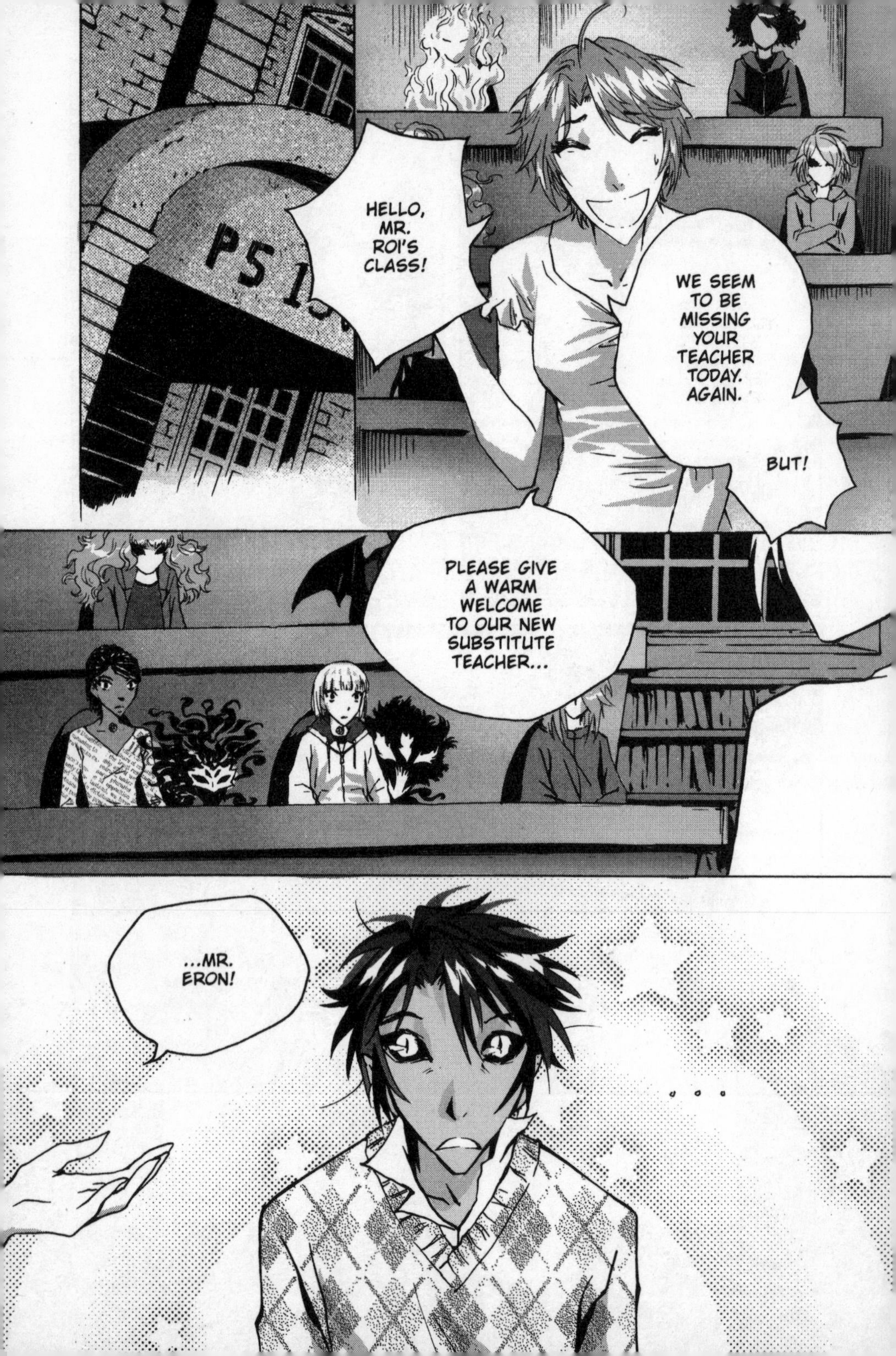
P5 1
HELLO, MR. ROI'S CLASS!
WE SEEM TO BE MISSING YOUR TEACHER TODAY. AGAIN.
BUT!
PLEASE GIVE A WARM WELCOME TO OUR NEW SUBSTITUTE TEACHER...
...MR. ERON!
...

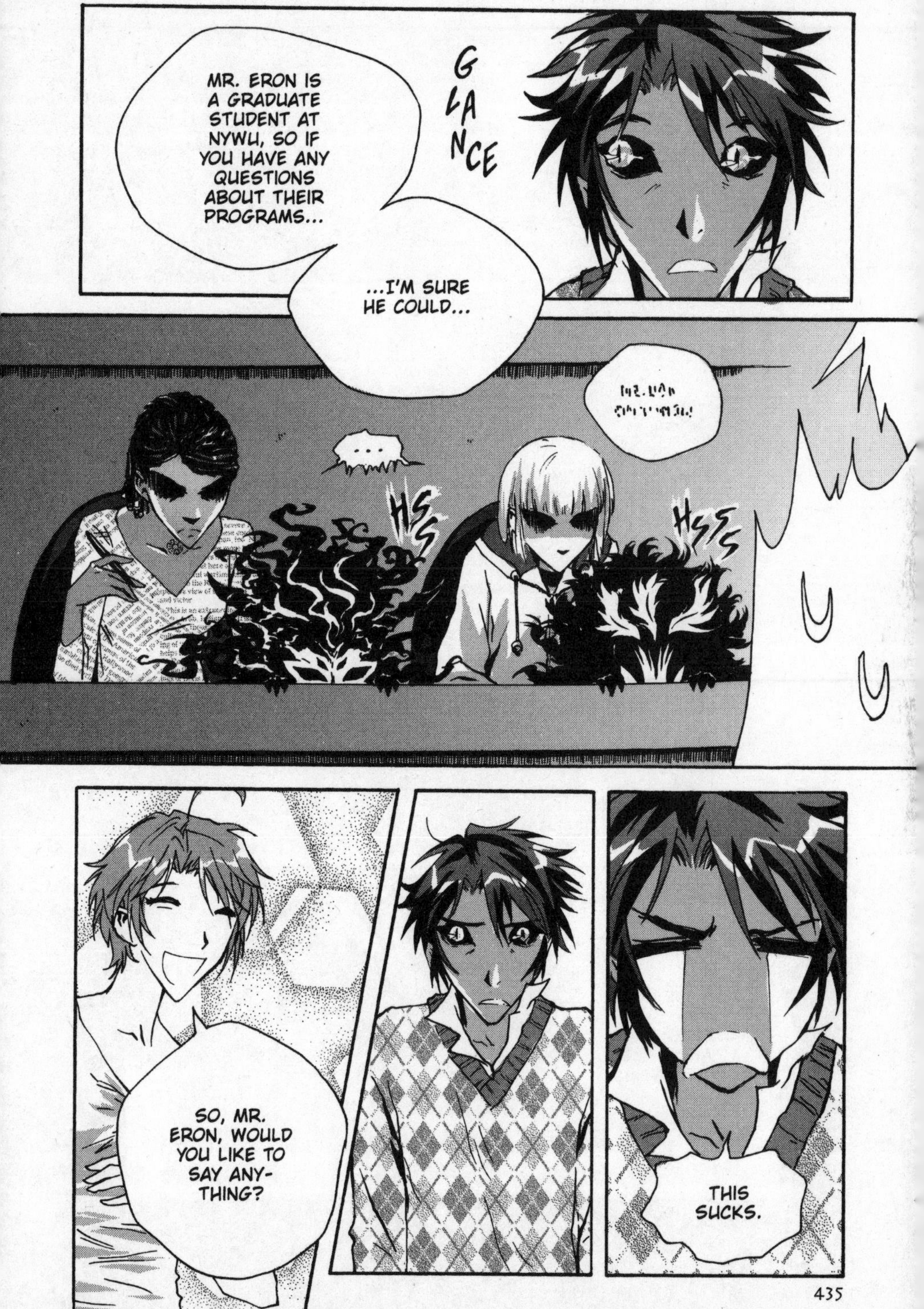
MR. ERON IS A GRADUATE STUDENT AT NYWU, SO IF YOU HAVE ANY QUESTIONS ABOUT THEIR PROGRAMS...
GLANCE
...I'M SURE HE COULD...
...
HSS
HSSS
SO, MR. ERON, WOULD YOU LIKE TO SAY ANY-THING?
THIS SUCKS.

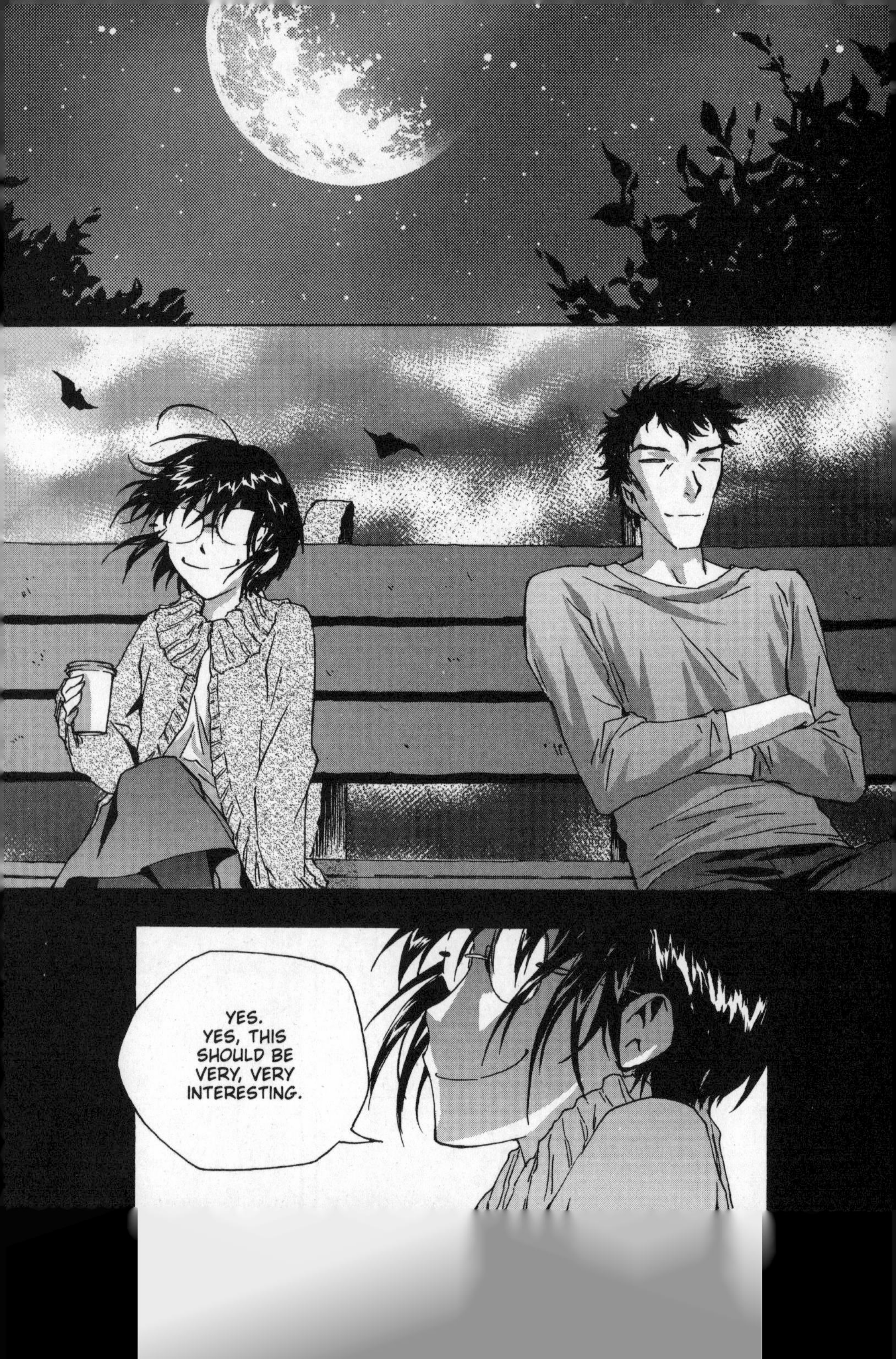
YES. YES, THIS SHOULD BE VERY, VERY INTERESTING.

THE END!

(... *for now* 😈)

BWAH HA HA
HA HA
H......

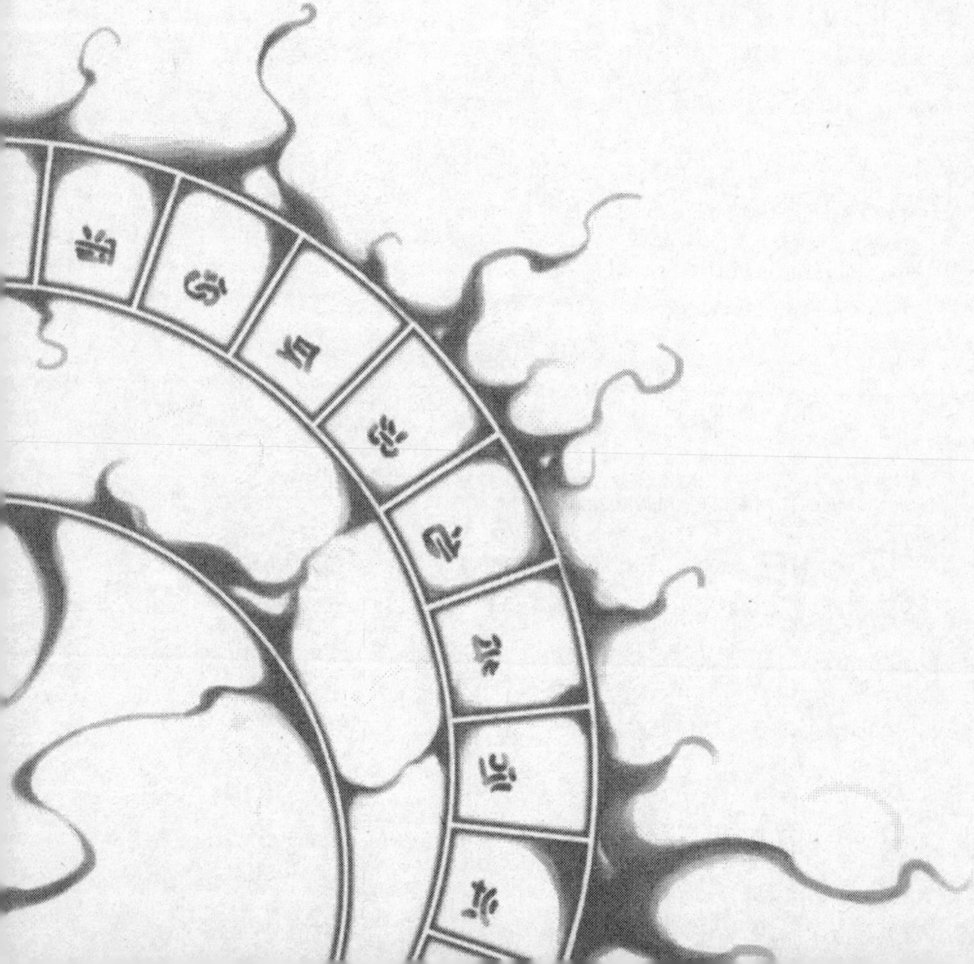

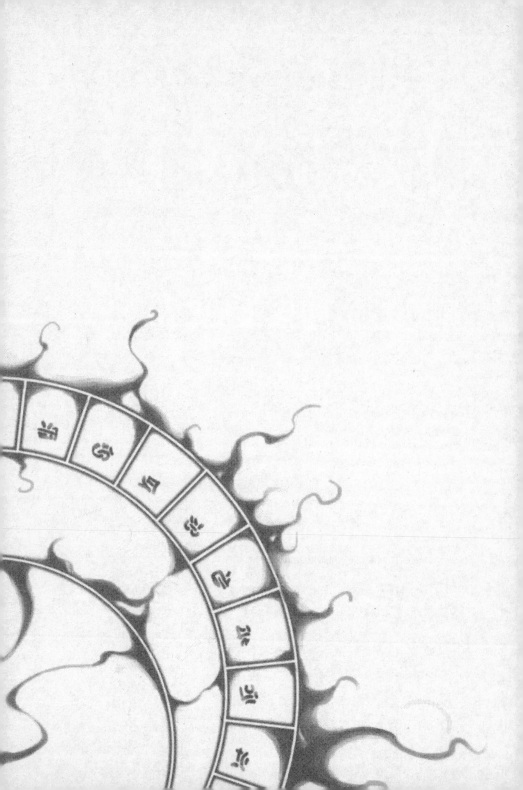

BONUS
AAAAAAAA

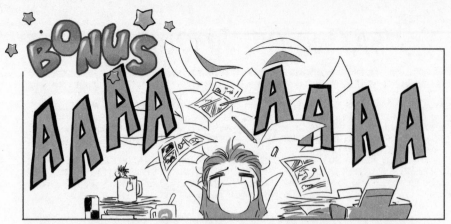

...SORRY, I HAD TO DO THE HAPPY FLINGING AND THE SCREAM, BECAUSE WOW, THE MARATHON TO FINISH THIS BOOK WAS EPIC!! EVEN MORE EPIC THAN USUAL, I DIDN'T THINK THINGS COULD GET THAT INTENSE, I THINK MY HAND FELL OFF SOMEWHERE IN CHAPTER 24 (IF YOU FIND IT, PLEASE RETURN TO OWNER, EVEN IF IT RESISTS AND TRIES TO RUN AWAY 8D!)

AND HOW ABOUT THAT ENDING, HUH?! BEFORE I AM PELTED WITH PRODUCE AND OTHER TOKENS OF, UH, APPRECIATION, I HASTEN TO SAY THAT NO! THIS IS NOT THE END OF THE SERIES! THIS STORY ARC IS DONE, BUT WE ARE PLANNING MORE BOOKS IN THE FUTURE.*

TO DISTRACT YOU FROM READING THE FOOTNOTE, I QUICKLY OFFER YOU VAGUELY AMUSING HIGHLIGHTS FROM THIS LAST MAD DEADLINE DASH! SOME OF THE THINGS I DID WHILE FINISHING:

ATTEMPT TO DRAW WITH THE WRONG END OF THE PEN:
...WAIT WHUT
X!
TRY ENERGY DRINKS TO ACHIEVE "MENTAL ALERTNESS."
...
Pit Bull
Z Z
(... IT DIDN'T WORK)
STAND ON THE BALCONY AND LOOK AT THE CITY STREETS, SMILING IN AN UNHINGED MANNER:
...SOON.
...YEAH, I DON'T KNOW WHY EITHER. XD

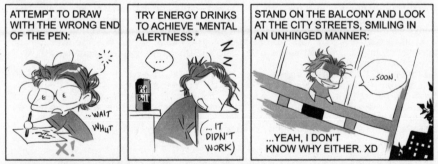

BUT I WAS NOT ALONE!! BIG THANKS AND HUGS GO OUT TO THESE KIND PEOPLE FOR HELPING ME OUT IN THE FINAL CRUNCH:

IRENE FLORES (for gorgeous inking help in the last 2 chapters ♥)

DEE! (for awesome tones, as always!)

JUYOUN! (for getting me every extension imaginable and cheering me on T_T)

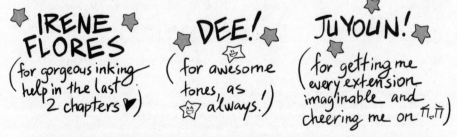

* ...H-HOWEVER, FIRST I HAVE TO TAKE A BREAK TO DO ANOTHER PROJECT *DUCKS AIRBORNE PRODUCE* WHICH IS SECRET AT THE TIME OF MY WRITING THIS, BUT SHOULD ALREADY BE ANNOUNCED AT THE TIME THIS BOOK HITS THE SHELVES!! FOR DETAILS, PLEASE CHECK MY WEBSITE: www.svetlania.com

...SPEAKING OF JUYOUN

I SOMETIMES GET QUESTIONS ABOUT WHAT IT'S LIKE TO WORK WITH AN EDITOR ON *NIGHTSCHOOL*; IS IT BETTER THAN WORKING ON MY OWN? MY ANSWER TO SAID QUESTION IS ALWAYS A RESOUNDING "YES." IT WOULD'VE BEEN HELL(!!) TO WRITE THIS SPRAWLING BEAST OF A STORYLINE IF I DIDN'T HAVE JUYOUN TO RUN TO WHEN I'VE STARED AT A SCRIPT FOR SO LONG IT NO LONGER LOOKS LIKE IT'S IN ENGLISH AND I CAN'T EVEN TELL IF IT WORKS OR NOT. @_@;; WHEN TIMES GET TOUGH LIKE THIS? THE TOUGH GO CRYING TO JUYOUN AND SPEND AN HOUR ON THE PHONE WITH HER UNTIL THINGS MAKE SENSE AGAIN!!

NOW, BESIDES BEING A BADASS EDITOR ALWAYS RESCUING CREATORS FROM DIRE PERIL, JUYOUN IS ALSO A REALLY COOL PERSON AND A FRIEND, SO I DECIDED IT IS MY DUTY TO THOROUGHLY EMBARRASS HER WITH A GUSHY INTERVIEW :3 SO HERE SHE IS, GENTLE READERS (AND THANK YOU FOR DOING THIS, EDITOR-SAN!!):

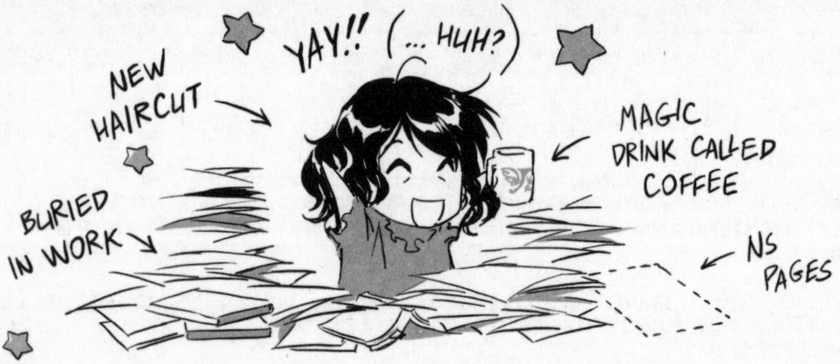
YAY!! (... HUH?)
NEW HAIRCUT
MAGIC DRINK CALLED COFFEE
BURIED IN WORK
NS PAGES

Svet: You are originally from Korea, where you edited and managed an impressive lineup of original books from Korean creators. Now you live in the U.S. and oversee original books from North American (and Russian-Canadian :D) creators as well! Has it been a difficult switch? What are some of the differences? (I know sometimes you wish Canada was next door...Like, when there is a deadline and the latest chapter pages are M.I.A....)

JuYoun: Oh, I do so wish Canada were next door! LOL. The switch itself was not as difficult as some might think, but to me, I guess the biggest difference is indeed the face time. It's not just when the deadline is close, but even at the earlier stages, I was used to sitting down and discussing things with creators, which I don't get to do a lot in the U.S. I still miss those times, but I wonder if I'm just reminiscing about the good old days, since technology has allowed many to work without actually having to be in the same room.

Svet: You fluently speak roughly a billion languages (...well, at least three that I know of). Is there any language you would really love to learn?

JuYoun: I feel like I'm fluent in none these days. LOL The motivation for learning a language (for me, of course) is my interest in the culture. These days, I really want to learn Chinese and French, since I feel like those two have a lot of influence on English, Japanese, and Korean, and I would love to learn more about those cultures.

Svet: How is it that you became an editor? Do you have a favorite part of the job? (That's not the weekend :3?)

JuYoun: Hmm. As anyone who works in publishing would say, I've always loved books, but the direct reason probably is that I worked for the school magazine while I was in college, and I found that I loved it. Comics, or manga, have always been my passion, so it felt only natural to get into this area of publishing. As far as favorite parts, while everything from finding talent to actually getting the books in my hand is exciting, I used to love getting to work on the artists' original pages, which felt like a privilege. But these days, I don't get that satisfaction, since everything's digital. :(

Svet: I found out you were an architecture major when I was working on the floor plans for Nightschool 13W in Volume 2. You helped me work out some of the problems with that (thank you!!), so now I wonder—if you could design any building in the world, fictional or real, what would it be?

JuYoun: What help are you talking about? It was already perfect! :D Yes, I was an architecture major, which was lots of fun, and it also involved a lot of art classes and whatnot. At the moment, I don't have any ambitions in that regard. (I hardly remember anything!) I do hope that someday, though, I'll design my dream house! Well, if I can't, I do still have many friends in that field whom I could hire. LOL

Svet: I know quite a few aspiring manga-ka read *Nightschool.* Would you like to say anything to any future Svetlanas out there? :D

JuYoun: An image of a little, chibi Svet popped into my head! LOL. Hmmm. Well, there's a lot to be said, like...practice a lot, always remember that the art and the text have to work together, etc. But I guess the one thing would be to always have passion and to always think about what's in your heart, what story you want to tell. That will give you the strength to try hard, to let you get to where you need to be in order to be a professional!

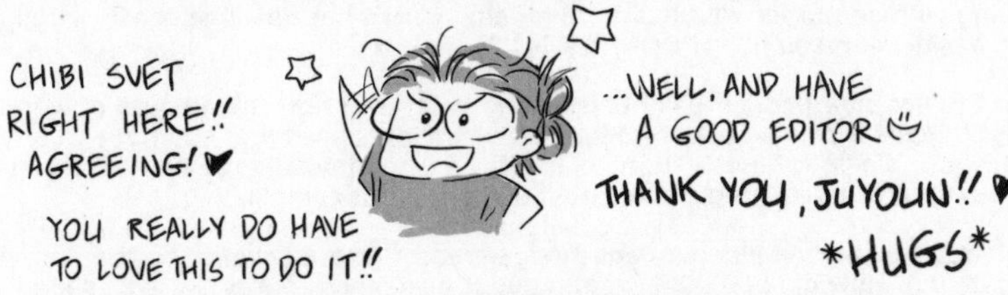
CHIBI SVET RIGHT HERE!! AGREEING! ♥
YOU REALLY DO HAVE TO LOVE THIS TO DO IT!!
...WELL, AND HAVE A GOOD EDITOR
THANK YOU, JUYOUN!! ♥
HUGS

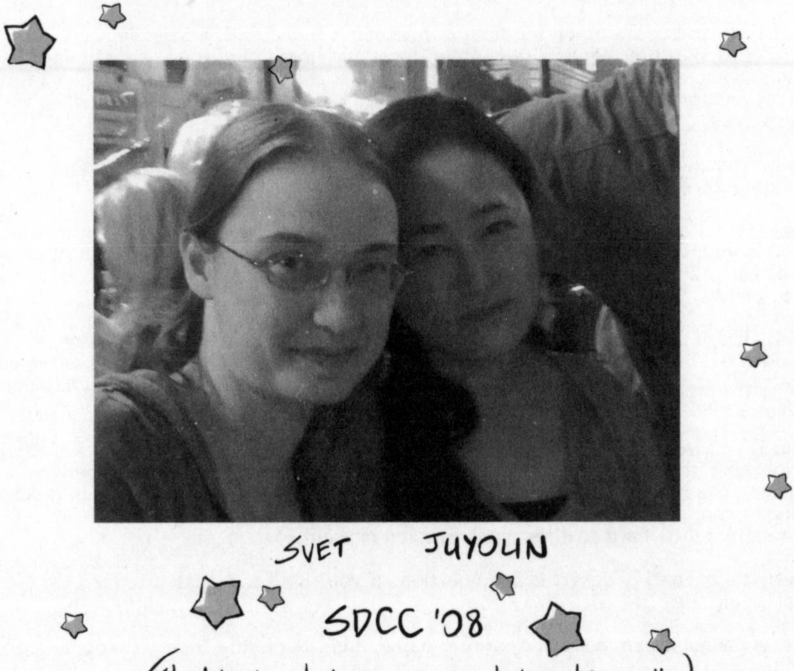
SVET
JUYOUN
SDCC '08
(Nightschool launch celebration)

AND FOR MY NEXT VICTIM...

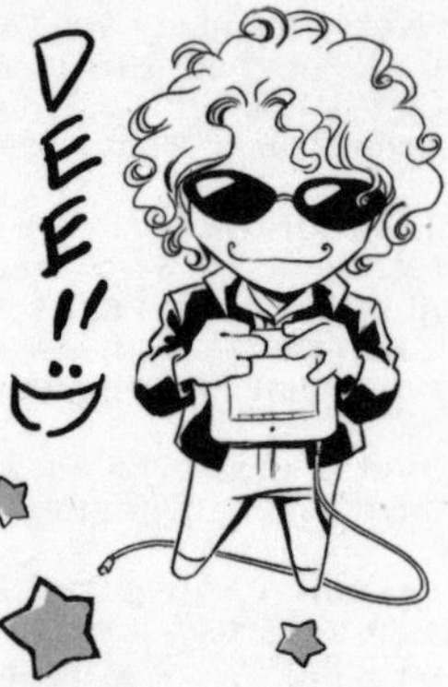
DEE!!

FOR THOSE WHO ARE UNAWARE, DEE IS TEN KINDS OF AWESOME AND ALSO THE TONE ARTIST ON *NIGHTSCHOOL*. WE'VE BEEN WORKING TOGETHER SINCE MY *DRAMACON* DAYS, AND IT'S A WORK RELATIONSHIP THAT STARTED ABOUT SIX YEARS AGO, APPROXIMATELY THUS...
DEE: SAY, SVET, YOU SOUND STRESSED. DO YOU NEED HELP WITH YOUR BOOK DEADLINE? SVET: YEEEEEES ;___;
...AND SINCE NO GOOD DEED GOES UNPUNISHED, I ENDED UP DRAGGING HER THROUGH ALL MY BOOK DEADLINES EVER SINCE :D;;; WE'VE BECOME GOOD FRIENDS ALONG THE WAY, DESPITE LIVING IN DIFFERENT PARTS OF THE WORLD, THUS I OWE HER AN EMBARRASSINGLY GUSHY INTERVIEW AS WELL! :D HEEEEEEERE IT IS:

Svet: You've been the long-suffering and patient tone artist for *Nightschool* for over two years now, on top of a full-time job, a move halfway across the world, and other miscellaneous things like life and stuff. Would you like to share any insights about working with an author who has a "durr" chip where her deadline sense should be? (...Er, besides a resounding "DON'T" XD;; ?)

Dee: I'm not sure people really understand just how crazy the amount of work is that it takes to make a comic book. And how crazy the deadlines are. You have to be insane to do this job. We both have a "durr" chip. :D I watched a truly remarkable series grow and a gifted creator make magic against all odds. I'm not complaining.

Svet: You are also an independent manga creator (more *OniKimono* chapters plz *begs* ;o;). How did you start creating your own stories? Was there a "spark" moment, a book, or an event that pushed you down that dark and winding path?

Dee: I remember sitting on the floor of my mom's house with a ballpoint pen and a stack of used printer paper. I remember drawing a horse. And then, without knowing why, drawing a vertical line. And then I drew what the horse did next. I think all the comics creators I know independently "invented" comics out of some place deep within themselves.

Svet: What tools did you use then, and what do you use now? Did anything change/evolve in your creative outlook?

Dee: From a ballpoint pen to Bristol board with a dip-pen to a Cintiq. The important evolution is your vision, not your tools, I think. And as for evolution of my toning technique, I fail, 'cause I'm still using the same battered copy of Deleter ComicWorks 1 on the same piece-of-crap PC I've been hauling all over the planet for eight years.

Svet: One of the many things I really love about *OniKimono* and *Shatterstone* (besides the fact that they are excellent stories) is that they both have hot, wisecracking detectives as main characters. You've mentioned that you are influenced by film noir; what are some must-watch titles that you would recommend?

Dee: If you watch *Casablanca* so many times that you can close your eyes and replay the entire thing in your head, read everything Dashiell Hammett ever wrote, spend your '80s watching *Miami Vice*, have the ANNOTATED Sherlock Holmes on your shelf, and listen to swing in your off-hours, you will find yourself writing a hard-boiled detective into all of your comics. The hard part becomes keeping him out of them.

Svet: The obligatory desert island question: If you could only take three things, etc., what would they be? :D

Dee: A ballpoint pen, a stack of printer paper, and...does "the Internet" count as one thing?

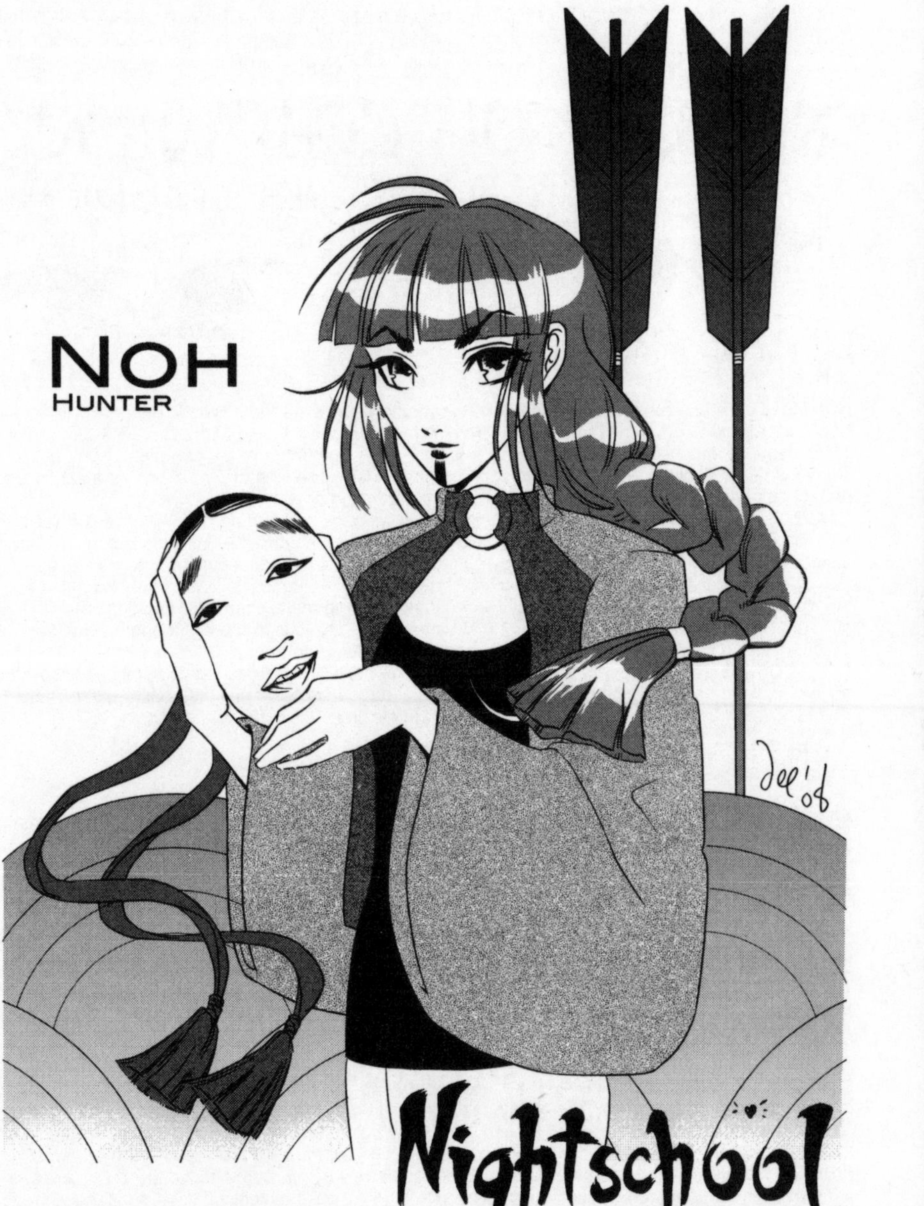
NOH
HUNTER
dee '08
Nightschool
FAN ART BY DEE!

THIS WAS DURING BOOK 1
(BEFORE NOH GOT KNOCKED OUT
AND MISSED ALL THE ACTION)
SUCH A GORGEOUS PIECE,
THANK YOU FOR EVERYTHING, DEE!!

AND LAST BUT NOT LEAST...

THE WORLD IN *NIGHTSCHOOL* IS VERY COMPLEX, AND I'VE ONLY BARELY SCRATCHED THE SURFACE IN THESE FOUR BOOKS... SO I LEAVE YOU WITH A VAIN ATTEMPT TO CLARIFY A FEW THINGS ABOUT SOME OF THE KEY GROUPS IN IT! BEHOLD THE...

NIGHTSCHOOL COMPANION!
(the really really short version ☺)

HUNTERS ٤٠)

HUNTERS—supernatural beings who are neither human nor of the Night World. They are very strong, fast, and can live a long time (but often die early in their line of work). Hunter bodies heal very rapidly, which makes it impossible for them to have tattoos or piercings (much to the chagrin of Hunters like Teresa, who really wants a salamander tattoo on her left leg.) The Hunters' initial natural function is to protect humans from Night Things, but things get complicated beyond that.

CLAVE—Hunters are brutally self-sufficient starting at an early age and don't really have families per se (many of them start out as abandoned children or orphans), so they have Claves instead. A Clave is a small group of young Hunters headed by an adult (or two or three, depending on the size of the Clave), who is usually referred to as "Teacher." Here they are homeschooled to know everything about the Hunter trade, the Night World, and the world in general (so math, chemistry, languages, etc.—there's no escape from those!) NOTE: Dating within a Clave is forbidden (though sometimes Teachers turn a blind eye, even if they know something's going on).

THE SCORING—a yearly event where many Claves meet and Hunters-in-training proceed to beat one another to a bloody pulp in moderated fights, with the purpose of furthering their battle skills. Those who repeatedly lose at The Scoring are most likely to die first back in the real world.

WEIRNS ⊚

WEIRNS—a special breed of witch who are born with demon guardian spirits (Astrals) bound to them. Each weirn has a spellbook that only they can open. (Alex carries hers around in the story.)

ASTRALS—demon guardian spirits (usually of limited intelligence, but nonetheless quite perceptive and clever in certain ways—like, cookie-stealing ways). Astrals are irrevocably bound to their Weirn hosts and have often been known to take on hidden traits of their hosts' personalities, sometimes even acting on the hosts' suppressed desires. Adult Astrals look very different from their younger incarnations. (Sarah has one, but it hasn't made an appearance yet.)

VAMPIRES ᵘᵘ⌐

TURNING—to become a vampire in the *Nightschool* world you need to a.) get bitten, and b.) lose a lot of blood, but not enough to die. The Turning is a gradual process that takes a few days, during which time your mortal body is actually still around, but slowly being devoured by the vampire persona. If you look in the mirror, you will see your reflection—but even if your vampire self is smiling, your mortal reflection will still look lost and terrified, as you are effectively dying. During these few days, you can still turn back into a human by subjecting yourself to a heavy dose of sunlight to burn out the vampire. (However, it's very painful.) After that, it's too late, and no mirror in the world will ever see you again.

RIPPERS—the future of any vampire—no exceptions—though many "live" a long time before they finally succumb. Rippers are vampires who've forgotten what it's like to be alive and can no longer maintain the illusion, which causes them to physically change into the dry, mindless, and perpetually hungry creatures portrayed in chapter 3 of Volume 1. If you want to scare a *Nightschool* vampire, tell them their skin is looking a little dry. None of them want to go that way anytime soon...

SHIFTERS ☆ ☆

THE SHAPESHIFTER community is incredibly diverse—there are wolves, foxes, ravens, and count-less other species. Even anacondas, I kid you not! These are all creatures of both the Night World and the wild—either people who turn into animals or animals who turn into people—who have claimed the city as their new dark and dangerous woods. Many of them are very urbane and have carved out new occupations for themselves in all areas of business. (For example, Gray and his buddies are basically muscle for hire... Too bad they didn't quite understand who they were messing with. 8D)

THE NERESHAI ☆

....are basically the resident badasses of the Night World who keep an eye on things. They are immensely powerful to the point where they don't posture or brag, they simply Take Care Of Business and move on. (...Well, unless they are Mr. Roi, who does like to indulge in a bit of posturing and self-congratulating. :D) Their job is largely thankless, incredibly demanding, and they'd all really love to quit, except that they can't for reasons that will be revealed later! Their individual histories are fasci-nating, especially for Daemon and Mr. Roi, who in fact are technically the same age and go way back. ...Did I mention that the Nereshai are my best, favorite people in this book? I could just draw them all day. I wish I could hang out with them. Madam Chen and I would have coffee, and Daemon and Mr. Roi would just sit there looking good and trying to not kill each other, and then I'd be be all "Hey, I know, let's go fight bad guys, lemme just get my Astral, brb! 8D"
/sad fantasy life...OTZ

THE WORLD ☆

LEYLINES—Jaq mentions these briefly in this volume. They are a net of energy lines weaving through the world and can be used for (barely reliable) communication. What you do is you give a piece of your voice to a Leyline in the form of a message as well as the name of the person you wish for it to reach. Such messages sometimes take the long way and may arrive a century later instead of, well, sooner. Giving a message to a Leyline will leave you hoarse for a couple of hours.
VOICES—voice messages that got lost on Leynet (and sometimes acquired a life of their own, or merged with others). If a person with a good feel for it were to stand in the middle of a Leysite (a place where a bunch of Leylines cross), they could hear all kinds of things from different times and places.
OLD WORLD VESTIGES—the Bogs of Lethe are one of them. They are very dangerous artifacts of a time past that lie in wait and only grow in power as the centuries roll on. Many try to use them for their own ends... When someone actually succeeds instead of becoming their sacrifice, well, that's when the Nereshai cancel all their meetings and wipe the floor with everyone involved.

... AAAAND THAT'S IT FOR NOW. ♡ THANK YOU EVERYONE FOR READING AND FOR YOUR SUPPORT, IT REALLY MAKES ALL THE DIFFERENCE WHEN I'M FACING OFF WITH THE BOOK PAGES IN THE STUDIO ALL BY MYSELF...
(... IT ALSO HELPS WHEN I FIGHT EVIL, SO IT'S JUST AN ALL-AROUND AWESOME BOON TO HAVE SUPPORTIVE READERS ⛧ ♭)

SEE YOU IN THE NEXT BOOK !!!
crawls off to sleep Svet ♥

Nightschool
THE WEIRN BOOKS
Collector's Edition

SVETLANA CHMAKOVA

Toning Artist: DEE DUPUY

• •

Lettering: JUYOUN LEE

NIGHTSCHOOL: The Weirn Books, Vols. 3 & 4 © 2010 Svetlana Chmakova.

Yen Press
150 West 30th Street, 19th Floor
New York, NY 10001

Visit us at yenpress.com
facebook.com/yenpress
twitter.com/yenpress
yenpress.tumblr.com
instagram.com/yenpress

First Yen Press Edition: May 2020

Yen Press is an imprint of Yen Press, LLC.
The Yen Press name and logo are trademarks of Yen Press, LLC.

The publisher is not responsible for websites (or their content) that are not owned by the publisher.

Library of Congress Control Number: 2020935039

ISBN: 978-1-9753-1290-9

10 9 8 7 6 5 4 3 2 1

WOR

Printed in the United States of America